P9-CFY-150

JIG

CAMPBELL ARMSTRONG

WILLIAM MORROW AND COMPANY, INC.
NEW YORK

Library of Congress Cataloging-in-Publication Data

Armstrong, Campbell.
    Jig.
    "A Thomas Congdon book."
    I. Title.
PR6051.R566J5   1987   823'.914   87-5735
ISBN 0-688-06879-0

A Thomas Congdon Book

Printed in the United States of America

First Edition

1 2 3 4 5 6 7 8 9 10

BOOK DESIGN BY BETH TONDREAU

Rebecca Armstrong co-piloted this book with me.
Her splendid insights and her fine judgment made her,
in every sense,
a full partner in this novel.

My gratitude is due to Tom Congdon, whose editorial wizardry approaches that magical condition—alchemy. And to Richard Pine, who encouraged and helped and offered all kinds of wonderful assistance from the start of the Irish dance. And to Arthur Pine, whose staunch, supportive feeling about this novel made a world of difference. I would also like to thank Dave Post of Computer Services, Sedona, Arizona, and Chief Engineer Mike Wilson for their kindness, as well as my English editor, Nick Sayers, for all his help and thoughtful consideration.

I am of Ireland
And of the holy land
    Of Ireland.
Good sir, pray I thee,
For of saint charity,
Come and dance with me
    In Ireland.

—"The Irish Dancer"
    Anonymous

JIG

ONE

LATITUDE 40N, LONGITUDE 70W

Captain Liam O'Reilly didn't enjoy the crossing whenever the Courier was on board. A funereal man who spoke in monosyllables, the Courier rarely moved from his tiny cabin all the way from the coast of Maine to the disembarkation point in the west of Ireland. He had no fewer than *three* briefcases this trip, each locked and chained to a single bracelet on his wrist. Usually he carried only one, which he clutched throughout the entire voyage. Three briefcases threw the man off balance. When he'd come aboard by launch eleven miles off the coast of Maine, he'd looked very clumsy, his skinny body listing to one side.

Why did he carry three this time? Liam O'Reilly turned the question over in his mind as he stood on the bridge and listened to the rattle of the ship's engines. He wondered how many more Atlantic crossings the two-thousand-ton *Connie O'Mara* was going to see unless she was completely stripped and refurbished. A rotting old tub, she'd begun her career in 1926, hauling various ores round the Cape of Good Hope.

When O'Reilly had won the old biddy in a drunken game of cut-throat poker with some dubious shipbrokers in Panama City in 1963, his first thought was to offer the ship to the Cause. Initially the

Cause had been reluctant to accept O'Reilly's generosity because of the costs involved in maintaining the vessel. But a ship was a ship, even if it did look like a great floating turd and leak like a colander. In twenty crossings she had carried automatic weapons, explosives and—when the Courier was on board—considerable sums of operating cash for the Cause. She'd done all this without mishap and O'Reilly was proud of the fact.

He smoked a small black cheroot. A moon appeared briefly, then the night was black again. O'Reilly wondered about going amidships to look in on the Courier, but it was an unwritten rule that the man was to be left alone, except when he needed cups of the weak Darjeeling he habitually drank.

The bloody man! O'Reilly thought. He had a detrimental influence on the small crew of the *Connie*. He carried doom around with him the way some people always have a supply of cigarettes. Or maybe it was just the way the Courier put people in mind of their own mortality. Somehow you just knew that a man who looked exactly like the Courier was the same fellow who'd greasepaint your face when you were dead and comb down your hair until you were suitable for boxed presentation at your wake.

O'Reilly strolled on the deck. The March night was very cold. He sucked icy sea air into his lungs. He looked at the black Atlantic. Friend, enemy. Wife, mistress. Life, death. Its dark, amorphous nature had a symmetry that only a man like Liam O'Reilly could understand. He tossed his dead cheroot overboard. There were footsteps along the deck.

O'Reilly recognized the young seaman Houlihan. This was Houlihan's second crossing on the *Connie*. Liam O'Reilly preferred age and experience, but there were times when you had to make do with what you got.

"The man just asked for some tea," Houlihan said.

O'Reilly placed the young seaman's accent as that of a Galway man. "Make it weak. It's the only way he'll have it. The closer it looks like piss, the better he likes it."

"Aye, Captain."

Houlihan vanished quietly along the deck. O'Reilly picked flakes of tobacco from his teeth and listened to the steady throb of the engines. He might have been listening to his own heartbeat, so well did he know the noises of his vessel. He walked a few paces, the engines seeming to throb inside his head, and then he understood there was something not quite right, something amiss in the great darkness around him.

THE second engineer was a small, sharp-faced man called Waddell. He wore an oil-stained pair of very old coveralls and a woolen hat pulled down over his ears. Although it was hot in the engine room, Waddell didn't feel it. He checked his watch. It was two minutes before nine o'clock, United States Eastern Standard Time.

At nine o'clock exactly, Waddell was going to cut the *Connie's* engines.

He ran one dirty hand across his oily face. He listened to the chug of the engines. He made a pretense of checking various valves and pressure gauges. Brannigan, the chief engineer, was drinking coffee out of a tin mug and flicking through the pages of an old copy of *The Irish Times*. From the pocket of his coveralls Waddell took a large wrench, which he weighed in the palm of one hand.

Brannigan, his back turned to the other man, slurped his coffee and remarked on something he was reading in his newspaper. Waddell wasn't listening to him. He was thinking about piracy, which was a word he didn't much care for. He had spent much of his life in the engine rooms of ships, and so, like a physician who must kill his own patient, Waddell disliked the task of shutting down the very system he was paid to keep running. He looked at the back of the chief engineer's head, thinking that he'd always gotten along well with Brannigan. It was a terrible pity.

Waddell stared at his wrench.

He lowered his head, ducked under an overhanging pipe, and hit Ollie Brannigan once right behind the ear. The chief engineer moaned but didn't go down. Instead, he twisted his face around in shock to look at Waddell.

Waddell grunted and struck Brannigan again, this time hammering the wrench down on the man's nose. Brannigan's face suddenly spurted blood. He dropped his tin mug and the newspaper and went down on his knees, groaning, covering his face with his hands.

Jesus God! Waddell had to hit him a *third* time.

He heard metal crush Brannigan's skull, then the chief engineer was silent, stretched back across the oily floor. Waddell, sweating now, dropped the wrench.

It was one minute past nine o'clock.

TO pass time during a crossing, the man known as the Courier often sang quietly to himself. He had a decent baritone voice, though this wasn't a fact known to many people since the Courier maintained a facade of strict anonymity. He came from a long line of men who could carry a decent tune. Hadn't his grandfather, Daniel Riordan, toured the music halls at the turn of the century, thrilling all Ireland with his voice? The Courier, who knew he'd never be in the same class as the Great Riordan, was proud of his voice just the same.

Even as there was a knock on the door of his cabin, the Courier was halfway through one of his personal favorites, "She Moved Through the Fair."

> *"Then she went her way homeward with one star awake*
> *"As the swan in the evening moves over the lake. . . ."*

The door opened. "Your tea, sir," the young seaman said.

"I don't recall asking for tea," the Courier answered. He wondered if the young man had heard him singing. The possibility embarrassed him a little. He watched the seaman place a tray on the bunk-side table.

"Captain's orders, sir. Will there be anything else?"

The Courier didn't reply. With a nod of his head he indicated that he wanted to be left alone. He noticed how the seaman—Houlihan, wasn't it?—let his eyes drift across the three briefcases just before he went out of the cabin. The chains tethered to the Courier's wrist jingled as he reached for the tea mug. Those bloody briefcases made him nervous. He was never happier than when he was rid of them. He didn't feel good until Finn took the briefcases from him in Ireland.

The Courier sipped his tea. He thought it was a little strange that O'Reilly had seen fit to send the tea in, because O'Reilly wasn't exactly Captain Congeniality.

It tasted odd. Was there too much sugar in it?

He took a second sip and he felt blood rush to his head and his eyeballs filled with moisture and his heart was squeezed in a painfully tight vise and his balance went all wrong. He felt he was going to explode. He couldn't breathe and there was something hard and very hot rising in his throat. He tried to stand up but his legs were a thousand miles away from him. He slithered from the edge of the bunk to the floor, hearing the tea tray clatter past him.

He lay gasping for air, trying to undo the knot of his dark tie even as he realized two things.

One, he was dying.

And two, the ship had become deathly quiet all around him and the sound of the churning engines had stilled.

THIS same sudden absence of noise chilled Captain O'Reilly. His first response was automatic. The fucking engines had broken down, which he'd been expecting to happen for a long time now. But then he realized something else.

Out there, a hundred yards or so from the *Connie*, the ghostly shape of a white yacht had materialized. It showed no lights and O'Reilly had the weird impression there was nobody on board the strange vessel, that it had come up out of the black like some kind of spirit ship bearing the bones of dead sailors. It lay in the darkness in a menacing way, seeming barely to move on the swell. O'Reilly could see no flag, no identifying marks, no name on the bow, no sign of life anywhere. It had appeared out of nowhere, hushed and anonymous. O'Reilly peered into the dark. The vessel looked to him like a sixty-foot diesel yacht, but he couldn't be sure unless the moon broke the cloud cover and gave him enough light so he wouldn't feel like a blind man. There was a knot of tension at the back of his throat.

Be careful, O'Reilly. Be cautious.

He went inside the bridge and opened the gun cabinet, which contained ten pistols and six semiautomatic rifles. He took out one of the semis. He saw the yacht drifting closer, as if whoever manned the damn thing wanted a collision and wouldn't be satisfied with anything less.

He rang the alarm. Within moments he heard the sound of his crewmen scurrying along the deck. Some of them, just wakened from sleep, wore only long thermal underwear. O'Reilly passed out his supply of weapons to the crewmen, urging them to hold their fire unless he gave them a signal. Then he went on watching the movement of the white yacht.

Seventy yards.

Sixty.

The appearance of the yacht might simply be accidental, some hapless nautical tourist veering too close to the *Connie*, a fancy Dan with a white cap and a double-breasted blazer and a fat wife in a bikini, except this wasn't the weather for casual seagoing. You couldn't be certain. O'Reilly had lived a long time with the fear that one of these crossings would end badly, terminated by either British or American authorities or some godless mixture of the two.

It was floating closer.

Fifty yards—

Forty—

O'Reilly narrowed his eyes. Momentarily he thought about the *Mary Celeste*. Maybe this yacht was something like that. An empty vessel. All signs of life inexplicably gone. One of the mysteries of an ocean that already had so many and all of them impenetrable.

Twenty-five yards.

Twenty.

He raised a hand in the air. There was no option now but to open fire. What else could he do, given the importance of the Courier's briefcases and the fear he suddenly felt, which made him so cold to his bones? And what had happened to the bloody engines?

Even before he could lower his hand to order his crew to fire, there was a white blaze of search lights from the yacht. Blinded, O'Reilly turned his face away from the glare.

As he did so, the gunfire began.

It lit up the Atlantic night with the brilliance of a thousand flares, slicing obscenely through the body of the *Connie*, smashing the glass of the bridge, battering the hull—and it went on and on, an indiscriminate kind of firing that seemed to have no end to it, as if whoever fired the guns did so with utter abandon. O'Reilly lay facedown on the floor of the bridge, listening to the air whine above his head. All around him he could hear the moans of those of his crewmen who were still alive. As for the rest, they had been cut down brutally and were in that place where only God or a good undertaker could help them.

O'Reilly, whose only wound was a glass cut in his forehead, lay very still. He was thinking of the Courier now. There was only one reason to attack the *Connie* like this—to steal what the Courier had in his possession. What else was worth taking on this big tub of rust? Madness, bloody madness.

Christ in heaven, how could he help the Courier when he couldn't even help himself? What was he supposed to do? Crawl down from the bridge and smuggle the Courier away in a lifeboat?

The gunfire stopped.

The silence filling the night was deep and complete.

O'Reilly blinked into the harsh white searchlights. He could hardly see the vessel because of the intensity of the lights. But he knew what it was—*a ringer, a viper in swan's feathers, a gunboat disguised as a very expensive pleasure craft.*

He rose to his knees. Here and there, blitzed where they'd come on deck, crewmen lay dead. One or two, wounded beyond medical assistance, crawled like rats across the deck. O'Reilly felt a great sadness for them. He thought about the widows and orphans this fucking yacht had suddenly created, and his sorrow became rage. *The hell with it! The hell with it all!*

He leveled his rifle and was about to spray the white boat with gunfire when he heard a voice from behind and something hard was pushed against the side of his skull.

"I'd be putting the gun away, sir."

O'Reilly turned, saw the young seaman standing behind him.

"Well, now," O'Reilly said. The young man's pistol was pressed directly at his head.

The seaman smiled. "It's all over."

"Houlihan. You double-crossing bastard."

Houlihan said nothing.

O'Reilly put his rifle down. "Do I have time to pray?" His mouth was very dry. Somewhere nearby, one of his crew members screamed out in agony. The awful sound of a man dying. Dear God.

"Of course you do, if you're a praying man," Houlihan answered, and he shot Liam O'Reilly twice in the skull.

HOULIHAN stepped inside the Courier's cabin. The dead man lay beside his bunk. His eyes were wide open and his mouth contorted in an expression of pain. One hand was at his neck and his face was a bright blood red. His legs had been drawn into a fetal position and Darjeeling tea stained his white shirt.

Houlihan bent over the body. He examined the briefcases. Each had a combination lock. He fingered the chain that was shackeled to the dead man's wrist. Then, from a pouch on his hip, Houlihan drew out a long, serrated knife.

He went to work.

T WO

LONDON

Frank Pagan stepped out of his 1982 Camaro and surveyed the dark street of terraced houses. Televisions flickered in windows, throwing out pale-blue lights. Now and again he could see a shadow pass in front of a curtain. It was a grubby street on the fringes of the Hammersmith district of London, and it reminded Pagan of his origins. He'd been born and raised on a street almost exactly like this one, except that in his memory the house where he'd been brought up didn't seem as small and grim as the houses facing him now. Terraces of narrow dwellings. A triumph of working-class architecture.

He closed the door of the car quietly and walked in the direction of number 43 Eagleton Street. He paused once and stared toward the end of the street, where an unmarked car of Scotland Yard's Special Branch was parked. Ostentatious bugger, Pagan thought. Nothing looks so much like a police car as one trying to appear inconspicuous. It was in the vicinity officially to provide what was called "backup," as if its occupants were gunslingers and Pagan an agent of the Wells Fargo Company.

Pagan found 43, a two-story terraced house that had been built in the late 1930s. He walked up the driveway and rapped on the door.

There was a shuffling from inside and the door was opened about two inches. A red face, which had the raw look of a badly peeled potato, appeared in the space.

Pagan stepped forward, shoving the door back briskly. The potato face scowled.

Pagan wandered inside a small living room that smelled of damp. A TV was playing. He switched it off at once, and the room was suddenly black.

"Find a light, Charlie," he said.

Charlie Locklin, in shirt sleeves and gray flannel pants, turned on a lamp. Its base was of yellow ceramic in the form of a mermaid. Pagan sat down, crossing his legs.

Charlie Locklin remained standing. With his TV dead, he looked uncertain about everything, a man who has lost his only map to reality. He shoved his hands inside the pockets of his flannel pants, which were held up by a frayed leather belt.

"We need to talk, Charlie," Pagan said.

"What would I have to say to you?" Charlie Locklin asked in a sullen way. He had a hybrid accent, part Dublin, suffused with some Cockney variations.

"This and that." Pagan gazed round the room. It was crowded with plastic furniture. "Class place, Charlie."

Charlie Locklin appeared wary, as well he might. There were half a dozen hand grenades under the floorboards, and an old Luger, in good working order, concealed beneath some boxes in the attic. Locklin was a stout man with a variety of tattoos on his bare arms. Hearts and flowers and serpents. They had a gangrenous tint, as if they'd been done by a half-blind tattoo artist at some decrepit seaside resort. Pagan had decided long ago that there was something essentially squalid about the Charlie Locklins of this world. They needed squalor to hatch out their violent little schemes the way a fly needs decay for its larvae.

"I don't like you coming here," Locklin said.

"I don't like *being* here, Charlie." Pagan rose, went to the window, parted the drapes. The mean little street with its blue windows winked back at him. About four miles away was Her Majesty's Prison at Wormwood Scrubs, a formidable place. "Blown anything up recently, Charlie? Been playing with any explosives?"

"I don't know what you're talking about, Pagan."

"Last night somebody blew up a car in Mayfair. Nice car. A Jaguar.

Unfortunately, there was a person in it at the time."

Charlie Locklin looked puzzled. "I'm not responsible for that."

There was a silence. Pagan looked at a clock on the mantelpiece. It was of imitation marble, and it had stopped at ten minutes past four. He had the impression that it had ceased working years ago, so that it was always 4:10 in this miserable little house.

"What I want, Charlie, is a little information. I want to pick your brain. Such as it is." A microscope might have been useful, Pagan thought.

Charlie Locklin took a cigarette from a battered pack and lit it, letting Pagan's insult float over his head. "I don't have anything to say to you, Pagan."

"Not very far from where we sit right now there's a jail called the Scrubs. It isn't pleasant, it isn't nice, it isn't even a *safe* place, especially for somebody with your particular political affiliations. The Scrubs wouldn't be beneficial to your health, Charlie boy."

"I know all about your Scrubs," Charlie Locklin said.

"I could throw away the key. Get you off the streets, Charlie. One less arsehole for me to worry about. I'm an inventive kind of man. I could come up with a decent reason. For example, if I was to search your house, Charlie, who knows what I might find? Our judicial system isn't charitable to men like you these days. The British don't think it's sociable for the Irish to be blowing up shops and hotels and planting bombs in cars."

"I've never blown up anything!"

"Come on, Charlie. What about Torquay?"

"What the fuck. All I had was some gelignite. I never used it. I was holding it for a friend."

"Charlie, when a known sympathizer of the IRA is found skulking down a basement in a slum in Torquay with nineteen pounds of gelignite on his person, it's a pretty fair deduction that he's not planning some simple weekend gardening. And when you add the fact that our beloved Prime Minister was in Torquay at the same time, well, it doesn't look like you're going in for a little sunbathing, does it?" Pagan took his hands out of his raincoat pockets and looked at them. They were big and blunt, like a couple of hammers. He had inherited his father's hands, a bricklayer's hands.

Charlie Locklin sat down on the arm of a sofa and peered at Frank Pagan through cigarette smoke. "I was holding the jelly for a friend."

"Sure you were."

"I could get a knee job for talking to you," Locklin said.

"Nobody's going to shoot your knees off, Charlie. We talk. I leave. It's dark outside. Who's going to know I've ever been here?" Pagan found himself wishing that Charlie Locklin *would* get his knees shot off because it would be one less scum to deal with, and that's what Locklin was as far as Pagan was concerned. *Scum.*

Charlie Locklin tossed his cigarette into the fireplace and watched it smolder. Then he looked at the useless clock on the mantelpiece. Pagan stirred in his seat. Whenever he plunged into the maze of Irish terrorism, he had the sensation of being locked within a labyrinth of mirrors. Images came at you, then receded. Truths were distorted, lies enlarged. And what you were left with at the end was a handful of broken glass, like something out of a child's ruined kaleidoscope.

"Let me throw you a name, Charlie."

"I'm listening."

"Jig." Pagan pronounced the word slowly.

Charlie Locklin smiled. "If you've come here to talk about Jig, you'd be a damn sight better off talking about the bloody wind. Jig! He's a fucking mystery."

"I know he's a mystery, Charlie. Point is, what do you know?"

"Nothing. Not a thing." Locklin laughed, as if the very idea of anyone knowing the *real* identity of Jig was too much of a joke to bear. Jig had all the reality of an Irish mist or one of those mythical figures of Celtic prehistory, like Cuchulain.

Pagan rose. "Give me a name, Charlie. Tell me the name of somebody who might know something."

"You're daft, Pagan. You know that? You come in here and you ask daft questions."

"Who's likely to know, Charlie? *Give me a name.*" Pagan leaned forward, pressing his face close to that of the Irishman. He had a way of making his jaw jut and the small veins in his temples bulge that changed his entire appearance. He could look dangerous and rough-edged, and when he rubbed his big hands together as he was doing now they appeared to Charlie Locklin like two flesh-colored mallets.

Charlie Locklin stepped away. "It's a closed shop."

"A closed shop, Charlie? Are you telling me that the Irish are capable of keeping secrets? You don't expect me to believe that, do you?"

"It's the gospel. I swear it—"

"Don't give me saints and your dear dead mother. I can't stand all that Irish sentimentality shit. I want Jig. And somebody must know where I can find him. Jesus Christ, he can't operate the way he does without some kind of support system. There's got to be *somebody*, Charlie." Did Pagan hear a tiny note of despair in his own voice just then? Or was it merely fatigue? He hadn't slept in twenty-four hours.

Charlie Locklin shook his head. "I'm not your man, Mr. Pagan."

Mister, Pagan thought. When Charlie Locklin called him Mister, it was almost certain he was being sincere. Pagan shoved his hands back into his pockets. He stared a moment at the mermaid table lamp. It struck him that it would be more plausible to locate a live mermaid in Hammersmith than a mysterious Irish terrorist who was known only as Jig, a shadowy figure forever on the farthest edges of his vision. Pagan sighed.

Last night in Mayfair, Jig had blown up a Jaguar driven by Walter Whiteford, the British ambassador to Ireland. Pagan recalled the debris, the broken glass, the shards of metal that had been scattered halfway down South Audley Street. But mainly it was Whiteford's head he remembered. It had been found lying twenty-five feet from the rest of his torso. How would you describe that look on the decapitated face? Surprise? Astonishment? Maybe it was disappointment for a career that had ended abruptly. Whiteford was going to be the new ambassador to the Republic of Ireland. He hadn't even started the job although he'd given press conferences during which he'd expressed his desire to see the death penalty brought back for Irish hoodlums who committed acts of terrorism. This had clearly endeared him to Jig, Pagan thought. Foolhardy man with a big mouth. Well, Walter wasn't shooting his mouth off anymore.

Pagan moved toward the door. The weariness he felt had a cutting edge to it. He wanted to get out of this dreary little house and into the cold street, where the wind might blow away all the cobwebs in his brain.

Charlie Locklin followed him to the door. "I swear to God, it's a closed shop," he said.

"I heard you the first time, Charlie." Pagan raised one finger in the air, a menacing little gesture. He flicked it beneath Charlie Locklin's nose. "If I ever find you've been lying to me, I'll have your Irish arse inside the Scrubs in quicker time than it takes you to fart. You understand me, Charlie?"

Locklin moved back from the wagging finger. "I swear, Mr. Pagan. None of the boys have ever known anything like it. I mean, usually you hear something. Some little thing, at least. But you don't even hear a *whisper* about this Jig. And that's the truth."

Pagan nodded. He was out in the darkened driveway now.

"Just remember," he said. "You hear anything, you call me. If you don't . . ."

He let the threat dangle in the night air. Threats were always more pointed when you didn't spell them out. He walked in the direction of his Camaro. The American car, parked among small British Fords and Hillmans, looked totally out of place in this narrow street. American cars were one of Pagan's weaknesses. He liked their style, their flash.

He turned back once when he reached the car, seeing the TV already flickering in the window of Charlie Locklin's living room. He had the intense urge to stride back to the house and put his fist through something. The TV, maybe. Or Charlie Locklin's skull.

He opened the door of the car and climbed in behind the wheel. He gunned the Camaro through the streets, aware of the car from Scotland Yard following him at a distance. He reached the M-4 motorway and slammed his foot down on the gas pedal, watching the speed rise. When he had the Camaro up to ninety he took a cassette tape from the glove compartment and punched it into the deck. Then he rolled the window down and cold air blasted his face. He was cutting across lanes, leaving gutless British sedans trailing behind him, honking their horns at the madman in the Yankee gas guzzler.

It was the only way to travel. He looked in the rearview mirror. He couldn't see the car from Scotland Yard but he knew it had to be somewhere at his back. The signs that said HEATHROW flashed past in a blur. Office buildings became streaks of dying light. A hundred. A hundred and five. The Camaro vibrated. The music filled the car at maximum volume.

Come on over, baby, whole lotta shakin' goin' on . . .

They didn't make rock and roll like this anymore. Now it was all pretension and posturing boys in makeup. It was a yawn these days.

Pagan beat his hands on the steering wheel.

I said now come on over, baby, we really got
the bull by the horn

"I ain't fakin'," Pagan sang at the top of his voice. One hundred and ten. The reality of speed. Everything was focused. Everything was crystal and hard. Speed and loud music and the wind making your face smart. *"There's a whole lotta shakin' goin' on!"*

He saw the flashing lights behind him. He smiled, drove the pedal as far to the floor as it would go, took the Camaro up to one hundred and fifteen, teased the Special Branch car a few miles more. This is it. This is the way to squash old pains. Let the poison drain out of your system at one hundred and twenty miles an hour with the Killer drowning all your thoughts.

He released the pedal. He pulled the car onto the shoulder and waited. The Rover from Scotland Yard drew in behind him. Pagan shut the music off, closed his eyes. The man from Special Branch was called Downey. He wore a soft felt hat, the brim of which he pulled down over his forehead. He had a waxed moustache and his breath smelled of spearmint. He stuck his head in the window of the Camaro and said, "Frank, for Christ's sake, why do you keep doing this?"

Pagan looked at the policeman, grinned. "Therapy, my old dear."

Downey shook his head. "You been drinking, Frank?"

Pagan blew into the man's face. "What do you think?"

"This is the third time in the last ten days," Downey said. "One day, you'll kill yourself. Bound to happen. Is that what you want, Frank?"

"Can I count on you, Downey?"

"Count on me for what?"

"To be a pallbearer. To bear my pall. You'd look good in black."

Downey stepped away from the Camaro. He said, "Funerals depress me. Yours might be different. Might be uplifting."

"Wall to wall merriment," Pagan said. "Would be quite a ceremony. Everybody from Scotland Yard would turn out and cheer."

"Right," Downey said.

Pagan smiled. He slid the Camaro forward a couple of yards, then stuck his head out of the window and looked back at Downey. "You been eating scrambled eggs, Downey?"

"Scrambled eggs?"

"You got some stuck in your wax there."

Downey's hand shot to his upper lip. He felt nothing. "Fuck off, Frank," he said.

But Pagan was already gone.

FRANK Pagan's office overlooked Golden Square on the edge of Soho. It was an impersonal place, filled with chrome-and-leather furniture. At night—and it was ten o'clock by the time he got there— you could catch a thin glimpse of the lights of Piccadilly, that garish heart of London.

Pagan had visited countless houses similar to Charlie Locklin's during the past twenty-four hours. He had talked with scores of people exactly like Charlie in Irish enclaves throughout London, such as Kilburn and Cricklewood and Chalk Farm, known IRA sympathizers and those with affiliations to that nebulous terrorist network. He'd talked with criminals who'd done time for bombings and other acts of what Pagan considered thuggery. He hadn't turned up anything on Jig. He hadn't expected to. What he'd encountered was a solid wall of silence and ignorance. Everybody had *heard* of Jig, of course, because the bloody man was notorious and his name was in all the tabloids, but nobody *knew* anything about him. Even those journalists who had written with sneaking respect for Jig's bravado, and who had sometimes seemed even to *glorify* the man in bold headlines, had never been able to uncover anything. It was as if Jig existed in a place far beyond the scope of all their investigative techniques, a place beyond probing, a fact that made him even more of a hero in certain quarters of Fleet Street. His name was mentioned often, in a tone that was almost reverent, in the wine bars and pubs of the newspaper district. Jig had become more than a terrorist. He was a star, the brightest entity in the whole constellation of terrorists. There were even some who thought the assassination of Walter Whiteford—an unpopular man with unpopular right-wing views—a justifiable act on a level with mercy killing. This prominence Jig enjoyed reflected badly on Pagan's section. That Jig could vanish after his killings without so much as a trace made Pagan feel useless— and yet at the same time all the more determined to catch the man.

Pagan had moments when he wondered if Jig actually existed. Then he'd think it all through again and he'd be struck by the fact that the acts of terrorism perpetrated by Jig were different in sheer quality from random bombings of hotels and busy stores and crowded streets—and he realized there was something about this character Jig he actually *admired*, albeit in the most grudging way. The man *never* did anything that would harm an innocent bystander. The man was *always* careful to select his victim and the proper circumstances, when there was nobody else around to be harmed by an explosive device or a badly aimed shot. It was a kind of tact, Pagan thought, a strange form of charity at the heart of violence.

Pagan peered down toward Piccadilly Circus now. Jig was almost an artist. It was as if he were signing his violent portraits, as if he were saying how unlike the regular IRA rabble he was, underlining a difference between himself and all the rest, those butchers who gave no thought to children and women and anybody else who just happened to get caught accidentally in the crossfire. It was a crude war, but Jig gave it his own civilized flourish.

For a second, Pagan thought about his boyhood, when he'd spent a couple of summers with his grandparents in County Cork. He'd developed a great fondness for the Irish and a sympathy for their plight as inhabitants of one of the most troubled countries in Europe, but he'd never seen a solution to their problems in the violence of the Irish Republican Army. He couldn't even imagine a situation in which the South, free of British sovereignty since 1921, would be reunited with the North. The Irish were a fractured people, polarized by religions, distanced by bigotries, and hammered to the cross of their history, which had given up more martyrs than there were holy saints in Rome.

Pagan moved away from the window. He turned his thoughts again to Jig and the sight of what was left of Walter Whiteford on South Audley Street. When Jig had first entered Pagan's lexicon of terrorism, it had been with the murder in 1982 of Lord Drumcannon, an old judge with a known hatred of the IRA and a propensity to sentence its members to long prison terms. Drumcannon had been shot once through the head by a sniper while walking his beagles on his country estate at Chiddingly in Sussex. The body, surrounded by yapping dogs, had been found by a gamekeeper. There was a solitary bullet hole in the center of the skull. One shot, which was all Jig ever seemed to need.

The next victim had been George Connaught, Member of Parliament for a district in Northern Ireland. Connaught was a hardline Protestant, the kind who thrived on the conflict between religious parties. He had been gunned down—and this was an example of Jig's talent, his daring, Pagan thought—in broad daylight in Westminster in the spring of 1983. The MP, who revered Queen and Country as if they were twin mistresses he kept in the same apartment, had been walking back to the House of Commons after lunch at his club. One shot had been fired from a passing car, piercing Connaught's heart.

And then sir Edward Shackleton, chief of the Royal Ulster Constabulary, a man of known paranoia concerning his personal safety, had been blown up in his bed in suburban Belfast one night by means of a high-tech explosive device triggered long distance, a sophisticated piece of equipment which, according to Pagan's analysts, had been manufactured in East Germany.

The list was growing long and it was going to grow longer still.

Frank Pagan shut his eyes. He thought about the phone calls after the killings. The taped voice. The accent seemed almost impossible to place, even though some of the best experts in dialects had analyzed it over and over.

This is Jig. I have just killed Walter Whiteford in the name of freedom for the people of Ireland. I am not finished yet. I have a long way to go. . . .

It was always that simple, always that deadly, the same dry, terrifying delivery. Pagan had listened to the tapes a hundred times. He had listened to the words and the silences between them, the quick intakes of breath, the pauses, as if he might one day be capable of imagining the man's face on the basis of his voice alone. The voice had sometimes even intruded on his dreams, where it echoed and reverberated like the sound of a man whispering in a large empty cathedral.

The door of his office opened and he looked up to see Foxworth there.

Robbie Foxworth—Foxie—was Pagan's assistant, a young man with a scalp of bright red hair, which gave some substance to his nickname. Foxie had been to Eton and Cambridge, and he talked with ball bearings in his mouth. What Pagan didn't know about Foxie was that the young man did a wicked impersonation of him at parties, right down to the South London accent and the way Pagan walked—his back straight and his long legs taking great strides. Foxie called this the Pagan Strut.

"Burning the old midnight oil?" Pagan asked.

Foxie smiled. He had one of those sly little smiles you can never quite recall later with any certainty. He sat down in the chair that faced Pagan. He had been with Pagan's section, which dealt exclusively with terrorism (Irish, or related thereto), for about eighteen months. On paper this section was supposed to work with Scotland Yard's Special Branch, but Pagan had eased his own people out from under the men at the Yard, whom he publicly called "good civil servants" and privately "all-round arseholes."

Consequently, the section operated with considerable freedom, answerable only to the Secretary whose office was responsible for Irish affairs. Foxie was related to the Secretary in a minor way—a fifteenth cousin three times removed, or something equally far-fetched that Pagan had trouble remembering. (The English were obsessed with bloodlines, to a point that lay somewhere off the coast of reason.)

Foxie said, "I have an item of some interest, Frank."

Pagan saw a slip of telex paper come across the desk toward him. He picked it up, scanned it, then read it a second time more slowly. He put the telex down and tipped his chair back. "Well, well," he said quietly.

Foxie gazed at his superior. There were moments when he thought Frank Pagan represented a triumph of incongruity. Pagan didn't *talk* the way anyone else in the section did because he hadn't been to an expensive public school. Pagan didn't *dress* like his colleagues either. He dispensed with three-piece pinstripe suits in favor of trendy loose-fitting clothes that seemed to have been purchased off the rack in secondhand stores, where they might have been hanging since the middle of the 1950s. Now and then Pagan even wore Hawaiian shirts that lit up a room like a light bulb. An odd bird, Foxie thought, with his tennis shoes and blue jeans and his jazzy American car.

Foxie sat back in his chair. He remembered there had been that awful business about Pagan's wife a few years ago. Foxie had no way of knowing how *that* might have affected his superior, but colleagues who had been with the section since its formation in 1979 whispered that Pagan had gone through a period of heavy drinking, which was understandable in the terrible circumstances.

"Somebody's been very busy," Pagan said.

"Do you think the Americans were behind it?"

"Does it sound like an American operation to you, Foxie?"

Foxie shrugged. "Who else could have done it?" He saw Pagan get up and walk to the window. In a certain light Frank Pagan looked younger than thirty-nine. It was only when you got up close you noticed the thin lines around his eyes and mouth. There were glints of gray in his short dark hair, which he wore brushed back across his head.

"I can't see them doing this kind of barbarism," Pagan said. "I can see the Yanks seizing the ship, but I can't see them getting this carried away."

"They sometimes get a little . . . overzealous," Foxie said. "Our cousins *are* fond of a little bloodletting, Frank. They think it's good for the soul."

Pagan stared at the telex. The *Connie O'Mara* had been found drifting in the North Atlantic by a Norwegian freighter, the *Trondheim*. Thirteen bodies had been discovered on board, eleven of them dead from gunshot wounds, one with a crushed skull, the other killed by means that hadn't yet been established. The *Connie* had been towed to New York City where U.S. Coast Guard officials and cops from the New York City Police Department had examined the carnage before calling in the FBI.

The telex, which was a duplicate, had been sent by the FBI to the Special Branch at Scotland Yard because the vessel was suspected of having had a longtime connection with the IRA. The FBI rather cheerfully considered Irish terrorism strictly a British problem. The *Connie* had been in Pagan's own computerized records for the last year or so and presumably in FBI records for at least that long because computers, which Pagan imbued with a malice of their own, had an uncanny way of tapping into one another's data banks. A lack of manpower for surveillance, and the vastness of the Atlantic Ocean, had contributed to the fact that the *Connie* hadn't been high on Pagan's list of priorities.

"I thought pirates had gone out of fashion," Pagan said. "We've got somebody out there doing a Long John Silver routine."

"If it wasn't us and it wasn't the Americans, Frank, who was it?"

Pagan touched his eyelids with his fingertips. The violent fate of one small boat, which might or might not have been ferrying arms to Ireland, didn't excite him. What he kept coming back to was the idea of catching Jig, and he couldn't see any kind of connection between the *Connie O'Mara* and the elusive killer. At some other time, maybe, the piracy might have intrigued him more than it did, but not now. Besides, whoever had hijacked the *Connie* had done Pagan's section a favor. It was one less problem, in the whole morass of Irish affairs, to worry about. He was under pressure from the press, the Secretary, and the public to put Jig out of business. So what did one small ship matter when you were working like hell to keep from buckling beneath the weight of clamorous demands?

He tossed the telex down. "Let Special Branch worry about it,

Foxie. Let them have this one. The commissioner used to be in the navy. He'd relish a mystery with a nautical flavor."

Foxie looked a little disappointed. He had expected a more enthusiastic reaction to the telex. He picked the piece of paper from Pagan's desk and said, "I adore that gruesome touch at the end, don't you?"

"Appeals to your darker side, does it, Foxie?"

"It does," Foxie said, grinning. "I mean, what's the point in hacking off a fellow's hand?"

Pagan was quiet for a moment. He was thinking of going home. He was thinking of sleep. The empty apartment. The hollows of his life.

"Presumably because something was attached to his wrist," Pagan answered, pressing a hand to his mouth to cover a yawn.

ENGLISH-WELSH BORDER

On the rare occasions when he drank, the man known as Jig preferred Jameson's Irish Whiskey. In the empty buffet car of the train that carried him from London to Holyhead in Wales—where he would take the ferry across the Irish Sea to Dublin—he sipped the whiskey slowly, occasionally swirling it around on the surface of his tongue. He looked the length of the car, conscious of his solitude.

He set his glass down on the table and the liquid shivered to the rhythms of the locomotive. He stared from the window at the darkness of the English countryside. The platforms of small stations whisked past as the train hammered through the night. Some of them, he noticed, were no longer in operation. They'd been closed down and boarded up, economy measures taken by an English government that nevertheless always seemed to have the means of funding a standing army in Northern Ireland.

He shut his eyes. He realized he wanted a cigarette, but he'd given up smoking several weeks ago although the desire was always there. It was a matter of will to deny yourself. And he had become accustomed to a life of such denials, a life lived in doorways and the dank rooms of cheap hotels, a life of watching and waiting, surrounded by shadows. It was an existence lived at one remove from yourself, as though you were nothing more than a transient in your own body.

He looked from the window again. He wouldn't sleep until he

was safely back in Dublin, even though he understood he wasn't ever safe anywhere these days. From his canvas bag he took out a copy of *The Daily Express* and saw the headline.

JIG'S DANCE OF DEATH

He turned to the inside pages. There was a shrill editorial about the inadequacy of British security forces. The writer posed the question: *Are we utterly incapable of catching this monster? Are we always to be victims of vicious Irish terrorism?*

A monster, Jig thought. He never thought of himself as either monster or terrorist. These were threadbare labels applied by the enemy, terms intended to elicit revulsion and horror from the British public and to obscure the real issue which, in Jig's mind at least, was that of a people fighting for the right of national unity, without British intervention.

There was a terse comment from an official called Frank Pagan, who was apparently in charge of the office conducting the investigation into the murder of Walter Whiteford. It said: *Every possible line of inquiry is being pursued.* Nothing else.

Jig tossed the paper aside. Every possible line of inquiry, he thought. It was the standard comment of any bewildered official. What did it actually mean? He wondered about this Pagan a moment. He imagined a tight-lipped humorless man, a somber bureaucrat who wore dark suits and overcoats. A man of plodding technique. Maybe he wasn't that way at all. Maybe he had moments of inspiration, little hunches he played now and again. It was interesting to know your adversary's name. It was like being one small point ahead in the game.

He rose from his seat, stepping out into the corridor of the car. Through open windows a cold night wind rushed against him and he shivered, drawing the collar of his unremarkable gray coat up against his face. He thought of Finn sitting inside the house in Dun Laoghaire, and he had a mental image of the gaunt old man smiling as he read about the death of Ambassador Whiteford in *The Irish Times.* Finn never showed any excitement when a mission was successfully accomplished. *You're a professional, boy,* he'd once said. *And professionals don't expect praise for success. Only criticism for failure.* Finn had other ways, quiet ways, of expressing his pleasure. A quick soldierly hug, a couple of glasses of the wretched peppermint schnapps he seemed to adore—often to his detriment—and a bright youthful light in his blue eyes, which belied his age and the exhausting years he'd given to a struggle that at times seemed endless.

Jig removed a thin thread from the lapel of his coat and let it drift out of the window into the darkness. Then he turned to look along the corridor, past the doorways of compartments lit by thin yellow-brown light bulbs. Three policemen, two in uniform and one dressed in a bulky gabardine raincoat, appeared at the end of the corridor. Jig watched them peer inside empty compartments as they approached him. The plainclothesman was enormous, his head almost reaching the ceiling. He had the smallest mouth Jig had ever seen on a human being. The two uniformed cops were ridiculously young, their bland faces covered with adolescent fuzz. Jig looked out through the open window just as the train plunged into a tunnel and the wheels roared in a deafening way and the carriages clacked and echoed. He had known that sooner or later cops would board the train, just as they would be swarming airports and seaports in the wake of Walter Whiteford's death.

The plainclothes policeman was clumsily polite and spoke with a Welsh accent, a kind of dull singsong. "Do you have any papers, sir?" he asked.

"Papers?" Jig asked.

"Passport. Identification. Anything like that."

The train came out of the tunnel and there was a slender crescent of moon in the black sky. "Are you looking for somebody in particular?" Jig asked. He opened his canvas bag and rummaged around inside. He felt no tension, no sense of danger. Whatever anxiety he might have experienced at the fear of discovery he kept under control. Any such feeling would have been irrational. The cops didn't know what he looked like, they had no description of him. They were operating in total darkness.

The plainclothesman looked into Jig's face. "You read the newspapers, sir?"

"Now and again."

"Then you'll have read about Whiteford, I expect."

Jig, who enjoyed this part of the game, who liked the sport of coming close to his pursuers, feigned a look of surprise. "You're looking for Jig?" he asked.

The cop nodded. He uttered a weary sigh. The two uniformed

officers, who might have been hatched out of the same pod, were staring at Jig's bag as if they expected it to contain bombs or grenades. Young and nervous and raw.

"I hope you find him," Jig said, removing a passport from his bag and handing it to the plainclothes cop.

The cop took the passport, which had been issued by the Republic of Ireland, and leafed through it. He glanced at the photograph, then at Jig's face before handing the document back. "You live in Dublin?"

Jig nodded.

"What kind of work do you do, Mr. Doyle?" he asked.

Jig took a small wooden toy out of his bag. It was a miniature rocking horse, immaculately carved, finely detailed. He watched the policeman take it and examine it.

"I sell toys," Jig said.

"Very pretty," the cop said.

"Danish. Sturdy. Won't break easily."

The policeman returned the miniature to Jig, who placed it back inside the bag.

"Thanks for your time," the policeman said.

"No problem, Officer."

Jig watched the three cops continue along the corridor. He wanted to call out to them. He wanted to tell them that he wished them luck in their hunt and that Jig was the kind of bastard who gave decent Irishmen a bad name and deserved the hangman's rope, but he restrained himself. Playing the game with them was one thing, but drawing attention to yourself was another. If they remembered anything about him later they'd mainly remember the small wooden horse, not his face nor how he was dressed nor the way he spoke. He saw them disappear through the door at the end of the corridor, and then he was alone again.

He caught a faint reflection of himself in glass and he had the thought that if he were to die now of some sudden ailment the only identification in his possession would be that of a certain John Doyle, commercial traveler in wooden toys imported from Scandinavia. His bag would yield up nothing more sinister than samples of his line— a small toy drummer, the miniature horse, a puppet tangled up in its own strings.

Of anyone called Jig, there would be absolutely no trace at all.

T HREE

Former United States Senator Harry Cairney stood at the window of his second-floor library, a room lined with books and filled with dark antique furniture that reflected everything with the accuracy of mirrors. He watched the helicopter come into view over the slate-colored waters of Roscommon Lake. There were four men in the chopper, three who had come to Roscommon to meet with Cairney, and a pilot who would unload his human cargo and fly promptly away, counting his improbably high fee and forgetting anything he ever knew about his passengers and their destination. Amnesia, Cairney thought, did not come cheaply.

The senator stared past the chopper now, out beyond the far shores of the lake where the trees were deep and secretive in the snow. When he had purchased this estate in 1958, it had been nine hundred acres of jungle and a rundown Victorian mansion owned by a senile German brewer who, in his madness, traveled the world collecting broken nude statues, most of them missing limbs and noses and, in extreme cases, their entire heads. The old German had been proud of his huge collection. *They remind me, Senator Cairney,* the brewer had said at the time of escrow, *of human infirmity.*

Cairney, forty-eight at the time, lacked any desire to be reminded of anything so undignified as human infirmity. He had removed the statues, renovated the big house, redesigned the gardens, and stocked the lake—known then as Lake Arthur—with rainbow trout and bass. Then he had renamed the property Roscommon, after the castle built in 1280 in Ireland by Robert de Ufford, although there were still old-timers in the nearby town of Rhinebeck who referred to the estate as Old Franz's place, Brewmeister Palace. Nine hundred acres of prime Dutchess County real estate—a mere ninety minutes up the leafy Taconic Parkway from Manhattan—surrounded by dense trees and rectangles of meadowland. A safe retreat from the problems of the world, except that the world had a tiresome tendency to intrude on the senator's sense of security.

He watched the chopper land slowly on the vast front lawn. Bare rosebushes shook from the power of the big whirring blades. Clouds, weighted with more snow, floated away over the lake. The senator watched three men get out of the chopper and saw them scurry beneath the beating blades in the direction of the house. He thought for a second of the telephone call he had received only some eight hours before from Ireland. He was going to have to convey the message to his visitors, an unpleasant prospect. But the whole thing was unpleasant, a calamity of enormous proportions. He caught his breath and heard a wheezing sound in the depths of his chest. Lately, he'd begun to experience human frailty for himself—waking in the night, struggling for oxygen, feeling himself skirt the edges of a panic, like a man who looks down from a great height to see below him the abyss of death.

He was reluctant to move from the window. The stereo, which he had built into the study walls, was playing one of his favorite records, John McCormack singing "The Rose of Tralee." He never tired of listening to it because it reminded him of his first wife, Kathleen, who had died some seventeen years before.

> She was lovely and fair as the rose of the summer,
> Yet 'twas not her beauty alone that won me. . . .

Harry Cairney closed his eyes a moment. It seemed to him that McCormack's voice on this old recording came from a place beyond the grave. He sighed, turning from the window, crossing the floor to the landing. Voices drifted up from below. He could hear Mulhaney over everyone else, because that was the big man's style, loud and blustery and forever dying to be heard. A little dizzy, Cairney looked down the long staircase. He was filled with dread. The meeting was necessary: no, more than that—it was urgent. But he didn't have the heart for it anymore. It was odd how age sucked the guts out of you, strange the way it eroded your fighting spirit. Age took away and, like some terrible miser, seemed to give nothing back. Not even wisdom. Not even that small consolation. Membership in the Fund-raisers, he reflected, was definitely a young man's game.

He moved to the stairs.

"Darling?"

Celestine stood in the door of the bedroom. Her beauty affected him as it always did. It made his heart roar inside his chest and chased his blood pressure up a ladder, and he wasn't old Harry Cairney anymore, he wasn't the retired senator from New York, he was a giddy young man enchanted by love, blinded by his own desires. *Celestine, his wife.* She had her yellow hair pulled back tight the way she sometimes wore it and it gave her beauty a rather gaunt quality, almost stark, as if her soul were laid bare. Her blue eyes were filled with all the electricity that might ever have been issued by lightning and trapped in conductors. Harry Cairney thanked the God in whom he'd lately come to believe for sending Celestine to him at this stage of his life.

And—wonder of wonders!—it was no classic case of a young woman marrying an old man for his money and esteem, no thirty-five-year-old fortune hunter, a power groupie, marrying a former United States senator for whatever cachet this might bestow upon her. She had married Harry Cairney the *man*, not the politician who had been part of the Kennedy inner circle and who'd known every major figure that had moved across the stage of the times and who'd had his picture taken with Jack and Lyndon and De Gaulle and Willy Brandt and Harold Macmillan and Eamon de Valera. It was, Harry Cairney thought, a miracle in a time when miracles were rare as unicorns. And this miracle was that Celestine, who might have been nothing more than a paid companion in the winter of his life, a mercenary, actually loved him. She *loved* him even in his age and frailty, and she drove him to moments of desire that would have been indecent in a much younger man.

"Do you have to meet these people?" she asked, and there was concern in the blue eyes that subtly altered their color, darkening the shade of cobalt to something no rainbow could ever register.

"Yes," the senator said. "I have to."

"Who are they anyhow?"

"Business associates." He smiled at his wife.

Celestine wore nothing more fancy than blue jeans and a plaid shirt, but she would have looked astonishingly lovely in an A & P grocery bag. She came across the hallway and laid her hand on his arm. "I don't want you to overdo it," she said. She pressed her mouth against the side of his face. Harry Cairney, who came alive whenever his wife touched him, patted her carefully on the cheek.

"I won't overdo anything. I promise," he said.

"Be sure," she said. "I love you."

Cairney moved away from his young wife reluctantly and began to go down the stairs where, around the long oval table in the dining room, the three men who had come to Roscommon by helicopter were already drinking shots of brandy poured from a crystal decanter.

MULHANEY, his face the color of a radish, was already on his second brandy when Harry Cairney stepped into the dining room. Mulhaney, who was a big man with enormous hands, crowded a room somehow, filling more space and sucking in more air than an individual had a right to. Harry Cairney moved to his place at the end of the oval table and sat down, smiling briefly at Mulhaney and then looking at the faces of the other men. Only young Kevin Dawson stood up at Cairney's entrance as a gesture of respect. God bless you, Kevin, the senator thought.

At the age of thirty-seven, Kevin Dawson had a sense of what Cairney considered decency. He was a conciliatory person, someone who seemed forever anxious not to give offense. *Nice* was a word that came to Cairney's mind. Kevin's brother Thomas, known to his political enemies as Grinning Tommy, was the President of the United States. Cairney often wondered if Kevin Dawson's membership in the Fund-raisers was the young man's way of compensating for the fact that his brother occupied the White House, as if Kevin were carving out his own special territory where his imposing brother couldn't and wouldn't go.

The other man in the room, Nicholas Linney, barely glanced at Cairney as he sat down. Linney was a man of the New Age, happy with spreadsheets and computerized data and satisfied, in a way that was almost sexual, with vast networks of interconnected intelligence. Linney's face had a peculiar hue, something like the color of an unroasted coffee bean. Maybe, the senator reflected, it came from staring at small green letters on screens all the day long. But there was a sense of controlled violence about Linney, hidden pressures. Harry Cairney always had the feeling that Linney would gladly have blown up his computers and torched his spreadsheets for a chance to go out into the direct line of battle. He could imagine Nick Linney skulking the alleys of Belfast with a rifle stuck underneath his overcoat and hatred for British soldiers in his heart. He was, in fact, a gun freak, and it was rumored that he took himself off to isolated beaches with his firearms and shot round after round into watermelons or pumpkins or any kind of fruit or vegetable that suggested, however remotely, a human skull.

"Gentlemen," Cairney said when he was seated. There was a breathless quality to his voice, the result of the simple act of coming down a flight of stairs. He felt as if his lungs were dried out and useless, withered inside his chest like two prunes.

The three men watched him now, each seemingly wary of what he might have to say. He clasped his hands on the table. "Big Jock" Mulhaney, as the press always called the man who led and allegedly mismanaged a branch of the most powerful trade union in the United States, puffed his lips out like a bloated goldfish and remarked, "Let's get down to it, Senator. Let's get down to the brass tacks. Let's just cut the fucking gentlemen shit."

The former senator winced. Mulhaney had been born with a talent for gracelessness, the way some people are cursed with muscular dystrophy.

Harry Cairney looked down at the polished surface of the table. He was aware of the sound of his young wife moving in the room immediately above.

"We've been ripped off," Mulhaney said. "Why don't we boil it down to that? We've been shafted."

"As you say," Harry Cairney agreed. "We've been shafted."

"So the only question is who the fuck did it," Mulhaney said.

There was a quietness in the room now, as if all sound had seeped out through a crack in the wall. Harry Cairney recognized what lay under the silence—there was mistrust, a sense of treachery, a certain lopsided tension that went back and forth among the four men in the room. This animus was sharp and cutting and fearful. The Fund-raisers had been contaminated. The suspicion in the room was as tangible as the presence of an uninvited guest.

Linney opened a folder and said, "The total loss is ten point two million dollars in used currency and negotiable bonds."

"I don't think figures are in dispute," Cairney said, and his voice was feeble.

"Damned right they're not in dispute," Mulhaney said. For a second he grinned his most charming grin, the one he always used when he walked in the vanguard of the St. Patrick's Day Parade on Fifth Avenue, his green sash across his big broad chest and his lips faintly green from the dye neighborhood bars introduced into their beers. "What we've got to consider here, friends, is a matter of betrayal."

Harry Cairney rubbed his eyes. "You don't imagine that somebody in this room is responsible for the piracy?" This idea shook him, but it was a possibility he knew he had to face even if the notion of a traitor in the ranks was a blasphemy. But if it hadn't been one of the Fund-raisers, then who the hell *had* taken the money? His eyes moved from one man to the next around the table, but what could he possibly tell from their faces? Mulhaney's accusative look, Dawson's tentative expression, Nick Linney's tightly drawn lips—appearances could hide almost anything.

Mulhaney ran a fingertip around the rim of his brandy glass. "There are four of us in this goddam room, and each one of us knew the destination of the ship as well as the route and the cargo she charried." The big man paused. "The conclusion's goddam obvious."

"We can't assume that one of us is responsible," Kevin Dawson said in his high-pitched voice. It was a voice that would keep Dawson out of public politics because it didn't fill a room and it couldn't be used to project anything solemn. Whenever he grew excited, he could sound like a man on helium gas. "I don't see any justification for that."

"Don't you now?" Mulhaney, who had always disliked anything to do with the Dawsons and resented what he thought of as Kevin Dawson's privileged world—old Connecticut money, the fucking landed gentry with all its feudal powers, big brother in the White House—was adopting one of his characteristic attitudes, a certain snide belligerence. "Do you have a better suggestion, Dawson?"

Kevin Dawson answered in a patient way. "I don't see any merit in leaping to conclusions, Jock. That's all."

"Conclusions," Mulhaney snorted. He had a habit of forcing words out through his nasal passages. "You're a fence-sitter, Dawson. You're never happy unless you're politely perched on some fucking fence."

Dawson tilted his chair back, said nothing.

Again silence. Cairney stared through the window at the waters of Roscommon Lake. He thought of a small dark ship gunned on the high seas. Blood on the waters. For too many years now, back as far as the old days of the Clan-na-Gael in Philadelphia and the Irish Republican Brotherhood, back as far as the times when the Cause had been glad to receive a few Thompson submachine guns and several thousand cartridges in the 1930s from their American sympathizers, he'd been promoting the Cause and raising funds secretively and nothing was more demanding, more exhausting, than secrecy, a darkly brooding mistress. Even Celestine, and Kathleen before her, had no idea about Cairney's activities.

He had first come to this country as a bright young man of eighteen in the spring of 1928 from Dublin, yet he'd never really left his homeland entirely, nor had he ever forgotten the Troubles that divided and ruptured his country. He might talk with an American accent and have served as a public figure during several administrations in Washington, but his heart was still through and through Irish. Now, as he looked at the faces of the men in the room and imagined the small dark ship machine-gunned, he realized that all he truly wanted was peace and privacy and a chance to spend his last years uninterrupted by the demands of the Cause. He wanted to spend this precious time with Celestine and nobody else. If the Fund-raisers were to continue, they would have to go on without him. But this wasn't the time to announce his retirement.

"Can the money be replaced?" he asked. He was trying to steer the meeting into less troubled areas. A little diplomatic sleight of hand, which he knew would be futile.

"Not through my sources," Linney said. "They're not going to be happy to invest again in the present circumstances. Besides, they're tightening the purse-strings these days."

Cairney knew that the millions of dollars that flowed through Linney's hands came mainly from Arab countries, especially from Libya, whose leadership was keen to promote revolution wherever it might be found. Linney also had access to funds from the Soviet bloc, from dour men who perceived the creation of a kind of Cuba off the coast of Great Britain, a socialist thorn in the pale white English thigh.

"And *my* people have given too much already," Mulhaney said.

"Hell, you all know that. I can't go back and dip into the funds. It's not like the old days when a union boss could treat union funds like his own private bank. I've got lawyers and shit-headed accountants to explain things to. I can't even get twenty bucks out of petty cash without signing in triplicate. As it stands, the membership of my union wouldn't be completely happy to know where their contributions go. Except the fellows from the old country." Mulhaney drew on a cigar and looked bleakly convincing.

Cairney stared across the table at young Kevin Dawson.

Dawson shook his head. "I don't think I would have very much luck either. The families are all tired of giving. And they're all getting weary of the bloodshed. It gets more difficult all the time."

Cairney stood up and walked to the window. The families Dawson had referred to were mainly New England Irish—third or fourth or even fifth generation—great clans of wealthy American-Irish who were happy to contribute money so long as they weren't involved by name. Most of them had returned once in their lifetimes to the old country to look at ancient parish records in obscure villages and come home clutching Irish lace or Waterford glass or Donegal tweed. And for most of them one sentimental journey to the motherland, the mythical Erin, was enough to last forever.

Cairney turned away from the window now. He was aware of the intricate complexities of financing the IRA, the networks that were made, the delicate interconnections of disparate elements, the secret cells and the chains invisibly linked. He was aware of how frail, how tenuous, everything was, and he knew that the lost money could not be replaced for many months, perhaps even years.

He moved slowly back to the table. He sat down. He poured himself one small shot of brandy. One beneficial little snifter he held in a hand noticeably shaking. The currents in this room upset him. Was there anything more destructive than unfocused paranoia?

"Let's get back to the biggie," Mulhaney said. "Let's get back to the missing money. Let's imagine that somebody in this room, somebody with total knowledge of the *Connie* and her cargo, decided to line his own pockets. Let's play with that notion."

Nicholas Linney looked up from an open folder that lay in front of him. "Which one of us do you have in mind, Jock?"

Mulhaney looked mysterious. "I have my own ideas," he said quietly.

"You want to share them with us?" Linney asked. An aggressive vein appeared in his forehead, a mauve cord. "You want to let us know the name of the person you suspect? Is it me? Do you think I had something to do with it? Say what you're thinking. Don't keep us in the fucking dark, Jock."

Harry Cairney cleared his throat and said, "It doesn't have to be one of us, Jock. The British could have seized the *Connie*."

"Which poses another question, Senator," Mulhaney replied. "If the British took the money, how the hell did they *know* what was aboard the *Connie*? Unless somebody in this goddam room told them. It keeps coming back to the same fucking thing. Somebody in this room." And Mulhaney turned his face slowly, gazing at each man in turn, as if he were privy to information he wasn't about to share with anyone else.

Kevin Dawson said, "The ship might have been taken by agents of our own federal government."

"And they'd slaughter the crew, would they?" Mulhaney made a scornful little noise. He didn't believe the feds capable of such carnage. He had a curiously naïve faith, common among self-made men, in the inherent fairness of law-and-order agencies.

"All I'm saying," Kevin Dawson answered, "is that the British aren't the only candidates. And it doesn't follow that somebody in this room betrayed us. We might have been under surveillance for a long time. The British, the feds—they have their own sources of intelligence. They wouldn't necessarily need the help of anybody here."

Harry Cairney held up one hand. "I really don't think it much matters who took the money, gentlemen. I really don't think that's the issue here."

"Of course it fucking matters," Mulhaney said.

Cairney shook his head. Mulhaney could be very tiresome. Cairney said nothing for a moment. He raised a finger to his dry lips and glanced around the faces in the room. They were all watching him and he felt exposed beneath their eyes.

"The point is, Ireland believes that *we're* responsible for the loss," he said, pronouncing his words very slowly. "Our Irish connection believes—rightly or wrongly—that one of us, perhaps even more than one, was behind the piracy."

Harry Cairney heard the sound of Celestine playing her piano overhead. It was very soft, distant, oddly moving. She was playing something baroque and intricate and it suggested tranquillity.

"And I have the very strong impression," he added, pausing, raising his eyes to the ceiling, "that they will send somebody to find the missing money because they're not going to sit back and shrug their shoulders over the loss. It's not their style."

"Did they say they were sending somebody?" Mulhaney wanted to know.

"I was led to believe so," Cairney answered, remembering the angry Irish voice over the transatlantic phone connection that had said, *We need that bloody money and we need it badly. And I have just the person to get it.* It had been an unpleasant conversation, one in which Cairney had been obliged to listen to a tirade that was no more palatable for being uttered in a lilting, musical accent.

Mulhaney asked, "And how is this *somebody* supposed to get the money back, for Christ's sake? If one of us in this room took the goddam stuff, how would this *somebody* even know where to *find* any one of us? How would he even know where to start looking?"

Cairney felt a little flutter in an eyelid, as if a moth had landed there. The sound of Celestine's piano had stopped. "I have no idea, Jock."

"Ireland doesn't even know our names. Our identities. So what do they think they'll accomplish by sending some asshole over here? What's he going to do? Huh? We've always operated in secrecy, Harry. Is this messenger boy going to unmask us?"

"I can't answer your questions, Jock. I don't have the answers. But my best guess is that they're not going to send any messenger boy. They'll send a man who knows his business. And whoever he is, he's going to be goddam determined to find out what happened to the entire operating budget of the Irish Republican Army for one whole year."

Nicholas Linney closed his buff-colored folder. He blinked his narrow eyes. "Let me get this straight. Are we meant to understand that this guy represents a *threat* to our personal safety? Is he going to come here armed?"

There was an unmistakable relish in Linney's voice. He sounded like a man who had been confined too long to the drudgery of paperwork and whose blood quickened at the possibility of physical menace. For a moment Cairney wondered if Linney had played a role in the murderous hijacking, but he dismissed the speculation as fruitless. Linney, Mulhaney, Dawson—any one of this trio might have had his own reasons for arranging the piracy. Cairney, who disliked the track of his own suspicions, pushed the thought out of his mind.

He said, "I can only assume this man would carry a weapon, Nick. But if you have nothing to hide, you have nothing to worry about."

Linney smiled. It was a humorless little movement of his mouth. "Believe me, Senator, I'm not remotely worried. I can take care of myself."

"I'm sure you can," Cairney said. "What really concerns me is the fact that we can't predict how this person will behave. We don't know how he operates—if he's rational, if he's given to violence. We're in the dark as much as he is. And since that's the case, it would be wise for each of us to take whatever precautions we think necessary. At least until the situation is resolved."

Kevin Dawson smiled uncertainly. "You don't really imagine we're in danger, do you?"

Cairney shrugged. "I don't know. Ireland sends a man who doesn't know our names, doesn't know if one of us is responsible for this terrible situation, a man whose only mission is the recovery of the money by whatever means. Put yourself in his shoes. How would you act if you had been entrusted with a task like this one? How would you behave?"

Cairney listened to the silence that followed his questions. He thought now of the faceless figure who would come from Ireland. He imagined somebody stalking the Fund-raisers, a shadowy man driven by his own sense of justice, of setting right a terrible wrong. He tried to envisage such a man, and even as he did so he experienced an unsettling chill. People who betrayed the Cause always paid an awful price because it was the one crime that was neither forgiven nor forgotten—and if somebody in this room *had* played a part in the seizure of the *Connie's* cargo, then Cairney could almost feel sorry for the culprit. Almost.

As he turned away from the window and the cold sight of the frozen trees around the lake, he wondered how this Irishman was going to proceed with his efforts. What if he did find out the identities of the Fund-raisers? What then? Was he going to come and knock on the front door and ask polite questions? Cairney severely doubted that approach. The Irishman would have other ways, quite possibly unpleasant ones, of getting to the truth. Cairney shivered slightly. He was too old to face the prospect of physical threats, even violence. But he understood one thing—that whoever came from Ireland was sure to be a man who was determined to get results, no matter what lengths he might have to go to achieve them.

"The whole thing's academic anyway," Mulhaney said, blowing smoke rings. "The guy has absolutely no way of finding us."

"I wish I could be as certain as you, Jock," Cairney said unhappily, staring down into the polished wood surface of the oval table where the reflected faces of the Fund-raisers, like men drowning in clear water, looked back at him.

FOUR

DUBLIN

The girl told Patrick Cairney he had the eyes of a devil, which he found amusing. She was called Rhiannon Canavan and she was a tall red-haired girl with wide hips and small sculpted breasts, and she lay in Cairney's bed in his tiny flat near the Fitzgibbon Street Garda Station, which was close to the main road between Swords and Dublin and not the quietest place in which to live. Cairney stretched out alongside her, feeling himself slip into that dreamy place at the end of intense lovemaking. He placed the flat of his hand against her belly, and she purred as a cat might, rolling her long body toward him and circling his legs with her own.

"The eyes of a devil," she said again, and she bit Cairney lightly on the side of his neck.

"And you're a vampire," he answered.

"A hussy is what I am. Or it's what you've made me anyhow. For the love of God, what am I doing here? Did you put something in my drink, Patrick Cairney?"

"I didn't think you noticed."

"I remember seeing this funny little envelope in your hand."

"Himalayan Fucking Powder," he said. "Ancient Tibetan secret recipe. Guaranteed."

"You say wicked things." She sat upright, straddling him. Her breasts swung slightly in the half light of the room. In the distance, the sound of a police car could be heard whining in the night.

"I don't think I'd personally like to live with the police on my doorstep," she said.

"Why? What have you got to hide?"

"Obviously nothing," and she arched her back, tilting her face away from him. She was, so she had told him in the pub, a nurse in the Richmond Hospital, and he wasn't to think that just because nurses had poor reputations she was going to hop into the sack with him straight off the bloody bat, even if he did have the eyes of a devil and his charming American manners into the bargain.

"Nurse Canavan," he said in a fraudulent Irish accent. "I am having this Jaysus of a pain between my legs. Can you do anything about it, out of daycent Christian kindness?"

"I think I have the prescription for you," and she swung her body around, lowering her face to his groin and taking him softly into her mouth. And then she moved away from him, rolling on her back, and he entered her even as he continued to hear the sirens of police cars outside in the night. There were depths here, Cairney thought, and he was afraid of them. In the half light of the room Rhiannon Canavan had her eyes closed and her mouth open, and she was holding on to Cairney as if he were a carnival ride that scared her. Spent, Cairney fell away from her, but she still held on to him.

"Are all Americans that loud?" she asked.

"I'm an average screamer," he told her.

Nurse Canavan reached for a cigarette and lit it, and her face was briefly illuminated by the flare of her Bic. She had a wonderfully straight Irish jaw, a fine generous mouth, and high cheekbones which gave her face a certain delicate strength.

"So tell me," she said. "You're at Trinity, did you say?"

"Trinity," Cairney answered.

"And you're one of them wealthy Americans that comes over here to study at Daddy's expense, is that it?"

Cairney shook his head. "Daddy's money can't buy happiness. Besides, he doesn't support me. I have a small income from teaching undergraduate classes at Trinity. He's never really approved of my studies. He doesn't see the point to them."

"I must say he has a case, Patrick Cairney. It seems to me a young man like yourself shouldn't be poking around so much in the past."

"And where should I be poking?"

"You know something? You're disgusting." She laughed again. She had one of those rich sincere laughs that change the temperature of rooms, like fine resonant music.

"Seriously now," she said. "Is archaeology a field for a young man?"

"We study the past to understand the future," Cairney intoned solemnly.

"You," and she nudged him with an elbow. "Are you never serious?"

"I have my moments."

Rhiannon crushed out her cigarette and lay back. "Does it really matter how much a loaf of bread cost in ancient Egypt?"

"I like to think it helps us understand inflation."

Cairney peered at the cinder of light that lay against the window, thrown on the glass by a faraway streetlamp. He felt both comfortable and secure with this lovely girl at his side. She offset something of the lonely edge he frequently experienced—a stranger in a strange country. And yet it wasn't alien at all because there was a sense in which he'd been familiar with it all his life, courtesy of his father, who had instilled in him the wonders of Irish culture and history. Harry Cairney, who for most of the year had been an absentee father in Washington, returned each summer to Roscommon to indoctrinate his son in the melancholic songs and stories that were part of the Irish tradition, tales of defeats and victories, old loves, poems about the Old Lammas Fair in Ballycastle and the headlands of Kerry and the braes of Strasala. When other kids were out in hot sandlots tossing baseballs at their fathers, Patrick Cairney would sit with a fishing pole on the bank of a river and listen to his father recite the last words of the patriot Robert Emmet on the eve of his execution. Even now the young man could remember Emmet's speech. *When my country takes her place among the nations of the earth, then and not till then, let my epitaph be written. I have done.* Harry Cairney had been less a father than a kind of history instructor whose view of the past was colored by the romanticism of the Irish exile. All through his childhood the boy had wished for a father like the one other kids had, those young vigorous men who'd throw a baseball at you or take you one-on-one on a basketball court or get down with you in a scrimmage. But Harry, who was fifty years older than his son, had seemed remote even then, removed from Patrick both by years and memories of a faraway island. As if he felt guilty about his absences, Harry forced himself on his son during the summer, but never quite in the way Patrick Cairney wanted. He was too old and too digni-fied, too *detached*, to get down in a sandlot and dirty his hands. He was too *sophisticated* to go inside a sporting-goods store and discuss the merits of this or that baseball bat. Consequently, when Patrick thought of his father now he felt a curious combination of admira-tion and pity, the former because Harry had occupied an exalted position in politics and was highly regarded by everyone—and the latter because the world Cairney had tried to foist on his son was an old man's dead reality and therefore pathetic.

Patrick Cairney got out of bed and went into the small kitchen, where he filled a glass with water. He carried it back to the bedroom and slipped under the sheets beside the girl. Once more through the night came the quick whine of a Garda car.

"You've gone very quiet all of a sudden," Rhiannon said.

"*I am Ireland: I am older than the Old Woman of Beare,*" he recited. "*Great my glory: I that bore Cuchulain the valiant.*"

"*Great my shame,*" the girl replied. "*My own children that sold their mother.*" She paused a second. "Patrick Pearse. Sure, I've known that since I was no higher than a blade of grass. Where did you learn it?"

"From my father," Cairney answered. "Didn't I mention he was born right here in Dublin? Above a shop at Number Twenty-nine Patrick Street, to be exact."

"And overseas he went to make his fortune," Rhiannon said.

Cairney nodded. "I don't think he ever really left this country."

The girl pressed her face into Cairney's shoulder, her damp lips against his skin. Something had changed in the room in the space of a few minutes. Somebody had left the door open, and that old Celtic wraith Melancholy had gate-crashed.

"The funny thing, as Irish as he still is, he's never been back here to visit," Cairney said. And he envisaged Harry Cairney as he'd last seen him two years ago, some months before the old man had un-expectedly married Celestine Cunningham of Boston in a private ceremony. Cairney had never met the woman but apparently the old man was overjoyed with the match. He'd written a couple of times to say so. When his letters weren't extolling the virtues of Celestine, they were urging Cairney to visit this place or that, as if the son might vicariously undertake a pilgrimage that the father had always meant to make for himself. *Take a walk through St. Anne's Park near the Dollymount Strand and smell the roses* or *Don't forget to have a jar in the Stag's Head at Dame's Court.* In these letters Cairney could still hear the strident voice of the man who had turned all his short boyhood summers, which should have been treasured times, into diatribes against the sheer perfidy of the English and the atrocities they had committed in Ireland.

Cairney said, "He wants to keep a memory of Ireland the way it was, not the way it is now. He romanticizes things that were never romantic to begin with."

"And I see nothing wrong in such a thing," Rhiannon said. "Why shouldn't old men have their illusions?"

Cairney nodded. Why not indeed? he wondered. Memories preserved in amber were inured to change. Harry Cairney's Ireland was the Dear Green Place, the *Sean-Bhean Bhocht*, the Old Woman of Sorrow. His was an Ireland of martyrs, a place of ghosts. It was the doomed Easter Rising of 1916, when Harry Cairney's heroes—Patrick Pearse and Eamon de Valera and James Connolly—had seized the General Post Office on O'Connell Street and Boland's Mills in the south of Dublin and the English had crushed the insurgency with field guns and a gunboat on the River Liffey, consequently creating a new generation of martyrs.

It was an Ireland where Harry Cairney's heroes were executed by the English. John MacBride, Pearse himself, James Connolly (wounded, carried by stretcher to the firing squad), Thomas Mac-Donagh, names that had echoed like bells through Patrick Cairney's formative years. And all the others—the glamorous Countess Markievicz who had stalked the streets of Dublin with a great plumed hat and a revolver, the beautiful Maud Gonne, who had captivated the heart of Yeats, running firearms into Ireland in defiance of the English, bold Rory O'Connor and his men who had dramatically seized the Four Courts Building in Dublin.

An old man's illusions . . .

What did they all come down to now, these clichés of glories lost and won? Patrick Cairney wondered. In what did all this romance and glamour and bravery distill itself?

The answer was simple. Squalor in Ulster, where courage had yielded to indiscriminate acts of terrorism and where, behind the walls of Her Majesty's Prison Maze—formerly Long Kesh Prison or, in convict terminology, The Lazy K—so-called political prisoners, members of the militant Provisional IRA, smeared their excrement on the walls of their cells and women did the same with their menstrual blood.

Patrick Cairney wondered if his father ever thought about that, the way courage had become eroded by sheer human indignity. He doubted the old man ever did: *memories preserved in amber* . . .

He propped himself up on one elbow. He stroked the side of the girl's face.

"For a student, Patrick Cairney, you've got a pretty fine physique," Rhiannon said. "What is it you do? Lift weights? Pump iron, as they say? Or is it just those old books you plow through are so heavy they build your muscles up?"

"I dig," he answered.

"Dig? With a shovel?"

He nodded. "I dig holes in the ground."

"Like a navvy."

"That's all I am, Nurse. A navvy with a purpose. When a laborer digs, he isn't looking for anything. But when I dig, I'm searching."

"And what have you ever found?"

"I once found a Coca-Cola bottle circa 1930."

"What treasure." *Traysure* was how she pronounced the word.

"You don't expect to find such a thing buried in the Egyptian desert," he said. It was best this way, he thought, best to keep everything at a level of flippancy he could handle. He stared at the darkened window. The silence of the night beyond the window was dense, impenetrable, as if it were the quiet left behind by all the lost causes of the world. He moved his body closer to the girl, holding her. For some reason the last stanza of Patrick Pearse's "Renunciation" went through his mind.

> *I have turned my face*
> *To this road before me,*
> *To the deed that I see*
> *And the death I shall die.*

Cheerful little ditty, he thought.

When he heard the sound of the telephone ringing from the kitchen, he wanted to freeze it out of his brain.

"It could be important," the girl said. "Why don't you answer it?"

Cairney said nothing. The telephone went on ringing.

"Good news. You never can tell."

"At midnight on a Saturday?" he asked.

After ten, twelve rings, the sound stopped.

Cairney's relief lasted only a moment, because the telephone started up again, and this time it seemed louder than before.

"Maybe it's a girl friend," Rhiannon said.

"I don't have one."

"And you expect me to believe that, do you?"

Cairney tossed the bed sheets aside. The room was cold around him. He went inside the kitchen and picked up the telephone and stood there shivering as he listened to the voice on the other end of the line. When he hung up he returned to the bedroom. He sat down on the mattress.

"Well?" the girl asked.

"You should never answer a telephone that rings after twelve o'clock."

Rhiannon crushed out her cigarette. "That bad?"

Cairney sighed. He looked slightly flustered. "A sickness in the family."

"I'm sorry."

Cairney reached out for the girl's hand, touching it softly. "My father," he said. "A mild heart attack."

FIVE

It was an old whitewashed house ten miles from the resort town of Dun Laoghaire on the south shore of Dublin Bay and in the gray dawn it appeared translucent. The house was surrounded by walls and thick trees. The only means of entrance was through a set of large iron gates, behind which a small gatehouse stood. Usually the gatehouse was occupied by a man who kept a nine-millimeter Brazilian Taurus semiautomatic pistol in his waistband and an FN assault rifle propped against the wall. On this morning, however, the gatehouse was empty and the iron gates were unlocked.

A beige VW came to a halt outside the whitewashed house. As it did so, a man appeared in the doorway. He was called Finn. Although he was in his late fifties, he carried himself in the erect manner of one who has been a soldier in his time. He was imposing —even in the pale dawn one could see the long white hair that fell over his shoulders and the suggestion of strength in his eyes. He came down the steps to greet the driver of the Volkswagen and together both men went inside the house. The driver, the young man known as Jig, noticed the empty gatehouse. It was never occupied when he came to this house because Finn required that his visits here take place with the utmost confidentiality. The guard was always sent away at such times. Even within the Association of the Wolfe secrets were stratified. No one person, other than Finn, knew everything that was going on. It was his way of maintaining control.

The sitting room was filled with harps. Finn collected them assiduously. He never played because he was tone deaf, but there were strange little moments when, with all the windows open and the wind coming in off the Irish Sea, he could hear a random music created by nature as the air stirred the strings and made them vibrate. Many of the thirty or so harps were gorgeous gilt creations, inlaid with mother-of-pearl carved with extraordinary care. Sometimes, Finn would reach out and pluck a string, setting up tiny quivering cacophonies as he crossed the room.

Finn sat down. He wore a simple fisherman's sweater and baggy cord pants and sneakers that looked as if they'd been chewed by a neurotic dog. He ran his fingers nervously through his long white hair, and for a moment Jig perceived Finn as a kind of aged hippie, an eccentric guru who'd been to the mountain and come back bearing a message—which, in one sense, was true enough. Today, though, Finn looked gaunt, almost hungry, his huge cheekbones prominent in the lean face.

He pulled a strand of hair from his head and held it up to the light at the window, examining it. "My bloody hair is beginning to fall out," he said. He had an actor's voice. It came booming out of his chest.

He stood up, moving toward one of the harps. He angrily ran his fingers over all the strings and the room rippled with sound.

"This bloody country!" Finn shouted suddenly, as if the climate of Ireland were responsible for his hair loss. "This godforsaken island of good intentions, dried-up old nuns, and bloody gossips! I tell you, there are times when I want nothing more than to just turn my back on the whole bloody place and let it sink into the ocean and see if I care!" Finn paused. "You know what the ocean would do? Eh? It would spit the bloody island back *up* again! And you know why, boy? Because it's too much fucking trouble, that's why! Besides, what ocean would want the taste of a man like Ivor McInnes in it?"

Ivor McInnes, a Protestant minister who until recently had had a parish in Belfast, was Finn's bête noire. McInnes, who specialized in sermons that were critical of Catholicism in general and the IRA in particular, was symptomatic, in Finn's mind, of the wrongs that plagued the island today. There were just too many hard-core Protestants, with views that were sometimes to the far right of bigotry, wandering the land. Finn thought all extremists should be incarcerated and the key thrown away. He brought up the name of McInnes at every opportunity, rather in the way a man with congested lungs might bring up phlegm.

The young man watched as Finn wandered around the room, plucking strings until the whole room was humming and singing.

Over the endless vibrations, Finn was talking rapidly. He moved backward and forward, waving his arms in an erratic fashion. He was ranting about how he'd struggled for supreme control of the finances of the Irish Republican Army, how he'd formed the ultra-secret innermost cell called the Association of the Wolfe precisely for the purpose of handling income. How, since 1981, he'd taken great pains to make sure that the money that came from "the friends overseas" was spread carefully and discreetly around, because he wanted to keep it out of the hands of the extremists. He wanted an end to the *atrocious* image the IRA had made for itself. What bloody good did it do to blow up a London bus, say? Wasn't that a waste of explosives and *terrible* PR into the bargain? If there was to be killing, it had to be selective. If there were to be assassinations, only hostile political targets were to be picked. Nothing else could ever be justified.

Finn shook his head from side to side. "Apart from the almighty dent that buying arms puts in our budget, do you know where our money goes, Jig?"

Jig shook his head. Finn had never talked about the particulars of finance before.

"I'll tell you. It goes to the Catholic families in the North when the man of the house is stuck in some bloody British jail because he was stupid enough to try and set off a bomb in the Tower of London and get himself caught. Do you know what this maintenance money costs us every year? Have you any idea? What will those women and children do if we can't get money to them?"

Santa Claus, Jig thought, dispensing banknotes from a sack.

"I'll tell you something else you didn't know," Finn continued. "Money gets plowed into keeping the Gaelic alive. It goes to finance teachers and students and the publication of works in Irish. How can we sit around and talk English if we're supposed to be an independent country? English is a barbaric tongue, Jig, a mishmash.

It doesn't have the sweetness of the Gaelic. Have you ever imagined what it would have sounded like if Bill Shakespeare had written in the Gaelic? Imagine *Hamlet* in Irish."

Finn smiled. The harps trembled and rattled. Jig stood very still. He'd never heard this kind of desperate note in Finn's voice before. The news of the *Connie O'Mara* had clearly wounded the old man in a deep place.

Finn stood at the window now, his hands folded behind his back. "She was a fine ship run by fine men," he said, his voice a whisper suddenly. "Liam O'Reilly grew up with me down in Bantry. A good man. And how he's dead and they're all dead and the bloody money's gone. Our money, boy. Our purse."

Jig said nothing.

Finn rubbed him lightly on the shoulder. "You're going to get it back for me, boy. Aren't you?"

The young man looked into Finn's eyes. What he saw there was a kind of madness, a needle-sharp single-mindedness. He imagined that the ancient saints who went out into the wilderness for months at a time had looked exactly like this. A manic light.

"If there's a way," Jig answered.

"No ifs, Jig. There's always a way." Finn moved back to the window. He stood looking out as if he anticipated enemies in the shrubbery. "The bloody Americans," he muttered.

"You think they're responsible?"

"For many years now, we've had sympathetic songbirds inside the New York City Police Department because that place is still basically an Irish colony. And the information that reached me late last night is that the *Connie's* crew was slaughtered by American weapons."

"American weapons are widely available," the young man said.

Finn spread his hands out. "There's more. I'm not quite finished. The same source was kind enough to mention the contents of a ballistics report conducted by the gentlemen of the Federal Bureau of Investigation."

"And?"

"The ammunition used was something called the SS109, which is manufactured by an American company called the Olin Corporation. This kind of ammunition, they tell me, is used in the Colt M-16A2 automatic rifle, also American."

Jig licked his lips, which were dry. "All right. Suppose the pirates were American. How do you narrow that down to specific individuals, Finn? The last time I heard, there were more than two hundred million people in the United States."

"Simple, simple," Finn answered. "Consider this. A group of men collects a large sum of money for the Cause. Imagine one of this group says to himself that the poor old *Connie O'Mara* is a sitting duck just waiting to be shot and plucked. This treacherous bastard sees gold in front of his eyes. He can taste it. He decides he's going to make his own arrangements and to hell with the Cause! He's going to make himself rich at our expense!"

There were little spots of saliva at the corners of Finn's mouth. "Only this group of men knew the cargo and destination of the *Connie*. Only *this* group, boy. Nobody else. And one of them is our fucking Judas. One of them *has* to be. It could only have been an inside job. I'll swear by that."

Jig absorbed all this for a second. "Who are the members of this group?" he asked. He knew what Finn's answer would be.

"Now right there you encounter your first obstacle," Finn said. "The lines of communication were established in such a way that the money always came from what we might call sources unknown. Even the telephone number I call in America is never the same one twice. All this was done in the sainted name of secrecy, of course, which we all know is a two-faced bastard that can easily work against you."

The young man spread his hands in a perplexed manner. "Where do you expect me to start?"

Finn narrowed his eyes. "I'll give you a name and that's all I can give you."

"Who?"

"A certain Father Tumulty in New York."

"What can a priest tell me?"

"I never said the man was a priest, did I now?" Finn looked faintly mischievous.

"How do you want me to handle all this?" Jig asked.

Finn studied the young man's face. It was a good face, handsome and strong, with eyes that suggested layers of inner conviction. *You chose this one well, Finn.* There was steel in this boy, there was backbone and guts and, best of all, a chill dedication to the Cause. He placed one hand on Jig's shoulder. "I'd be the happiest man on God's earth if I could tell you the names of the men who call themselves the Fund-raisers, because if I knew that we could sit down the way we usually do and devise a blueprint of action for you. I can tell you the *kind* of men they are. I can tell you they're the sort of men who've always been drawn to the Cause because it brings a small sense of danger into their otherwise drab lives. It gives them the illusion of *purpose,* boy. They send large sums of money over here, then they sit back on their fat Yankee arses and feel very Irish. They've paid their dues. They think they belong. They think they *understand.* They think they're part of the whole bloody struggle. But they're not. They're money men, and *they* don't have any blood on their lovely white hands. They have silly little dreams in their heads, but the only dream worth a damn is the one you're prepared to die for. And these men aren't ready to die for anything just yet, thank you very much. They're not Irish. They're Americans. They beat their chests and call themselves *Irish*-Americans, and they put on a big green production every St. Patrick's Day, but they're about as Irish as the Queen of England. Personally I long for the day when we won't need such men. . . ." Finn, who had a moment of uneasiness, a sense of uncertainty, a sudden nagging doubt, glanced at the boy. "I know the kind of men they are, but I don't know their names, and I don't know how many of them are in the group. Three, four, six, I just don't know. Consequently . . ." And here he took a deep breath. "We don't have a blueprint, boy. Only a burning bloody need for *that money.*"

The young man knew the kind of American Finn was talking about. He didn't care for them any more than Finn did, but his private feelings were irrelevant to him right then. He said, "You still haven't answered my question, Finn. How do you want me to handle this?"

Finn rubbed the tip of his long straight nose. "You have to keep several things in mind. One, the members of this group are going to be more than a little paranoid right now. The money's gone. They're going to be accusing one another and suspecting one another. They're going to be nervous, boy. And a nervous man isn't altogether a predictable one. Remember that. Two, when you find out who is involved in the Fund-raisers, you've got to proceed on the possibility that each and every one of them is the traitor. None of them is going to be happy to see you, because they're going to think that you *suspect* each of them of this awful crime. None of them will want to be your friend." Finn looked suddenly exasperated. "Ah, Jesus, it's a tricky situation."

The young man blinked at the morning light climbing against the window. *None of them will want to be your friend.* He had no friends other than Finn, nor did he imagine ever needing any. He could have made friends if he'd wanted to, because he had an easy charm he was able to turn on and off and he had the kind of looks that others found attractive. But friendships were for other people. They were part of ordinary lives.

Finn put his hands in the pockets of his pants. "Approach them carefully. Try to take them off guard if you can. But expect them to lie to you. Expect them to shift suspicions onto other members. Expect them to deny they have anything to do with sending money to Ireland. And don't be surprised if some of them treat you with outright animosity. As I said, these are nervous men. Push them a little if you feel you have to, but bear in mind this sorry fact—we'll probably need the services of some of these men in the future."

The young man said nothing. He hadn't anticipated making a trip to America, and he found the prospect just a little unsettling. When he operated on the British mainland or in Northern Ireland, he always did so with a specific plan in mind, a detailed map of what he was supposed to do and how it was going to be achieved. Now, though, it seemed as if Finn expected him to go into America blind, which was an idea he didn't like. When you didn't have a plan, it was difficult to maintain control. And if one thing was anathema to him, it was the loss of control. He didn't want to go to America, but if Finn commanded him, then he'd obey. It would never have occurred to him to question Finn's orders.

The harp strings in the big room had all stilled now, and there was only a pale lingering echo of any noise.

Finn sat down, crossing his long legs and adjusting his baggy cord pants as if they had a razor-sharp crease that needed to be preserved. He was a man of small, endearing vanities. "You'll need a gun, although I hope with all my heart you don't have to use it. But it would be downright foolish to go into this without one. Tumulty can help you there. I don't want you going into one of those bloody Irish bars in Queens and picking up what our American friends call a Saturday Night Special, Jig. I don't want you making any kind of contact with the Irish rabble that collects money in tin cans and sends cheap handguns to post-office boxes in Belfast or Derry. They mean well, no doubt, but they drink too much and they talk too bloody much, and we don't need any kind of gossip about you."

Jig nodded. What he suddenly wished was that Finn were going to the United States with him. For a moment he felt a twinge of loneliness, but he put the sensation out of his mind. He had chosen this life. Nobody had selected it for him. Finn, certainly, had nudged him in the direction of this existence, but finally the choice had been entirely his own.

"One other thing," Finn said, regretting his anger when he'd talked on the telephone with his anonymous American contact. He'd blurted out some threat about sending a man over, and now he was sorry about it. Quick to rage and say things he wished he hadn't—would he never change? "They'll be expecting you over there."

"Somebody's always expecting me, Finn."

The old man didn't speak for a time. He reached for the bottle of peppermint schnapps that sat on a table against the wall, then changed his mind about drinking. He wanted to be cold sober. "You did a fine job with Whiteford," he said in a low voice.

Jig shrugged. The compliment was unexpected and quite uncharacteristic of Finn. He wasn't sure how to take it. "It went off as we planned." It was all he could think of to say.

"And you'll do a fine job in America too, because I want you *and* our money back here in one piece. That money means a lot, boy. Without it . . ."

"I understand," Jig said.

Finn clapped the palm of his hand against the young man's shoulder. "Remember this. If it becomes unpleasant at any time in America—and you know what I mean by that—your life is more important to me than any one of the Fund-raisers." And then, as if this confession were something he regretted, he turned away from Jig.

"Let's talk about the cash you'll need for this trip," he said, and once again set the harp strings dancing with flourishes of his hands.

FINN slept for thirty minutes after Jig had gone. It was troubled sleep and he woke with the feeling of having dreamed something disastrous that he couldn't recall on waking. Something to do with Jig.

When he got up, he went into the bathroom to shave. He studied his face in the mirror awhile. It was a lean, chiseled face, crisscrossed by lines and filled with small hollows under the cheekbones. What Finn saw looking back at him from the mirror was a man who had a special sense of history at a special time.

The idea of founding the Association of the Wolfe had come to him when he perceived the general disunity of the Cause, when he had seen the need for strong hands on the financial reins. Secretive centralized planning was the answer to the outrages of the *eedjit* rabble. If you didn't give the hotheads money, how could they buy weapons and explosives for their little sorties in Belfast and on the English mainland, when all they ever got was a damned bad press?

The ultimate goal of the Association was that old dream—to get the British out of the North and unite Ireland once and for all. Two separate Irelands was as much a travesty of history as two separate Germanies. An artificial border, created by the English and maintained by its soldiers, was a farce, a rupture inflicted by the politics of hatred. The Association was named after Wolfe Tone who in 1796 had attempted to land twelve thousand French soldiers on Bantry Bay to help overthrow English supremacy. When the mission failed and Tone was captured, he asked for death before a firing squad, cutting his own throat when this request was denied.

Finn believed in selective assassination. He had a list of intended victims, which was composed mainly of British politicians who were against the prospect of a united Ireland. The list also included several Northern Irish diehards, those iron-skulled morons, like Ivor McInnes, who swore on their own lives that the Union Jack would always fly over Belfast, that Ulster would always belong to the Queen. If you systematically assassinated enough of these jackasses, sooner or later the cost in blood was going to prove too expensive to the English. They'd be happy to leave Ulster, which was something they should have done years ago if they'd had any decency—which they clearly did not have.

Finn turned away from the mirror. He had a sense of things slipping away from him. Without control of the purse, how could he control the extremists? But now the purse was gone, and the thought brought a bitter taste into his mouth. Liam O'Reilly was dead. So was the Courier. Finn closed his eyes and observed a quiet moment of mourning for old comrades, both members of the Association.

He went down the stairs. In his small office, a spartan room with a desk and a chair and bare white walls, he picked up the telephone. He began to dial a number but stopped halfway through and set the phone back. What was he going to say? What was he going to tell the Saint? He stood at the window, stroking his jaw. What in God's name was he supposed to say? The Saint didn't believe in credit. He was always in a hurry to deliver his goods and get paid.

Finn picked up the telephone a second time. He dialed nervously. It was a number in the port city of Rostock in East Germany. It rang only once before it was picked up. Finn spoke his name.

The voice at the other end was guttural New York City. "I got tired waiting, Finn."

Finn said nothing a moment. The connection was poor. "There's been a problem. A cash problem."

"Maybe for you, Finn. I ain't got problems."

Finn saw a blackbird fly past his window. *Pack up all my cares and woe,* he thought. "Listen to me. I need some time."

"Time's run out, fella. You know how much it costs when you got a Greek boat to rent? When you got an Arab crew that sits around on its duff all day and they still gotta get paid? Then you add the fact I got harbor personnel to grease here. You know how much that runs, Finn?"

Finn's throat was dry. "I need a week. Maybe more than a week."

"Tough titty," the guy said. "I'm trying to tell ya, Finn. You're shit outta luck, man."

"What do you mean? What do you mean I'm out of luck?"

"I got tired waiting. I already sold the cargo, Finn."

"You did what?" Finn shouted. *"You did what?"*

"Guy came up with a good offer. I said sure thing. What the hell. I wanna sit round in Rostock for the rest of my life, Finn? Wait for you?"

"This is a joke," Finn said. His voice was very low, even. A nerve had begun to work at the side of his head.

"No joke. I don't joke about my cargo—"

"You sold it! How could you *do* a thing like that, in the name of Jesus!"

"Hey, it ain't like you and me had a written contract, pal. You wanna sue? Be my guest."

Finn shut his eyes tightly. First the money. Now a whole boatload of arms and explosives. The very air he breathed seemed poisoned with treacheries.

"You're trying to tell me a buyer just came along? Out of the bloody blue?"

"Right," the Saint said. "I'm a businessman, Finn. This is a business. I gotta sell. I gotta eat."

"Who was this buyer?"

"I can't answer a dumb question like that."

"Who was he?" Finn trembled with rage.

"Hey, Finn. I don't ask questions. Guy paid, I delivered. Simple and clean. Now I just wanna get my ass outta this town, which I intend to do in the next few hours. This ain't exactly a day at the beach, Finn. You ever been in Rostock?"

"I'd like to know the name of this person."

There was a crackling sound over the line. The Saint said, "Listen, Finn. I keep confidences. Unnerstand? The guy who took delivery of the cargo, he was a South American. A Venezuelan or something. He waved cold cash and I took it. That's all I'm saying."

Finn said, "I'll go elsewhere! I'll find another supplier! Damn you—"

The line was already dead. Finn slammed down the receiver. He sat, dismayed, spreading his arms on his desk and laying his face against them.

The shipment was gone.

He raised his face. A bloody Venezuelan! A bloody Venezuelan had purchased the whole boatload of arms and high-tech explosives, for Christ's sake! Probably to waste them in some fucking futile border skirmish that didn't matter a damn in the scheme of things. An arms shipment like that took *months* to put together. If Jig recovered the missing money, Finn thought he could set up another deal, but not through the Saint, who, like most of his mercenary kind, didn't have much in the way of honor and loyalty. But it would take time to make another deal, and Finn wasn't very patient. God in heaven, he'd lived all his life with his dream of a free Ireland, from the time he was a small boy in Bantry and all through his years of service with the IRA, when he'd done everything a man could do. He'd planted bombs in England. He'd robbed mail trains. During the Second World War he'd gone into Northern Ireland to sabotage a British troop ship that was carrying soldiers to fight in Europe. A lot of blood had been spilled in pursuit of the dream. A lot of fine men had died.

But without weapons and explosives, you might as well hang a CLOSED sign on your door. If Jig didn't recover the money, it was back to homemade hand grenades and other dubious devices that were absolutely undependable. Which meant he couldn't keep up the pressure on the English to get out of Ulster. If Finn was truly afraid of anything, it was the idea of dying before he saw his dream come true.

He turned his thoughts to Jig.

There was a lot riding on that young man's shoulders. Jig had never let him down in the past, no matter how difficult or complicated the task. But this was something altogether different. Apart from Tumulty, Jig would have no support in America. There was no network in place to assist him if he needed help over there. And there was no network for the simple reason that Finn had never imagined the need for Jig to operate in the U.S.A. Scoundrels, he thought. All of them, from the Fund-raisers to the Saint, a scurvy blackhearted bunch.

It was more than the lack of a network, though, that troubled Finn now. And it was more than the treachery of men. It was the fact that Jig, who had been highly trained to kill men, was going into a situation where his particular form of expertise wasn't going to be of any damned use to him. He wasn't going to be called upon to plant explosive devices or track some potential victim through the scope of a sniper's rifle. He was being asked to do something in which he had utterly no experience. He was being asked to *investigate* a crime. To solve a specific problem. *To sleuth.*

Finn had a strange lurching sensation around his heart. *You're sending an assassin into a situation that calls for a detective's talents.* In the name of God, Finn, what have you done? Have you asked the impossible of that boy? Have you packed him off to be devoured by bloody Yankee vultures?

But there was nobody else to send. There was no other man Finn could trust. It was really that simple. He could have enlisted some young hothead who would have gone blundering into America, but what good would that have done? If anybody could get that money back, it was Jig. From the very start of their association Finn had seen a dark streak in the boy, an unrelenting determination in his heart. He was the stuff of an assassin. He had nerves of marble and a hawk's fastidious eye for detail. He had required careful shaping, of course. He had needed the rough edges smoothed away. Some of his political notions had been naïve and idealistic back when the young man had first been brought to Finn's attention. Finn remembered now how Jig had hung around the fringes of political action groups in Dublin, acquiring a certain notoriety for his habit of espousing extremism and advocating grand gestures—such as the bombing of Buckingham Palace or the Houses of Parliament. For security reasons, Finn never attended such meetings himself. They were too easily infiltrated by plainclothes Garda and other enemies of the Cause, but the old man had a network of people who brought him reports—who was saying what, the kinds of schemes being plotted, anything that might intrigue Finn. In enthusiasms and energy, in the stark apocalyptic suggestions he carelessly made, Jig had put Finn in mind of his own younger self—the raw boy from Bantry who wanted to change the world with one grand stroke. Ah, the innocence of it all! The sheer unfettered naïveté! But the possibilities inherent in the young man—these were the things that had interested Finn most.

His first private meeting with the boy took place in an isolated bird sanctuary at Booterstown on Dublin Bay where, surrounded by squalls of gulls and anxiously watchful wading birds, Finn had talked of the need for patience and careful judgment when it came to the problem of getting the British out. He had deliberately circled his real purpose in interviewing the young man, which was his own need for a person who could become the kind of assassin required by the Association of the Wolfe. Was this boy the one? Or was his impulsive streak unharnessable? These were the early days of the Association and Finn, disgusted by the outbreak of IRA bombings and killings on the British mainland, spoke of the importance of selective assassination. There, at Booterstown, knocked by a harsh wind and the cuffs of his pants caked with soft mud, Finn made his distinction between an ordinary IRA gunman, a hothead, and the kind of dedicated assassin the Cause really needed.

The young man had listened, his mind seemingly elsewhere, his eyes distant and unresponsive. Each of Finn's questions had been answered in short, unrevealing sentences. The boy's background, his interests—these were dismissed, as if they had absolutely no relevance and Finn was impertinent to ask so many questions. Finn had the feeling that the young man thought his time was being unforgivably wasted. Dragged out in the first light of dawn to some bloody bird sanctuary and for what? So that a nosy old man could pose silly questions?

What's the point of all this? the boy had asked.

Finn, a little irritated by the young man's abrasive edge, had answered this question with one of his own. *Why do you hate the English so much?*

Does it matter? Jig asked.

Finn had watched a flock of seagulls rise up and go screaming toward the ocean, which was barely visible in the muffled fog of the early morning. *Answer my question,* he'd said.

The young man had replied tersely, almost as if he were editing his own material in his head. He had been in the North about two years ago, he said, and in Belfast, that ruined city, he had come across the bagged bodies of two infant children on the sidewalk outside a house that had been ravaged by British soldiers because they suspected the place was filled with arms. Armored cars and tanks and soldiers milled around in confusion. It transpired that the two children had been alone in the house when the British assault took place. But what Jig remembered most were the two bundles on the sidewalk and the way blood soaked through the material of the bags and the sounds of old women sobbing, like the somber women of Greek tragedies, in the doorways of the street.

Finn had thought there was something unconvincing about this story. He didn't doubt that it was true, but atrocities were alas commonplace in Belfast. Everybody and his uncle had at least one horror story to tell. By itself, it wasn't enough to produce the kind of venom that was present in Jig whenever he spoke of the English. Was the young man simply trying to say that he was a humanitarian outraged by the casual and utterly useless deaths of small children? Finn didn't buy that. It was too easy, facile. He had the strong feeling that Jig, for whatever reasons, was going through his memory on a highly selective basis. That something was being left out of the narrative. He flirted briefly with the notion that perhaps Jig was one of those psychopathic types that were unfortunately drawn to the Cause because it offered a justification for their violent tendencies, but he dismissed this because there was a certain authenticity in the way the boy had delivered his story. Just the same, Finn still felt dissatisfied. If he was going to find a use for this young man, he needed to be absolutely certain of him.

It's not enough, boy, Finn said.

What more do you want? Jig asked.

Hatred doesn't spring from one isolated incident.

Doesn't it?

Finn shook his head. *There's got to be more.*

The young man had smiled then, which was something he apparently didn't do very often. His normal expression was one of grimness, an unrelaxed look that suggested a life of forever being tense.

Wary, maybe that was the word Finn had wanted. It was a good quality in a killer. An assassin had to have an edge. But Finn needed more than what this young man had told him before he could recruit him.

Do you want a history lesson, Finn? Is that it? Do you want me to tell you how the British presence in this country sickens me?

You can't tell me anything about bloody history, boy.

I didn't think so.

Together, they had walked silently through the sanctuary, scaring birds out of the rushes and puddles and mudbanks. When they paused beneath some trees, Finn asked, *Do you know your way around a gun?*

Jig said he did.

Finn paused for a second. *We'll talk again* was what he had finally said, drifting under the trees and away from the boy, who watched him sullenly.

When Finn had gone several yards the young man had called out. *I'm tired of talk. Is that all anybody ever does in this country?*

Finn had smiled to himself but hadn't looked back.

N O W , staring at the telephone on his desk, Finn felt despair. All the work, all the planning—and the Saint turns around and sells to the first fucking buyer that comes along with a stuffed wallet!

Dear God. He needed to get out of this house for a time. He wanted the sharp morning air on his face and the sea breezes blowing at him and the chance to get his thoughts straight. Maybe he'd go into Dublin. He always had a relaxing time there. Maybe he'd go and see Molly, who had a flat in the suburb of Palmerstown. Molly had ways of unwinding him and God! he needed that now.

He dressed himself slowly in his best suit, a three-piece black worsted with squared shoulders. It was an old-fashioned suit and it looked peculiarly Irish. He dabbed his underarms with deodorant. Then he piled his long hair up on top of his head and covered it with an old black felt hat. He put on a pair of sunglasses. Without these small precautions, his long hair would have drawn attention, and he believed in a low profile when he had to go out in public. He didn't want to look eccentric on the streets, not even in these times when there were punk rockers on Grafton Street with their hair dyed pink and safety pins hanging from their nostrils.

He picked up the telephone and called a number. It was that of the man who usually sat armed out in the gatehouse and who lived nearby.

"George," Finn said. "Will you bring the car around now?"

George said, "Certainly. Where are we headed?"

Finn hesitated a second. "Dublin. I think Dublin would be very nice."

He stepped out of the house and walked down the driveway toward the gatehouse. The March morning was unusually sunny and the only clouds in the sky lay somewhere out in the middle of the Irish Sea—drifting, he hoped, over to England. He sat inside the gatehouse for five minutes; then he saw the old Daimler approach. He hoped America would be kind to Jig. If Jig couldn't get that money back . . . Finn didn't want to think the worst.

The tires of the Daimler crunched on gravel. Finn opened the rear door, climbed inside.

"Palmerstown," Finn said.

The driver nodded. He had driven the Old Man to Palmerstown many times before.

DUBLIN

"No good-byes," Patrick Cairney told the girl.

"I want to drive you to the airport. What's wrong with that?"

"I hate airports. I hate farewells. I get a lump in my throat. My eyes water. I fall to pieces."

Rhiannon Canavan was dressed in her nurse's uniform, over which she wore a green coat with the sleeves dangling empty. Cairney thought she looked particularly lovely.

"Didn't I slip away from the hospital just so I could take you to the airport?"

"I'll call you from the States," he said.

"Oh, sure you will."

"Why do you doubt that?"

She shrugged. "Maybe there's something just a wee bit thrust-and-run about you, Cairney. I don't see you calling me at all."

"Cross my heart."

"I'll drop you off. I won't even come with you *inside* the blasted place!"

Cairney relented. "Promise?"

"I give you my word."

Cairney reached out to touch her face.

"Will you come back to me when your father's better?"

"Or worse."

Rhiannon put a fingertip against his mouth. "Don't say that. I'm sure he's going to be just fine."

Cairney looked at the sky from the window. There was somewhere a weak suggestion of the sun that had been in the heavens earlier but that now lay behind a clutch of miserly clouds. He took Rhiannon Canavan in his arms and held her tightly.

She said, "Some people make complete recoveries from mild heart attacks, you know. I've seen it happen hundreds of time."

Cairney didn't speak.

There was a dryness at the back of his throat. He played with the idea that it would be perfect to stay right here where he was. Just him and this lovely girl in this small apartment. Their own uninterrupted love nest. Silence and exhaustion and the sweetness of flesh. They could lie here and make love and die of malnutrition.

"I've never been in America," the girl said. "Sure, I have millions of aunts and uncles and cousins I've never seen. I think most of them live in Union City, New Jersey. Is it pretty there?"

"In New Jersey?"

"Yeh. Is it pretty?"

"It has its moments. I don't think Union City is one of them, though."

Rhiannon Canavan looked at her small wristwatch. "Are you packed?" she asked, all at once practical. "You don't have a lot of time, Patrick."

"I'm packed."

"We don't even have time for a quickie, do we?"

"How quick's a quickie?" he asked.

"Now that depends entirely on you, doesn't it?"

Patrick Cairney smiled. He wondered if he could lose himself a moment in sheer blind passion, if there was an oxygen bubble inside the vacuum he felt.

Rhiannon kissed him on the lips. It was a warm kiss and he was drawn down into it where he found himself in a well-lit place where there existed neither airplanes nor schedules nor long journeys to make. It was like drowning in tepid, scented water, peacefully and without panic, watching yourself circle and go down and circle and go down again, until there was no further place left to sink to and you were blissfully on the bottom. He slid his hands between the buttons of her uniform, feeling the small breasts under his palms. Her nipples were hard. He worked the uniform open, pushing it back from her shoulders. Her green coat fell to the floor. He traced a line with his fingertips from her breasts to her navel and then down across her smooth stomach, which had a lustrous silken texture.

Afterward, Rhiannon said, "I hate heart attacks."

GEORGE SCULLY, the driver of the Daimler that dropped Finn off in Palmerstown, parked the car on St. Stephen's Green and walked until he came to the large covered marketplace known as the Powerscourt Townhouse, which he entered from South William Street. He passed stalls selling earrings and lace items and Celtic crosses carved in stone and recordings of the Clancy Brothers, and he rose to the upper tier where he entered a coffee shop. He bought a milky coffee, took it to a table, sat down, drummed his fingers impatiently. He knew he didn't have very much time before he would have to get back to the car and pick up the Old Man.

Presently, he heard the sound of somebody whistling tunelessly and a shadow fell across the table. The driver looked up and smiled. The newcomer wore a navy-blue seaman's coat and a woolen hat drawn down over his ears.

"I'll be quick," George Scully said.

The other man nodded. He sat down, looking around the coffee shop.

The driver leaned across the table. "It's just like we thought it would be. He's sending Jig."

"Is he now?"

George Scully said, "I couldn't hear this very well because the Old Man takes precautions like nobody's business, but he's definitely sending Jig." Scully paused and ran the tip of a finger round the rim of his cup. "Sometimes Jig uses a passport in the name of John Doyle. Sometimes not. I happened to be the one who picked up the passport for him, so what I'm telling you is reliable."

The man in the seaman's jacket nodded. "Jig," he said quietly. "Well now. Isn't that something?"

Scully said, "The New York connection is a certain Father Tu-

multy. Your friends in Belfast will want to know that, I'm sure."
Scully was silent a second. He bit uncertainly on his lower lip. "Come
to Dun Laoghaire around ten. The Old Man's with his fancy woman
right now, and he's going to be drunk when he gets home."

"We'll be there."

"The gates will be unlocked. I won't be in the gatehouse."

"Fine," the man in the seaman's jacket said.

George Scully stared into his coffee. He said, "Ten years I've been
with the Old Man. Ten years of guarding him, running his bloody
errands. Long before he started getting all his grand ideas. He wasn't
always the way he is now, a bloody big shot. And what have I got
to show for it? Sweet fuck all."

The man in the seaman's jacket took a brown envelope from inside his shirt and pressed it down on the table and George Scully
picked it up quickly, hiding it under his coat.

"It's all there, Scully. Twenty-five thousand English pounds."

George Scully looked unhappy. "I never thought I'd see this day,"
he remarked.

"You've earned the cash," the other man said.

"There's a bad name for what I'm doing," Scully said solemnly.

"Aye. But you could think of it another way. You're making your
own little contribution to ending the Troubles, aren't you?"

Scully placed a hand around his coffee cup. "We'll see, won't we?"

The other man went back out through the Powerscourt Townhouse to the streets. He walked rapidly, pausing only at the Market
Arcade to place a coin in the can of a blind penny-whistle player.

The blind man was playing "The Minstrel Boy."

> The Minstrel Boy to the war is gone,
> In the ranks of death you'll find him.

The ranks of death.

Jesus, there was going to be a lot of dying.

The man, whose name was Seamus Houlihan and who four nights
ago had been employed as an ordinary seaman on the *Connie O'Mara*,
found a taxi to take him to Connolly Street Station, where he'd be
in time to meet Waddell coming off the train from Belfast.

S IX

LONDON

"Vile," said Sir John Foulkes, who had a flamboyant handlebar moustache and Edwardian sideburns. "This business with Walter Whiteford. Utterly vile, Frank."

Frank Pagan looked from the window of the Under-Secretary's office. A barge was making its way up the River Thames, leaving a wake like a water beetle.

"Why are these assassinations always so vile?" the Under-Secretary asked. It was not so much a question as a reflection on the lack of common decency in the world. The Under-Secretary defined decency in terms of the right breeding, the right schools, and ultimately something that was called "good form," itself a consequence of being expensively raised and expensively educated. It was a vicious circle of privilege, and Pagan sometimes resented it.

Pagan was surrounded every day of his working life with members of the Old School Tie Network, characters who talked casually about going up to Scotland where they had property reserved entirely for grouse shooting or salmon fishing. It was hard at times for Pagan to believe that this was the late twentieth century. He had moments when he leaned toward a form of primitive socialism in which there wouldn't be an aristocracy and the land would belong to everybody. Dream on.

The Under-Secretary fidgeted with the cuffs of his white shirt. Pagan turned away from the view of the Thames. Today, because he knew he was meeting the Under-Secretary, Pagan had made a few concessions. He'd left his blue jeans and sneakers at home. He wore an olive-colored suit and brown slip-on shoes and his slim silk necktie was pale green. All good earth tones, he thought, and by his own standards subdued.

"I am certain to figure somewhere in a future assassination plan," the Under-Secretary said. He swept a hand through the air. "It's not a prospect I relish."

Pagan moved his head slightly. The Under-Secretary was new to Irish affairs. Previously, he had been considered an expert on trade unions. Pagan wondered about his credentials. A knowledge of wage negotiations and how to talk with mining or railway leaders—tasks at which he hadn't been very successful, a fact that perhaps explained his present posting (which was more of a punishment than a job)—wouldn't help him in the quicksands of Irish matters. Pagan understood how these unsuitable appointments happened. It was pal helping pal, one Old Boy to another, and to hell with credentials. Only your school background mattered. Incompetence in the higher echelons of power, Pagan thought, could always be traced back to the fact that unqualified men had gone to the right public schools. It was a good way to run a country.

Sir John had his cuffs to his liking now. "Ireland is a nightmare to me, Frank. I have times when I *think* I've penetrated its various complexities. But then it seems to slip away from me." He stroked his enormous moustache. The satirical magazine *Private Eye* had christened him Furry Jake.

"It does that," Pagan agreed.

"Why in the name of God are we still in Northern Ireland?"

Pagan smiled. He wondered if the Under-Secretary really wanted an answer or whether he'd just asked another of those rhetorical questions in which, like all politicians, he specialized. Pagan decided he'd answer anyway. "Because it's what the Protestant majority wants, Sir John."

"We should just get the hell out of Ulster and say 'There, chaps, go work out your own differences with the South.' "

Pagan laid a hand on the Under-Secretary's huge desk. There wasn't a piece of paper anywhere. He glanced at the bookshelves. Several histories of Ireland were stacked there. They looked as if they hadn't been opened. "We can't let them settle their own differences so long as the Protestant majority in the North wants to remain a part of the United Kingdom," he said. "If the day comes when the North wants to be a part of a unified Ireland, fine. Personally I don't see that happening. There's too much hatred between Catholic and Protestant."

The Under-Secretary leaned back in his padded leather chair.

"And there are too many suspicions on both sides," Pagan continued, wondering if it was easier for Furry Jake to get his history in small doses like this instead of having to crack open the tomes on the bookshelf. Sometimes Pagan encountered an almost willful simple-mindedness in the higher reaches of power that appalled him. People like the Under-Secretary, in defiance of the tenets of Darwinism, hadn't evolved since the days when the British Empire could put down a Zulu uprising with a handful of rifles and some good men.

Pagan said, "The Protestants in the North are scared shitless by the predominance of the Catholic Church in the South. They think that in a unified Ireland they'd be discriminated against because then *they'd* be in a minority. They don't like giving up their present status. Right now they're the lords of all they survey, but there's a tide rising against them."

The Under-Secretary didn't look very interested. He had the expression of an unwilling participant in a crammer course. There was also the fact that he wasn't absolutely sure of Frank Pagan's loyalties. Some said Pagan was just a little too *soft* on the South.

Pagan went on regardless. There was a certain wicked enjoyment in the idea of instructing the Under-Secretary in his job and knowing that he was causing him a minor irritation. "The Catholics in the Republic don't trust the Protestants in the North because of their allegiance with England. And there's been too much English misbehavior in the past." *Misbehavior*, he thought. There was a neat little euphemism. "People don't forget quickly. They can't forget how the English have treated Ireland over the centuries. They can't put aside the fact that the English have gone periodically into Ireland and filled the streets with Irish blood."

"That's ancient history, Frank." Sir John made a small gesture of impatience.

"To you, maybe. But England has a dirty name over there. It stands for Oliver Cromwell slaughtering the inhabitants of Wexford in 1649 and then as a gesture of *real* goodwill, committing atrocities on priests of the Roman Catholic Church. It's a potato famine and starvation, which was exploited by English landowners who didn't exactly shed tears when they saw Irishmen either starve to death or be packed into emigrant ships—coffin ships—because it meant they didn't have to rent their land to the bloody peasants. It's the fact that in six miserable years in the late 1840s, one million people died as a result of famine, while the English landlords didn't suffer a bit. Quite the opposite; the buggers prospered."

The Under-Secretary frowned. Pagan leaned against the bookshelves. Instant history, he thought.

"And the Irish can't forget that in our own century the English crushed the Easter Rising of 1916 with more enthusiasm than the event merited. Somehow we managed to kill about five hundred men of the Irish Volunteers, a militant group of *really* dangerous men who were poorly armed and badly trained and were never any match for English field guns. And then we went on to execute the leaders of the Rising in front of firing squads. We did a wonderful job all around, didn't we?"

Sir John stood up. A joint cracked in his leg. He didn't say anything for a time. With his back to Pagan he looked down at the river. "You sound rather sympathetic to the Irish, Frank."

"I've tried to understand them, that's all." You might give it a shot yourself, Sir John. Open a book or two. Do yourself a favor.

The Under-Secretary stared at him curiously. He wasn't happy with Pagan's tone, but then he wasn't sure if Pagan was really the right man for the job anyway. His search for Jig, for example, hadn't exactly been a resounding success. "IRA gunmen wander the streets of Belfast," he said after a while. "They shoot British soldiers. Protestants arm themselves in basements to fight against the Catholics and the IRA. And we've got this lunatic fellow Jig doing all kinds of damage." The Under-Secretary fingered his moustache and quietly suppressed a belch, pulling his chin down into his neck. It was all very polite, Pagan thought.

The Under-Secretary went on, "Damned troublesome island, Frank. Hardly worth the bother. It's not as if we actually *get* anything out of it save for a great deal of grief, is it? It's not as if they're one of the OPEC nations sitting on millions of barrels of oil or something like that. Sooner we're out of it, the better."

Pagan said nothing. Furry Jake's ignorance and insensitivity was really quite impressive.

"How do you propose to catch Jig, Frank?"

This question echoed inside Pagan like a minor chord struck on piano keys. "I wish I had the answer to that," he said, a bleak little response to the problem that dogged him constantly.

The Under-Secretary turned. "It has to be given top priority, Frank."

"It has," Pagan replied.

"I mean *top*, Frank."

Pagan nodded. The Under-Secretary annoyed him the way all his kind did. They issued their orders and then went out to lunch at their clubs. Fine old sherry and quail eggs and men dozing in leather armchairs behind copies of *The Daily Telegraph*. The death of the British Empire in microcosm in the fancy clubs of Pall Mall, where you needed a pedigree from Debrett's *Peerage* before you could actually breath the air.

"What about this business with the ship?" the Under-Secretary asked.

Only that morning Foxie had brought Pagan another telex on the matter, this time one sent from the FBI to Scotland Yard. Pagan had read the thing quickly.

"Special Branch is handling that," he said. "My whole section is busy with Jig. Exclusively."

"Mmmm," the Under-Secretary said. "Just the same, Frank, I wish you had paid it some attention yourself. It does come under your domain, after all."

The little arsehole was scolding him. Pagan studied his fingernails a moment. "My latest information is that we've had a positive ID of the individual whose hand was severed at the wrist. One Sean Riordan, aka the Courier, a resident of Philadelphia. His function was the delivery of capital to his sources in Ireland from sources unknown in the United States. So it's fair to assume the *Connie* was carrying an amount of cash."

"Why do the Americans insist on sending money to those brutes?"

Pagan shrugged. He could have made an easy answer: historic ties. But it went deeper than that, down into the mists of darker emotions and old sentiments and an idealized conception of Ireland that was aroused in many Irish-Americans whenever they heard the first few bars of "Danny Boy." This sedimentary yearning had a way of opening wallets.

The Under-Secretary asked, "Do you have any opinion on who seized this money?"

"No, I don't. But you can bet that the IRA will be more than unhappy about the whole thing. What I wonder is how they're going to react."

Furry Jake smiled. The idea of the IRA suffering a setback pleased him hugely. "One other thing, Frank. I don't much care for the press we've been getting. I don't think you should say anything to reporters. Let the commissioner do any talking that has to be done. He likes to see his name in print."

"All I ever said was 'No comment.' "

"I know that, but some of our journalists take that as an admission of defeat. The commissioner has more . . . experience in handling the press than you, Frank." The Under-Secretary looked at his watch. "Well, Frank. Keep me posted, will you?"

"I will, Sir John."

"And will you make sure Special Branch keeps its vigilance?"

"I've already requested that security at your home be doubled," Pagan said.

"My wife worries," said the Under-Secretary, smiling thinly.

And you don't, of course. Pagan went to the door. He heard Sir John clear his throat.

"Catch him, Frank. Catch Jig."

Pagan stopped at the door.

The Under-Secretary said, "No matter what it takes, you have to catch this fellow."

"Exactly how do you want him?" Pagan asked. There was a faint hint of sarcasm in his voice, which the Under-Secretary didn't notice. *Catch Jig.* Just like that. What the hell did the Under-Secretary think Frank Pagan had been trying to do?

The Under-Secretary looked a little puzzled. "What do you mean, how do I want him?"

"Dead or alive?" Pagan asked. Poached? Toasted? Pickled? Take your pick, Sir John.

"Ah." The Under-Secretary was quiet a moment. "I don't think it matters one way or another with scum like that, do you?"

"Quite," Pagan said and stepped out into a carpeted corridor. *Catch Jig.*

The Under-Secretary called out to him, "Been meaning to ask. Who's your tailor, Frank?"

Pagan stopped. He looked back into the office. "Nobody in particular. Sometimes Harry's Nostalgia Boutique on the Portobello Road. Sometimes Crolla on Dover Street. Why? You want the addresses?"

"Not really," said the Under-Secretary.

DUBLIN

The man known as Jig did not leave the Republic of Ireland from Dublin Airport, although he went there initially. He was accustomed to creating a maze of his own movements. At the terminal he went inside the men's room and locked himself in a cubicle where he changed his clothes.

He did this as an ordinary, everyday precaution, something that had become second nature to him. He removed his suit and shoes, stuffed them inside his canvas bag, then put on an old pair of faded cord pants and a heavy sweater. He placed a cap firmly on his head and pulled it down over his brow. On his feet he wore the kind of sturdy boots a casual laborer might have worn. Anyone who saw him emerge from the men's room would have seen a man on his way to look for work somewhere—a man who shuffled a little, like somebody defeated by the prospects of ever finding employment. He wore a money belt concealed beneath his sweater. It contained ten thousand American dollars, one thousand pounds in sterling and five hundred Irish *punts*.

He walked out of the terminal and into the parking lot. The car he chose was a drab brown Hillman Minx. In the old days, a car might have been left there for him on purpose but now, with all Finn's mania for secrecy, cars were stolen, not supplied. A supplied car had the distinct disadvantage of being arranged in *advance*, which afforded one's enemies the chance and the time to find out about it. Stealing, Finn always reasoned, was less risky because it was random.

The Minx spluttered and hacked like an old man in a terminal ward. Jig drove it as far as the Connolly Street Station in Dublin, where he bought a train ticket for Belfast. Once there, he would fly to Glasgow and take a bus to Prestwick Airport on the Ayrshire coast, where he'd catch a flight to New York City.

It was a circuitous and time-consuming route, but it was one of Finn's maxims that you saved time by spending some, that when you were in a hurry you were always prone to that evil demon Carelessness. Survival, Finn always said, is a matter of attention to the mundane. A matter, boyo, of *detail*.

Jig opened a newspaper on the train and read an editorial that referred to Walter Whiteford's decapitation. It was funny, though. He couldn't make a mental picture of a headless man, couldn't see the head tearing away from the body and rolling down a cobble-stoned street. He had a gift for abstraction. He didn't think in particulars when it came to violence. He always tried to make his acts of violence swift and clean and painless. Finn had drummed this into him. Even now Jig could hear the old man's melodic voice in his head. *You only need to kill. You don't need to make your victims suffer. In and out with precision, boy, never needless cruelty. This is a war, not a torture chamber.* Walter Whiteford wouldn't have had the time to feel anything. Gone. Like that. Like a candle blown out on an empty Mayfair street. *You don't kill the meek, and you don't kill the innocent. You only kill the harmful, and even then you do it with economy and speed and grace.*

Economy, speed, grace. Jig remembered how Finn, at the point of farewell, had forgone his usual firm handshake in favor of an embrace, which had been tight and almost painful as if the old man were reluctant at the last to send Jig on such an unmapped errand. There had been none of the usual last-minute instructions, no quiet encouragement, just an odd imploring look in Finn's eyes which had put Jig in mind of a man facing the impossibilities of ever seeing his ambitions realized. It wasn't a look Jig liked to see. For a second it hadn't been Finn's face at all, it had lost buoyancy and strength and resilience, like a mask cast suddenly aside by its wearer. It was more than the loss of the money, Jig knew that. It was the loss of all the schemes and plans and uses that the money was good for.

Jig had a sense of sleep coming in on a dark cloud, so he rose and stood in the corridor with the window open and the rainy air blowing against his face. The fresh smell of the nearby sea came rushing toward him.

He had left Dublin before on other missions. But this time, with the wind blowing at his face and the rain on his skin, this time was different for reasons he didn't altogether understand.

He stood at the window and he thought about the great love he had for this country. He thought of the valleys of Glendalough and lmaal and Clara. The bewitching landscape of Kerry and the great peninsulas of lveragh and Dingle. The towns of Tralee and Inch and Kenmare and that strange uninhabited group of islands called the Blaskets, which sat lonely in the Atlantic tide. Once, the largest of the Blaskets had been called the next parish to America.

America. And good-bye, Mr. Pagan.

He watched the rails slide past under the March sky, and he wondered when he'd see Ireland and Finn again.

LONDON

Frank Pagan lived alone in a flat at the top of a Victorian house in Holland Park. There had been a time in his life when he had enjoyed the place, when he'd found himself hurrying home from the office and taking the steps two at a time in his haste. Now when the street door closed behind him, he went up through the dark slowly.

He took out his key when he reached the apartment.

Inside, the air was trapped and stale. He turned on the living-room lamp and poured himself a glass of scotch, which he carried inside the bedroom. The bed was unmade, the room cold. He sat on the edge of the bed without taking off his raincoat. Bleak House, he thought.

His usual method of cutting back the edge of bleakness was to play rock music loudly. He liked it full blast and raucous enough for dainty Miss Gabler in the flat below to rush upstairs complaining about that "dreadful Negro music" and Pagan would say, Now, now, Hedda (even though her name was Cynthia), we mustn't criticize music on racial grounds, must we? A dose of Little Richard or some early Jerry Lee Lewis usually worked for him, but tonight he didn't want to play the stereo.

His condition was paralysis of the heart.

He reached out across the clutter of the bedside table and touched a framed photograph of his wife, Roxanne, then drew his hand away as if it had been scalded. There was still too much pain here. Sometimes he wondered if it would ever go away entirely. It had been more than two years now and there was still the same old nightmare, there were still times when he'd sit up in the darkened bedroom and smoke cigarettes and imagine he heard the sounds of Roxanne moving in the other rooms.

Once, when he'd drunk too much Chivas Regal, he stumbled through the apartment calling out her name. Banging doors open, slamming them shut, saying his wife's name over and over like some incantation, he stalked her. The rooms were all empty, all dark. He'd never encountered anything like that kind of emptiness before. It was worse than any pain he could ever have imagined.

Dreams, Pagan thought. Roxanne was gone. He glanced at the photograph. It was a fine face with wide bright eyes that were filled with an amused intelligence. The mouth suggested great depths of humor. It was the kind of mouth that had been built for smiling. Sweet Christ, how he had loved her! Even now, he loved her. *But Roxanne was gone.* Then why in the name of God did he keep sensing her presence in this bloody apartment?

He got up from the bed and wandered inside the kitchen. There were eggshells in the sink and coffee stains on the surface of the stove. He sat at the kitchen table and finished his drink and his eyes brimmed with moisture. He wiped them with the sleeve of his coat. Maudlin behavior. He was being drawn down into the morbid center of himself. He poured a second drink.

"Roxanne," Pagan whispered. "Dear Roxanne."

Outside, a March wind came rushing out of the night, springing through the shrubbery. He heard the branch of a tree knock against the side of the house.

Pagan sat down, fidgeted with his glass. He liked to think of himself as a practical man living in a practical world, one without psychic interference. He liked to think his personal radio was tuned only to what was broadcast in reality, not to ghosts, not to dreams. But what was this presence of Roxanne he kept feeling? Why did he keep talking aloud to a woman who was no longer alive?

Pagan closed his eyes tightly. He didn't need to remember any of this.

Roxanne Pagan, twenty-seven years of age, had died at Christmas, 1984, killed on a Kensington street. She had been doing some last-minute Christmas shopping. She didn't know that a man called Eddie Rattigan had planted a bomb inside a wastebasket beside a bus stop. She didn't know that her own life was destined to collide with the violent longing of Eddie Rattigan, who later told the police he wanted to make a political statement on behalf of all IRA soldiers held in Northern Irish jails.

Roxanne Pagan had been passing the wastebasket when the explosion took place. Eddie Rattigan's bomb killed seven people and injured a dozen others. Eddie Rattigan's "political statement" killed Roxanne and tore the heart out of Frank Pagan's life, shattering his world in a matter of a second.

Pagan blinked at the window. He remembered Eddie Rattigan's

trial. He recalled the small man's interminable smirk during the whole proceedings. Rattigan was *pleased* with himself. *Pleased* that his bomb had actually worked! After Rattigan was sentenced to life imprisonment Pagan had worked for months on a wild plan to get inside Wormwood Scrubs and kill the man. But the notion of vengeance passed, and he was left with an emptiness that had been with him ever since.

Pagan went into the bedroom. He wanted to sleep but he didn't want to close his eyes because he knew the nightmare would rush in at him again. In this awful dream he was running down that Kensington street toward Roxanne and he was always too late to warn her. He shouted her name until his throat ached but she never heard him, never turned in his direction. Turn! For God's sake, turn! Pagan would scream. Screaming, running. And then the explosion came. Which was when Pagan always woke, shivering and afraid and wracked by unspeakable grief.

He removed his coat and tossed it across a chair. Then he kicked off his shoes and sat with his back to a pillow, his glass in his hand. He understood that he was a lonely man, but he'd come to terms with that. Once or twice since Roxanne's death he'd gone out, hitting a couple of bars where single people stared morosely at one another and casual sexual assignations were made with all the passion of people selecting lamb chops out of a butcher's window. The whole scene depressed Pagan. If he didn't belong there, where did he belong? Here in this apartment with a phantom? Was that his future?

He smoked a cigarette. He had a third drink. Halfway through it his front doorbell rang. He glanced at the bedside clock: 9:45. He went inside the living room, where he switched on the intercom button.

"Who is it?" he said.

"Drummond, Mr. Pagan. It's Jerry Drummond." The voice crackled up from the street.

"What do you want?"

"I have a message for you."

"I'm listening, Jerry."

"Not like this. Let me come up, Mr. Pagan."

Pagan sighed. He pressed the buzzer that opened the street door. He heard the sound of footsteps on the stairs. Then Drummond's soft knock at the door.

A small man with pointed ears, Jerry Drummond wore long side-whiskers and invariably had a green silk scarf knotted at his throat. His nickname, perhaps predictably, was the Leprechaun.

"I'm not meaning to disturb you, Mr. Pagan," Drummond said as he came into the room.

"It's late, Jerry."

"So it is, so it is." Jerry Drummond sat down, taking a flat tin from his overcoat. There would be, Pagan knew, the usual elaborate performance of rolling a cigarette, which Drummond did with all the intensity of an architect designing a cathedral.

"And how is yerself today?" the Leprechaun asked.

Pagan nodded. "I've known better days, Jerry."

The little man lit his cigarette and his cheeks subsided into huge hollows as he puffed. "Haven't we all known better days?"

"What do you have for me, Jerry?" Pagan asked.

"Oh," said the Leprechaun mysteriously, twinkling like a Christmas tree light.

"I don't have all night. You said you had a message, Jerry."

The little man smoked furiously. At one time, he'd been a promising apprentice jockey at a stable in Newmarket, but a fondness for alcohol and a lack of discipline had finished his career quickly. Now, he was an odd-job man who was also one of Pagan's many connections to the puzzle known as Ireland.

"It's from some of the boys," the Leprechaun said.

"Which boys?"

"I'm not at liberty to say, Mr. Pagan."

"Then I don't want to hear, Jerry. You know what I think about anonymous messages."

Jerry Drummond was using his open left hand as an ashtray. "I do, I do," he said. "But I'm just a simple messenger. I can't tell you everything you think you want to know, can I? A messenger has only limited information, after all. He's like a walk-on part in a play, when you think about it—"

Sighing, Pagan interrupted. He knew the little man could gab all night long, going off at tangents. "Who sent you, Jerry?"

Drummond was quiet for a time. "Shall we just say it's a certain party interested in bringing Jig to justice?"

"Jig?"

"Right."

"What about Jig?" A tiny flutter went through Pagan's heart.

Drummond leaned forward, looking conspiratorial. "I'm to tell you that Jig is on his way to the United States of America, Mr. Pagan."

"And why would Jig be going to the United States, Jerry?"

"I understand there's a small matter of some missing money to be settled, Mr. Pagan."

Pagan finished his scotch and set the glass down. "How do you know this, Jerry?"

"Tut-tut," Drummond said, his eyes wide.

Pagan said, "If you expect me to believe your story, Jerry, you better tell me its source. Otherwise, I'm going to throw you out of here. Bodily."

"Ah, the English don't know the meaning of hospitality, do they now?" the Leprechaun smiled. He tilted his tiny pear-shaped face back and stared at the ceiling. "Let me say this much, seeing as how you threatened me with physical violence just then and me being a peaceable sort of fellow and all. Let me just say the message comes from members of the Free Ulster Volunteers, Mr. Pagan."

"That bunch of scum?"

"They're fine men, Mr. Pagan. They believe in keeping Northern Ireland for Britain. Could anybody have a finer goal than that, eh?"

The Free Ulster Volunteers. In recent years Frank Pagan had become bewildered by the proliferation of groups and sects that had arisen in Ireland. There was a thicket of them, each with its own initials. And they spawned themselves on almost a daily basis. Even with the help of computers, it was impossible to keep track. On the Protestant side, Pagan had heard such names as the Tartan Hand, Tara (an allegedly homosexual group of anti-Catholics), the Ulster Defense Association, the Ulster Freedom Fighters, the New Apprentice Boys, the Free Ulster Liberation Army. The Catholic IRA had split into cells and groups, some of them of a religious nature, some with Marxist objectives, others with ties to terrorists groups in Germany and Italy. Disenchanted IRA members had formed their own outfits. The Irish Liberation Army. The New Sinn Fein. The Catholic Brotherhood. More recently Pagan had heard whispers concerning something called the Association of the Wolfe, supposedly run by a man named Finn, who appeared nowhere in Pagan's data banks. Some of these organizations were chimerical. Others exaggerated their membership. A few had power. Finn was said to have his hands on the bankbooks, but whoever Finn was—and Pagan suspected the name was a pseudonym—he obviously led a secluded life, far removed from the conflicts of Belfast and Derry. Certainly, none of Pagan's sources knew the man.

Pagan sighed. Irish goulash. Rich, impenetrable, inedible, filled as it was with alphabet macaroni.

The Free Ulster Volunteers was a Belfast-based clandestine group of Protestant thugs who specialized in torturing and killing anybody with a connection to the IRA. When they couldn't find a bona fide IRA member, any passing Catholic would do. Now and then, they slipped over the border into the Republic to make a hit.

The FUV was allegedly connected, in tenuous ways, with a Belfast zealot called the Reverend Ivor McInnes, a pastor without a church. He'd been ejected from the official Presbyterian Church for preaching sermons designed to encourage his congregation in the belief that Catholicism, like cigarettes, was bad for your health and should therefore be abolished. McInnes still wore his dog collar and drew huge crowds of Ulster Loyalists to hear him speak in public places. He was one of those fire and brimstone shouters who could raise the temperature of a mob to boiling point. He was a man of many gifts—charm, eloquence, and that nebulous quality called charisma—but Pagan considered them wasted ones. Ivor was utterly committed, some would say blindly so, to a Northern Ireland free of any Catholic influence. He didn't want his own little domain, all five thousand square miles of. it, all one million and a half souls, tainted by popery, dogged by priests and nuns. Pagan had never been able to prove conclusively that Ivor was the power behind the FUV. If he was, he somehow contrived cunningly to keep himself removed from the organization.

"Exactly who in the Free Ulster Volunteers sent you here? Ivor McInnes?"

"Now, Mr. Pagan. We all know the Reverend isn't associated with the FUV, don't we?"

"Don't make me laugh, Jerry."

The Leprechaun smoothed out the folds in his coat. "Can't we just say the FUV sent me here and leave it at that?"

"It's not precise enough, Jerry. Give me a name. Give me something authentic."

The Leprechaun sighed. It was a long-drawn-out sound. "One name, that's all."

"One's enough," Pagan said.

"John Waddell."

"Waddell?" Frank Pagan brought an image of Waddell to mind.

He was a short man with a sharp face that was practically all snout. Eight months ago Pagan had interviewed John Waddell in connection with the killing of an IRA man in the London suburb of Chalk Farm. At the time, Pagan hadn't been impressed by Waddell, who struck him as strangely timid and not at all the kind of material the FUV would use in an assassination. He'd released Waddell for lack of evidence, convinced that the man hadn't had anything to do with the murder. Too scared. Too gun-shy. Now he wasn't so certain. The FUV absorbed all types, especially the meek and the cowardly, who found the courage to act only when they were concealed under the umbrella of a movement. "Your information came *directly* from John Waddell?"

"I'm not saying," Drummond answered.

"But he's involved."

"Mr. Pagan, you asked for a name, I gave you one. Don't be pressing me for more than I can give you."

Pagan thought for a second. "Why would the Free Ulster Volunteers want me to have this message, Jerry?"

"You're looking for Jig, are you not?"

Pagan nodded. His mouth was dry. He filled two glasses with scotch and gave one to Drummond.

Drummond smacked his lips and said, "You've got the resources to find him. You and the Yanks between you. You can find him before he kills somebody else." The word "kills" came out of the Leprechaun's mouth as *culls*. Pagan disliked the hard accent of Belfast. The Dublin lilt, by contrast, could be musical and hypnotic.

"How does the FUV come by this information?" Pagan asked.

"That's something I wouldn't know," Drummond answered. "I'm only told so much, Mr. Pagan, and it would be fruitless for me to speculate, wouldn't it now? But the members of the FUV would like for you to get your hands on Jig and hang the bastard. They don't like seeing somebody going around killing politicians who are sympathetic to the free Protestants of the North."

Pagan sipped his drink. "We don't hang people in this country, Jerry."

"More's the pity."

"I almost agree with you," Pagan said.

There was a silence in the room. The missing money the Leprechaun had mentioned was presumably the same that had been on the *Connie O'Mara*. Attached, Pagan guessed, to the Courier's wrist. But there was something here that didn't quite fit, and he felt faintly uneasy. How the hell did the Free Ulster Volunteers get this information? How did they get so close to Jig that they knew his movements? Or had Jerry Drummond been sent here to convey false information? But that made absolutely no sense. Why would the little man come here with a pack of lies?

He looked at the Leprechaun. "What else can you tell me, Jerry?"

"I've already told you a wee bit more than I intended, Mr. Pagan. What else is there?"

"America's a big place."

Drummond finished his drink and stood up. He was twinkling again and there was a certain mischief in his eyes. "Oh, didn't I mention New York, Mr. Pagan?"

"No, you didn't mention New York."

"And Father Tumulty? Did I mention him?"

Pagan shook his head. This was so typical of Drummond. He'd dole his message out in fragments, getting as much mileage out of it as he possibly could. He was like a comedian taking a tortuous, suspenseful route to his punch line.

"Who's Father Tumulty?" Pagan asked.

"Sounds like a priest to me," and Drummond smiled.

Pagan heard the night wind spring up again. "Is that the complete message now, Jerry?"

"Aye." Drummond seemed hesitant. "Wait. There's one other thing. Jig sometimes uses a passport made out in the name of John Doyle."

Pagan took the empty glass out of Drummond's hand. "Why don't your friends in the FUV go after Jig themselves?"

"All the way to New York, Mr. Pagan? They couldn't afford that kind of expense. You, on the other hand, you travel all expenses paid, don't you? Besides, they don't have your resources, Mr. Pagan. Nor your expertise. And you'd have the Americans to help you out, with their computers and all. The only computer I ever saw belonging to a member of the FUV was a small Japanese thing he used for playing Pac-Man. Then it went on the blink."

Pagan watched the little man a moment. "You really expect me to drop everything and transport myself to New York on your say-so, Jerry?"

The Leprechaun looked hurt. "Mr. Pagan, have I ever given you false information? Have I ever done that?"

"No."

"Didn't I tell you about that shipment of rifles in Ostend? The ones in wooden crates marked BUTTER that were destined for Dublin? Didn't I do that for you? And wasn't that true?"

Pagan nodded his head.

"And didn't I tell you about a small IRA bomb factory right here in Fulham? Right here on your own doorstep? Was that a lie?"

"Jerry, your information has always been high quality. But this is something quite different."

"I don't see why you would disbelieve me now."

"Maybe because I don't exactly trust your FUV friends, Jerry."

The Leprechaun got out of his chair. "Cross my heart, Mr. Pagan. This is all on the level. Jig is on his way to New York City. And you'd be a fool to ignore that fact." "Fool" pronounced *fule.*

Pagan watched the little man go out. Alone again, he found the apartment smaller than before. The walls pressed in on him. It made sense, he thought, that Jig would be the one to track down the missing capital. The man was a hunter. He had predatory instincts and the capability of vanishing on the wind. But how did the FUV get hold of this information?

The question turned over in his mind again, and he had the feeling he was missing something, something important. Puzzled, he went back inside the bedroom and sat down. For a moment he tried to imagine Jig's face. A young man, an unremarkable face you wouldn't look twice at in the street, drab unassuming clothes. Perhaps a nervous mannerism. A tic in the jaw. A fingernail biter. A way of smoking cigarettes right down to the filter. Nicotine stains. Slightly discolored teeth. And maybe there was a light in his eye, something that suggested intensity. He had to be intense, committed to his purpose. Highly trained too. The kind of training that wasn't available in Ireland. The kind you went abroad to get in places like Libya and Cuba.

Pagan lay back across the bed. Had the American suppliers of the money somehow turned their thinking around and seized their capital back on the high seas?

Pagan sat up now. The sense of being perplexed wouldn't leave him. There was something a little askew, out of joint. He couldn't think what except that there were small threads he couldn't quite stitch together. They kept unraveling in his mind.

He reached for the photograph of Roxanne and held it tilted under the bedside lamp so that the glass caught the yellow glow of electricity.

"New York City," Pagan said to his ghost. "It's been a long time."

SEVEN

Finn woke in his dark bedroom, his throat dry. He pushed himself into an upright position, and there was a pain at the back of his head. It was the whiskey he'd drunk at Molly's. Now he had one hell of a hangover. He should have known better—his old body couldn't take the drink the way it used to. Sweet Jesus! He could remember times when he'd wake with a big black dog of a hangover and start drinking right away and go on for three or four days at a time.

He left the room and stepped out onto the landing.

Halfway down the stairs he stopped. He listened to the darkness. He had a fine instinct for the night. He thought sometimes he had a personal angel who whispered nocturnal warnings in his ear. In the distance he heard the cry of an owl. But there was some other thing too, something he couldn't altogether place, like the soft sound of an animal moving in the undergrowth.

He reached the bottom step and looked across the room filled with harps. There was thin crystal moonlight falling through the window. He stood motionless, listening. The owl had gone. But there was still something else, an undercurrent.

Finn padded inside the kitchen, bare feet slapping floorboards. He drew a glass of water from the tap and devoured it quickly. He rinsed the glass because he was a tidy man and had always been fastidious in his way, perhaps because he'd lived a solitary life without a wife to help him. He was married to the Cause like a bloody nun married to Christ. If he could turn back the clocks of his life, what he'd do was marry Molly Newbigging and get a decent job and settle down with a big brood of kids. He thought of Molly's white thighs and her large rounded breasts and that way she had of seeing straight through to the bones of him.

He left the kitchen, moving along a narrow hallway in the direction of his small study. There was a loaded pistol in his desk. It was a Mauser that dated from the 1920s and it had once belonged to old Dan Breen, commandant of the Third Tipperary Brigade of the IRA. The pistol was of great sentimental value to Finn because it had been given to him personally by Breen shortly before the old fellow died in 1969.

Finn stepped inside his study. He stared at the gun, then reached down for it and picked it up, holding it loosely in his right hand. The feel of the weapon made him think of the first time he'd ever entrusted Jig with a task. It had happened during their third or fourth meeting, which had taken place on a cold morning at Glasnevin Cemetery.

Finn, who was invariably spooked by places of death because he resented anything as disruptive as the act of dying, had stared for a long time into the boy's eyes. What the hell did he really know about this young man anyway? After a few clandestine encounters, what could he really say he'd learned about the young man's history? The boy constantly dismissed his past as irrelevant. He was as much a mystery as he'd been in the beginning, and the only thing Finn didn't doubt was his commitment to justice and his yearning for action. These were real enough. But there were walls around him still, and Finn was uneasy with men who erected barricades. If he was ever to know this young man, if he was ever to cross the wall, he was going to have to take the first step himself. A big step—because its only basis was Finn's own hunch, his instinct that the boy could prove valuable to the Association of the Wolfe and the Cause in general. There were times in one's life when intuition overrode the dictates of sweet reason, and this was going to be one of them. And Finn, who had an almost arrogant pride in his ability to judge character, had an instinct about the boy that was almost as clear as a melody in his head.

A certain man has to be eliminated.

Who and where? Jig asked.

Don't you want to know the why of it, boy?

Jig shook his head and looked between rows of tombstones. *I know what you stand for. If you consider this man your enemy, what else do I need to know?*

I'm flattered by your trust in me, Finn had answered. *But you've got a lot to learn. You trust too easily. You react too quickly. You're too bloody impatient.*

Maybe I need a teacher, Finn.

Finn had strolled among ancient graves, noticing broken crosses and moss climbing over stone and a bedraggled cat asleep on a fallen marker. He'd studied the names of the dead. O'Hara. Ryan. Corcoran. Fine Irish names. Brendan Behan, whom Finn remembered as a hot-blooded young IRA recruit, was buried somewhere at Glasnevin, dead and wasted by drink.

Teach me, Finn, the boy said.

Finn had turned to look at the young man again. He'd seen it then in the boy's face, almost as if a guard had slipped and fallen away. It was the face of a kid anxious to please an elder, a vulnerable look that Finn wouldn't have thought belonged in the boy's repertoire of expressions. It was uncharacteristic and eager, without a hint of toughness, and it was Finn's first real encounter with what he thought of as the young man's inner self. For the first time, too, Finn felt a strong affection for the boy, a sensation that took him by surprise. It was this moment, in which he perceived Jig's naked enthusiasm, that made Finn take the revolver from the pocket of his overcoat and pass it slowly to the young man.

There's no pleasure in killing, boy. If you're after thrills, I don't need you. Let's get that straight from the start. I don't need a vandal or a hooligan. I want somebody who understands the reasons behind his actions.

I'm not looking for thrills, Finn.

And when you work for me there's no money in it. You'll get enough to keep yourself in food and shelter, but nobody ever got rich from the Cause.

I don't remember ever asking for money, Finn.

It was the answer Finn had expected. *You'd have to go to Belfast,* he said. *A man called Cassidy is doing some damage to us.*

That was all. Cassidy's offense, which the boy hadn't asked about, hadn't even seemed to *care* about, was that he had been talking too freely with the British Army about IRA operations. Jig had gone to Belfast before the end of that same week and shot Cassidy as he was stepping out of a public house called the Butcher's Arms at closing time. One shot, delivered with accuracy. One shot, then Jig was gone. He had the eye of a natural marksman and the affinity of a night creature for the crevices of darkness in which to hide. Later, when the young man had returned to the Republic, Finn had told him that in future he'd need a nom de guerre. *We'll call you Jig,* he'd said. *If you're the dancer I think you might be, it's a damn good name.* I molded you, Jig, he thought. You gave me the basic edifice and I improved it. And somewhere along the way we came to understand and maybe even love one another a little bit too. And where are you now, Jig? *Where the hell have I sent you?*

He wished Jig were beside him in this house. He needed the young man's nerve, because his own wasn't what it had been in the old days when he'd been as sharp as a razor and as daring as anything that ever cavorted on a trapeze. The old days! Jesus, the old days had been fine, but they were gone, and what faced him now was the stark reality of danger. With his pistol in front of him, he stepped back into the hallway and moved toward the room with the harps. He went to the window and looked in the direction of the gatehouse.

George Scully, reliable George, was on guard tonight.

Finn breathed on the windowpane. The guardhouse was in darkness, which meant nothing in itself because Scully might have turned out the light simply to enjoy the quiet of the night. George, who had been with Finn for years, had been known to turn the light off and lean against the wall and prop up his feet and breathe the Atlantic air into his lungs while he recited the poems of W. B. Yeats quietly to himself.

A shiver went through Finn. The hairs on the back of his neck bristled. Something was going on out there. Something that pressed upon the whitewashed house and set up a vibration audible only to his ears. He shut his eyes, listened. He thought suddenly of that poor boat hijacked on the high seas, he thought of the dead men and the missing money, and the shipload of arms that had slipped away from him. He was sick to his heart.

Eyes open now, pistol forward. *Beware, Finn.* It was the voice of his angel. He could hear it clearly.

He moved among the harps, his pistol trained on the doorway.

He held his breath and stood very still. It was always possible, he supposed, that someone had overpowered Scully down there in the gatehouse. But there would have been shooting, wouldn't there? Scully would have fired off one of his weapons, wouldn't he? Unless he'd been taken out suddenly, with no warning and no time to defend himself.

Finn moved very slightly.

His heart, his bloody heart, thumped upon his ribs like a rabbit stuck in a snare. He moved an inch, two inches, edging between harps, going in the direction of the doorway. Dan Breen's Mauser was heavy in his hand.

Out in the hallway now. Facing the front door. Waiting.

Was that the wind that rattled the shrubbery and set it shaking?

He moved slowly down the narrow hallway.

He placed one hand on the door handle.

Then he drew the door open and peered out into the night, his Mauser raised for action.

There were two men outside, both holding automatic weapons. Finn barely had time to register this fact before he heard the first few rounds. He thought it strange that he felt nothing although he knew he'd been hit.

He staggered backward down the corridor into the room of harps, aware of blood seeping out of his body, conscious of the hushed voice that said, *I told you, Finn. Beware. I told you that.* Finn skidded across the floor of the big room, his legs abruptly cut out from beneath his body, his feet slithering over pools of his own lost blood, and he stumbled against a harp, his head tipping forward between the strings of the instrument so that he was stuck there like some beast cruelly trapped, aware of death coming in on wings. Finn gazed at the window where the halfhearted moon floated in the terrible night sky. There were footsteps behind him. There were other voices in the room. They made sounds he was beyond understanding because he was listening to something else.

He was listening to his angel, whom he had come to recognize as Death.

Come to me, Finn.

He blinked his eyes.

Then the room was filled with more gunfire, which he heard as a deaf man might hear thunder. Vibrations, not sounds. His face slid between harp strings, and the pistol dropped from his hand, and he went down slowly into his own blood where he lay very still.

W A D D E L L placed the Stoeger Max II rifle on the floor. He was shaking violently, and when he looked down at Finn's body, the long white hair covered with great scarlet slashes, he wanted to be sick. He put one hand up to his mouth. Houlihan came into the room and stared at the wasted body and there was no expression at all on his face.

"I thought he'd never die," Houlihan said. "Did you see the way he was bouncing like a rubber ball about this fucking room? I thought he'd never go down! Tough old shit."

Waddell nodded his head. There was excitement in Houlihan's voice.

"He had a lot of heart," Houlihan remarked.

Waddell wanted to be elsewhere. Another city. Another galaxy. He needed a drink, something to settle him down. Something to calm him. He looked around the room, found a bottle of schnapps and drank from it quickly.

"Ah, John, you need to develop an attitude," Houlihan said. "You need to be hard as a nail."

Waddell said nothing.

"Finn's a casualty of war. That's all," Houlihan said. He took the bottle from Waddell. He didn't drink. Instead, he turned the cap over in the palm of his hand so that Waddell could see several tiny perforations in the metal.

"Tricky," Houlihan said. "But we won't be needing this anymore."

"Is that what I think it is?" Waddell asked.

"A small microchip listening device. The blessings of Yankee technology. But our man Scully won't be listening to Finn anymore, will he?" Houlihan stuck the cap in his pocket. "For one thing, Scully's probably a thousand miles away by this time. And God knows, *nobody* will be listening to Finn anymore." Houlihan laughed. It was an empty, mirthless sound, like a cough.

Waddell felt the schnapps heat his chest. He looked into his companion's eyes, which were hard and cold.

Houlihan said, "Call Belfast, John. Tell them we succeeded. They're waiting to hear. Take your share of the credit."

Waddell went out of the room. Credit, he thought. He didn't need credit like this. He found a telephone in Finn's office. Houlihan came into the room behind him.

"What are you waiting for, John? We don't have all night."

Waddell put his hand on the receiver. He felt weak all of a sudden.

"Go on," Houlihan said. "I know they'll be anxious to hear Finn's out of the way. It means the green light for America."

America, Waddell thought.

He picked up the telephone.

"It's a strange thing about blood," Houlihan was saying. "It's all the same, John. Black man or white man. Protestant or Catholic. It's the same taste. No difference. English blood or American. It all looks and tastes the same."

American blood, Waddell thought. He wondered how Houlihan knew about the taste of the stuff.

He dialed the number in Belfast, and after a few moments it was answered by the Reverend Ivor McInnes, who spoke with a pronounced English mainland accent that Waddell knew was Liverpool.

"It's done," Waddell said.

"On the contrary," the voice answered. "It's only just beginning."

E IGHT

NEW YORK CITY

J oseph X. Tumulty couldn't quite believe that he had received the call after all this time. He had lived with the knowledge that there was always some slight possibility of such a thing, a shadow that lay over the life he had built for himself here, but he'd never actually believed it. But there it was. *The call from Ireland.* Now he was nervous and tense and possessed with the uneasy feeling that threads were being pulled in the night, that his destiny was being woven by hands he couldn't see. It wasn't a good feeling at all. He was a man who liked to be in charge of his own affairs.

He stood in the doorway of St. Finbar's Mission on Canal Street in the grubby southern part of Manhattan, his black coat drawn up at the collar, his fighter's nose made red by a chill river wind. From the kitchen behind him came the smell of food and the sounds of hungry men, quite beyond the dictates of good manners, attacking their plates of stew. To many people it might have been an unpleasant noise, but to Joe Tumulty it had a gladdening effect.

He looked along the sidewalk. He'd been thinking about the call ever since he'd received it twenty-four hours ago. He was listening still to the voice of Finn on the telephone—that mellifluous singing voice that could seduce and flatter and cajole and make any man believe that there were indeed fairies at the bottom of his garden. But this time there had been something else in Finn's voice, and Joe Tumulty had been trying to pin the quality down for almost a day now. What was it? Sometimes Tumulty thought it was weariness, at other times fear. He wasn't sure. All he knew was that Finn's call had disturbed the equilibrium of his life and that he didn't want any conflict between the work he was doing on Canal Street and the demands of the Cause.

A drunk lay about fifteen feet down the sidewalk. Tumulty had been watching him for the last couple of minutes. The man lay face down, arms outstretched. He wore a pair of pants at least three sizes too large for him. His threadbare overcoat was pulled up around his waist, revealing a thin cotton shirt that was no protection from the bitter wind. The man could die there and nobody would care. He could die among the plastic bags of trash and the roaches. But Joseph Tumulty wasn't about to let any man die within shouting distance of St. Finbar's, which was named after the sixth century founder of the City of Cork.

"Are you going to help him, Father Joe?"

Tumulty turned. The man who'd asked the question was known only as Scissors, which was said to be a reference to the trade of barber he'd once carried on. Now, five nights out of seven, Scissors was drunk. Tonight he happened to be sober. He had a ravaged face and the kind of luminescent eyes you sometimes see on street people—a result of nutritional deficiency, a lack of vitamins, and a totally depleted body. It was a look Joe Tumulty had come to know very well on Canal Street.

"Of course I am," Tumulty said. He put out one hand and squeezed Scissors' frail shoulder. There was misfortune everywhere, Tumulty thought. And most of it seemed to congregate here at the southern tip of Manhattan. Tumulty attacked human misery wherever he found it. Father Joe, crusader. The point was, if he didn't do it, then people like the man who lay there right now would probably perish.

The former barber blinked at the body on the sidewalk. "He's a young one," Scissors said.

Tumulty moved down the steps. He knew that alcohol was no great respecter of age. All kinds of people found their way to St. Finbar's Mission, young and old, skilled and unskilled—and what they had in common was a descent from society, from lives that might have been useful. Tumulty liked to think he could give them back some form of hope. He fed them, often clothed them, prayed for them, counseled them. He entered their broken lives and applied the only salve he knew, which was to care for them even when they had forgotten how to care for themselves.

As he crossed the sidewalk he was conscious of a tan-colored car parked about half a block away. It had been parked there for the past two hours. The man who sat behind the wheel appeared to be engrossed in a book. The whole thing made Tumulty nervous. It wasn't exactly the kind of place where a man would station his car to do a quiet spot of reading. His first response was that the car contained an agent of the bloody Internal Revenue Service. The IRS was always on his back these days, ever since he had split from the official Catholic Church to create his own mission on Canal Street. The tax-exempt status of charities and religious orders had been coming under a lot of scrutiny lately. It wasn't that the government was after Tumulty's income, because that was laughably small. But they could cause all kinds of nuisances by examining his accounts and asking to see canceled checks, just to make sure St. Finbar's was what it claimed to be—a nonprofit venture. Besides—and this was something he didn't like to think about, something he'd chosen to ignore—there was a certain bank account, held in his own name, that contained money Finn had given him and that he had absolutely no way of explaining.

Maybe he was being paranoid. Maybe Finn's phone call had made him that way. He suddenly felt that the night was filled with things he couldn't trust.

He crossed the sidewalk. He bent down beside the young man and very lightly placed a hand on the man's arm. The young man didn't move. Joe Tumulty moved his hand to touch the side of the man's face. The smell of booze was strong, as if it had been stitched into the threads of the man's coat. Tumulty turned his face to one side a moment. His eyes watered.

"Get up," Tumulty said.

The man was still.

Tumulty slipped his hand under the man's face and raised it slowly up from the hard sidewalk. He was about thirty and appeared to be in good health. His face was pale but showed none of the usual signs of decay Tumulty had come to expect on people like this. The lips were open a little way, and the teeth were good. Whoever this drunk was, he hadn't been on the streets for very long. Tumulty stared a moment in the direction of the parked car. The shadowy figure inside had his head tilted back and appeared now to be asleep.

"Can you get up?" Tumulty asked. "I'll help you."

The young man's eyes opened.

"Put your arm around my shoulder," Tumulty said. "We'll get you indoors."

"Who are you?" the young man asked.

"Joseph Tumulty. They sometimes call me Father Joe."

The young man closed his eyes again. There was a faint smile on his lips.

"Is it safe?" he asked.

"Safe?"

"Is it safe to come inside?"

"Of course it is. What do you—" Tumulty didn't finish his question because the young man's eyes opened again, and they were clear, bright, with no bleariness, no bloodshot quality. Joseph Tumulty was remembering Finn's phone call again. He was remembering Finn saying *Take good care of him, Joe. He's a fine lad.* This is the one, Tumulty thought, and he felt a strange little sensation around his heart. He had a slight difficulty in catching his breath.

"You can never be too sure," the young man said. He slung his arm around Joe Tumulty's shoulder and raised himself to a standing position.

"You're from Finn," Tumulty said, and his voice had become a whisper.

The young man nodded.

Tumulty stared at the light falling from the doorway of St. Finbar's and the outline of the man known as Scissors who stood at the top of the steps, then he glanced once in the direction of the parked car.

Take good care of him, Joe.

"You're Jig," Tumulty said.

"The very same."

THE wind that blew off the Hudson brought ice with it, hardening dead branches and imparting a spare look to the skyscrapers. Frank Pagan thought the city resembled a large ice palace. He had a room at the Parker Meridien on West Fifty-seventh Street, a costly hotel that his per diem expenses didn't cover. When he'd last been in

New York he'd stayed with Roxanne at the Gotham, which was now a hollow locked shell with boarded-up windows on the corner of Fifty-fifth and Fifth. A deserted hotel was fitting somehow. A black epitaph.

Four years ago. The first year of their marriage. An anniversary trip. What he recalled now was Roxanne's flushed excitement in Manhattan, how like a small child she'd been, going down Fifth Avenue and strolling through Tiffany's and Cartier's and Harry Winston's, asking endless questions of patient sales clerks. Pagan had bought her a silver locket at Fortunoff's, which she'd been wearing the day she died. Pagan wore the locket now. City of Memories. How could he feel anything but uneasy in this town?

On his first night at the Parker, when he was still groggy from jet lag, Pagan had a meeting with an FBI agent called Arthur Zuboric in the piano bar. Zuboric, a squat man with a Zapata moustache and a suntan achieved under the lamps of a health spa, had the look of a mournful bandit. He wasn't exactly happy with the notion of helping Frank Pagan since he had a caseload up to here, but the order had come down from Bureau headquarters in Washington, so what could he do? Reciprocity was the catchword here. I'll scratch your back, sometime in the future you'll scratch mine. So here he was scratching Frank Pagan and listening to Broadway show tunes on a piano and wondering about the limey's clothes.

Baggy tweed jacket, bright shirt, blue jeans, no tie. The casual look. Zuboric had the feeling, though, that there wasn't anything casual about Frank Pagan himself. The face was too intense. The mouth reminded Zuboric of a tight rubber band, and the gray eyes had a fierce quality. The word Zuboric had heard about Frank Pagan was *determined*.

The guy had built himself a solid reputation in the Special Branch at Scotland Yard, where he'd specialized in antiterrorist tactics. Once, Pagan had been involved in a shootout with Libyan terrorists in a London street. He killed three that day. On another occasion, he'd captured some Italian anarchists after a chase through London Airport. Somewhere along the way he'd been given his own section, practically independent of the Yard, thus causing some resentment among the older hands, who didn't like Frank Pagan's style or the way he dressed or the fact he wasn't quite forty yet. They envied his autonomy. The term for Frank Pagan, Zuboric decided, was *maverick*. All this stuff was in the file Washington had hurriedly put together for Zuboric. It was impressive material, but he wished the English wouldn't go dragging their Irish problem into the United States. Who the fuck needed that? Bunch of micks with guns, spouting shit about freedom.

He stuffed some peanuts in his mouth. The piano was giving him a royal headache. "We ran your Father Tumulty through the computer, Frank. Mind if I call you Frank? Call me Artie. Arthur's an old man's name, I always think."

Pagan didn't mind what the agent called him. He was only interested in Tumulty.

"Clean as a whistle," Zuboric went on. "So I put a field agent on it who tells me there's only one priest in the whole of New York City called Tumulty. Joseph X."

Zuboric tasted his rum and Coke and made a face. "Uncommon name," he said. "The thing is, this Joseph X. Tumulty isn't a priest anymore. Seems he either left the RC Church or got himself thrown out for some reason. Whatever, Tumulty runs a mission called St. Finbar's down on Canal Street."

Pagan looked at the pianist absently, then turned his thoughts to the idea of a lapsed priest having a connection with Jig. Irish labyrinths, little connections between this person and that, this furtive group with some other, on and on into the maze. Pagan thought a moment about the Leprechaun and the Free Ulster Volunteers and their alleged leader, the Reverend Ivor McInnes. Now there was a strange link, a failed jockey and a Presbyterian minister. And here was another, a lapsed priest and an assassin. Only in the murky world of Irish terrorism, Pagan thought. Only there could you find these weird bonds.

Zuboric said, "The Immigration and Naturalization Service records say that Father Tumulty entered the United States in October 1978 from Ireland. He came complete with permanent residence status as a priest. His church was Our Lady of the Sorrows on Staten Island, where he stayed two years. Since then he's been caring for broken souls on Canal Street."

Zuboric drained his glass. "According to INS records, Joseph Tumulty came fresh out of a seminary in Bantry to the United States. The INS always runs a police check on potential immigrants in their country of origin. Tumulty was clean in Ireland too, Frank."

"Clean or very clandestine," Pagan said. "I've known priests sympathetic to the IRA. They get involved in a little gunrunning on the side. Or they skim the collection plate to make contributions. A little adventure compensates for the stresses of celibacy."

"No doubt," Zuboric remarked. "Maybe this Tumulty is a sympathizer. But if he is, he's playing his cards pretty close to his chest."

Pagan sat back in his chair. "If he's Jig's contact in the United States, then he can't be Mr. Clean altogether."

Zuboric fidgeted with his empty glass. "I guess," he said. "I put a man on Canal Street. But what am I supposed to tell him, Frank? Keep your eyes open for a guy you don't know what he looks like?"

"Has your man talked to Tumulty?"

Zuboric shook his head. "I didn't want to take that step before I talked to you."

"Good," Pagan said. He didn't like the idea of some FBI field agent trudging over territory he thought of as his own.

Zuboric said, "So far as somebody using a passport in the name of John Doyle, Immigration has no record of anyone by that name. It doesn't mean much. Your man could have entered illegally through Canada, or he could have come into the U.S. under another name." Zuboric paused. "What's your next move?"

"Canal Street. Talk to Tumulty."

Zuboric sighed. He wondered what kind of metal Frank Pagan was made of. Guy gets off a plane after a five-hour flight through time zones and wants to start work right away. Zuboric played with the word *obsessed* for a moment. He'd seen obsessed law enforcement officers before. He'd seen how something unsolved just nibbled away at them until they were completely devoured and more than somewhat insane. Maybe Frank Pagan was wandering toward the abyss.

Zuboric said nothing for a moment. His present caseload involved a kidnapping in White Plains, a group of Communist dissidents suspected of illegal arms purchases in the Bronx, and a Lebanese diplomat who was smuggling dope in the diplomatic pouch. He didn't need Frank Pagan's problems. He didn't need a priest who might be an IRA sleeper. He didn't need some Irish assassin wandering around his turf. There were times in Artie Zuboric's life when he wondered what it was that he did *need*, periods of uncertainty when he played with such notions as "career moves" and "upward mobility," neither of which seemed appropriate within the structure of the Bureau, where promotion depended on the incomprehensible whim of the Director. Zuboric often longed for a life where the pressures were less weighty and the rewards somewhat more tangible. What had the goddam Bureau ever done for him anyhow? He had one broken marriage behind him and now he was in love with a girl called Charity who danced in a topless bar, a girl whom he wanted to marry but who had continually spurned him because she wanted no part of any man gung ho enough to be associated with the feds. Zuboric spent a lot of time thinking about ways of getting Charity to accept him. Money and good prospects might have helped. It galled Zuboric to think of his beloved Charity flashing her tits in front of drooling strangers. He wanted to take her away from all that.

"I don't understand why you can't settle this Irish crap once and for all, Frank. Why don't you just pull your soldiers out of Ulster and tell the Irish to go fuck themselves? What is it? Some colonial hangover?"

Frank Pagan smiled. "Why don't *you* do something about stopping the flow of American money into IRA coffers?" he asked.

Zuboric said, "Tell me how I can dictate what private citizens do with their money, Frank. Then maybe I can help you. Besides, we have a President who's a stage Irishman, and he's got an enormous Irish-American vote around here, which he isn't going to throw away by legislating against mick fund-raisers. And if they choose to send bucks to some rebels, what's he gonna do? Anyhow, I'm not absolutely convinced there's much more than chump change flowing from here to Ireland."

Chump change, Pagan thought. Colorful Americanism. But Zuboric was quite wrong. There was far more than chump change leaving the United States. Both men went outside. The wind off the East River blew scraps of paper along the sidewalks. Zuboric shivered. He thought Pagan looked immune to the cold.

"You got a weapon, Frank?"

"I brought a Bernardelli in my luggage," Pagan replied.

Zuboric shivered again. "Don't go waving it in public. The local cops frown on that kind of ostentation. They don't like foreigners with guns, even if your business here is lawful."

"It's a precaution," Pagan said. "I don't like guns."

"Yeah," Zuboric said. He whistled for a cab. A dirty yellow vehicle slid toward the sidewalk. Zuboric told the driver Canal Street.

"You're coming with me?" Pagan asked.

"I'm instructed to extend to you every courtesy, et cetera et cetera. But my orders don't stop there, Frank. I go where you go."

"It isn't necessary," Pagan replied. "I work better alone."

"Yeah, I bet you do." Zuboric settled down in the back of the cab. "But as long as this character Jig is on U.S. territory, your problem is my problem. I wish it was otherwise, believe me. I don't care about the Bog People, Frank. They can blow one another up every hour on the hour, so long as they don't do it in the United States of America. And if Jig has it in mind to track down some missing money, there's probably a good chance of bloodshed. In which case, I want to be around."

Pagan watched the lights of Broadway flicker past. He didn't like the notion of being dogged by an FBI agent. He liked to work on his own. He had never been a team player, which was why he hadn't fitted in at Special Branch. Too many team players. Too much paperwork. He supposed the FBI was exactly the same. Compartments. People in boxes. Rivalries and grudges and tiny jealousies.

Zuboric said, "You think this Tumulty guy is going to talk to you, Frank?"

Pagan looked at the agent a moment. Zuboric's suntanned face was incongruous in a wintry city. "I'm an optimist, Artie."

"Priests take vows of silence. They're pretty good at keeping secrets."

"We'll see," Pagan said.

THERE were fifty or sixty men inside St. Finbar's Mission. They sat at tables or wandered aimlessly around trying to scrounge cigarettes from one another. The kitchen was a large room with an enormous stove located at one side. Stacked against one wall was a large pile of thin mattresses enveloped in sheets of clear plastic. Smoke and cooking smells and the sweaty aroma of despair mingled in the air. A crucifix hung on the wall. Here and there were slogans from Alcoholics Anonymous. THE TWELVE STEPS OF AA. EASY DOES IT. ONE DAY AT A TIME.

Frank Pagan stood on the threshhold of the room, gazing in the direction of the counter that surrounded the stove. Faces turned toward him, then away again. They had the nervously furtive expressions of men who have reached the bottom and can't find their way up from the pits.

Pagan moved to the cooking area. Soups and stews were simmering in big aluminum urns. He raised a lid and peered at carrots and onions floating on a greasy brown surface. He realized he hadn't eaten anything since the alleged beef Wellington on the flight, but his hunger was at one remove from himself, like somebody else's sensation.

He looked around the room. What he felt in the air was mainly a sense of hopelessness that came in waves toward him. Casualties of the system. The unemployed. The alcoholic. The mentally defective. He glanced at Zuboric, who was clearly uneasy here. Pagan leaned against the wall, folding his arms. All those faces: He wondered if any one of them could be Jig.

"Can I be of assistance?"

Pagan turned. The man who asked the question was probably in his early thirties, unshaven, his dark blue coat covered with scuff marks, his dark curly hair uncombed. There was a smell of liquor on his breath and dark circles under his eyes.

"I'm looking for Father Tumulty," Pagan said.

The man looked quickly in Zuboric's direction, then back at Pagan. "Who shall I say is asking for him?"

Pagan hesitated. "He wouldn't know my name."

Zuboric stepped forward and said, "Just point us in Tumulty's direction."

The man rubbed his hands together. "Father Joe's pretty busy right now."

"Look," Zuboric said. "Either you go get him or we'll go looking for him. It's all the same to me."

The big-stick approach, Pagan thought. It wasn't always the most fruitful. He watched the man go across the room and out through a door into a hallway. The door closed behind him. Without hesitation, Pagan headed after the man. Zuboric, sighing, followed. The corridor was narrow, badly lit, the air even more stale than inside the kitchen.

There was a flight of stairs at the end of the hallway. Pagan saw the man disappear into the gloom at the top. He went after him. Zuboric, his overcoat flapping, came up behind. When they reached the landing, which was lit by a solitary bare light bulb, they saw a halfway open door in front of them. Through the crack Pagan observed a desk and a lamp. There was no sign of the man they had followed. Instead, another figure appeared in the doorway, a squat man with crewcut hair and powerful arms that hung from rolled-up shirt sleeves.

"Is it taxes?" the man asked.

"Taxes?" Pagan said. He shook his head.

"Only I'm having trouble with the IRS, you see. They questioned my nonprofit status. They're always sending people around to see me. People that look a lot like you," and the man gestured toward Zuboric. "All I do is feed those poor folk downstairs. I don't see why the IRS would bother me. Are you sure you're not with them?"

"Positive," Zuboric said.

"I'm Joe Tumulty," the man said. He looked at Zuboric warily. "What can I do for you?"

"Let's go in your office," Zuboric said.

"Certainly, certainly."

It was a small room. The walls were covered with religious portraits, the desk strewn with papers. Mostly bills, Pagan noticed. He had the impression that St. Finbar's Mission wasn't exactly a solvent concern. Many of the invoices had demands stamped on them in red ink. There were several envelopes from the Internal Revenue Service, pale brown and unopened. If Father Joe was a conduit for American money going to Ireland, he certainly wasn't skimming any off the top for himself.

"Please sit," Tumulty said. He had short blunt fingers. His face was not the kind you'd automatically associate with anything as ethereal as the priesthood. He reminded Frank Pagan of the kind of priest who liked to get down in the dirt with his parishioners or instruct street urchins in the arts of pugilism. There was a quiet toughness about the man, a quality of having been seasoned on the streets. He'd need that kind of quality working in a place like this. "I don't know your names, gentlemen." His accent was Irish, but it had become refined. There were small American inflections.

"Zuboric. Arthur Zuboric. Federal Bureau of Investigation." The agent flipped a wallet open, showing his ID.

Tumulty said, "Impressive." Then he looked at Pagan. "And you?"

"Frank Pagan."

"London. Am I right?"

"Right."

"I have an ear for accents," Tumulty said. He took the IRS envelopes and stacked them in a small pile.

Pagan said, "You're doing good work downstairs."

"God's work," Tumulty said. "Which you can't always do within the confines of the established church, alas. It isn't easy either. I locked heads with my church to create this place. And ever since then I believe the bishop has been pulling all kinds of delicate little threads behind the scenes to make life more difficult for me. Sometimes there are inexplicable shortages of food from the city's food banks. Delays in delivery that don't make sense. I often think the bloody bishop is behind this business with the IRS. Spiteful little man."

"Is that why you left the Church? To do God's work?"

Tumulty nodded. "I grew dissatisfied. Bishops play golf with realtors. They belong to country clubs. I didn't join the Church to develop a taste for sherry and a knack for parish politics." He smiled. When he did so the face, which had a slightly battered look, resembled a baseball glove that has seen one season too many. Pagan guessed Tumulty was somewhere in his late forties.

"So you know I left the Church, do you? It doesn't surprise me. I heard somebody had been asking questions on the street. I thought it was a tax snoop. The FBI indeed! Should I be flattered or afraid?"

Zuboric tapped a foot impatiently. "You don't have anything to be afraid of, do you?"

"Now that depends." Tumulty leaned forward into the direct light of the desk lamp and said, "Since you gentlemen know a little something about me, isn't it fair that you tell me something of yourselves? What brings you to St. Finbar's? It can't be the cuisine, I'm sure."

"Your name cropped up in connection with an investigation—"

"My name?" Tumulty laughed. "I can't imagine my name coming up in the context of any investigation unless it's something to do with the bloody IRS. What are you investigating anyway?"

"Murder," Zuboric said.

"Ahhh." Tumulty sat back in his chair. "And who's been killed?"

Frank Pagan stood up. Instead of answering Tumulty's question, he asked one of his own. "What connections do you have in Ireland, Joe?"

"By connections, d'you mean family? Friends? I have a great many—"

Pagan shook his head. "I'm talking about political contacts."

"I'm not a political animal."

Zuboric hunched over in his chair and said, "That's not what we hear, Joe."

"You've got poor information then."

Pagan walked around the room. He paused under a garish portrait of the Virgin Mary, who regarded him with technicolor sorrow.

"The taste in art isn't very sophisticated, is it?" Tumulty said. "I'd especially throw that one out except some of my patrons here are devout men in a simplistic way. Icons console them."

Zuboric asked, "What does the name Jig mean to you?"

Pagan was annoyed. He wanted to play this more slowly, wanted to wander around the subject of Jig in an indirect way before deciding whether to spring the name on Tumulty, but Artie Zuboric, an apparent graduate from the bulldozer school of questioning, was off and running in his own direction. Pagan could see that it was going to be difficult to work with the FBI agent.

"It's a dance, of course," Tumulty said.

"Can it," Zuboric said. His tone was one of irritation. Pagan thought Zuboric looked like a heavy in some low-budget Spanish western with his Mexican-style moustache and drooping eyelids. All he needed was a toothpick, something to dangle from his lips.

"Should it mean anything else?" Tumulty blinked.

Frank Pagan went back across the room and sat on the priest's desk. "Not a dance exactly. Not this time, Joe."

"Tell me then. If it isn't a dance, then what are you talking about?"

"A killer," Pagan said.

"Preposterous," Tumulty said. "A killer! What would I be doing with a killer, for God's sake?"

"We understand he has plans to visit you. Maybe he's already done so. Has he? Has Jig been here *already*, Joe?" Zuboric asked.

Pagan rubbed his eyes. He was feeling fuzzy, fatigued. He had one of those waking moments when the lack of sleep causes a slight hallucination. Joseph Tumulty's desk lamp seemed to shimmer in front of his eyes and the walls of the room became darker beyond the reaches of electricity.

"Why would this killer come to see me?" Tumulty asked.

"Suppose you tell me, Joe."

Tumulty stood up. "I think this has gone far enough, gentlemen. I've got hungry people waiting. If you don't mind." He took a step toward the door, and Zuboric reached out, fastening his hand round the Irishman's wrist.

"Stick around," Zuboric said.

Pagan looked at the FBI man's hand clamped on the priest's wrist. Tumulty didn't look unduly concerned about being grabbed and held. The expression on the Irishman's face was one of pity. It might have been the look of a priest listening to something especially pathetic in the confessional.

"Is it a nightstick next?" Tumulty asked. "Or have nightsticks gone out of fashion? Do you use the butt of your pistols these days?"

"No nightsticks. No guns." Pagan shrugged. "All we want is a little information."

Tumulty said, "Which I don't have. Sorry and all that. How often do I have to say it, Mr. Pagan?" Zuboric let his hand fall back to his side.

"Now can I go and feed my people?" Tumulty asked. "They expect that of me downstairs."

Pagan nodded wearily. "We'll talk again, Joe."

"I don't doubt that. But you'll keep getting the same answers."

Pagan watched him a moment, thinking about the small things that gave a man away. A little sweat. The nervous motion of an eyelid. A flutter of hands. The human body as lie detector. He moved toward the door. "What would your people have to eat if you weren't around to care for them? If, for example, you were to find yourself lodging in Attica?"

Tumulty said, "They might starve. They might end up sleeping on the streets. God knows, the kind of people I take in here aren't always welcome at some of the more genteel missions. But then I don't have any plans to abandon them, Pagan. And I most certainly don't plan on Attica."

Frank Pagan smiled. "The best-laid plans, and so forth," he said. "You know how it goes, don't you?" He pushed the door open and stepped out onto the landing. He turned back to Tumulty and added, "Be seeing you."

IT was very cold in the attic. Jig huddled deep inside his overcoat. For a time he'd been listening to the sounds of voices that floated up through an air-conditioning vent, but then there had been silence, followed by footsteps. When the attic door opened a little way he found himself looking into the yellow beam of a flashlight. Tumulty stood there.

"You live dangerously," Tumulty said.

Jig stared into the light. He smelled food. Tumulty was carrying a plate in one hand. Jig took the plate and the plastic fork and started to eat. He hadn't eaten in a long time. With his mouth full, he said, "All I did was go downstairs for food. When I saw those characters, I couldn't resist the impulse."

Tumulty sat cross-legged on the floor. He produced a pack of cigarettes and lit one.

"Suppose they'd somehow gotten hold of a picture of you?" Tumulty said. "Suppose they had a description from somewhere?"

"But they didn't."

Tumulty sighed. "How did they know you were coming here anyhow?"

Jig set the plate aside. "Good stew," he said.

"I asked a question."

"I don't have the answer," Jig said.

"It doesn't worry you?"

"I came to America to do a job. Nothing else."

Tumulty sighed again. "How did they find out about me? Only myself and Finn knew you were coming here. Since I didn't tell anybody, there's only one conclusion. Something went wrong at Finn's end."

Jig thought a moment about Finn. He couldn't afford to worry about the old man. The money had to be found. Nothing changed that. The only thing of any importance was the task he'd been sent to do. Despite himself, he felt a small chord of concern echo in his head, but he rejected it. Finn would have been the first to tell him that worry only weakened a man's concentration, disrupted his single-mindedness. Worry was a peripheral pastime and an unworthy one.

He adjusted his grubby overcoat, which smelled of alcohol. He had soaked the material of the coat with a half pint of very cheap rum, and now the pungent aroma was irritating him.

"They'll come back," Tumulty said.

"And you'll tell them nothing."

"I've never been tested," Tumulty said. "I don't know my limits."

"You'll tell them nothing," Jig said again.

Tumulty rubbed his leg. He had a cramp suddenly. "I think they've got a man outside on the street."

Jig nodded. "I saw him before. He was a cinch to spot. Looks like a boy in the marines, all short hair and jaw. He's sitting inside a tan Chrysler. He looks very conspicuous and very bored, Joe. Anyway, what did he see? Another bum staggering along the pavement, that's all. Another drunk falling down."

Tumulty said, "You look like a derelict, I'll grant you that." He stood up, still clawing at his leg. "But this whole situation worries me. What happened at Finn's end? And how much does this Pagan know?"

"Worry about something else, Joe. Worry about how you're going to help me."

Tumulty was quiet. From the kitchen far below came the noise of a drunk singing. "The Irish members of the flock think they're the Mormon Tabernacle Choir sometimes. I better get back down there. It's a bloody zoo."

Jig reached out and touched Tumulty's arm. "I'll need a decent pistol."

Tumulty nodded but said nothing.

"And if it can be done, I'll feel better if I have a collapsible rifle as well. Just in case."

"It's going to take a little time."

"I don't have much time."

"I can't hurry a thing like this," Tumulty said. "Especially now, when I've got those two characters breathing down my neck."

Tumulty turned toward the attic door. The singing from below was growing louder.

> "My feet are here on Broadway this blessed
> harvest morn
> "But O the ache that's in them for the spot
> where I was born. . . ."

Jig said, "I'll also need names, Joe. Names of anyone connected with the Fund-raisers."

"Of course you will. Otherwise, how will you know who to shoot?"

"Do I detect disapproval in your voice?"

Tumulty said nothing.

"I never shoot anybody unless I have to," Jig said. "Does that ease your conscience?"

"Sometimes the Cause overrides conscience," Tumulty said. "If it didn't, I'd still be a priest." He waved the flashlight. The beam illuminated the attic, picking out various objects. A dressmaker's dummy. A heap of old hatboxes. Piles of newspapers. "I suggest you vanish from here and come back in two days. I also suggest you don't use the telephone to get in contact with me."

"Two days," Jig said.

"I can't do anything in less," Tumulty said.

Jig watched Tumulty move toward the door.

Tumulty said, "I still think you took an unnecessary risk."

Jig replied, "At least I know what my enemy looks like, Joe. Which is more than Frank Pagan knows about me."

Jig saw the door shut. Tumulty had taken the flashlight with him and the attic was once again completely dark. Jig sat with his back to the wall. Frank Pagan, he thought. A tall straight-backed man with a strong jaw and a face that might have been handsome if it hadn't looked like it was cast in cement. Frank Pagan. Here in America. Well, well.

Jig listened to the song rising up from the kitchen.

> "When I was young and restless, my mind was
> ill at ease
> "Through dreaming of America and gold beyond
> the seas. . . ."

He closed his eyes. What difference did it make to him if the Englishman was here in the United States? Since Frank Pagan hadn't identified him, it meant that the Englishman was operating in the dark. Which in turn meant that Finn, no matter what might have happened to him in Ireland, no matter how any information had been leaked to Pagan, hadn't revealed Jig's identity. It was the one thing that Finn, whom Jig had come to perceive as being somehow immune to harm and danger, an indestructible embodiment of the Cause, would never do. He'd cut out his tongue before he revealed any of the secrets he kept. Anyway, the old man knew how to look after himself.

Jig got up and wandered around the attic, trying to keep warm. He dismissed Frank Pagan from his mind and instead turned his thoughts to the business of passing the next couple of days. He was impatient to do what he'd come to America for, but he was at the mercy of Joseph Tumulty, and he didn't like the feeling of having to rely on anyone but himself.

He stopped moving.

The maudlin song continued to float up toward him and, even though he disliked the sensation, he felt a prickling of homesickness, a faint longing for the things he'd left behind.

IN the back of the cab that headed in the direction of the Parker Meridien, Zuboric said, "I think the fucker knows."

"Of course he knows. But what would you do, Artie? Beat information out of him? Take him down into a dungeon and kick the shit out of him until he talks?" Pagan asked.

"Yeah." Zuboric spread his hands, gazed at his fingernails. "It's your ball game, Frank. You want to play it softly, that's your business. You want to be Mr. Nice, fine by me."

Pagan thought: Mr. Nice. He could have threatened Tumulty directly. He could have menaced him with a variety of pressures, including physical violence. But what would that have achieved? If Tumulty was IRA, then he'd embrace martyrdom happily. Broken ribs and bruises would be like badges of merit to Father Joe. No, it was better to leave threats hanging in the air, unspoken, veiled, and let Tumulty's imagination go to work on them. He was still a little unhappy with Zuboric's blunderbuss attitude and the way the whole interview had been conducted, but he decided not to criticize directly for the moment. He didn't want to alienate Zuboric, and with him the whole FBI, unless it was completely unavoidable.

Zuboric said, "I'll keep my man in place. Maybe get a tap on the guy's phone. Maybe."

"Which he'll expect," Pagan remarked. He watched the streets. Times Square. He'd photographed Roxanne here, right outside a HoJo's. She wanted her picture taken there, because the place looked wonderfully sleazy. He had overworked the camera that summer. Roxanne outside the CBS building. Roxanne eating a huge pretzel at the Statue of Liberty. That's what this place suggested to Pagan. A series of old snapshots. Pictures of another life lived by another man. He remembered suddenly a detail of Roxanne: the way her lips felt when they touched his own. The taste of her. The warmth.

It was details like this that killed him. He felt empty. Restless.

He learned forward and told the cab driver to pull over.

Zuboric said, "Where you going, Frank?"

Pagan stepped out on to the sidewalk. "I need a little exorcism," he said.

Arthur Zuboric frowned in puzzlement. "Whatever," he said.

N INE

ROSCOMMON, NEW YORK

Former United States Senator Harry Cairney rose very slowly from his bed and looked from the window at Roscommon Lake, which was sullen and utterly still in the windless morning. Cairney found himself longing for spring, true spring, which sometimes at nights he smelled on the cold air. When each spring came he wondered if it might be his last. Morbid speculations.

He pressed his forehead against the windowpane and saw Celestine riding her black mare, Jasmine, along the shore. Celestine's yellow hair floated out behind her, and her body rose and fell with the rhythms of the animal. Cairney watched this fluent amalgam of woman and horse until Celestine had galloped out of sight. Then a black four-wheel-drive vehicle appeared between the trees. The jeep had the words DUTCHESS SECURITY painted on it. Cairney had hired them immediately after the emergency meeting with Kevin Dawson and the others a few days ago. Now the black vehicle was always out there, occupied by two men who carried automatic pistols and rifles.

Celestine hadn't questioned him about the presence of the security men. If she thought about them at all, she presumably attributed them to an old man's groundless fears for his home and property. He watched a pall of exhaust hang in the wintry air, then he turned from the window.

The light in the bedroom was poor. Misshapen clouds, leaden and dreadful, filled the sky. Sighing, Cairney reflected on the fact that he'd recently fallen into the habit of reminiscing, ransacking his memory and speaking his recollections aloud, even though he knew he was sometimes repeating himself. He'd say, *I remember the time when Lyndon decided he didn't want the presidency. I remember he told me he didn't give a rat's fuck for the job anymore, even though he'd lusted after it all his life, and now here he was with his ambition realized except it was goddam empty,* and Celestine would nod her head sweetly and smile, as if she'd never heard Harry's stories before. Softening of the brain, Cairney thought. A shiver of senility. Old age and death terrified him. He thought nothing could be lonelier than death.

The door of the bedroom opened. Celestine, in blue jeans and a heavy plaid jacket, stepped inside. Her pale skin had been buffed by the cold air. Her cheeks were faintly red and her eyes bright, and she looked to Cairney like something that winter, at its most artful, had created especially for him. Young. So goddam young. He touched her face with his palm. All his morose thoughts dissolved. Celestine was life and vitality—a light that pierced his gloom.

She spread her hands in front of the fire. "Why are you out of bed, Harry?"

Cairney coughed loudly, then popped a Kleenex from the box on the bedside table and raised it to the tip of his nose. "God, I hate lying in bed, Cel," he complained.

"How the devil are you going to get well if you don't rest?"

Scolding him. Smiling as she did so. Cairney sometimes felt like a small boy caught raiding the cookie jar. He liked the feeling. "Nag, nag," he said. His voice sounded strange to him. Thick, coming from a distance. He wondered about the condition of his lungs. It had to be a swamp in there.

"For you own good, old man," Celestine said. She sat on the bed and removed the riding boots from her long legs. She tossed her hair back. Cairney watched her. He had loved his first wife, Kathleen, but not with this kind of intensity. He absorbed every little detail of Celestine, as if he were afraid of her somehow slipping away from him. He made orbits around her sun, like some satellite planet. With Kathleen, the relationship had evolved through the years into one of comfortable friendship, lacking passion but filled just the same with mutual understanding. With Kathleen, Cairney had always been in control. He had no control at all when it came to Celestine. He'd relinquished it cheerfully.

"Lie down," she said, and she patted the bed.

Cairney did as he was told. He made a great show of moaning about her commands. She propped herself up on an elbow and looked at him, tracing a line down his cheek with her fingernail.

"Are we going to work at getting better, Harry?" she asked.

"Yes," he answered.

"Doctor's orders, Harry. Listen to your physician."

"Tully's a broken-down old Irish sawbones."

"Stop being irascible. It doesn't become you."

Cairney smiled. The nearness of his wife was like a cocoon, a place to shelter. "Well, he is."

"He's highly experienced—"

"That's a euphemism for over the hill."

"Harry, Harry, Harry." Celestine tapped a fingernail on his lip. "I think you like playing the role of an old codger, don't you?"

"An old codger is what I am, sweetheart."

Celestine pressed her face against Harry Cairney's cheek. "You're not so bad, Harry. You're not so bad." She rolled away from him, staring up at the ceiling.

He glanced at her. She was wearing what he thought of as her secretive expression. It was the look she always had when she was about to surprise him with a birthday present or something unexpected at Christmas. He always saw through it because Celestine, no matter how damn hard she tried, didn't have the knack for guile.

"Out with it," he said.

"Out with what?"

"Whatever it is that's making you look so smug."

"Smug? Me?"

"Yeah. You."

She sat up, clutching her knees and smiling.

"I don't know if you're well enough for surprises, Harry. Tully said you needed peace and rest."

"Jesus Christ," Cairney grumbled. "Are you going to tell me what it is that makes you look like a cat that's swallowed the bloody canary whole?"

"Patrick called early this morning."

"Patrick? My Patrick?"

"The very same."

Cairney reached for another Kleenex and sneezed into it, causing a tiny pain in the center of his chest. "Why didn't you wake me, for God's sake?"

"Tully said you needed your sleep."

Cairney dismissed Tully with a gesture of his hand. "I haven't spoken with Patrick since God knows when."

Celestine ran her fingers through her hair. "You'll get the chance soon enough, Harry."

"What do you mean?"

"He called from Albany. From the airport. He's on his way to Roscommon, even as we sit here."

Cairney laid a hand against his chest. "Patrick!" he said. "Why the hell didn't he let me know he was coming?"

"Don't get excited, Harry."

"He could've called. I'd have made arrangements to have him picked up, Cel."

Celestine massaged Cairney's shoulders. "He said he was going to rent a car in Albany and drive here."

Cairney sat up, swinging his feet to the floor.

"Lie down, Harry."

"And have my son come here and see me like an invalid?"

"Which is what you are."

Cairney wandered to the fireplace. Patrick. His only child. The boy who left Boston University to go to Dublin and study archaeology. When he wasn't off digging in some ridiculous desert, he was deep inside books and old documents and God knows what. He was thirty years old, and Harry Cairney thought it was time his son stopped being the eternal student and did something useful with his life. He wasn't going to say so to Patrick because all the arguments were old and had been used up years ago and Patrick was an independent soul who'd go his own way anyhow. What Cairney couldn't understand was the boy's infatuation with ancient things. He loved his son fiercely. Differences of opinion didn't inhibit that feeling. Just the same, he wished Patrick would come back to America permanently and take up something less . . . esoteric than digging in the graves of long-dead men. But Patrick had never expressed the desire to leave Dublin nor any interest in anything other than useless archaeology. Now he was coming home to a sick father and security men crawling over the estate. Terrific.

Celestine stood behind him, blowing warm breath on the back of his neck. "Shouldn't we be killing the fatted calf or something?" she asked.

Cairney turned to her with a smile. "You'll like him. I know you will."

"I hope he likes me," Celestine said. She was quiet a moment. "I'll make you a deal. I'll let you get dressed and come downstairs on the condition you don't do anything strenuous and you limit your intake to one glass of brandy. A small one."

Cairney coughed again. "You drive a hard bargain, woman."

Celestine said, "I want a husband who's healthy, Harry."

"Okay," Cairney said. "It's a deal."

Celestine removed her plaid jacket and tossed it over a chair. "I'm going to take a shower and dress in something suitable for my stepson." She paused, laughed quietly. "He's only five years younger than I am, Harry! How can I possibly be somebody's stepmother?"

She moved toward the bathroom, pausing in the doorway.

"You really ought to tell your guard dogs out there that we're expecting company, Harry. You wouldn't want them shooting at your own son, would you?"

Cairney nodded. He watched his wife discard her shirt, saw how it slipped from her body as she stepped inside the bathroom. The door shut and then there was the rattle of water falling inside the shower stall and after a moment the sound of Celestine singing.

P A T R I C K C a i r n e y parked his rented Dodge Colt at the side of the road and stepped out, leaving the engine running. He'd come off the Taconic Parkway near Rhinebeck where a minor road branched in the direction of Roscommon. Out here, miles from any major city, the air smelled good and he took it into his lungs deeply. The landscape was covered with crusted snow. He stared across the frozen fields and the stark clumps of woodland. It was the landscape of his childhood and he knew it thoroughly, all the tracks, the hiding places, the best trees to climb. When he considered his boyhood now, the recollection was touched by a strange little sense of emptiness, as if his only memories were forlorn ones—which wasn't entirely true. Harry had provided a few good things to look back on—a camping trip one summer to the deep woods of Maine, or the time one humid August when they'd gone together up into the Adirondacks and fished Sacandaga Lake. Even there, though, Harry had never strayed too far from civilization and the nearest phone booth because he always wanted to keep in touch, which to Senator Cairney meant placing one call every day to his Washington office.

Patrick Cairney stepped back inside his car. He drove carefully on slippery pavement. When he reached the gates of the estate he got out and pushed them open. A black jeep came out of the trees toward him. There were two men inside. One carried a rifle across his knees, the other climbed out and approached Cairney. He was a stocky man with a pistol strapped to his belt and he came over the snow cautiously. Across the side panel of the vehicle were the words DUTCHESS SECURITY.

"You Patrick?" the man asked.

Cairney nodded.

The man hitched up his belt. "Okay. You're expected."

Cairney studied the man a second. He had the look of security guards everywhere. His face had become pinched from years of scrutinizing people. Around his eyes was a dense mass of wrinkles. "What's with all the security?" Cairney asked.

The man shrugged. He didn't answer Cairney's question. He turned and went back to the jeep, where he climbed in beside his partner. Cairney returned to the Dodge Colt and watched the black jeep reverse. It vanished behind a clump of trees. Security guards. What was Harry worried about? His collection of old Celtic manuscripts he'd gathered over the years? Or was it those moldy first editions of Yeats and George Bernard Shaw and Joyce that bothered him? Cairney wondered if there were burglars of a literary persuasion in the area, masked men planning to heist the precious scrap of beer-stained paper on which Brendan Behan had written: *To my pal Harry Cairney, may he colonize Amerika.* The old man had that one framed and prominently displayed on the desk in his office.

The house came into view. Patrick Cairney had always thought of it as a monstrosity, sprawling across the landscape like an immense mausoleum. Given a smokestack, it might have passed as a crematorium. It wasn't a house that invited you inside. It lacked any welcoming warmth. Cairney pulled up at the foot of the steps, glancing a moment at Roscommon Lake, then he got out of the car. He marveled at it all—the mansion, the estate, everything that one poor but overwhelmingly ambitious Irish immigrant had pulled together in his lifetime. There was something to be said, after all, for making your career one of public service in Amerika.

The door at the top of the steps opened. Celestine Cunningham Cairney stood there, looking down at him. She wore tailored tan slacks, a chocolate-brown sweater, a peach-colored chiffon scarf. Her soft blond hair hung at her shoulders. Patrick Cairney, who had always thought his father must exaggerate Celestine's beauty in his letters because he was blinded by love, felt astonishment. The woman had the kind of loveliness that stopped men dead in their tracks, that made all heads turn in crowded rooms and silenced cocktail-party conversations. She moved down the steps without any of the self-consciousness of beautiful women, as if she were quite unaware of the way she looked.

She reached the bottom step and she laid one hand on her stepson's arm. "Welcome," she said. "Harry's told me a lot about you."

She leaned forward and kissed Cairney on the cheek. A stepmother's kiss, tentative and quick and just a little awkward. Cairney wasn't sure what to say. He was still trying to recover from his surprise. What had he expected anyhow? A good-looking matronly woman, maybe, somebody with the face and body of a sympathetic head nurse. Somebody, at best, handsome. But not this. This vision. And, although he didn't like the question, it entered his mind anyway: *What did she see in an old man like Harry Cairney?*

"Harry's waiting for you."

Patrick Cairney looked over Celestine's shoulder. His father appeared in the doorway, smaller than Cairney remembered him, shrunken, his silver hair thinner than before and his eyes, under the great overhanging forehead, set in deep shadow.

"Let me hear it, Pat," Harry Cairney called out in a voice that was curiously cracked.

Patrick Cairney hesitated before he sang, *"You haven't an arm and you haven't a leg,/You're an eyeless, noseless, chickenless egg—"*

His father sang the next two lines hoarsely. *"You'll have to be put with a bowl to beg,/O Johnny, we hardly knew ye!"*

"With drums and guns, and guns and drums,/The enemy nearly slew ye—"

"My darling dear, you look so queer,/O Johnny, I hardly knew ye!"

Then the old man was laughing, and Patrick Cairney climbed the steps quickly, thinking how the way they greeted each other never changed. It was a ritual as well preserved as his father's mythical vision of Ireland. And Patrick found it empty and meaningless, a routine first developed in his childhood. It had been embarrassing even back then. Now it was worse because it was forced and ridiculous. Both men embraced, then Harry Cairney stepped back and said, "Let me look at you, Pat. Let me take a good long look at you. You've put on some muscles since I last saw you. It must be all those Irish potatoes you've been eating."

Patrick Cairney glanced at Celestine, who was coming up the steps. She said, "Did somebody give you permission to come out here into the cold, Harry?"

Cairney winked at his son. "She never lets up," he said. "She keeps an old man in check."

"Somebody has to," Celestine said. She slipped her arm through Harry's and she smiled at her stepson. It was a good smile, the kind Patrick Cairney thought you could bask in on a chilly winter's day. Like having your own private sun.

"Now let's all go indoors," Celestine said. She shivered as she ushered Harry inside the house.

"I'll fetch my luggage," Patrick Cairney said.

He went back down the steps to the Dodge Colt. He reached inside and lifted his bag from the rear seat. He closed the door. He saw the black security jeep appear on the shore of Roscommon Lake, idling between bare trees.

JOHN F. KENNEDY AIRPORT, NEW YORK

The man from the State Department was called J. W. Sweeting. He wore a three-piece suit and his hair was immaculately brushed over his broad skull. He had a brown leather briefcase with his initials embossed on it. He sat in the arrivals lounge at John F. Kennedy Airport and studied the man he'd just met from the London flight. The Reverend Ivor McInnes was big, weighed somewhere in the region of two hundred and twenty pounds, none of it flab. He had a large, craggy face that was handsome in a fleshy way. He was about fifty, Sweeting reckoned. The eyes were green and lively and burned into you whenever you looked at them. The British press called him Ivor the Terrible, which Sweeting thought he understood. There was the scent of brimstone hanging all around the Reverend McInnes. Sweeting knew he wouldn't like to sit through one of McInnes's sermons, which would be all thunder and spit. And yet like many people before him, J. W. Sweeting realized that there was something attractive about McInnes, a certain quality of roguish charm, which, as a political tool, could be extremely useful. It was easy to imagine Ivor swaying large crowds, shaping them any way he wanted.

Sweeting tapped his briefcase. "I'll go over the conditions of entry for you," he said.

McInnes smiled. "No need, no need," he said in an accent that reminded Sweeting of a Liverpool rock singer. "I know them all. Your embassy people in London, the gargoyles of Grosvenor Square, already put me through their wire-mesh procedures."

Sweeting rubbed his embossed initials with a fingertip. "In case there's any misunderstanding, Reverend, you were granted an entry visa on the condition that you refrain from speaking in public places or giving inflammatory interviews to the press. State is adamant about that."

McInnes swiveled his green eyes up to the high ceiling and looked very impatient. "I know all this, young man."

Sweeting sighed. It was the sigh of a man carrying out his duty regardless. "You are to refrain from all and any public assemblies. You are also ordered to refrain from addressing any private assemblies, clubs, associations, organizations, and the like, which are considered partisan in nature. You are prohibited from activities designed to raise funds for any partisan organizations with which you might be associated in Northern Ireland."

"Can I actually breathe?" McInnes asked. "Or am I forbidden the use of your air as well?"

Sweeting ignored this. "You are also deterred from making political statements concerning British or American policy in Ireland, the Irish Republican Army, the conditions of Irish political prisoners in British jails, and any remarks, ambiguous or otherwise, about the Roman Catholic Church."

"Did somebody tear up your Constitution? Did somebody just decide to disregard that wonderful document in my case?" McInnes was looking amused rather than annoyed.

Sweeting went on, "Your stay is limited to ten days and restricted to New York City and its environs. Any other movements must be cleared in advance with a representative of the State Department. To wit, me. And I'll turn down any and all requests you might make. Is all this clear?"

McInnes nodded. "Loud and clear."

"Any violation of these conditions will result in your expulsion from the United States. Between you and me, I think you're lucky to get this visa. The fact is, State pursues a policy of fairness toward both sides in the Irish question. If we let in, say, a priest from Tipperary, then we can't keep out a minister from Belfast. Even one whose own church has rejected him."

"Are you a Catholic?" McInnes asked.

"Is that relevant?"

McInnes grinned. He had strong white teeth. He brought his face very close to Sweeting's. It was a characteristic of his, this closing of the distance between himself and his listener, and it forced an uneasy intimacy on whomever Ivor was talking to. "I have this reputation, Mr. Sweeting. They say I hate Roman Catholics. I admit I have my differences with the Church of Rome, friend, but as far as individual Catholics are concerned, I don't hate them. They're misguided people, that's all." McInnes paused. His grin created little squares of puckered flesh all across the expanse of his face. "My own church failed to understand that, Mr. Sweeting. They interpreted my objections to Rome as attacks on individual Catholics. Which wasn't what I intended. Far from it."

Sweeting stepped back a pace. McInnes had been talking very loudly and several people were staring at him.

"You're misunderstood, is that what you're saying?" Sweeting asked.

"I'm damned in certain quarters whenever I open my mouth."

"Maybe you should keep it shut more often," J. W. Sweeting said.

Ivor McInnes smiled. He placed one of his big hands on Sweeting's shoulder and rocked the man from the State Department very slightly back and forth. Sweeting once more stepped away. McInnes reminded him of one of those TV salesmen who pitched Herbalife or urged you to send your dollars to some church beamed into your living room from a satellite in the sky. He made you feel you were the most important thing in his life when he talked to you. It was the way the green eyes concentrated on your face and the easy manner, the quiet little touches, the familiarity. He was convincing, Sweeting thought, but so were all the blow-dried evangelists of the airwaves. Where McInnes had the edge over his electronic rivals was in the way he looked—he was rumpled instead of embalmed in polyester, and his silver hair had never been styled beneath a dryer but was unkempt and grew down over his collar.

"You're not a stuffy little man, are you, Mr. Sweeting?" McInnes said. "I thought everybody in the State Department had had their sense of humor expunged at birth. I thought they had their wit circumcised along with their foreskins."

J. W. Sweeting passed the palm of one hand over his forehead. He was inexplicably nervous all at once. In theory, he should have loathed a man like McInnes. In practice, he was finding it difficult. The green eyes suggested amusement and a benign tolerance for the sorrows of the human condition, and the smile, that big wide-mouthed expression, was magnetic. What Sweeting had expected to encounter was a hateful bigot, which would have been easy to handle. McInnes didn't come across that way at all. Indeed, he appeared reasonable and easygoing, a man given to instant friendships, huge handshakes, intimate gestures. A man who played on your sympathies by insisting, with a downturned mouth, that he was misunderstood by his enemies, which was a terrible cross he had to carry. He was goddam *likable*.

McInnes rubbed his chin. "You're not a bad fellow, Sweeting. And because I like you I'll make life easy for you. I'll go along with all your restrictions. I'll whistle any tune you care to hear whether I like it or not, because I'm not here on any political mission. I'll tell you something else. I smell the White House behind all these conditions of yours. I smell Tommy Dawson at work."

"Like the State Department, the President is neutral in the Irish question," Sweeting said.

McInnes laughed. It was a curious sound, a throaty wheeze. "Neutral?" Tommy Dawson's a black-hearted Catholic Irishman who makes pilgrimages to the dear little town of Ardare in the Republic of Ireland where his grandparents were born. He's about as neutral as the pope, Mr. Sweeting. And he hates anybody from the North. He hates Ulster."

Sweeting wasn't going to be drawn into the question of Thomas Dawson's Irish heritage or the matter of his sympathies. He returned to the only subject he was interested in. "If you restrict yourself to the research you say you want to do here, then we'll get along just famously."

McInnes nodded his head. "What could be more peaceful and worthy than writing the saga of Ulster laborers in the history of the American railroad? All that sweat and toil. All the sadness of the immigrant worker. The longings. The hopes. The dreams. By God, it's a rich tale. And a complicated one. Besides, I'm a minister without a congregation, and a man has to make a living somehow."

"Indeed," Sweeting said. He thought of how, in support of his visa application, McInnes had submitted a copy of a contract with a small university press for his projected history. It was one book Sweeting would manage not to read, if indeed it was ever likely to see the light of publication.

McInnes picked up his suitcase from the floor. "I'm booked into the Essex House on Central Park, Mr. Sweeting."

"I know," Sweeting said.

McInnes winked at the man. "I thought you might."

WILDWOOD, LONG ISLAND

Big Jock Mulhaney drove his four-wheel-drive vehicle slowly over damp sands. He had a view of Long Island Sound, which looked dismal and abandoned in the sullen light of afternoon. He wore a thick flannel jacket and waterproof pants, and he had a baseball cap pulled down squarely on his head. It wasn't the kind of clothing he usually favored. His tastes ran to rather bright three-piece suits, large checks and flashy herringbones, accompanied by wide-knotted neckties. But today he wasn't traveling in his usual environment either, which was bounded by his penthouse over union headquarters in Brooklyn and the midtown Manhattan clubs he patronized, where his fellow members regarded him with all the suspicion Old Money has for the nouveau riche. He was viewed, he knew, as an upstart, a man who didn't belong in the more rarified heights of society. He was a brawler, a climber, a loudmouth, and he suffered from the most heinous condition of all—which was naked ambition—but there was a certain shrewdness to him that nobody disrespected.

Now, as the four-wheel-drive vehicle slithered into ruts and a vicious wind stirred the waters of the sound, Mulhaney wondered if it was bad judgment to be out here at all. For one thing, expanses of nature made him nervous. He couldn't take too many trees. He couldn't stand silences and great spaces. For another, he wasn't sure he should be meeting with Nicholas Linney anyhow, but who else was he going to confide in? He couldn't go to Harry Cairney with his theory unless he had some backing. So he needed Linney's approval and support.

Besides, there was another reason for his uneasiness, one he didn't want to think about. It was the simple fact that he had recently been obliged to cover some very bad investments with money that had been earmarked for Ireland. It wasn't any great sum, a mere $450,000 skimmed from his total contribution of $1.9 million, and he was going to return it next time funds were raised, and nobody was going to find out about it anyway—but just the same the mere prospect of discovery made him feel apprehensive. What if one of the other Fundraisers found out about the shortage? Hell, that would make Big Jock the prime suspect in the hijacking of the *Connie*. How could it not? A man who could "borrow" from Irish funds for his own private purposes wasn't a man who could be trusted. It had been a stupid thing to do, admittedly, but he'd been pressured by creditors, and he hadn't been thinking clearly, and he didn't want any kind of public scandal attached to his name. Thomas Dawson had recently announced a committee of inquiry into the financial practices of unions, and Mulhaney didn't like the idea of coming under the scrutiny of a bunch of congressional jerk-offs who were bound to ask tough questions. He'd covered his shortage this time, and so had spared himself some potential embarrassment, but he'd done it only at the expense of the Irish. But it wasn't something he intended to continue doing. *Fuck Tommy Dawson,* he thought. Always pointing a mighty finger at the unions, slinging accusations, digging for dirt.

Mulhaney's vehicle became bogged down in the soft wet sands. He switched off the engine and stared the length of the beach. *What if this Irishman they were all so goddam afraid of found out about the shortage?* He shook his head. The Irishman wasn't going to get within a hundred miles of him, so he wasn't going to worry about that notion.

He got out of the vehicle and turned the collar of his jacket up against the whining wind. In the distance there was the sound of gunfire, a constant rapid knocking that was muted by the churning waters. He walked a little way. He moved awkwardly because the heavy sands inhibited his progress, and every now and again spray splashed up and blinded him. Christ, he hated this place. He stopped and removed a small silver flask from his hip pocket. He opened it, sipped some cognac, then stuck the flask away again. Ahead, a hundred or so yards along the seafront, he could see Linney's Land-Rover, which had been painted in camouflage colors. The trouble with Nickie Linney, Mulhaney thought, was the guy was some kind of nut. He read *Soldier of Fortune* and believed every word of it. He was into weaponry and combat and guerrilla techniques, and he went through the pages of *Soldier of Fortune* with a big yellow marker in his fist, circling stories and advertisements that interested him.

Mulhaney kept walking. Now he could see Linney lying flat on the sand. The sound of gunfire was constant. Blap-blap-blap. As he got closer, Mulhaney noticed the targets Linney was using. Close to the shoreline, the guy had set up row after row of cantaloupes, and he was currently blasting away at them. Every now and then one of them would explode and rise up in the air in pulpy smithereens. Linney was from outer space, Mulhaney thought.

"Nick!" he called out.

Linney stood up, raised one arm in greeting. He was dressed in combat clothing. He even had a beret, which he wore at a precarious angle. Mulhaney noticed the heavy army boots. Grenades lay on the sand alongside an assortment of weapons. Jesus, the guy was a one-man militia.

Linney stared in the direction of the cantaloupes. Then he held out the weapon he'd been using as if he wanted Mulhaney to inspect it and give it some seal of approval. Mulhaney wasn't happy around firearms.

"The M-16A2," Linney said proudly.

Jock Mulhaney nodded. The melons, most of them shattered, were being sucked at by the tide.

"Feel it, Jock." Linney thrust the weapon out in the manner used by gun freaks the world over when they're in apprehensive company. Cavalier. A little too casual.

Mulhaney held the gun for a moment before returning it. He wondered how Linney got hold of weapons that private citizens weren't supposed to have. "Yeah. Feels solid" was all he could say.

"Excellent piece," Linney said. He pointed out some features, such as the new muzzle brake/compensator and the integral brass deflector, and Mulhaney made humming sounds, as if he might be remotely interested. Mulhaney hoped that if any one of the Fundraisers ever found out about the "borrowed" cash it wouldn't be Nick Linney.

Linney swung the weapon back toward the rows of cantaloupes and fired off a couple of shots. Mulhaney watched one of the melons explode and then hit the water, carried away like a mutant jellyfish.

"Very nice, Nick," Mulhaney said.

Linney smiled, then put the gun inside his Land-Rover and lit a cigarette. There were oil stains on the backs of his fingers. He smoked in silence for a time, his face turned out toward the waters, before he tossed the cigarette away and looked at Mulhaney.

"What's on your mind, Jock?" he asked.

"You have to ask?"

Nicholas Linney beat the palm of one hand upon the panel of his vehicle. "I get the impression you suspect me, Jock. I got that feeling when we were at Roscommon."

Mulhaney shook his head. "I considered it, I admit."

"And you changed your mind?"

Mulhaney took his flask out again. He wished he'd brought a cigar with him to complement the flavor of the cognac, but he'd left his case behind. He swallowed, offered the flask to Linney, who declined.

Mulhaney said, "Yeah. I changed my mind. Which is why I drove all the fucking way out here to see you."

Linney pulled a pair of sunglasses over his eyes even though the sky was gloomy and overcast. "I'm listening, Jock."

"Okay. First, I ruled out Cairney. He's been in this business for nearly fifty goddam years and I can't see him screwing the Irish at this stage of the game. He's been on the Cause's side since I was in fucking diapers and you weren't even born, so why would he dump on it now?"

Linney said, "I'll go along with that. It wasn't Cairney."

"Okay. I ruled out myself because I *know* I didn't have anything to do with the *Connie.*"

Linney smiled. "I'm supposed to take your word for this, Jock?"

"Hear me out," Mulhaney said. "Okay. I eliminated Cairney and myself. Leaving you and Kev Dawson."

"Don't keep me in suspense, Jock."

"First, I figured it might be you. You wanna know why? Because you're the guy that *physically* takes the money to the Courier—"

"I never saw the Courier in my life," Linney said.

"Okay. Let me put it another way. You give the money to a guy who gives the money to the Courier. Right?"

Linney adjusted his dark glasses. "Something like that."

"Fine," Mulhaney said. He glanced at the demolished melons, understanding now why Nick Linney had an effect on him. It was more than just the gun thing, it was something in Linney's physical qualities that unsettled him. That strangely colored face, which reminded Mulhaney of a lime. The guy's general air of self-confidence and the feeling you got that when a nuclear holocaust came, Linney was going to be among the survivors, bottled up in some fucking concrete cellar with his guns and dried fruits and astronaut foods. Linney always looked as if he knew something the rest of the human race had either ignored or forgotten.

Mulhaney played with the surface of his flask. "I ruled you out, Nick, because I couldn't see you turning against the Cause. I couldn't quite get a fix on that. I mean, you bring in more money than the rest of us put together, and if you wanted to steal it you'd find an easier way than going to the trouble of hijacking a fucking ship. You could have stolen the money at the source, for Christ's sake! You could have pocketed the money you raised and then told us that your donors just couldn't come through and who the hell would have been any the wiser?"

Nicholas Linney crossed his arms on his chest. He looked like some tinpot general in a South American jungle army. "And that leaves Kevin Dawson," he said.

"Kevin Dawson." Mulhaney gouged out a pattern in the damp sands with the heel of his shoe.

"He's got money coming out his ears. Why would he want more?"

Mulhaney smiled now. "It wasn't the cash he was after, Nick. His family owns about half of fucking Connecticut, so he wasn't looking for financial gain. You wanna know what I think?"

Linney took off his sunglasses. "Tell me, Jock."

"Okay. I see it happening like this. Let's say he gets a call from Tom Dawson in the White House. Big Brother's unhappy. He doesn't like money flowing out of America and into Ireland. He's in a flap because all that money coming from the States makes him look bad with his bosom buddies in London, who are about the only fucking allies he's got in the world, and they've been bitching about American aid to Irish terrorists. He says to Kev that it's got to stop. And Kev, who's never been a man to deny Big Brother anything, tells him about a certain shipment aboard a certain small vessel. Wonderful, Tommy thinks. We'll put a stop to that one. He gets on the phone, talks to some of his cronies, and these cronies put together a bunch of fucking killers. Vets. Former marines who've been twiddling their thumbs since the Bay of Pigs. Whatever. The money's taken, Tommy is happy, Kev hasn't let Big Brother down, the crew isn't around to point the finger at anyone, and there's no awkward publicity."

Nicholas Linney reached for the M-16A2 and held it against his side. He fired off two shots, missing the cantaloupes both times. Mulhaney's ears rang from the noise of the gunfire. Linney studied the barrel of the weapon for a moment, then turned to look at Mulhaney.

"What kind of proof do you have that Kev Dawson went running off to the White House, Jock?"

Mulhaney shrugged. He had been so convinced by his own theory that the matter of proof hadn't occurred to him. To him it was blatantly obvious that Kevin Dawson was the turncoat, and even if he had constructed a scenario that might or might not have been correct, that alone didn't detract from the basic feeling of rightness he had. And he wasn't accustomed, in the world of ass-kissers and yes-men in which he insulated himself, to having his judgments questioned because proof was lacking. Kevin Dawson was the one. The only candidate. Everyone *knew* that the Dawsons weren't a trustworthy bunch.

Linney said, "For all I know you could have come out here to tell me this story because you wanted to avert suspicion from yourself."

Mulhaney was quiet. *Does this bastard suspect me of something?* he wondered. The speculation filled him with a cold fear. He said, "I could have. But I didn't."

"I've only got your word for that, Jock. Which leaves us right back where we started." Linney looked out toward Long Island Sound. "What makes you so sure that *I* didn't arrange the whole thing anyhow?"

Mulhaney felt spray rise up against his face as the wind forced itself over the tide. "Because I know it was Kev Dawson, for Christ's sake," he said. "A process of simple elimination, Nick."

"It's not so simple, Jock. Show me proof. I need to see proof before I can go along with your story. From where I stand, Kev Dawson's always been reliable when it comes to raising funds. I need something that might convince me otherwise. I need a smoking gun, friend. Right now, I'm thinking that you dislike Kevin Dawson so intensely you'd hang anything on him. Jesus, you hate that whole goddam family."

"There's nothing personal in any of this," Mulhaney said. He sipped from his flask again. Coming out here to talk to Linney—a waste of time. He had hoped that Linney would become an ally and together they'd go see Cairney and lay the story in front of the old man and let him decide how to deal with Dawson. Now Linney was asking for proof, for God's sake. What did he want? Taped conversations? Transcripts?

"It's not exactly the kind of thing where proof's easy to come by," he said, a little deflated. He had revealed himself to Linney and now, having been rebuffed by the man, he felt very defensive. "Okay.

So maybe my theory isn't correct. Maybe it happened some other way and Kev Dawson had motives I haven't even thought about. Maybe the family empire is strapped for cash, I don't know. But I *know* he's the one."

Linney said, "Let me tell you what I think. The money's gone and that's a mystery. I've never been happy with mysteries, Jock. Detective stories, bodies inside locked rooms, that kind of thing never appealed to me. I like facts. The harder the better. This gun, for instance. It's a hard fact. Right?"

Mulhaney nodded in a sullen way.

Linney ran the palm of one hand over the weapon. It was almost a lover's caress. The gun might have been the leg of a mistress. "I don't give a shit right now about who took the money because the only hard fact I can see is that some guy is coming here from Ireland. And that makes me very unhappy. Do you think he's going to sit down and discuss the missing money over a friendly cup of tea?"

Mulhaney said nothing. He hadn't given a lot of thought to this shadowy Irishman who seemed to terrify everybody but himself.

"The fuck he is," Linney went on. "If I was that guy I'd have a bad attitude. I wouldn't be disposed toward kindness. I wouldn't make polite inquiries. I wouldn't trust a fucking soul. If I was him, I'd be ready to do violence." Linney paused, gazing at Mulhaney's florid face. "Suppose this character runs you down, Jock. What would you tell him?"

"I'd give him Kevin Dawson," Mulhaney said quickly.

"What if he doesn't believe you? Who would you give him next? Cairney? Me?"

Mulhaney shuffled his feet in the sand. He was always out of his depth when it came to hypothetical matters. Ifs played no role in Mulhaney's world. He didn't answer Linney's question.

"This guy isn't going to be your friend, Jock. You better understand that."

Mulhaney smiled now. He was uncomfortable with the way Linney was talking. "How would you behave if he came to you?" he asked.

Linney made a gesture with the weapon. "I'm ready for anything," he answered.

"Jesus," Mulhaney said. "You talk as if this guy's going to find us. I think you're paranoid."

"Is there another way to be?" Nicholas Linney asked.

T EN

F rank Pagan was very cold on the rooftop. He wore a heavy overcoat and a plaid scarf and thick gloves, but even so the wind
squeezed through his clothing. He sometimes walked in circles,
stamping his feet for warmth, but he never strayed far from the
view overlooking the entrance to St. Finbar's Mission. It was just
after 8:30 A.M., and the frozen wind, which had been blowing all
night, hadn't died with daylight.

He could see Zuboric's field agent parked down the block a little
way, a young man called Orson Cone, a graduate of Brigham Young
University in Utah. He was keen, bright-eyed. He'd been with the
agency for only eighteen months and he was still fresh enough to
think stakeouts were a big deal. Earlier, when Pagan had talked with
Orson Cone, he'd noticed a copy of *The Book of Mormon* lying facedown on the backseat of the car. With his straight white teeth and
closely cropped fair hair, Cone reminded Pagan of a surfer, one who'd
had an encounter with Jesus out on the waves.

Cone had nothing to report. He'd been sitting inside his car for
about ten hours and, apart from the clientele that drifted in and out
of St. Finbar's, he'd seen nothing of interest. Since there was only
one exit, and Cone hadn't seen Tumulty leave the place, it was a
safe assumption the Irishman was still inside. Pagan, still dislocated

by the change of clocks, went into a rundown building that housed two import-export companies, a shabby PR outfit called Images, and a telephone answering service, and climbed the unlit stairs to the roof. There, surrounded by scrawny city pigeons, he watched the street.

Frank Pagan yawned. Last night, when he left Zuboric, he'd walked several blocks back to the Parker Meridien. He'd stood for a while in the bar, nursing a scotch and soda and studying one of the waitresses, an attractive young girl with a certain airheaded approach to things, a giggler who was forever making the wrong change or dropping glasses. Her name, she told him, was Mandi with an *i*. He'd wondered about introducing himself, just to see where it might lead. But he couldn't imagine performing an act of sexual exorcism with somebody called Mandi with an *i*, so he'd gone up to his room. Sleep hadn't exactly come in like an angel. He tossed around restlessly for hours; then, tired of being tired, he dressed and returned to Canal Street, walking all the way down Broadway to the edge of Chinatown.

Now he beat his gloved hands together and watched his breath mist on the frigid air and concentrated on St. Finbar's Mission, wondering about Joseph X. Tumulty. Sooner or later, the man would step outside. Eventually, he'd have to go somewhere. And Frank Pagan wanted to know where.

His eyes stung as the wind scoured the rooftops, making TV antennas tremble. He huddled deeper inside his coat, trying to shrink himself down into a place where the wind wouldn't hurt him. Hopeless. He blinked at the street. Inside his car Orson Cone sat motionless, no doubt drawing his patience from *The Book of Mormon*. A simple faith. Frank Pagan had always envied simple faiths. His own God was a different kind of joker altogether—complicated and brooding, seating masked at the inaccessible center of some intricate labyrinth. A totally whimsical character with more than a touch of cruelty. He never returned your calls.

Pagan looked along the sidewalk, where the wind skirted across plastic trash bags, making them ripple. He propped his elbows on the top of the wall, leaned forward a little way.

"If you fall, don't expect me to catch you," Zuboric said.

Pagan turned around. Artie Zuboric was coming across the roof, his coat flapping behind him. His nose was red from the cold. There was an angry expression on his face.

"I know," Pagan said. "I didn't call you."

"Damn right you didn't call me," Zuboric said. "Next time you move, I want to know about it."

"Cone told you I was here."

"Cone called me as soon as he saw you."

Pagan shrugged. "I couldn't sleep. I came back here."

"I'm mildly pissed off, Frank. I don't care what time it is; when you have the urge to hit the streets, you let me know."

Pagan said, "I assumed you'd need your beauty sleep, Artie."

Zuboric grunted and glanced toward St. Finbar's Mission. He checked the FBI car, then turned back to Pagan, his anger subsided. "By the way, I couldn't get authorization for a phone tap."

"No?" Pagan thought he detected a tiny note of pleasure in Artie Zuboric's voice.

"Insufficient reason," Zuboric said. "Happens."

Pagan said nothing for a moment. He had the feeling that a telephone tap wouldn't have yielded anything anyway. Not if Joe Tumulty was a careful man. Besides, if Joe *thought* there was a tap on his phone, then that suspicion was as good as any eavesdropping device might have been.

"Something bothers me." Zuboric cupped his hands and lit a cigarette. "You're betting on Jig getting in touch with Tumulty. But I keep coming back to the possibility that your man's been and gone, Frank. In which event, you're freezing your ass off on this godforsaken roof for nothing."

Pagan had already considered this. "I'm betting on another possibility altogether, Artie. I'm betting Jig needs something only Tumulty can get for him."

"Like what?"

"The tools of his trade," Pagan said. "I don't see Jig trying to score an ordinary gun someplace, Artie. And the chances are he didn't arrive in this country carrying anything. He's too careful. If Joe's been an IRA connection here all along, he's bound to have contacts in the kind of specialty weapon Jig might need. When you boil it right down, I think Joe's the only chance we've got."

"And what makes you think he hasn't already supplied Jig?"

"Unless Tumulty keeps weapons on his premises, which I doubt, they'd have to be specially ordered. That takes time."

Pagan looked at the grimy windows of St. Finbar's. They were impossible to see through. Whoever said cleanliness was next to godliness hadn't tried to peer inside Tumulty's soup kitchen.

Zuboric said, "Tumulty's going to have his eyes open, Frank. He isn't going to walk through the streets without looking over his shoulder a whole lot. He won't be an easy tail."

Pagan smiled. He said, "Tailing's one of my good points. If I do it alone."

"Christ, you keep trying, don't you?" Zuboric said.

"He'll spot a pair, Artie. You know that. If we work this together, he's going to spot us as quickly as I spotted you last night."

Zuboric looked pained. He didn't say anything. He stared down into the traffic going along Canal Street. Last night, when Pagan had stepped abruptly out of the cab, Zuboric had taken the taxi one block farther before getting out; then he'd followed Pagan back to his hotel. His orders were specific. Washington was going to be very unhappy if Frank Pagan was turned loose in the city. The possibility of bloodshed had them worried. What it meant for Zuboric was a terrific pain in the ass. He had to keep a lid on Frank Pagan and make sure the Englishman didn't do anything drastic to attract attention. Especially violence.

It was a can of fucking worms, and Zuboric was very unhappy.

"I can't do it, Frank. I can't let you out of my sight."

"Suppose I just slipped away when you weren't looking?"

"No can do."

Pagan put his gloves back on. "Fuck it, Artie. If I choose to go out on my own, what the hell are you going to do to stop me?"

Zuboric looked at the Englishman. "Tell you the truth, Frank, I don't know what I'd do if you were just to take a hike," he said. "I know Washington would have my balls for paperweights, though."

Pagan went to the edge of the roof and leaned against the wall. There was a movement in the doorway of St. Finbar's Mission. Joseph X. Tumulty appeared, the collar of his priestly black coat drawn up to his face.

"There he is, Artie," Pagan said.

Zuboric peered into the street.

"Now what?" Frank Pagan asked. "Do I go alone?"

"No way."

JOSEPH TUMULTY didn't feel the cold. He walked in the direction of Lafayette Street. He passed the FBI car, the tan Chrysler with the fair-haired young man inside. The agent had his face in a book, trying to appear inconspicuous. Tumulty barely noted him. He was concentrating on reaching Lafayette. He knew there were others, that the solitary agent in the Chrysler wasn't alone. When he reached the corner of Lafayette, he looked back. There were several people on the sidewalk, but he saw neither Frank Pagan nor the FBI agent with the Slavic name.

Tumulty, who had been recruited by Padraic Finn while still at the seminary in Bantry, tried to remain calm. Years ago, before he'd come to the United States, membership in an IRA cell had seemed gloriously romantic to him. The adventurer-priest. The swashbuckler behind the dog collar. He'd been swept away by Finn's persuasive tongue, carried along on old glories. Finn's Ireland was going to be a paradise, a land of unity where the old hatreds were demolished forever.

The idea of being an IRA connection in New York City was, quite simply, a thrill. It was also a part of his heritage, his background. Tumulty men had been associated with one or other of the Free Ireland movements ever since the nineteenth century. But, as it turned out, it had seemed an abstraction to him, like having membership in a club he never attended. Even the annual chore he was instructed to perform had never felt remotely dangerous. Once a year he received a telephone call from an anonymous person instructing him to travel to Augusta, Maine, and check into a motel, which was always a different one each time.

There, he'd wait in his room until he was contacted by the same individual informing him to proceed to a certain place, sometimes an abandoned gasoline station, sometimes a deserted factory, and once even the football field of a local high school. Tumulty would do as he was told. It was always at night when the encounters took place. The man would appear, seemingly out of nowhere, and give Tumulty a briefcase, which Tumulty would then deliver to another man known as the Courier in one of the small towns along the Maine coast. Cutler, Vinalhaven, and on the last occasion—when there had been three briefcases—Jonesport. After the Courier took possession of the cases, Tumulty's job was finished. He never asked questions. He knew what the cases contained, and he understood the Courier transported them to Ireland, but that was the extent of it.

It was only by accident that he'd discovered the identity of the man who supplied him with the briefcases.

He went north on Lafayette, heading in the direction of Little Italy. Outside a small produce store he stopped to examine a basket
of apples. He looked back the way he'd come. There was still no
sign of either the Englishman or the FBI character. Tumulty paid for
an apple and crunched into it as he turned right toward Mulberry
Street. He passed an Italian social club, then a flashy new trattoria,
and the smells of espresso and pastries drifted out to him. Beneath
his heavy overcoat he was perspiring and his heart was hammering
at his ribs. Somebody *had* to be following him.

He reached Mulberry Street. His throat was very dry and he had
difficulty swallowing. There was a quiet sense of panic inside him.
It wasn't so much the idea of being followed that troubled him, rather
it was the realization that he was uncertain of how much he could
stand if he was caught. He didn't know his own limits or the extent
of his endurance if it came down to threats like the one he'd heard
last night about Attica. The idea of incarceration wasn't so terrible
in itself—after all, many good men had been jailed for their work in
the Cause—it was the prospect of being removed from St. Finbar's
Mission that clawed at him. Who would run the place if he was
gone? Who would care for those men? Who would be as interested
in saving their lives as he was? They were the lowest characters in
the whole social hierarchy. Many of them were of the kind that other
missions didn't like to accept—the obviously deranged, the potentially violent, men who were beyond the reaches of polite social
agencies. It was a vanity, he knew, to think of himself as indispens-
able, but when it came to St. Finbar's he sidestepped his own hu-
mility. Why shouldn't he be proud of himself?

He tossed the apple away and went inside a delicatessen where
he pretended to examine the salami that hung in the window. There
was a fine layer of sweat on his forehead. St. Finbar's Mission would
fall apart without him, he was convinced of that. Hadn't he carved
the place out of practically nothing anyhow? Hadn't he begged and
borrowed money to renovate the building and buy bedding and
cooking equipment and then gone out into the drab streets looking
for clients, sometimes having to drag them to the kitchen when they
appeared reluctant? He'd given all his energies to the project. But
more than that, more than time and effort and sweat, he'd brought
to the place his own form of love and charity—which the established
church hadn't needed. Shaping St. Finbar's had seemed to Tumulty
a holy thing to do, and a practical expression of Christian love. Christ's

love wasn't to be found in the chicanery of parish politics or out on golf courses where bishops rode their little fringed carts and discussed stock options. God didn't thrive in upper-class social settings. If He was anywhere, He was down there on the streets with the poor and needy, and Tumulty was nothing more than an instrument for God's work. God's world wasn't stained glass and velvet cushions and hypocrisy. He existed wherever hearts were breaking and men cried out in terrible need. St. Finbar's Mission had become Joseph Tumulty's personal cathedral, the place where he felt spiritually closest to his deity.

From his coat pocket Tumulty removed a small black notebook Finn had given him the day he left Ireland. It was a cheap little book, perhaps thirty pages in all, and it contained only one name and address, written in Finn's flamboyant hand. The pages fell open at the center because Tumulty had studied the name many times, wondering if and when he might have to use it. He'd tried on several occasions to commit it to memory, but somehow he hadn't trusted himself to do so. He stared at the writing, then shut the book and returned it to his coat pocket.

Go to this man, Finn had said. *Only when you need something badly, something you don't know how to get on your own.*

Tumulty went back onto the street. He reached the corner of Mulberry and Kenmare, and there he paused. He remembered now the last trip to Maine and the man who'd given him the briefcases in the snowbound parking lot of an old filling station. The man who never gave his name, who kept his conversation to an absolute minimum and who was always in a hurry to leave. The man with the peculiar unhealthy color to his face. The man whose photograph Tumulty had accidentally come across in the pages of *The New York Times,* in an article concerning those mysterious brokers whose specialty was that of arranging mergers between corporations who didn't want the values of their stocks affected by advance publicity of their plans. A middleman, someone who operated in the fiscal shadows. His name was Nicholas Linney and he operated a company called Urrisbeg International.

Tumulty understood he wasn't meant to know Nicholas Linney's identity. But the fact was he *did* know it. There was no way of forgetting he knew it. And he was going to give it to Jig because Jig needed a name.

He turned onto Kenmare. Halfway along the block he stopped,

turning to check the sidewalk behind him. Even though he saw nobody who looked as if he might be following him, his instincts told
him otherwise. People like Frank Pagan were smarter at this kind of
thing than he could ever be. People like Pagan knew the tricks of
this trade. Tumulty, rubbing a hand over his clammy forehead, looked
across the street. He found himself gazing at the window of a small
shop that sold religious artifacts. It had to be wrong. He took out
his book and checked the address again. How could this possibly be
the right place?

Plaster virgins looked mournfully out at him from behind the dirt-
streaked window. Gaudy prints depicted the crucifixion. There were
crosses and rosaries draped all over the place. There were Shroud
of Turin souvenirs. It was a joyless window display. Tumulty went
in the direction of the shop, walked a few paces beyond it to the
corner, then stopped. This was the critical part. This was the moment.

He had a sudden inspiration. He'd call the shop, tell his contact
to meet him somewhere. He went inside a phone booth and flipped
through the pages of a ragged directory, looking for an entry under
Santacroce, which was the name Finn had written in the notebook.
He didn't find any name that corresponded with the address. Damn.
Tumulty pressed his face wearily against the cold glass of the phone
booth. He looked back the way he'd come. Cars. Pedestrians. How
could he possibly tell if *anyone* was following him?

He stepped out of the phone booth. He took a handkerchief from
his coat pocket and blew his nose. He examined the front of the
shop again. It had no name. Inside the window, everything was
covered in dust. The place looked as if it hadn't had customers in
years. There were even framed paintings of the old pope, Pius XII.

Dear God, Tumulty said to himself. He'd go in. He had to. What
did it matter if anyone saw him? He wanted to buy a religious picture for St. Finbar's Mission. There. It was as simple as that, if anybody asked. He had the perfect excuse for being in a shop like this,
didn't he?

He pushed the door open. A small bell rang over his head. It was
gloomy inside and the air smelled stale, a mixture of sandalwood
and dampness. He approached the counter and a curtain was parted
at the back of the room. A man appeared.

"Santacroce?" Tumulty asked. There was a crack in his voice.

THE old guy said to Frank Pagan, "This is kinda exciting. This kinda thing don't happen to me every day."

Pagan and Zuboric sat hunched in the narrow backseat of the old man's 1973 Opel. It was a shabby car with great chunks torn out of the upholstery. The floor was covered with discarded fast-food wrappers and moldy french fries that looked like blunt pencils. Bumper stickers were plastered all over the back of the car, attesting to the man's extensive travels.

"I'd never a done this if it hadn't been for that FBI badge," the man said. His name was Fogarty, and he'd been parked on Canal Street when Pagan had suggested that he might like to help in a "confidential government investigation." Fogarty was scouring missions and soup kitchens up and down the East Coast in the quest for some long-lost alcoholic brother. Pagan was sure it was a sad tale, but he didn't encourage Fogarty to tell it.

The old man was delighted by the diversion. It was odd, Pagan reflected, how quickly the average citizen could slip into an undercover role. Fogarty narrowed his eyes and watched the street, and when he spoke his voice was hushed. It was the way he'd seen it in the movies. It was something to tell the folks back in Sunbury, Pennsylvania.

"What's this guy done anyhow?" Fogarty asked.

Zuboric said nothing. Commandeering a car and involving a private citizen hadn't been his idea. But he had to admit that this battered old jalopy was perfect because nobody would ever expect the FBI to travel with such a marked absence of style.

"Can't tell me, right?" Fogarty asked.

"Right," Pagan said. Up the block a way Tumulty had disappeared inside a shop.

"Confidential stuff, right?"

Pagan nodded. The old man chuckled. "I'll be damned," he said.

Pagan told him to drive forward slowly and park at the end of the block. The only available space was alongside a fire hydrant. Fogarty took it, even though it was illegal.

Pagan turned round in his seat. The store into which Tumulty had gone was the kind that sold tawdry religious items.

Zuboric took out a notebook and scribbled down the address of the store, then tucked the book away. The smell of ancient fried foods was getting to him. Under his feet Big Mac wrappers made crinkling noises.

"He's taking his time," Zuboric said.

Fogarty twisted around to look at the FBI man. "Whyn't you just bust into that joint and go for broke?"

Zuboric smiled politely, said nothing.

"I get it," Fogarty remarked. "You want the whole syndicate, don't you? It ain't just one guy. Right?"

"Right," Pagan said, wondering which particular movie was playing in the old man's head.

"I'll be damned," Fogarty said.

Tumulty stepped out into the street now. He was carrying a large crucifix, unwrapped. He held it clutched against his side. He looked this way and that, then he began moving along the sidewalk.

"An ostentatious display of holiness," Pagan said.

Zuboric nodded. "He wants to be seen looking innocent."

"You think he's afraid of vampires, Artie?"

"I think he's afraid period."

SAINT ANDRÉ DES MONTS, QUEBEC

The old DC-4 landed awkwardly on an airstrip located several miles from the village of Saint André des Monts, east of Saint Hyacinthe in southeast Quebec. The airfield had been used by the Royal Canadian Air Force during World War II, and then abandoned. The hangars had rotted and become overgrown with weeds, and the landing strip had subsided here and there, cracked by severe winters. The plane bounced a couple of times before it slid to a halt in front of a hangar. A man in a ski mask and goggles came out and, leaning his face away from the sharp wind that blew across the field, walked toward the DC-4.

The door of the plane opened. Including pilot and copilot, there were six men on board. The man in the ski mask watched them disembark, scurrying down a rope ladder. They had been airborne for a little more than thirteen hours, and they moved wearily. But before any of them could rest there was cargo to be unloaded.

The man, who was called Fitzjohn, took his goggles off and rubbed his eyes. It had been his responsibility to find a suitable airfield as close as possible to the Canadian border with New York State. Posing as a businessman interested in opening a flying school, he'd searched for a location for months. This field was the best he'd found.

Its present owner lived in Montreal and rarely visited the place, so Fitzjohn had considered it safe for his purpose.

Fitzjohn greeted Seamus Houlihan, who was the first man off the plane.

"You could've laid on better weather, Fitz," Houlihan said, covering his face with the collar of his seaman's jacket.

"You're lucky it isn't snowing," Fitzjohn replied.

Houlihan looked across the bleak airfield. In the distance there was ragged barbed wire and a couple of bleached signs that at one time had read NO ADMITTANCE. Bare trees grew beyond the fence. A Ryder rental truck sat alongside a hangar.

"Some place," Houlihan said, shivering. "The arsehole of the world."

"It's everything you asked for." Fitzjohn wanted to say something about how long it had taken him to locate this spot, he wanted to mention how many weeks he'd spent away from his home in Camden, New Jersey, but Houlihan was never interested in that kind of detail.

Houlihan stepped toward the nearest hangar and looked beyond the broken door at the dark interior. Fitzjohn had forgotten how suspicious Houlihan was. Every dark place contained the possibility of menace for Seamus Houlihan. The inside of the young man's mind had to be like the interconnected tunnels of a gloomy sewer. Fitzjohn was glad that his own role was coming to an end. After the border crossing he'd go back to New Jersey and sink into his own anonymous life and hope he'd never hear from the Free Ulster Volunteers again. He wasn't cut out for this kind of life. He had an American wife and two small kids and Armagh Jail, in Northern Ireland, where he'd spent two years for possession of hand grenades, was just an unpleasant memory now. Aside from the deprivation of liberty, what he resented most about Armagh was the fact that it was a British jail, and he was a British subject who'd armed himself against possible attacks from the IRA. A man protecting himself, that was all. He had always been loyal to Queen and Country. The trouble was, Britain wasn't winning the struggle against the IRA. British policy in Northern Ireland was chicken-hearted. The army didn't crush the IRA with enough force.

John Waddell and the other men stood close to the plane. Fitzjohn smiled at them. He knew Waddell from the old days in Belfast, but the other characters were unfamiliar to him. He thought John Waddell looked like a dying rat, pale and shuddering in the cold air.

Houlihan made introductions. One of the men, a stocky figure with a scar running from the corner of his ear to his upper lip, was called Rorke. Another was named McGrath, a tense individual with the nervous eyes of a street fighter and a mouth that had very few teeth. They looked, Fitzjohn thought, seasoned in violence. Houlihan then introduced the pilot and the copilot, both of whom appeared anxious to be back inside the plane and out of this forsaken place. They'd delivered their cargo, which was the extent of their commitment, and they wanted to go home. The pilot was called Braxton and the copilot Lessingham. They were both English, both former air force pilots. Their last employment had been to airlift Libyan troops into Chad.

Braxton smiled in a pale way, then turned his face upward, checking the sky. "I'd like to be on my way, Seamus." He pronounced the name correctly. *Shaymus.* Englishmen sometimes couldn't get their tongues around Irish names.

"And so you will, Braxton," Houlihan said. "Just as soon as we get this beast unloaded."

Houlihan scanned the inside of the hangar again, as if his first examination of the place hadn't satisfied him. "Have you found us a crossing?"

Fitzjohn said, "I have."

"Good, good," Houlihan remarked.

There was silence. In the distance wind rattled the rusted barbed wire and shook the ancient signs. Fitzjohn looked at Houlihan. There was an odd expression on the young man's face. He appeared to be staring inward, into his own black mind. He licked his lips, shifted his weight from one foot to the other. Fitzjohn had a premonitory moment, a sense of something unpleasant about to happen. He glanced at the pilot, Braxton, then looked back at Houlihan, who had one hand inside the deep pocket of his navy-blue jacket.

Fitzjohn *knew.*

He watched Houlihan take a pistol out of the pocket and turn very slowly toward the pilot, who stepped back a pace, his mouth open, a hand extended in front of his face.

The explosion of the gun roared in Fitzjohn's ears. He saw Braxton's face blown apart, the impact of the bullet throwing the body back several feet. Braxton lay facedown under the fuselage of the DC-4, his arms pressed beneath his body. From the opening in his skull there was blood and gray fluid creating a puddle under his cheek. The copilot, Lessingham, stared at Houlihan in utter disbelief and then turned away, hurrying toward the rope ladder that hung from the door of the plane. He began to scramble upward and the ladder swayed back and forth with the movements of his body.

Houlihan shot him in the back of the skull. Lessingham, caught in the strands of rope, twisted around, his face turning toward the hangar. One of his eyes was gone.

"Jesus God," Fitzjohn whispered.

Houlihan smiled. He went over to Braxton's body and kicked it gently. "Mercenary bastards," he said. "You can't trust people who do things only for the money."

NEW YORK CITY

In his hotel room Frank Pagan had found a radio station that played nothing but old rock and roll. He was lying on the bed and listening to the late Gene Vincent hiccuping through "Be-Bop-a-Lula," when the telephone rang. It was Foxworth calling from London.

"How are things in the land where people say Hi and Have a Nice Day?" Foxie asked.

Pagan turned Gene Vincent down. The connection with London was bad and Foxie's voice echoed.

"Cold," Pagan said. "Brass-monkey weather."

"I have a tiny snippet of info for you, Frank. It may interest you."

Pagan massaged a bare foot. He stared at the window where the midday light, filtered by a drape, was pallid.

Foxie said, "Our old chum Ivor the Terrible is practically your next-door neighbor. Did you know that?"

"McInnes is here? In New York?"

"I am reliably informed by a young gal who works at the American fortress in Grosvenor Square that the Reverend Ivor McInnes obtained a temporary visa for research purposes."

"What's he researching? New ways to boil Catholics?"

"Would you believe a book? A work of history?"

"Didn't know he could read," Pagan said.

"He's staying at the Essex House," Foxie said. "Thought you might like to know."

Later, when he'd replaced the telephone and turned up the volume of the radio to catch Buddy Holly's "Rock Around with Ollie Vee," he sat cross-legged on the bed and closed his eyes and turned Foxie's news around in his mind. It was the familiar old labyrinth again. It was the Irish version of Join the Dots. Why was McInnes in New York at this particular time? Pagan didn't buy the idea of Ivor writing a book unless it was a polemic concerning the satanic ideology of the Roman Catholic Church and nobody was going to issue him a visa for that kind of lunacy. So why was he here? Coincidence? Pagan never trusted coincidence.

He opened his eyes. There was a knock on his door. He went across the room, undid the lock. Zuboric came inside, rubbing his cold hands together. He sat down in an armchair and made a face at the music that filled the room.

"Does it have to be that loud?" the agent asked.

"Is there any other way, Artie? Great rock was intended to be deafening." Pagan made no move to adjust the volume. Quite the contrary. He wished he could make it even louder, but the tiny radio was already at maximum.

"What is with you and this music, Frank? You caught in a time warp?" Zuboric took a notebook out of his coat.

"They don't make music like this anymore. It's all so bloody humorless these days. People with pink and green hair taking themselves seriously, spouting messages I don't want to hear." Pagan sat on the edge of the bed. The music had changed to Chuck Berry. "Maybelline."

Zuboric had to raise his voice to be heard over the noise. "The shop in Little Italy belongs to a certain Michelangelo 'The Saint' Santacroce."

"The Saint?"

"That's what they call him. He doesn't exactly live up to it, though. Two terms in Attica. One for tampering with a jury. The second for illegal possession of automatic weapons." Zuboric paused, looking over the top of his notebook. "Here's the kicker, Frank. The weapons were all nicely crated when Santacroce was busted. Crated *and* labeled. Guess where they were going?"

"Ireland," Pagan said.

"You got it."

"What did the crates say? Butter?"

"Holy Bibles."

Frank Pagan lay back across the bed and inspected the ceiling. "What will they think of next?" he asked.

ELEVEN

ROSCOMMON, NEW YORK

It was seven o'clock before Celestine persuaded Harry Cairney he should retire. She escorted him upstairs, helped him undress. He was already sound asleep when she left the bedroom and went back down to the library, where Patrick Cairney sat in front of the log fire with a brandy glass in his hand. There was music playing on the stereo, Harry's music, the old Irish stuff he loved. Celestine turned the record player off. She sat down in the chair facing her stepson and picked up her own brandy from the coffee table.

"Don't tell your father," she said. "But I can take Irish music only in small doses. He's been playing it all afternoon. Too much."

Patrick Cairney smiled. He'd been pleased to see his father leave the room because Harry had been headed in the direction of garrulous reminiscence, induced no doubt by the music. The entire afternoon had been filled with Irish tunes, ranging from "If You Ever Go Across the Sea to Ireland" to the inevitable rebel song "Kevin Barry." Too much indeed, Patrick Cairney thought. An onslaught that dulled the senses after a while. Only Harry himself had been animated by the music, tapping his feet, rapping his fingertips on his knees, sitting sometimes with eyes closed and mouth half open, and old man traveling in old realms.

Once or twice, Patrick Cairney had felt so irritated that he'd wanted to turn the music off and go grab his father and shake him, as if to impress upon the old man the fact that all the songs in the world couldn't bring his private Ireland back to him. The same damn music, the same damn memories, and Patrick Cairney had heard them all a hundred times before. The brainwashed childhood, he thought. The childhood riddled through and rotted by Harry Cairney's nostalgia, his fake dreams. If Harry loved Ireland the way he claimed, then why had he never done anything about the troubles there? Why had he never—not *once* in all his years in Washington—gone on record as condemning sectarian violence and supporting some kind of acceptable solution? The answer was simple—it was enough for Harry to sit with his eyes shut and his foot tapping and listen to the same old goddam songs. His dreams were safe things, retreats from a world where men and women and children died needlessly, and torture and terror were a part of every child's vocabulary.

In the glow from the fire, which was the only source of light in the large paneled room, Celestine's face was half hidden by rippling shadows. Cairney thought the firelight gave her beauty a mysterious quality. She sipped some brandy, then set the glass down and extended her long fingers in front of the flames. She continued to look at Cairney, her stare disarming.

"You don't understand this marriage, do you? You see a relatively young woman married to a man much older, and you wonder why."

Cairney made a small sound of protest, but the truth was otherwise. He *had* been wondering.

"Maybe you're even thinking I married Harry for money and security," she said.

Again Cairney protested. "It never crossed my mind."

"I love him," she said. "It's really that simple."

Cairney finished his drink. "And he dotes on you."

Celestine settled back in her armchair, crossing her legs. "I met your father quite by chance. I was doing PR work for one of those companies he lends his name to, a textile concern in Boston. They like to have Senator Harry Cairney on their stationery. He came to visit the company, and there was a luncheon in his honor, and we talked, and we met again the next day. He proposed to me within the week. I accepted."

A whirlwind, Cairney thought. All during the afternoon he'd watched Celestine and Harry's mutual adoration society, the little touches between them, the long looks of affection they shared. And still, somehow, it didn't sit right with him except he wasn't sure why. The age difference, that was all. The curious contrast between this obviously healthy young woman and Harry Cairney's frailty. The other question that had gone through his mind was why a woman as vivacious as Celestine would want to lock herself away in the isolation of Roscommon. He had underestimated love, nothing more. It was an emotion he always underestimated.

Celestine stood up. "I wasn't looking for anybody, Patrick. Marriage was the very last thing on my mind. I'd already been through one, and I wasn't enchanted by the experience. And I'm not interested in Harry's money. I want you to know that."

Celestine's shadow was large on the wall behind her. She stretched her arms, then ran her fingers through hair that settled back in place immediately, as if it hadn't been disturbed at all.

"He charmed the heart out of me, Patrick. He's capable of that. He paid so much attention to me—he still does—that I felt like the center of his universe. I was never in awe of him or his position. I didn't even *notice* the difference in our ages. It was all perfectly natural. I don't think anything in my entire life has ever been so natural." She was quiet a moment, staring at Cairney with a frank look on her face. "Why do I feel I have to explain myself to you?"

"You don't," Cairney said.

"Maybe I want you to like me. Maybe I don't want you to have any doubts about me. Maybe all I really need is for you to understand that I love your father and that I'll take care of him. He's a wonderful man, Patrick, and I want him to be really healthy again. It's just such a heartache to see him sick." She smiled now and the expression of concern that had appeared on her lovely face dissolved. "Do you like to walk?"

"Sure."

"I always take a stroll about this time," she said. "Want to keep me company?"

Cairney got up. He turned to look from the window. Roscommon was in darkness. The moon lay under thick clouds.

They went downstairs. Cairney put on his overcoat, and Celestine dressed in a fur jacket. Outside, they crossed the expanse of front lawn in silence until they reached the shore of Roscommon Lake, a dark disk stretching in front of them.

They walked the shoreline to a stand of bare trees. There, Celestine paused and looked out across the water. The lake made a soft knocking sound, a whisper of reeds. Cairney glanced back the way they'd come, seeing the black outline of the house. He had a brief image of his mother, Kathleen, a tall, round-faced woman with the kindest eyes he'd ever seen on any human being. Kathleen, who had never really been at home in Roscommon because she disliked its size and location, had presided over the big house like some unwilling empress whose emperor was constantly elsewhere. Cairney smiled to himself because the memory was warm and good. It had about it the tranquillity of recollected love.

The sound of a vehicle broke the stillness. Headlights appeared through the trees. It was the security jeep, which parked some yards away. A man came toward them, carrying a flashlight. He was the same man Cairney had seen that afternoon.

"Cold enough for you, Mrs. Cairney?" the man asked.

Celestine didn't answer. In the beam of the flashlight she looked unhappy. The man stood very still, shining the beam toward the shore of the lake.

"Just the routine check," the guard said.

Celestine turned away. When the man had returned to the jeep and the vehicle had moved off in a southerly direction, she said, "I hate them. They're always nearby. Even when I can't see them, I feel them."

"Why are they here?" Cairney asked.

"Harry's idea. He mumbled something about protecting his valuables. He thinks somebody is going to rob this place. I pretend the security goons don't bother me. But they're a nuisance."

She moved along the shore. Cairney followed. The moon broke free from clouds and showered the lake with silver. Celestine stopped, turned to him, laid a hand on his arm.

"The trouble with your father is he thinks he's a young man all over again," she said. "He thinks he can do all the things he used to do when he was in his twenties. I can't get him to stay in bed. He won't follow his physician's orders." She sighed. She dropped her hand to her side. "I'm tired of telling him things for his own good."

"He's a stubborn man," Cairney said.

"Maybe he'd listen to you."

"I doubt it. The Senator's never been much of a listener."

"Why do you call him that?" she asked.

"The Senator?" Cairney shrugged. "I'm not absolutely sure. I guess

I've always thought of him that way. The Senator from New York."

"It's just the way you say it. It's almost as if you resent the sound of the word. Or the man behind it."

"I don't resent him," Cairney replied. "And I don't mean to sound that way either." He paused now, listening to the rustle of some night creature foraging nearby. If you listened closely, as he always did, even the most superficially placid nights were alive with undercurrents of noise. Resentment, he thought. That was only a part of it. It was more, the sense of being locked constantly in a relationship that was composed of conflicting emotions. Pity and love. Annoyance and admiration. It was a deep conflict and there were times—especially in Ireland, where he felt as if he were stalked by the ghost of Harry Cairney's younger self, a specter who had the knowledgeable persistence of a tour guide—when it twisted inside him with the certainty of a knife.

Celestine turned her face around to him just as the moon poked through cloud again. Staring at her, looking at the moonlight in her hair and the shadows under her cheekbones and the silvery flecks in her eyes, Cairney felt a little flicker of attraction that he pushed away almost as soon as it touched him. He moved back from Celestine. Your stepmother, for God's sake. Your father's wife. He wondered if she'd noticed, if his expression had betrayed anything. He was annoyed with himself. He didn't like unwanted feelings coming up out of nowhere and startling him. They suggested hidden places inside himself that he didn't know about, unmapped territory within his own psyche.

She went on talking about Harry's health. How his bronchial condition had recently worsened. How sometimes in the night she'd sit listening to his breathing, actually *waiting* in dread for the sound to stop. Cairney was hardly listening. Her words swept past him. He wanted to go back indoors. Get out of this moonlight, which was affecting him in uncomfortable ways. He shivered and looked toward the house. He thought of his father asleep in the upstairs bedroom.

"I don't want anything to happen to him," she said.

"He's made of old shoe leather," Cairney said. "As a kid, I used to think he was indestructible."

"That's the trouble, Patrick. He isn't."

Cairney was silent. He put his hands into the pockets of his coat. A wind rose off Roscommon Lake. Cairney started to move in the direction of the house. Celestine followed.

"You're tired," she said.

"A little."

They walked back. Celestine paused on the steps of the house. Cairney, who had reached the door, looked back down at her.

She said, "I don't want to lose him, Patrick. But Tully says his lungs are badly congested. This last bronchial attack really hit him where it hurts."

Cairney didn't say anything. He gazed at the expression of concern on Celestine's face. He wanted to reach out and comfort her. Instead, he ushered her inside the entrance room, where it was warm.

Celestine removed her fur jacket. "At least there's one consolation, Patrick. His doctor says he has a heart like an ox. That's something."

Cairney smiled. "What do you expect? It's a good Irish heart. They don't make them that way anymore."

Celestine laughed. She pushed open the door that led to the sitting room. She hesitated in the doorway a moment, watching Cairney's face. Then she said, "Let's have a nightcap."

THE WHITE HOUSE,
WASHINGTON, D.C.

Thomas Dawson, President of the United States, former senator from Connecticut, ate only yogurt and raisins for his evening meal. He had a phobia about putting on weight, and he monitored his caloric intake carefully, using a small calculator he carried with him everywhere. He stuck his plastic spoon inside the yogurt carton and sat back in his chair, punching the buttons of his calculator.

When he was through he looked up at his brother Kevin, who was standing on the other side of the desk. Kevin was pale and nervous and his voice a little higher than usual on this particular evening. With damn good reason, the President thought.

Thomas Dawson stood up. He fixed Kevin with the Dawson Grin, which had been patented years before during the first Senate campaign. It was a bright expression suggesting honesty and easy confidence. It appealed to women and it didn't threaten men, and it was perhaps the most important expression any politician could be blessed with, attractive and unmenacing. It was the smile of a man from whom you would buy a used car and go home feeling good about it, and you'd never think to complain when it started to leak oil on the second day.

"Kevin," he said, using the tone of one brother to another, reassuring and almost conspiratorial.

Kevin Dawson shifted his feet. Whenever he visited his brother in the Oval Office, he felt the weight of history pressing down on him, and he was overawed like a schoolboy. Jesus, this was his own brother! They'd been brought up together, played together, shared a bedroom—and he could hardly talk to the man! Even now, when he'd come here to speak about his fears and look for a little support, words hadn't come easily. This meekness, which often took the form of a rather elaborate politeness, had long been the fatal flaw in his character. He was a man who found it easy to be overcome, whose arguments were always the first to be swept aside in any debate. Sometimes he wished he had the heart for confronting the world face on.

"The Irish question's a delicate one for me," Thomas Dawson said. "My general policy, at least in public, has been to ignore it. Leave it to the British. We pump in a few bucks to Belfast every now and then, and we do considerable trade with Dublin. But we don't play favorites. Don't take sides. Keep everybody happy. It's a balancing act and it's goddam tricky."

Kevin Dawson watched his brother come around the large desk. He reflected on the fact that the politics of the presidency changed a man. Thomas Dawson had become somber, more serious, and at the same time somewhat devious. Even the Dawson Grin seemed jaded, little more than a reflex.

"Privately, it's another matter. You know that as well as anyone, Kevin. God, it's only been a hundred years since old Noel Dawson sailed from Killarney. How could I not feel some kind of attachment to the old country? How could I not take sides?" The President smiled sadly. "The trouble is, I'm not a private person anymore. It's one of the first things you find out in this job. Every damn thing you do is public. Even my diet, Kevin. I had a publisher offer me a ridiculous sum of money for my goddam diet! Can you imagine that? Wanted to call it the White House Diet or some such thing."

He spread his hands on the desk. Finely manicured nails glinted under the green lampshade. "Consider this, Kevin. There's a large Irish vote out there. Right now, I have it in my pocket the way no American president outside of Kennedy ever had it. I can count on it and that's a nice feeling in politics because usually the only thing you can take for granted is the electorate being fickle." The President sat up on the edge of his desk and played with the empty yogurt carton. "I'd be pretty damn stupid to screw around with this support. It would be suicidal to alienate it."

Kevin Dawson bit the inside of his cheek. What was his brother trying to tell him? He remembered Thomas Dawson when he'd been plain old Tommy, eighteen years of age and a halfway decent quarterback at Princeton. Simple unadulterated Tommy, without a devious bone in his body. He failed to make the connection between the President and that young man who had loved nothing more than football, beer, and cheerleaders, in any order you liked. Now Thomas Dawson watched his weight, didn't drink beer, paid no attention to football, and—instead of dallying with cheerleaders—was married to a glacial woman called Eleanor, who was always traveling the country in her relentless and entirely manic crusade against the indiscriminate dumping of radioactive wastes. Mrs. Radioactivity, Kevin thought. Eleanor Dawson was an ice princess, a woman with all the sexual charm of cake frosting. Kevin could never imagine his brother in bed with her. With her high cheekbones and her fashionable demeanor and the calm way she handled herself with press and public, she was an absolutely perfect wife for a president.

Thomas Dawson examined his fingernails. "I've always turned a blind eye to your little gang of fund-raisers, Kevin. I've always considered that side of you your own private business. Despite the potential embarrassment you represent, I've never told you what to do. Have I?"

Kevin Dawson shook his head.

"I've let you run as you please," the President said. He reached out and clapped his brother on the shoulder and all at once Kevin Dawson was sixteen years old again, confiding to his big brother that he'd gotten a girl into trouble and what the hell should he do about it. He felt small.

The President sat down behind his desk. He had a red-covered folder in front of him. He flipped it open. "Maybe I should have kept a firmer hand on you," he said. He shrugged, stared at the several sheets of paper inside the folder. "And now you come here and tell me that some Irishman might be a menace to your life. Which wouldn't have been the case if you'd quit hanging around with those Irish fanatics." The President was careful enough not to name them, even if he knew who they were. His was a life of sometimes pretending ignorance of things he knew. It was a way of thinking in which he became two distinct people, and then two more, splitting and multiplying his personalities like some primitive cell.

"Yes," Kevin Dawson said quietly. His face assumed an expression of regret. His cheeks sagged and his lips turned down and his eyes seemed to shrink into his head.

The President said, "The problem is, he's not just *some* Irishman, Kevin. The man who's got you steamed up is none other than Jig. Ring a bell?"

"Jig?" Kevin's throat constricted. *"They sent Jig?"*

The President nodded his head. "I'm told he entered the United States within the last forty-eight hours, give or take a few. He's suspected to be in the New York City area. We're not sure."

Kevin Dawson sat down, something he didn't usually do in this particular office. He felt something very cold settle on his heart. He stared at his brother, as if he were expecting the President to tell him that he'd been joking about Jig, but Thomas Dawson's expression didn't change and the seriousness in his eyes didn't go away. Kevin realized that a small nerve had begun to beat in his throat and his hands were suddenly trembling. In a million years he could never have imagined Jig's orbit touching his own. What the hell did *his* life have to do with that of the famous Irish assassin? They were worlds apart. But here was Thomas Dawson telling him otherwise. Kevin closed his eyes.

"You're not *sure?*" he asked. "What the hell does that mean?"

The President was quiet for a long time. "I've been trying to explain something to you, Kevin. I've been trying to instruct you in the realities of my position."

Realities, Kevin Dawson thought. The only reality that concerned him right then was the notion of Jig lurking out there in the shadows of his life. It had been bad enough to imagine a faceless Irishman, but now that this figure had been identified, it was much worse. For the first time since he'd become associated with the Fund-raisers he felt a sense of fear. He tried to remember Jock Mulhaney's reassurances about how this Irishman would never find them in any case, but how could the big man's bluster console him now? Even Harry Cairney hadn't seemed very convinced that the group's anonymity was inviolate. Cairney had given the opposite impression, that the secrecy in which the group had always operated was goddam *fragile*. Kevin Dawson leaned forward in his chair, clenching his hands between his knees. "You must be doing *something* to catch this guy, Tom."

Thomas Dawson closed the red-covered file. "You're not listening to me. You're not paying attention. Jig's become something of a folk hero in every Irish bar from Boston to Philadelphia and back again. They sing songs about him. They adulate him. He's the Irish Pimpernel, Kevin. And you know how the Irish love their heroes. The daring of the man. The mystery. He kills English politicians and disappears as if he doesn't exist! They just adore all that. He's been written up in *Newsweek* and *Time*. The guy's a goddam savior as far as the Irish are concerned."

Kevin Dawson watched his brother stroll round the office. It dawned on him now. "You're not going out of your way to catch him, is that it? You're going to give this killer a free rein. Are you telling me that?"

"Not exactly."

"I'm lost, Tommy. Enlighten me."

"The votes," Thomas Dawson said. "If I place myself firmly behind a massive effort to catch this man, how are the votes going to go? How are the Irish going to mark their ballots next time around? Are they going to pull their little levers for the man who approved of a massive manhunt to catch their hero?" He looked at his younger brother seriously. "I have a number of promises to keep while I occupy this office. And the only currency a president has is the vote of the people. In my case, Kevin, the Irish-American community constitutes a sizable proportion of that vote. It's like having money in the bank. And I don't want to squander it. I don't want to take the risk of tossing it all away. Have you seen the opinion polls lately, Kevin? It seems like I'm having what the pros call an image problem. Some people out there perceive their President as a man who doesn't make decisions quickly enough. I don't like that."

Kevin Dawson didn't speak. He heard the sound of a door closing at the back of his brain.

"I'm not going to give them a martyr, Kevin. I'm not going to be the one to take their folk hero away from them." Thomas Dawson looked up at the ceiling. When he spoke again his voice was low. "Besides, it's my understanding he's only looking for the men in your little group, Kevin. It's not as if he's a threat to the population at large, who don't even know the man's in the country. And I intend to keep it that way."

Kevin Dawson shook his head. "I can't believe I'm hearing this."

"Try," the President said. "Try a little harder."

"You'll sit here and do absolutely nothing about him?"

"I didn't say that, Kevin. At this moment there's an English agent called Frank Pagan in New York City who's getting some assistance from the FBI."

"How much is 'some'?" Kevin asked.

The President shrugged. "Just enough."

Kevin Dawson tried to see inside his brother's head. There was a cynical balance sheet in that skull. The President was weighing four men, one of whom was his own brother, against his precious Irish-American vote. "Doesn't it matter to you that *my* life might be in danger? Jig kills people, for Christ's sake! It's his profession. And they aren't sending a professional assassin from Ireland for the good of his goddam health. If he doesn't recover the money . . ." He didn't finish this sentence.

"I don't think for one moment that Jig is going to find you. I know how your little gang covers its tracks."

"Yeah, I keep hearing how good we are at secrecy," Kevin Dawson said. "Pardon me if I'm not convinced."

Thomas Dawson laid a hand on his brother's arm. "I'm prepared to put a couple of Secret Service men at your disposal."

Kevin Dawson looked at his brother. For a moment the touch of the President's hand on his arm reminded him of the man he used to have as a brother, when life had been carefree and political ambition hadn't taken total control of Tommy's personality. "I've got a Secret Service man already," he said.

"One man who does nothing but escort your daughters to school," the President said. "You need your protection beefed up, Kevin. And you'll have it before the end of the night."

Kevin Dawson looked suitably grateful. "Suppose this Frank Pagan character gets lucky? Suppose he captures Jig? What will you do with the guy if you catch him?"

"I don't think I can answer that."

"A Jimmy Hoffa style disappearance? The Irish hero simply vanishes off the face of the earth and nobody knows where or why?"

The President didn't answer his brother's questions. He sat back down behind his desk and put the red file inside a drawer. "Let me ask *you* something, Kev. Who really took the money from that ship?"

"I haven't got a clue."

"No ideas?"

Kevin Dawson shrugged. It was a question he'd asked himself

frequently. His immediate impulse was to suspect Mulhaney, but this was totally unfair, a suspicion motivated by a personal dislike for the man. It could have been Mulhaney. It could have been Linney. Even Harry Cairney. The problem was that all four men, himself included, would come under Jig's suspicion. What if Jig somehow reached the conclusion that he, Kevin Dawson, was responsible for the affair? What if Jig got to Mulhaney, say, and Big Jock, to divert suspicion from himself, managed to convince the Irishman that the guilty party was Dawson? Kevin Dawson's fear intensified. Suspicions created other suspicions. Possibilities led to other possibilities. He had the feeling of a man locked within a complex hall of mirrors, images reflecting themselves to an inscrutable infinity so that you could never find the true source of them. *And there was no way out.* He didn't like thinking this way, didn't like the panic rising in him.

The President placed his feet up on the desk and crumpled his empty yogurt carton, flipping it toward a wastebasket. "If there's a next time, Kevin, you ought to be a tad more careful."

"I don't think there will be a next time," Kevin Dawson said.

He went toward the door. He thought of going out into the darkness of the city and the prospect didn't appeal to him. Despite its floodlights, its illuminated tourist attractions, Washington was a city of too many dark places.

"What about the others?" he asked, turning in the doorway.

"Others?"

"My associates. I don't imagine they can count on your protection as well."

"They're not exactly my blood relations, are they?"

There was a small indifferent light in Thomas Dawson's eyes. Callous, Kevin thought. Maybe that came with the territory. With the subterfuges of the office. The great numbers game the President played. The numbers justified anything. Everything.

Kevin Dawson opened the door.

The President said, "Two things, Kevin. The first, you don't mention Jig to any of your . . . associates. So far as I'm concerned, Jig isn't in this country. I don't want anybody saying otherwise."

"What's the second?" Kevin Dawson asked.

"We never had this conversation."

SAINT BERNARD DES BOIS,
QUEBEC

The Ryder truck was parked in the forecourt of a gas station. Fitzjohn sat behind the wheel. The other men in the cab were Houlihan and Waddell. Rorke and McGrath traveled in the back with the cargo that had been unloaded from the DC-4. Houlihan squinted through the windshield at the unlit gasoline sign that hung like a small deflated moon over the pumps; then he glanced at his watch.

"Am I right, Fitz? Is it seven-thirty in New York City?"

Fitzjohn looked at his Rolex and nodded.

"All these bloody time zones confuse the hell out of a man," Houlihan said. He slumped back in his seat and closed his eyes. "Let's hear about the route, Fitz."

Fitzjohn stared at the sign in the gas-station window, which read FERMÉ/CLOSED. He was still thinking about what had happened at the airfield, and no matter how hard he tried he couldn't get rid of the images. The weird look on Houlihan's face. The dead bodies of the pilots. In fucking cold blood, without even so much as a blink of an eye. Houlihan hadn't mentioned the incident since they'd left the airstrip. It was over and done with. Already ancient history. Two dead airmen whose only crime, so far as Fitzjohn could tell, was that Houlihan hadn't trusted them. Seamus Houlihan, judge and jury and executioner, all rolled into one.

"There's an old road twelve miles from here," he said without turning to Houlihan. He couldn't look at the man. "It's a dirt road that leads to a fishery. The fishery's closed this time of the year because of the weather, which suits us fine. Nobody travels that way."

"And where does your road lead?" Houlihan asked.

"Beyond the fishery, it turns into a narrow path that goes between some trees; then it passes an abandoned farmhouse. There are fields after that."

"Open fields?"

Fitzjohn nodded. "We cross the fields for about two miles. On the other side there's a track that comes out just north of Highway Twenty-seven."

"Highway Twenty-seven?" Houlihan opened his eyes. "That doesn't mean a thing to me, Fitz."

"It's in the State of Maine."

"What about the Border Patrol?" Waddell spoke for the first time since they'd left the airfield. He'd become pale and totally withdrawn, gazing speechlessly out of the window for mile after mile. He moved only when he lit cigarettes, chain-smoking them in silence. His brown-stained fingers trembled in his lap.

"The nearest port of entry is at a place called Coburn Gore. It's about two miles away from the spot where we join Highway Twenty-seven. I don't think we're likely to encounter any Border Patrol." Fitzjohn paused. "It's not as if we're coming in from Mexico, after all. The Border Patrol down there are fanatics. Anyway, this truck has New Jersey plates, and that helps."

Houlihan asked, "Can we get across the fields without getting stuck?"

Fitzjohn said, "I don't see why not. The snow's hard and there haven't been any fresh falls in more than a week."

"And this Highway Twenty-seven, where does it lead us?"

"All the way to Interstate Ninety-five."

Nobody spoke for a time. Fitzjohn could hardly wait to get inside the United States, because it meant he would leave the truck to Houlihan and the others, then make his own way back to New Jersey. Relief. An end to this damned business as far as he was concerned. He didn't want to know what Houlihan planned to do in America. He didn't need to have that kind of knowledge.

"I've got a phone call to make," Houlihan said.

Houlihan climbed out of the cab. He moved across the forecourt of the gas station, then went inside the phone booth and picked up the receiver.

Fitzjohn watched him from the cab. He was about to say to Waddell that he thought Seamus Houlihan might benefit from being locked up in a padded room, but why bother? For one thing, Waddell might take it into his head to pass such a remark on to Houlihan, which wasn't a marvelous prospect. For another, everybody involved in this escapade had to be a little mad, himself included. Except Houlihan was more than that. He was lethal.

T WELVE

J oseph X. Tumulty looked from the window of his office down into the darkened street. Earlier, a navy-blue Ford had parked halfway along the block, and the tan Chrysler that had been stationed there drove off. It was the changing of the guard. He peered across the way. There was a light in the office building opposite St. Finbar's Mission. Tumulty could see a fat man sitting behind a desk. He was counting papers, flicking them back and licking his thumb every so often.

Tumulty turned from the window and went to his desk. He sat down, adjusting the lamp so that the light didn't shine directly into his face. He unlocked the middle drawer and took out a leather pouch, which he unzipped. There was seven thousand five hundred dollars inside. This money had been given to him by Padraic Finn more than three years ago. A contingency fund, which Finn, with the canniness of a man who understood that money *worked* for you, had placed in an interest-bearing account under Tumulty's name. When Tumulty had gone just before closing time to make the withdrawal—a tense moment, standing in a line that never seemed to move—he had the feeling he'd been followed to the bank. He'd withdrawn all the money and closed the account. Santacroce wanted six thousand dollars. Six thousand would have fed the clientele of St. Finbar's for about four months.

Tumulty absently regarded the religious artifacts on the walls. The Mexican cross he'd bought that day in Santacroce's store lay propped against the wall near the window. The Christ figure nailed to the wood was gory in the way Latin Americans loved. Blood filled up the eyes and dripped from the most unlikely places in the wooden body. Tumulty thought Jesus looked more perplexed than sorrowful. It was a distasteful piece but he hadn't wanted to leave Santacroce's store empty-handed. For appearance's sake.

Santacroce had said the merchandise might take some time to get together. Arrangements had to be made. He estimated twenty-four hours maximum, maybe a whole lot sooner. It depended on a variety of factors, none of which the gun merchant volunteered to explain. Tumulty hadn't asked either. He'd been very anxious to get out of that stifling little shop with its smell of old sandalwood and lacquer and dust. And away from Santacroce too, whose white puffy face and slitlike eyes seemed to suggest he was in the business, plain and simple, of death.

Twenty-four hours. Tumulty wondered a moment about Jig. When was he coming back? He couldn't remember if he'd told Jig two days or three. And then there was the unpleasant prospect of picking up a package from Santacroce and getting it back to this place. He knew it was crazy to bring weapons inside St. Finbar's, but what was his alternative? He couldn't think of a place where he might safely stash guns.

He hated the feeling of St. Finbar's being under siege like this. The idea scared him. And if came down to a choice between the Cause and his own little mission here on Canal Street, the desperate souls he cared for, which way would he go? That was the Big One. Would he go to jail before giving up Jig? Or would he quietly surrender the assassin to Frank Pagan so that he might get on with his life's work in peace?—if indeed peace was attainable after an act of treachery.

From the kitchen below there came the sound of voices. Babble. The smell of cooking floated inside his office. It was time, he thought, for prayer, the quest for guidance. He folded his hands together and closed his eyes, inclining his forehead to the tips of his fingers. For most of his life this act had been invigorating for him, although at times God's responses were difficult to catch. Sometimes Tumulty felt he was pursuing a sweet, silvery thread through empty reaches of the ether, fumbling toward a divine light. But there were other moments when he achieved the light, and then a great calm would come over him and he would glimpse a way through the mysteries of the divinity.

He sat very still. He tried to concentrate on the inner voice that was for him his means of communication when it came to prayer. A secretive little voice, which sometimes sounded like a tiny whisper in the vastness of the cosmos. He opened his eyes, frustrated. It wasn't happening today. There were crossed wires in his brain, and other thoughts kept intruding. Guns and politics, secular matters. He made fists of his thick hands and clenched them on the surface of the desk. *Guidance, dear God. Show me.* He stood up and wandered to the window, looked down into the street, saw that the navy-blue Ford was still in place down there. *Guidance,* he thought again. Instead of God's voice, what he heard was Finn saying, *The Cause is a holy one, Joe. And God knows that. There's no conflict, none at all, between serving God and the Cause. You wouldn't be the first man of the cloth to embrace them both.*

Tumulty wanted to believe this. The problem lay in violence and murder, neither of which he could possibly condone. It seemed to him that the Cause and God were diametrically opposed to each other. The former promoted death, the latter life. It was the difference between a total eclipse and the warming light of the sun. Dear Christ, how had he ever stumbled into this dilemma? More to the point, was there any way to resolve it? To square his religious beliefs with the demands of the Cause?

A sound in the doorway of his office made him turn around. The tall, skinny figure who stood there was a man called McCune, who blinked into the room with watery blue eyes. McCune wore a flannel shirt, open at the neck so that his large Adam's apple was visible, like some kind of growth, in his scrawny throat.

"We're wondering when you're coming down, Father Joe," the man said.

Tumulty stared at the man. McCune had been one of his earliest successes. When he'd first encountered him, McCune had been a suicidal drunk with violent tendencies, a former railway engineer canned by the railroad for hauling eight hundred tons of coal through Pennsylvania while extremely intoxicated. McCune had lost wife and kids, home, and any sense of his own dignity. It had taken time and patience, but Tumulty had given him back the dignity at least. McCune had been sober for almost a year and worked as a night clerk in a hotel on Eleventh Avenue. It wasn't much—but self-worth, Tumulty knew, was a quality you retrieved only in small stages.

"I almost forgot," Tumulty said.

McCune looked a little surprised. "You've never forgotten before."

Tumulty nodded, smiling at McCune. *This man trusts me*, he thought. *This man thinks he owes his life to me.*

"I'll be down in a minute," Tumulty said. Every night at the same time he conducted an Alcoholics Anonymous meeting in the kitchen. It was an event for which he was always punctual because he believed that one of the basic ingredients for sobriety was commitment to responsibility. And he had to show the men at the meeting that he took his own responsibilities in earnest. He had to set examples. You could show how much you cared only by your actions.

"I'll tell the others," McCune said, then hesitated. "Is something troubling you?"

Tumulty was about to answer when the telephone on his desk rang.

He started at the sound. Two rings, then silence. Followed by two more rings. It was Santacroce's signal.

So soon.

Too soon. He hadn't expected to hear from Santacroce until next morning at the earliest. He felt panicked. He stared at McCune, then at the Christ on the Mexican cross, but all he found in the eyes was an impossible blankness.

"I'm fine," he said to McCune. It was the first time he'd ever lied to any of his clients at St. Finbar's.

FRANK PAGAN sat behind the wheel of a rented 1974 Eldorado convertible. He'd found a place in the Village that specialized in renting old convertibles and, since he'd always wanted to drive a Cadillac, he'd hired this big dark-green monster with battered upholstery and a cracked dash and a rusted-out body. The radio worked. Pagan had it tuned to an FM rock station that was playing the entire cycle of Fats Domino's hits.

Zuboric, who felt in the Eldorado like a pimp fallen on hard times, said, "I grew out of that music. When the sixties came to an end, I was more into jazz. Modern jazz. Dizzie Gillespie, like that."

Pagan looked at the FBI man. The tone in Zuboric's voice was admonitory, as if he were really advising Frank Pagan to grow up. Rock and roll was for kids. Pagan had come to think of Artie Zuboric as an appendage he couldn't shake, a hump on his back, a growth attached to his body. He might not have minded so much if Zuboric had simply been a tail, someone who followed his movements unobtrusively, but the FBI man was a constant physical presence.

Pagan rubbed his gloved hands together. The chill inside the car was pervasive, bleeding through his bulky leather jacket. Along Canal Street, where he was parked, was a navy-blue Ford occupied by Orson Cone's relief, an older man called Tyson Bruno. Tyson Bruno was taciturn and morose. He had one of those wooden faces upon which expressions have a very hard time. He sat inside his Ford like a block of cement, defined by his duty, which was simply that of observing the comings and goings at St. Finbar's. Like Orson Cone, Tyson Bruno was also a kind of decoy, somebody in place for Tumulty to spot. Orson Cone and Tyson Bruno. Americans had the most peculiar names. When he'd been in New York before with Roxanne, they'd drunk too much champagne one night and in a hilarious mood they'd gone through the pages of the Manhattan phone book, discovering such oddities as Neddy Bummer and Bobbi Plapp, which Roxanne had laughed over, saying it sounded like a baby farting into a diaper. Harmless times, he thought now. Laughter before dying.

"We should've put somebody outside Santacroce's," Pagan said. It wasn't the first time he'd made the suggestion. He recalled what he'd said that afternoon when they'd tracked Tumulty to a bank. *Nobody is watching Santacroce.* Artie Zuboric hadn't seemed very interested.

"I told you. Lack of manpower, Frank." Zuboric shrugged. Pagan had still to learn that his problems got low priority here.

"Lack of manpower. No phone tap. One agent in the street. This is a shoestring operation. If you and I split up, one of us could watch Tumulty, the other Santacroce. Manpower problem solved in one swoop. Maybe that's a little too logical for you, though."

Zuboric wasn't going to respond to this. He wasn't going to be drawn into another argument with Pagan over human resources. He lit a cigarette and coughed a couple of times. The trouble with Frank Pagan was his sheer fucking persistence. He wouldn't let something go once he'd taken a bite out of it. He kept digging, kept trying to operate on his own. He was the same goddam way with Jig. He was consumed by Jig. Probably he dreamed Jig at nights. Had Jig for breakfast.

Zuboric sighed. What he really wanted to do was bust Tumulty and Santacroce both, because that was one way of putting Jig out of circulation. Deprive the guy of his connections. Isolate him. He'd mentioned this briefly to Pagan but good old Frank dismissed it. It was clear Frank Pagan wanted to run this show his own way, which was something Zuboric couldn't allow. He shut his eyes, let his cigarette dangle from his lip, and thought about Charity, and wondered where she was right this moment and whether she'd ever consent to marry him. The last time he'd asked, Charity told him she'd think about it when he wasn't married to the goddam Bureau and his prospects had improved. Prospects, he thought now. Sitting in a drafty Eldorado with a cop who was manic and argumentative—his prospects didn't seem entirely *rosy*. Maybe he should never have fallen quite this heavily for a gorgeous girl in a topless bar, but that was the way the cards had been dealt and what could you do but pick them up, see if you could play them? The trouble was, Charity was used to high rollers, and Artie Zuboric couldn't compete on that level.

Pagan stuck the key in the ignition. He played with the power switches. He made his seat go backward and forward, then he had the windows going up and down. There was a certain kind of limey, Zuboric reflected, who was enchanted by American flash. Big cars and loud music and Hawaiian shirts. Pagan was one of them. Zuboric attributed it to a kind of insecurity, cultural inferiority, as if the Tower of London and Shakespeare and Stonehenge weren't enough to be going on with. They had to immerse themselves in things American. Pagan was like a kid in a whole new playground. Zuboric suddenly wondered if Frank Pagan was afraid of the threshhold of forty, if the way he dressed and behaved had something to do with his reluctance to face the big four-oh.

Pagan leaned forward against the steering wheel.

"Ah-hah," he said. "There goes our boy."

Zuboric looked along the street at the sight of Joe Tumulty coming out of St. Finbar's. Here we go again, he thought, as Frank Pagan slid the huge car slowly forward.

IVOR MCINNES stepped out of the Essex House and walked along Central Park South. It was eight o'clock and he'd just eaten a satisfying dinner in the hotel. He turned onto Fifth Avenue, looking at the lights along the thoroughfare. He had in mind a specific destination, but first he intended to walk as far as Forty-ninth Street. He looked at his wristwatch and checked the time; then he thought a moment about J. W. Sweeting, the lackey from the State Department. McInnes had fought a great many battles with bureaucracy in his life, most recently with the asinine leaders of his own Presbyterian Church, who were dismayed by the controversy that always surrounded him and had stripped him of his parish. They were men of limited imagination. What the hell did it matter? McInnes had never been a truly *religious* man. All along he'd seen the Presbyterian pulpit as a convenient place from which to influence the politics of Northern Ireland, an attitude that had embarrassed Presbyterian churchmen, who failed to notice a very obvious fact of life in the country—that churches weren't just places where people went to sing hymns and hear sermons, they were instruments of social and political usefulness. The Catholic Church, cunning as ever, had always known that. Priests hid IRA members in their chapels or carried weapons back and forth. The Protestant clergy, on the other hand, had been slow on the uptake, immersed in the drudgery of committees and do-good schemes. For Ivor McInnes, that simply wasn't enough. And now the time for talking, the time for conciliation, had passed.

He stopped outside St. Patrick's Cathedral. A priest appeared on the steps, said something to a tourist with a camera, then agreed to have his picture taken with the cathedral in the background. McInnes saw a flashbulb pop. St. Patrick's made him uneasy. It was a vast stronghold of Catholicism, and in McInnes's world anything remotely connected to the Vatican was distasteful. He thought that any church that took ordinary tap water and did some abracadabra over it and called it holy was still locked into the superstitions of the Dark Ages. Therefore backward. Therefore a breeding ground for ignorance. There were times when he felt sorry for people who had been indoctrinated by the Roman Catholic Church, which he placed at the level of a cult, with its brainwashing tactics and Latinate mumbo jumbo and the highly curious notion of confession. It wasn't that he detested individual Catholics as such—he considered them merely misguided, suckers swayed by a holy carnival of stained-glass mysteries and enthralled by the stigmata and prone to the hysteria of seeing wooden effigies shed salt tears. No, it was more the fact that he completely resented the enormous power and riches and influence of the Vatican, from whence all Catholic conspiracies emanated—including the one that threatened to engulf Northern Ireland.

He reached Forty-ninth Street. He was in love with New York. It was a city with a delightfully sinful face. Every human weakness was pandered to somehow here. There was a sense of freedom that didn't exist in Belfast. Poor dear Belfast, a broken-hearted city with its military checkpoints and burned-out buildings. A city of fear. McInnes mainly blamed the Catholics for the atmosphere. They bred like flies in such RC ghettos as Ballymurphy and Turf Lodge and Andersontown, which were nothing more than nurseries for future IRA gunmen. A time would come, McInnes had warned his congregation in his parting sermon, when Catholics would outnumber Protestants in Northern Ireland—and then what? It would be like bloody South Africa, a minority straining to hold on to power in the face of a hostile majority. A prescription for doom. A prescription Ivor McInnes wasn't going to see filled.

He left Fifth Avenue and walked until he came to a phone booth located outside a bar called Lonnigan's, one of those Irish pubs scattered around Manhattan. Posters in the window advertised *ceilidhs*, nights of folk singing and dancing. McInnes went inside the booth. He checked his watch again. He felt apprehensive now. A taste of the duck he'd eaten came back into his mouth, a film of scum on the surface of his tongue. What if something had gone very wrong? What then? He laid his hand on the receiver and inclined his forehead on the glass. By nature he was a relentless optimist, and like others of this persuasion he was sometimes prey to a certain brief dread of failure.

He drummed his fingers on the receiver.

The telephone rang. He picked it up immediately.

He heard Seamus Houlihan's voice.

"We're crossing tonight," Houlihan said. He sounded as if he were trapped inside a tunnel.

"Fine," McInnes said. He was flooded with relief that Houlihan had at least arrived. At the same time, the idea that the border crossing was yet to take place pricked his capacity for dread again. Tension made a nerve move in his eyelid. "Has Fitzjohn found a place to cross?"

"He says so."

McInnes looked into the street. A high-stepping girl went past, and he tracked her with his eyes. "The flight was uneventful?"

"It was," Houlihan said.

McInnes paused. He wasn't exactly happy about Seamus Houlihan having any responsibility. Seamus was the kind of man who'd kill somebody if they happened to look at him with any trace of hostility. He didn't have much going on in the brain department. People like Houlihan were useful, but only up to a point. When they'd outlived their functions, they could become utterly embarrassing.

"Same time tomorrow night, Seamus. And good luck."

McInnes put the receiver back. He moved out of the phone booth and went along the sidewalk. The girl was just ahead of him, her hips swaying beneath her overcoat. On other trips to this city, at a time when he hadn't been banned by his own church and harassed by the State Department, he'd been struck by the number of beautiful women here. It seemed to him they came dropping out of the sky like bright pennies.

He reached the Hotel Strasbourg, stopping only a moment outside the dimly lit lobby. He looked up and down the sidewalk, then he went inside the hotel and moved toward the stairway, passing the night clerk who didn't even glance up at him. The carpet under his feet was threadbare and elaborately stained. On the second floor McInnes looked for Room 220. When he found it he knocked quietly on the door. He heard the girl's voice call out to him. He stepped into the room, which was lit only by a weak bulb in a lamp on the bedside table.

"Am I on time?" he asked. He felt only the smallest misgiving. He had needs, and they had to be satisfied, and this was nothing more than a transaction of skin—although he knew he would change it, by an act of his imagination, into something more than that.

The girl, who wore only the underwear McInnes had requested by telephone, smiled at him. "You're the one talks like John Lennon," she said. "It's cute. You're kinda cute yourself."

McInnes moved to the bed. He looked down at the girl. In a moment he was going to take the shortcut out of his tension, but right then he just wanted to look. She was skinny and her breasts were very small, and she must have been just sixteen. McInnes took off his coat and laid a hand on the girl's thin thigh. The girl didn't move. She stared at him coolly. Then she slid languidly down the pillow and stretched her long legs, parting them a little as she moved. He brought his hand up to the edge of her red panties. He continued up to the cups of her red bra, which fastened in the front. He undid the clip, pushed the bra aside.

"Tell me your name," he said.

"Elva."

"Elva." McInnes wove her long fair hair between his fingers. It was a moment that took his breath away. Here, in this shabby room, touching this delightful yellow-haired girl, he could pretend. Pretend he was elsewhere in another room at another time and that he held somebody else in his arms, and then there wouldn't be any sense of shame or treachery.

"Elva," he said again. It was the wrong name and it had the wrong number of syllables, but he could still pretend anyhow. He closed his eyes and lowered his mouth to her nipples, lost in the pungent scent of her perfume and her supple young flesh.

The girl held on to the big man tightly. She couldn't know that this same man who whimpered in her ear and pretended that she was another woman altogether had set in motion a sequence of events she'd read about in the newspapers in the days ahead. She thought he was just another weirdo who liked to fuck with a dog collar around his neck.

IF Joseph Tumulty knew there was a big green car tracking him a block away, he gave no indication of it. He walked slowly, calmly, pausing every now and then to study menus in the windows of Chinese restaurants along Mott Street. Frank Pagan, who had to concentrate on a variety of driving problems—stop lights, impatient drivers behind him, kamikaze pedestrians in front, and the fact he was driving on the wrong side of the road—found the Cadillac as unresponsive as a broken-down horse. Something clanked under the hood and the vehicle had a tendency to stray to the left. There was also an ominous smell of burning oil.

Zuboric said, "You should've let me drive."

"Why should you get all the fun, Artie?"

"Fun?"

Zuboric leaned out of the window and flipped his middle finger at the honking car immediately behind. It was a standard sign of the road in New York City. Pagan hunched over the wheel and tried to keep an eye on Tumulty, who was lingering too long this time outside a place called Yang. Was he going inside to eat? Was this outing nothing more than an innocent Chinese dinner? Frank Pagan braked as a couple of teenage Chinese boys walked directly in front of the Cadillac. Ahead, almost a block away, Tumulty was moving again. Pagan let the car roll slowly forward, knowing it was only a matter of time before Tumulty would become aware of the vehicle, if he hadn't done so already.

Tumulty kept walking. He had begun to move a little faster. Then, quite suddenly, he disappeared. It was almost as if he'd vaporized right there on the street. Pagan pressed his foot down hard on the gas and drove to the place where the Irishman had vanished. It was a narrow alley, a crevice between two buildings. Even if he'd wanted to, he couldn't have taken the Cadillac into that tiny space. There was only one thing to do.

Bye-bye, Arthur.

He pushed his door open and stepped out into the street. He said to Zuboric, "You wanted to drive, Artie. She's all yours," and he headed toward the alley, ignoring Zuboric, who was shouting at him to get back in the car. Behind the Cadillac there was a knot of cars occupied by impatient drivers, every one of them hammering on horns. Pagan smiled and felt a pleasant sense of liberation as he went into the alley and saw Joe Tumulty turning a corner at the far end.

Pagan made his way past piles of garbage in plastic bags, trash cans, old cardboard boxes jettisoned by restaurants and stores. He reached the corner where Tumulty had turned, and he saw Joe moving along the street about a block ahead, his black coat flapping around his ankles. Tumulty hesitated, looked back. Pagan stepped into the doorway of a store that sold electronic gadgets. Fuzz-busters. Listening devices. There was, as yet, no gadgetry that could render you invisible. Tumulty, on the move again, went around a corner. Pagan followed. If he had his geography correct, the Irishman was going toward Mulberry Street.

On Mulberry, Tumulty didn't head for Kenmare Street and Santacroce's store as Pagan had expected. Instead, he went inside a tenement whose ground floor was occupied by an Italian restaurant and whose upper floors appeared to be apartments. The restaurant, called Il Tevere, was one of those chintzy places with red-checkered tableclothes and candles stuck in Chianti bottles, a whole style Pagan thought had gone out of fashion. A smell of garlic and tomato sauce poured out into the cold air. Pagan gazed up at the windows over the restaurant, wondering how many apartments were in the building and which one Joe Tumulty might have entered.

He moved toward the door through which Tumulty had gone. It wasn't locked. It opened into a long very narrow hallway covered with faded black-and-white linoleum like some ancient, cracked chessboard. There was a flight of stairs at the end. They faded up into gloom at the top. Pagan went quietly along the corridor. At the foot of the stairs he stopped, tilting his head and listening, but the building was quiet save for music coming through the wall from the next-door restaurant. "O Sole Mio." Accordion music yet. There was something intrinsically absurd about any instrument you had to squeeze. He climbed the stairs, pausing only when he reached a landing.

A single closed door faced him. At the end of the landing there was a second flight of stairs. Pagan ignored the door for the moment and climbed upward. He reached another landing, another door. This one was halfway open, revealing an unlit apartment beyond. Removing his gun from the holster he wore in the small of his back, he went inside cautiously. He saw total disarray—bags of cement, bricks, stacks of wood, stepladders, all kinds of building materials. He noticed that the walls of the apartment had been ripped out, exposing old beams. Somebody was renovating this place. Room after room had been torn apart. Windows were covered with sheets of thick plastic, and there was the smell of fresh paint in the air.

He turned, went back to the stairs, descended slowly. When he reached the first landing again he looked at the closed door. There were only two apartments in the building, and if one of them was empty, then Tumulty had to be in the other.

He waited. He had no way of knowing how many people were inside the place. He glanced down the stairway into the hall. The music from the Italian restaurant was louder now. "Funiculi, Funicula." It was a song he particularly disliked. If that kind of music continued to assail him, he wasn't sure how long he could stand it before he took a chance and kicked the door down. Screw waiting. Screw the torture of Italian opera. The only thing worse than Italian opera was probably Vic Damone or Al Martino. It was a tossup.

He heard a sound from behind the door. The creak of a floorboard, it was hard to say. Then there was silence again. What the hell was Tumulty doing in there? What if he was simply visiting a friend? Pagan frowned. He wished Tumulty had gone back to Santacroce's little shop, because then at least he'd have guessed that a gun transaction was under way. Here, it could be anything.

He wasn't very good at waiting. His concentration slackened. He moved a little, back to the stairs going upward. He had the protection of shadows there. If somebody were to open the door quite suddenly, he wouldn't see Frank Pagan. There was another sound now from the apartment, and he brought his gun up again. He tensed, filled with a sense of expectancy. He saw the door open a little way. A bar of pale light from the room caused him to blink.

A figure appeared. Pagan made out the shape of a fat man in a navy-blue three-piece suit. A jeweled tiepin glinted against the man's white shirt, and his cuff links sparkled. He went to the edge of the landing and looked down into the hallway. Then he turned and stood on the threshhold of the apartment. He made a curious grinding noise with his teeth, and he wheezed as he moved, as if his bulk were a little too much for his lungs. His eyes were tiny, surrounded by mounds of pallid flesh. Pagan, hidden by shadow, watched him.

The fat man called back into the apartment, "Thought I heard something." Whoever he'd spoken to inside didn't answer. The fat man waddled back to the top of the stairs again.

Pagan felt perspiration form between his skin and the surface of his pistol. Fattie took a handkerchief out of his pocket and pressed it between his plump hands as he peered down into the hallway. There was an expression of doubt on his face. He turned toward the apartment.

"Say, did you lock that door down there when you came in?"

Again there was no answer from inside. The fat man shook his head.

"Hey, you deaf in there? I asked you a fucking question."

Irritated by the lack of response from inside, the fat man pushed the door wide open. Pagan had a glimpse of the interior. A lamp, a coffee table, and an armchair occupied by Joseph X. Tumulty, who looked pale and rather unhappy.

The fat man turned to shut the door behind him. Pagan moved. In four quick steps he was across the landing before Fattie had a chance to react. The fat man swore in surprise and tried to slam the door but Pagan kicked it back and heard the wood strike the man's head. It was a satisfying noise, like the whack of a cricket bat on a ball. The fat man slumped against the wall, holding a hand to his forehead. Joe Tumulty, whose astonishment had frozen him into the armchair, made a small moaning sound. He stared at Pagan blankly.

The fat man, bleeding from his brow, managed a mirthless smile. "You the law?"

"Joe knows who I am. Don't you, Joe?" Pagan said.

Tumulty nodded. There was no color in his face.

The fat man looked at Tumulty with disgust. "Fucking Irish," he said. "I always get problems when it comes to the fucking Irish. Goddam."

"Welcome to the club," Pagan said. "Are you Santacroce?"

The fat man nodded and wiped his brow with his handkerchief. "You let this fucker follow you, Joey? Not smart. Not at all smart."

Pagan moved toward Tumulty's armchair. There was a leather attaché case on the floor. "Open it," he said to Tumulty, jerking the hand that held the gun.

Trembling, Tumulty set the case on his lap and flipped it open. It contained a pistol, a rifle with a collapsible stock and three sets of sights. Everything had been neatly packed inside the case, fitted into compartments that had been specially made to hold the weapons. They were handcrafted weapons, tailored for the needs of a professional killer.

"Very nice, Joe," Pagan said. "Jig would love them."

"What happens to me now?" Tumulty asked in a hoarse voice.

"You oughta have your fucking head blown off," Santacroce said.

"It's a consideration," Pagan said. He looked across the room at Santacroce. The man was calm, unreasonably so in the circumstances. But he knew the score. He knew the jeopardies of his trade. He'd been here before. Even so, he was too acquiescent, and Pagan didn't like it.

"So," Santacroce said. "They sending the English in these days to help out?"

"Something like that," Pagan said.

Tumulty asked his question again. "What happens to me?"

"You're going to fucking jail," Santacroce said.

"Is that right?" Tumulty asked Pagan.

Pagan said, "It doesn't look too good, Joe."

Santacroce laughed. "Amateurs. Jesus. I shoulda known better. I gotta call my fucking lawyer. Awright with you?"

The fat man walked calmly across the room to the telephone, which was located on a small desk beneath the window. Pagan, suddenly uncertain about the legality of criminals making phone calls in this country, saw him apply the handkerchief to his forehead as he moved. Santacroce picked up the receiver and started to punch in numbers. Without really thinking, Pagan was mentally counting the digits the fat man pressed on the push buttons. The count wasn't right. It came only to six. On a level of awareness that was instinctive more than anything else, Pagan realized the Saint was talking into a dead phone.

Santacroce said, "Sam? I got a problem."

Pagan saw the fat man turn away so that he was facing the window with his back to the room.

"Yeah," Santacroce mumbled. "I'll hold."

Pagan tightened his grip on his pistol. What the hell was the fat man doing? Did he take Pagan for a complete fool?

"Yeah, I'm still holding," Santacroce said. "Don't leave me hanging too long, Sam."

"Put the phone down," Pagan said. "Put the fucking phone down."

Santacroce turned with a cold smile on his face.

Pagan didn't know where it came from, but there was a gun in the fat man's hand, a weapon that must have been concealed somewhere in his clothing. It caught the light, flared as Santacroce started to go into a defensive crouch, his big body bending at the hips, the gun hand held out in front of him, his other arm raised in the air for balance. For a fat man he seemed almost dainty right then, his whole body coordinated delicately as if in some dance.

Frank Pagan fired one shot.

Santacroce clutched his arm and cried out in pain, dropping his gun and falling backward, the drapes at the window coming loose from their clips in a series of harsh little *clicks* and folding all around him like a collapsed tent. And then he was gone in a confusion of shattered glass and buckled frames. Pagan rushed to the window and looked down. The fat man lay on the sidewalk, the curtains still covering his body in the fashion of a shroud. People were emerging from the restaurant, crowding around the corpse, then staring up and pointing at the broken window.

Joe Tumulty asked, "Is he dead?"

Pagan said nothing. He backed away from the window.

"Oh, God." Tumulty got up from the armchair.

Pagan wondered what Artie Zuboric was going to say about all this. He speculated on the depths of Artie's wrath. What was he supposed to have done anyhow? Let Santacroce shoot him?

Tumulty said, "I can't go to jail, Pagan."

Frank Pagan stared a moment at the broken glass, feeling the cold wind blow in off Mulberry Street. The curtain rings rattled on the brass rod. The idea of Santacroce lying down there on the concrete depressed him. He turned his gun over in his hand. The death-maker. The eliminator. He had no rapport with guns the way some cops had, cleaning them endlessly, refining them, always reading gun literature, even naming their guns as if they were pets. He put the weapon back inside his holster and looked at Tumulty.

"There may be a way out for you, Joe."

"How?"

"I can't promise anything," Pagan said. "But a little cooperation on your part could be beneficial."

Tumulty straightened his back and looked for all the world like a prizefighter coming out for a round in which he knew he was going to be demolished. "I'm listening."

ROSCOMMON, NEW YORK

Patrick Cairney wasn't able to sleep. He lay in the second-floor bedroom, staring at the darkened window and listening to the old house. He recognized familiar little noises. The way a stair creaked. The sound made by the wind thrusting an elm against a downstairs window. They were echoes of the childhood he'd spent here when he'd convinced himself that a house as large and as old as Roscom-mon had to be haunted. Back then, his imagination fired, he'd seen all kinds of apparitions—ghostly hands upon the windows, odd monsters slinking through shrubbery. Harry had conspired with him in this creation of a netherworld. *Of course there's ghosts, boy. Don't let anybody tell you otherwise. What would the Irish be without their banshees?*

He hated this house now as he'd hated it then. It was big and cold and furtive, and he always had the very odd impression that it contained undiscovered rooms, hidden chambers he could never quite locate. He remembered Harry's answer when, around the age of nine, he'd mentioned this suspicion to his father. *Sure there are secret passages, Paddy. Where else would I hide fine Irish gunmen on the run from the bloody British?*

Fine Irish gunmen, Patrick Cairney thought. Why could he find so few memories of his own goddam father that weren't related in one way or another to Ireland? When he ransacked his own past, when he rummaged his recollections, all he ever heard was the same monotonous drumbeat that was Harry's voice.

Patrick turned on the bedside lamp. Along the hallway was the bedroom his father shared with Celestine. He'd watched Celestine drift along the landing about thirty minutes ago. At the door of her bedroom she'd looked back and smiled and said good night to him and then, disappearing with a languid wave of her hand, she'd left him feeling suddenly lonely there, as if he were the only occupant of the house.

He stepped out of bed. This room was the one he'd had as a kid. All his old books were still stacked on the shelves. He ran a fingertip over the spines. *The Call of the Wild. A Treasury of Irish Legends. Kidnapped.* Relics of a lost boy. In another mood, he might have yielded to the brief comfort of nostalgia. He might have wallowed in that place where a young man sees the child he used to be and wonders about the direction his life has taken since, the crossroads missed, the paths ignored, the fragmented geography of his movements. He was sure that if the boy could talk to the man he'd say how surprised he was that things had turned out like they had. And yet— was it so surprising when you considered the father who had raised the child?

He sat on the edge of the mattress. He looked at his overnight bag, situated on the top of the dressing table. He hadn't even unpacked. Restless, he thought about Rhiannon Canavan, but that kind of image, lascivious as it was, didn't cut into his loneliness. It only underlined it. He remembered the way he'd last seen Rhiannon Canavan at Dublin Airport and how she'd watched him cross the terminal building. He'd looked around at her once and for a moment wanted to go back and hold her one final time. Weaknesses, he thought. All his longings were faults.

He shut his eyes, clenched his hands, pictured the way Celestine had raised her fingers in the air at the moment of her departure, and thought he'd never seen any gesture so innocently sexual in all his life. Innocence, he reflected, was the keyword. Sexuality was in the beholder's eye, and he'd done just a little too much beholding, that was all. You didn't go around being attracted to your own step-mother.

He lay back across the bed. The nightcap with Celestine had been two generous brandies, the second of which he'd left unfinished. She'd talked about herself, her first marriage to an architect called Webster. It was closed kind of talk, not very revealing, nothing about her family, her background. Polite chat. A stepmother eager to befriend the son she'd suddenly inherited. Now and then he'd seen a kind of glaze go over her eyes like blinds drawn down on windows, as if she were afraid of getting too close to revealing her own personality. Was that coyness? If so, it was a rare quality and endearing.

He heard the sound of someone knocking at his door, and at first he thought it was just the elm tree rattling again on the downstairs window. But when he realized it wasn't he rose from the bed and quickly took a robe out of his bag, tying the cord and stepping toward the door in one hurried movement.

"I couldn't sleep," she said.

Cairney felt awkward. He made a meaningless gesture with one hand. Celestine entered the room. She wore a pink satin robe, floor-length, and her yellow hair was tied up at the back of her head.

"Am I disturbing you, Pat?"

"No," and Cairney closed the door, glancing along the hallway as he did so.

Celestine looked around the room. "I've often wondered about the boy whose room this used to be."

"Now you know."

"I don't really know," she answered him. She fiddled with the cord of her robe, working the knot with her finger. Cairney didn't move. He had the uneasy feeling that any movement on his part could be misconstrued. He didn't want this woman in his bedroom. He didn't want any of the odd little responses she caused him to have.

"I see a boy's books, but that's all," she said. Her blue eyes seemed stark and glassy in the light from the lamp. "You needn't look so pale, Patrick."

"Pale?"

"When I was a child I had this fish that died by jumping out of the bowl. When I found it, it was exactly the color you are right now. Does my presence in this room upset you?"

Cairney watched Celestine wander around the room, touching

things as she moved. The edge of the drapes. The spines of books. She stopped at the dressing table. Lamplight made small delicate shadows in the folds of her robe, which clung to her flat stomach. She was lean, and Cairney knew that the body beneath the robe was hard and taut and yet that it would yield in the right places. *Harry's wife*, he thought. *The Senator's wife.* He tried to absent himself from his responses to her, to step away from his own reactions. God, it was difficult. It was just so damned hard to shut your eyes and ignore this woman's compelling beauty and her nearness and the faint notion he had that he could go to her now and slip the robe from her body and draw her down to the bed with him. Was her presence here telling him that? Was she saying she was available?

She was standing very close to his canvas bag. "The truth is, Harry's been snoring worse than usual since this recent attack. I know he can't help it but it drives me up the wall." She put the palm of her hand on top of his bag, which was lying open. He felt a tension in his throat.

"So here I am," she said. "I thought we might go down and have one last nightcap. It might help me sleep. And I don't like to drink alone. There's something a little pathetic about it."

He couldn't take his eyes away from her hand. He realized he should have closed the bag after removing his robe, but he'd been hurried. It was a mistake. He saw that now. He should have taken the time.

"I like this room," Celestine said. "It gets a lot of light in summer. It must have been a pleasant room for you, Patrick."

"I have some good memories," Cairney said, and turned toward the door. "Shall we go downstairs?"

"Are you rushing me, Patrick? It just so happens that this is one of my favorite rooms in the entire house. Sometimes I come here and I sit. I just sit in the chair by the window. There's a good view of the lake. Sixteen rooms in this big house and this is the one I like best."

Cairney realized something then. The two brandies Celestine had drunk before had affected her more than he'd realized. Her speech was just a little slurred. Not much, just enough to notice. There were red flushes on her cheeks.

He reached out, turned the door handle. "A nightcap sounds like a great idea," he said.

"You're in such a hurry," Celestine said. She looked at him, her mouth open a little way, the tip of one finger pressed to her lower lip. There was something mischievous in the gesture.

Then Cairney saw her palm slide along the top of the bag. He started toward her, thinking he'd slip the bag away from her, perhaps pretend there was something in it he needed, but before he could make his move she was lifting an object out and turning it over in her hand, her expression one of interest.

He could feel his blood turn cold.

"Where did you get this?" she asked.

"It's just a souvenir I picked up at the airport."

Celestine fingered the object, stroking it with the tips of her fingers. "It's very pretty," she said.

Cairney shivered. A draft came up the staircase and moved along the hallway through the open door of the bedroom. He stepped toward Celestine, took the object from her hand, then dropped it back inside the bag, where it lay on top of his passport.

It was a miniature wooden horse, a Scandinavian import.

"Let's have that drink," he said, and he was conscious of an awkward tone in his own voice. He clasped her arm and led her gently out of the room. On the landing, the relief he felt was intense. She had come within a mere half inch of the passport made out in the name of John Doyle.

T HIRTEEN

NEW YORK CITY

A rthur Zuboric's office was located in lower Manhattan in a building that had absolutely no distinguishing features. Frank Pagan thought he'd never been inside a place with less personality. It was a testimonial to bureaucratic blandness, erected in the sky by architects who lacked any kind of taste. Zuboric, looking very pale beneath his sunlamp tan, stared across the room at a wall where there was a college diploma with his name on it. Pagan imagined he heard Artie ticking like an overwound watch.

Zuboric sighed, then said, "First you split, leaving me stranded in that goddam pimpmobile you rented. Then you shoot a guy. You actually *shoot* a guy, which is a mess I had to clean up with the local cops, which I needed like a hemorrhoid. Jesus Christ. I mean, Jesus *Christ*, Pagan."

Pagan tilted his chair back at the wall. There wasn't a great deal to say in the circumstances. He folded his arms against his chest. It was best to let Zuboric continue to tick until his clockwork had run down.

"Don't get me wrong, Pagan. Santacroce's death is no loss to the civilized world. There's not going to be a great weeping and gnashing of teeth. And his criminal connections aren't going to cause a run on Kleenex—but holy shit, there was a fucking corpse on the goddam sidewalk and a whole *gang* of diners with napkins tucked in their shirts, and they *saw* him lying there."

"It probably put them off their osso buco," Pagan remarked. Bad timing. A look of pain crossed Zuboric's face.

The FBI man got up from behind his desk and strolled around the small room. There was a window looking down over the towers of Manhattan, and Artie Zuboric paused there a moment, surveying the night with a miserable expression. Not more than an hour ago he'd had the Director on the telephone from D.C. The Director never raised his voice, had never been heard to shout, but he had a way with anger like nobody else Zuboric knew. He spoke quietly, clipping his words. Leonard M. Korn terrified Arthur Zuboric. Sometimes Artie had nightmares in which he was alone in an interrogation room with the man and he felt so paralyzed, so overawed, he couldn't answer any of his superior's questions, including the one concerning his own name. *Is there no way, Zuboric, of keeping this Englishman under lock and key? Is he to be allowed to run through the streets as he pleases?* There had been a very long pause after which the Director had spoken the most ominous sentence Zuboric had ever heard in his life. *For your sake, Zuboric, let us hope that not one word of this unfortunate incident ever reaches a newspaper.* This chilled Zuboric to his bones. Suddenly whatever meager prospects he'd had before appeared to dwindle and then finally disappear in front of his eyes.

Now Zuboric said, "You landed me in the shit."

"Santacroce drew a gun," Pagan answered. "It was either him or me."

Zuboric touched his moustache in a thoughtful way. It was obvious to Pagan whom Zuboric would have preferred between those alternatives.

Artie sat down. There were papers littered across his desk and a computer terminal attached to a printer. Every now and then the printer would hiccup into action and paper would roll out of the device, but Zuboric paid it no attention. He buried his face in his hands a second, then sighed again, looking across the room at the Englishman.

"And now you tell me you've got some cockeyed plan for that mick."

In the time that had passed since the shooting of Santacroce, Pagan had gone over the scheme a couple of times, approaching it from all the angles he could think of, testing it and weighing it and then giving it his private seal of approval. It wasn't watertight and he wouldn't trust it in a storm, but it was the best he could do.

"Joe Tumulty doesn't want to go to jail, Artie. It's a powerful incentive."

"What did you do, Pagan? Offer him immunity? Huh? Just take the law into your own hands and tell him he's walking away scot-free if he plays a little game for you?"

Frank Pagan gazed at the window. Out there in the night sky there were the lights of a passing plane. He felt a small homesick longing. Wintry London. Somehow it seemed farther away than a six-hour plane ride, like an impossible city of his own imagination.

Zuboric said, "You can't just fuck around with the laws of this country, Frank. I don't know what it's like where you come from, but here you can't promise a guy something that's not in your power to give him."

Pagan stood up. He studied the college diploma on the wall. It had been issued by the University of Michigan at Ann Arbor. He wondered a moment about the pathways of a man's life that led from a degree in business administration to the Federal Bureau of Investigation; then he thought of Joe Tumulty, who sat along the corridor in a locked room, presumably staring at the blank walls and worrying about his sorry predicament. With a man like Tumulty, whose political affiliation threatened the ruin of his charity work, his shot at sainthood, you couldn't ever really be sure of anything.

"He'll give us Jig," Pagan said. Was that a small lack of conviction in his own voice? Confidence, Frank.

"What makes you think he won't call Jig and warn him?"

Pagan put his hands in his pockets. "He doesn't know how to get in touch with him. He doesn't have a phone number. He doesn't have an address. He doesn't know where Jig is."

"He isn't exactly a mine of information, is he?"

"Do you expect him to know more? Do you think Jig goes around giving out personal information, Artie? You think he passes out a nice little business card embossed with his name and number? Occupation, assassin?"

"Did Tumulty at least give you a description?"

"Nothing that's going to help. Thirtyish. Five eleven. A hundred and sixty pounds. Dark curly hair."

"That's terrific," Zuboric said. "You know what I really think, Frank? Father Joe is jerking you off."

Pagan smiled now. "I think Father Joe and myself have come to an understanding."

Zuboric lit a cigarette and narrowed his eyes against the smoke. "When's Jig supposed to show?"

"Tomorrow, the next day. Tumulty isn't certain."

"Tumulty's a fucking mine of uncertainty."

Zuboric shook his head. Frank Pagan had given up that one thing any cop should have considered his greatest asset: objectivity. His peripheral vision was severely damaged. Zuboric, for his part, wouldn't trust the mick as far as he could throw a crucifix, and as a reasonably good Catholic he'd never have thrown one anyhow. He sighed again, unhappy with the condition of his life. Was he really supposed to let this character Tumulty walk away from here with a loaded attaché case? What was he going to say to the Director? These questions hung bleakly in his mind.

Frank Pagan was still studying Zuboric's diploma. He was very tired all at once. He covered a yawn with the palm of his hand. "I'm going back to my hotel," he said.

"I'll ride with you."

"Of course." Pagan turned away from the diploma. "We should keep Joe here overnight and release him in the morning. A small taste of imprisonment might be a useful reminder to him."

Zuboric agreed halfheartedly.

Frank Pagan moved to the center of the room and stood directly under a strip of fluorescent light. "Before we release Joe, there's a couple of things we ought to do. First, there's a certain Englishman I'd like to talk to. And second, we ought to pay a visit to a tailor."

An Englishman and a tailor. Zuboric felt he had just been asked to solve an impossible riddle. "What Englishman? What tailor?"

Frank Pagan smiled in the knowing way that so infuriated Zuboric. "It can wait until morning," he replied.

QUEBEC-MAINE BORDER

A freezing rain had begun to fall all along the border country from Lake Champlain to Edmundston. It pounded on the roof of the Ryder truck with such ferocity that the two man who sat in the back with the cargo—McGrath and Rorke—felt they were trapped inside a very large yellow drum. The headlights of the vehicle faintly picked out trees obscured by the torrent. Behind the wheel Fitzjohn could see hardly a thing save for great drops of moisture illuminated by the lights. He was nearly blinded. Every now and then the wheels of the truck would spin on old snow that was turning to slush. Waddell slept with his head tilted against the window, his mouth hanging open. Houlihan, who sat in the center, was truly alert, turning his pistol around every so often in his hands, like a man anxious to keep checking reality.

"How much farther is it?" Houlihan wanted to know.

Fitzjohn wasn't sure but he lied because it was best to appease Houlihan whenever you could. "Five, six miles."

The Ryder truck rattled and shook. Fitzjohn was a proficient driver who'd made scores of nocturnal runs from Northern Ireland over the border into the Republic, driving through some hostile terrain to do so, but he'd had no experience of anything quite like this. The wipers worked furiously backward and forward but they couldn't keep up with the deluge. How in the name of God could John Waddell sleep through all this?

Trees and more trees and nothing beyond the feeble reach of the lights except a darkness the like of which Fitzjohn had never known. If there was a God, he'd forsaken this stretch of country for sure.

Houlihan whistled quietly for a time. Fitzjohn recognized the tune as that Protestant anthem, "The Battle of the Boyne," which celebrated the defeat of Catholic forces by King William of Orange in July 1690. Old hatreds. Very old hatreds.

In a tuneless voice Houlihan sang a couple of lines. *"With blow and shout put our foes to the rout/The day we crossed the water."* And then he was silent, which made Fitzjohn nervous. He understood something he'd known all along but had refused to acknowledge—that Seamus Houlihan could quite casually blow off the top of his head and dump him by the side of the road, if such a whim ever moved him. It was a numbing insight.

"Are you sure you know where you're going, Fitz?" Houlihan asked.

Fitzjohn nodded and said, "I didn't expect this kind of weather. It's a bad time of year for country like this."

"Aye," Houlihan said. Something in the way he used simple words, little negatives and affirmatives, suggested that Seamus Houlihan was a man to whom language had all the firmness of quicksand. It was as if everything he uttered could be construed in different ways on different levels. Treacherous and shifting, Fitzjohn thought.

Ahead, quite suddenly, there were lights.

Houlihan leaned forward, straining to see through the rain. "What's that?" he asked, and the gun was back out in his hand, the barrel propped against the dash.

Fitzjohn braked. The yellow truck slowed. The lights disappeared, then returned a second later. In a nervous voice Fitzjohn said it was the highway, that the lights were those of passing cars.

"America," Houlihan said. He nudged Waddell, who woke suddenly and peered out into the dark.

"Here we are, John. Here we are in America."

Waddell mumbled something. Ever since the airfield he'd been either asleep or ashen and withdrawn, and Fitzjohn suspected that the man had no stomach for any of this business. But John Waddell had always gone along with Houlihan, no matter what. It was almost as if Houlihan had cast a spell over the man. Or was it some form of hero worship, with Waddell always tagging along behind?

"Well?" Houlihan asked Fitzjohn. "Are we going to sit here and wait for the bloody weather to change?"

Fitzjohn took his foot from the brake and the truck, its hood steaming with rain, rolled in the direction of the highway. This was the worst part, Fitzjohn knew that. Although he understood that an illicit border crossing at this godforsaken point was simpler, say, than crossing from Mexico, just the same his nerves were abruptly shrill. The concept had seemed easier than the reality, which was cold and wet, dreamlike and menacing.

The disaster happened about fifty yards from the pavement. The faint track along which the truck had been moving suddenly ended and the land dipped into a basin before rising up a slope to the highway. The hollow was muddy and impossible, and the truck, straining as hard as it might, didn't make it up the incline. It slithered, then slid back down through slush, wheels spinning noisily and dense exhaust rising into the icy rain. Dear Christ, Fitzjohn thought. This was the last thing he'd anticipated. He'd imagined only a clear run onto the highway, not this, not anything like this bloody great ditch.

Seamus Houlihan angrily slapped his pistol on the dash. Fitzjohn swore, shoved his foot down hard on the gas pedal, and tried to ram the truck back up the slope again but failed a second time as the Ryder slipped down into the hollow, where it sat with its big wheels uselessly turning.

"Try it again!" Houlihan shouted.

Fitzjohn plunged the truck into first gear, thrust the gas pedal to the floor, and tried a third time to force the heavy vehicle up the incline to the highway, which was suddenly lit by the lights of a passing car. He turned off his own headlights and prayed for invisibility even as he felt the truck lose traction about halfway up the slope. It rolled down again with a terrible inevitability. Fitzjohn shut his eyes and wanted to weep out of sheer bloody frustration. Beside him in the cab, Seamus Houlihan was very quiet all of a sudden. It was the kind of brooding silence in which Fitzjohn could sense the man's capacity for danger.

"I'll give it another shot," Fitzjohn said.

"No. We'll push. We'll push this bastard up onto the road. Waddell, get behind the wheel. Fitz, get McGrath and Rorke out of the back," and Houlihan shoved the door open quickly, thrusting Fitzjohn out into the freezing rain, then following him around to the back of the truck. Fitzjohn opened the rear door.

"Is it a breakdown or what?" McGrath asked from the dark interior.

"Push! Get your shoulder behind this fucker and push!" Houlihan, who seemed immune to the cold and the relentless rain, was already pressing his body against the back of the truck. All four men strained in the numbing rain, inching the truck up the slope. Fitzjohn, his skull like a block of ice, felt utterly hopeless. How could four of them get this truck up a slushy slope? Maybe on a dry day with no mind-splitting rain to blind you and ruin your footing, maybe you could do it then, maybe. He felt his lungs turn to crystal. There was absolutely no feeling in his ungloved hands. Push! Houlihan was screaming. *Push! Fucking push!* The truck edged upward, then Houlihan was screaming again, like some creature who wasn't flesh and blood at all but a creation of the harsh elements. *Push! Push! Push! Waddell, give it some bloody petrol, man!*

John Waddell, dragged out of sleep and unhappy at the controls of an unfamiliar vehicle, eased his foot down on the gas pedal. He brought the clutch halfway up from the floor. The rough grinding of the gears sent a series of little shock waves through his body. There was a cramp in his foot, and he wasn't sure if he could handle this strange vehicle.

For fuck's sake, Waddy! Give it more petrol!

Waddell's foot slipped on the clutch. He heard the engine stall and die. He turned the key in the ignition quickly, heard the motor come back to life, then he let out the clutch, but the truck didn't move. The wheels churned and dense exhaust spumed out into the freezing rain, but the bloody truck *wasn't going anywhere!* Pray, Waddell thought. Pray it gets up this damned slope.

Then he was suddenly dazzled, suddenly terrified, by headlights that came lancing down through the rain. He blinked his eyes furiously against the constant glare of the lights. As he did so, the truck died under him again and he had to shove his foot down hard on the brake to stop the thing from rolling back down the incline.

Outside, Fitzjohn wiped water from his eyes and peered into the same bright lights that had startled Waddell. He thought, Jesus, not now, not now. There was the brief glow of the car's interior light, then a door was slammed and a figure moved in front of the beams with a flashlight that he shone toward the Ryder truck. "Don't move!" the man from the car shouted in an authoritative voice. "Don't any one of you move or I'll blow your fucking heads off!"

Houlihan did the strangest thing then. He tossed his head back and laughed, and it was a weird noise that managed to override the pounding rain. The figure started down the incline toward the truck, his flashlight making the rainy air sparkle. Houlihan laughed a second time and shouted, "We're stuck! We ran straight off the bloody road!"

Fitzjohn shut his eyes and pressed his face against the metal panel of the truck. God, if the figure from the car was an agent of the Border Patrol he was going to find Seamus Houlihan's thick accent very strange indeed. And if he was a cop it was going to be just as bad, because he was surely going to insist on a search of the vehicle, and then what? Fitzjohn stared at the movement of the flashlight. The figure was approaching the truck, and Fitzjohn saw for the first time that the man held a shotgun pressed against his side.

When he was almost level with the Ryder the man said, "Let's see some identification."

It was the wrong request to make of Seamus Houlihan, who knew only one way to identify himself. Fitzjohn opened his mouth and was about to speak—anything, a lie, anything at all to fill the horrible void—when he noticed Seamus Houlihan's hand going toward the pocket of his jacket. The man with the shotgun made a gesture with his flashlight.

"You move that hand too fast and you can kiss it good-bye," he said.

"I was only going to show you my papers," Houlihan responded. "Reach for them slowly. Very slowly. Slow as you know how. The rest of you characters back off from the truck. The guy behind the wheel—put your brake on and step outside."

Waddell climbed down from the cab. In his anxiety, he hadn't checked to make certain that the emergency brake was firmly in place and so the truck, swaying slightly from side to side in the slicing rain, began to drift slowly back down the incline.

The man with the shotgun shouted at Waddell. "Get back in there and put the fucking brake on, asshole!"

Waddell moved toward the cab and was reaching up to the door handle when Houlihan—always the opportunist, always seizing the unguarded moment and twisting it to his own advantage—took out his pistol and fired off two shots. The flashlight fell, and the man cried out in pain before going down into the slush, where he lay with his face pressed into the ground. Houlihan walked to the place where the flashlight was located. He picked it up, turning the beam on the man's face.

Fitzjohn stared at the scene.

A glare of rainy light.

Houlihan standing over the man.

The echo of gunfire.

The runaway truck slithering to a half in the mud.

John Waddell was the first to speak, and his voice trembled. "Who was he?"

Seamus Houlihan turned away from the body. "According to his pretty uniform, he was a gentleman from the United States Border Patrol."

Fitzjohn had a sour taste in his mouth. Even after they had labored to push the truck onto the highway, after they had shoved the agent's car down into the hollow and hastily covered the corpse with frozen slush, the taste was still with him, mile after rainy mile.

ROSCOMMON, NEW YORK

It was early morning and the sky over Roscommon was the color of salmon flesh, a pale pink sun slatting through the cloud cover. An unusual day, neither winter nor spring but some uncharted hiatus between the two. Even the snow that covered the landscape was a curious rose tint. Harry Cairney, walking with the help of a cane, stopped at the edge of the lake. He said nothing for a time, then turned to his son, and there was a small look of expectation in his eyes.

"What do you make of her, Patrick?"

Patrick Cairney tossed a flat stone out across the water, watching it skip three times before sinking. "She's a beautiful woman," he answered.

The old man smiled. "After your mother died, I thought that was it. End of the ball game. Well, that didn't happen." The senator poked the tip of his stick into the snow. "You think God figured he owed me a favor? You think he said there's one old Paddy needs a good turn?"

Patrick Cairney gazed across the lake. He had spent a restless night after the final brandy with Celestine. What he saw when he lay in bed later and shut his eyes was Celestine's robe clinging to her body by firelight and the way she sat with her legs spread in front of her, so that there were shadows deepening the length of her thighs. What he couldn't decide was whether it was the unconscious physical gesture of a woman who'd had too much brandy or something else— and when he reached that borderline, a place of sheer discomfort, he stopped speculating.

"I was surprised by joy," Harry Cairney said. "It crept up on me."

"I can understand that." Patrick Cairney wasn't sure that he could, though. Joy wasn't a feeling with which he had any regular acquaintance.

The old man clapped his son on the shoulder. "Dear God, it does me good to see you again, Pat. You should come back more often. You shouldn't be traipsing all over the goddam world digging in tombs or whatever it is you do. What's the point to all that anyhow? You think it matters to an Appalachian dirt farmer or some Boston longshoreman if King Tut was left-handed or had rotten teeth? It's not going to change any lives, is it? And what do we live for if it isn't to try and *change* a few things?"

This was an old argument. Whenever he heard it, Patrick was always beset by the feeling that he'd somehow disappointed Harry, let him down in some unforgivable way. That he was to be blamed for failing to meet Harry's expectations for him. What the hell did the old man want anyhow? A younger copy of himself? A nice buttoned-down young man happy to go into politics, which Harry had made the family business? Patrick Cairney had given law a try once some years back simply to please the old man, and he'd been utterly miserable. It was the last time he'd ever even attempted to gratify his father. If Harry still entertained ambitions on his son's behalf, they were well and truly doomed to failure. And if this fact disappointed him, then that was a burden the old man had to carry. Patrick couldn't be responsible for his father's feelings about him.

Patrick Cairney tossed another stone out on the lake. A wintry bird rose up out of the trees. Both men moved a little way along the shore. For a moment Patrick wanted to tell the old man that he *was* trying to change a few things but in his *own* way.

Harry Cairney caught his son's arm. "Tell me about Dublin. I want to hear about Ireland."

Patrick Cairney knew what the old man wanted to hear and it wasn't the hard brutal world of northern cities like Belfast and Derry with their burned-out buildings and bloody casualties. He wanted to hear only the same unchanging litany of heroes and martyrs. Patrick Cairney said nothing. It was cowardly of Harry to dream his time away in the comfort and security of Roscommon, to hide behind his record collection and his Celtic documents, and ignore the real troubles in his homeland. Patrick—who had gone to Ireland expecting to find the glowing island of song and poetry that Harry had always pictured for him, only to discover something relentlessly terrible behind the romance and the myth—felt contempt for the old man and everything he represented.

"I used to meet a pretty young girl under Waterhouse's clock on Dame Street in Dublin," the old man remarked. "I sometimes wonder if that clock's still there. She was very fond of a shop called Butler's on O'Connell Bridge. It sold musical instruments. Polly liked to browse in that place for hours. Sweet girl."

Patrick Cairney smiled thinly. He wanted to say that it was gone, it was all gone, that another world had taken the place of everything the old man remembered. He glanced across the lawn at the house, which had a pink tint in the hallucinogenic morning light. He was thinking of Celestine moving through the rooms of that big house. He was thinking of the lithe way she moved, the slight forward thrust of hips and the fair hair bouncing against her shoulders and that strange little electric light in her eyes, which he found indefinable and puzzling. He didn't need these thoughts, for God's sake. He didn't need to wander in this direction. He had come to the

United States for one reason only and nothing, not a goddam thing in the world, was going to interfere with his purpose.

Harry Cairney let his hand fall from his son's arm. He drew a sinewy line in the snow with the tip of his cane. "When are you going to this symposium of yours?"

"Tomorrow," Patrick Cairney replied.

"And after that—will you come back here?"

"I hadn't planned on it."

"You don't need the excuse of a symposium to visit me. This is still your home, Patrick."

"I know," Patrick said. He thought how remarkable it was that he had developed a knack for believing in his own fictions. It was the simplest thing in the world to believe that there really *was* a symposium of archaeologists in New York City he was going to attend. He could picture the room in which the event would take place. He could invent faces, and he could give those faces names. Afterward he could describe, if anyone asked, how the room smelled and the kind of cigarettes Professor So-and-So smoked and what the lecturer from Oxford had to say about Etruscan pottery. When you lived a life grounded in lies and deception, all the lines of reality became blurred.

He remembered the simple lie he'd told Rhiannon Canavan about his father's heart attack the night Padraic Finn had telephoned with the news of the *Connie*. Had he known that his father was really unwell, he might have chosen a different fabrication, but in the end it made no difference at all. Even his identities were lies. He was no longer Patrick Cairney. Neither was he John Doyle, traveler in Scandinavian trinkets.

He was Jig and all his experiences were Jig's.

The months spent training in the savage wasteland of the Libyan desert with Qaddafi's mad guerrillas, who valued human life as much as a match flame. The endless days crawling over burning sand when you had nothing to drink and your throat had the texture of sandpaper and the gun and backpack you carried became the heaviest burden in all your experience. Freezing nights when you slept naked under a moon of relentless ice and shivered so badly you felt your skin was coming loose from your skeleton. These were Jig's experiences. And it was Jig who had become the hardened professional under Padraic Finn's guidance, who had sworn allegiance to the Association of the Wolfe and the goal of Irish unity, achieved through a program of political assassination. A program carried out by professionals who had no desire for the old ways of martyrdom and considered self-destruction beneath contempt. It wasn't a dreamer's Ireland. It was a hard place, and there were hard goals to accomplish, and these couldn't be left to the amateurs, the home-made grenade groups, the desperate little losers who tossed bottles of fiery gasoline at British soldiers and thought they were brave for doing so. Sad, misguided men who dreamed the dreams of hooligans. Finn's program would eventually change everything. Jig had a complete belief that in the end, weary of death and the assassinations of its political figures, the British would have no choice but to withdraw.

It was Padraic Finn who had smoothed the abrasive surface of Patrick Cairney. It was Finn, surrogate father, mentor, who had insisted on Libyan training and then, in a further process of refinement, six months at the Patrice Lumumba University in Moscow where Cairney had learned the uses of high-tech explosives. If Harry had provided the early, relentless indoctrination, then it was Finn who had carried this out of the realm of vague impracticality and vapid rhetoric into the real world. He thought of Finn now, and the remote possibility that something might have happened to the old man in Ireland caused him fleeting concern—but what he came back to was Finn's own maxim. *I'm expendable. You're expendable. Only the Cause has permanence.* Cairney lifted his face and looked up at the sky. He could still picture Finn, in baggy cord pants and fisherman's sweater, standing at the window in the room of harps. He could still hear Finn say, *The Cause is a killing mistress. It seeks your total devotion and never excuses your weaknesses. It demands your complete commitment and it rewards your infidelity, not with forgiveness and understanding, but with death. . . .*

"Let's walk back," Harry Cairney said. "It's damn cold out here. Besides, we shouldn't neglect Celestine. You ought to get to know her a little better."

A harmless suggestion, Patrick Cairney thought. But there was no such thing in his life anymore. He couldn't make the ordinary connections other people made. He lived in the shadows he'd created for himself.

They moved across the lawn in the direction of the house. The young man clutched his father's elbow when they reached the steps, which were slick underfoot. He noticed how his father puffed as he climbed. Inside the house Celestine appeared at the foot of the stairs.

"Did you walk far?" she asked.

"Just to the lake," the old man said. He started to take off his coat. Celestine helped, fussing around him.

Patrick Cairney watched her. She had her yellow hair pulled back tightly, making her sky-blue eyes prominent in her face. She wore faded blue jeans and a red silk shirt and she was barefoot. She looked impossibly young. She might have been a young girl strolling through the grass at an open-air rock concert, someone you followed with your eyes and wondered who was lucky enough to be screwing her. And then you might track her through the crowd and lose her, knowing you'd never seen her again.

She moved toward him now. There was a scent of perfume in the air around her. She laid her fingertips on his wrist and said, "I'll make breakfast. I expect you're both hungry."

Patrick Cairney hung his coat on the rack, turning his face away from Celestine. He had developed a sense of danger that was like having some kind of internal compass whose needle would vibrate whenever danger was near, and he had the awareness now of that needle swinging madly inside his brain—and it had nothing to do with the idea that a man called Frank Pagan was in New York City looking for him, it had nothing to do with whatever calamity might have happened to Finn in Ireland, it had nothing to do with his reason for being in the United States. It was connected entirely to the touch of this woman's fingertips on his bare skin, which provoked a warm and unsettling physical response inside him. Sometimes there was an inexplicable chemistry between two people, instant, like a small Polaroid of emotion. If that was the thing happening between himself and Celestine, he had no room for it in his world.

He said, "I could eat."

But he still didn't look at her because he knew he had absolutely no mastery right then over his own expression. He didn't like that. He didn't like yielding up any of his control over himself. Without control he was a dead man. Finn had told him once that Jig was an instrument, a very fine instrument of destruction. But what Patrick Cairney felt as he avoided Celestine's eyes was a distressing knowledge of flaws in the structure of this instrument—a damaged reed, a faulty valve, something he'd have to repair in such a way that it would never fail him again.

NEW ROCKFORD, CONNECTICUT

The two Secret Service agents were of Hispanic descent. One was called Lopez, the other Garcina. They sat motionless and squat in a blue car parked in the driveway beneath Kevin Dawson's study. Now and again Dawson would walk to the window and look out at them. They never seemed to move. What did they do down there in the car? he wondered.

Dawson went toward his desk. It was strewn with papers. Many of them were invitations of the kind routinely extended to a brother of the President of the United States. The opening of a new office block in Manhattan. A fund-raising banquet on behalf of scientific research in Antarctica. Kevin Dawson attended as many of these functions as he could because he considered it his duty to wave the Dawson flag in public whenever possible. Duty was an important word in the Dawson lexicon. Sometimes Kevin thought that the entire Dawson clan had been selectively bred with public service in mind.

He sat down and pushed his chair back against the wall. From another part of this large Victorian house, which had been in the Dawson family for more than eighty years, he could hear the sounds of his daughters, Louise and Kitty, getting ready for school. Running water. The rattle of a spoon in a bowl. Kitty's high-pitched laughter. Martha, Kevin's wife, drove the girls every morning to the stop where they boarded the big yellow bus that took them to a grade school in New Rockford. At one time Martha had argued that the girls ought to attend a private school, but Kevin, pressured somewhat by his own brother who saw the chance to score some points for democracy and egalitarianism, insisted they go to a public school like normal kids. Thomas Dawson, locked into a marriage that seemed destined to be childless, was always bringing such minor pressures to bear on the family, the kids especially. He saw them, Kevin Dawson thought at times, as the children he didn't have himself.

There was the sound of footsteps on the stairs and then Louise and Kitty came running into his office to say good-bye to him. Kevin Dawson embraced his daughters, hugging them hard. A small ritual of family. Sometimes, when he stood in the doorway of their bedroom and watched them sleep, he was filled with an awesome love.

Louise, grown-up at eleven and graceful in the way of a ballet dancer with her long skinny body, wanted to know about the men parked in the driveway. Dawson stepped back from his daughters. They had a way of scrutinizing him that made him feel as though he were made of glass. The eyes of innocence, he thought.

"The President ordered those men to be here," he said slowly. "For our protection."

"Protection from what?" Kitty asked. She was balanced on one foot like a stork. At the age of nine, Kitty resembled her mother in a manner that could take Kevin's breath away.

"Well, the President has enemies. And because we're part of the President's family, we have the same enemies." He let this casual lie hang in the air, wondering if the girls were really buying it the way Martha had done. He had muttered vaguely about a rash of Dawson hate mail when he'd explained the presence of the Secret Service agents to his wife. Apart from Martyns, the agent who accompanied the kids to school and remained there all day long, Kevin had always refused Secret Service protection in the past even if, as the President's brother, he was entitled to it.

"It isn't anything that should worry you guys, though. It's a precaution, that's all."

Louise said to her sister, "It's politics as usual."

Kitty looked thoughtful. "Politics is a dirty game." Her small oval face was earnest.

"Where did you hear that?" he asked.

"*Everybody* knows *that*, Daddy," Kitty said.

"Everybody," Louise agreed. "Didn't you know that about politics, Daddy?"

There were moments when Dawson understood that his daughters liked to bait him in tiny ways. Affectionate little jibes, jokes, verbal conspiracies.

Martha appeared in the doorway. She was a small woman whose looks had deteriorated since the birth of Kitty. Kevin, who adored his wife beyond any means of measurement, didn't notice changes in her. He didn't see the wrinkles edging the eyes. He didn't see the thin lines that stretched from the corners of her mouth, nor did he notice the streaks of silver that had appeared in her black hair. All he ever saw was the girl he'd proposed to one wet afternoon in Bayville when a summer storm had raked the waters of Long Island

Sound and Martha had pressed her lips against the back of his hand and whispered *Yes*. Kevin had built his whole life around that whisper of acceptance.

"Let's go, girls," she said. "We don't want to miss the bus, do we?"

"I don't think you want an honest answer to that question, Mom," Louise said.

Martha kissed Kevin. "I'll be right back," she said, herding the girls out of the room. She blew another kiss at her husband as she drew the door shut.

From the window Kevin watched his family get inside the station wagon. Martyns followed in the blue sedan. Kevin gazed until both cars had gone out of sight down the long curve of the driveway and the stand of ancient elms. He went to his desk and began to sift through the papers.

He was searching for the file that contained a monthly computerized printout detailing the ebb and flow of the Dawson family fortune, which came from such diverse sources as condominiums in Dallas and Houston, dairy farms in Wisconsin, New York, and Ohio, a chain of small-town newspapers that extended from Oregon to Florida, and a pineapple plantation in Hawaii. The whole thing was a maze of corporations, and it was Kevin Dawson's function to manage this labyrinth, which grew more complex every month.

He found the file and flipped it open. He stared at the columns of figures, prepared by a centralized computer bank in Jersey City, which recorded every business transaction in the Dawson empire from the purchase of paper clips to the financial lubrication of some local politician. It was difficult to concentrate. His mind kept drifting to Jig and to the crazy idea that he was in danger. He tried to persuade himself he was safe—after all, there were Secret Service men stationed outside—but he couldn't still the anxiety he felt.

He closed the file and stood up, stretching his arms. He disliked being vulnerable. All Kevin Dawson had ever really craved was a peaceful life, the life of a family man. Wife and kids. Dogs and roses. But destiny, that crooked schemer, had arranged for him to be born into the Dawson clan with all its political ambitions, its history of ruthless business intrigues. His grandfather had been impeached by the House of Representatives in 1929 for "immoral and unacceptable" trading in the stock market. His father, the one-time United States ambassador to Italy, had been maligned in the late 1930s for his uncritical attitude toward Mussolini and criticized even more strongly in the fifties for having a tumultuous affair with a Greek opera singer, a histrionic woman the press called "Dawson's Diva." It was as if the Dawson clan went out of its way to court turbulence and self-destruction. What chance did he have for a peaceful life with a background like that?

His telephone rang. He picked up the receiver and heard the voice of Nicholas Linney.

"Mulhaney thinks he's got it all figured out," Linney said.

Dawson pinched the bridge of his nose. "Figured what, Nick?"

"Who took the money." Linney had a flat nasal accent, like that of a man with stuffed sinuses. "He figures you."

"Me? Why me?"

"He's got some cockeyed reasons of his own."

"I'm sure he has," Kevin Dawson said. "Do I want to hear them?"

Linney was quiet a moment. "I didn't find them convincing. He's full of shit. I think he's laying down smokescreens, if you want my opinion."

"Smokescreens?"

"Yeah. He makes an accusation like that, it takes the heat off him."

"Why would *he* feel any heat, Nick?"

"If he had a hand in the hijacking he would," Linney answered.

"You think he did?"

"I hear rumors. I hear things about Mulhaney privately investing union funds and losing some hefty change on Wall Street. I hear things about auditors moving in on his union, wanting to check the books. I think maybe he's been skimming. Chipping away at the Irish money. Mending fences."

There was a long silence. Dawson thought about the wholesale paranoia that the hijacking of the *Connie O'Mara* had brought, and he doubted that the Fund-raisers could ever function as a unit again. He realized he welcomed this prospect. It was a step in the direction of the untroubled life he sought. His ambitions for Ireland belonged to another time in his life, to his youth when he'd been less prudent than he was now. Dawson turned his thoughts briefly to Mulhaney. If Jig ever got to Big Jock, then it was a pretty sure bet that Mulhaney *would* send the killer here to Connecticut. *Kev Dawson's the one*, Mulhaney would say. *Kev Dawson took the money.* Mulhaney hated the Dawson family, and Thomas especially, ever since the President had created a commission to look into union funds. Big Jock would love to create problems for the Dawsons. Kevin Dawson understood that he feared Mulhaney almost as much Jig. Mulhaney, dictated to by blind hatreds and prejudice and the fear of seeing his power eroded by a presidential commission, would go out of his way to make life difficult for anyone connected to the Dawson family. If he couldn't get Tommy directly, then Kevin would do.

"You really believe any of this, Nick?"

"It's a possibility, that's all. Guy's got a cash-flow problem."

"Here's something else to consider, Nick. Maybe you're the one setting up a smokescreen."

"I like that," Linney said.

"My point is, Nick, when this kind of suspicion starts, where the hell does it stop? Where do we draw the line, for God's sake? None of this mutual accusation shit is going to get the money back. It's sick to go around blaming somebody when there isn't a goddam shred of evidence."

"I'm not accusing anybody," Linney answered calmly. "I'm examining options, that's all."

"Examining options," Dawson said. He had always found Nick Linney to be a cold character, somebody whose personality seemed indefinable at bottom. A human enigma. His encounters with Linney invariably left him feeling faintly depressed, as if he'd run into somebody hovering on the sociopathic margin of things. For a second Dawson had the urge to mention Jig, but he'd promised his brother—and Kevin, no matter what, always tried to keep his word.

"You come up with any bright ideas, you call me," Linney said.

"Immediately," Dawson replied.

"And if you see any strange-looking Irishmen hanging around, you be careful."

"Is that supposed to be funny?"

"Take it any way you like," Nicholas Linney said.

When Dawson had hung up he opened the bottom drawer of his desk and took out a bottle of Dewar's White Label. He poured himself a small shot and sipped it. Drinking just after breakfast. A bad sign, he thought.

Carrying his shot glass, he got up and wandered to the window. The hills on the other side of the road appeared secretive and barren. He looked across the lawn at the wrought-iron fence that faced the narrow road. It seemed oddly flimsy to Kevin Dawson just then, as if even the slightest breeze might flatten it.

He finished his drink.

He saw the station wagon come up the driveway. Martha stepped out. She looked tiny to Dawson. Vulnerable and pale beneath the monochrome of the sky. He raised one hand and waved, but she didn't see him. When she'd passed out of his sight in the direction of the house, a wave of cold fear ran through him. It wasn't just the wrought-iron fence that was fragile. It was his whole life.

FOURTEEN

NEW YORK CITY

In his room at the Essex House Ivor McInnes woke at seven-thirty A.M. as he usually did. He shaved and showered and had breakfast sent up by room service. He ate at the window, chewing on streaky pieces of what passed for bacon in America, pausing every now and then to look in the direction of Central Park. He perused *The New York Times* casually, then set it aside and continued to gaze out into the park. He drank several cups of coffee, then left his room and rode the elevator down into the lobby where he wandered toward the telephones.

Today, he thought, would have to be spent in the New York Public Library. Taking notes, reading, satisfying those morons at the State Department on the chance that he was being observed. He glanced across the crowded lobby before he dialed the number in White Plains. He punched in a handful of change at the operator's request and after a moment he heard a voice saying, "Memorial Presbyterian Church. This is the Reverend Duncanson speaking."

"I would like to know the times of your Sunday services," McInnes said.

"Seven A.M. and ten," Duncanson answered. He had a firm oratorical voice, a voice made for pulpits. "I can tell from your accent you're a long way from home. Do you want to attend one of our services?"

"I'd like to," McInnes answered.

"We always welcome guests at Memorial. Especially those from overseas."

A nice man, McInnes thought. A decent man. "Which is the more popular service?" he asked.

Duncanson laughed quietly. "Oddly enough, my congregation prefers the sunrise service. They tell me my sermon is more mellow at that time of day. Can we expect you?"

"You can."

"Introduce yourself to me after," Duncanson said. "I know your lovely country well." He paused a moment. "My text this coming Sunday is First John, chapter one, verse nine."

"Ah," McInnes said. " 'If we confess our sins, he is faithful and just to forgive us our sins and to cleanse us from all unrighteousness.' "

"You know your Bible," Duncanson said.

"Some of it," Ivor McInnes answered.

When he'd hung up he stood in the lobby for a time and rattled coins in the pockets of his pants. The Memorial Presbyterian Church, which he had visited during his last trip to the U.S.A. in 1983, was one of those picture-postcard American churches, white framed and steepled and looking as if it were a Norman Rockwell construct. Its congregation was rich and influential, consisting mainly of well-heeled commuters who held executive positions in New York City. It was a hive of the American WASP. Unlike his own church in the Shankill district of Belfast, Memorial Presbyterian would never have any difficulty raising funds for new pews or a stained-glass window or an elaborate organ.

He rode the elevator back up to the seventeenth floor, still caressing the coins in his pockets. He strolled along the corridor to his room. When he saw the two men framed against the window at the end of the corridor he didn't break his stride. Instead, he took out his room key and inserted it into the lock of the door as the pair approached him. He turned to look at them. He had met Frank Pagan briefly once before, during an Irish peace conference in Westminster in the winter of 1984. Pagan had talked that day about the need for cooperation between the law enforcement agencies of both Irelands, if terrorism was ever to be destroyed. A touching little speech, McInnes had thought at the time. Liberal, fair-minded and totally impractical. He remembered now how the conference had broken down into a shambles, a slanging match between himself and the bishop of Dublin, who'd droned on for hours about the violation of Catholic civil rights in Ulster. McInnes had always regarded the bishop as a cousin of the Prince of Darkness anyway.

"Frank Pagan! This *is* a surprise," McInnes said, suppressing the terrible temptation to ask Pagan if he'd had any luck in catching up with Jig. There were moments in McInnes's life when he had to struggle fiercely with his sense of mischief, and this was one of them. He wondered if he looked suitably surprised by Pagan's appearance.

Frank Pagan had the kind of face that was difficult to read. He'd be a hell of a man to play cards against, McInnes thought. He stared into Pagan's gray eyes, which reminded him of cinders.

"This is Arthur Zuboric," Pagan said. "FBI."

The suntanned man with the drooping moustache nodded his head. McInnes looked at him a second, then back to Pagan.

"What brings you to New York City?" McInnes asked. He stepped into his room and the two men followed him.

"Funny," Pagan said. "You took the words right out of my mouth, Ivor."

McInnes sat in the armchair by the window. "You must know why *I'm* here," he said. "Your bloody people in London know just about everything."

"I understand you're writing a book," Pagan said.

"Correct." McInnes noticed a muscle working in the Englishman's jaw.

Pagan smiled. "What's the title?"

"I haven't made up my mind yet." McInnes saw the FBI man move to the window where he slid the curtain back and looked out, as if he suspected all manner of nefarious events to be taking place in Central Park.

Pagan picked up a Gideon Bible and flipped the pages for a time. McInnes drummed the tips of his fingers against the table. He was ready for anything Frank Pagan might ask.

"You know, of course, that I'm looking for Jig."

"Now how would *I* know something like that?" McInnes, like any good actor, had all kinds of facial expressions at his command. The one he chose to assume right then was innocence. His large eyelids rose and his eyes widened.

"Because my information came from *you*, courtesy of that merry band of yours, the Free Ulster Volunteers."

"Because members of the FUV belonged to my former congregation, Frank, doesn't mean I'm a card-carrying member myself," McInnes said. "I categorically deny any association with that organization, and I challenge you to prove otherwise. I don't deny *knowing* members of the FUV, Frank. It would be difficult not to. But as for myself, I've always steered clear of involvement."

"Ivor, Ivor." Pagan sighed. "I didn't just come up the Thames on a water biscuit. I wasn't exactly born yesterday. You, or a representative of yours called John Waddell, sent the Leprechaun to see me in London with the information that Jig had come to the U.S.A."

"The Leprechaun?" McInnes stood up. He looked at Zuboric and said, "Your English friend here has a fanciful imagination. Next thing he'll be telling me he converses with gnomes and counts elves among his dearest chums."

"You're a droll fellow, Ivor," Pagan said.

McInnes laughed again, a big throaty sound. It was as if he had an untuned accordion lodged in his larynx. "As for John Waddell, well, you've lost me."

"How did you find out Jig was coming to America, Ivor?"

"You're barking up the wrong tree."

"I don't really think so," Pagan said. "Every time the Free Ulster Volunteers move, it's because you're sitting backstage pulling their strings."

"You're on shaky ground, Frank."

McInnes gazed at the blank TV. For a moment he considered the complicated mosaic of this whole operation, and it filled him with a dizzy sense of achievement. It had taken three years to get this far, three years of planning and scheming and infiltrating and carefully sliding each delicate part into its correct place. And now, even with Pagan and his American sidekick in his hotel room, he could almost taste the triumph in everything that had been assembled. In a life filled with strife and dissension and disappointment, victory was a new flavor for him and he enjoyed it. What he also enjoyed was playing a little game with Frank Pagan, who was laboring in a blind place indeed.

"Did you come to my hotel just to harangue me, Frank?" he asked. "Did you come here to make false accusations?"

Pagan rose from the bed. "I've got a problem, Ivor. Let me see if I can explain it to you. First, I get this snippet of information about

Jig. No matter how hard you deny it, I know it comes from you. The horse's mouth. I get on a plane. *Voilà.* New York. Second, as coincidence would have it, I find my old pal Ivor in the same city, researching a book. I don't put a lot of faith in coincidence, Ivor, and since I've had the miserable fortune to actually struggle through some of your writing in pamphlet form, I don't put much faith in your literary talents either. Do you see where I'm going?"

McInnes shook his head. "You're still barking, Frank."

"Something's going on. Something's happening." Pagan's eyes, which McInnes had thought cindery before, appeared to have caught fire.

Ivor McInnes looked out at Central Park. A watery sun, the color of sulfur, hung over bare trees. He had a sudden image of the girl in the Hotel Strasbourg, and he felt a weird little outbreak of guilt at the memory. It was one of the drawbacks of Presbyterianism, this smoldering guilt that sometimes attacked you unawares.

"Check with my publisher if you want to know about my book, Frank," he said. "I'm sure he'd tell you the book's no sham."

Pagan glanced at his wristwatch, then looked in the direction of the FBI man, whose silence had been faintly disturbing to McInnes. After a lifetime of speechmaking and pulpit thumping, McInnes abhorred silences.

McInnes said, "I hope you find your man, Frank. Jig's a bloody menace to peaceful people everywhere. Especially to the Loyalists in Ireland. If he keeps killing, the British are going to think very carefully about the cost of maintaining a presence in the province. And what would happen to the Loyalists then?"

"What exactly are you loyal to?" Pagan asked. "Enlighten me."

"Queen and Country of course," McInnes replied.

"Your patriotism's touching. But you left something out, Ivor."

"What?"

"You forgot your *overriding* loyalty, didn't you? The only one in your life. To yourself. To Ivor McInnes. That's the only true allegiance *you* understand."

"Frank, Frank," McInnes said, his voice filled with the weariness of a man who is tired of being vilified unjustly. "You're beginning to believe all the things you read about me in the newspapers. I credited you with more sense than that, my friend. Aren't you being just a trifle hasty in your character assassination? Besides, you forget something. Something important."

"What's that?"

"We're on the *same* side. We both want to see Jig behind bars, don't we? We both want to see an end to IRA terrorism, don't we? You forget, Frank, that I'm an ardent supporter of the government you work for. You shouldn't let something that bloody important slip your mind. Whether you like it or not, we're *allies*." And here McInnes placed one of his large hands on Pagan's shoulder and squeezed it in a confidential way.

Frank Pagan stared at McInnes. His face was hard and cold again, and there was a distance in his eyes. McInnes wondered about the reservoirs of anger inside the man. He let his hand drop to his side.

"You overlook a major difference," Pagan said, his voice flat, words clipped. "I don't play on bigotry and fear, McInnes. I don't incite people to meaningless acts of violence. And I don't use scum like the Free Ulster Volunteers to do my dirty work for me."

McInnes, who realized he'd struck a vibrant chord here, simply shrugged. "I've been accused of bigotry before, Frank, and I daresay I'll be accused again. I challenge you to find anything in my speeches or my writing to support that charge. You'll find that *nowhere* have I ever uttered or written a single word that could justifiably be construed as bigotry. What I have done, and what I'll continue to do"—and here McInnes flashed his widest smile—"is to criticize the policies of the Roman Catholic Church, which I consider an impediment to any kind of progress. You look at any poor country, you'll find the Catholic Church somewhere in the picture. You look at any poor country wracked by a runaway birthrate and you'll find priests and nuns holding total dominion over the peasants. The Vatican doesn't want adherents and converts, it wants prisoners. It wants people who are scared to ask questions. It wants numbers, and it dangles the threat of excommunication over anybody who has the guts to ask straightforward questions. Take something dead simple, Frank. Take your average parish priest. What in the name of God does he know about women and marriage and raising children? Nothing! He leads a celibate life, with his head stuck up his arse. And yet he's the man who's supposed to give *guidance* to people whose marriages are falling apart or husbands who are impotent? It's this same church that has kept the Republic of Ireland in bondage for centuries, with its censorship and its damned laws of contraception and its attitude to divorce."

McInnes paused now. His voice, which had been kept at a constant, restrained pitch, had filled the small hotel room like air blown into a balloon. "It's the same church that has been behind the troubles in Ulster. Do you think Ulster would be in its present pitiful condition if the Catholic Church weren't there? We're an impoverished, backward society, Frank. We should be in the vanguard of European life, but instead what do we get? Bloody handouts from British politicians. A little charity from Westminster. And you can say what you like about the FUV, Frank, but it's people like them that keep the Catholic IRA from turning Northern Ireland into a complete bloodbath."

Pagan shook his head. There was something just a little mesmerizing about McInnes when he was in full flight. He could make even the most irrational arguments sound forcibly convincing. What you had to do when you confronted Ivor was to keep in mind that his arguments appealed only to unanalytical audiences already predisposed to his point of view. If you didn't, you ran the risk of having your head addled. He was annoyed with himself for having allowed Ivor to launch into a speech. He was also annoyed that his own composure was slipping. "You make the FUV sound like a peace-keeping force. What's your big dream, McInnes? A Nobel Peace Prize?"

McInnes was determined not to be drawn by insults. He found it remarkable how blind Frank Pagan could be. Why didn't the man accept the fact that they were both on the same side when you got right down to it? What was so difficult about that notion?

"My aim's simple," McInnes said. "I've said it many times before and I'll say it again. I want an end to the IRA. Can you deny you want the same thing?"

"The problem with talking to somebody like you is the feeling I get of hammering my head against a bloody great brick wall," Pagan said. "You have a bad habit, Ivor, of twisting things around so that they'll fit your thesis."

"You didn't answer my question, Frank."

"Okay. I don't deny it. I want to see terrorism finished. But are you sure that's what *you* really want?"

"What is that supposed to mean?"

"It's simple. Without having the Catholics and the IRA to rant about, what would you do with your time, Ivor? Just think how bloody bored you'd be."

McInnes smiled. "Bored but at peace, Frank."

Pagan looked at his wristwatch. "It's been fun talking to you and

I'm sorry we have to run. In the meantime, Ivor, keep out of trouble and try to have a nice day."

"I always have nice days," McInnes said.

He watched Pagan close the door quietly. Alone, he moved to the window and saw two brightly dressed joggers pounding through Central Park. He placed the palm of his hand upon the glass, leaving a print. Pagan, of course, was mistaken. Without the IRA, the Catholics in the North would have no real protection, which meant they would migrate to the South—that medieval, Church-choked country where they belonged—leaving Ulster in the hands of the Protestants. And McInnes, whose vision encompassed an Ulster free of sectarian violence, would have a major role to play in the formation of this shining new society. It was really very simple. There would be a great many things to keep him occupied in the future.

He put on his overcoat. He'd spend the afternoon in the public library, leafing through old records and documents and making sure he took notes conscientiously. It would be difficult, though. He knew his mind would keep drifting to the Memorial Presbyterian Church in White Plains.

Sunday at seven. Two days from now. The first step. He felt suddenly excited and anxious. It had been a long road, and it had been filled with deprivation for him. But now at least, he could read the signs along the way. He put his hand on the telephone but then drew it away again quickly. This urge to speak, to make contact, to utter aloud the excitement he felt—he had to let it subside. To make any kind of contact now would be to break rules. And the rules had been observed stringently ever since the beginning. Even in times of the utmost difficulty.

He stepped out into the corridor just in time to see Frank Pagan and Zuboric get into the elevator. Pagan looked briefly in his direction, raised a hand in the air, then the elevator doors slid shut behind him.

FRANK PAGAN was depressed in the thrift shop. Old clothing had its own peculiar smell, reminiscent of locked attics and damp chests filled with moldering papers. It wasn't the sleazy ambience of the store that brought him down, though. It was the encounter with McInnes. To be drawn into an argument with Ivor was like trying to do a butterfly stroke in a small bathtub. You never got anywhere.

Pagan picked out a very old black overcoat and tried it on. He turned to Artie Zuboric. "How do I look?"

"Sensational," Zuboric said, looking at an enormous Hawaiian shirt, which might have housed the entire Barnum and Bailey Circus. He examined the pattern, a nightmare of pineapples and Venus fly-traps.

Pagan took off the overcoat. It wasn't grubby enough for St. Finbar's. He found a more likely garment on the next rack, an old raincoat with tattered epaulettes and faded stains tattooing the sleeves.

Frank Pagan tried on the overcoat. He wandered toward a cracked wall mirror at the far end of the store and stared at his own reflection. "The trouble with Ivor is he shapes the world to suit himself. It's a common trait among megalomaniacs."

Zuboric lifted a red and black checked suit from a rack and held it up. He'd seen another side of Frank Pagan in the room at the Essex House. He'd caught the distinct vibrations of the man's capacity for anger. It was enjoyable to see the fault lines in Pagan's surface. "*Are* you on the same side, Frank?"

Frank Pagan turned away from his reflection and looked at Zuboric, wondering if the agent was trying to goad him. "The Irish problem turns up some strange companions," he said. "Maybe McInnes and I have a common enemy. And maybe our goals overlap. But what McInnes loves is strife. He feeds on it. If there weren't any trouble, he'd go out and manufacture some."

"He says he's writing a book—"

Pagan snorted. "McInnes spews out pamphlets that make *The Protocols of the Elders of Zion* seem positively charitable. If you've ever got a few minutes to waste and you want some insight into Ivor's mind, I suggest you read the one entitled *The Roman Catholic Conspiracy in Northern Ireland.* In that priceless work he actually advocates sterilization for the Roman Catholic women of Ulster after they've had two babies. So the idea of him writing a book is fucking laughable. Unless he's found a publisher who specializes in madness. Which isn't *altogether* an impossibility."

Zuboric said, "So what's he doing here then?"

Pagan shrugged. "I wish I knew. The only thing I know for certain is I don't trust him. And I don't trust the coincidence of him being here. What you have to keep remembering about Ivor is that he's clever and he's cunning. You might disagree with the things he says, but you don't underestimate him. And there are thousands of people in Ulster who agree with his every word. That kind of support shouldn't be overlooked either."

"You said he was involved with the Free Ulster Volunteers. He denied that. What's the score there?"

"We've had him watched and we've had him followed, and we've never been able to pin that connection on him directly. The chances are that he's behind the FUV, but he's very careful. If he ever makes contact with them, we don't know about it. I've got sources that say he meets with FUV members secretly, but when it comes down to documented proof, I can never get my hands on any. I work on the assumption that he's the leader, but I can't guarantee it." Pagan paused a second, casting an eye around the store. "Ulster's filled with secrets. And Ivor knows a whole lot of them, but he isn't telling."

Zuboric watched Pagan plunge into a mountain of old shoes now. There was footwear of every variety. Sandals, battered slippers, two-tone horrors, beat-up climbing boots. A sweaty odor arose from the heap. There was no way in the world he'd try on any of the shoes himself, but Pagan, who'd already removed his own casual leather jobs, was plucking a dilapidated pair of brown brogues from the heap. He sat on the floor and placed one of the shoes on his left foot. He suddenly reminded Zuboric of a kid getting dressed up for Halloween. He had this quality of enthusiasm.

"Fine, don't you think?" Pagan asked.

"Yeah. Terrific."

"Now I need a shirt and a pair of pants." Pagan wandered off to another pile of clothing and Zuboric followed. Pagan chose an antique flannel shirt that was missing several buttons. The cuffs were frayed. Pants next, a pair of crumpled old flannels with enormous fly buttons and broken belt loops. When he had his wardrobe assembled Pagan said, "It's a pity about that suntan of yours."

Zuboric was unhappy with the notion of Pagan infiltrating St. Finbar's. At first, Artie had wanted to dress up the way Pagan was planning to do, and position himself inside the soup kitchen dressed as one of its clientele. But this notion had disintegrated as soon as he'd tried on an old tweed coat and looked at himself in the mirror. There was absolutely *no way* he could pass himself off as a derelict with a complexion as healthy as his. He looked too good to carry off a charade like the one Pagan was going to play. Instead, Zuboric planned to conceal himself in Tumulty's office while Pagan mingled with the deadbeats downstairs. There was a certain ironic symbolism in this arrangement that Zuboric enjoyed.

"You should stay out of spas," Pagan said. "And avoid suntan lamps in future. They're unnatural."

"And look as white as you? No thanks."

"Didn't I tell you, Artie? The way I look is all the rage in London this winter. Everybody's trying it."

Pagan took his purchases to the desk where a frail old man with a face that resembled a spider's web operated an ancient cash register.

When they were outside on the street, Pagan said, "It's time to release Father Joe."

Zuboric looked across the street at Pagan's big green Cadillac. There was a tiny knot in his stomach, a vague tension. He wanted a tidy conclusion to this whole murky business. He wanted to escort Frank Pagan to Kennedy Airport and watch him step aboard a flight to London, which would thankfully be the last of the guy. But first there was the uncertainty of Jig.

They crossed the street to the car. Pagan took the key out of his pocket, and as he was about to insert it into the door of the vehicle he saw a girl come out of a delicatessen half a block away, and his heart jumped as if electricity had coursed through his body.

Roxanne.

He dropped the bag of secondhand clothes. His lungs were tight in his chest and his hands trembled.

"Something wrong?" Zuboric asked.

Pagan said nothing. He watched the girl move along the sidewalk, her thick black hair floating behind her. The way she walked. The way her hair flew up from her neck and shoulders. He shut his eyes a moment, and when he opened them again the girl was already turning the corner at the end of the block. *Fool.* Deceived by resemblances. Misled by impressions. He felt weak. He had to lean against the side of the car.

"Frank?" Zuboric asked.

"It's nothing. I thought I saw somebody I used to know. That's all."

Zuboric picked up the bag of clothing from the pavement and gave it to Pagan, who clutched it in an absentminded way against his chest. Pagan looked along the empty sidewalk. He had the depressing realization that if he lived a million years, if he lived long enough to see the sun shrivel in the sky and the earth freeze and wither and the planets plunge into eternal darkness, he'd never see Roxanne again. He'd see resemblances in a hundred places, but never again the real person. It was quite a thought.

He opened the car door, his hand still trembling. He got in behind the wheel. What he needed was something desperately simple. He needed to fuck the specter of Roxanne out of existence. It came down to that. But what were you supposed to do if that particular appetite had died? If all the women you ever saw didn't match the memory of a dead woman? If your heart was empty?

"You sure you're okay?" Zuboric asked.

Pagan smiled. "I'm in great shape."

ROSCOMMON, NEW YORK

Celestine Cairney listened to Harry's Irish music float out through the open door of his study. She paused on the threshold of the room, watching Harry and his son sit close together near the fire. A flask of brandy and two glasses stood on the coffee table. It was late afternoon and the sun had gone behind the trees, and the only light in the study was the glow of the log fire. Harry leaned toward his son and said something, and the young man laughed, perhaps a little too politely. It was the laughter of somebody who hadn't quite learned the language of mirth. An artificial sound.

Celestine leaned against the door jamb. The Irish music made her uneasy at times because it was the music of ghosts, the music of Harry's first marriage, with all its comfortable intimacies. She had mental pictures of Harry and his first wife sitting by the fire while this music wove through the air around them.

She moved very slightly. Neither man was aware of her presence. She liked the idea of observing people when they didn't know she was watching. She studied Patrick. He was a good-looking man in an intense way. He had serious eyes and a certain strength about him, but there was an aura of privacy, almost a force field, that one couldn't get through easily. She had the impression of somebody who lived in his own secret fortress. He wasn't like Harry at all, outgoing and gregarious with that facile Irish charm he could trot out whenever it suited him. These were the gifts of a politician. The necessary equipment.

Come back, Paddy Reilly, to Ballyjamesduff,
Come home, Paddy Reilly, to me.

All Harry's music was like this. It was all drenched with yearning.
Now there was a break in the song and the thin notes of a fiddle
filled the room.

Patrick Cairney had seen her. He rose from his chair. Harry smiled
and stretched out a hand in her direction.

"She's been spying on us," he said.

Celestine moved into the room. "Why would I do that, Harry?
You don't have any secrets from me, love."

Harry stood up now too. "Want a brandy?" he asked.

"I don't want to interrupt this reunion," she said. "Besides, I was
on my way to take a shower before dinner."

She gazed at Patrick Cairney. She found his awkwardness in her
presence a little touching. The way he'd reacted last night when
she'd gone to his bedroom was amusing. He'd been like a kid who'd
smuggled a girl inside his dormitory against all the school rules. He
seemed now like a man who wished he were someplace else. She
knew exactly what kind of effect she had on him. In her lifetime,
she'd come to understand that her beauty often devastated people.
Certain men didn't know how to react to her. She had had her share
of flowers and lovers' poems and men who stuttered and fumbled
around her. She considered her appearance a genetic accident, useful but finally transient. She never saw in the mirror what other
people saw when they beheld her, almost as if her appearance were
something apart from what she thought of as her inner self, her
reality. Extremely good looks, such as her own, were often interpreted wrongly. Men looked at her and they couldn't get beyond
her appearance and down into the place where she really lived. They
couldn't begin to think their way beyond her surfaces.

Most men anyway.

"You could never interrupt anything, my dear," Harry said.

He had that look on his face. Total devotion. Utter bliss. There
were moments when her husband's love made her feel uncomfortable. Harry gave it so wholeheartedly and without qualification that
it was like a light he was forever shining into her eyes. Sometimes
she felt blinded by it.

She warmed her hands in front of the fire. Patrick Cairney moved
out of her way, but there was a second of contact between them, a

tiny friction as her body touched his. She liked the connection. She liked the expression on Patrick's face, the effort he made to conceal his discomfort.

"I was riding and I'm grubby," she said. She spread her legs in front of the fire. "I can't sit down to dinner in this condition."

Harry reached for her hand. His skin had the feel of rice paper. She took his fingers in her palm. They were cold with that unfathomable coldness of age. She took her hand away and walked back across the room to the door. What she frequently longed for was warmth—another climate altogether, where she wouldn't be confronted by the chills of a long winter. What was she doing in this big house located on this huge frozen estate? Why in the name of God had she ever agreed to come here to this place of isolation and snow and security guards who watched her lasciviously through their binoculars whenever she went outside?

She reached the doorway. She shivered slightly. "Dinner will be ready in about thirty minutes," she said. "I'll meet you in the dining room."

"What are we having?" Harry asked.

"The specialty of the house. Corned beef and cabbage. What else?" If there had been such a thing as Irish wine, a Cabernet Killarney or a Château Galway, say, she would have served that as well. She disliked the stodge of Irish food.

"Ah," Harry said, delighted. He was showing off his wife for the benefit of his son. "Didn't I tell you, Pat? Didn't I tell you she knows how to warm an old man's heart?"

Patrick nodded. He fiddled with the stopper of the crystal brandy flask. He wasn't looking at Celestine. She left the room and moved along the landing. She paused outside the door of Patrick's bedroom. What she remembered was how furtive he'd been last night about his canvas bag and the small wooden horse, which he'd practically seized from her hand and stuffed back inside the bag as if it were a souvenir too precious for anyone else to sully. Curious. She was tempted to sneak inside the room and explore it in his absence. Instead, she continued toward her own bedroom.

She went inside the bathroom and removed her clothes, catching glimpses of herself in the mirror. She had small breasts and a flat stomach. She thought her hips were probably a little too narrow, but otherwise it was a good body, firm and smooth and untouched as yet by age. She let her hair fall over her shoulders as she turned to the shower stall. The water was very hot, the way she liked it. Steam rose against her flesh, glistened in her hair, filled her nostrils. She took soap from the dish and made lather all over her body, smoothing the soap slowly over her breasts and across the surface of her stomach. She tilted her head back against the tiled wall, closing her eyes.

She slid the soap between her inner thighs to her pubic hair, as though it were a lover's hand she was directing. She moved it backward and forward slowly between her legs and then the bar slipped from her hand and now there was nothing between herself and her body. With the tips of her fingers she stroked herself gently, very gently, anticipating the pleasure. Her fantasies were always tropical. There were always exotic flowers and a suffocating humidity and a hint of danger, like an indistinct presence just beyond her field of vision. Her imaginary lover's face kept changing, first one of the men she'd known in her life, then another and another coming at her in quick succession until she settled on the one who could please her fantasies best. But this time the face that finally came before her was that of a man who'd never been her lover, and this realization excited her, this new perspective made her nerves tingle.

He remained stubbornly fixed in her mind.

Faster now. Faster. She had a sense of something warm flowing through her body, something molten that was located deep inside her. She heard herself moan. She bit the knuckles of her left hand and she gasped, and for a second her whole body was rigid before she fell apart inside, as if she were destroyed by the astonishing ferocity of pleasure. She slid down slowly against the tiled wall to a sitting position, her eyes still shut against the pounding water, her hand limp between her thighs.

She didn't move for a long time.

She thought it weird she'd allowed Patrick Cairney to participate in her fantasy. Out of all the men she'd known in her life, she'd selected one who was off limits, who was forbidden by the fact of her marriage. She stood up, reached for a towel, started to dry herself carefully.

Patrick Cairney, she thought. My fantasy lover.

She rubbed condensation from the mirror, making a small space in which she could see her face. Her smile was enigmatic, even to herself.

NEW YORK CITY

Dressed in the clothes he'd purchased at the thrift shop, Frank Pagan put down the half-empty bowl and said, "It's pretty bland, Joe. It needs a dash of something. Tarragon. Paprika. Something to spice it up. Some Worcestershire sauce would do it."

Joseph X. Tumulty wore a crucifix about his neck, a small flash of gold against his black shirt. Every now and then his hand went to it, his ungainly fingers fumbling with the miniature Jesus. "The men here are better served by nutrition than haute cuisine, Mr. Pagan."

"You may have a point." Pagan stared into the bowl, which sat on Tumulty's desk. "Have you got everything straight in your mind, Joe?"

Tumulty nodded. These men were playing with him, and he resented them for it. He laid his hands in front of him and saw how the skin glistened with sweat. He was beginning to discover that fear had various strata of intensity. The fear he'd felt before when Frank Pagan had burst into the room on Mulberry Street and shot Santacroce was nothing to what he was going through now at the prospect of facing Jig again.

Lying to him. Entrapping him. Setting him up. He felt very small and very weak. But a promise had been held out to him like a carrot to a donkey. If he did what was asked of him, he wouldn't go to jail. It was that simple. Who would run this place if he was incarcerated? He couldn't depend on volunteers to keep the whole thing going, and he couldn't stand the idea of St. Finbar's being shut down, his people having to go hungry. God knows, they had little enough in their lives as it was. They *relied* on him and how could he deprive them of that? And what would happen to people like McCune, people he had saved, if their mentor went to prison? Tumulty saw only sheer disaster. His night of solitude in a cell had convinced him that he could stand the strain of being locked up, but he couldn't take the notion of being removed from Canal Street. He had prayed in the small cell. He had gone down on his knees and searched his mind for God. God, the great problem solver, the unlocker of puzzles, had responded only with a roaring silence, as if He had abdicated his place in the firmament. And Tumulty understood what the absences were saying to him. *He was on his own in this situation.*

"When Jig comes into the kitchen," he told Pagan in a monotone, "I'll say a specific blessing when we sit down to eat. *The Lord hath done great things for us, whereof we are glad.* After we've eaten, I'll signal for Jig to follow me up to my office. You'll come up behind to block his retreat. Jig and I will come in here. Mr. Zuboric will be waiting."

Pagan thought there was something incongruous about Psalm 126, verse 3 when you spoke it aloud inside a soup kitchen, but the choice of phrase had come from Arthur Zuboric who didn't believe Tumulty could be trusted to devise his own code. Pagan suspected there was some spiteful part of Artie that wanted to see this whole scheme fall to pieces so he could quietly gloat. A gloating discontent was apparently built into Artie's circuitry.

Tumulty asked, "Do you enjoy this, Mr. Pagan? Do you enjoy seeing me squirm?"

Pagan didn't answer. He hardly heard the question. He was wondering about fear. He was wondering whether Joe Tumulty's fear was going to be strong enough to lead him into betraying Jig. Or whether at the last moment the priest might experience some spasm of courage. He was sure that Tumulty had courage inside him—otherwise he wouldn't have gone to the meeting with Santacroce in the first place. Pagan glanced at the attaché case that sat on the floor beside the desk. It contained the two customized weapons, but as a precaution all the ammunition had been removed.

Tumulty looked at Frank Pagan. "It's a hell of a thing you're asking me to do. You know that?"

"You got yourself into it in the first place, Joe. I didn't enroll you in the IRA, did I?" Pagan asked. "Just remember this. Don't fuck around with me when it comes to Jig. Don't even think about it."

Tumulty wandered in the direction of a painting of the Virgin Mary that hung at the back of the room. He looked up at it for a moment, drawn into the eyes. He was being asked to betray more than an individual called Jig. He was being asked to betray the Cause and himself along with it. He found a little consolation in the fact he hadn't exactly told his captors very much. He hadn't said anything about the deliveries in Maine, and he hadn't mentioned Nicholas Linney, and his description of Jig had been vague at best. Small consolations. He turned away from the Virgin.

Something else occurred to him for the first time. The notion of reprisals. If he gave these men Jig, he might just as well be signing his own execution order, because a day would come when another gunman would be sent from Ireland to even the score. There was nothing more terrible than a traitor so far as the Cause was concerned. No crime was greater than treason.

A rock, Tumulty thought. And a very hard place. Somewhere, if only he could find it, there had to be a solution, a compromise. *Guidance*, he thought. But he knew that God wasn't about to show him the way. Prayer, this time, was a dead connection.

He said, "I'll do it. You don't need to worry." Even as he committed himself, he was still frantically searching. How could he even *think* of betraying the Cause? He'd been raised with a belief in the sanctity of the Cause, just as he'd been brought up in the seminary to believe that God's authority was the only one. Little divisions of the heart. Pangs. If he couldn't get the weapons to Jig—and he was certain that that was out of the question now—then what small thing could he do to help the man? Think, Joseph. Think hard. There has to be a way.

"I'm not worried," Pagan said. He managed to keep the tension out of his voice. But he *was* concerned. When you backed a man into a corner, any man, there were sometimes reserves of surprising defiance. Was Joe going to find that nerve of resistance?

Tumulty sat down. He experienced a moment of calm. What he realized was that Jig, who had seen Frank Pagan before, was going to recognize the man, no matter Pagan's ridiculous old clothes and his unkempt hair. Jig was going to know.

Then what?

FIFTEEN

It was a cheap joint at the edge of the Interstate—unpainted cinderblock, a flamingo-colored neon sign with the words CAPITOL CITY MOTEL, a cracked swimming pool, drained for the winter. Fitzjohn walked round the pool, Waddell in tow. He paused when they reached the diving board. On the other side of the pool was the motel bar, where Rorke and McGrath had gone for a drink. Seamus Houlihan was up in his room—resting, he'd said. Seamus always looked as if he were carrying the bloody world on his shoulders and enjoying its weight regardless.

The five merry men, Fitzjohn thought. He heard Rorke's weird laughter float out of the bar. It had the staccato quality of a pneumatic drill. Fitzjohn put his hands in the pockets of his pants and shivered in the night wind. The lights that hung around the entrance to the bar gave the place all the cheer of a pauper's Christmas.

Waddell said, "I suppose you'll be leaving tomorrow, Fitz."

Fitzjohn nodded. "After I drive you to Tarrytown, I'm going home to New Jersey. That's my arrangement."

Waddell raised his sharp little face and smiled. "Back to the family, eh?"

"Back to the family," Fitzjohn said.

"You'll be looking forward to it, I expect."

"You don't know how much."

Waddell moved to the rim of the pool. He made a funny little plunging gesture with his hands, then stepped back. "I had a wife and a kid once," he said. "About ten years ago. We had a small house in Ballysillen. I was second engineer on a ship at that time. The day they died I was on board a Liberian vessel called the *Masurado,* somewhere in the Gulf of Oman. I'm working in the engine room when the captain himself comes down to see me. He says to me he just received a message. My wife and kid are dead." Waddell's voice was very flat, unemotional.

"What happened was they got burned to death," he went on. "They were trapped inside the house when some soldiers and the local IRA started a gun battle. Snipers everywhere. Explosions. Somehow the house started to burn. Nobody ever told me who was responsible for that. I don't suppose it matters much."

"I'm sorry," Fitzjohn said. Another waste, another tragedy in the ongoing horror that was Ulster. He wondered how Waddell coped with the pain.

"It's a fucking long time ago." Waddell looked very sad as he turned his face to Fitzjohn. "It's best to bury it."

"Yes," Fitzjohn said.

Waddell ran the back of his hand over his lips. "About a month after it happened, I ran into Seamus Houlihan. I'd known him for years. I told him about the wife and kid. You know what Seamus did?"

Fitzjohn shook his head.

"Seamus went out that same night and killed two men. One was a high-up in the IRA, a man called Costello. The other was a British soldier. Seamus said it was retribution."

"Retribution?" Fitzjohn asked.

"It was to help even the score, you see." Waddell reached out to touch the diving board. "I never asked him to do anything like that, you understand." He took a cigarette out of his coat pocket, a Woodbine. He lit it in a furtive way, cupping both hands against the wind. "I always felt I owed him something for that."

Fitzjohn thought it was a strange kind of debt, a murderous obligation. "You didn't ask him to do anything for you, so how can you owe him?"

Waddell shrugged. "It's the way I see it." He sucked the Woodbine deeply in the manner of a man who has spent time deprived of tobacco. "I know Seamus and I know what his faults are, you see. But he's been a bloody good friend to me."

The emphasis was on "bloody," Fitzjohn thought. He wondered how many victims Houlihan had left strewn behind him. He had the sudden desire to leave Albany tonight and get away from the madman and whatever atrocities he was planning, because he was afraid. Maybe, after the work he'd done finding the airfield and the long hours spent driving the Ryder, Houlihan would be understanding. Jesus, that was a contradiction in terms! Houlihan would probably shoot him if he mentioned anything about leaving. On the other hand, he didn't exactly relish the idea of driving this gang to Tarrytown and discovering there that he'd outlived his usefulness, that he was destined to stare down the barrel of Seamus's gun. He had no intention of being pressed into premature retirement.

"What are the plans after Tarrytown?" he asked Waddell.

Waddell said, "That's not for me to say."

Fitzjohn thought about the crates inside the rental truck. In a hesitant way he asked, "Don't you get sick of it all, John? Don't you want an end to all the killing?" As soon as he'd phrased the questions, he wondered if Waddell would report them to his bloody good friend. Houlihan, a product of Protestant Belfast street gangs and Armagh Jail, which was where Fitzjohn had first encountered him, would regard such questions as a sign of unacceptable weakness. In Houlihan's world, chaos and violence were moral constants, necessities.

Waddell didn't answer immediately. He tossed his Woodbine away and turned up the collar of his coat. "Sometimes I think a peaceful life would be very pleasant," he said. "I suppose that's what you've got for yourself in New Jersey?"

Fitzjohn said that it was.

"Then why did you agree to be a part of all this if your life's so bloody wonderful?" Waddell asked.

Fitzjohn answered quietly. "You know what they say, John. Once you're in the FUV, you're always in."

A slight despair touched Fitzjohn just then. Here he was in the United States of America, a new life, and when he'd been asked to do a job for the FUV he'd jumped at it without consideration, like a man programmed into the ruts of old hatreds. He hadn't known the nature of the job, nor had he ever stopped to ask. It was only now that he truly realized the FUV was the culmination of feelings he should have left behind in Northern Ireland, otherwise he was doing nothing more than hauling used baggage into his new life.

He wondered if he could sneak away in the night, if he could wait until the others were asleep and then vanish swiftly. Maybe he could hitch a ride to Albany County Airport and fly back to New Jersey. Home. He'd forget he ever participated in any of this insanity. He didn't belong with people like Seamus Houlihan these days, or with thugs like Rorke and McGrath. They stood for the old world and the senselessness of a war whose roots were buried in a history that should have been forgotten long ago. He turned the prospect of departure around in his mind. A risky business. Maybe. But waiting might prove fatal.

A movement on the balcony caught his eye and he looked up. Houlihan was standing there, legs apart, hands on the rail.

"Waddell, Fitz," Houlihan called down. "I'd like to see you and the others in my room right away."

"Right, Seamus," Waddell replied.

Fitzjohn started toward the stairway, looking back once at the empty swimming pool. He wondered how long Houlihan had been standing on the balcony and whether he'd heard any of the conversation with Waddell.

ROSCOMMON, NEW YORK

Patrick Cairney had drunk just a little more of his father's brandy than he intended. When he went inside his bedroom and lay down, his head was spinning. He didn't close his eyes because that way the spinning was worse. He had to sit up and concentrate on something inside the room, an object he could focus on until the nausea had passed. He stared hard at his canvas bag, which sat locked on the dresser. After dinner there had been several toasts proposed by Harry. Sentimental toasts, tributes to the composers of the Proclamation of the Irish Republic written at Easter, 1916, at the time of the Rising.

All Harry's heroes had been signatories of the Proclamation, and he could recite the entire document by heart. Certain words came back to Cairney. *Supported by her exiled children in America . . . Ireland strikes in full confidence of victory. . . . We pledge our lives and the lives of our comrades-in-arms to the cause of Irish freedom. . . . We* pledge our lives, Cairney thought, though not necessarily our brains or our skills. During the toasts he'd fought with the urge to silence Harry and stuff the empty words down his throat and tell him how little significance they had, how meaningless they really were. This streak of cruelty inside himself wasn't surprising, but what astounded him was the forceful way it had suddenly risen. Harry's beatific expression, the way he sniffed as he recited the sacrosanct old sentiments—Patrick Cairney despised it all, the facile nature of Harry's words, the easy emotions. He despised a life given over to talk, endless talk, and no action.

The Cause needed action. Not the empty rattling of old men.

He let his thoughts drift back to the beginning, the very beginning, when he had first come to Finn's attention. In those days he'd gone around the fringes of clandestine political groups in Dublin as if his head were going to explode. Here he was in a divided country where injustice was a commonplace event and, if you excluded the mad bombers and the angry snipers, nothing much was being done to correct the situation and get the English out. Here he was on an island whose northern section was constantly on the edge of apocalypse. When he'd visited Ulster he'd been sickened by the flames and the raddled buildings and the rubber bullets fired by British soldiers and the checkpoints and the Saracen cars and tanks and the kids who mindlessly parroted a hatred they had inherited, a whole desolate world galaxies removed from Harry's green dreams that had been spoon-fed to him throughout childhood. And he'd been impatient back then, insanely so, driven by an urge to transform his emotions into direct physical action. People were suspicious of him because he was American. Because he hadn't been born and raised in Ireland. He wanted to tell them he knew more about Ireland and its history than any of them.

But it wasn't until he'd gravitated into Finn's orbit that the opportunity came up to serve the Cause. He remembered now the precise moment in Glasnevin Cemetery when Finn had given him a gun and a mission to accomplish. It was the most perfect moment of his life. He'd stepped through a door into a different world where justice was something you pursued outside courts of law, where you moved beyond the realms of the Queen's laws and her lawyers and judges, those bewigged fools whose only interest lay in the maintenance of a status quo that had always protected them and their privileges. You created your own justice. And it was fair, the way it was supposed to be.

Finn said once, *It's a monastic life this. There's no glamour and no comfort. You can't have a family and kids. You can't hold down some regular job. You're always going to be standing outside of things, and every bloody shadow you see will make you wonder if there's a gun concealed in it. You want that, Jig?*

Yes. Yes, he wanted that. He wanted that the way he had never wanted anything else. He had given up his life for the Cause. *But where would the Cause be if he didn't get that missing money back?*

Now he pushed the window open, hoping the cold air would clear his brain. Four brandies had brought him to this condition, but then he wasn't accustomed to alcohol. He looked out at the shadowy waters of Roscommon Lake. The night was intensely cold, moonless. He drew the window shut. He was suddenly anxious to get away from Roscommon, anxious for action, anxious to locate Finn's money.

He was thirsty. He opened the door and gazed down the flight of stairs to the first floor. The house was silent and dark, save for a thin light that burned dimly somewhere below. He moved toward the stairs and went down. He stepped inside the large kitchen—stainless-steel surfaces and high-tech appliances, he noticed, which meant Celestine had redecorated the room since Kathleen's time, when the kitchen had been chintzy and floral. He found a glass and pressed it against the ice dispenser, then he filled it with water from the faucet. He drained the glass quickly, and stood with his back pressed against the sink. Once, this kitchen had been the warm heart of the house. Now it seemed more like a transplant, a triumph of the new technology. What did it tell him about the difference between Kathleen and Celestine? he wondered.

He became conscious of a voice drifting very faintly toward him through the open door. It was Celestine's. For a moment he wondered if she and Harry had come back downstairs for a nightcap, but as he strained to listen he realized he heard only one voice. He set his glass down inside the sink and went out of the kitchen. There was a thin light that burned through the crack of a doorway at the end of the hall. He moved toward it, even as he realized that he should have gone the other way to the stairs and back up to his bedroom. This was none of his business. Nothing that happened at Roscommon had anything to do with him.

He stopped outside the sitting room. Celestine was standing with her back to the door, a telephone receiver held in place between shoulder and jaw. She wore a blue silk robe that shimmered in the light from a nearby lamp and in one hand she held a glass of whiskey. Cairney heard her say, "I'm not making it up," and then she turned around and saw him in the doorway, and her expression was one of restrained surprise, almost as though she'd expected to find him standing there. She put the receiver down, perhaps a little too quickly, and the first thing Cairney thought was that she had a lover somewhere, somebody she talked to when Harry was fast asleep upstairs. He didn't like the idea, but it made some kind of sense. How could Harry satisfy her at his age and in his health? Why *wouldn't* she look elsewhere for consolation? *I'm not making it up.* He wondered what she was referring to.

"I spy," she said lightly, like a child involved in a game of hide-and-seek.

He pushed the door open. "I didn't mean to creep up on you."

"Enter." She gestured with her glass. It was an expansive motion, a little careless. She was slightly drunk. Cairney had a small insight into her life. A beautiful young woman married to a man forty years older than she was, probably lonely in the isolation of Roscommon—what was there to do at times but blur her life with liquor? And perhaps a lover she met now and again.

"Harry's physician," she said, pointing to the phone. "I make my daily progress report. Dutifully."

Patrick Cairney wondered if that was a lie. He'd become so good at telling them himself, he should have been expert at detecting them in others, but he wasn't. She had hung up so quickly, though, without any farewell, and it was so late in the evening for a routine medical report, that he assumed it wasn't Harry's physician on the other end of the line. He watched her go to an armchair and sit, crossing her legs. Between the folds of the robe a stretch of pale thigh was visible briefly before she rearranged the garment.

"Want a drink?" she asked.

"I've had too much already."

"People talk about the Irish Problem, but they miss the point," she said. She indicated her drink. "*This* is the Irish Problem. Jameson's elixir of life."

Cairney smiled. Maybe he was mistaken. Maybe there wasn't any man in Celestine's life other than Harry. He was so accustomed to paranoid thinking, to looking for levels of meaning beneath the superficial, that it was difficult to regard things in any normal fashion. An assassin's habit. You came to think that every situation was fraught with hidden significances. Nothing was every ordinary, nothing innocent.

Celestine put her glass down on the coffee table. She let her hands fall into her lap. "Why don't you sit down, Patrick?"

He didn't move. "I was thinking of going back upstairs. I need some sleep."

She turned her face slowly toward him. At a certain angle, her beauty seemed to have been sculpted in delicate detail. The fine mouth, the perfectly straight nose, the strong jaw that suggested a streak of determination. "Harry told me he wanted you to go into politics."

"He had some notion I'd follow him into the Senate, I guess."

"Why didn't you?"

"I'm not a committee man," he answered. "I don't work well in collaboration with others."

"A loner. Or was it rebellion against Daddy?"

Cairney shrugged. "Maybe both."

Celestine reached out for her glass. She raised it to her lips but didn't drink. "Why archaeology?" She said this last word in a manner that might almost have been mocking, as if she couldn't bring herself to believe that he was really what he said he was.

"Why not?"

"It just seems so quaint, that's all. I have this image of you in khaki shorts and a pith helmet, directing a bunch of Arabs to dig holes in the sand. You never wanted to be famous like Harry? You never wanted your name to become a household word?"

"Never." Cairney moved toward the door. The security of the unlit hallway. *I never wanted to be anything like my father.*

"Why is it I always get the impression you're running away from me? What is it? Don't you care for my company?" she asked.

"I'm just tired."

She stood up. She drained her glass, set it down. "Don't go. Stay a little longer."

Her hands were stretched out toward him, and the expression on her face was one he couldn't quite read. A look of anxiety? He wasn't certain. But he recognized one thing beyond any doubt—his compass was going crazy again. He couldn't cross the space between himself and Celestine, couldn't possibly move toward her and clasp those hands in his own. Couldn't touch her. And then he thought: *I could, I could go to her so goddam easily.* He felt like a man flirting with the notion of his own ruin. Yet it appealed, the whole idea caught his fancy. *There, Harry. I had your wonderful wife. How does that affect your gorgeous dreams? Your infallibly beautiful wife and your cozy little world at Roscommon where you live your life falsely?*

He stared at her. He imagined how readily his father must have fallen in love with this woman. He could see the old man losing his heart like a bird deliriously set free.

"Please stay," she said.

He looked at the paleness of her shoulders and the way the silk robe hung loosely against her body.

"You're leaving in the morning, I understand," she said.

Cairney nodded his head. Why was he still here in this room, this danger zone? He had no business in this place.

Her hands were still held out to him. "I have the feeling you won't be coming back."

"Maybe," he said.

She lowered her hands slowly to her side. "You're afraid of me," she said.

He wanted to say he was more afraid of himself than anything else. But he didn't speak.

"You don't have to be," she said. "Why are you always so twitchy around me?"

"I didn't notice."

"I come near you, you jump. I ought to get one of those little bells lepers used to carry. I'd ring it whenever I moved within ten feet of you."

Cairney pressed his fingertips to his eyelids to ease his headache. Harry's wife, he thought. Keep remembering that.

"I make you tense," she said.

"No—"

"Look at yourself, Patrick. You can't wait to get away from me, can you? Can't wait to hurry upstairs to your little bedroom." She picked up her empty glass and sighed. She looked very fragile just then. "I'm sorry. I shouldn't be talking to you like this. Forget I ever said anything. I drink too much sometimes and say things I don't mean, that's all. My mouth has a mind of its own. Change the subject."

He leaned against the wall. "I think you're unhappy," he said.

Jesus, it was the wrong thing to say. It was provocative, which meant it needed explanation. He should have simply said good night and gone upstairs, but now, in a sense, he'd committed himself.

Celestine poured herself another shot of Jameson's. "Is that how you see me?"

"I think so."

"And I thought I kept it hidden."

"Not very well."

She passed her glass from one hand to the other. "Certain days. Certain moods. I'm not unhappy all the time. You catch me on a bad day, that's all."

"Maybe it's Roscommon at winter. I remember how it used to drive me stir-crazy as a kid."

"Maybe." She sipped the whiskey. "I try to be cheerful for your father's sake, but it isn't easy. Sometimes I feel I've buried myself here in a large gray tomb and my whole life's come to a dead stop. But this is his home. How can I tell him I can't stand it here at times? How can I say that to him? It's not his fault I get into these moods. He tries very hard to make me happy." She paused. "I didn't use to drink this way."

Cairney said, "When Harry's better, why don't you get him to take you on a trip? Maybe you could talk him into a Caribbean cruise on that boat of his."

"I get seasick and I don't like ocean cruises," she said. She raised the glass to her mouth and then, changing her mind, stuck it down on the table. "The last time we went anywhere I kept throwing up all the way from Maine to Saint-Barthélmy. I don't *want* to be unhappy. It seems so goddam ungrateful somehow."

"Harry wouldn't think so. You only have to tell him you'd like a change of scenery, that's all."

She was quiet for a very long time before she said, "I took a trip to Boston last fall. Alone. The whole New England in fall bit. I drove through Maine and Vermont and Connecticut. Harry understood I needed to get away. I missed him, so I came home after a couple of days. But I need more than just getting away, Patrick. I don't think a change of scenery's going to cut it."

She came very close to him now, looking at him in a searching way. He felt the air around him change. It was suddenly charged with electricity. He thought, *No, it's wrong, it doesn't happen like this*, but he didn't move out of her way.

"There," she said. "You're doing it again."

"Doing what again?"

"Looking tense."

She placed one hand against the side of his face. Her flesh was surprisingly cool. There was a fragrance from her skin suggestive of lime. Cairney didn't move. He shut his eyes. He felt the silk of her robe against his arms, the pressure of her small breasts against his chest, her hair upon the side of his face. He expected it, he knew it was coming, and he knew he ought to resist it, but the kiss took him by surprise anyhow, the movement of her lips against his and the way her fingers touched the back of his neck and the contact of her tongue against his. Dear God, it was easy to drift out into a dream, into an unreal world where there were no rules to govern this kind of situation, a place where Celestine was a perfect stranger to him.

Suddenly she stepped back from him. "Forgive me," she said. "I didn't mean that to happen. I'm more drunk than I thought."

He opened his eyes. The yearning he felt was intolerable.

"I'm sorry" was all he could think to say, cursing himself for his own weakness. He heard one of Finn's old warnings. *If you lose concentration, you're history.* He remembered the day Finn had said this. They'd been walking together close to the Martello Tower in Sandycove, where James Joyce had once lived. He remembered the seriousness in Finn's voice. *Concentration will save your life one day.*

He turned away from her and went quickly out into the hallway. What the hell was he *doing*? What was he playing at? He climbed the stairs and when he reached the landing he stopped, listening to the silences of the big house all around him. He had a driving urge to go back down again. Instead he went inside his bedroom and closed the door.

He checked his wristwatch. It was almost midnight. In a few hours he'd be gone from Roscommon. He'd be out of Celestine Cairney's life.

He took off his clothes and lay down with his hands tucked behind his head and just before he drifted into sleep it all came back to him, the touch of silk, her scent, the feel of her hair and the intimate warmth of her mouth. He realized, with an awareness that was painfully sharp and very depressing, that he desired the woman as much as he'd ever desired anyone.

He wanted his father's wife.

NEW YORK CITY

Joseph X. Tumulty stepped inside his office. He saw Zuboric dozing in an armchair. The FBI man opened his eyes as soon as Tumulty came in and squinted into the light from the desk lamp.

"What time is it?" Zuboric asked.

"Twenty past midnight." Tumulty moved to his desk and sat down. He was glad to notice that his hands didn't tremble, that he'd somehow managed to control his nervousness. The idea that had come to him was inspired less by God than his own desperation. But he was in a position where the question *Why not?* didn't merit an answer. He simply had to do *something*.

"Is Pagan downstairs?" Zuboric asked.

"Yes." Tumulty thought of Frank Pagan, dressed like a hobo and propped against the kitchen wall downstairs. When Tumulty had been shelling eggs to scramble for the morning breakfast, he'd been aware of Pagan watching him intently, his eyes two keen scanning instruments that constantly measured and analyzed, studying the other men in the big room as they spread mattresses on the floor and started settling down for the night.

Tumulty leafed through a variety of invoices. He was conscious of the FBI agent observing him.

He said to Zuboric, "Paperwork. I used to imagine God's work would have nothing to do with bureaucracy."

Zuboric grunted. He wasn't very interested.

Tumulty picked up a pen and began to make calculations on a scratch pad. When he'd written a column of figures that were utterly meaningless, he glanced at Zuboric again. The agent was looking at him blankly.

"I'm hopeless at math," Tumulty said, in what he assumed was a lighthearted kind of voice. "I need a calculator. But all I could probably afford is an abacus, and I don't know how to work those things."

The agent looked glum and uncomfortable in the armchair. Tumulty scribbled again. He hoped he looked like a man struggling over figures that would never add up no matter how hard he worked. He tore off the top sheet and began to write on the one underneath, conscious all the time of Zuboric watching him.

"I don't know how the Chinese manage," the priest said, smiling.

Was this silly banter convincing the agent? It was hard to tell anything from Zuboric's face, except that the man was vigilant.

Tumulty pressed the pen down on the new sheet of paper. He would have to do this quickly. He muttered in the manner of somebody calculating as he wrote, but what he set down on the paper had nothing to do with sums of money. He ripped the sheet from the pad and crumpled it, setting it to one side. Then he tossed his pen down and stood up, scooping up the crumpled paper and smuggling it into the pocket of his pants. He felt pretty damn good, but was he going to get away with it?

"Ah, well," he said. "I'm too tired to go on."

He was sure Zuboric hadn't noticed anything, hadn't seen the writing on the piece of paper, hadn't caught him slipping the sheet into his pocket. The real problem would come later when he tried to pass the paper to Jig. But at least he'd committed himself to a course of action, a move designed to appease his conscience. Perhaps it was possible, after all, to serve both God and the Cause provided you fudged round some delicate ethical questions. And if God disapproved, Joseph Tumulty trusted that he could win forgiveness somehow.

At best, the piece of paper would be helpful to Jig. At worst, like an atheist on his deathbed turning to prayer, Tumulty felt he had covered all his bets.

ALBANY, NEW YORK

Houlihan's allocation of rooms at the Capitol City Motel meant that Fitzjohn shared with Waddell, while Rorke and McGrath were together in the next room. Only Houlihan had a place to himself. Fitzjohn wished it had been otherwise. It was going to be difficult to leave because he wasn't sure that Waddell was sound asleep yet. Fitzjohn turned over on his narrow bed and looked across the room at his companion. Waddell's mouth was open and his eyes were closed, but every now and then he'd mumble and change the position of his body.

Earlier, Houlihan had convened a brief meeting in which he talked about an early morning departure. The destination was White Plains, New York. He wanted everybody to be up and ready to leave by six A.M., which caused Rorke to grumble briefly. Houlihan had pointed out that this was no bloody vacation they were on and when he said six A.M. sharp he meant *sharp*. After that, Rorke had been very quiet.

"What's in White Plains?" Fitzjohn had asked.

"What does it matter to you, Fitz? You get off in Tarrytown, don't you?" Houlihan had pronounced the word Tarrytown as though it were a bad taste in his mouth. "You're going to be out of it. You've done your work. And we're all grateful."

Houlihan hadn't looked remotely grateful, Fitzjohn thought. There was something just a little guarded in the man's eyes. The expression had struck a chord of concern inside Fitzjohn, and now he was glad he'd committed himself to leaving. If he didn't go now, he knew he wouldn't get another chance. The prospect of dying in Tarrytown, or anywhere else for that matter, didn't enthrall him. And he didn't trust Houlihan to let him go with a cheery farewell. Cheery farewells were not exactly Houlihan's style. The best you could find to say about Seamus was that he wasn't big on the social graces.

Fitzjohn sat upright. He stared at Waddell, whose hands were limp on his chest. Waddell's breathing was regular and deep, but he still made occasional sounds suggestive of someone deprived of oxygen on the ocean floor. Fitzjohn moved from the bed. He went to the closet and very quietly took out his holdall. Waddell chose that moment to kick his legs so abruptly that the blanket flew from his bed.

Fitzjohn saw Waddell sit up, grope for the blanket like a blind man, then draw it over his body once more. For a long time Fitzjohn didn't move. He listened to the sound of Waddell's shallow breathing. When he was absolutely certain the man was asleep, Fitzjohn reached for the door handle and turned it gently, then he stepped out onto the balcony. He noticed that the window of Houlihan's room was dark as he moved cautiously toward the stairs.

The motel bar was still open below. He turned up the collar of his coat against the biting chill of the night air, then he started to descend slowly. He looked toward the swimming pool. A cat slunk around the rim, then was gone with a rattle of leaves into the shrubbery. The whole night around him seemed like some large dark satellite dish that caught every noise, every movement, and amplified them.

At the bottom of the stairs he shifted his bag from one hand to the other. Now he had only to cross the pool area and he was gone.

He moved away from the stairs, passed the door of the bar, walked around the edge of the empty pool. He could see the road beyond the pink neon sign. The highway to freedom. New Jersey and home. He'd be safe there. Nobody would bother him again. Nobody would come looking for him.

He slid between a couple of parked cars and reached the spot where earlier he'd parked the Ryder truck. It looked luminously yellow under the pale lamps of the motel. Grinding his teeth nervously, he started to pick up his pace, walking away from the truck and heading for the road.

"What's your hurry, Fitz?"

Fitzjohn froze. He heard the noise of something inside him slipping and crumbling.

Houlihan climbed down from the cab of the Ryder. Fitzjohn, filled with bottomless dread, watched him. It had never occurred to him that Houlihan would be in the truck. Such a possibility hadn't crossed his mind. But then he hadn't thought *any* of this through. He'd been impetuous instead of careful. Fool.

"I just came down to fetch a map," Houlihan said. "Wasn't that a stroke of good fortune?"

Fitzjohn's tongue was cold lead in his mouth. He wanted to speak, couldn't think of anything to say. The dread was worse now. It was a sensation into which he sank like a man swallowed by swamp. As he looked at Houlihan he was conscious of the highway at his back. He could run. He could just drop the bloody bag and turn and run because the darkness out there would cover him.

"I thought you seemed a wee bit uncomfortable with all this." Houlihan, smiling, made a gesture with his hand. "Marriage does that to some people. Makes them forget where they started out from. Puts soft ideas into their heads. You're not the man you used to be, Fitz. I've been thinking that ever since Quebec. You're soft. It's amazing you lasted this long."

Fitzjohn had never felt this paralyzed in his life. Why the hell couldn't he *run*? "This isn't what you think, Seamus."

"No? I see my man leaving in the middle of the night with his bag packed and all—what am I supposed to think?"

Fitzjohn put the bag down. It occurred to him that a swift movement might take Houlihan off guard, a sudden kick, a punch. It might buy him a little extra time. The problem was how to get within striking range of Houlihan without making him suspicious. If it came down to a fair test of strength, Fitzjohn knew it wouldn't take Seamus long to overpower him. The key lay in speed and accuracy and surprise.

"Are you going to tell me you didn't like this fine motel, Fitz? Eh? Are you going to tell me you decided to find yourself something more comfortable?"

Fitzjohn moved nearer to Houlihan. One swing, he thought. One almighty swing. "Let me explain," he heard himself say.

Houlihan laughed. "Save your fucking breath."

Fitzjohn lunged. It was a sad effort. Houlihan sidestepped and tripped him and Fitzjohn went sprawling, colliding with the side of the truck. Dizzy, he slid to the ground and lay there looking up at the other man. Somehow his mouth had filled with blood. He must have split his gum when he hit the truck.

"You don't cross me," Houlihan said. "Nobody crosses me, Fitz."

Houlihan bent down. He had his gun in his hand now. With the other hand he took a length of wire from the pocket of his seaman's jacket.

"Get inside the truck, Fitz. I think we ought to discuss your future in private."

Fitzjohn pushed himself to a standing position. He couldn't take his eyes away from the wire in Seamus's hand. "I don't want to go into the truck," he said.

"The way I see it, you don't have a fucking choice, Fitz."

ROSCOMMON, NEW YORK

Celestine stepped inside the bedroom, which was dark and cold, and she stood motionless until her eyes had become accustomed to the absence of light. Now she could make out the window and the moonless sky beyond and the branches of black trees. Her body was chill under the silk robe and her nipples hard and there were goose bumps all over her flesh. She went toward the bed, where she hesitated again. Then, reaching out, she caught the sheet and drew it back quietly. He didn't move. She could make out the dim shape of his naked body. He lay fast asleep in a fetal position.

She sat on the edge of the mattress. With the tips of her fingers she traced a line on his thigh and then moved her hand, light as air, to the flat hard surface of his belly. It had been too long a time since she'd touched flesh as firm as her own, and it took her breath away.

She shut her eyes and remembered the kiss, wondering if her drunken act had really fooled him. She'd been drinking, but not enough to make her do anything she hadn't wanted to. She ran her fingers up his side, then pressed them softly on his lips, feeling the warmth of his breath. She lowered her face and brushed her lips against the curve of his hip and the desire she felt was unbearable, as if all her self-awareness had crystallized in this one thing, a beautiful naked young man stretched out before her.

"Wake," she whispered. She leaned close to his face and ran her tongue in the folds of his ear, whispering over and over, "Wake, wake."

He stirred and moaned quietly and she drew her hand down to his cock, which was hard almost as soon as she began to stroke it. She could feel the veins beneath the skin. She touched the tip, the opening, which was moist under her finger.

"There's nothing wrong," she said. "There's nothing wrong in any of this. It's right, Patrick. It's very right. You know that, don't you?"

He turned his body, lying now on the flat of his back. She felt his hands press down on her shoulders, as if he wanted to force her head into his groin, force her to take him in her mouth, but he didn't need force because she was more than willing. She licked the pubic hair that grew up around the navel and then she started to move her face down slowly, feeling his cock stiff against her cheek. She took strands of her hair and made a web around the penis, stroking it slowly, feeling it grow harder and harder as she touched it. She parted her lips and sucked him for a moment, then she drew her body up over his so that she was straddling him, climbing him, struggling out of her robe at the same time. She wanted all of him, wanted everything he could possibly give of his strength and his youth, she wanted to feel his mouth upon her cunt, and then she'd take him deep inside her, far into the privacy of herself where it was warm and black and nothing that lived in the outside world mattered.

She said his name over and over. It came to have a mystical sound the more she repeated it, the syllables of some magical ritual. She felt his lips against her navel, and she squeezed her eyes tightly shut because she was no longer interested in anything she might see in this dim bedroom. This was the world, here and now, this blind place where she burrowed and where her blood rushed.

And then he was limp and motionless and she thought he must

have come prematurely in his excitement, but that wasn't it because she didn't feel any wetness on her.

"What's wrong?"

He moved out from under her without saying anything. She reached over him and turned on the bedside lamp as he rolled away from her.

"What is it?" she asked.

He looked around for his robe, found it, put it on.

"Get dressed," he said. He picked up her blue silk robe from the floor and tossed it at her.

"Just like that?"

"Just like that, Celestine."

"What is it, Patrick? An attack of conscience?"

He turned his back on her, walked to the window, looked out. He was shaking his head.

"Look at me," she said.

She went to him, laid her face against his spine. He shivered.

"You think it's wrong, don't you?" she asked.

"I don't think it. I *know*," he replied. His voice was cold and life-less. "Why the hell did you marry him? That's what I don't understand."

"Because I love him."

"You'll pardon me if suddenly I find that hard to believe," Cairney said.

"I don't care what you believe! I love him as well as I can. Which is how he loves me, Patrick. *As well as he can.* And in certain departments that unfortunately isn't enough."

"You didn't think about that before, did you?"

She had a sense of her life pressing in on her, the barren trees of this huge estate, the unattractive waters of the lake, the forlornness of it all. "I didn't have choices, Patrick." She hadn't meant to utter this sentence. It was bound to puzzle him and she couldn't begin to explain. She drew her robe around her.

"You could have chosen *not* to marry him."

She shook her head. "It wasn't like that. You don't know what you're saying."

"Enlighten me then."

Celestine went toward the door, leaving Cairney's question un-answered. She turned and smiled at him. "It's in your eyes. It's in all your behavior since you came here. You want me. I want you. It's undeniable. So what happens next?"

"Nothing," Cairney said. "Nothing can happen."

"We'll see."

She went out of the room, closing the door quietly.

I T was one A.M. and bitterly cold when Patrick Cairney left the house and walked along the shore. He picked up stones and tossed them out across the water, listening to them hit out there in the darkness. He was angry with himself. He could make petty, unconvincing excuses—he was half asleep when he first felt Celestine touch him. He hadn't fully understood what she was doing and how he was responding because at first the experience had had the texture of a dream in which he had absolutely no control over events. Excuses, excuses. He couldn't brush aside the hard animal thing that possessed him or the amazing desire that had almost consumed him. He could wrestle it, certainly, but he couldn't pin it.

It was only a small consolation that he'd pulled himself back at the last possible moment when he'd encountered the weak phantom of his own conscience. His private policeman, the one that stopped the flow of traffic inside his head. But that was no consolation to him at all the more he thought about it. The desire was still there. The longing was still strong. His own sense of shame was intact. He picked up a heavy stone, turning it around in his hand, and he remembered her smell, the touch of her fingers on his body, her mouth. The clarity of the recollection shook him. What he suddenly wished for was another world, an alternative reality, in which Celestine wasn't his father's wife and Jig didn't exist. Wishing was a game for fools. It wasn't going to change the world. And he hadn't come to America to be embroiled in the sexual dissatisfactions of Celestine Cairney.

He took a deep breath of the cold air. There was a certain madness in the night, an insanity of the heart. He drew his arm back as far as it would go and released the stone and he heard it strike out in the middle of the lake. He wished sensations could be released as easily.

He turned from the lake and went back through the trees. He'd leave Roscommon tonight. He'd drive away now. It was the simplest solution he could think of. Distance was a benefactor. A salve.

Halfway back across the frozen lawn he stopped, looking up at the black house. Upstairs, a light was burning in one of the windows. It was the window of his own room. It could only mean that

Celestine had gone back in there. Suddenly he wasn't thinking about her anymore. He was thinking instead of the canvas bag with the cheap lock and Celestine's curiosity about the small wooden horse.

He hurried inside the house and climbed the stairs quickly. When he reached his own room he pushed the door open and stepped inside. The place was in blackness but he had an intuition that she'd been there only moments before. He switched on the bedside lamp. The room felt different to him, violated in some fashion, and yet nothing had been moved, nothing changed. The bag still sat on the dresser where he'd left it. He stepped closer to look at it. He took out the key from his pocket and turned it in the lock.

Nothing had been touched inside the bag. Nothing had been moved. The wooden horse, the passports, the clothing, everything was the same as it had been. He closed the bag, locked it, wondering about the fear he'd suddenly felt. What possible reason could Celestine have for going through his belongings anyway?

He turned to the bed, where a sheet of violet notepaper was propped against his pillow. This was the reason she'd come back to his room. To leave a message. He picked up the paper and read,

Next time

There wasn't going to be a next time, he thought.

He picked up his bag, stuffed the note inside his pocket, gazed at the rumpled bedsheets, which suggested a consummation rather than an interruption, then switched off the lamp. He made his way quietly down the stairs. Once outside, he walked in the direction of his rented Dodge.

He wouldn't be so careless in New York as he had been here at Roscommon. He wouldn't be so careless, in both heart and action, ever again.

SIXTEEN

NEW YORK CITY

Dressed in thrift-store garments, Frank Pagan woke in a cramped position, every muscle in his body locked. He opened his eyes and checked his watch. It was five-fifty A.M. and still dark, and he was propped up against the wall of the dining room in St. Finbar's Mission, where he had spent the most uncomfortable night of his life. He stared at the outlines of sleeping men who lay on mattresses all across the floor and he thought of how the entire night had been filled with the strangest sounds—men coughing, wheezing, snoring, wandering blindly around in a manner Pagan found vaguely menacing (he had an image at one point of somebody trying to cut his throat), men stumbling, cursing, spitting, striking matches for surreptitious cigarettes, men hacking their larynxes to shreds, men rattling while they slept as if marbles rolled back and forth in their rib cages, men crying out, sobbing, uttering incomprehensible phrases in the language of sleep. Once, Pagan had been startled into wakefulness by the cry *Don't leave me, Ma!* Now the air inside St. Finbar's was filled with the odor of tooth decay, gum disease, old booze, greasy clothing, yesterday's smoke, and the incongruous and almost shocking antiseptic scent of air deodorant that Joseph X. Tumulty, awake before anyone else, had sprayed through the room.

Pagan stood up and cautiously stretched. His first conscious thought was always of coffee.

He moved carefully around the mattresses and into the kitchen where he found a jar of instant Maxwell House. He boiled some water in a saucepan, poured it into a large mug, dumped in a tablespoon of the crystals, and sipped. The brew was as subtle as crank oil, but it had the effect of starting his heart.

Joseph Tumulty appeared in the doorway. He looked brisk and freshly showered, hair wet and eyes shining. The priest nodded to Pagan, then went to the refrigerator, where he removed a huge bowl of eggs ready for scrambling. Pagan, anxious about Joe's mood, his frame of mind, and the depth of his commitment when it came to fingering Jig, watched the priest carefully. He thought that Tumulty looked a little too composed, and he wondered why.

"Sleep well?" Pagan asked.

"Very." Tumulty set the bowl of eggs on the table. Then he laid out rashers of bacon, enough to feed an army. He struck a match and lit the burners on the huge stove. After he'd done this he took six loaves of bread from a bin and peeled the cellophane wrapping away.

"I couldn't get used to sharing my bedroom," Pagan said. Joe Tumulty had spent the night on a mattress by the door. "Especially with noisy strangers."

"I don't notice it anymore," Tumulty replied. "Besides, a lot of these men have become my best friends. They're a mixed crew, but you'll find that even the worst of them have some small redeeming quality that's worth exploring."

My best friends, Pagan thought. There was something about Joe Tumulty to admire. His dedication. His selflessness. He felt sorry that Joe had become ensnared in this whole affair. He could see how it happened—growing up in Ireland, listening to the legends, drifting into a cause almost before he had time to understand what he was doing.

"How many people do you get for breakfast?" Pagan asked.

"Fifty. Sixty. I've had as many as a hundred in here and as few as twenty-five."

"What time do you serve?"

"Seven."

Pagan drained his mug of coffee. "You haven't changed your mind?"

"About Jig?" Tumulty was pulling skillets and broiling pans out of a cupboard. "I gave you my word, didn't I?"

Pagan wondered about Tumulty's word. There had been a change, some small and almost indefinable alteration in the man, and it perplexed him. He watched the priest go about the business of preparing breakfast. There were undercurrents here that Pagan caught, only he couldn't understand them, couldn't arrange them into a meaningful alignment. Was Joe planning something? Had he come up with something devious?

"I'd be very unhappy if you backed out now," Pagan said. Which was to phrase it mildly. "We understand one another, don't we?"

"I think we do," Tumulty answered.

"There's no going back, Joe."

"I haven't changed my mind, Mr. Pagan. I'll do *exactly* as you asked."

There. A very tiny tone of irritation in Tumulty's voice. A quick little flash of light in the eyes that was almost a defiance. What are you up to? Pagan wondered. Maybe nothing. Maybe the expectation of Jig had simply raised Pagan's own anxieties and now he saw shadows where he should have seen only light.

Tumulty was laying out slices of bread in a tray. Pagan wandered around the kitchen.

"Jig might not come today," Tumulty said. "Nothing's certain. He might not even choose to come at mealtime, in which case my saying the grace you want me to say is going to sound very strange."

"He's going to think mealtime is the safest time. In Jig's trade, crowds mean security."

Tumulty looked up from the tray of bread. "Shouldn't you be out there at a table, Mr. Pagan? I don't allow my customers inside the kitchen. You'll stand out like a sore thumb."

Pagan walked into the dining room. Men were waking, sitting on their beds or struggling to their feet, folding the mattresses away, stashing pillows inside the cupboards that lined the walls. There was a great deal of throat clearing and hawking and already the air was thick with cigarette smoke. Pagan sat down at an empty table and took a very crumpled cigarette out of his coat pocket, lighting it and coughing in what he hoped was an authentic way. He looked around the room, watching men stagger into the emptiness of a new day that was going to be exactly like the one before. The debris of the Great Society. It was odd that in the richest country on the planet, and not very far from Wall Street, where the great money machine cranked daily, men were forced to eat and sleep in a slough like St. Finbar's. Pagan's old socialism found such a contrast inhuman. What democracy and capitalism really needed, he thought, was a conscience. In a world like that, though, pigs could fly.

He put out his cigarette and thought about Artie Zuboric sitting upstairs in Tumulty's office, then about the two agents on Canal Street. Orson Cone was located on the roof across the street. Tyson Bruno sat inside an all-night coffee hangout on the corner. Everything was in place, everything was set. It only needed Jig to step into this room for the picture to be complete. Pagan took a deep breath. Something troubled him, something he couldn't quite define. A sensation of unease. He felt enmeshed by two different strands of spider-webbing. One, sticky and mysterious, led back to Ivor the Terrible and his enigmatic purpose in New York. The other was directly linked to Joseph X. Tumulty and that quietly upbeat mood of his.

Pagan shook his head. He couldn't allow himself any kind of misgiving. He had no room in his head for anything else except Jig. He stared in the direction of the kitchen. Tumulty turned to look at him.

The priest smiled and winked, then went back work.

The smile was one thing, Pagan thought. The wink was quite another. How the fuck could Joe Tumulty, who was on the point of betraying a man, look so bloody secretive and confident?

PATRICK CAIRNEY left his rented Dodge in an underground parking lot at Broadway and Grand. Every mile he'd traveled from Roscommon had taken him farther from Celestine and closer to his own purpose, and so he'd driven at speeds far in excess of the limit, a curious adrenaline rushing through him. He realized he could put Celestine out of his mind, and all the turmoil she caused, only if he didn't forget—even for a fraction of time—that he was Jig and Jig had only one reason for being in America.

What Celestine had accomplished was the arousal of an appetite he couldn't afford to have. She'd succeeded in breaking his concentration, diffusing his energies. It was beyond the consideration of any morality now, beyond the ugly idea that what had almost happened between him and Celestine was akin to some kind of incest. It came down to something more practical, the unsettling realization of a weakness inside himself, an odd awareness like something left over from another life. He needed strength, singularity of purpose, total focus. He had no use for the distraction of a beautiful young woman locked in a frustrating marriage to an unhealthy old man. What he really sought was that ideal state for a man who had purposely chosen a lonely life—immunity against feelings and the confusion they produced.

When you had that kind of immunity, you had control. Over your urges, your flaws, your limitations. Over yourself.

He'd stopped briefly near Peekskill, changing his clothes in a public rest room. Now he wore the shabby coat and shapeless flannels he'd worn on his first visit to St. Finbar's, and, as he emerged from the parking lot, he had the appearance of a deadbeat, even to the fashion in which he walked—unsteadily, like a drunk whose whole mind is consumed by the idea of the next drink. He felt comfortable in disguise. He liked the idea of melting into any background he chose. Only at Roscommon had his disguise felt awkward. It was increasingly difficult to be Patrick Cairney, Harry's boy, the kid who lived in the sad shadows of the Senator.

When he turned onto Canal Street it was barely daylight, a somber morning with a scavenging wind pushing itself through the gulleys of Manhattan. He shuffled along, a pitiful figure to anyone who observed him. But this was New York and nobody who passed paid him any attention other than the cursory one of steering away from his path. He paused to look at himself in the window of a store. Almost perfect. The oversized coat concealed the muscularity of his body and the gray flannel shirt, worn outside the pants, hid the money belt. Only the face and hands bothered him. Too clean. He stepped into an alley and plunged his hands inside a trash can, bringing out an assortment of garbage. Damp newspapers were best for what he wanted because the ink came off on his fingers and he could rub it lightly over his face. When he came out of the alley back into Canal Street his face was smudged and his hands black.

It was about six blocks to St. Finbar's. He crossed Centre Street, then he stopped. He bent to tie his lace. It was more than a matter of being vigilant now. He had to listen to his own keen instincts and keep his eyes on the internal compass. There were factors involved he didn't like. For one thing, he was uncertain of Tumulty. Had the priest obtained the weapons yet? Or had he collapsed under pressure? For another, there was the distinct possibility that Frank Pagan was still around. Cairney felt he was weighing intangibles, like a man placing feathers on scales that didn't register.

He continued to the next corner. Carefully, his eyes swept along Canal Street. Among the parked vehicles there was none that immediately suggested the presence of the FBI. This meant nothing, though. It might only indicate that agents had taken the trouble to conceal themselves more thoroughly in the neighborhood. He had the feeling he was walking through a minefield. A man with few choices. He needed the weapons. Even more, he needed information from Tumulty. A name, an address, anything at all that would lead him in the direction of the stolen money. If Tumulty let him down on that score, where else could he possibly turn? He'd go back to Ireland with nothing achieved. He'd be letting Padraic Finn down, which was something he hadn't ever done. Something he intended never to do.

He kept moving.

Outside the entrance to St. Finbar's there were half a dozen or so derelicts standing on the steps. A faint aroma of fried food drifted toward Cairney, and he stopped again. He had an inherent suspicion of anything that looked normal, the way St. Finbar's did right now. He might have been staring at a painting whose detail seemed bland and absolutely right, but at the same time this very banality suggested a sinister occurrence just under the surface.

He scanned the parked cars again, then the windows of the street, rooftops, doorways, but he saw nothing out of the ordinary. Swaying like a man who had just stepped out of a wrecked train, he kept walking. When he reached the steps he paused. He stuffed his hands in the pockets of his coat and glanced quickly at the faces around him. They were stunned, glazed by defeat. One or two had the desperate hardened look of men who have had a lifetime of crime imposed upon them. Cairney felt a kind of affinity for them.

"What time's breakfast here?" he asked.

One of the men, a gnarled character with a silvery beard, said "Seven. If you turn up at seven-oh-five, you miss grace. Don't matter none. You eat anyways."

Cairney peered inside the dining room. He saw groups of men at tables, but no sign of Tumulty.

"Religion and breakfast, they don't mix so good for me," the man with the beard said.

Cairney nodded. He guessed it was probably close to seven by now.

"You new around here?" the man asked.

"Yeah."

"Seems I seen you one time before."

Cairney said nothing. Inside the dining room men were shuffling in the direction of the serving area. Still no Tumulty. It crossed Cairney's mind that if he could somehow catch the priest's eye Tumulty might give him a sign, a gesture to reassure him that it was safe to enter.

"Last week maybe," the man was saying. "Was you here last week?"

"Could be."

The little group was silent now, as if they were weighing information of a vital nature. One of them, a short man with a face mottled by alcohol, eventually said, "I had a Rolex one time. Good timepiece."

Somebody laughed at this, and Cairney smiled. There was a certain incoherence about these men, conversational leaps difficult to follow. The death of synapses, he thought. He moved closer to the threshhold of the dining room. The smell of bacon was strong, nauseating. He experienced a familiar tingling in his nervous system. It was what he'd come to think of as the Moment, that point in time when either he committed himself or he stepped back. It was that place where he could choose to pull the trigger or press the detonating device or else abort his plans entirely. He listened to himself, the sound of his blood, the way his heart thumped. His body, in that peculiar vocabulary it had developed, was talking to him.

He quickly scanned the street again. He saw nothing unusual. It occurred to him that if anything *had* gone wrong, Joe Tumulty would have managed to give him a sign of some kind. In the absence of any warning, what else could he assume except that everything was fine? Like a swimmer cautiously testing water, he put one foot inside the dining room. And then he had momentum going and was moving toward the serving area, picking up a tray, a plate, cutlery, shuffling in line behind the other men. He faced Joe Tumulty, who stood behind trays of simmering food with a large spatula in his hand. There was nothing on the priest's face, no recognition, no surprise, nothing. Cairney watched two strips of bacon, a slab of toast and a spoonful of scrambled eggs fall on his plate, and then he turned away, carrying his tray in the direction of a table.

When he sat down he saw Frank Pagan on the other side of the room.

Calmly, Cairney cut one of the bacon strips in half. He didn't let his eyes linger long on Pagan. He stared at his food as he chewed on the rasher. He tasted absolutely nothing. In one sense, now, he seemed to stand in a place outside himself, figuring, assessing possibilities like a meteorologist studying a cloud formation. Objectively. Coolly. If Frank Pagan had infiltrated the place, there was the chance that he wasn't alone. Perhaps others, dressed as Pagan was, sat in the dining room at this very moment. This was the first consideration. The second was even more bleak. Tumulty must have known that Pagan was here. Why then hadn't the priest warned him? Had Tumulty sold out? Had Tumulty *betrayed* him? Be still, he told himself. Be very still. To run now would bring Frank Pagan chasing after him. Besides, there was always another possibility, that Tumulty was simply playing along with Pagan's game and had no intention of betraying Jig.

Cairney sought the quiet center of himself. The place of supreme calm, detachment. It had always been easy to locate in the past but now, as if Celestine had tampered with it and damaged it, he couldn't quite find the correct frame of mind. He came close, but there was an uneasiness that made clear thinking difficult. He worked at suppressing his nerves, his heartbeat, the way his thoughts were beginning to race.

Tumulty had come to the middle of the room. He was calling for prayer. He held his hands up in the air but he didn't turn his face in Jig's direction.

"You all know the rules," Tumulty was saying, over the clacking of forks and knives. "You all know we say grace at St. Finbar's before we eat." Nobody was paying much attention to him. "Silence, please," Tumulty said.

When he had some semblance of quiet, which was broken by coughing and the occasional belch, Joseph X. Tumulty closed his eyes and inclined his head.

He said, "We thank Thee, Heavenly Father, for what we are about to receive."

A long silence. Tumulty looked as if he were locked in some internal struggle. Then he added, "The Lord hath done great things for us, whereof we are glad. Amen."

Cairney glanced at Frank Pagan, who was digging heartily into his breakfast. Tumulty, after his quick little prayer, was threading his way between tables, finally approaching the one where Cairney sat. Cairney looked up at the priest. Tumulty made a small gesture with his head, indicating that Cairney should follow him. The young man rose just as Tumulty disappeared through the doorway in the direction of the stairs. Cairney walked very slowly, turning to glance at Frank Pagan again. The Englishman had stopped eating. He was staring bleakly at his empty plate.

Cairney stood very still on the threshhold of the dark hallway. He'd caught something just then. A vibration. Something in the way Frank Pagan gazed at his plate. It was the look of a person *pretending* to study, when his mind was elsewhere. The sideways movement of the eyes. The apparent absentmindedness of expression that was an attempt to conceal a highly focused brain. Cairney knew that look. Supressed excitement. Hidden tension. He understood that Frank Pagan was going to get up from the table at any moment and follow him out into the hallway.

Tumulty, balanced on the bottom step, had a finger to his mouth for silence.

"You've sold me," Cairney whispered.

"Will you please shut up?'" Tumulty said.

"You bastard, you sold me."

Tumulty shook his head. "They forced me. It's not what you think."

Cairney said nothing. He wondered how much force it had taken to turn Joe Tumulty around.

"Is Pagan alone?" he asked.

Tumulty said, "There's another one in my office upstairs."

"I'm in a hell of a spot then," Cairney said. He looked up the stairway. He was thinking wildly now, which wasn't the way Jig had been trained to react. But all the placebos his instructors had drummed into him about turning adversity to your own advantage meant absolutely nothing right then. He had walked straight into this.

"There's one way out," Tumulty said.

"How?"

Tumulty was moving quietly up the stairs. Cairney, who felt he had little to lose, followed. They reached the landing. The door of Tumulty's office stood open. On the other side of the landing was a second door.

"In there," Tumulty whispered. "The bathroom window."

As Cairney moved toward the door, Tumulty pressed a piece of paper into his hand like an uncle surreptitiously passing a five-dollar bill to a favorite nephew.

"They took the weapons away from me," Tumulty said, his quiet voice filled with apprehension. "This is the best I can do. Now go. For God's sake, go."

Before Cairney could open the bathroom door he heard Frank Pagan coming up the stairs. At the same time he was conscious of a man standing in the door of Tumulty's office. He had a pistol in his hand. It was clear from the expression on the man's face that he'd use the gun without weighing ethical questions beforehand. Indeed, he had his arm extended now and was going into the kind of crouch universally favored by law enforcement officers. Only Joe Tumulty stood between Cairney and the weapon.

"Stand very still," the man said. "Don't even breathe."

Cairney, shielded by the priest, saw Frank Pagan rushing upward. From the folds of his clothing Pagan had produced a weapon. There was a curious little smile on Pagan's face that wasn't quite triumph. It contained fatigue.

Pagan reached the landing. With the gun held out in front of him, he approached cautiously. "I want a damn good look at what we've caught."

Cairney turned his face away. There was one slender chance left to him. It would take a quick smooth movement, a moment of sudden imbalance in the group of people around him, temporary confusion. He concentrated hard, reaching down into the depths of himself for the answer. One perfect motion. That was all. He felt elated all at once, anticipating the moment of action, his entire being consumed by the notion of movement. He was alert now, and sharp, and his senses had the efficiency of surgical instruments. Tumulty's frightened face, Pagan's smile, the other man's hard little eyes—all these things made a heightened impression on him. And then he was out in a place where there was no thinking, no rationalizing, nothing but pure movement and the overwhelming instinct to survive, a place that was quicksilver, where he ceased to exist except as an embodiment of action.

He did two things at once in a movement so fluid, so swift, that it was a blur to the other people around him. He pushed Tumulty forward, thrusting him forcefully across the landing in the direction of the man with the Mexican moustache, and he simultaneously swung his leg upward at a right angle to his body, his foot connecting with Frank Pagan's hand. Pagan didn't drop the gun and the blow barely affected him, but it was the opening Cairney knew he had to achieve, the fraction in time when the concentration all around him was punctured, the only time he'd ever have.

He lunged toward the bathroom door, which swung away from him, and then he was inside, kicking the door shut at his back and sliding the bolt in place hurriedly before he ran toward the window at the far end. He heard two gunshots, wood tearing, the rattle of a bullet on the lock, all sounds from another world. He lashed at the window with his foot. Glass shattered and the rotted wood frame collapsed, creating a jagged opening out on to the roofs above Canal Street. He squeezed through to the roof. He heard, distantly, the bathroom door being kicked open, and then Frank Pagan was shouting, but Cairney wasn't about to stop and listen. He scampered gracelessly along the roof, struggling to maintain his balance on a surface made slick by morning frost.

The sound of a gunshot split the air around his head. He heard the bullet burst into the concrete casing of a chimney just beyond him. The shot had come from across Canal Street, not from behind as he'd expected. He glanced at the other side of the street, seeing a figure on the roof opposite. Crouching low, he crossed the roof. The firing continued, kicking up fragments of asphalt and brick. He kept his head down as he moved in the direction of the next building. How many men had Pagan planted in the vicinity? When he leaped the narrow space from one rooftop to the next, he heard Pagan call out again and he turned to look. The Englishman was two buildings behind and running, and his breath left small clouds on the chill air.

"Jig!" Pagan shouted.

Cairney smiled and slithered down the incline of the roof that faced away from Canal Street so that at least he was out of the line of fire from across the way. He heard Pagan grunting, and then there was the sound of gunfire coming from Pagan's direction. The first shot was erratic, whining several feet from Cairney's head and crashing uselessly into brickwork. The second, closer and more urgent, cleaved the air about three feet from his shoulder. Either Frank Pagan wasn't a very good shot or else he wasn't shooting to kill.

Why would he want to kill Jig anyhow? Cairney wondered. Like the curator of a zoo who has coveted a certain exotic animal for years, Pagan wanted to *capture* the creature that had tantalized him for so long—he didn't want a corpse. He couldn't put a dead man on display. Where was the satisfaction in that? Pagan wasn't going to shoot his own prize.

Cairney found something amusing in this perception. He took a deep breath, listened to Pagan calling out his name, then he ran. He reached the roof of the next building, a flat expanse of concrete with a couple of wooden tubs in which the brown wreckage of dead plants wilted in hard soil. Two deck chairs and a plastic table. Somebody's summer aerie dead in the grip of winter. At the center of the roof there was a door. He dashed toward it. A season of moisture had swollen the wood, jamming the door tightly. Cairney kicked at the handle, then thrust his shoulder against the wood and the door flew backward, revealing a flight of steps. He plunged down into the darkness below. It was an empty office building, a shabby place that seemed to house a variety of small companies.

On the first landing Cairney stopped. He looked back up the way he'd come. He heard the sound of Frank Pagan on the rooftop. Then he moved to the next flight of steps and went down quickly. Now, free from the exposure of the roof, he thought about his predicament. Unless there was a rear exit to this building he'd have to leave by the front door, which would lead him straight back onto Canal Street. A sorry prospect. Another alternative, which he rejected immediately, was to conceal himself somewhere inside the building and wait the whole thing out—but that was a trap he wasn't going to encourage. The building would be sealed off and thoroughly ransacked, and he'd be discovered sooner or later. There was one other possibility, also rejected, and that was to confront Frank Pagan, somehow overpower him and get the gun away, but he knew that the Englishman, taken by surprise once, wasn't going to allow himself to be caught off balance a second time.

He heard Pagan on the floor above. He took the next flight of stairs and found himself on the first floor, a hallway with a glass door to Canal Street. He turned in the opposite direction, back along the hall. Pagan was directly overhead and coming down loudly, his feet clattering on the wooden steps. Cairney ran to the end of the corridor. There, the only possible route he could take was down to the basement. If there was no rear exit from the basement, then his chance of escape was screwed. He shoved the basement door open and found himself going down into the dark heart of the building. It was a large room of angular steam pipes and the kind of dampness no boiler could ever dispel, and the air, like that inside a box locked for years, was still and rancid and unbreathable. He could see nothing save for a slot of pale light in the distance. It had to come from a window, and if there was a window then there might also be a door if the original architect, in his infinite wisdom, had included both in his plans. Moving, hands outstretched in the dark like a blind man, he crossed the basement floor, which was strewn with objects—boxes, rags, bundles of papers, tools.

He heard Pagan call out to him again. The man's voice sounded muffled down here in this stifling space.

"You can't get away, Jig. There's no place for you to go. Even if you got out of here, there are twenty or thirty men outside. Think about it."

Cairney said nothing in reply. He went toward the source of light. He heard Pagan come after him. The man was moving with great caution, measuring his steps.

"In your situation, Jig, I'd call it a day," Pagan said.

Cairney put his ear toward the origin of the sound. How far, how near, was Frank Pagan? He cursed this abominable darkness that prevented him from estimating distances. Pagan could be thirty feet away, or a lot closer. He just couldn't tell.

He ducked his head beneath an overhanging pipe and saw, just ahead of him, the rectangle of a window, light filtering in from outside. It was perhaps fifteen feet from where he stood. The problem with light was the fact that, as soon as he reached the window, he'd create a silhouette for Frank Pagan to see. A cobweb brushed his forehead and he wiped it aside. Still keeping his head low and his shoulders hunched, he approached the source of the light.

There was no goddam door, only the window, ridiculously small and streaked with dirt, impossible for him to squeeze through.

"Jig," Pagan called out. "You don't have a chance, man."

Cairney wanted to tell Pagan that he could talk all day and it would make no difference because Jig hadn't been programmed to surrender, but he said nothing. He went down on the floor now, crawling toward the light. Tilting his head up, he stared at the pane of glass. He'd have to be a midget to get out through that space. He pressed his face into the dirt of the floor, thinking, thinking. Finn had once told him that there was no box a man couldn't get out of except despair, and it was despair, like a cold-gloved hand, that touched the fringes of his mind now.

Twenty or thirty men. Was Frank Pagan lying? Cairney had seen only three, Pagan included.

He went forward on his hands and knees.

Out of the dark he heard Pagan's voice again. "Jig? Why don't you talk to me?"

Cairney, flat against the wall under the window, moved his head slightly. Pagan was very close now. He could hear the man breathing.

Cairney stretched his hand along the wall. His fingers encountered a hollow rectangle of metal, an opening that puzzled him only a moment before he understood what it was.

A coal chute.

Unused probably for forty, fifty years, filled with dirt and stuffed with garbage, it was a goddam coal chute, a way out! He gripped the inside of the metal opening and drew himself slowly up into the black funnel, which ran at a sloping angle toward the street. There would be a lid, of course, but beyond that cover there would be air and daylight and opportunity. He climbed, shoving aside the assorted detritus of whoever had used this basement over the years, through the dank narrow tube where the trapped air was even worse than in the basement itself. Beer bottles and cans and ancient newspapers and the pervasive stench of cat urine. Straining, he reached the cover and thumped it desperately with the heel of his hand, and it yielded in a shower of rusted flakes that fell into his eyes, but at the same time there was daylight, glorious daylight, streaming against his face from the alley behind the building.

A few more feet. That was all. A few more feet and he'd be clear.

He felt Frank Pagan's hand clutch his ankle. It was a ferocious grip, powerful, and it threatened to bring him down out of his precarious position inside the chute and back into the basement. He freed his other leg from the cramped space and kicked out as hard as he could, bringing his foot down on Pagan's fingers. He heard Pagan say *Bastard* then felt his fingers slacken. He was free. With one last thrust, he shoved his face up beyond the lid of the chute and hauled himself out into the alley. It was empty. No men. No cars. Nothing. He reached down and slammed the cover shut before he turned and ran.

WASHINGTON, D.C.

The Director of the FBI was a small man called Leonard M. Korn. He wore rimless glasses to correct his notorious short-sightedness, and he shaved his head so that it resembled a blunt little bullet. He spoke always quietly, never raising his voice, not even when angry. To his subordinates, he was perhaps the most frightening man on the face of the planet. His sense of control, both of himself and the Bureau, was awesome. His taste for punishment, when an agent had disappointed him, was absolutely merciless. Many good agents, with otherwise meticulous records, had found themselves posted to places like Nebraska and South Dakota because they had made a single slip. With more bitterness than affection, some said the middle initial of his name stood for Magoo, the cartoon character Korn resembled in appearance though not in action.

About an hour after Jig had vanished in an alley behind Canal Street, Leonard M. Korn was seated behind his desk at Bureau headquarters staring at his special deputy, a man named Walter Bull. Bull had been with the Bureau all through the Hoover years and was known to be a big-league survivor around whom administrations came and went. A plump man with a face that resembled a used khaki handkerchief, Bull perspired regularly and copiously, no matter the temperature of the day. He was sweating as he stood in front of Korn's desk right then. His associates called him B. O. Bull.

Korn folded his small white hands on his blotter. He had been listening very carefully to his special deputy, and now Bull was quiet, waiting for a response. Korn manipulated silences, an old ploy in the power game. He knew how to use them, how long to let them last. He let this particular silence linger for almost a minute before he said, "I think it's a hoax, frankly."

Bull didn't say anything in reply. He was staring at Korn's bald head, where an enormous vein pulsed just under the skin.

Korn unfolded his little hands. They looked like baby albino rodents to Walter Bull. "A man can pick up a telephone and say anything he likes under the cover of anonymity, Walter. He can lay the blame for a certain event on anyone or any party he chooses because he knows he can hang up the phone and disappear without a trace. And nobody is any the wiser."

Walter Bull nodded. His penchant for longevity within the Bureau came from his natural gift for servility. He had spent many years agreeing with the different men who occupied the chair in which Leonard Magoo Korn now sat. Like a good call girl, he knew how to give pleasing service.

Korn continued. "There are certain people in our society, Walter, who have nothing better to do than send the Bureau off on wild-goose chases. This caller in Albany seems to fit that particular category."

Bull said, "I wondered if it might be connected with Jig."

Korn narrowed his eyes. The whole subject of Jig was supposed to be secret, the way the White House wanted it. But Korn knew that in the grapevine of the Bureau nothing remained concealed very long, especially from a man like Bull, who had access to almost everything.

"Jig is persona non grata, Walter," Korn said. "We ought to keep that clearly in mind. Officially, Jig doesn't exist."

"Of course, sir." Bull turned toward the door, stopped. "What'll I tell Albany?"

"I'll take care of that," Korn replied.

Walter Bull went out, leaving his trademark aroma behind, thick cologne and sweat.

Alone, Leonard Korn realized he would have to place two telephone calls. The first would be to the field office in Albany, giving strict instructions that the crime was to be handled discreetly and that no information was to be given either to the Albany PD or to the newspapers. The second and more important call would be to the White House.

Korn wasn't altogether sure that it *was* Jig who had committed this crime in Albany and then called the local FBI office to claim responsibility on behalf of the Irish Republican Army. But why take any chances? President Thomas Dawson, deeply concerned as he was with the Irish assassin, would want to be informed anyway. Korn didn't plan to place this call at once, though. He wanted to wait until he had heard from Agent Arthur J. Zuboric that the Englishman's scheme in New York City had worked. It would be very gratifying to tell Thomas Dawson that Jig was safely in custody and that the Bureau, somewhat maligned in recent years, could be counted on to come through in the end. If there was one obsession in Leonard Korn's life, it was the reputation of the Bureau. He had neither wife nor mistress. Nor had he any intimate friends. The Bureau was all things to him, and he loved it with more passion than he was ever capable of showing to a human being. He loved its computers, its chicanery, its internecine power struggles. But more than anything else, he adored the possibility of its omniscience. He liked to think that a day would come when a sneeze in the Oval Office would register on the Bureau's data banks before it even tickled the President's nostrils. Leonard M. Korn's ideal of the FBI was a huge cyclopean entity made of stainless steel, unblemished, all-seeing, its bloodstream composed of infinite corpuscles of information, its heart one enormous muscle forever pumping data, its brain an insomniac scanning device classifying all this data day and night.

If the plan in New York City worked, excellent. And if it didn't—well, the blame could always be laid on Frank Pagan, a perfect scapegoat, thus sparing the Bureau any presidential wrath.

Leonard M. Korn smiled. He liked having things both ways.

SEVENTEEN

Artie Zuboric said, "It was a brilliant plan, Frank. It was probably the most billiant plan I've ever been associated with. When I'm an old man looking back I'll remember it with total fucking admiration. I'll gather my grandchildren up on my lap and tell them about the day Frank Pagan tried to catch an Irish gunman."

Pagan flexed his bruised fingers. He didn't like sarcasm at the best of times and he found Zuboric's brand particularly juvenile. His hand stung. He rubbed it gently, then stared from the window of Zuboric's office.

"You had a clear shot at him," Zuboric said. "When he was standing there on that landing, Frank, you could have taken him out. You had all the time in the world."

And on the rooftop too, Pagan thought. But he hadn't narrated the chase to Zuboric in any detail. He'd fogged the pursuit through the basement, not because he thought it embarrassing but because he wasn't about to throw more fuel on Artie's little bonfire of sarcasm.

"Granted he moved like lightning," Zuboric said. "Granted it was unexpected. But that doesn't excuse you, Frank. If I'd had the same opportunity, I'd have pulled my trigger. But I was knocked on my ass when Tumulty crashed into me. So I didn't have a shot. You bombed, Frank. You screwed up."

Pagan watched the street, where a shaft of gloomy March sunlight penetrated the grayness of things. What he kept coming back to was Jig's smile on the rooftop, the moment when the man had turned and glanced back and the smile on his lips was somehow knowing, as if Jig understood that Frank Pagan wasn't going to shoot him in the back. But that wasn't it either, it wasn't anything so sentimental, so *nice*, as an unwillingness to shoot a defenseless human being. It was something else. It had nothing to do with any concept of fair play.

He had never *dreamed* of taking Jig dead, that's what it came down to. Even if he had never admitted it to himself before now, he had always imagined Jig alive, intact. He had always envisaged himself looking Jig straight in the eye and taking the measure of the man, talking with him, questioning him, as if there were some revelation to be found in the mystery of Jig's soul. He wanted an *understanding* of the assassin, something you couldn't get from a dead man. He wanted to *know* Jig, who played the game of terrorism according to his own meticulous rules. It was his appreciation of Jig's calculated acts of violence, so economical and accurate, that made it difficult to gun the man down in cold blood. And if there was irony in this, in his unwillingness to meet Jig's violence with violence of his own, Pagan wasn't going to recognize it. He wanted Jig badly, but not dead. Not shipped back to England in a bloody box, which would have been an empty triumph.

There was even something admirable, Pagan thought, in the fact that Jig, during that first visit to St. Finbar's, had actually *approached* Pagan to ask if he could help. There was gall in the man, and bravado, and surely an overwhelming sense of confidence. To come straight up to Pagan and look him in the eye the way he'd done—it was quite an act.

Pagan rubbed his aching hand again. He wondered if he was simply trying to rationalize his own failure, trying to explain it away in manageable sentiments. He thought suddenly of Eddie Rattigan's bomb and how it had destroyed Roxanne, and he realized that what he felt toward Jig was almost a kind of gratitude for the fact that the assassin had introduced *dignity* into the whole Irish conflict, that he had transcended the brutal behavior of the Eddie Rattigans of this world. He thought of the enormous gulf that separated somebody like Rattigan from Jig. Rattigan killed the innocent, the blameless, the harmless bystander. Jig would never have casually detonated a bomb at a public bus stop. He would never have indulged in such mindless destruction. He would never have taken Roxanne away. You didn't shoot a man like Jig in the back. "I want him alive. That's all."

"You could've shot to wound," Zuboric snapped. "You ever think about that?"

Pagan didn't respond. He considered the two shots he'd fired at Jig on the rooftops. The first had been a warning, fired in the vague chance that Jig would stop running. Vague indeed. The second had gone close to Jig, but Pagan wasn't sure now if that bullet had been intended to wound the man. In the heat of the moment, in the confusion of the chase, he hadn't had time to take careful aim.

Zuboric said, "I get this sneaky feeling you've been after Jig too long. I think you've actually begun to admire the sonofabitch. You want him alive because you can't understand what makes you admire him, so you'd like to sit down with him over tea and crumpets and tell him what a jolly good fight he's fought. It wouldn't be the first time that's happened to a cop."

"Call me unpatriotic, but I don't eat crumpets," Pagan said. He was remembering the basement, the moment of contact when Jig, finding the means of escape in a coal chute, had finally lunged out at him with his foot. He'd almost had Jig then. Almost. A coal chute! It was extraordinary how people who wanted desperately to survive somehow always managed to find the means of survival in the basic material around them. Somebody other than Jig, somebody with less of the sharp instinct to escape, might never have found that opening in the basement. Chalk up another point for the man, Pagan thought. Did that wonderment at Jig's ability, his slipperiness, constitute admiration?

Zuboric stared at Pagan. He was beginning to perceive his life in terms of how much the Englishman irritated him. The prospect of calling the Director with news of the Canal Street Fuck-up, which was like a newspaper headline in his mind, made him very unhappy. He had been putting it off ever since they'd come back to his office. Why had he ever listened to Pagan anyway? He was suddenly very weary. Of his office, his job, the Bureau, the whole ball of wax. And last night, when he'd been in bed with Charity, who always made the act of sex seem like an enormous favor on her part, she'd once again reiterated her determination never to marry anyone who didn't have two cents to rub together. Especially a man connected with any law enforcement outfit. She'd had her share, she said, of deadbeats in the past. Zuboric hadn't wanted to hear about her past particularly. It was the future he was interested in, and it was going to be a wintry future if Charity wasn't in it. She had driven him last night to the limits of sexual bliss. He didn't like to wonder how she'd learned some of the tricks she knew.

He picked up a pen and rapped it on his desk, still staring at the Englishman. "As for Tumulty, I knew that cocksucker couldn't be trusted," Zuboric said. "I knew it all along."

"You told me that," Pagan answered. "You were very *happy* to tell me that, Arthur."

"Jesus, Frank. I saw the guy slip something into Jig's hand. I don't know what exactly. A piece of paper. Something. I was standing in the goddam doorway watching."

Pagan closed his eyes. His entire body hurt from the exertion of rooftop acrobatics. He was thinking of Tumulty now, whom they had brought back to Zuboric's office from Canal Street. Father Joe was locked inside a cell along the corridor. He claimed that Zuboric was imagining things, there was no piece of paper, nothing. Maybe it was time to turn the screws on Joe a little tighter.

"I'll talk to him again," Pagan said.

Zuboric shrugged and tossed a key into Pagan's hand. "Be my guest. In the meantime, I've got the unpleasant task of reporting this failure, Frank. If you don't see me again, it's because I've been abruptly transferred to Carlsbad, New Mexico."

"I'll come visit you," Pagan said in the doorway. "I've always wanted to see the bat caves."

"I bet," Zuboric replied, thinking that the caves of Carlsbad would be a perfectly fitting place for Frank Pagan to die and be buried in, under a million tons of bat shit. "After you've talked to Tumulty, do me a favor and make sure you lock the door behind you, huh? We wouldn't want to lose two Irishmen in one day, would we?"

F R A N K P A G A N slid the key in the lock and stepped inside the room where Joe Tumulty sat propped up in the corner. Zuboric's last remark niggled him. He suddenly wished he'd shot Jig on the roof when he'd had the chance. Who the hell would have cared anyhow in the long run other than himself? He'd have been a hero. The Man Who Killed Jig. So what the fuck was he doing, dickering with this appreciation of his prey? What was this bullshit about wanting Jig alive? If he'd gunned the Irishman down he wouldn't have had to put up with Zuboric's snide comments.

"You really let me down, Joe." He spoke between clenched teeth. He felt confined inside a triangle whose sides consisted of Zuboric's criticism, Tumulty's pigheadedness, and his own failure to apprehend Jig. He wasn't in the mood to fart around with Tumulty.

Tumulty didn't speak. Pagan squatted alongside him. The priest blinked, then closed his eyes slowly.

"What was written on the paper, Joe?"

"There was no bloody paper."

"My arse. Zuboric saw you."

"Look. I said the grace you wanted. I put the finger on your man. Don't blame me if he slipped out of your hands. I did everything you expected, so why the hell am I locked up like this?"

Pagan placed his hand on Tumulty's shoulder. "You're locked up because you're a fucking criminal, Joe. You impeded the investigation of a federal agency. I bet you just loved it when Jig pushed you into Zuboric, didn't you? I bet you loved making that little contribution to Jig's escape."

"I made no contribution," Tumulty said.

"What was on the paper?"

"I'd like to call a lawyer."

"No lawyer," Pagan said.

"It's my constitutional right."

"What right? What Constitution? You don't have any rights, Joe. You signed them all away when you helped Jig."

"There's something to the effect that a man's innocent until he's proven guilty—"

"Where did you hear a fairy tale like that?"

Tumulty sighed. "Thank God this is a country of litigation and hungry lawyers. I'll sue. You'll see."

Pagan smiled. "What was on the paper, Joe?"

Tumulty shut his eyes again. He tipped his face to one side, away from Pagan. Pagan reached out and deftly took Joe's cheek between thumb and forefinger and pinched very hard. Tumulty's eyes watered before Pagan released his grip.

Pagan stood up. "I'll tell you what really bothers me about all this, Joe. It isn't the fact that you'll most likely go to jail. It's the end of the road for all that good work you've been doing down on Canal Street. It's curtain time, folks. No more good works. No more charity. You've lost your little bid for sainthood, Joe. Pity."

"There isn't a court in the country that would send me to jail," Tumulty said, rubbing his cheek and looking annoyed.

Pagan shrugged. "Even if you don't go to jail, your life's going to be sheer hell, Joe. You know what Zuboric is planning?"

Tumulty shook his head.

"First, he's contacting some friends in the IRS who owe him a favor. You know how that works. Zuboric reckons his tax pals can hassle you so much you'll *wish* you'd been sent to prison. That's for starters. Second, he's going to arrange for the local health department to go through your establishment hunting for sanitary violations. They also owe Zuboric favors. In other words, they're going to be hard on you." Pagan paused. He wasn't absolutely sure if Tumulty was absorbing this. "I'm not finished yet. He's also making arrangements to bring the local cops down on you."

"He can't do that."

"He can do anything he likes. The Director of the FBI is God, which makes Artie Zuboric a minor kind of deity by association. He asks for something in this town, everybody is ready to just bloody jump for him. You'll see. As far as the cops coming in, it seems they're going to suspect some of your clients of carrying narcotic contraband and using your place as the source, as it were, of their deals. Suddenly, no more St. Finbar's. Big headlines. Lapsed Priest Runs Drug Ring. Tabloids love anything to do with lapsed priests, don't they?"

Tumulty said, "This is blackmail."

"Hardly, Joe. All I'm doing is painting you a picture of your dilemma. Bleak days lie ahead. Unless, of course, you decide that cooperation is the best way to go."

The priest stood up. He studied Frank Pagan a moment. Then, very deliberately, he said, "There was no paper. I gave Jig absolutely nothing."

"I admire a man who sticks to his story," Pagan said. He turned to the door. "Don't let anybody convince you to change it."

He went out. He drew a cup of water from the cooler in the corridor and drank it, leaning against the wall and staring at a portrait of Thomas Dawson. He thought Dawson looked vapid, homogenized. But these were the very qualities the American electorate found endearing in its presidents.

He crumpled his little wax cup. He wondered if Joseph X. Tumulty was pondering the exaggerated portrait of doom Pagan had painted for him. Maybe. God knows, he had to do something to shake Tumulty loose from his posture of innocence.

Pagan moved back in the direction of Zuboric's office just as the agent, looking as if the heavens had parted and God had roared angrily at him, stepped out into the corridor.

"I thought you'd be in Carlsbad by now," Pagan said.

Zuboric had a sheet of paper in his hand. "I just talked with the Director."

"And?"

"He's angry. He's angry and goddam impatient. He doesn't think a whole lot of you, Frank. Quote. If the limey doesn't shape up, I'll have him shipped back to England so fast his feet won't touch the ground. Unquote."

"Harsh words," Pagan said. He didn't remotely care what Leonard M. Korn had to say about him.

Zuboric waved the sheet of paper. "Which brings me to this tidbit of information he gave me. It seems that a man was murdered early this morning in Albany. He'd been garroted by a length of wire and dumped in a culvert. A very nasty death."

"Garroting can be unpleasant," Pagan agreed.

"The killer called the local FBI office at two A.M. and claimed that the killing had been carried out by the Irish Republican Army."

"In Albany? *New York?*"

Zuboric nodded. "My precise reaction, Frank."

"It's a hoax. It has to be."

"Also my own first reaction. But it becomes more plausible when you hear about the victim." Zuboric read from the paper. "*Alexander Fitzjohn, aged thirty-eight, resident of Camden, New Jersey. Entered the United States legally from Belfast in August 1984.*"

"Belfast?" Pagan said. He wondered where this was leading.

"According to what I've got here, Frank, Fitzjohn had once been a member of the Free Ulster Volunteers."

Pagan reached quickly for the paper. It was covered in Zuboric's scrawl. He must have taken it all down very quickly over the telephone. "It doesn't add up. It doesn't make any sense at all. Even if it was some old score being settled, since when has the IRA started to make hits overseas? The Libyans, yes. The Bulgarians, sometimes. But I've never heard of the IRA playing that kind of long-distance game."

"Maybe there's a local cell," Zuboric said.

"Maybe."

Pagan handed the paper back. Zuboric said, "There's another possibility."

"Which is?"

"It could have been Jig."

Pagan opened his mouth to reply when he heard the sound of Joseph Tumulty banging on the locked door of his room.

PATRICK CAIRNEY drove his rented Dodge through the streets of Lower Manhattan. Dressed still in the clothes he'd worn at St. Finbar's, he realized he'd have to change into something more in keeping with the brand-new vehicle he was driving. When he came to Battery Park he found a secluded place where he could change without being seen. Even when he'd discarded the dirty old clothes and dumped them in a trash container, he felt unclean.

He took out the piece of paper Joe Tumulty had given him. He read it quickly, memorized it, tore the sheet into thin ribbons, and tossed them into the wind, which ferried them carelessly down toward the river. *The name,* he thought. It was all he had. No guns. Nothing but the name. What was he supposed to do without a weapon?

As he looked out over Battery Park, he was conscious of the great expanse of the Atlantic beyond Gowanus Bay and the Narrows, and it occurred to him that the tide that rimmed the shores of Staten Island was the same that eventually found its way back to Dingle and Castletown, Galway and Donegal. He listened a moment to the squealing of gulls in the distance, and he wondered about this upsurge of longing that filled him. He'd been in Ireland too long, he thought. It had rubbed off on him, the sentimentality, the emigrant's yearning.

He didn't move for a time. His body still shook from the recent effort on the rooftops of Canal Street. It was the first time in his life he'd ever come close to capture, and he didn't like the feeling. He'd evaded Frank Pagan in the end, but it was a situation he should never have encountered in the first place. He blamed Tumulty. It should have been possible for Tumulty to warn him *not* to come inside that bloody soup kitchen. It ought to have been possible for the priest to get some kind of sign to him before he'd taken that first fateful step into the place. But Joe Tumulty, who must have been playing both ends against the middle, had behaved like the deplorable amateur he really was. Why the fuck had Finn put a man like

Tumulty in America anyway? Bad judgment on Finn's part? Or was Tumulty just rusted from inactivity? Cairney, who couldn't believe that Finn would ever show careless judgment, had no answers to these questions. But he knew one thing for sure—the worst outcome of the whole thing was that Frank Pagan now knew what Jig looked like and the exposure worried Cairney. Suddenly Jig had a face. He had features. Characteristics. He was no longer just a name. His anonymity was gone.

Goddam. Patrick Cairney shut his eyes and let the breeze blow against his skin. For a second he considered aborting the whole thing right then and going back to Ireland and Finn. He thought about telling Finn that his cover, so laboriously assembled and protected, had been shattered. The game could no longer be played by the same rules. What would Finn say? Would Finn simply retire Jig? Put him out to pasture? Patrick Cairney loathed that prospect. He couldn't stand the idea of Finn patting him on the shoulder and saying that he'd had a good inning but now it was time to close up shop. He'd *get* the goddam money back! He'd get it back and to hell with the fact that he'd been seen and was now neatly stored in Frank Pagan's memory. He opened his eyes and took several deep breaths. He realized then that he needed control over his thoughts as much as his actions. What had he been thinking about, for Christ's sake? Defeat? Retirement? He smiled these notions away. He'd complete the task he'd been sent all this way to do, and nothing, *nothing* was going to stop him.

He walked back to his car, jammed the key in the ignition and drove away from the park. He went back down through the streets of Lower Manhattan, heading for the Brooklyn Battery Tunnel. He was acutely aware of time pressing down on him now. What if Joe Tumulty had given the name to Frank Pagan as well? Inside the tunnel, as if enclosed spaces troubled him, he felt apprehensive. It was the lack of a blueprint that unnerved him, the absence of a concrete plan that concerned him. It was also the realization that he had no way of knowing what this Nicholas Linney was like and how he was going to receive a caller who had some hard questions to ask and who wanted quick truthful answers.

He was going in blind.

And he didn't like that idea at all, because every success he'd had in the past had come about as a result of good planning, the kind of planning you did with your eyes wide open and your vision uncluttered.

BRIDGEHAMPTON, LONG ISLAND

Nicholas Linney lobbed the tennis ball over the net to where the plump East German, absurd in white shorts and Nike sneakers and a baggy white shirt, lunged with his racket and missed. It was the East German's habit to stamp his feet petulantly on the concrete court every time he missed an easy return. Linney, playing at half throttle, was bored. But it was necessary every so often, for purely commercial purposes, to entertain these yahoos from behind the Iron Curtain.

"I think I call quits," the East German said.

"Fine," Linney answered.

He walked off the court back toward the house. The East German, Gustav Rasch, came flopping alongside him, his mammaries bouncing up and down.

"I am perhaps too old a little," Rasch said, breathing very hard.

"You're not old," Linney lied. "A little out of shape, maybe."

Linney stepped on to the terrace. The house he owned in Bridgehampton had cost him $2.7 million three years ago. It was a sprawling structure, the result of various owners adding whimsies of their own to the original dwelling—a greenhouse, a glass-walled breakfast room, servant quarters at the rear. Linney sprawled in a deck chair. The East German, who had heard that Nicholas Linney's hospitality was always exciting, plopped into a chaise longue.

Linney offered him a drink. Grapefruit juice and Tanqueray gin spiked with chopped mint leaves. The breakfast specialty of the house. For quite some time neither man spoke. Linney lit a cigarette and looked across the tennis court.

"Is a nice house," Rasch said.

"Thank you." Linney filled two glasses from a flask, passing one to the East German, who drank as if his life were running out.

Linney put his glass down. Rasch had already finished his drink and was helping himself to another.

"Now," Rasch said, and licked his thick lips. "Is important we talk money."

Linney wanted to talk money, but only on his own terms, and only after Rasch had sampled the pleasures of the house. "Later," he said, "If you're agreeable, that is."

Rasch crossed his arms on his large chest. He was still smiling. "Perhaps we touch on subject briefly now. Then later more?"

"Very well," Linney said.

"My people are unhappy," Rasch remarked.

"So are mine."

"Of course. We are all unhappy. My people see their money go on board a ship and then *zoom*, no more money. Swallowed up by the sea, no?"

Linney sipped his drink. He had invited Rasch out here to Bridgehampton for the sole purpose of exploring further fund-raising opportunities. It looked, as he'd told Harry Cairney at Roscommon, very bleak. The East Germans and their Soviet overlords could be very tight when it came to disbursing money.

"There are some of us who do not like this kind of investment," Rasch went on. "Is money wasted, they say. Bad policy to throw money into Ireland. What is Ireland, they ask, but a wart in the Irish Sea? Now, these people are very, very happy because they can . . ." Rasch faltered.

"Gloat?" Linney suggested.

"Indeed." Rasch put his empty glass down. "They gloat. They say security is bad and Ireland is unworthy of money anyway and why spend more?"

Linney made a little gesture with his hand. This business about the missing money nagged at him. He'd always enjoyed a good working relationship with his contributors but now, because one of the Fund-raisers had committed an act of treachery, all that was threatened. So far as Linney was concerned, the most likely candidate was Mulhaney. But in the absence of any hard evidence, what could he do about his suspicions? Big Jock was devious and greedy and he'd been plundering Teamster funds in the Northeast for years. Linney would have liked to get Big Jock in some white-tiled, soundproofed cellar and hammer the fucking truth out of him.

Something else crossed his mind now. It was the two M-16A2s he had inside the house. It was no *major* deal, but about six months ago he'd come into possession of the two automatic rifles as well as a half dozen Fabrique Nationale assault rifles, those lovely Belgian babies, from a gun dealer he'd met at a survivalist training camp in the Poconos. The dealer, who was the kind of man Linney ran into at these camps, where quiet machismo and boastful innuendo were the common currency of conversation, claimed he had a shipment of a hundred guns he wanted to sell to any interested party, if such a thing could be arranged. Linney, with more bravado than prudence, had allowed—with a small show of self-importance—that he was at least in the position of *exploring* the possibility of sending the guns to a buyer he knew in Ireland. He offered to transport the two automatic rifles and the six FN weapons as samples, and if there was interest he'd get back to the dealer. All this was discussed discreetly, and it had intrigued Linney enormously to be involved in the clandestine business of running guns.

He'd taken the weapons, and sent the FN rifles to the address of an acquaintance in Cork, but he'd kept the M-16A2s for himself because they were prized weapons and difficult to acquire. Linney had paid cash for all the guns and hadn't heard from the gun merchant again. Nor had he been surprised, because those kinds of deals fell through more frequently than they ever came to fruition. But the thing that worried him slightly now was the possibility of this business coming to light. He hadn't done anything dishonest. He'd simply kept the guns he wanted for himself and sent the rest. And he hadn't screwed the Irish out of any money to do so, which was something he'd never dream of doing. But they were a sensitive, touchy crew in the old country, and if they heard that two precious samples of the M-16A2 had been diverted, they could quite possibly be upset. When it came to the Cause, the people in Ireland hated the idea of anybody fucking with it. And Linney's decision to keep the two guns could be interpreted as interference. It wasn't much—but it bothered Linney. What if they'd heard over in Ireland about the two samples they never received? What if, in the murky world of gun dealing, information had come up? What if the gun dealer asked some Irish acquaintance, *By the way, what did you think of the M-16A2s?*

It wasn't likely. But Nicholas Linney's mind had a twist that often exaggerated possibilities. He had the thought that if they found out about the two guns, they could leap to the conclusion that Linney wasn't altogether loyal—and that could perhaps lead to more stinging accusations. Such as the hijacking of a small ship. The idea of being falsely accused filled him with a certain little jolt of excitement. It wasn't going to happen that way, of course, but the possibility was enough to increase the voltage of his adrenaline.

"More contributions are conditional," Rasch was saying. He beamed as if he were pleased with his mastery of English. "One, your security measures in the future we must approve."

"In triplicate?" Linney asked.

Rasch didn't know the word so he ignored it. "And two, no more money will be donated until you have catched the criminals and they are very punished."

Nicholas Linney pulled a sliver of mint leaf from his glass and rolled it between his hands. How could security plans be submitted to some fucking committee in East Berlin? Apart from the fact that such a process would take forever, Linney realized that with so many people involved, agreements could never be reached. The whole business of raising money would become bogged down in forms, those fucking forms of which the East Europeans were so fond and which seemed to Linney the paper foundation on which all Communism was built. If the Arab patrons were going to be as difficult as the East Europeans, you could practically kiss everything off. Linney sniffed mint on the palms of his hands. He was suddenly very impatient and restless and more than a little annoyed by the way things were turning out.

Rasch settled back in the chaise longue. "I must know if you are soon catching the pirates. Is expected of me."

"That's a police matter, Gustav." Even as he said this Linney knew that no American agency, neither the FBI nor the cops nor the Coast Guard, gave a flying fuck about a ship with Liberian registry and an Irish crew that had been attacked in international waters.

"No," Rasch said. "Is a matter of your own house being in order, Nicholas."

Linney said nothing. He was thinking of the two M-16A2s he had in his study.

Your own house in order, he thought.

He looked down over the tennis court at the willow trees that marked his property line. There was an iron fence beyond the trees. It wasn't going to keep anyone out who was determined to get in, such as this Irishman old Harry had mentioned. Let him show his face around here, Linney thought. *Let him try.* He had enough weapons stashed inside the house to keep a goddam army at bay for days. And for quite some time now, in fact ever since he'd been rejected by the draft board for Vietnam because of fallen arches, he'd been frustrated by the fact that all he ever got to shoot were watermelons and cantaloupes and plastic bottles filled with water. It was time to ponder a different kind of target.

The Irishman. Linney had spent some time trying to imagine the guy's state of mind. He'd reached the conclusion that the Irishman was going to treat each one of the Fund-raisers as a suspect. He wasn't going to come off like some tightly wrapped detective with a few penetrating questions to ask and leave it at that. No, this fucker was going to be hard and menacing, which was a prospect Nicholas Linney enjoyed. Besides, Linney didn't put a whole lot of faith in the value of the Fund-raisers' anonymity. Secrecy always had a weakness in it somewhere. And the weakness here was the priest, Joseph Tumulty, who was the liasion between the Americans and the IRA. Sometimes Linney got the impression that Tumulty knew a little more than he ever said. He'd always meant to get rid of Tumulty and strengthen that weak link in the chain, but he'd never quite done it—and he knew why. It was simply that he *liked* the vulnerability in the chain because it gave everything a delicious edge, a little tinge of danger in the otherwise mundane chore of delivering large sums of cash. He enjoyed that. It provided spice during the cold nights when you were skulking around Maine with briefcases stuffed with dough.

Nicholas Linney finished his drink. *This Irishman is going to suspect everybody,* he thought. *Including me.* Let him come here. Let him show his face.

He turned to Rasch and smiled. "Let's go indoors," he said. "We can talk about all this later."

Rasch stood up hastily. "I have been waiting."

Linney draped an arm loosely around Rasch's shoulder as they moved across the terrace. Sliding glass doors opened into a lounge the length of the house. It was furnished in pastels, the minimalist look, lean chairs and low-slung coffee tables and a couple of sparse paintings of the Anemic School. Linney liked understatement. He had no taste for the brash. He liked clean lines and crisp angles. Even in his politics he favored simple alignments and economy. His activities on behalf of the Fund-raisers, for example, served two purposes at once. They satisfied his Irishness, handed down to him from his father, Brigadier Mad Jack Linney of the IRA, a dashing figure with a black eye patch who had been shot to death in Belfast in October 1955, and they created useful bonds with the Arabs and the East Europeans, which helped in his other commercial enterprises. He often steered foreign capital into foundering Western businesses threatened by either bankruptcy or takeover. It was amazing sometimes to Linney how much Eastern European money had been used to help pump new blood into the arteries of capitalism.

Passing a large saltwater fish tank in which a variety of exotic species flickered back and forth, Linney walked across the floor to a door on the other side of the room. It opened into a very large bedroom. Two girls, neither of whom was more than fifteen, sat listening to rock music. They were easily corrupted, Linney thought. When he first brought them to this country, they had been shy and retiring, delicate little things who understood nothing about Western ways. Now Linney wondered how long he could keep them before they wanted their freedom, a Western concept that, like rock music and whirlpool baths and TV, they'd grasped all too quickly.

Linney indicated for them to come out into the lounge. They wore simple pastel dresses, so that they were coordinated with the room they entered. Their hair, shiny and black and long, lay in an uncluttered way over their shoulders, exactly as Linney liked it. Each girl was long-legged and lithe and small-breasted. When they smiled they did so in a shy manner, turning their dark brown eyes down. They were beautiful and still acquiescent in a way one rarely found among Western girls these days.

"Ah," Rasch said. "Supreme."

"I'm glad you approve," Linney said.

"Will they undress?" Rasch asked.

The girls took off their dresses and stood in white underwear that made their skin seem starkly ochre.

"They have names?" Rasch asked.

Linney shrugged. "I call them Dancer and Prancer."

"Pardon?" Rasch said.

"Not their real names. I bought them in Phnom Penh."

"A fine purchase," Rasch said. "Very fine. Is no problem to bring them to United States?"

"There were visa considerations," Linney answered.

"Paperwork." Rasch looked as if he understood the labyrinthine requirements of bureaucracy.

"Which one do you favor?" Linney asked.

The East German strolled around the girls, nodding his head. This was precisely what he had come to Nicholas Linney's home for, the satisfaction of appetites that went undernourished in East Berlin, where he had a wife who resembled a sumo wrestler. He weighed a delicate breast in his hand, fingered a fine hip, patted a lean buttock. The girls didn't move. They were accustomed to being assessed by Linney's associates, men of Western culture who regarded them like oxen.

Rasch turned to Linney with a grin on his face. "Such pretty little birds," he said. "I like them both."

PATCHOGUE, LONG ISLAND

"It's not Jig's style," Frank Pagan said. "For one thing, he *never* claims he's made a kill on behalf of the Irish Republican Army. He never says *anything* like that. If he had reason to kill somebody in Albany, why would he change his usual message?"

Zuboric, sitting in the passenger seat of Pagan's Cadillac, had his hands clenched tensely in his lap because he didn't like Pagan's idea of driving, which was to occupy the fast lane at around ninety-five miles an hour and keep a leaden foot on the gas pedal, ignoring anything in his way. Pagan was a fast man on the horn, thrusting his palm down and holding it there until the driver in front switched lanes.

"If it wasn't Jig, who was it?" Zuboric asked.

Pagan shrugged. He had the alarming habit of not looking where he was going. He forced the Cadillac up to a shaky eighty-five and turned his face to Zuboric. "I don't have an answer to that. None of it makes sense. I can't imagine some local IRA cell in Albany doing anything like this. I can't even imagine the *existence* of a cell in Albany. Christ, what would they do anyhow in the middle of New York State? Hold bake sales to raise funds for weapons? Lemonade stands? Sell little flags you can stick in your lapel?"

"Watch the road, Frank," Zuboric said.

Pagan banged his horn again, and the car in front, a canary-yellow Corvette, moved into the slow lane. "Another thing that bothers me is the connection. An old FUV man turns up dead in Albany at the same time as Ivor McInnes is here in New York."

"They don't have to be connected," Zuboric said. He favored the Jig hypothesis plain and simple. It was the only logical one and besides he was tired of bird-dogging Pagan. How sweet it would be to have a quick wrap on this whole business and be rid of Frank fucking Pagan once and for all. Then he could go back to the tangled affair that was his own life. *A topless bar, for Chrissakes. Shaking her wonderful tits for all and sundry to see. Drooling men with hard-ons under their overcoats.* Zuboric couldn't take any of this. He had to get Charity away from that life.

"Maybe not," Pagan answered.

"Jig had time to kill a man in Albany and then get to New York."

"He had time, certainly," Pagan said. "I don't know why he'd want to kill Fitzjohn, though."

"Consider this." Zuboric opened his eyes. "Jig finds out this character Fitzjohn had something to do with the missing money. Fitzjohn won't tell him anything. Jig kills him."

Pagan was unconvinced. "Why kill somebody who might have information you want? What sense does that make? If Fitzjohn knew something, Jig wouldn't kill him. He'd try everything he could to get the information out of the man, but he wouldn't kill him. That would be a sheer waste of resources." Pagan rubbed his eyes, taking both hands off the wheel to do so. Zuboric sat straight forward in his seat like a drowning man looking for something to clutch.

"Frank, for Chrissakes."

Pagan returned his hands to the wheel. "It just doesn't add up. Jig came back to St. Finbar's for two reasons. One was guns. The other was a name. And Tumulty knew only one name. Nicholas Linney. He said he never heard of Fitzjohn, so he couldn't tell Jig that one."

"Maybe Jig brought the name with him from Ireland," Zuboric said. He felt weary. It seemed to him that the whole Irish situation, at least so far as it had been imported into the United States, was too complex to contemplate. Complicated allegiances, obscure motivations. He understood it was best to keep it all simple in his mind. It was Catholic against Protestant, basically. Any side issues, any sudden tributaries, were not worth exploring if you wanted to retain your sanity, a possession Frank Pagan had almost relinquished.

"If he knew of Fitzjohn before he left Ireland, why would he go to all the trouble of getting a name from Tumulty? He understood the risks involved in going to Canal Street. Why take those risks if he already had a lead to the missing money? And if he did have a lead, why kill it?" Pagan peered into the rearview mirror. He changed lanes abruptly, overtook a large Mayflower van, then swung back out into the fast lane and gave the big Caddie more gas.

Zuboric had an image of the Cadillac, and all who sailed in her, crashing off the highway and plummeting down an embankment. A fiery death. This whole trip across Long Island wouldn't have been necessary if Pagan had used his gun on Jig the first time around, a perception that made Zuboric resentful.

"Maybe we're going to Bridgehampton for nothing."

Pagan didn't think so. He had the feeling that poor Joe Tumulty, faced with premature eviction from St. Finbar's and the end of all his humanitarian labors, had finally been truthful. And if it hadn't been for Artie Zuboric blurting out Jig's name at that first meeting with Tumulty, if Pagan had been given the chance to take slower steps, more circumspect ones, the chance to run things his own way, then Tumulty would have been less defensive and more easily caught unawares. And perhaps Jig would have been simpler to snare. Hindsight, blessed hindsight, Pagan thought. It was an overrated quality.

"We'll find out soon enough," he said.

"What if Jig's already been there?" Zuboric asked.

"That's something else we'll find out," Pagan replied.

He pressed the gas pedal to the floor, rolled his window down, turned on the radio just as the town of Patchogue slipped past on the edge of Highway 27, and heard the sound of Freddie Cannon singing "Palisades Park," an anthem from an innocent time.

ROSCOMMON, NEW YORK

Celestine Cairney listened to her husband's music drift out through the open door of his library. It seemed more melancholy than usual this morning. It fitted Harry's mood, certainly. Ever since he'd learned that his son had gone abruptly in the middle of the night he'd retreated behind the wall of his music, his silence chilly and his face pale and haunted. Patrick's manner of departure had disappointed him. No farewell. No final hug. No promises to keep in touch.

She stood on the threshhold of the room, looking across the floor at her husband. He sat in a large wing chair besides the fireplace, unaware of her. He appeared very frail, his skinny white hands clasped in his lap, his eyes closed under white lids, his head moving very slightly in time to the music. She didn't have the heart to talk with him. She had no way of explaining Patrick's departure to him, even if she'd wanted to.

She went down the long flight of stairs to the hallway below. Inside the sitting room she stood at the window and looked out over the expanse of land that sloped down to the shore of the lake. She twisted her fingers together. When she tried to remember her visit to Patrick Cairney's bedroom her memories were evasive. The taste of the man, the way he felt—these things came back to her with a clarity. But there was something else that eluded her. What did she want to call it? His essence? His private self? Perhaps it was the simple mystery of the unattainable, longing for the thing you can never have.

No. It had nothing to do with the ache of remembered desire or the way it clawed at her heart or the fact that Patrick Cairney was her husband's son.

It was another kind of mystery altogether, concrete and tangible.

She pressed her cheek against the cold glass. Outside, the early morning sun had a faint mist hanging around it. A veil. Like the veil Patrick Cairney drew over himself.

She turned away from the window. Her hand went out to the telephone and lingered over it. The obvious place to begin was with the archaeological departments of universities, but today was Saturday and those offices would be shut. It would have to wait, she thought. She sat down, struggling with her impatience and the sense of excitement she suddenly felt. She knew she was on to something, but precisely what she couldn't quite say. It was almost as if Patrick Cairney were a book she had somehow opened in the middle at a suspenseful part, a tease that would compel her to read to the end where everything enigmatic would be clarified in one stunning revelation.

Harry came inside the room, moving slowly. Celestine took his hand and held it against her breasts.

"I can't understand it," he said. "Why did he leave like that?"

Celestine didn't speak.

Cairney inclined his head so that it touched his wife's shoulder. "Did he strike you as being unhappy about something? Did I say something to upset him?"

She shook her head and said no, he hadn't.

"There's something restless about that boy," Cairney said. "There's always been this restless center to him. It's like he's never fully at ease anywhere."

"I can't imagine why," Celestine replied.

Harry Cairney, who felt very old this morning, closed his eyes. His sense of unhappiness was strong, like a blade in his chest. He'd been looking forward to spending the morning with his son, talking of his favorite subject, Ireland, reminiscing, reliving a past that was going to die when he did. He'd awakened that morning with old memories vitally refreshed, things he wanted to tell Patrick, sights and sounds he wanted to convey to the boy—the clattering old trams that used to run all over the city with their Amstel Lager Beer and Bovril and Neaves Food signs, along the North Circular Road and Rathmines Road and Sackville Street out to Phoenix Park (although he couldn't remember the exact routes now, as if the geography of his beloved Dublin had collapsed in his memory), the smells of loose tea in Sheridan's on North Earl Street, how he'd bought his first real pair of shoes at the Popular Boot Emporium on South Great George's Street, and Croke Park where on March 14, 1921, the British had surrounded a crowd of ten thousand at a football game and opened fire, volley after volley, wounding and killing the blameless. Fourteen dead. Fifty-seven injured. His memory had become all at once a crowded place, but what goddam good were memories when you didn't have your boy to share them with? Patrick would have been interested in hearing these things. He was always interested in his father's recollections. He loved Ireland just as the old man did.

Celestine put her arms around Harry and drew him against her body. "I'm sure he'll call," she said.

She stroked the side of his face very deliberately, almost as if she were seeking resemblances between the old man to whom she was married and the young man who had left her, in the dead of night, with enigmas.

"Love me," Harry Cairney said.

"Here? Now?"

"Here and now."

She put her hand between the folds of his robe, cupping his testicles in her palm. His skin was cold. She worked her fingers over the shaft of his penis, which was infirm and soft until she began to stroke it energetically. She listened to the low sound he made as he grew excited—a quiet moaning, a whispering of words she could never quite catch. His breath quickened and there was rasping from his tired lungs.

She parted his robe and went down on her knees. Looking upward once at the whiteness of his body, the sagging pectoral muscles, the folds of his neck, she shut her eyes and transported herself to an imagined place and time, where she kneeled, exactly as she was doing now, at the feet of another man, whose body was Patrick Cairney's.

EIGHTEEN

Patrick Cairney parked his car on Ocean Road at the edge of Bridgehampton. Like the other small resorts in the area known as the Hamptons, Bridgehampton had the feel of a place abandoned for the winter. Empty cafés, closed bars, gulls squabbling in a forlornly quarrelsome way in the cloudy sky over the beach. The man known as Nicholas Linney lived in this village. Earlier, in Southampton, Cairney had consulted a local telephone directory and learned that Linney lived at number 19 Wood Lane. When he'd been inside the phone booth, he'd experienced an urge to call Finn, just to pick up the telephone and make the transatlantic connection and hear Finn's voice. He'd let his fingertips linger on the black receiver. He had nothing to report to Finn yet.

Wood Lane, a private estate of the kind that suggested wealthy inhabitants and the likelihood of a private security patrol, was a narrow thoroughfare running at a right angle from Ocean Road. In summer, the lane would have been leafy and dense and green, but now the trees were barren, affording him absolutely no cover. He left his car on Ocean Road, the canvas bag locked inside the trunk.

He began to walk. He felt conspicuous even though he understood that many of the houses on the lane, hidden behind shrubbery and walls, had been vacated for the winter. Once, he heard the sound of a child shouting, followed by the noise of a ball bouncing against stone. After that, nothing.

He had no idea of what he was going to do when he found number 19. A great deal depended on the attitude of Nicholas Linney, which was an unpredictable factor. In an ideal world, Linney would be a reasonable man who would discuss the problem of the money calmly, rationally. In this same world Nicholas Linney would know precisely what had happened to the *Connie*'s cargo and he'd tell Cairney at once. But Finn had talked of the need for caution. *Expect them to lie to you. Expect outright animosity toward you.*

Take them off guard, if you can.

When he reached number 19 he kept moving, noticing a wrought-iron fence and, some distance beyond, a one-story house surrounded by sycamores. There were three vehicles parked in the driveway. A Mercedes, a BMW, and a Land-Rover painted in camouflage. He came to the place where the iron fence ended, and he stopped. A house built on one level was good because it meant he didn't have to worry about anybody concealed in upstairs rooms. A small bonus. The cars suggested two things. Either Nicholas Linney collected foreign autos or else he had a visitor.

What Cairney wished for right then was the obscurity of night, darkness. His best plan was to wait for nightfall and hope that Nicholas Linney would emerge alone from the house at some point. But he couldn't afford to wait. It was really that simple. He couldn't afford the luxury of time because he had absolutely no way of knowing what Joe Tumulty might have told Pagan. If the priest had pointed Pagan in this direction, then time was truly of the essence. He might be trapped inside an hourglass and slipping with the sands.

He studied the fence. He considered a direct approach, straight up to the front door like a Jehovah's Witness or a man from the Fuller Brush Company, but he decided against that. It came back again to the fact he couldn't *predict* anything in this situation. Linney might be reasonable. Or he might not be. Stealth was the most prudent approach to the house. And if he was going to climb this fence he'd have to do it at the corner where a small stand of pine trees would conceal him from the windows of the place.

The fence was easy. He hauled himself up, dropped quickly down on the other side. As he stood under the pines he was conscious of music issuing from the house. There was a harsh sound of a man laughing. The music stopped. The house was silent again.

It was perhaps fifty feet from the pines to the side of the house where an empty terrace overlooked a concrete tennis court. For that distance he would have no cover. A man stepped out of the house and moved onto the terrace, where he sat down at a table and propped his feet up and poured himself a drink. Cairney, seeking invisibility, pressed himself against the trunk of a tree. He had the thought that if this were some other situation, the kind he was used to, the kind where it was a matter of bringing down a particular target you fixed through the scope of a rifle, then he wouldn't feel this uncertain. The man on the terrace, for example. How simple it would have been, in other circumstances, to shoot him. But even if he *had* been armed, Finn hadn't given him a mandate for violence.

Now there was more laughter from the house. A girl's laugh this time, high-pitched. False and polite. Cairney stood very still. Then, tensing his body, he moved out from under his cover and headed in the direction of the front door, passing the parked cars quickly.

He reached out and turned the door handle. The door wasn't locked. He opened it an inch, two inches, seeing a square of hallway beyond. He stepped into the house, closed the door softly, then stood very still in the center of the hall, listening, concentrating, wondering about the next step. Other doors, each of them closed, faced him. Which one to try?

Then, suddenly, one of the doors opened and a beautiful Oriental girl stood there wrapped in a large white towel, her black hair hanging on her shoulders and her dark eyes wide with surprise.

Cairney stared at her. The girl must have assumed he was a guest in the house because she did something that amazed him then. She let the towel slip from her body, stepped over it and, with her arms held out, came toward him. Cairney reached for her wrist, twisted it, swung her around so that she had her back to him, then held her tightly against him like a shield. The girl's reaction surprised him. She giggled, almost as if force were a regular occurrence in her life. She *expected* men to treat her this way. He clamped his hand across her lips.

"Linney," he said. "Show me where Linney is."

The girl made a small sound into Cairney's palm. He could feel her wet lips, her teeth, the tiny tip of her tongue. She moved forward. Cairney kept his hold on her, following her toward the doorway from which she'd emerged. There was a large bedroom beyond.

A plump man, who wasn't the one Cairney had seen on the terrace, lay naked on the bed while another girl, remarkably similar to the one Cairney grasped, attended to his needs. She had her face buried deep in the man's groin. The man sat upright quickly, staring at Cairney with an expression of stunned vulnerability. He shoved the girl away from himself and he grabbed the bedsheet, hauling it quickly up over his body.

"Who are you?" the man asked. He had a foreign accent, European of some kind.

Cairney still held the girl tightly. "Linney?" he asked.

The plump man shook his head and looked angry. The girl who'd been shoved so rudely aside gazed at Cairney as if she didn't know quite what to make of him. There was a dull defensive quality in her face.

"Who are you?" the plump man asked again and then started to rise from the bed, his expression now one of alarm. He began to make for the door, the bedsheet hanging loosely from his body. Cairney hesitated only a moment over his options. He could let this man leave the bedroom—but then what? The look on the man's face suggested that of some outraged burgher searching for the nearest telephone to call the police. And that was a complication Patrick Cairney didn't need.

"Don't go any farther," Cairney said. "Stop right where you are."

The plump man paid no attention. He was about six feet from the door and still hurrying when Cairney said, "Don't take another step."

The man ignored him.

Cairney clenched his fist and struck the man on the side of the head. It wasn't the fiercest of blows but it had an immediate effect. The plump man's eyes rolled and he gasped and then appeared to implode as he staggered back across the floor onto the bed. The bedsheet, like some outsized shroud, collapsed around him. It was crude and Cairney regretted having to do it, but there was no way he could have let the man stroll out of here. He looked down at the unconscious figure, feeling curiously depressed by the sight of the open mouth and the broken skin on the side of the scalp. It shouldn't have been necessary, it should have been simple and smooth and uneventful. Instead, he'd been drawn into an act of violence that seemed all the more upsetting to him because of its very intimacy, the connection of his flesh with that of another, the moment of harsh contact, bone on bone. It wasn't violence from a distance, the kind he was accustomed to. It was close up and personal, and it made him unhappy. He was still holding the girl, still staring at the inert figure on the bed, when he heard a man's voice from beyond the bedroom door.

Rasch? Are you finished in there?

And then the door opened and the man from the terrace stood on the threshold. He appeared only slightly surprised by Cairney's presence. There was a momentary widening of the eyes, and then he was smiling, as if the unexpected appearance of a total stranger were an everyday event.

"You can let the girl go," he said. "I don't like having my property mistreated."

Cairney didn't release the girl. He ran his eye over the man, but he didn't notice the presence of any weapon. Besides, since the man was dressed only in shorts and a sweatshirt, there were no obvious hiding places for a gun.

"Linney," Cairney said.

Nicholas Linney nodded. He gazed a moment at Gustav Rasch on the bed. Then he turned his face back to Cairney.

"You're the one they sent from Ireland," Linney said. *This was the one everybody was so worried about. This was the man Harry Cairney had said was going to be so fucking good at his business.* Nicholas Linney felt a rush of pleasure to his head, a keen anticipation, an awareness of combat. He'd find out how good this guy was supposed to be. This guy was about to discover that Nick Linney wasn't some overweight German clerk. All at once Linney's chest was tight and his heartbeat had the persistence of a funeral drum.

Cairney let the girl go. She sat on the edge of the bed, pushing her glossy black hair out of her eyes. The other girl reached for her friend's hand and held it.

"I'm the one," Cairney said.

Nicholas Linney took a step back out of the bedroom. Cairney moved after him. Linney glanced at the man's overcoat, seeing how one hand was thrust inside a pocket now. *He has a gun in there.* And he wouldn't carry one unless he intended to use it somewhere down the line. Linney thought of all the weapons he had inside his office. He'd play along, he'd wait for the moment, the opening. It was bound to come. There was a wonderful irony in the idea of killing this hotshot with one of the M-16A2s that had been intended for Ireland. Linney was enormously pleased by it.

Both men stood inside a large living room. There was a massive fish tank where small electric colors darted back and forth.

Cairney said, "We need to talk. You know what I've come for."

Linney smiled. His goddam heart wouldn't stop hammering. Here was a situation he'd wanted all along, his own private little war. Right here in his own living room. He could already feel the stark warmth of the automatic rifle between his hands.

"Suppose I tell you what I know. What guarantees can you give me you won't shoot me when you've heard everything I have to say?"

"I don't give guarantees," Cairney said. He wondered why Linney had talked about shooting, and then it dawned on him that the man imagined there was a gun in his pocket. Fine. Let him think so.

"You pump me dry of information, what fucking good am I to you after that?" Linney asked. "I need something. I gotta have a guarantee. Something."

Cairney, who saw on Linney's face a desperation that lay beneath the intensity, felt suddenly relaxed. With barely any effort he'd established control here. He'd taken command. The game was his and he could play it however he liked. Whatever uncertainty he'd felt before fell away from him. He felt the way he had when he'd assassinated Lord Drumcannon, that elation when the man had appeared in the sight of his rifle, that moment when you knew the game was over and the result already sealed beyond doubt and all that was left was the mere bloody formality of the victim falling. *You've got this one*, he told himself. *You've cornered this one.* And all because he thinks you've got a gun concealed in your pocket.

"Somebody broke a contract," he said. "Somebody screwed the Cause. It's not the kind of situation where I can offer you immunity, Linney. For all I know, you might be the man I'm looking for."

Linney shook his head. It was just as he'd expected. This fucker suspected *him*. "Not me, friend."

Cairney moved forward. He was very close to Linney now.

"Who gave you my name anyway?" Linney asked. He glanced a second at the half-open door of his office. He could turn quickly, he could make it inside, slam the door hard behind him. He could do it. He could get to a weapon. It all depended on letting this fucker think everything was going his way. "It was that scumbag priest, wasn't it? He sent you here."

Cairney said nothing. He had a tremor, a fleeting doubt, that Nicholas Linney was preoccupied with something, that his mind was feverishly working in some other direction. Cairney bunched his hand in his coat pocket and moved it very slightly to emphasize the phantom gun.

Linney saw the gesture. He'd never been faced with a gunman before, and he felt the vibrancy of the challenge. His mind was astonishingly clear and sharp. He had a sense of a steel spring coiled deep inside him. Play along with the guy, he thought. Lull him. Then *move*.

"What is it you want? Names? Addresses?"

"I want everything you can give me, Linney."

Nicholas Linney had his back flush to the wall now. He looked at the man a moment, then said, "In my office. I got all the information there." Linney indicated a door to his right.

"After you," Cairney said.

Linney took a step toward his office. He sucked air deeply into his lungs and felt that spring inside him suddenly unwind.

Now!

He shoved the door open and slammed it hard behind him and before Cairney could get a foot in he heard Nicholas Linney bolting the door. And then there was another sound from within the locked room, one that Cairney recognized only too well. It was the click of a magazine being shoved hurriedly into a rifle. And then Nicholas Linney roared aloud, the strange cry of a man exalted by the prospect of battle.

Cairney reacted immediately.

He threw himself to one side, rolling over and over in the direction of the sliding glass doors, so that he was out of the line of fire. When the sound of automatic gunfire started, he heard it split the silence of the house like a hammer smashing glass, and then the two girls were screaming and grabbing one another for protection against the random, blind assault of bullets that traversed the living room and buried themselves in plaster.

Cairney blinked involuntarily. Linney was shooting wildly through the door of his office, his bullets tearing huge holes in the wood and spraying the air with splinters. It was desperate stuff and Cairney, cursing himself for having been misled by his own sense of supremacy, closed his eyes and pressed his face down into the floor. Linney kept firing madly, the door shook and vibrated, the splinters flew, the girls screamed. It was insane, a world that had only a moment ago been regulated and under control turned totally upside down and gone berserk.

One of the Oriental girls was struck by the spray inside the bedroom and was screaming because there was an enormous hole in her stomach. The other girl, covered by her blood, lay flat on the floor and cried for a time until she became quiet. The gunfire pierced woodwork and mirrors and windows, creating chaos and debris. A stereo blew up in a violent plume of smoke and sparks, and the chandelier threw out tiny shards of crystal that created a glassy rain. The fish tank exploded like a dynamited kaleidoscope, showering the room with yellow and blue and red fish.

Cairney saw the plump man on the bed slither to the floor in a tangle of bedsheets and a snowstorm of feathers released from a punctured pillow. He lay beside the two girls, both of whom had been hit.

And then abruptly the firing stopped and the silence was the most profoundly unsettling Cairney had ever heard. He raised his face and looked at the door, which was buckled and split and hanging precariously from its hinges. What was Linney doing now? Reloading?

Listening, Cairney heard the sound of dying fish flapping desperately in puddles of shallow water. He crawled through the sliding glass doors to the terrace where a rough wind rising up off the ocean scoured his face. The carnage, so sudden, so unexpected, had shaken him. It wasn't supposed to be like this, he thought. It wasn't supposed to get away from him like this. He had had *goddam* Linney right where he wanted him—and now, Christ, it had fallen apart.

He heard the noise of the broken door being kicked down, then the sound of Linney moving in the room, feet squelching through the water from the fish tank.

Cairney peered through the glass doors. Linney, his back to Cairney, was holding a pistol out in front of himself as he moved. He walked hesitantly toward the bedroom, trying to keep his balance on the slippery floor. Cairney watched. He knew Linney could turn around at any second and see him framed in the glass doors, a perfect target.

There were twenty feet, twenty-five at most, separating Cairney from Linney, who was standing now in the threshold of the bedroom. It might be the only chance Cairney would ever have. He would have to move now or not at all.

He stepped through the glass doors back inside the room, moving with all the stealth he'd learned in the desert, moving as the Libyans always said, "like a man whose feet are the wind," watching Linney who was regarding the girls inside the bedroom. Fifteen feet, ten. How far could he travel across this watery floor before Linney heard him and turned around and fired his pistol? Ten feet. Nine. Eight.

When Cairney was a mere six feet away, some instinct made Linney swing quickly around, firing one shot that was unfocused and wild and went flying past Cairney's cheek into the glass panel of the door. Cairney bent low, shoulders hunched, every muscle in his body relaxed and ready now for the move he'd have to make before Linney found his range and fired again. He threw himself across the room with neither grace nor elegance, an anxious linebacker, his shoulder crunching into the man's face. There was the sound of bone breaking as the man slithered on the watery floor and tumbled back against the wall. The blow confused and pained Linney but didn't render him unconscious. The pistol clattered across the ceramic tile of the floor and Cairney, turning away from the other man, picked it up.

Linney watched him grimly. Then, using the wall for support, he made it to his feet. "I gave it a good fucking shot, didn't I?" He seemed very pleased with himself. "You're not bad. You know that?"

Cairney shook his head. None of this should ever have happened. *This chaos and destruction. None of it.* He could think of nothing to say. He felt brutalized. This was so far removed from any sequence of events he could possibly have anticipated. He couldn't have dreamed this even if he'd dreamed a hundred years. *There's no thrill in killing*, Finn had said once. But there was, if you were a man like Nicholas Linney. What did Linney resemble anyhow but the kind of random killer that Finn had always loathed? A lover of easy death and casual destruction?

"Mulhaney took the money," Linney said. His jaw must have been broken because he spoke as if he had a mouth filled with old socks.

"Mulhaney?" Cairney asked.

Linney grimaced in pain. He raised one hand to his lips and probed the inside of his mouth and removed a filling, a small gold nugget that lay in his palm. Cairney glanced a second inside the bedroom. The plump man, whose nakedness in death seemed oddly childlike, like that of an unnaturally huge baby, was surrounded by feathers from the wrecked pillow. The girls, who lay beneath him, looked only mildly surprised.

Nicholas Linney's face had already begun to swell. "Mulhaney runs the Northeastern branch of the Teamsters. Big Bad Jock."

Cairney knew the name now. It was one he always associated with questionable labor practices, slush funds, Las Vegas intrigues.

"What makes you think Mulhaney has the money?"

Nicholas Linney said, "Take my word for it. I thought at first it had to be Dawson, but what would he want money for? He's got it coming out of his ass."

Dawson. Another name now. "Who's Dawson?"

Linney smiled. The expression caused him obvious pain. His face contorted. "You don't know anything, do you? They really sent you here blind, didn't they?"

"I asked about Dawson." Cairney made a gesture with the pistol.

"Kevin Dawson," Linney said. "Big brother Tommy occupies the White House."

Kevin Dawson, the quiet member of the Dawson clan, the background figure whose family was sometimes trotted out for the edification of wholesome America. They just adored Kevin and his wife and kids in the heartland. Cairney was surprised by the names Linney tossed out. But how could he trust a man like Linney, who was capable of doing and saying anything?

Linney said, "You got my word. You want Mulhaney."

Your word. "Where do I find him?"

Linney shuffled toward the broken door, beyond which was a room whose walls were stacked with gun racks. There were all kinds of weapons, competition rifles, shotguns, black-powder muskets, handguns. On the floor lay the automatic rifle that had been used to blast through the door. Linney, who was thinking about the pistol he kept in the center drawer of his desk, slumped into a chair and punched some buttons on a computer console. A small amber screen lit up and a disc drive whirred.

"There," Linney said.

A name, an address. Cairney studied them. He committed them to memory. He felt strangely removed from himself now, like somebody going through the motions. He concentrated on pulling himself together. It didn't matter what had happened here, he still had his work to do. He still had Finn's task to carry out. He couldn't afford to dwell on the outrage perpetrated by Nicholas Linney. He stared at the shimmering little letters. His eyes began to hurt. He looked at Linney, who had his hands in his lap.

Linney said, "You're thinking I'll call Mulhaney, right? If you let me live, I'll call him. Isn't that what's on your mind? Hey, I give you my word, I won't warn him. Why should I? If he stole the goddam money, he deserves to die."

"What do you deserve?" Cairney asked with contempt. "You think *you* deserve to live?"

Linney forced a little smile. He moved one hand toward the center drawer of his desk. *Nobody beats Nicholas Linney*, he thought. *Nobody leaves my house thinking I'm some fucking loser. I trained myself for exactly this kind of situation.* "I gave you what you wanted, guy. That merits some consideration."

"The price was high, Linney."

Linney shrugged. He drummed his fingertips on the handle of the drawer. This guy was fast, but Linney believed he could be even quicker. "Sometimes you have to pay it."

Cairney felt the weight of the pistol in his hand. It would be the simplest thing in the world to turn the gun on Linney. If he left Linney alive, who could predict what the man would do then? He couldn't afford to step out of this house and walk away from Linney, who could start making frantic little calls. It was a strange moment for Cairney. He could see a vein throb in Linney's head. He had an unsettling sense of Linney's life, the blood coursing through the man's body. This was a living presence, not a distant figure fixed in the heart of a scope. There were only a couple of inches between Cairney and the man, and he found himself longing for space, longing for the lens of a scope, longing for *distance*. If he had that kind of separation from this monster, he'd kill him without blinking an eye.

Linney stared at the gun. He curled one finger around the handle of the drawer. Go for it, Nick. Just go for it. *You got nothing to lose because this fucker is going to kill you anyway.* "Mulhaney's in bad shape financially. He needed money more than the rest of us."

The rest of us. "How many are there, Linney?"

"Come on, guy. I gave you what you wanted. Don't get greedy."

"How many, Linney?"

Linney did something desperate then. He swiveled his chair around, a gesture that was meant to be casual, easygoing, just a man turning his chair in preparation for getting up out of it—but it was a feint, a sorry kind of deception, because all at once there was a pistol in the center of his hand, a weapon he'd slipped from the desk in a very smooth motion, and he was bringing it around very quickly in Cairney's direction—

Cairney shot him once through the side of his face. Linney was knocked backward and out of the chair, one hand uplifted to his cheek as if death were a sudden facial blemish, and then the hand dropped like a stone and Linney followed its downward path to the floor. He lay looking up at the ceiling of his gun room, seeing nothing.

Cairney stared at the body. *Jesus Christ*. There was a terrible slippage going on here, a downhill slope into destruction. His hand shook. He couldn't find his own private center. He couldn't find the place of calm retreat. It was as if a storm had broken out inside himself. Four people had died in this goddam house and all because he'd come here looking for information. Looking for Finn's money. He shut his eyes a moment. The death of Linney shouldn't have touched him. He was accustomed to killing. But he'd never shot anyone at such close range before. Okay, Linney had sought death, Linney had manufactured that destiny for himself, but what about the two girls? What was their role in this? Had they ever even *heard* about the Cause?

He opened his eyes. He heard a car crunch into the driveway. He stepped to the window, saw a dark-green Cadillac. Quickly, he moved into the living room and went to the sliding doors, then out onto the terrace where he saw Frank Pagan climb from the big green car. Nimble and silent, unseen by Pagan, Cairney vaulted the terrace wall and skipped across the tennis court to the fence, which he climbed swiftly. And then he was back in the lane, hurrying away.

NEW YORK CITY

Ivor McInnes left the Essex House and walked south on fifth Avenue. He went along Fifty-seventh Street, checking his watch, looking in shop windows. The whole array of American consumer goods dazzled him as it always did, the flash and the glitter and the sheer availability of things. He spotted a thrift shop that sold only furs, and he thought that only in America could such a place exist. Did the rich dames on Central Park toss their used lynx coats this way? Did those blue-rinsed old biddies you saw walking their poodles, manicured little dogs that seemed to shit politely on sidewalks, bring their weary minks to the fur thrift shop? Amazing America!

When he reached Broadway he headed south. Broadway disappointed. He always expected the Great White Way, showgirls stepping out of limos and maybe the sight of some great actress hurrying inside a theater, last-minute rehearsals. But it was all sleazy little restaurants and an atmosphere of congealed grease. At Times Square he found the public telephone he needed, then he went inside the booth and checked his watch again. The phone rang almost immediately. Seamus Houlihan was nothing if not punctual.

McInnes picked up the receiver.

"We're in place," Houlihan said.

"Good man." McInnes ran the tip of a finger between his dog collar and his neck.

"I had to take out Fitz," Houlihan said. "He was trying to skip."

The disposal of Fitzjohn was of no real concern to McInnes, who had long ago understood that human life, a tenuous business at best, was nothing when you weighed it against ultimate victory. Fitzjohn had been a mere foot soldier, and they were always the first casualties. "What did you do with the body?"

Houlihan told him.

McInnes listened closely. He couldn't believe what Houlihan was telling him. When Houlihan was through with his story, McInnes was quiet for a while, drumming his fingertips on a filthy pane of glass. If he hated anything, if anything in the world aroused his ire beyond the dangerous philosophies of the Catholic Church, it was when a meticulous plan was interrupted by needless variations, such as the variation Houlihan had introduced in Albany.

"What the hell did you expect to *achieve* by calling the bloody FBI?" McInnes asked. "Jesus in heaven, Seamus, what the hell were you *thinking* about?"

"It seemed like a good idea to set the ball rolling," Houlihan said in a curt voice.

"The ball, Seamus, was not supposed to be set rolling until tomorrow. Sunday, Seamus. White Plains. Remember?"

Houlihan was quiet on the other end of the line. McInnes, who experienced a stricture around his heart, had the feeling of a man who has completed an elaborate jigsaw only to find a piece removed during his absence by a willful hand.

"Don't you see it, Seamus? It's too bloody soon."

Houlihan still didn't speak. What McInnes felt down the line was the young man's hostility. The killing of Fitzjohn had presumably been necessary in Houlihan's questionable judgment, but the next step—which Seamus had taken without consultation—was not very bright. But then you couldn't expect anything bright out of Seamus. He was great when it came to demolition work. Beyond that he was useless. McInnes thought about Houlihan's unhappy background. Perhaps allowances could be made for a man who was the offspring of an absentee Catholic father and a Protestant mother who had become a drunken bigot of the worst kind. Houlihan must have spent years hating the man who had fathered and abandoned him.

McInnes said, "It removes the element of surprise, Seamus. Don't you see that? It's like sending them a bloody telegraph. You were instructed to wait until you'd done your work in White Plains before calling."

Sweet Jesus Christ, McInnes thought. It had long been one of the problems of the Free Ulster Volunteers, this lack of good responsible men and the need to draft street scum who killed for the joy of killing and who were misled, by their own acts of violence, into thinking they were actually *smart*. McInnes had always been troubled by this. For every good man he brought into the FUV, there was always a psychopath with a terrible need for blood. What McInnes longed for was a figure like Jig, somebody who killed but who always obeyed instructions. Somebody who didn't step outside the limits of his authority. Jig, he thought. Even somebody like Jig was running out of time. And luck. And sometimes luck, that erratic barometer, swung away from you in the direction of your enemies. Jig's time was coming.

"Now they're going to be out beating the fields with sticks," McInnes said. "And all because you took it into your thick head to make a bloody phone call, Seamus. God in heaven, I didn't want them to have an inkling until the work in White Plains is done with."

Houlihan was heard to clear his throat. "They can beat the fields with sticks all they want. They're not going to find us, are they?"

McInnes stared across the street at a movie-house marquee. There was a double feature. *Pussies in Boots* and *G-string Follies*. Somewhat incongruously, two nuns went past the theater, hobbling in their black boots. McInnes watched them, two middle-aged brides of Christ, their juices all dried up. A lifetime of celibacy was likely to drive you mad, he thought. It was no wonder they believed in such unlikely things as holy water and the infallibility of the pope and that philo-

sophical absurdity the Holy Ghost. And these women ran schools
and influenced the minds of small children, venting all their accu-
mulated frustrations on the souls of infants. Dear God! McInnes
turned his thoughts to what he perceived as the final solution for
Ulster, and it had nothing to do with the persecution of Catholics or
denial of their rights to their own schools and churches. The answer
was so bloody simple nobody had ever thought it could work. You
repatriated the Catholics, that's what you did. You sent them to the
Republic of Ireland. There they could pursue their religious beliefs
until doomsday in a society already priest-soaked and dominated by
his Holiness, the Gaffer of the Vatican. There would be no more civil
strife, no more violence. Ulster would be free, and the Catholics
happy. *So damned simple.*

"No, they're probably not going to find you, Seamus. All I'm saying is you didn't follow my instructions. I didn't just sit down and
make everything up on the spur of the moment. I worked bloody
hard and I planned a long bloody time, Seamus. And I won't have
it bollixed up by somebody who takes it into his head to change my
plans."

McInnes fell silent. What good did it do to scream at Houlihan,
whose temperament was unpredictable at best? If you didn't butter
up people like Seamus, they were likely to fold their tents. And then
where would you be? McInnes controlled himself. When the time
was ripe, he'd find a way to dispose of Houlihan and the others. In
the future he perceived for himself, there was no room for thugs.

"We'll forget it this time," he said. "But next time follow the blueprint, Seamus."

Houlihan said nothing.

"Good luck tomorrow," McInnes said.

He stepped out of the stale phone booth and wandered through
Times Square. He had a slippery sense of his own fate lying in the
clumsy hands of a man like Seamus Houlihan. By calling the FBI,
what Seamus had done was to set that whole federal machine in
motion too soon. McInnes thought he could already hear the wheels
grinding away, the cogs clicking. If they ran a check on Fitz, they'd
discover his affiliation with the Free Ulster Volunteers, which might
in turn lead them directly to himself. Naturally, he'd deny everything, but just the same he saw little connecting threads here he
didn't remotely like. The whole point of the exercise had been to
keep the FUV name out of everything. But now it was likely to come

up, and there was nothing he could do about it except look totally innocent if anyone asked about Fitzjohn. There was Frank Pagan to consider as well. When Pagan learned about the death of Fitzjohn, if he hadn't already done so, he'd be back sniffing around like some big bloodhound. Pagan was desperate to pin something, *anything*, on the Reverend Ivor McInnes.

There was another possibility, of course, that the FBI might automatically associate Jig with the slaying of Fitzjohn, which would fit McInnes's scheme of things very nicely indeed. Jig was a pain in the arse, but he wasn't the whole IRA by any stretch of the imagination.

Bloody Houlihan. What a nuisance.

McInnes stopped in front of a movie poster. The star of *Pussies in Boots* was a girl with the unlikely name of Mysterioso McCall. She had breasts that suggested two of God's more inspired miracles. Either that or silicone. For a second McInnes experienced a terrible pang of longing.

He took a last look at the poster and turned north on Broadway, stepping back in the general direction of his hotel. On the corner of Fifty-second Street he stopped, looked back the way he'd come, saw no sign of anyone following him, then he made a right turn. Inside a darkened cocktail bar on Fifty-second he ordered a ginger ale, which he took to a corner table by the telephone.

He checked his watch again. Almost noon. He sipped his drink, waited, staring now and again at the phone. He was in the right place at the right time, but when the phone hadn't rung by twenty past twelve he finished his ginger ale and went back out on to the street again, a little lonely suddenly, a little forlorn, thinking of warm flesh and the consolations of love and how a silent telephone could bring a very special dismay all its own.

BRIDGEHAMPTON, LONG ISLAND

Frank Pagan stared at a gorgeous angelfish that expired in the middle of the floor, slowly flapping its body and looking for all the world like the wing of an exotic bird. The fish hypnotized him, held him captive. If he didn't take his eyes away from the sight of the pathetic thing shuddering down into its own doom, then he wouldn't have to look again at the wreckage of this house. Having gone once from room to room, he had no desire to do so again. It was best left to somebody like Artie Zuboric, who seemingly had the stomach for this kind of wholesale destruction. Businesslike, brisk, Zuboric was flitting here and there and his Italian shoes squelched on the sodden floor.

"Two men, two girls," Zuboric said, bending to look at the dying fish.

Two men, two girls. Zuboric could make this tally of death sound like a football result. Pagan took his eyes from the fish and moved toward the room that was filled with guns. In there lay one of the dead men, minus a major portion of his face. There was something depressing in the sight of so much death. It ate at your spirit, filled your mind with darkness, numbed you. There was an automatic rifle on the floor.

Zuboric came into the gun room. He was holding an imitation leather wallet, flicking it open and checking the various cards inside.

"I guess this belonged to the guy in the bedroom," Zuboric said. "A certain Gustav Rasch. There's a bunch of stuff here in German. Can you read kraut?"

Pagan, who had an elementary knowledge of German, took the wallet. He scanned the cards, each sealed inside a plastic window. There was a Carte Blanche, a Communist party membership card issued in East Berlin, a Visa—a mixture of gritty socialism and suave capitalism. At the back of the wallet was a small plastic card identifying Gustav Rasch as a member of the East Berlin Trades and Cultural Mission, which was one of those meaningless societies they were forever inventing to send men into the West. Trade and culture, Pagan thought. Tractors and Tolstoy. Plutonium and Prokofiev. Pagan closed the wallet. The smell of death was overwhelming to him. He shoved a window open and caught a scent of the sea, good cleansing ozone with a dash of salt. There was blood on his fingertips, which he wiped clean against the curtains.

Zuboric took the wallet back. "What was Gustav Rasch doing here?" he asked. "What's the connection between an East German and Nicholas Linney?"

Pagan shook his head. The bizarre bedfellows of terrorism again, odd couples coming together in the night like hungry lovers, consuming each other before parting as total strangers. He didn't feel up to discussing the nebulous terrorist connections that were made in all the dark corners of the planet.

"If the guy in the bedroom's Rasch, this character lying here must be Nicholas Linney," Zuboric said.

Pagan said nothing

"Our friend Jig," Zuboric said. "He had a field day here."

Pagan stepped around the body on the floor. He tried to imagine Jig coming here and going through this house and leaving such wreckage behind him. Pagan's imagination wasn't functioning well. All the pictures he received were shadowy transmissions. If Jig had been responsible for all this, then the man's style had undergone drastic changes. Whoever had shot this place up had done so indiscriminately. Jig's violence had never been like this in the past. Why would he change now? What kind of circumstances would force him to perpetrate these horrors? There was nowhere in all of this a trace of Jig's signature. There was no elegance here.

Pagan watched Zuboric go out across the living room to the bedroom, saw him bend over the body of one of the dead girls whose stomach had been ripped open. A wave of pain coursed through Pagan's head. He thought, perhaps inevitably, of Roxanne, whose body they had not allowed him to see after her death. He had yearned for a sight of her back then, driven by a sickness to look one last time at what was left of the woman he'd loved. That desire struck him now as mad and morbid, but grief derailed you, leaving you empty and haunted and bewildered.

Pagan gazed at the racks of guns. He tried to reconstruct the events that had taken place here, but it was a maze with an impossible center. He looked at the door, which was riddled and splintered and lay off its hinges. This damage had obviously been done by the M-16, but who the hell had been firing the thing? Had Jig somehow been trapped inside this room and forced to shoot his way out?

Pagan could hear Zuboric sloshing around in the living room. The aquatic sleuth. What the hell did he think he was going to find amidst puddles of salt water and slivers of broken glass and the demolished innards of an expensive stereo system?

Pagan turned his attention to the surface of the desk. A variety of papers lay around in disarray, most of them computer printouts with references to ostmarks, rubles and zlotys. If Linney dabbled in Communist currencies, what Pagan wondered was just how much of this funny money found its way, via the United States, into Ireland. Nicholas Linney gathered rubles here, coaxed ostmarks there, and sent them, suitably converted into U.S. currency, to the IRA, using Joseph X. Tumulty as a link in the chain. But how long was that chain? And where did it reach?

Pagan looked at the illuminated screen of a computer console. There was a name and address in amber letters. Pagan stared at it in wonderment. Jock Mulhaney. Mulhaney was known even in Britain for his goodwill publicity tour of Ireland, both North and South, when he'd made a tour of what the press called "the trouble spots," giving impressive speeches in small border towns about how the real tragedy of Ireland was unemployment. At the time, carried away by his own rhetoric, Big Jock had pledged to do what he could about steering U.S. industry into Ireland, which was a promise he could never deliver. Ignoring the fact that he had a vested interest in keeping jobs in America, the Irish considered Big Jock something of a proletarian hero. And here he was on Linney's little screen. Well, well.

Connections.

Pagan stared at the keyboard. There was a scroll key, which he touched rather gingerly, because he didn't have an easy rapport with the new technology. The screen whisked Big Jock's name away, replacing it suddenly with two others.

Pagan gazed at the letters with astonishment. The amber treasure trove of information. He felt a sudden quickening of his nerves as he recognized the names that glimmered in front of him. More connections. Lovely connections. He scribbled them down on a piece of paper torn from Linney's printer, then put the paper inside his pocket. He heard the sound of Zuboric coming back across the living room. He quickly scanned the keyboard, looking for an off key, anything to kill the screen before Zuboric came inside the room. There was no way he was going to share this stuff with the FBI agent. He couldn't find an appropriate key so he yanked the plug out of the wall and the screen went wonderfully blank, carrying the names of Kevin Dawson and Harry Cairney off into some electronic limbo. With a look of innocence, Frank Pagan turned to see Zuboric enter.

"Here's the way I see it," Zuboric said. "Jig comes in. He gets inside the gun room somehow. Something goes wrong. Maybe Linney says he doesn't know anything about the money. Who knows? Jig becomes more than a little upset and decides to vent some spleen, the results of which are obvious," and Zuboric made a loose gesture with his hand. "Put it another way, Frank. Your cunning, clever assassin, the guy you seem to admire so much, is no better than a fucking fruitcake going berserk inside a crowded tenement on a hot summer evening in Harlem with a cheap twenty-two in his hand."

"It's one scenario," Pagan answered, still thinking about the names on Linney's computer. Connections, threads linking one powerful name with another. "It's not the only one, Artie. Even if you're half in love with it."

"Frank Pagan, attorney for the defense," Zuboric said.

Pagan clenched his large hands. There was this terrible urge to hit Zuboric. Nothing damaging, nothing that would leave an ungodly bruise or break a bone, just a straight solid punch that would silence the guy for a time. Zuboric's attitudes, his way of doing business, were beginning to pall.

Zuboric, who didn't like the expression on Pagan's face, turned away. "You can also assume Jig's armed by now," he said. "He sure as hell wouldn't leave without helping himself to a gun or two. Don't you wish you'd shot the fucker when you had the chance?"

Pagan understood the process going on here. Jig was going to be blamed for this massacre, and he, Pagan, was standing nicely in line to take some of the heat as well. That was the Bureau's tactic. When things go wrong, blame Frank Pagan. And all the blue-eyed boys in Leonard Korn's army stayed Kleenex-fresh.

"Jig didn't do this," he said.

Zuboric had a thin smile on his face. "You say. How do you know what Jig did or didn't do?"

It was a fair question and one Frank Pagan had no specific answer for.

"And that killing in Albany," Zuboric said. "How can you say it wasn't Jig?" The agent shook his head. "I'll tell you. He's on a goddam rampage, Frank. He's got the taste of blood in his mouth."

"And that's what you'll tell Washington?"

"I'll give them my considered opinion," Zuboric said.

Pagan saw Zuboric step out of the room, heard him move inside the kitchen. There was the sound of the telephone being lifted. Then Zuboric was talking in a low voice.

Pagan looked at the body of Nicholas Linney. He wished somebody in this house could come back, even on a temporary basis, from death, and tell him the exact truth about what had happened here. But there were only stilled pulses and hearts that no longer beat and voices forever silenced.

CAMP DAVID, MARYLAND

It was five o'clock in the afternoon before Thomas Dawson finally met with Leonard M. Korn. The President didn't like to conduct business on a Saturday, which was the day he habitually set aside for reading, catching up on the voluminous amount of material his aides and cabinet members prepared for him. It was a bleak afternoon, already dark, and there was a nasty rain slicing through the trees around the presidential compound at Camp David. Leonard M. Korn, who arrived in a black limousine, had the kind of presence that made a dark day darker still. What was it about him? Dawson wondered. He somehow seemed to absorb all the light around him and never release it, like a black mirror.

When Korn stepped inside the presidential quarters, Dawson was lounging on a sofa wearing blue jeans and boots and a plaid flannel shirt, all purchased from L. L. Bean. He sat upright, shuffled some papers, smiled coldly at Korn. Korn was a leftover from the previous administration, an appointee made by Dawson's predecessor who'd been a Republican in the cowboy tradition, an old man who dreamed nights of a world policed by U.S. gunboats.

"Take a pew," the President said.

Korn sat stiffly in his black gabardine overcoat. He removed several sheets of paper from his briefcase.

"Here is the information we've gathered on the casualties," he said, thrusting the sheets toward Thomas Dawson, who waved them aside.

"Suppose you give me the details briefly, Len," Dawson said. His eyes were tired from reading reports on such arcane matters as the butter glut in the Midwest, farm foreclosures on the Great Plains, proposals to alter corporate tax structures.

"Nicholas Linney ran a company called Urrisbeg International," Korn said. "Linney had fingers in a great many pies, Mr. President."

Korn paused. Dawson had grown immune to the clichés of language that surrounded him on a daily basis. A great many pies. Too many cooks. People in glass houses. Imaginative language was the first casualty of any bureaucracy.

"He had been investigated by Treasury two years ago. There was some suspicion of illegal dealing in foreign currencies," Korn said. "East European mainly. He was cleared."

Thomas Dawson nodded. He remembered Nicholas Linney well, and the recollection troubled him. He stood up. Once or twice, in the years before he had become President, he had played tennis with Nick Linney at fund-raising tournaments that were described under the general umbrella of Celebrity Invitationals. The celebrities were always ambitious politicians, game-show hosts, bargain-basement actors and tired comedians who had bought real estate in Palm Springs when that place was just a stopover in the desert. He squeezed his eyes shut very tightly. He was thinking of his brother now. He wished he'd never heard of the Fund-raisers. He wished even more that Kevin had stuck to running the family empire, keeping his nose out of Irish matters, and staying away from people like Linney.

"The second male victim was Gustav Rasch," Korn said. "An East Berlin party hack. He came to the U.S. periodically. General gofer. Sometimes he wanted to buy a piece of U.S. technology. Sometimes he wanted to tout a touring ballet company."

Leonard M. Korn placed the sheets flat on the briefcase that lay on his lap. The expression on the presidential face struck him as a little queasy, seasick.

"Linney was involved in raising funds to be sent to Ireland," Korn continued. "This much we've learned. As for Rasch, perhaps he was an investor, perhaps not. It doesn't matter very much at this stage, especially to Gustav Rasch. The two dead girls were probably Linney's personal harlots. He imported them from Cambodia as housemaids. They simply got in Jig's way."

Harlots, Dawson thought. Quaint puritanical word. He remembered Nick Linney's fondness for Oriental girls. He coughed quietly into his hand, then asked, "Can we assume Jig retrieved the stolen money and has returned to Ireland?" It was the kind of question a man asked with his fingers crossed.

Leonard M. Korn shook his head, as if the question were too naïve to contemplate. "We can't assume anything, Mr. President. If Linney didn't have the money, Jig would go looking elsewhere for it. It's that simple. Until we have evidence to the contrary we have to work on the understanding that he's still in the country, still actively searching. And the killing isn't going to stop. One man in Albany isn't very significant. But four people in Bridgehampton—well, that's a different kettle of fish."

Dawson walked to the window. He'd never seen fish in a kettle in his whole life. Outside, under the rainy trees, Secret Service agents stood around like drenched though vigilant birds. He thought of the two men he had supplied to brother Kevin. He wondered if, in the circumstances, two was enough.

"Do you have any suggestions?" Dawson turned to look at Korn.

Leonard M. Korn stood up. In his platform shoes, which were made especially for him by a discreet shoemaker on Atlantic Avenue in Virginia Beach, he stood five feet nine inches tall. That wasn't imposing but the shaved head added a quality of menace to his appearance.

Korn took a deep breath. "Thus far, my agency has had only minimal involvement. As per your own instructions, sir. And thus far the show has been run, so to speak, by the Englishman Pagan. With marked lack of success." He lowered his voice on this last sentence, a tone he hoped would not presume to question the President's judgment. "I'd advise a full-scale manhunt," he went on. "I could activate every available agent in and around New York. That way, I firmly believe we could see conclusive results, which is something we haven't been getting from Frank Pagan."

Thomas Dawson returned to the sofa and sat down. He understood Korn's need to blame this character Pagan, but the idea of a full-scale manhunt was totally unacceptable. Given the Bureau's heavy-handedness, there would inevitably be publicity. And where you had publicity you also had public reaction, which was a scandalously fickle barometer.

He was certain of only one thing. He was not about to alienate his precious, dependable Irish-American Catholic vote. So slender was the margin between further residency in the White House and the unseemly role of useless ex-president, fitted out in pathetic plaid knickerbockers and paraded on the golf circuit, that Dawson needed all the support he could muster. Publicity would be fine for Korn and his Bureau, especially if Jig was landed in the FBI net. But it could well be another matter for Thomas Dawson. Things were getting out of hand, admittedly, but he was going to turn down Korn's gung-ho suggestion.

"I'll think about it," he finally said.

An objection formed on Korn's lips, but he said nothing. He understood the meeting was over. He was waiting only for the President to dismiss him.

"In the meantime," Dawson said, "we continue to play it all very quietly. Sotto voce."

Korn nodded. Although he wondered how long it could continue to be played sotto voce, he wasn't going to voice this aloud. Presidents, like sticks of dynamite, had to be handled with care. They needed flattery, reassurance, agreement.

"Thanks for coming, Len," Dawson said. "Remember. Quietly. Very quietly. And keep me informed."

When Korn had gone, Thomas Dawson lay down on the sofa and stared at the rain sweeping the window. He thought again of Kevin. If Jig had found his way to Linney, how long before he reached Kevin?

He pondered the prospect of calling Kevin. He had given his brother two seasoned Secret Service men—what else could he possibly do? If he stepped up the Secret Service detachment at his brother's house, for example, sooner or later somebody was going to notice. There was always somebody, deep in a Washington cellar, who kept tabs on such things. There were always gossip columnists as well, who were drawn like doomed little moths to the Dawson flame and who were never very far from the center of Kevin's life. Dawson-Watchers who reported each and every Dawson social engagement with a shrill passion and who knew, courtesy of their sensitive antennae and inside informers, the things that went on around Kevin's household. And if these snoops observed a goddam battalion of Secret Service men lingering in New Rockford, they'd be pecking away at their portable Olivettis like a crowd of clucking birds.

The trouble with being President of the United States, he thought, was the sheer weight of the secrets you felt you had to keep. Jig's presence in the country, the murder of Nicholas Linney, Kevin's fund-raising activities. It was all just a little too much.

There was one simple solution to the immediate problem of Kevin's safety, and when it occurred to him he picked up the telephone and dialed his brother's number in Connecticut. It was answered by the woman who ran the Dawson household in New Rockford, an old family retainer named Agatha Bates. Agatha, ageless and humorless, was one of those stiff-backed examples of New England spinster who were bred less frequently these days. She had been connected with the Dawson family one way or another for most of her life.

"Kevin's gone," she said. She wasn't impressed by young Tommy being President. He'd always been the least of the Dawsons in her mind. Too ambitious. Too sneaky. Character flaws.

"Gone?"

"Took the family," she said.

"Where?"

"Up to the cabin."

The cabin was a primitive wooden shack located thirty miles from Lake Candlewood. It was a place without electricity. No telephone. No amenities. It was where Kevin took his wife and kids when he wanted privacy, when he felt the need to retreat. Kevin had this notion, which Thomas Dawson found quaint and yet politically useful at times, about family unity, togetherness. He was always dragging Martha and the girls out into the wilderness. Backpacking, camping, fishing, communing with nature.

"Did he say when he was coming back, Agatha?"

"Sunday night," she answered.

"What time?"

"Didn't say. And I didn't ask. Just threw some stuff into the station wagon and left. The two men from Washington went up there with him."

"Fine," Dawson said. "I'll call him Sunday night."

He put the receiver down. At least Kevin would be safe up at Lake Candlewood with the Secret Service protecting him. At least he'd be safe until he returned to New Rockford, which was when Thomas Dawson was going to suggest that Hawaii or the Virgin Islands would be a pleasant change of pace this time of year.

NINETEEN

Frank Pagan did not get the chance to think about the information he'd taken from Nicholas Linney's computer until nine o'clock in the evening. There had been delays in Bridgehampton while Zuboric, looking extremely secretive, hung around waiting for the telephone to ring with instructions from God in Washington. There had also been a visit from two men who drove a rather anonymous van and who carted the corpses away in plastic bags. When the phone finally rang at approximately seven-thirty, hours after they'd first arrived in Bridgehampton, Zuboric spoke into it briefly, then hung up. It was apparent that no new instructions were forthcoming from Washington, at least for the time being.

They drove back into the city in the green Cadillac, Zuboric subdued and thoughtful. He escorted Pagan inside the Parker Meridien, his manner that of a male nurse attending a certifiable lunatic.

"Stay home, Frank. I'll be in touch."

Pagan stepped inside an elevator and was glad when the doors slid shut. He locked himself inside his room and lay for a while on the bed. He took the piece of paper out of his coat and stared at it, smiling at the idea of slipping something past the vigilant Arthur. As his eyes scanned his scrawled handwriting, he couldn't help thinking of the dead girls again. The direction of his thoughts irked him. You could see everything through a prism of grief if you wanted to, you could dwell on morbid associations, but it was a hell of a way to live a life.

He called room service and had them send up a bottle of Vat 69, a scotch sometimes referred to as the pope's phone number. He half hoped that Mandi with an "i" would appear in the doorway, but the scotch was finally delivered by a young Greek whose English was riddled with fault lines.

Pagan poured himself a generous glass, dropped in some ice. Harry Cairney. Kevin Dawson. Jock Mulhaney. All good Irish lads and perfect candidates for raising and dispersing IRA funds. Who else could they be but Nicholas Linney's comrades? Harry Cairney, the retired senator from New York, had been part of that Irish Mafia in Washington that included Congressman Tip O'Neill and Senator Moynihan. He had served on various committees that had pumped funds into the Republic of Ireland. It seemed perfectly natural that the retired senator, under the surface of his public persona, would be involved in something a little darker than political gestures of goodwill. And Kevin Dawson, the President's baby brother, had made several trips to Ireland to pay homage to the Dawson ancestry. The visits were always surrounded by tight security and excessive publicity. The Irish loved Kevin and his family and adored Kevin's loyalty to the country of his heritage. He was shown such adulation in Ireland that it must have gone straight to his brain and perhaps compensated somewhat for any sense of inferiority he might have felt about his brother's prominence. Sigmund Pagan.

Pagan closed his eyes. The next step was the question of what to do with his knowledge. He wasn't going to enlist the help of Zuboric, he was sure of that. Their reluctant marriage of convenience was heading down the slipway to divorce. Artie's problem was obvious—he accepted as gospel the first solution he thought of, and nothing could make a dent. For example, his unshakable conviction that Jig was responsible for the slaughter in Bridgehampton—there was just no way in the world to make Artie consider alternatives. He didn't have the imagination for them. Besides, it was easier to lay the blame on Jig than go to the trouble of exploring other possibilities. There was something of lazy discontent in Artie's makeup, the death of natural curiosity, a dangerous thing for a man licensed to carry a gun and use it.

Pagan thought of the zigzagging geographical patterns involved here. New Rockford. Brooklyn. Rhinebeck. Why couldn't it have been convenient—Cairney and Dawson and Mulhaney all under one roof right here next door to the Russian Tea Room? Sure. But what then? Would he have gone to them and sat them all down nicely and talked to them of Jig? *If you happen to run into Jig, be a sport and let me know?* They would deny any association with the act of collecting funds for Ireland. They were secretive men accustomed to operating furtively, and each was a public figure. They weren't going to want their Irish activities made common knowledge. If you even broached the subject with them, they were bound to look as if they'd never heard of Ireland, let alone the Irish Republican Army.

What the fuck had really happened in that Bridgehampton house anyhow? He wondered now if Jig had discovered the same names from the same source, Linney's wonderful computer. If he had, there was no way of knowing which of the three men he would visit next. Besides, there was also no way of knowing if Nicholas Linney had been able to point Jig in the direction of the missing money. *It's buried under a tree in my backyard, Jig. It's banked in Zurich and here's the account number.* You had to work on the assumption that Jig was out there still hunting and that sooner or later he would pay a visit to the names on Linney's list. But when? To guess Jig's movements was close to impossible, even for Frank Pagan who had made a study of his prey like a meteorologist examining shifts in the wind. Finally, there was just no certainty.

He stood up, moved absently around the room. Problems had a habit of multiplying. Now he thought of the man called Fitzjohn garroted in Albany. And Ivor the Terrible sitting cosily over in the Essex House. You could play with these threads all the goddamn day. You could ruin your health. The link he especially didn't like was the one that seemingly connected Fitzjohn with Ivor. That whole FUV thing troubled him. Ivor McInnes's presence nagged him. Why the *hell* was he here at the same time as Jig? And why had the FUV informed Pagan that Jig was in the U.S. anyway? He kept returning to this particular conundrum, although now it had become more complicated with the murder of Fitzjohn. He was irritable and antsy and filled with the urge to cut through all the mystifying shit at one stroke, as if all the various questions in his mind were in reality one huge question, something that could be resolved with one equally huge answer. *Give me the simple life.*

What was Fitzjohn doing in Albany? Why had he been murdered? What came back to Pagan again and again was the notion that Ivor McInnes was the key to these questions. That if you could get inside Ivor's head the mysteries would begin to dissolve. The idea of the descent into Ivor's mind wasn't an exactly pleasant prospect, but then nothing about this whole business was what you might call delightful. Pagan picked up the telephone, called Foxworth's home number in Fulham, rousing the young man from inebriated sleep. Foxworth loved to dig into the data banks, which he did with all the enthusiasm of a fanatical mechanic getting inside the engine of a car.

"Get your arse over to the office," Pagan said. "I need some information. The name is Alex Fitzjohn. Got it?"

"My arse is hung over," Foxie complained, his voice made small by distance and drink.

"Move it, sonny. I'll call you back in a couple of hours."

"Yes, master."

Pagan hung up. He was tired but the inside of his head had come to resemble a pinball machine in which balls ricocheted maddeningly back and forth. He looked at his precious piece of paper again. Mulhaney wasn't far away. Brooklyn was nearer than either Rhinebeck or New Rockford, Connecticut. Would it do any good to go talk to Mulhaney? Or simply to stake out the place where Mulhaney lived? Pagan was undecided. If Jig decided not to go to Brooklyn but went instead to either Rhinebeck or New Rockford, you would be wasting a great deal of time. This whole dilemma needed a small army of men, and Pagan knew he wasn't going to get them from Zuboric. Nor did he want them, not if they were afflicted by Zuboric's lack of insight. It wasn't the first time in Frank Pagan's career that he wished he were more than one individual. Three or four Pagans, clones, would have been useful.

Where now? he wondered. What next? He couldn't just *sit* here in his room. And it made no sense to visit Ivor until he had some word on Fitzjohn.

He wondered what Brooklyn looked like at night.

He put his overcoat on and stepped out into the corridor. He rode the elevator to the third floor, got out, took the stairs. He knew Zuboric would have a man nearby, maybe Orson Cone or good old Tyson Bruno, probably seated right now in the piano bar, chewing peanuts and nursing a Virgin Mary and watching for a sight of the tricky Pagan. Crossing the lobby, Pagan found himself surrounded by a jabbering party of fashionable French tourists who were seemingly agitated about the nonarrival of their luggage from Air France and were talking litigation, in the intensely shrill way of excited Parisians. Pagan merged smoothly with the French party. It was good cover—though not absolutely good enough. He saw Tyson Bruno come hurrying across the lobby toward him, coat flapping, face anxious. Pagan smiled and gave Bruno a victory sign even as Tyson, looking altogether unhappy with the course of events, collided with one of the Parisians, a woman who might have stepped from the pages of *Elle*.

Pagan hurried past the front desk and out onto Fifty-seventh Street and then he was lost in the inscrutable Manhattan night as he headed, with a bright feeling of truancy, toward the place where he'd parked his Cadillac.

WHITE PLAINS, NEW YORK

The Memorial Presbyterian Church dated from the early years of the twentieth century. A large white frame construction with a steeple and a cast-iron bell that hadn't yet been replaced by an electronic sound system, it occupied a huge corner lot of prime White Plains real estate. Its congregation had dwindled steadily over the years and now numbered about three hundred and fifty, of whom two hundred or so were active churchgoers. Adorned by stained-glass windows, an enormous organ, and polished mahogany pews, it was a rich church, a highly profitable enterprise that received generous endowments from the estates of past members. During the hours of darkness, a solitary floodlight shone upward at the steeple, bathing the front of the church in a white light that suggested purity and cleanliness. One might imagine God himself perched up there in a place beyond the light, a materialization of spirit just out of the range of the human eye.

John Waddell, who had always been a religious man despite the violent deaths of his wife and child—which might have damaged any man's faith—thought that Memorial Presbyterian was like no other church he'd ever seen. He was accustomed to grubby little halls, joylessly dark places of worship in Belfast, where the hymn-books fell apart in your hands and the congregation sang in a dirge-like way and everything smelled of gloomy dampness. Memorial, on the other hand, might have passed as God's private residence. Waddell was awed by the artful floodlight and the shadows up there in the belfry. Inside, after McGrath had forced a rear door open, Waddell was overwhelmed by the beauty of stained glass and the rich reflective wood of pews and pulpit and the way the pipes of the vast organ rose up into vaulted shadows. He felt humbled. He had an urge to sit in one of the pews and pray. Only Houlihan's impatient glance prevented him.

All day long Seamus had been in a grim mood. It was connected, Waddell guessed, with the disappearance of Fitzjohn. Suddenly, in the night, Fitzjohn had gone. Nobody asked questions, though. Nobody went up to Houlihan to inquire about Fitz, because Seamus had that look on his face that meant *don't fuck with me*. Now, as he ran a hand over the smooth surface of a pew, Waddell watched Houlihan move toward the pulpit. McGrath was standing and staring at the reaches of the organ pipes. Rorke, fingering the scar on his face, looked bewildered by the whole display of Presbyterian opulence. Wasn't Presbyterianism meant to be a grim little religion with no display of ostentation? Not here in America. Nobody in the Land of Plenty wanted to buy the original Scottish package, which was spare and hard and gritty and had been exported intact to Northern Ireland by the fervent followers of John Knox and Calvin. But Americans preferred a little comfort with their God. There were even pillows lining the pews!

"It's like a chapel," Rorke said, referring to Roman Catholic churches. "It's like a fucking Fenian chapel."

Houlihan stood in the pulpit. Waddell thought he looked satanic up there.

"Get over to the organ," Houlihan said to Rorke, who moved immediately, stopping only when he reached the keyboard.

Waddell, raised in a tradition where the authority of the Protestant church was unquestionable, sacrosanct, thought it odd to hear voices raised beyond a whisper. And Rorke's earlier profanity was wildly out of place. But there was a whole uncharted area here that confused John Waddell. On the one hand, there was the Ulster cause. On the other, the authority of the Protestant church. Normally, these went hand in hand without causing him any kind of dilemma. But now, now that he knew what Houlihan was planning to do in this place, he felt a curious sense of division. In the end he knew he'd go along with Seamus, because that was what he always did, but the doubts he entertained were not easily cast off. The work Seamus planned to do here was something unusual for the FUV, something that ran at a right angle to Waddell's understanding of the Volunteers. If Memorial were a Catholic church—no problem. But it wasn't. It wasn't a Roman church.

Houlihan came down from the pulpit. "We don't have all fucking night," he said. "I'd like to get this done and get the hell out of here."

Waddell listened to the vague echo made by the sound of Houlihan's sneakers. Every small sound was amplified inside this place. As a kid he'd imagined that if you swore in church God's long finger—a huge talon in the boy's mind—would come down out of the sky and pierce you. He wasn't so very far removed from this kind of image now. He felt dread. The thing they were doing here was wrong, no matter how you looked at it. And God was still up there, sinister and birdlike, His claw ready to strike.

Houlihan approached. He seemed very tall in the dim interior of the church. "What's *your* problem?" he asked.

Waddell said, "I just don't like being here, that's all."

Houlihan smiled. "You're a superstitious wee fart, Waddy. Because I like you as much as I do, I'm going to let you in on a secret." Houlihan brought his face very close. "There's no such thing as God. Or if there is, he fell asleep a long time ago."

Waddell returned the young man's smile although rather nervously. He would have followed Houlihan to the gates of hell and back, but this was the first time Seamus had ever spoken so openly about his religious attitudes. Waddell traced the line of the organ pipes up into the ceiling. You could imagine Something stirring up there in the darkness, no matter what Seamus thought.

"God's for nuns, John," Houlihan said. "God's for priests and nuns and RCs. And if he exists he's become so bloody addicted to incense fumes by this time his mind's addled. So let's get this fucking show on the road. Okay?"

John Waddell nodded. Across the vast stretches of the pew saw Rorke bent under the keyboard of the organ. McGrath close to Rorke, wore a backpack from which he took he passed down to Rorke. The scarfaced man

"Are we ready?" Houlihan asked.

"Aye. Just about," McGrath called

John Waddell held his breath

a place so badly in all his life. There was the sudden sound of air escaping from the organ pipes. It was a single musical note that echoed briefly.

"Jesus Christ," Houlihan said.

"Sorry," Rorke mumbled. "Accident."

"Clumsy bastard," Houlihan said.

Waddell could hear the echo of that single note, so deep, so profound, long after it was inaudible to anyone else inside the church. He had the distinct feeling that Somebody was trying to tell him something.

BROOKLYN, NEW YORK

Big Jock Mulhaney had spent his professional life pumping flesh and slapping backs and eating chicken dinners at fund-raisers. He was a gregarious animal, at home in the company of men, sharing a confidence here, eliciting a favor there, joking, smoking, and yet always scanning the company for the important faces the way a bat will use radar to seek out prey.

Mulhaney, who sipped a glass of wine and chomped on his cigar, was seated at the head table in his own banquet hall, a very large room inside his union's headquarters in Brooklyn. Teamster Tower had been constructed in 1975 to Jock's specifications. Apart from the banquet hall, it contained a dancehall, five reception rooms, six floors of offices, and perched at the very top, Jock's private quarters, a two-story penthouse decorated in what Jock's fag designer called "oatmeal," but which Mulhaney referred to as "porridge." He adjusted his cummerbund and stared across the diners at the other tables.

The event taking place was the annual March bash, a stag affair Jock threw for the prominent Irish members of the union the week before St. Patrick's Day. In the course of the year, the Italians, Poles, Scandies, and Latinos would all have dinners of their own, but the Irish one was closest to Mulhaney's heart. The diners, some three hundred of them, had eaten their way through a menu of Dublin coddle, imported Dublin prawn, french fries and mint-green *gelato*, and now they were embarking on the important course of the meal, Irish coffee.

The Irish-Americans in the banquet hall belonged to scores of dif-

ferent organizations. The Loyal Order of Hibernia, the Sons of Killarney, the Ancient Order of St. Patrick, the Society of Galwaymen,
the Loyal Boys of Wexford, the Clans of Kilkenny. Some of them
wore green sashes with gold lettering attesting to their particular
affiliation. There were even a couple of local priests, men made red-
facedly benign by brandy. Mulhaney, who was a member of every
society, who joined clubs and fraternities like a man with no tomor-
rows, had a simple green shamrock in the lapel of his tux.

The waiters moved swiftly around dispensing Irish coffee when it
was time for Jock's speech. Six brandies and a bottle of fine claret
inside him, he stood up and acknowledged the round of applause
from the tables. His people were blindly loyal to him. He gazed
cheerfully across the faces, cleared his throat, held up his hands for
silence. He had a standard speech he made every year at the same
time with only minor variations.

He rambled on awhile about union solidarity, made a token reference to the state of unionism in the Soviet countries, spoke with
embarrassing nostalgia about his mother and the way she had with
Irish stew back in the old days in Boston, and then asked for a moment of prayer for peace in the Old Country. After that, he suggested everyone adjourn to the bar and listen to the live music, which
was provided every year by three middle-aged men from Cork who
called themselves the Paul Street Brothers, after a famous thoroughfare in their native city. The room cleared out. The corridors became
clogged with men seeking fresh drinks in the commodious bar established in one of the reception rooms, where the musicians were
already singing "If You Ever Go Across the Sea To Oireland . . ."

Patrick Cairney, who sat at the back of the room alongside the
contingent from Union City, New Jersey, considered the speech the
tiresome kind of thing Harry might have loved. He went out into
the corridor, pressed on all sides by men wearing green sashes. The
cigar smoke and brandy fumes created an altogether dizzying perfume that suggested the complacency of affluence. They were all
affluent men here with soft hands. There was nobody in this assem-
bly who laid bricks or carried hods or dug ditches these days. Cairney, who had a plastic shamrock fixed to the lapel of his dark blue
suit, watched Mulhaney work the crowd.

Big Jock pumped flesh vigorously, traded jokes, heard secrets
whispered in his ear, promised a favor here, a favor there. He was
like some pontiff strolling through a herd of lowly cardinals. It

wouldn't have been surprising to see somebody's mouth pressed against his ring.

Now Jock shoved his way toward the bar where a waiter immediately served him a double brandy on a silver tray. Unlike the lesser prelates, the minor bishops and the insignificant abbots, Mulhaney didn't have to stand in line. He had a confidential conversation with a member from Buffalo, he made expansive promises to a man from Schuylerville, and he swore on his mother's grave he'd hammer certain fuckers to the wall when it came time to negotiate a new contract on behalf of his members in Wilmington, Delaware. He was basking in warmth, smoke, adulation, and the glow of good drink in his body. There was a narcotic effect here he couldn't get anywhere else. It was the life of Riley, and he'd worked damn hard to get here, and what he felt now was that he deserved every second of it. This was his world, and he dominated it like a large red sun.

"How did my speech go?" Mulhaney asked one of the priests, knowing the answer in advance.

"It was *choost* delightful. Delightful," the priest answered, happy to fawn on Mulhaney, who provided the best free cuisine in the whole diocese.

Patrick Cairney stood against the wall. The music was deafening. The hubbub of voices droned in his head relentlessly. He lightly touched the gun he carried inside the waistband of his pants. The problem here was to get Mulhaney alone. It would come. Even if he had to conceal himself inside the building until the party was finally over, the moment would come. He continued to observe Mulhaney, who was now standing face to face with a priest. Both men had clearly drunk too much.

Cairney closed his eyes a moment. He was thinking about Nicholas Linney and trying not to. And those two dead girls. That whole thing in Bridgehampton had been a disaster. No, it was more, disaster was too feeble, too mild for the carnage that had gone on in that house. He remembered Linney's face at the moment when he'd blown half the head off, the torrent of blood, the abrupt searing of the man's scalp, the splinters of bone and gristle that hurled themselves against the wall.

He couldn't let these images plague him now. He couldn't afford to. He wanted to salvage something here in Brooklyn, provided Mulhaney didn't go in for amateur heroics. He didn't look as if he had the kind of *edge* Linney had had. Just the same, Cairney was thankful he was armed. He opened his eyes, remembering Frank Pagan arriving in Bridgehampton and wondering if the Englishman was somewhere nearby now. If so, he'd have to work fast. He'd have to get information out of Mulhaney quickly if he could, which was where the gun would be useful to him.

There was a tension inside him, when what he needed most was cool. *Don't be your own worst enemy,* Finn said once. *A man like Jig has so many real enemies, he doesn't need to make himself one.*

Jock Mulhaney drained his brandy glass and, still shaking outstretched hands, rubbing shoulders, exchanging pleasantries, made his way out along the hallway. His bladder ached from all the drink he'd consumed. He walked quickly in the direction of the toilets. The first one he came to was jammed. Standing room only and an atmosphere heady with urine and cigars. He backed out of it. He went toward the reception area, passing silent desks and covered typewriters and unlit lamps. There was a bathroom here the receptionists used. He liked the notion of skipping inside a woman's john.

Cairney saw the big man slip along the corridor and followed quietly. The band was playing "Kitty of Coleraine." Mulhaney had paused outside a door marked LADIES. He appeared uncertain about whether to go inside or not. Cairney was conscious of the vast expanse of the reception area and the black street beyond the plateglass windows and the limousines parked out there. *Go inside, Mulhaney. Open the door, go in. Let's be alone a moment, you and I.* The moment he wanted was coming sooner than he'd expected.

Mulhaney stepped into the toilet, noticing a tampon machine and a dispenser of packaged colognes and the fact that all the cubicles were empty, their doors lying open. He moved inside one of the cubicles. He unzipped, emptied his bladder, flushed his cigar butt away. He rinsed his hands, dried them under a hot-air machine that roared inside the empty toilet, and hummed the tune the band was playing.

He was leaning toward the mirror and fluffing his thick hairpiece with a comb when the door swung open behind him. He saw a young man come in. Dark hair, blue suit, well-built, unknown to Mulhaney. But with three hundred guests here, how could he know everybody?

"Good speech," the young man said.

Mulhaney smiled. He slapped the young man on the back.

"We've met before," Mulhaney said. He had a practiced way of pretending to remember everyone, as if names were forever on the tip of his tongue. "Aren't you with the Syracuse continent?"

The young man shook his head. "I don't think we've ever met."

"I never forget a face." Mulhaney farted very quietly just then, and looked cheerful. "Better an empty house than a bad tenant, huh?"

"Right." Cairney turned on the cold-water faucet full blast but made no move to dip his hand in the stream.

Mulhaney gazed into the fast-running stream of water a second. He was conscious of the way the young man stared at him in the mirror. What was it about the intensity in those hard brown eyes that disturbed Mulhaney just then? He turned away from the young man, which was when he felt a circle of pressure against the base of his spine and the warmth of the man's breath upon the back of his neck. Glancing into the mirror, Mulhaney saw the gleam of the pistol pressed into his back. Horrified, he heard himself gasp, felt his body slacken. In his entire lifetime it was the first time anyone had ever pulled a gun on him. How did some fucking mugger find his way inside this place?

"My inside pocket," he said. "The wallet. Take the whole fucking wallet. There's probably a couple hundred bucks in it."

The young man jammed the gun hard against the backbone. "I'm looking for more than that, Jock," he said.

Pain brought moisture into Mulhaney's eyes. There was an awful moment here when he felt himself slip into cracks of darkness, saw his own hearse roll through the streets of Brooklyn, heard Father Donovan of All Saints deliver the graveside eulogy in that hollow voice of his—*He was a flawed man, but a good one.* Even imagined the *wake*, for Chrissakes, boiled ham and stale sandwiches curling and flat Guinness and drunks babbling over his open coffin.

"Jesus Christ," Mulhaney said. Darkness had become realization. And realization brought him a sense of horror. *This young man was The One.*

"Linney said you took the cash."

"Linney?"

"Don't bluff it out with me, Jock. Just point me to the money."

"I don't have it, Linney's a fucking liar."

The gun went deeper this time. Mulhaney, catching a glimpse of his face in the mirror, barely recognized himself. His big red face had turned pale like a skinless beet boiled in angry water.

"Where is it?" the young man asked.

"I told you, I don't know," and Mulhaney wondered why nobody was looking for him, why his goons weren't stalking the goddamn corridors for him right now. God knows, they were paid enough to take care of him.

The pressure of the gun was enormous. Mulhaney thought it would bore a hole in his spine. The young man sighed. "I'm tired, Jock. And I don't have a whole lot of time."

"I don't know where the money is, I swear it."

Cairney thought about bringing the gun up, smacking it against Mulhaney's head. Something to underline his seriousness. Some token violence. It was tempting, and he felt pressured, but he didn't do it, didn't like the idea of it. He just kept the pistol riveted to Mulhaney's spine and hoped he wouldn't have to use force.

"Linney said you took it. Talk to me, Jock. Talk fast. Don't make me hurt you."

Mulhaney twisted his head around, looked at the young man. It occurred to him that he could play for time here. Sooner or later somebody was going to come looking for him. He could stall, though the hard light in the man's eyes suggested that stalling was a precarious business. But he didn't like the position he was in and he didn't care for being at someone else's mercy and his pride, that cavernous place where he lived his life, was hurt. And he hadn't scratched his way to the top of the union without having more than his share of sheer Irish pigheadedness.

"You're not going to walk out of here," he said, and his voice was stronger now. "You're not going to walk away from this, friend. I've got a small army out there. I've got people who take care of me."

Cairney rammed the pistol deeper into Mulhaney's flesh and the big man moaned. "I don't have time for this, Jock. Tell me what I need to know and I'm gone."

"Look, Linney's a liar. Linney wouldn't know the truth if it hit him in the goddamn eyes. He makes shit up all the goddam time. If he sent you here it was to make a fucking idiot out of you."

Cairney felt the intensity of fluorescent light against the top of his head. *"Where's the money?"* There was a note of desperation in the sound of his question. He didn't like it, didn't like the way he had begun to sound and feel. He knew that at any moment somebody was bound to come inside this room, that his time alone with Mulhaney was very limited.

"I won't ask you again, Jock."

Mulhaney thought he had seen something in the young man's eyes. A certain indecision. The signs of some inner turmoil. He said, "Even if I knew anything, do you honestly think I'd fucking tell *you*?"

Cairney brought the gun up and smacked it against Mulhaney's mouth. Blood flowed out of Big Jock's lips and over the small shamrock he wore in his lapel. The pain Mulhaney felt was more humiliating than insufferable. He lost his balance and went down on his knees. His expensive bridgework, three thousand dollars worth of dental artistry, slid from his mouth and lay cracked on the tiled floor. He reached for it, but Cairney kicked it away, and the pink plate with the gold inlays and the plastic teeth went slithering toward one of the cubicles where it struck the pedestal of a toilet and broke completely apart.

"Jesus Christ," Mulhaney muttered.

Cairney was trembling slightly. He felt sweat under his collar. He shoved the gun against Mulhaney's forehead and pressed it hard upon the bone. "Talk, Mulhaney. And make it fast."

Mulhaney, whose vanity was as enormous as his pride, covered his empty mouth with his hand. There were streaks of blood between his fingers. He blurted his words out from behind his hand. "Kev Dawson. You're looking for Kevin Dawson. He's the only one who could have taken it. It couldn't have been the Old Man."

"The Old Man?"

"He's been at this game too long to start thieving now," Mulhaney said. He was conscious of the pistol on his brow. It was a terrible feeling.

"Tell me about the Old Man, Jock."

Mulhaney looked down at his blood on the white-tiled floor. "The Old Man had nothing to do with this," he said, and his voice sounded funny to him when he spoke. Without his teeth, the inside of his mouth felt like a stranger's mouth. He'd give this bastard Dawson, but he wasn't about to give him the Old Man immediately. He'd do it in the end, he'd be a damn fool not to, but meantime he'd hand Dawson over gladly. "My bet is Kev took some heat from his big brother. There was pressure. Something like that. It had to be politically too tricky for Tommy. The Old Man couldn't have had a goddam thing to do with it."

As Mulhaney spoke, the toilet door swung open and a middle-aged man in a black tuxedo stepped inside from the hallway. He wore a frilly pink shirt and matching cummerbund, into which was tucked a pistol. The man was called Keefe and he was one of Mulhaney's bodyguards, a union heavy who was paid a hefty fee to protect his boss.

"Keefe," Mulhaney cried out.

Keefe, formerly a bouncer in a Las Vegas nightclub, was a tough man but slow. He reached inside his cummerbund for his gun and even as he did so Cairney, possessed with a feeling of inevitability, with a sense of things sliding away from him in a manner he couldn't stop, shot Keefe once through the center of his chest. The sound of the gun roared in the white-tilted, windowless room. Keefe staggered across the slippery floor, his legs buckling and his hands stretched out in front of him. He collided with a cubicle door and he fell forward against the john. His gun dropped to the floor and slipped across the slick tiles to Mulhaney's feet. Cairney watched Big Jock's hand hover above the gun a moment.

"Don't," Cairney said. *"Don't even think about it."*

Jock Mulhaney pulled his hand back to his side. It wasn't worth it. The young guy would shoot him if he even moved an inch toward Keefe's weapon. And Jock had no appetite for violent death.

Cairney kicked the gun away. The music had stopped. The whole building had become quiet. The only sound he registered was Mulhaney's heavy breathing.

Mulhaney said, "You got a problem, kid. In about ten seconds three hundred guys are gonna descend on this room."

Cairney looked at the door. Three hundred guys. The suddenness of silence was unsettling to him. He glanced at Mulhaney, who was still on his knees. Blood ran down from the big man's mouth.

Cairney opened the toilet door a little way. He stared across the reception room. Drawn by the sound of gunfire, men in tuxedoes were emerging slowly from the banquet room. Cairney bit his lower lip. If he acted now, if he moved promptly, he could get out of this toilet and through the reception area to the street before any of the men could reach him. *Provided none of them was armed.* He glanced back at Mulhaney, who was staring at him openmouthed.

"Get up on your feet, Jock."

Mulhaney gripped the rim of the washbasin and hauled himself to a standing position.

"Now move over here," Cairney said.

Mulhaney came across the floor.

"In front of me, Jock. You're about to be useful."

Cairney pressed his gun into the small of Mulhaney's back and pushed the big man through the door, out into the reception area.

Men were still coming down the corridor that opened into the reception room.

"Tell them, Jock. They move and you're dead. They call the cops and you're history."

Mulhaney, whose vanity caused him to keep a hand up against his toothless mouth, mumbled. "You hear that, you guys?"

Cairney, moving sideways toward the front doors with Mulhaney as a shield, stared at the faces that watched him. Each one had the slightest imbalanced look of a man wrenched suddenly out of inebriation into sobriety. Their eyes bored into him, and Cairney realized he'd never felt quite this exposed before. It didn't matter now. It didn't matter because his anonymity had already been shattered by Frank Pagan. The only important thing was to get out of here in one piece. He felt fragmented, though, as if the whole reason for coming to America had broken and, like smashed glass, lay in shards all about him. He was halfway across the reception room now and none of the watchers had moved and Mulhaney, he knew, wasn't brave enough to try and break away. He was going to get out of here, but he was leaving empty-handed, and the perception depressed him. Finn had entrusted him with a task and he wasn't even *close* to achieving it. Maybe it was luck. Maybe that was it. Maybe he'd been lucky in the past and now that vein had run completely dry. And maybe he wasn't the man Finn thought he was, maybe all his achievements in the past had been purely fortunate. Jig, the dancer. *Why am I not dancing now?* he wondered. He didn't feel like the man who had assassinated Lord Drumcannon and had blown up Walter Whiteford on a Mayfair street. He didn't feel daring and carefree and composed and cold-blooded. His past actions seemed like those of some other man.

"Keep moving, Jock." Six feet to the plate-glass doors. The street.

He pressed the gun into Jock's spine and heard the big man grunt quietly.

"Only a few more feet, Jock," he said.

"Fuck you," Mulhaney said. He was playing to his audience. He was showing that he was still a brave man who could talk back even when the pressure was on. And if he could talk to some fucking hoodlum like this, think how he could ram it home to builders and contractors when he didn't have a goddamn gun in his back!

Cairney reached the doors and knocked them open with his foot. The air in the street was cold and sharp. He wondered how much time he had before the cops arrived. He knew it was inevitable that somebody inside the building had sneaked away into an office to place a quiet call, that pretty soon the street would be filled with patrol cars.

"Okay," Mulhaney said. "You've made it out of the building. What now?"

Cairney said, "We've got unfinished business. You were going to tell me about the Old Man, Jock."

"I gave you Kev Dawson."

Cairney shoved the gun into the nape of Mulhaney's neck. "Don't stall, Jock." He looked the length of the dark street in both directions. It was silent now, but it wasn't going to stay that way for very long. Through the glass doors he was conscious of the men inside. They stood around indecisively, but that was a situation that could change at any moment. They were Irish and they'd been drinking, and they might decide to move into boisterous action, regardless of the fact that Mulhaney had a gun at his head.

"*Hurry,*" Cairney said. And even as he said this he heard footsteps along the sidewalk and turned his face quickly, seeing somebody move in the soft shadows between the parked limousines and the wall of the building. The figure stopped suddenly and dropped to the sidewalk. There was the sound of a gun going off and a flash of light from the place where the man lay and the plate-glass doors shattered, showering the air with bright splinters.

Surprised, Cairney moved back, pressing himself against the wall. He was aware of Mulhaney lunging away from him, the glass doors swinging, Big Jock thrusting himself inside the safety of the building. Cairney fired his weapon at the man along the sidewalk and heard the sound of the bullet knock upon the hood of a limousine. He backed away, sliding against the wall and out of the light that fell from the building. He sought darkness, places where he couldn't be seen. He fired his gun again. This time the shot slashed concrete. The man returned the fire, and the air around Cairney's head screamed.

Cairney kept moving away. He was about ten feet from the corner of the building and conscious of the need to get the hell out of this place. He saw the figure move now, scampering behind one of the parked limousines. The man's face passed momentarily under the light that fell from the reception room.

It was Frank Pagan.

Cairney reached the corner of the building, where there was a badly lit side street and rows of shuttered little shops. He was seized by the impulse to stay exactly where he was and fight it out with Frank Pagan, as if what he wanted to prove to the Englishman was that he didn't have to run away as he had done on Canal Street, but how would that have taken him any closer to the money? Priorities, he thought. And Frank Pagan—despite the fact that the man was always just behind him like some kind of dogged specter—wasn't top of his list.

He stared a moment at the car behind which Pagan was crouched. Then he turned and sprinted into the darkness of the side street, weaving between parked cars and trash cans, zigzagging under weak streetlamps, like a man following a maze of his own creation. He could hear Pagan coming after him, but the Englishman wasn't fast enough to close the gap that Cairney was widening with every stride. The echoes of Pagan's movements grew quieter and quieter until there was no sound at all. When he was absolutely certain he'd lost Pagan, he lay down beneath a railroad bridge and closed his eyes, listening to his own heart rage against his ribs.

Pagan had known about Linney. Then about Mulhaney.

Cairney opened his eyes, staring up into the black underside of the bridge. *Was it safe to assume that Pagan also knew about Kevin Dawson?*

Cairney sat with his back to the brickwork now. He felt the most curious emptiness he had ever experienced. It drained his heart and created vacuums throughout his mind. He knew he had to get up and make his way back to the place where he'd left his car, but he sat numb and motionless. There was an uncharacteristic need inside him to make contact, a connection with somebody *somewhere*. He thought he'd call Finn, but he couldn't see any point in relating failure to the man. He didn't want Finn to be disappointed in him. And he didn't want Finn to think he'd sent the wrong man from Ireland. That he'd send a man who wasn't equipped for this task. He couldn't bear the idea of Finn thinking badly of him.

He shut his eyes again. The face that floated up through his mind, a warped, pellucid image like something refracted in shallow water, was Celestine's.

FRANK PAGAN went back in the direction of the union building. He was breathless, and his whole body, jarred by the effort of running, was a mass of disconnected pulses. Jig's speed hadn't surprised him. He'd seen Jig in action before. But this time it was the manner of the man's disappearance that impressed him. It was almost as if Jig had vaporized down one of the narrow streets. Stepped out of this dimension and into another one. For a time, Pagan had managed to keep the man in his sight, but with every corner Jig turned, Pagan realized that his hope of catching up was dwindling. Then, finally, somewhere between a canal and weedy old railroad track, Jig had disappeared in the blackness, with the deftness of a rodent.

Goddam. Pagan resented the idea that Jig was swifter than he, more agile, more attuned to the hiding places offered by the night. He envied Jig's affinity for invisibility. Now he had the feeling that even if he were to seal off the surrounding twenty blocks, he still wouldn't find the man. *Goddam again.* These close encounters only frustrated him. What also bothered him, even if he didn't like to admit it, was the insurmountable fact that Jig must have at least ten years on him, that his own youth had long ago begun to recede, and time—the dreaded erosion of clocks—was making impatient claims on his body.

He walked slowly, like a man skirting the blades of open razors. When he reached the broken glass doors he paused, making one huge, concentrated effort to catch his breath. He stepped inside the reception room and saw Mulhaney sitting on one of the huge black-leather sofas, surrounded by anxious men in evening wear and green sashes. Mulhaney had a bloodied handkerchief up to his mouth.

Pagan pushed his way toward the sofa, elbowing men out of the way. Mulhaney, enjoying the attention he was getting, peered over the top of the handkerchief at him. Pagan showed his ID in a swift way, sweeping it in front of Mulhaney's eyes before the union boss had time to register it.

"I've got a few questions," Pagan said.

Mulhaney dabbed at his lip. His bare gums were pink and bloody. "What kind of ID was that?"

Pagan ignored the question. "You have a private office some-place? I'd like to talk to you alone."

Mulhaney looked puzzled. "I'm perfectly happy where I am," he said.

"Okay." Pagan shrugged and lowered himself on to the arm of the sofa. "What did the guy want with you, Jock?"

"He was a mugger, for Christ's sake. What the fuck you think he wanted?"

Pagan shook his head. "He was sent here from Ireland. You know that. I know that."

"Ireland?" Mulhaney looked blank. He appealed to the other men around him. "Who is this guy? Who let him in here?"

"What did you tell him?" Pagan asked.

"Hey," Mulhaney said. "Let's see that ID again, fellah."

"Did you tell him where he could find the money? Or did you send him someplace else?"

Mulhaney stood up. His eyes had a bruised, angry look. "I don't know what the hell you're talking about. Somebody toss this knucklehead outta here. Ireland, for Christ's sake! My man Keefe's been shot dead and you're babbling about fucking Ireland!"

"Keefe?"

"My bodyguard. Mugger shot him."

Another corpse. One way or another, Jig was leaving bodies strewn behind him. What had happened to the fastidious assassin? Pagan hesitated a second before reaching out to grip Mulhaney's wrist tightly. "What did you tell him, Jock? Did you sent him to Dawson? Did you tell him Cairney was the man to see? Or did you tell him something else altogether? What did you say to him?"

Mulhaney made a gesture of exasperation. "Out," he said.

Pagan felt various hands grab him. It hadn't been terrific strategy to come in here and confront Jock, but on the other hand there was always the chance that Mulhaney might be taken off guard and give Pagan the answers he was looking for. Big Jock, though, was set on a course of complete denial, which wasn't entirely surprising. Pagan wished he could have had time alone with the man. It might have made a difference in Mulhaney's attitude. Surrounded by his sycophants, Big Jock was forceful and stubborn.

Pagan pulled himself free of his assailants. He stepped to one side. "It's important, Jock. I need to know."

"I've had it with you," Mulhaney said. He looked at the faces of the men. "Toss this nut."

Pagan was still struggling to catch his breath. "If I leave here, I walk. Under my own steam."

"Walk then," Mulhaney said.

Pagan pushed his way back through the crowd toward the glass doors. He moved out onto the street, where he turned and glanced back through broken glass at the sight of Mulhaney holding forth for his audience. *I hit the guy a couple of times,* he was saying. *Then he pulls this piece on me, which is when poor Keefe walks in.*

I bet you hit him, Pagan thought.

He moved away from the building, just as two patrol cars turned the corner into the street, their lamps slashing holes in the darkness and their sirens screaming like voices in purgatory.

NEW YORK CITY

"It's raining in Piccadilly Circus," Foxie said, his voice unusually crisp and clear, given the great distances of the Atlantic. "Doesn't that make you homesick?"

"Why? I'm having a ball here," Pagan replied. The muscles in his legs throbbed from running. He lay on the bed and stared up at the ceiling of his room in the Parker Meridien. "What have you got for me?"

"Straight to the point, eh?" Foxie's voice faded a second. "According to my little screen, Alex Fitzjohn did time in Armagh Jail in 1977 for posession of grenades. Six months. Somewhere in this period he must have thrown in his lot with the FUV. They recruit in jails, of course." Foxie paused. "My head hurts and my throat's dry. There are gremlins inside my brain doing things with dental drills."

"Don't drink until you're grown up," Pagan said.

"Whenever. Back to Fitz. Suspected of participation in at least three border incidents. One, the bombing of a pub. Two, the attempted assassination of a priest. A failure, that one. Three, a brief shootout with the Garda. An inconclusive affair, it would seem."

Pagan was suddenly impatient. "Is there anything that ties him directly with McInnes?"

"Ivor's a careful sort of chap," Foxie said. "You know how damned hard it is to get reliable documentation on whether he's running the FUV or not. However . . ." and here Foxworth paused.

"I'm all ears," Pagan said.

"There is one very grubby photograph in our possession. It's about seven years old. Somebody stored it in Fitzjohn's file, which is on the inactive list. It really ought to have been put in Ivor's. There's a lot of clerical idiocy around here, Frank."

"Foxie, please," Pagan said.

"One description coming right up. The picture shows Ivor stepping out of his church. He's robed up to sermonize, so we can assume he's just delivered himself of one of his brimstone jobs. Around Ivor are a few other people. There's a lot of smiling going on. Somebody is reaching out to shake Ivor's hand. Maybe to congratulate him on his words of wisdom? Whatever. In the midst of the people gathered on the steps of the church is one Alex Fitzjohn. He's about five feet away from Ivor, and he's smiling. But Ivor isn't looking at him. Ivor's staring at the man offering the handshake." Foxie paused. "That's it, Frank."

Pagan massaged the side of his head, which had begun to ache. It had been a long day, and he was exhausted now. A peculiar kind of exhaustion too, as if a rainy mist were crawling through his brain. He was thinking of Jig and how the man had managed to slide away from him once again on the streets of Brooklyn. *What had Mulhaney told Jig?*

"It's not a hell of a lot, is it?" Pagan said. "I'm looking for a connection and all we've got is a photograph that doesn't even show Ivor and Alex making *eye*-contact."

"It doesn't exactly confirm that they're bosom buddies," Foxworth agreed. "The best case you could make is that they probably knew each other. Probably."

Pagan sat down on the edge of his bed. He'd hoped for something more substantial than an old inconclusive photograph. Something definitive. Something Ivor couldn't posssibly deny. But all he really had was a weak hand that was useful for a couple of bluffs, nothing more.

"By the way, Frank. The Under-Secretary popped into the office."

"That's a first," Pagan said. "Did you call the *Guiness Book of World Records?*"

"He came in the day after you left. Quite the grand tour. He expressed some—shall we say misgivings?—about your sojourn in the Americas. Doesn't think you should be gallivanting about over there. Thinks your information from the FUV about Jig is spotty and doesn't justify your trip. People don't say *spotty* much these days, do they?"

"Tell him to stuff it," Pagan said.

"I think I hear the quiet sharpening of the ax, Frank. Furry Jake is no friend of yours. And you've got all those delicious enemies at the Yard who love the idea of you being away because, heaven forbid, they can make waves. Get the Sec's ear and whisper anti-Pagan slogans into it. It's not a glowing horoscope, is it?"

"In other words, if I don't get Jig, don't come home."

"It's what I'm hearing, Frank. Apropos of Jig, how goes it?"

"I haven't quite booked my return flight, Foxie."

"When you do, I very much hope you won't be traveling unaccompanied."

"Take aspirins for your hangover," Pagan said. "And go back to bed."

Pagan put the receiver down. The sharpening of the ax, he thought. You leave your desk and the vultures start to circle. You step away and suddenly it's the Night of the Long Knives. What else could you expect? People were unhappy with him. People didn't like the way he ran his section. People like Furry Jake thought little of Pagan's tailor and, by extension, little of Pagan too. Scotland Yard wanted control over him. They didn't like an upstart having power. And they reveled, *God, did they ever*, in the idea of Jig's eluding Pagan's grasp.

Pagan poured another scotch. Jesus Christ, was this job *that* important to him? He could run security in the private sector and earn twice as much as he was paid now. But what he hated was the idea of scumbags waiting for him to fall, waiting for him to come home empty-handed because then they could pounce on him and denigrate him with that particularly wicked smugness certain pencil pushers have for those who work out in the field, the real world.

He was agitated by the confinement of his room. He wanted to get out of the narrow little rectangle in which he was trapped. He put on a jacket and went down in the elevator to the piano bar.

Silence. The pianist had gone. The bar was almost empty. Pagan sat up on a stool and ordered a Drambuie. Mindi with an "i" was cleaning the surface of a table in the corner. When she saw Pagan she smiled and drifted over to him. She was small and she moved with economy, like a dancer. It was all an illusion of coordination. Halfway toward him she dropped her order pad and pencil and giggled as she bent to pick them up because loose change tumbled out of her pocket and went off in a series of little wheels across the floor.

He wondered what she'd be like in bed. It was the first time he'd entertained this notion quite so clearly in years and it took him by surprise. There was something else too—a small shiver of ridiculous guilt, almost as if the thought of having sex with this girl were somehow a betrayal of Roxanne. And he wondered at the tenacious hold the dead could sometimes have over the living. Could he ever shake himself free?

"I drop things," she said.

"I never noticed."

The giggle was high pitched and, although he wasn't a man enamored of giggling, he did find something endearing it in.

"Palsy," she said. "Or is it dropsy?"

Pagan sipped his Drambuie. He studied her over the rim of his glass. She had dark hair naturally curled, creating an overall effect of a head covered with bubbles. She had a small heart-shaped mouth and straight teeth. There was humor in the face. Mindi was a woman who liked to laugh at herself. Going to bed with her would be some kind of romp through innocence, with no serious attachments, no kinks, no entanglements. Quick rapture and a fond good-bye.

"Enjoying your stay?" she asked.

Pagan shrugged. "It's a bewildering city."

The girl placed her hands on the surface of the bar. She had chubby, cherubic hands, dimpled. Straightforward, good-natured Mindi. An uncomplicated girl. It was all there in the hands and the brightness of the eyes. Simplicity. The uncluttered life.

"You need a guide," she said. "If you want to see the place properly."

There was an opening here, but Pagan was slow to move toward it. He was out of touch, rusty.

"I'm Mindi, by the way."

He nodded. He was going to say he knew that already but why bother? "Frank Pagan."

"Good to know you, Frank. You're from London, right?"

"Does it show?"

"It's the way you talk. It's like Michael Caine in that picture. God, what was it called?" She pursed her small lips and concentrated. "I'm hopeless when it comes to remembering names."

No memory. Forever dropping things. Why did he find her clumsiness sweet? She must go through her life in a sweet-natured daze. She wouldn't need drugs or alcohol because reality made her dizzy enough.

"*Alfie!*" she said. "That's the one."

"I remember it vaguely."

"Are you on your own?" she asked. Another opening.

Pagan was about to say that he was, he was about to say that he was weary of his own company, that he needed a bout of companionship and would she be interested, when he noticed Tyson Bruno sitting in a dark corner of the bar. Whatever nascent appetite he'd begun to feel abruptly shriveled inside him. The mood was spoiled, sullied. He pushed his glass away and got down from the stool, glancing at Bruno's hardened wooden face.

"I'd like to be," he said. The waitress looked puzzled.

Pagan moved across the thick carpet of the bar and out into the lobby toward the banks of elevators. For a moment there he'd felt an old mood returning, a need rising inside him, a desire to do something simple and natural, like touching a woman, like bringing quickness back into his circulation, yesterday's heats, yesterday's passions, something that would slash away at his ghost. But Tyson Bruno's face had risen out of the darkness to spoil things, reminding Pagan of the contrast between his own sorry little world where men and women died painfully and treachery was a viable currency, and the world of a cocktail waitress in a Fifty-seventh Street hotel who dropped things and laughed at herself and lived an uncomplicated life. Two planets, different orbits.

He traveled up in the empty elevator, thinking of himself as perhaps the first man in history to suffer from a case of premature exorcism. When the car reached his floor, the doors slid open and he looked down the long corridor toward his room. Fuck it, he thought. He needed life and liveliness. And the real trick to that was to say no to self-analysis and no to your history. If you wanted to live, you just went out and did it.

He stepped back into the elevator and returned to the bar.

Mindi was gone.

But Tyson Bruno was still there, coming across the floor with an ape's grace.

"Don't run out on me again, Pagan," Bruno said. "I don't like being made to look stupid."

"That takes no great effort, Tyson." Pagan felt weary.

"I hate smartasses," Bruno said. "Where did you go anyhow?"

"I always wanted to see Brooklyn by moonlight."

"Sure." Tyson Bruno folded his thick arms across his chest. He had a mean, dangerous look all at once, that of a man who lives with violent solutions to tough questions. Pagan stared at the tiny eyes, which resembled the pits of a cherry.

"See it doesn't happen again," Tyson Bruno said.

"I never promise the impossible, Tyson."

Pagan turned away and headed back toward the elevators.

WHITE PLAINS, NEW YORK

It was eight minutes past seven A.M. when the Reverend Duncanson began his Sunday morning sermon in Memorial Presbyterian Church. The congregation numbered about two hundred people, and

Duncanson was pleased to see so many young people in attendance. He wondered if the Englishman who had telephoned was among the worshipers. His sermon, perhaps a little too heavy for the spring weather that had suddenly surfaced this day, concerned the confession of sins and God's ability to refresh and cleanse the sinner. It was a dark, wintry speech, and it tended, like most of Duncanson's sermons, to ramble through thickets of personal anecdote, non sequiturs, and erudite attempts at wordplay.

His eyes scanned the congregation as he spoke. A bright March sun fell upon the stained-glass windows, creating a nice dappled effect along the central pews. He spoke of confessional needs, carefully making a distinction between the *inner* need of man to ask forgiveness, and the *outer* compulsion, a Catholic notion that would bring momentary uneasiness to some of his members. The very word *confession* was loaded.

The Reverend Duncanson glanced at his watch, which he always took from his wrist and laid alongside his notes. He had been speaking now for thirteen minutes. He needed to pick up the pace and bring everything to a conclusion within the next two minutes. After years of sermonizing he had the ability to edit his own material in his head. He sometimes thought he was like a stand-up comic who intuited his audience's mood and shuffled his material accordingly.

Seven-twenty-one.

The second hand of Duncanson's watch swept forward.

He closed his sermon after he'd talked for fifteen minutes. He nodded in the direction of the organist, a middle-aged woman who raised her hands above the keyboard, ready to strike. The congregation rose, hymnbooks open.

"We will now sing the Twenty-third Psalm," Duncanson announced. " 'The Lord Is My Shepherd.' "

The organist rippled off the introductory chords.

The great pipes took the sound, transformed it, scattered it through the uppermost parts of the church. It swelled, died, then came back again, a vast flood of music. As Duncanson opened his mouth to sing, he saw a sudden ball of flame rise up from the keyboard and engulf the organist, surrounding her with a wall of fire that spread upward with a horrific crackling. The force of released heat was so intense he felt it burn the skin at the side of his face. Then there was an explosion from the dead center of the church, a blast that shook the entire building and blew out the stained-glass windows.

Duncanson rushed down from the pulpit, unaware in all the smoke and screaming and confusion that his robe had caught fire. Another blast rocked the area around the pulpit, a violent outburst of flame and dark smoke that suggested something released from the fissures of hell. By this time, the ceiling was ablaze, wooden beams consumed by flame. The hymnbooks were burning. The pews were burning. People were burning too, screaming as they tried to rush through the suffocating smoke toward doorways they couldn't find. Babies. Young men and women. The fire attacked everything.

And then there was still another explosion, the last one Duncanson heard. It brought the organ pipes down out of the walls, a tumble of plaster and bolts and woodwork and electrical wires, which conveyed flame down into the basement of the church where the oil-fueled central-heating system was located. When the oil caught fire the air became dead air, unbreathable, filling lungs with a searing poison.

Some people made it out through the madness and the panic to the lawn in front of the church where they saw that the steeple was one ragged mass of blue flame whipped by breeze and spreading in a series of fiery licks across the entire roof. Others, trapped and suffocated inside, barely heard the final explosion as the oil tank went up, because the world of fire had become a silent place for them, all noise sucked out by a vacuum of intense heat, a scorched epicenter where no sound penetrated, no air stirred, the vast parched heart of destruction.

STAMFORD, CONNECTICUT

Seamus Houlihan dialed a telephone number in New York City from a phone booth beside an industrial park in Stamford. It was eight-thirty on a sunlit Sunday morning. As he listened to the sound of the phone ringing, he looked across the street at John Waddell, who sat in the driver's seat of the yellow rental truck. The truck had begun to bother Houlihan. It was too big, too conspicuous. They'd have to ditch it soon. McInnes had said he wanted them to dump the truck after Connecticut, but Houlihan thought it might be a damn good thing to be rid of it right now, before the next stage. Maybe he'd steal a smaller vehicle, though it would need to have a large trunk to keep the weapons in.

He winked at Waddell, who looked white. A stolen vehicle was a fucking risk, that was the snag. People actively looked for them. Their numbers and descriptions were put on lists. Cops, who wouldn't blink at a rented truck, would be on your arse quick enough if they spotted you in a stolen car.

It was all right for McInnes, Houlihan thought. He sat in his fancy hotel and called all the shots. He wasn't out here getting himself grubby, doing the deeds, *working*. McInnes was terrific at organization, Houlihan had to admit that much, but the man was always at one remove from the center of it all, the place where things really happened. And he was always getting his name in the papers, always basking in publicity, another thing Houlihan resented.

Over the phone, Houlihan listened to the ringing tones and wondered if anybody was ever going to answer. Thinking of McInnes irritated him. He hadn't felt good about McInnes ever since the man had scolded him for the action in Albany. *Stick to the blueprint, Seamus. Be a good boy, Seamus. Keep your nose clean, Seamus.* Yessir and up yours.

What McInnes resembled at times was one of those figures of authority from Houlihan's past. A judge. A cop. A screw. A counselor. All the fuckers who either sent you to jail or spoke softly to you about taking your place in society. They had you coming and going, those characters did. McInnes couldn't stand the idea of anyone else showing some initiative, some imagination. That's what it all boiled down to. McInnes didn't like the idea of Seamus Houlihan doing something on his own.

Fuck him, Houlihan thought. McInnes thinks he knows it all.

The phone was finally answered.

A man said, "Federal Bureau of Investigation. Please hold."

"I won't hold," Houlihan said.

"Sorry, sir. I have to ask you to wait."

"I've waited long enough, shithead."

"Sir—"

"Listen close. You'll hear this only once." And here Seamus paused, enjoying himself. He winked at wee Waddy again and smiled.

T WENTY

Patrick Cairney woke in a hotel room on Eighth Avenue. It was called the Hotel Glasgow, a peeling old crone of a place with murky hallways and dampness. When he checked his watch he saw that it was almost eight-thirty in the morning, and a frigid New York spring sun was streaming through the brown window blind. He'd come to this place very late last night, after Brooklyn, and fallen asleep immediately on the narrow bed, a long sleep filled toward its end with a dream.

He'd dreamed he was back in the Libyan desert where he was trying to dismantle and clean an automatic rifle. An odd weapon Cairney had never seen before. It was composed of parts that didn't fit. Once you had the gun stripped down, you couldn't put it back together again no matter how much you pushed and maneuvered and tried to force things. The damn gun, a trick weapon, wouldn't be reassembled. It was a distressing dream, panicky, inexact, one of those insanely catered affairs of the unconscious when streams of incongruous people gate-crash.

Celestine had been in there somewhere toward the end. She'd picked up the befuddling gun, and with three or four quick movements of her hands she had the whole thing snapped back together again. *There,* she kept saying to him. *There, there, there.* What the hell was she doing in his dream anyhow?

Cairney got out of the hard little bed. He dismissed dreams as messages from nowhere, sediment stirred by the uncontrolled brain. He didn't see in dreams the things soothsayers did, prophecies and portents, future disasters. He went inside the small shower stall and drummed tepid water all over his body. When he was finished he dressed quickly. He packed his canvas bag, locked it, left the room. But the dream, as if it were a narrative in a seductive tongue, still whispered in his mind.

He traveled down to the lobby by the stairs because elevators were always too claustrophobic for him. Outside, where the sun was cold, he crossed the street and walked in the direction of the garage where he'd parked the Dodge. It was a sleazy stretch of Eighth Avenue, pawnshops and fast-food places and porno stores. He entered the dimly lit garage cautiously, distrustful of dark places. He found the car on the second level exactly as he'd left it. Unmolested, unvandalized. He unlocked it, drove it past the ticket booth, paid his fee, and then he was out into harsh white sunshine, heading north. By the time he reached Columbus Circle he was hungry but he didn't want to stop until he was clear of the city.

Finally, when he was close to Yonkers, he pulled into a twenty-four-hour place that served the whole staggering array of American roadside cuisine. He took a table near a window and chewed on a strange red hot dog, which he left half eaten. He drank two cups of coffee, and for the first time that day his brain, which had been numb and unresponsive, kicked into gear. Low gear.

You'll have times when you can do nothing but abort, boy. You'll have times when circumstances are stacked up against you. The trick then is to step away without despair.

Without despair, Cairney thought. But he could feel a certain sickness in his heart. Ever since he'd entered the United States, he'd encountered one set of circumstances after another that provoked nothing but despair in him. But he wouldn't abort. Not now. Not ever. Was it his fault that Tumulty had been playing both ends against the middle? Was it his fault that Linney had turned out to be some kind of frantic madman? Was it his fault that Mulhaney's bodyguard had chosen to come through the door of the rest room when he did and then draw his goddam gun? You were sometimes faced with extremely limited choices. And sometimes you had no choices at all, because events narrowed all around you and went off at their own uncontrollable speed, and the only thing you could do was follow the track of chaos and make the best of what you had.

Finn's money, the Cause's money, had taken on a graillike quality in his mind. It shimmered and tantalized and then, as though it were a mirage, vanished even as you thought you were close to it. He had moments now when he wondered if it even existed or, if it did, whether it was buried forever in some inaccessible place beyond human reach. All he knew was that the money was surrounded by accusations and treacheries and suspicions. People told lies. They made up stories. Linney had been sure that Mulhaney was responsible for the theft. Mulhaney had pointed to Kevin Dawson. And he'd also mentioned somebody enigmatically known as the Old Man, who appeared to occupy a position of authority that put him in a place beyond suspicion.

What Cairney suddenly wondered was how a man like Frank Pagan would have gone about the task of searching for the money. Pagan, presumably, had been trained in investigative skills, quietly gathering data, knowing the questions to ask, knowing how to assess the answers. Frank Pagan, perhaps, had insights that were denied Jig, a deeper human understanding, an ability to cut through lies and deceptions and misleading statements. Frank Pagan *understood* people because he lived in their midst. Jig didn't. Jig didn't know people. Jig had cut himself off from ordinary society by his own choice. Cairney could imagine Pagan operating on some intuitive level, knowing when he was hearing bullshit and when he was hearing the truth. Cairney, trained to assassinate, trained to track, to plant explosive devices, to use rifles, to survive in extreme conditions, in arctic cold and desert heat—Cairney had never learned a goddam thing, in all his training, about the puzzlingly intricate clockwork of the human heart. And it was hurting him now.

He picked up the half-eaten hot dog and shredded it surgically into fragments between his fingers. It was useless to speculate on what gifts he had and didn't have. It was the wrong time. It was the wrong time to entertain even the smallest kind of doubt. To think that Finn—in his anger and frustration—had sent the wrong kind of man to America.

Cairney pushed the dissected hot dog aside.

I'll get the money, he thought.

I'll get it and take it back to Finn and say, There, there's your money.

And Finn would receive it with a small smile of pleasure, the smile Cairney liked, the one that made him feel as if he were basking in his own private sunlight. The kind of smile he'd never seen on his own father's face. *I knew you'd do it, boy. I never had any doubt. And the Cause is forever grateful to you.*

Kevin Dawson. He had to concentrate on Kevin Dawson. Given the amount of documentation on the private lives of the Dawson clan, given all the reams of publicity so loved by the tabloids, it wasn't going to be very difficult to locate the Dawson home. But Cairney knew that Dawson was going to be surrounded by the kind of protection afforded brothers of the President. Which meant extreme caution. And then there was always Frank Pagan to consider.

Cairney stared through the window at a stream of traffic sliding north. Hundreds of Sunday afternoon travelers, whole families complete with dogs, hurrying to dinners with in-laws or visits to the zoo or places of worship. He watched them with solemn detachment for a time.

He stood up, paid for his food, then moved in the direction of the door. There was a pay phone in the lobby. He stopped. Glancing through the glass door at his small red Dodge, he was seized by an impulse to pick up the receiver. He dialed a number, punched in coins.

Celestine's voice was thin when she answered. "Hello?"

Cairney listened. Didn't speak. Why the hell had he made this call? It wasn't as if he needed to hear his father's voice, was it? It was something else, something he didn't want to think about it.

"Hello?"

Cairney opened his mouth, but he remained silent.

"Is anyone there?" she asked.

He took the receiver away from his ear. He pictured her standing with the telephone pressed to the side of her face, perhaps a lank of fair hair falling across a cheekbone, her slim legs set slightly apart. The image was strong in his mind, and teasing, and desirable. The sound of her voice brought back to him the night she'd come to his bedroom, and he trembled very slightly.

"Patrick? Is that you?"

Now why would she think that? Why would she think of *his* name? He replaced the receiver and went outside to the parking lot. He unlocked his car, stepped in behind the wheel. He drove away from the restaurant, the sun laying a white film over his rear window.

.

THE WHITE HOUSE,
WASHINGTON, D.C.

Shortly after Seamus Houlihan's anonymous phone call had been logged by the FBI in New York City, Leonard M. Korn stepped inside the Oval Office like a man with a mission in life. Thomas Dawson saw this at once. Magoo had fire in his myopic eyes. If it was any hotter there, his contact lenses would melt. The President understood Korn's manner. The man had come here looking for a free hand. He wanted to hear Dawson say that the wolves could be released now, the pack liberated, the time was ripe. The FBI could tear apart the whole goddam eastern seaboard, if that's what it took to catch one Irish terrorist.

Korn saw indecision in Thomas Dawson. Indecision and subterfuge. But how could Dawson explain away the bombing of a church in White Plains to the soothed satisfaction of the public? A faulty boiler? Or would he go with some natural phenomenon, like spontaneous combustion? Korn's Bureau, his agency, his love, was like a caged leopard clawing bars, ready to pounce. This time it wasn't four casualties in a house in Bridgehampton. This one couldn't be kept under wraps.

Dawson ran a fingertip over his lower lip and said, "It doesn't make any sense to me, Len. Why come to the United States and blow up a goddam church, for Christ's sake?"

Korn enjoyed Dawson's discomfort. The changing currents of international terrorist policy meant nothing to the Director. He was interested only in apprehending the culprit. More specifically, he was interested in being *seen* to do it.

"I can understand the death of Linney," Dawson continued. "He was involved in these clandestine Irish affairs. But a whole church-load of people? Come on. Why the hell this escalation?"

"Jig may have been after just one person in that church," Korn suggested. "It's possible."

Dawson sighed. "If it was Jig," he said. "Do we have any really *hard* evidence that he's responsible?"

Korn considered this a naïve question. "He's our only candidate, Mr. President."

Thomas Dawson stood up. He could hear Korn panting at the leash.

"Jig only came here to recover money," the President said. "I don't see where bombing churches fits on his agenda."

"Terrorists aren't like you and me," Korn said. "They don't function with normal motives. They aren't driven by normal impulses. We know absolutely nothing about Jig, so how can we say what he is or isn't capable of doing?"

Dawson poked his blotter with the tip of a silver paper knife. "The latest count is seventy-eight," he said. "Seventy-eight, for Christ's sake!"

"It may rise," Korn said.

Dawson ignored what he felt was a rather distasteful eagerness in Korn's voice. Seventy-eight people was a hell of a tally. What was he going to tell America? What would he announce into that great ear out there? So far, the only information it had received was of an explosion inside a church. No explanation given, a simple headline on news programs. But by this time the journalists would be scavenging the disaster site like vultures. Sometimes Dawson thought that freedom of the press was the enemy of democracy. Why couldn't it be muzzled?

All at once he felt a real need to draw people around him, cabinet members, image makers, advisers, counselors, poll takers, speech writers, he wanted every possible scenario thoroughly analyzed before he did anything. Would this act of Jig's alienate the Irish from their hero when—and if—they learned about it? Would there be outrage? Or would it somehow draw the clans tighter together? Imponderable questions.

He stared at Korn who gazed back at him with expectation.

The American public could wait, the journalists could dig, the rumors could fly and multiply with the speed of maggots in a rancid stew, Korn could pop some blood vessels. But Thomas Dawson wasn't going to drop the starter's flag for the FBI until he'd consulted with his own policymakers.

He saw he had savaged his blotter with the letter opener. "It's not my decision alone, Len. I can't tell you to go ahead with this manhunt of yours until I've talked with my Cabinet."

Korn was annoyed, but not absolutely surprised. He'd always thought Tom Dawson the wrong man for number 1600. He was in too many people's pockets, for one thing. This whole love affair he conducted with the Irish-Americans was way out of whack. There was one group that had him by the balls. And the Irish-Americans weren't the only ones. He was in deep with the Italians, the Puerto Ricans, the farmers. If it moved in sufficient numbers, if it had the capability to organize itself and knew how to pull a voting lever, then Tommy Dawson was probably obligated to it.

"While you *consult*, Mr. President, an Irish terrorist is out there, planning God knows what next move, and we have a total of four men on the case—*four*, count them—one of whom is an Englishman that two of the remaining three spend most of their time watching, for God's sake."

Dawson held a hand in the air. "You'll have a decision soon."

"How soon is soon?" Korn asked. "And will it be soon enough?"

Korn moved to the door. He had a flair at times for melodramatic exit lines. He enjoyed the one he left hanging on the air as he reached for the door handle.

Dawson was damned if he was going to give Korn the satisfaction of the last word. Angered by Korn's manner, he said, "If your god-dam Bureau wasn't like some goddam elephant that hollers because it fears extinction, if it knew how to conduct an investigation with any kind of tact and discretion, if it wasn't manned by so many fuck-ups and psychopaths, I'd say go ahead. I'd give you my bless-ing. But we know what it would really be like, don't we, Len? There would be inexplicable leaks to the press. There would be interviews with Len Korn, master of counterterrorist tactics. It would become a full-blown media circus for the glorification of King Korn and his personal adversary, Jig. Black and white! Good guys and bad guys! All the lines of conflict nicely drawn for the masses to understand! God bless the FBI and good night!"

Leonard Korn had the dark sensation that he'd overstepped the mark. He turned to the President with a small insincere smile on his face. "I spoke out of turn," he said.

"Damn right you did."

"Sorry."

Dawson smiled back with an equal lack of warmth. "Too much tension, Len. Too much stress. And stress kills."

"So they say, Mr. President."

When Korn had gone, Thomas Dawson did something he never did in public. He lit a cigarette, a Winston, and sucked the smoke deeply inside his lungs. It was the most satisfying thing he'd done in a long time. He put the cigarette out carefully, dropped the butt in a wastebasket, then sprayed the air with a small can of Ozium he kept in his desk. He sat back and shut his eyes. It wasn't just the violence done against the Memorial Presbyterian Church in White Plains that troubled him. It was also the old Irish thread, that dark-green blood-soaked thread, linking the late Nicholas Linney to brother Kevin.

He tried to get Kevin on the telephone again, only to learn from Agatha Bates that the family hadn't returned yet from their cabin at Lake Candlewood. And no, she wasn't precisely sure when to expect them either. What was this goddam urge Kevin felt every now and again to take his family into inaccessible places? This fondness for the rough outdoors and kerosene lights and dried foods?

Thomas Dawson hung up, frustrated, tense, and for the first time in his entire presidency, truly afraid. Kevin, he felt, was going to be okay because he had the Secret Service men around him. But as for himself and his presidency—that could be quite another matter.

NEW YORK CITY

It was the pounding on the door of his room that woke Frank Pagan at five minutes past nine. He hadn't meant to sleep this late. Last night, when he'd walked away from Tyson Bruno, he had intended to sleep four hours, maybe even less, but he still hadn't quite recovered from the ravages of jet lag. He pulled on a robe, opened the door, saw Artie Zuboric outside. Zuboric swept inside the room immediately. Pagan saw at once that something was up. Artie looked both driven and yet rather pleased with himself. The agent drifted to the window, pulled back the drape, let the room fill with wintry sunlight. Pagan wondered if he was about to be lectured for slipping the leash last night and leaving Tyson Bruno stranded. But it wasn't that.

"A church has been bombed," Artie said at once. "A Presbyterian church in White Plains, New York."

"Bombed? With a *b*?"

"With a big *b*," Zuboric said. "Somebody planted explosives in the place. Seventy-eight people are dead. The explosives went off in the middle of the sunrise service. Nice timing, huh?"

Pagan absorbed this information, feeling tense as he did so. Zuboric wasn't telling him this for nothing. There was something else coming. Pagan waited, seeing how Zuboric enjoyed dispensing this information.

"The bombing happened around seven-twenty this morning. At approximately eight-thirty a man called my office in New York City and claimed responsibility on behalf of the Irish Republican Army."

Pagan licked his lips, suddenly dry. "Which you attributed to Jig, of course."

Zuboric eased into sarcasm. "I don't see a whole busload of Irish terrorists running around New York State, do you?"

"It's damned convenient to blame Jig," Pagan replied. "It's so nicely packaged and wrapped for you. It's so fucking American. If you can wrap it, you can also buy it. And I don't buy it any more than I buy the incident at Bridgehampton."

"Why? Because you think you've got Jig pegged as a Boy Scout? The honorable terrorist? Helps old ladies cross streets before he blows them up? Grow up, Pagan. He doesn't have any scruples. He doesn't give a shit who he hurts."

Pagan sat on the bed. He could tell Zuboric that Jig operated differently, that Jig was a new refinement in a very old conflict, that there was no way in the world, given Jig's past acts of terrorism, he was going to blow up a whole church and the people in it. He could tell Zuboric that Jig wasn't in the habit of murdering the innocent. But he saw no point in saying such things because he could smell the lust for blood, Jig's blood, coming from Zuboric. He could smell the sweat of the lynch mob eager to hang a victim in a public place for the intense gratification of the masses. Hang first, ask questions later. People in Zuboric's frame of mind were notoriously narrow in their vision, and decidedly uncharitable.

"Face it, Frank," Zuboric said. "Your man's an animal. And the sooner you realize this, the sooner we can catch him. You've been playing it as if this cocksucker was civilized, which he isn't. He's a fucking *beast*. He ought to be shot on sight."

Pagan looked for a calm controlled corner of himself, and found it. He had the thought that if only he'd captured Jig last night in Brooklyn, if only that chase through mean streets had ended differently, then Jig would be in custody now and beyond suspicion of any terrorism in White Plains. If. Pagan had a very bad relationship with conditionals. He considered them the lepers of English grammar. He hadn't caught Jig, and it was pointless now to have regrets.

"What exactly did the caller say?"

"You can hear the tape."

"I'd like that," Pagan said. He remembered all the hours he'd spent in London listening to Jig's voice, that strange flat drone that announced each new assassination in a cold detached way. He'd even brought in two professors of dialect to analyze the accent. One said it was British West Country, the other that Jig had obviously spent time in America but was working to disguise the fact. Academic dispute, and totally useless.

"I'll come down to your office," Pagan said.

"Be my guest." Zuboric had gloves on his hands and he rubbed them together. He watched Pagan step toward the bathroom and he said, "I also hear you split last night."

Pagan nodded.

"Like to tell me where you went?"

"No," Pagan said.

Zuboric raised one of his fingers in the air, shaking it from side to side. "I'm fucking sick of you, Frank. I'm fucking sick and tired of the way you want to do things."

"It's mutual," Pagan replied.

"You think you can go after this Irish moron on your own. You think your way's the only way. Let me remind you, Pagan. This isn't your country. You don't have any jurisdiction here except what we choose to give you. If we withdrew our support, you'd be nothing. And if we want to kick you out unceremoniously and go after this Jig ourselves, what the hell can you do about it?"

Pagan stood in the bathroom doorway, flicking a towel idly against the wall. He wondered if there was any sense in getting angry. At whom would it be directed anyhow? Artie and the FBI? Furry Jake and the butchers of Scotland Yard? Or at the barbaric nature of those who set off explosives in a church? He decided to say nothing. Zuboric's head was a Ziploc bag, deeply refrigerated and impossible to open and colder than hell once you managed to tear it apart. He went inside the bathroom, closing the door quietly.

He looked at his pale face in the mirror. Eyes slightly bloodshot. Small dark circles. *The IRA blows up a church in White Plains, New York. The IRA kills a man called Fitzjohn in Albany. Fitzjohn almost certainly had a connection with Ivor McInnes, though not one that would stand up in a court of law.* What was going on? He brushed his teeth and made a horrible face at himself, mouth open and jaw thrust forward and tongue sticking out. You look your age, Frankie, he thought. This morning, finally, you can see the effects of Old Father Time's facial. Even inside the body, in the places you couldn't see, his organs felt ancient and sluggish and all used up.

He plunged his face into a basin filled with cold water and opened his eyes, thinking of puzzles and their solutions. And what it came down to, somehow, was that Ivor had the key to Fitzjohn in Albany and—perhaps, perhaps—the bombing in White Plains too. If only he could be made to give it up.

ROSCOMMON, NEW YORK

Harry Cairney answered the telephone on the second ring. He heard the familiar voice of Jock Mulhaney.

"He was here, Harry. Last night," Mulhaney said.

Cairney didn't ask who. He knew. He gazed silently out of the window, seeing the security jeep move between stands of bare trees. He felt a small tic under his eye and he put a hand to the place.

"He came right here, Harry," Mulhaney was saying. "Are you listening?"

"Yes," Cairney said. "I'm listening." If the man sent from Ireland could get inside Mulhaney's headquarters, how could one small jeep keep him at bay if he found his way here? It was an appalling thought.

"He killed one of my people," Big Jock said. "He threatened me."

"What did you tell him?"

"Harry, what the fuck you think I told him? Nothing, for Christ's sake."

Nothing, the old man thought. He wondered about that. "And he left? He just left after you said you had nothing to tell him?"

"That was when he shot Keefe."

"Keefe?"

"A bodyguard."

Cairney watched the jeep travel along the shore of Roscommon Lake, then it was gone.

"Then another guy showed up. An English guy. He was looking for our crazy Irish friend."

An Englishman. Harry Cairney looked at his wife, who was sitting cross-legged before the fire. By firelight she seemed frail, composed of porcelain. He hated the idea of anyone coming here and putting her in a situation of menace because of something that he himself was responsible for. He couldn't stand the notion of that. He watched Celestine stretch her legs, reach for her toes, absent-minded exercise. Cairney observed this fluid gesture with the expression of a connoisseur absorbing a particular lovely painting, then opened the center drawer of his desk. He looked inside at the handgun, an old Browning. He might not be a young man anymore, but by God, he hadn't forgotten how to fight. And he would, if it came to that.

Mulhaney was still talking. "This English character asked some questions, Harry. He mentioned your name."

"My name?" Harry Cairney's heart skipped one small telling beat. "Who was this man?"

"I don't know."

"Have you any idea where he is now?"

"Uh-uh."

Cairney was silent. "Do you think he might be coming this way?"

Mulhaney didn't answer at once. "I don't know if he knows about you, Harry. I really don't."

"Does he know Linney?"

"He mentioned Nick's name."

"Dawson?"

"He knows about Dawson too."

Cairney closed the drawer. Celestine was watching him. Cairney turned his back to her and quietly said, "Then I imagine there's a damn good chance he knows about me."

Mulhaney said, "I don't know what he knows, Harry. All I can say is he's young and he's quick and he's ruthless."

"It's a ruthless business." Cairney turned once more to his wife and smiled. "Thanks for calling, Jock."

He put the receiver down. It was over, then. The secrecy had been more fragile than he'd ever realized. He went toward his wife, laid his hand on her scalp.

"What was all that about?" Celestine asked. "What's a ruthless business?"

Cairney didn't answer. He didn't want her involved. He couldn't bring himself to make up a lie either.

"I'd like a drink," he said. "Am I allowed one?"

"Very tiny."

She kissed his cheek as she went out of the room. Downstairs in the kitchen she poured a small shot of brandy and mixed a vodka martini for herself. She glanced at the kitchen clock. It was just after noon. She sampled her drink, arranged the glasses on a tray, then headed back upstairs. She didn't go inside the study at once. Instead she entered Patrick's room, set the tray on the bedside table, and looked at the various photographs of Cairney as a boy. There was one that depicted him at thirteen, maybe fourteen, sitting cross-legged among other members of a school football team. He had a helmet in his lap. Another showed him in shorts and sweatshirt, poised to release a discus. He was well-muscled and taut even then, but it was the face she stared at. She saw only that eager open quality of youth, the smile of innocence, nothing of the secret darkness in the eyes he had as a man. What do you know? she asked the face. What do you really know?

Old pictures yielded nothing. They were interesting only as history, mileposts on the road to somewhere else. She touched the surface of a photograph with her fingertips, imagining she felt Cairney's skin under glass. Some hours ago, when the telephone had rung and nobody had talked, she was convinced that the person on the other end of the line was Patrick. Now she wasn't so sure. Some instinct had suggested it at the time, but now she wondered if it had been just the blindly hopeful reaction of a woman intrigued. Intrigued, she thought. There was a word belonging to the cheap romances. Intrigue was for lady librarians vacationing in Corsica or swanning about the Taj Mahal by moonlight. Intrigue wasn't a good word when it came to serious business. And what else was all this but serious?

She heard Harry coughing along the landing. She switched off the bedside lamp, picked up the tray, left Patrick's room quickly. Harry was standing in the door of the study, watching her.

"Wrong room," he said.

She laughed his remark away. She kissed him and together they went inside the study. She sat in front of the fire and sipped her drink and listened to a log slip in the flames. Harry sat down beside her eventually, and she laid her head in his lap, closing her eyes.

"He was quite a sportsman," she said lazily.

He looked at her in a puzzled way. His mind was elsewhere.

She opened her eyes, looking up at him. "Your son."

"Oh." Cairney, held captive in his wife's blue eyes, made a small mental adjustment. The curse of age, this difficulty in focusing. "He had one year, I remember, when sports became an obsession. He slept and dreamed sports. He had the makings of a fair quarterback. You were looking at the old photographs?"

She nodded. Firelight made her hair very gold.

Cairney stared at the window. "He was always like that, always picking up on something. Then he'd become obsessed with it for a while, before he moved along to something else. He wouldn't stick with a thing. He'd overdose on it when he was interested, but when the interest went flat he'd just move on. Compulsive behavior. Always searching."

"Archaeology must have been different for him then," she said. "He's been doing it for years now, hasn't he?"

"It's the damnedest thing," the old man said. "I sent him to Yale. He was going to do law, he said. He spent a year at Yale, then suddenly I received a postcard from him. He's in Ireland, for God's sake!"

"Just like that?"

"Dropped law. Dropped Yale. Wanted to learn more about the past, he said. Wanted to enroll in Trinity College. I didn't mind that. After all, I suppose I'm the one who gave him a taste of the past in the first place—but archaeology!"

Harry gazed into firelight. There was an ache inside him. He realized he was hurting from the way Patrick had so abruptly left. When you were old, even small emotional slights became exaggerated inside you. You wanted to look toward death without that kind of pain.

"He went overseas a lot," he continued. "This desert. That desert. He was always sending me postcards from strange places."

Celestine was very quiet for a time. She was trying to imagine Patrick Cairney turning brown under a desert sun. It was a fine image, and it was exact. Where else would he have gone but to the deserts of the Middle East?

"For long periods, I'd hear absolutely nothing from him. Then there'd be a flurry of postcards from places with Arab names. I worried at first, but then I had to let go of that. He was grown-up. It was his life. I couldn't influence him anymore."

"Did you ever influence him?"

Harry laughed quietly. "He's the only one who could answer that."

Celestine raised her head, sipped some of her drink. She wanted to know more about Patrick Cairney. Tomorrow morning, first thing.

That's when she'd know something Harry couldn't possibly tell her. Maybe. Or maybe she was simply tracking a mystery that didn't exist, a construct of her own mind, something to pass the time with the way people whittled on sticks or took up watercolors. *No. She was sure. Damned sure.*

"Are you proud of him?" she asked.

"Proud?" Harry Cairney smiled. "I never asked myself that."

Celestine pressed the palms of her hands against her thighs. The loose-fitting cotton robe she wore slipped up to her knees, and she could feel the heat from the fire lay a band of warmth against her calves.

"Why all these questions?" the old man asked.

"He's my stepson, don't forget. You don't have a monopoly on him. I want to know him better, that's all."

Cairney looked suddenly rather solemn. "Be warned," he said. "He's not so easy to know."

Celestine closed her eyes again. "I don't believe he's as difficult as you suggest," she answered.

Cairney patted the back of her hand. It was all right to talk about Patrick, it was fine, but finally it only produced in him an illusion of normality. Sitting here by firelight, his wife's head in his lap. The surfaces of the very ordinary. The taste of brandy. Family chatter. He turned his face back toward the window. Out there the world was quite a different place. But he would maintain a front of calm because he was good at that. He had a lifetime of self-control in public office behind him, a decent support system. He wasn't given to easy panic or impulsive acts. Everything would go on as it had done before the *Connie* was stricken at sea. Life, marriage, love.

"We need music," he said, starting to rise.

She shook her head. "Let's enjoy the peace, Harry."

He rose anyhow. He walked to his desk and looked at the Browning once more. It was years since he'd fired the gun.

Celestine, propped up on her elbows, was watching him. "What's the big attraction there, Harry?"

He closed the drawer slowly.

He came back across the room and sat down beside her. "Nothing will ever happen to you," he said. "I want you to know that."

Celestine looked surprised. "Why would anything happen to me, Harry? This is Roscommon. And nothing ever happens here."

Harry Cairney closed his eyes. He thought he felt it in the very air around him, a shiver, as if the atmosphere of this house had changed with Mulhaney's phone call. It was a sinister feeling, and he didn't like it. It resembled those disquieting moments when you felt that somebody, somewhere, was walking on your grave.

NEW ROCKFORD, CONNECTICUT

It was two o'clock in the afternoon when Kevin Dawson received a telephone call from his brother in the White House. Thomas Dawson sounded very weary when he spoke.

"How was Candlewood?"

"Candlewood was terrific," Kevin Dawson replied. "You ought to try it some time. That place never lets me down. I always come back feeling refreshed."

"My idea of roughing it is to watch black-and-white TV," the President said. "One Boy Scout to a family is okay. Two would be a travesty of genetic theory."

Kevin Dawson heard the sounds of his daughters from the foot of the stairs. They were involved in a game of what they'd described as "cutthroat poker," which they played to rules of their own random making. It was altogether incomprehensible.

Thomas Dawson said, "It's been a long winter."

Puzzled, Kevin reached out and closed the door of his office with his knee. "You didn't call to discuss the length of the seasons," he said.

"True."

Another pause.

Kevin sat down, tilting his chair back against the wall. With one hand he managed to pour himself a scotch. He heard the door of the Secret Service vehicle open and close in the driveway below. Both agents, whom the kids had christened Cisco and Pancho, had spent the weekend in obvious discomfort, sleeping in a two-man tent because there was no extra room in the small cabin. They took their meals alone, laboriously burning things over a Coleman stove and filling the cold, sharp air with a dark-brown pollution that smelled, Kitty said, like skunk on a spit.

"It's been a long winter, and you're about ready for a vacation," Thomas Dawson said.

"It's that bad, huh?"

"It's that bad. Nicholas Linney has been murdered."

"Linney?" Kevin felt an odd tightness in his throat. His voice sounded very high, even to himself.

"I don't have to spell out the implications."

"Was it Jig?" Kevin asked.

"Almost certainly. By the way, I don't want this news bruited about, Kev. You understand me?"

Kevin Dawson drained his glass. He reached for the bottle, poured himself a second shot. All the invigoration he'd brought back with him from Candlewood was draining away. He had the very strange feeling he'd just been kicked in the stomach and couldn't breathe properly. How in God's name had Jig managed to track Linney down? Kevin curled the telephone cord tightly around his wrist.

He heard Martha and the kids coming up the stairs. Their voices echoed in this great sprawling house.

"I don't think you're seriously in danger, Kevin. You've got protection there. But why take any needless chances?"

Protection, Kevin thought. What it came down to was the fact that all the security in the world couldn't prevent somebody getting to you, if he was determined enough, and crazy enough, to find a way.

"What do you suggest?" Kevin asked.

"Hawaii. Make it a business trip with a little R and R on the side. Check into the family interests out there, but take Martha and the kids as well. Stay until Jig's been caught. How soon can you get out of there?"

Kevin Dawson wasn't sure. There were business meetings of one kind or another on Monday morning and Martha was the guest of honor at a breakfast in Stamford sponsored by the Make-a-Wish Foundation, which was her favorite charity. It would take more than a terrorist threat to make her cancel. "Tomorrow afternoon," he said. "I can't see getting away from here before that."

"I'd like it if you left earlier, Kevin."

"I don't see how."

Kevin heard his brother light up one of his infrequent cigarettes.

"I've just been talking with what the press always calls 'my closest advisers,' Kevin. Terrorists are the new bogeymen. They've replaced Communists in the American nightmare. If I lose some of the Irish vote by sicking the full fury of the FBI on somebody as famous as Jig, I'm advised I'll pick it up again with the rednecks who have orgasms when they know there's a firm presidential hand on the old helm of state. The Law and Order Ticket. The Jerry Falwell Brigade. Imagine a Catholic climbing into bed beside those polyester gangsters!"

Kevin Dawson couldn't imagine anything like that. But his brother had gone so far into cynicism that nothing was surprising these days. Thomas Dawson, human being, was almost a lost cause. Not quite gone, but fading fast. Tom would climb into bed with any group that could deliver votes. He was less a president than a calculating machine. If the Irish couldn't be counted on, you dumped them and looked around for substitutes. The politics of expediency, of numbers. Tommy would have sat down to supper with a consortium of the KKK, the John Birchers, the Posse Comitatus and the Unification Church, if he thought this crew could deliver.

"We were weak on law and order during the campaign," Thomas Dawson said. "I know it lost us the Midwest and the South. Maybe my advisers are smarter than I think."

"Maybe," Kevin said.

"Call me from Hawaii."

"I'll do that."

"Good night, Kevin."

Kevin Dawson put the telephone down. The door of his office swung open and Martha stood there. She was dressed in faded blue jeans and an old red parka. There were streaks of mud on her hiking boots. Her Candlewood Collection. Kevin loved it.

"The girls and I are going to watch some Disney thing on TV," she said. "Wanna join us?"

Kevin Dawson nodded. He reached for his wife, held her wrists in his hands. "Later," he said.

Martha smiled. "I want you to know I had a wonderful weekend. I didn't even mind Pancho and Cisco and their awful cooking. I just had a terrific time."

"Me too."

Kevin wondered how to approach the subject of a trip to Hawaii. Martha hated to travel very far from her home. A day trip to Stamford was as far as she liked to go.

"Why don't you watch your movie, then we'll put the kids to bed as early as possible. You can slip, as they say, into something more comfortable, and I'll open a bottle of wine." Kevin thought that a couple of glasses of Burgundy would make the notion of Hawaii palatable to her. She might not cancel her luncheon in Stamford, but she might be persuaded that Waikiki was a good idea. Sometimes you had to coax Martha along, seduce her into acceptance. Besides, nothing was more pleasurable in Kevin Dawson's world than the act of making love to his own wife.

"You've got a funny look in your eyes," she said.

"Don't I."

"I know that look, Kevin Dawson."

"You should. You're the one who put it there."

She raised her face up and kissed him, standing on tiptoes. "I look like somebody from the combat zone," she said. She went to the door, turned back to him. "Next time you see me I'll be gorgeous."

"You always are," Kevin Dawson said, but his wife had already gone.

He sat alone in his room, staring absently at a pile of business papers. He couldn't keep Nicholas Linney out of his mind. He kept seeing Nick as he'd seen him last at Roscommon, kept hearing Linney say he could take care of himself. Well, he hadn't. He hadn't taken care of himself at all. He thought now of Harry Cairney and Mulhaney and he considered calling them. But what was there to say? And neither of them had troubled to call him, which meant they had nothing to say either.

Kevin Dawson walked to the window. He looked down at the Secret Service men. One of them—Cisco, Pancho, Kevin wasn't sure—stared up at him and smiled. A fleeting little expression, then it was gone. Kevin stared across the meadowlands that stretched all the way from his house to the road. Beyond the ribbon of concrete the hills rose up, pocked with mysterious shadows and dark trees. It was a landscape he had been familiar with all his life, except that now it appeared strange to him, and threatening, as if it might conceal the Irishman somewhere in its crevices.

NEW YORK CITY

The voice on the tape said: *I'm claiming responsibility on behalf of the Irish Republican Army for the explosions in the Memorial Church at White Plains. Have you got that, shithead? I don't intend to repeat it.* And then the tape went silent, the line dead. Frank Pagan pressed the rewind button on the Grundig and listened for the third time. Zuboric drummed a lead pencil on the surface of his desk, watching Pagan carefully. You couldn't tell, from the surfaces of the Englishman's face, what he might be thinking.

The voice filled the room again. Pagan pushed the stop button. He looked at Zuboric.

"It's Irish. There's no mistaking that," Pagan said.

Zuboric stroked his moustache. There was something in Pagan's eyes he didn't like. He wasn't quite sure what it was, but a strange little film had appeared in the ashen grayness. A sneaky quality. It was as if Pagan's eyes were being bleached of what color they possessed. Zuboric wished he had a passport valid for entry into the Englishman's mind.

"Is it Jig?" the FBI agent asked.

Pagan stared down at the reels of the Grundig. "It could be," he said.

"You're not convinced, naturally."

"I'm just not sure. There's distortion. And maybe he's disguising the voice. It could be Jig."

Zuboric appeared satisfied with this. Frank Pagan walked up and down the office and then returned to the Grundig, as if he needed to hear the voice one last time to be absolutely sure. He pushed the play button, listened, killed the machine.

"I'm still not one hundred percent certain," Pagan said.

"We don't *need* one hundred percent certainty, Frank."

No, Pagan thought. You don't. He looked at Zuboric's college diploma which hung just over his head and wondered what Institution of Higher Learning had been so foolish as to bestow any kind of degree on Zuboric. Obviously it was one that didn't specialize in imaginative pursuits.

"I'd like to have the original Jig tapes relayed from England," Pagan said. "A comparison would erase any doubt."

Zuboric was about to make an answer to this when the telephone rang. Pagan watched the agent pick up the receiver. Zuboric's body was suddenly tense, at attention, which meant only one thing. Leonard M. Korn was on the other end of the line. Pagan listened to the occasional "Yes, sir" that Zuboric dropped into a conversation that was otherwise one-sided. Yessir, yessir, three bags full, sir.

Zuboric put the receiver down. "Well, well." He was positively beaming. Pagan thought ships could guide themselves by the beacon that was Zuboric's face right then.

"As of eight o'clock tonight," Zuboric said, glancing at his wrist-watch, "the Director is placing himself in charge of the Jig opera-tion."

"Ah," Pagan said. "Divine Intervention."

Zuboric rubbed his hands together. "Tomorrow morning, one hundred agents will be working full time on Jig. *One hundred.*" Zu-boric laughed in an excited way. He was like a lottery winner, Pagan thought. Blue-collar, worked hard all his days, liked the occasional sixer of Schlitz, a game of bowling Fridays—and lo and behold! his number has just come up and he doesn't know what to say. I'm happy for you, Artie, Pagan thought. Spend it wisely.

"The Director estimates we'll have Jig in a matter of days."

Pagan said nothing. He mistrusted the optimism of law enforce-ment officers, especially those who dwelt on Olympian heights the way Korn did. Probably the guy in charge of the Jack the Ripper investigation had said much the same kind of thing a hundred years ago, and *he* was still searching.

"I'm going back to my hotel," Pagan said. "I'm tired."

"I'll keep you company, Frank."

"Of course you will."

Pagan did up the buttons of his overcoat. He glanced once at the Grundig machine. He thought again of repeating his proposal to have the original tapes of Jig relayed from London, but suddenly it was redundant, suddenly those tapes wouldn't make a damn bit of difference. The hunt was on and the night was filled with baying hounds. And there was going to be noise, so much noise that no-body was going to stop and listen to tapes of the real Jig. Even if they did, they wouldn't hear them anyhow because blood had a way of singing into your ears, making you deaf. The hunt mentality, whether it was federal agents thrashing around for Jig or plump-rumped English squires intent on diminishing the evil fox pop-lation, was akin to insanity. It was blinded, and restricted, and obsessive.

Whoever had called the FBI about White Plains wasn't Jig. He didn't sound *remotely* like Jig. There was no way in the world Jig had made that phone call. Pagan had hoped to use his apparent uncertainty as a ploy, a way of winning a little time and getting the real tapes played. But he saw further maneuvers as totally useless now. There was no future in arguing, in trying to convince Zuboric. For his own part, he knew what he was going to do. It wasn't the smartest move he'd ever contemplated, but at the same time he couldn't see any alternatives. He had tried to play this whole thing by FBI rules and regulations, but that time was long past. He hadn't come all this way to America to have his quarry trapped in some bloody corner by morons like Zuboric. He hadn't made this trip to see that kind of travesty happen. He wanted Jig, but not on the sort of terms dictated by the hangmen of Federal Bureau of Investigation.

PAGAN locked the door of his room at the Parker Meridien. He sat for a time on the edge of the bed. He was motionless, like a man in the still center of meditation. Then, when he moved, he did so with the economy of somebody driven by a solitary purpose. He checked his gun, stuck it in the waistband of his pants at the back. He left the room. It was all movement now. Down in the elevator. Out into the lobby. Heading for the street.

Tyson Bruno came across the lobby toward him.

Pagan swept past the agent into the street, but Bruno came after him swiftly. It was interesting, Pagan thought. There was no effort on Bruno's part to conceal himself, no shadow work going on. It was out in the open. Maybe Bruno had been surprised by Pagan's sudden appearance and the quickness of his stride and hadn't had time to hide himself. What the hell, it was completely academic now.

Pagan stopped, turned around, waited until Bruno was level with him. Tyson Bruno, who was built like an outhouse, looked very solid in the dusk of Fifty-seventh Street.

"Before you even ask me one question, Bruno old boy, the answer is dead simple. I'm going for a walk and I don't want you on my arse. Is that clear enough for you?"

Tyson Bruno grinned. He was a man who enjoyed adversity. If he hadn't stepped inside the labyrinthine clasp of the FBI, he would have been a happy bouncer in a sleazy strip joint. "I go where you go, Pagan. This time, you don't take a hike on me."

Pagan turned, continued to walk. Bruno was still coming up behind him. On Fifth Avenue, Pagan made a right. Bruno was still behind him.

"Your last warning, Ty," Pagan said, looking back at the man.

"You shouldn't be doing this," Bruno said.

Pagan moved away. He was tired of boxes. Tired of restrictions.

Tired by fools who, left to their own devices, courted lunacy. He paused at a stoplight. Bruno was right behind him, still grinning. Pagan glanced at him.

"I just keep coming," Bruno said.

Pagan made as if to step off the sidewalk and cross the street. He moved an inch or two, then stopped abruptly, bunching his hands together and swinging them as if he held a hammer. The connection with Bruno's jaw made a delicious crunching sound. Reverberations created ripples, like tiny springs, all the way up Pagan's arms to his shoulders. Tyson, off balance, hopeless, sat down on the edge of the curb and said, "Hey!" He was bleeding from the lip, and his eyes looked like two glazed pinballs under the bleak glow of the streetlamps.

Pagan didn't stop. He ran to the other side of the street and began to move along Fifty-sixth, past the windows of closed restaurants and travel agencies, past the plastic sacks of garbage and a solitary sleeping wino, a failed candidate for St. Finbar's Mission. Pagan stopped running only when he had reached Fifty-fifth and Broadway and was certain that Tyson Bruno was nowhere near him. Winded, he paused in the doorway of a closed Greek sandwich shop, where the scent of yesterday's fried lamb filled his nostrils.

It occurred to him that he had done more than burn his bridges. He had exploded them in such a way that the whole bloody river was on fire.

T WENTY-ONE

With a newspaper rolled up under his arm Ivor McInnes stepped into Central Park. It was barely dawn and the sky above Manhattan was the color of milk. McInnes followed a narrow pathway between the trees until he came to an unoccupied bench. He wiped a layer of thin frost from the wooden slats, then sat down and unfolded his newspaper.

Photographs, headlines. They leaped out at him. For a moment he couldn't read because his eyes watered and his hand trembled. But there it was! McInnes had the feeling, given to very few men, that something he'd long dreamed was finally taking form in reality.

He stared at the newspaper again. He didn't see what other men might see there, a story of outrageous vandalism. He saw glory instead. He looked at the pictures of the smoking church, the tight little crowds of people gathered on the sidewalk, the shots of firemen aiming their hoses into the carnage. He felt for the victims, of course. It was only natural. A man without feelings was a dead man. But these feelings were small considerations compared with the balance of history. And it was history, or rather his personal piece of it, that enthralled Ivor McInnes.

He folded the newspaper over. For a while he stared into the trees.

There was a breath of spring in the chill early morning around him. A sense of fresh breakthroughs, newness. He spread the newspaper flat on the bench and read the story through, unable to control the excitement that overcame him.

There was of course no mention yet of the IRA. Nobody was going to release that information to the public so soon. There hadn't been time to analyze Houlihan's call, there hadn't been time in Washington to prepare a public face or concoct a feasible story to cover this incident. A church had blown up. Why? What had caused it? The paper didn't say. The reporter didn't know. There wasn't even speculation. McInnes smiled and rubbed his face with the palm of a hand. The powers of law and order could sit on this one, he realized. They could stall and prevaricate, if they didn't want to alarm the public with the news that IRA terrorists were suddenly operating within the continental United States. But they couldn't stall forever.

After today, they couldn't even stall for a moment.

McInnes folded the newspaper again and was about to rise when he became conscious of somebody sitting down on the bench beside him.

Frank Pagan said, "Interesting reading."

"A damn tragedy," McInnes said and glanced at Pagan's big hands, which were bone-white and tense on the man's knees. There was a sense of power about Pagan, a force held narrowly in check as if by some enormous inner effort. What had he come for at this time of the bloody morning? McInnes wondered.

"What do you think caused it, Ivor? A whole church gone in a flash. I mean, what do you think really caused such a thing to happen?"

"The paper doesn't say," McInnes answered. Was Frank Pagan baiting him? McInnes dismissed the suspicion. Pagan was groping in the dark.

"Your opinion, Ivor. You must have one. You usually do."

McInnes shrugged.

"God works in mysterious ways," Pagan remarked.

"Isn't that the truth."

A jogger went past. A potbellied middle-aged man with a scarlet headband and expensive sneakers. There was total desperation in his eyes.

Pagan said, "Somebody told me the IRA claimed the job in White Plains."

"The IRA?"

"Strikes me as farfetched," Pagan said. "How does it strike you?"

"Hard to believe," McInnes answered. "They'd be operating pretty far from home, wouldn't they?"

Pagan smiled. He stared at McInnes for a while. "It's not their style, is it?" he asked.

"Styles change. Anything's possible."

"Anything's possible. But why bring their war into the United States?"

"You're asking me? I've always found the Catholic mind unfathomable, Frank. I know this much, though. If it's the IRA, it's not going to end with some church. Once those fellows get a taste of blood, they don't know when to stop."

Pagan was quiet now. McInnes was conscious of the man's cold stare, which made him uncomfortable. Frank Pagan, with his inside track, would of course know about the IRA story. But why would he casually mention this? McInnes wondered. Pagan was like a bloody submarine, operating way below the surface in a place where the waters were murky. You could never tell where the man was headed or what torpedoes he might fire.

Pagan draped an arm across the back of the bench. "It's funny," he said quietly. "Now it's the church. Before that it was Alex Fitzjohn."

"Fitzjohn?" So here it was at last. Fitzjohn's name, as McInnes had expected, had finally cropped up. He tried not to appear defensive.

Pagan nodded. "Alex Fitzjohn was murdered in Albany, New York. The IRA claimed responsibility for that one too."

"I didn't hear anything about that," McInnes said.

"It wasn't in the papers, Ivor."

McInnes, who had the gift of supreme detachment when he needed it, stared blankly into Pagan's face. "Well," was all he said. He tapped the bench with his newspaper.

"You ever hear of Alex Fitzjohn, Ivor?"

McInnes shook his head.

Pagan said, "He was a member of the Free Ulster Volunteers. I thought you might have run into him along the way somewhere."

"We're back at that again, are we?" McInnes said. "We're back at the FUV again?"

"Why not," Pagan said. "Do you deny knowing Alex Fitzjohn?"

"I know a lot of people in Ulster, Frank. I know a lot of Fitzes. Fitzthis, Fitzthat. I told you before, I have absolutely no connection with the Volunteers. To suggest otherwise is a falsehood. I can't remember anyone by the name of Alex Fitzjohn." McInnes smiled and stared across the park. In the milky light of dawn the trees appeared to have been brushed lightly with an off-white enamel paint. "I have enemies, Frank. You know that. Certain people in Ulster have always tried to discredit me. Certain Catholics." McInnes crossed his legs and leaned closer to Frank Pagan. "For years the Catholic Church has been putting out stories about me. Incredible lies. They say I'm the leader of the FUV, among other things. The reason's very simple. They don't like what I have to say, Frank. They don't like my criticisms. They've been in a cave of superstition for centuries. And they don't like what I do. *I shine some light into that cave. I attack their idolatry.* They fight back the only way they know how, which is dirty."

McInnes paused. His large handsome face was intense now. The light in his eyes, like some laser, could have bored two neat holes in a plank of wood.

"What I really object to, Frank, isn't just the Roman Catholic attitude to social issues. It's bad enough when they tell some unemployed laborer with nine kids that he can't get his wife on the pill. Keep on breeding, they say, and to hell with the misery. You'll get your rewards in the afterlife, sonny. It's bad enough when they tell people they can erase their sins by mumbo-jumboing over some set of bloody beads, Frank. But what I truly find deplorable is the damned backwardness of it all. It's late in the twentieth century and we're in the throes of a vast technological revolution and the Catholic Church belongs to another time. It doesn't like progress because it means that people have more information. And more information, as we well know, leads to freedoms. And that's what the Catholic Church doesn't like. People who are free to think, Frank. *They want men and women in bondage.*" McInnes shut his eyes a moment. He moved one hand through the air, inscribing a pattern of some kind. "It keeps Ulster in the Dark Ages, Frank. It keeps my country from going forward. It hates the new technology. It doesn't know what to do with it. It wants its adherents to live in blind obedience to the dictates of the Vatican. Consider this, Frank. *In Dublin priests actually bless the fleet of Aer Lingus!* Can you believe that? Priests bless the planes! What does that tell you about the Catholic Church? It's trying to impose superstition upon high technology! It makes me uneasy and it makes me angry because, with the present Catholic birthrate, it won't be long before Ulster is dominated by the Vatican the way the Republic is. Then we kiss the whole of Ireland good-bye. And back to the Dark Ages with *all* of us."

There was a certain hypnotic effect in the cadences of McInnes's voice. It lulled and it soothed even as it provoked. Pagan could see how thousands of people in Ulster were swayed by the man. You had to give it to Ivor. He put on a damn good show. Even the hand movements, which were expressive and sinewy, must have impressed people in a society not known for great conversational use of the hands. There was something Mediterranean about it all, something exotic. And in drab, burned-out Belfast it must have had enormous appeal.

Now Pagan wanted to bring this conversation, which Ivor had taken up to roof level, back to the ground floor. "We were talking about Fitzjohn."

"I was talking about my enemies," McInnes said.

Pagan sighed. "You claim you don't know Fitzjohn. But my London office has different information. We have a photograph of yourself and Fitzjohn together taken outside your church. It's quite a chummy little composition."

A photograph? McInnes couldn't recall ever having a picture taken with Fitz, whom he hadn't seen since the man had emigrated. "You're bluffing me," he said.

"Hardly, Ivor."

McInnes thought of Houlihan. Bloody Seamus, who had to go and kill a man and then turn around and call the FBI! It was the one flaw in the whole mosaic, the one tile that didn't quite fit right, and it could so easily have been avoided. Damn. Damn Houlihan. Everything should have been perfect. Now there was one spidery crack. And it wouldn't be sealed because bloody Pagan wasn't going to leave it alone.

"Do you have the photograph, Frank?"

"Not in my possession. But I can get it."

"I wouldn't mind seeing it. I'm sure there's some mistake."

"I don't really think so, Ivor. This picture shows you and Fitzjohn standing side by side. You have an arm round Fitz's shoulder and he's looking happy as the day is long."

McInnes blinked. "I don't deny I may have *met* the man, but I don't remember the encounter. As for the photograph, I'd have to see it before I could comment. If there is such a picture, which I doubt."

He stood up, but Frank Pagan caught him by the wrist and tugged. Pagan's grip was very strong.

"Don't run away, Ivor. Stay and chat."

"I've got work to do, Frank."

"What kind of work?"

"Research." McInnes saw that Pagan's eyes, which were hard and distant, resembled the small gray moons of some icy planet. It was a look he didn't like.

"Why was Fitzjohn in Albany?" Pagan asked. His tone of voice was chilly now, and harsh. It was the voice of an interrogator demanding answers in some basement room.

"How the hell would I know?"

"Who killed him?"

McInnes made a flustered movement with his hands. "Frank, for God's sake. You keep harping."

"Did you know the IRA was in America?"

"How could I know something like that?"

"*Did you know they planned to bomb the church?*"

McInnes shook his head. "You're losing control, Frank."

Pagan stood up. He released McInnes now. Ivor took a couple of steps away.

"You're scared of something, Ivor. What is it?"

McInnes smiled thinly. His wrist hurt from Pagan's tight grip. "Irrational people upset me, Frank."

Irrational people. Pagan thought that was pretty good, coming from McInnes.

"It's the photograph, isn't it?" Pagan asked. "That's what's worrying you now. You can't remember where or when it was taken, and you're desperately trying to think up some lie to cover it."

McInnes shook his head. "I don't even believe in this photograph, Frank. So how could it worry me?"

Pagan came very close to McInnes now. There was hardly an inch separating the two men. "You and Fitzjohn," Pagan said. "You must have been close, Ivor. Two good pals."

McInnes stepped back. He rapped his rolled-up newspaper against his leg. Bloody man, he thought. Hard man with his tough talk. But Pagan knew absolutely nothing. He was all bluster, all empty performance. A man on a fishing expedition, that was Frank Pagan. There was no photograph. There couldn't have been.

"Why don't you do something important, Frank? You said Jig was here in America, didn't you? Why don't you go out and *catch* him?"

Frank Pagan smiled, but barely. The expression was little more than a slit on his face. "Nice comeback, Ivor. Very nice," he said in a grim way. "But remember this. Whatever it is you're doing here, I'll find out. I'm good at finding things out. In other words, Ivor, keep looking over your shoulder."

"I'm used to that, Frank."

"You may be used to it, Ivor. But you better be good at it."

McInnes turned away. He moved in the direction of his hotel, walking without glancing back, even though he knew Pagan was still watching him. He wasn't going to let Pagan shake him. Damn the man! But today of all days he wasn't going to be upset by Pagan. He entered his hotel, passed the telephone banks, tempted to make one call, *aching* to make one call, longing to hear the voice of reassurance that would tell him his plane was fine, that it wasn't going to go wrong, that Frank Pagan couldn't stop it.

He kept moving.

When he entered his room, he locked the door. He opened his briefcase and searched the lining for the street map of New Rockford. He spread the map on the bed and stared at the thick black pen marks, meticulously drawn arrows that indicated the route the bus always traveled. He concentrated on the arrows but what he kept hearing was Frank Pagan's bloody voice saying *I'm good at finding things out.*

Not this time, McInnes thought. Not now.

PAGAN exited from Central Park on Fifth Avenue at Sixtieth Street and walked to the place where he'd parked his rental car, a very mundane Cutlass. He'd abandoned the Cadillac because it was too conspicuous. The Olds, on the other hand, was the color of excrement and melted into the background, which was the kind of camouflage he wanted. Last night, when he'd dumped the whole FBI in the shape of Tyson Bruno, he'd walked all the way to the Village, where he'd checked into a rundown hotel and passed a bad night on a mattress that felt like the surface of Mars. He had half expected Zuboric to break down the door.

He drove up Sixth Avenue, clogged with bad-tempered Monday morning drivers. There was a great deal of rage on the streets of New York City. At a stoplight, he pressed the scan button on the digital radio and found a rock station with which he felt comfortable. He listened to the Mersey Beats singing "Sorrow," and although he wasn't a big fan of the old Mersey sound, the music was restful. More restful, certainly, than the little scene with Ivor, which had proved only that the Reverend was a man with a secret he was grimly determined to keep even when confronted by a potentially damaging photograph.

A secret, Pagan thought.

Was it *possible* Ivor knew of an IRA presence in the U.S.A.?

Was it possible that he had come to America *knowing* the IRA was about to launch a mysterious offensive?

And was it Ivor's intention to direct covert operations against the IRA, using America as a battlefield? Had Fitzjohn been one of Ivor's foot soldiers who came to grief in a skirmish with the IRA?

Pagan shook his head. He wasn't sure where this line of speculation was going. If it was true, it would mean that both the FUV and the IRA had forces present inside America. But why would the IRA *suddenly* export its violence? Why bring it to America in the first place? That made no sense. The only foreign soil on which the IRA had ever operated was England. And there was nothing to be gained from acts of terrorism inside America because they would certainly alienate the Irish-Americans who provided both sympathy and money. The main attraction of the Cause, after all, was that it conducted its affairs at a distance of some three thousand miles and was therefore not something to sully your own backyard. The Irish-Americans appreciated that, and the IRA understood it, and there was agreement on that basis. So why the hell spoil a decent understanding by blowing up a church, even a Protestant one?

It was all wrong. It was all out of balance.

Pagan braked at another stoplight. Ivor wasn't a stupid man. He had a cunning capable of creating Byzantine situations. Jig, for instance. McInnes had surely known all along Jig was in the country, but he'd consistently denied it. Just as he denied any association with the Free Ulster Volunteers. These links and connections, these skinny threads, made painful knots inside Pagan's brain. And he had the feeling that it was all utterly simple, something so damned obvious it was staring him in the face only he couldn't see it.

He squeezed the Olds between a taxicab and a garbage truck, a maneuver that caused several cars behind him to brake quickly. He made a right turn, sliding away from the chaos he left in his wake. He wondered what Artie Zuboric was doing right now. But he didn't wonder for very long.

NEW ROCKFORD, CONNECTICUT

Patrick Cairney lay flat on his stomach. The long blades of grass around him were coated with a thin film of ice. Overhead, the branches of bare trees were illuminated by a weak sun, a frosted disk with no color. Cairney edged forward through the grass until he could go no farther because the hill became sheer suddenly, a grassy cliff, a long drop to the road below. He blinked into the sun.

He'd seen such a sun before and he remembered it, remembered participating in a raid with Libyans inside the border of Chad. Twenty men, himself included, had attacked a convoy of trucks about two hundred miles from Sebra, the last Libyan command post before Chad territory. It was a dawn attack, filled with surprise. The Chad drivers, their trucks loaded with old machine guns, had been traveling straight into the sun and they hadn't seen the small force descend on them, weapons blazing. It was over in a matter of minutes, and what Cairney recalled best was the sense of anticlimax after the long night of anticipation.

He peered across the road below at the big house, which was located at the end of a narrow driveway. It was a sprawling house, additions made here and there with no particular theme in mind. He brought his binoculars up to his eyes and swept the grounds. A car sat in the driveway. Earlier, a woman had escorted two children into a station wagon and, followed by a pale-blue sedan, had driven down the driveway and vanished along the road. Neither the wagon nor the sedan had returned.

Before coming to New Rockford, Cairney had gone to a newspaper office in Stamford, Connecticut, which had an entire section in its morgue dedicated to the adventures of the Dawson family. America, it appeared, couldn't get enough of the Dawsons. Tons of newsprint were devoted to Tommy and Kevin and Martha and the daughters. The daughters especially. In the absence of presidential offspring, Kitty and Louise Dawson were the next best thing. They went to a local school. They were ordinary kids, the kids next door. Unspoiled, nicely flawed. Little princesses, the Republic's answer to the royalty it had cast off two hundred years ago and still pined for.

Cairney assumed that the big dark car was a Secret Service vehicle. The grounds, so far as he could see, offered very little opportunity for any kind of cover. Winter had stripped the trees with the result that anybody traveling up the driveway could be seen clearly from the windows of the house. He realized that if he was to get to Kevin Dawson without being seen he'd have to wait until nightfall. His coat was damp from the grass and his feet were cold. His breath hung on the chill air. This wasn't going to be a snap. This wasn't going to be anything simple, like slipping inside Nicholas Linney's home or mingling with the half-drunk crowds at Jock Mulhaney's court.

He brought the binoculars back up to his eyes. He saw a tall, dark-haired man get out of the big car and light a cigarette. The man crossed the lawn slowly in front of the house, surveyed the grounds, stubbed his cigarette underfoot, then returned to the car. Cairney lowered the glasses. Nightfall, which was many hours away, many dead hours away, was going to be his only chance. He crawled backward from the edge of the hill and when the house was no longer in view he stood up, shivering. He was tense, and his sense of solitude strong.

Hours to kill. He was thirsty and hungry now. He walked back down the slope to the place where, behind a stand of trees at the end of a faded path, he had parked his car. He'd seen a diner some miles back near the freeway. He'd go there, eat and drink quickly, then come back here to his post on the hill. He drove through the somber Connecticut landscape, which reminded him more than a little of certain parts of Ireland in winter.

The diner was an aluminum tube with an air of the Depression about it. Cairney parked the Dodge and went inside, where he sat up on a stool and ordered coffee and a sandwich. He picked at the sandwich, no longer as hungry as he thought he was. Then he looked around the diner. A married couple with a child sat near the window. Two linemen for the phone company occupied a back booth. It was all very ordinary. For a moment he wondered about conventional lives, little acts of love and hatred, commitments and belongings and yearnings. He wondered about the bricks of everyday life and how people managed to balance them. Mortgages and library books and envelopes with cellophane windows in them and alarm clocks ringing on chilly mornings. He wouldn't have been very good at such a life. He was alone the way Finn had always been alone, married to an abstraction called the Cause. And the only freedom from the marriage lay quite simply in the last divorce of all, which was death.

The Cause, he thought. What would become of it if he didn't get the money back? The blood would cease in the veins of the Cause, and the heart would stop pumping, and the brain would atrophy and die. And what would he have given his life to if the Cause withered on his account—*because he couldn't get the money back?* There was a small, panicked voice in his head now.

He stepped down from the stool. He was anxious to get back to the hill overlooking Kevin Dawson's house. He had the strong intuition that the money was there, maybe because he wanted it to be there. Maybe because he longed for the end of this particular road.

He moved toward the front door of the diner. Then paused. There was a telephone in a small alcove to one side. He stared at it. Then he was going toward it even as he resisted. Even as he thought, *No, I don't need this now. I don't need this ever.*

JOHN WADDELL sat at the wheel of the rental truck. He had braked at an intersection where there was a four-way stop sign, an American traffic peculiarity to which he was unaccustomed. He was reluctant to edge the vehicle forward because he was uncertain of what the sign meant exactly. Did he or did he not have right-of-way? There was no other traffic in sight, just rows of frame houses and porches. On one porch an elderly woman was watering a potted plant, bent like a worshiper at a shrine. She looked up once, glanced at the truck, then went back to her watering can.

"What are you waiting for?" Houlihan asked. "The fucking weather to change?"

Waddell eased the truck forward. He was flustered by the unfamiliarity of the vehicle and the strangeness of driving on the right side of the road. Houlihan, who sat beside him, was extremely impatient this morning, more so than usual, always snapping when he talked. On his lap Houlihan had a sheet of paper on which he'd scrawled the directions he'd been given over the telephone. He'd been in the phone booth a long time and when he emerged he'd looked dark-faced and determined, the muscles clenched furiously in his long Irish jaw. The sheet was a mess of black lines and scribbled words.

Waddell reached the other side of the intersection. The old lady raised a hand and waved, and he thought, *Missus, you wouldn't be waving if you knew, if you really knew*. He drove slowly for a block, then Houlihan said, "This is Makepeace Street. Turn right."

Makepeace Street, Waddell thought. If ever a street was wrongly named. He swung the truck right and followed the street, which looked the same as all the back streets of New Rockford, until Houlihan instructed him to turn left. Nantucket Street. Here the houses were starting to thin out. At the end of the block there was a school behind a wire fence. Three yellow school buses were parked just inside the fence. Waddell glanced at a playground with basketball hoops, a soccer field, and a set of wooden swings. In the distance, at the end of the field, a group of small kids chased a ball around, and the sound of their play reached Waddell's ears. It was a sound he found particularly unsettling because it reminded him of his own history, of a time when he'd stand on the sidelines of muddy fields and watch his boy play soccer, when his nerves would be taut on behalf of the kid who played with the clumsy determination of a child with two left feet but an enormous heart. The kid had heart all right.

Waddell held his breath. He hadn't really thought about the boy in a long time. There wasn't much point in bringing all that up again, because he'd buried the pain along with the bodies, but you never really buried pain, did you? He blinked out across the field. He just wanted to be away from this place.

Houlihan looked at his notes. "Keep going," he said. "When you get to the end of this road, turn left."

Waddell put his foot on the gas pedal. He followed Seamus's instructions. Now, beyond the school, there were no more houses and the road was very narrow, barely wide enough for one vehicle to pass. Trees grew on either side, mature trees whose lower trunks were covered with deep green moss. The branches made a bare arch overhead, reaching out to touch other trees, creating all manner of shadows. Waddell kept driving until Houlihan told him to pull over. There was a flat area, grass worn by old tire tracks, at the side of the road. It was a rectangular patch of land surrounded on three sides by woodland. Waddell thought there was something forlorn about the place.

Seamus Houlihan opened the door and jumped down. He went to the back of the truck and released Rorke and McGrath, who had obviously been sleeping because they emerged unsteadily, rubbing their eyes and yawning. Rorke cleared his throat and spat out a ball of phlegm and looked very satisfied with his output.

Houlihan walked over the rectangle of land. Here and there candy wrappers lay around. A kid's discarded sneaker, weatherbeaten and abused, was caught in the tangled branches of a bush. Waddell stepped down from the cab and watched Houlihan, who stood with his hands on his hips, his face turned toward the woods beyond the clearing. John Waddell shuddered. The wind blowing out of the trees was biting.

"Over that way," Houlihan said, directing Rorke and McGrath into the trees. The two men moved between the trunks, waiting for Houlihan to tell them when to stop. When they were about twenty yards away, Seamus told them to halt. "That's far enough," he said.

Waddell looked at Rorke and McGrath. They were hardly visible there in the woods. If they were to bend down you couldn't see them at all. Houlihan whistled tunelessly a few seconds, then approached Waddell and slung his big arm round Waddell's shoulders.

"You'll be over there with me, Waddy," Houlihan said.

Waddell licked his lips. The surface of his tongue was very dry. He was trying to make his mind go far away, sending it off on a journey, as if it were a javelin he could toss through the air at will. Anywhere but here.

He followed Houlihan into the trees, then stopped when the big man came to a halt. Waddell wanted to ask why they were out here, what it was that Houlihan was planning now, but he didn't want to know. Something was going to come this way, he understood that much. And it was going to be ambushed.

"This is where we'll be," Houlihan said, squinting back the way they'd come. He dug the heel of his boot into the ground, making a mark. Waddell wanted to think it was a game, kids playing in the woods, cowboys and Indians, a game of hiding, anything at all but what it really was.

Waddell turned up the collar of his jacket. The wind blew into his eyes and made the branches overhead rustle. It had to be pleasant here in the summer, he thought, leafy lanes, bowers, a romantic spot. But it wasn't pleasant now, not even with the yellowy sun streaming behind the threadbare trees.

"When the time comes, we'll have the weapons in our hands," Houlihan said. "The real thing, Waddy."

Waddell shifted his head slightly. He peered through the trees to where Rorke and McGrath were situated. The real thing, he thought.

"Are you up for it, Waddy?"

Waddell tried to imagine standing here, hidden from the road, with a machine gun in his hands. The prospect alarmed him.

"What are we going to be shooting at?" he asked.

Houlihan smiled. He tapped his nose with his index finger, a gesture indicating secrecy. "You'll know when the time comes."

"Is it a vehicle of some kind?" Waddell asked.

"You're an inquisitive wee bugger, Waddy."

"Do we just stand here and open fire on it?"

Houlihan nodded. "That's all you have to do."

Waddell stared up into Houlihan's eyes. The look he saw there was the same he'd seen that night in Finn's house when the old man lay trapped and dying between the strings of a bloody harp. It was beyond cold, more than the mere absence of light. There was nothing in the big man's eyes but a vacancy, a frightening void where everything that breathed and had life perished.

"What chance will this vehicle have?" Waddell asked.

Houlihan said, "None."

Waddell was quiet a moment. What was it Houlihan wanted to ambush? A truck? A car? "How many people will be inside it?"

Without answering, Seamus Houlihan walked away. When he'd gone about ten yards, the big man turned back and said, "Let's get the hell out of here. It's time get some lunch."

NEW YORK CITY

Leonard M. Korn looked at the huge wall map that had been hung in Zuboric's office. A few colored pins, each indicating a place where Jig had either been seen or had allegedly operated, were stuck into the surface. There was one for Lower Manhattan, another for Bridgehampton, one for Albany, and a fourth for White Plains. Since coming to New York City by helicopter from Washington, Korn had dispatched six field agents to each of these locations to do what he called follow-up, which consisted mainly of going over the territory and asking questions of inhabitants who might have seen Jig without actually knowing it. It was a blunderbuss operation, in fact. You scattered men all over the place, compiled hundreds of pages of notes, fed the raw information into computers and hoped that some kind of pattern, capable of predicting Jig's movements, capable of sketching a variety of scenarios, would emerge from deep within the electronic brain after a process of analysis, comparison, and collation. In addition to the twenty-four agents in the field at present, Korn had also sent six explosives experts to White Plains to sift through the charred remains of the church. A further ten agents were involved in checking the backgrounds, movements, and financial records of Nicholas Linney. All in all, it was exactly the kind of operation the Director enjoyed because it gave him the opportunity to leave his mark everywhere.

Korn turned in his chair to look at Arthur Zuboric over the bank of special telephones, each a different color, that had hurriedly been installed since his arrival. Agents came and went along the corridors, rushing to feed data by direct computer link to Washington, making phone calls, keeping tabs of the men in the field. Zuboric, who no longer recognized his own office, was impressed.

Korn said, "This should all have been done before, of course."

Zuboric nodded slightly.

"Still," and Korn rose in his platform shoes. "Better late than never. Our President's motto." A small smile played on Korn's mouth. He folded his hands in front of his body and swayed back and forth on his heels a moment. "But we're not here to criticize our elected officials, are we?"

"No, sir," Zuboric said in a dry voice.

Korn turned to the window and looked out at Manhattan with disapproval on his face. He was a Washington man through and through and generally unhappy with any city that wasn't the Nation's Hub.

"Frank Pagan," he said.

Zuboric had been waiting for this. The full wrath of the Director could come down on him now. It crossed his mind that this would be a highly appropriate moment to suddenly say that he'd decided to resign from the Bureau. The perfect time to run away. He caught a tantalizing glimpse of freedom beyond the reach of Korn's mighty arm. Out there, away from the Bureau, was another country, a pleasant sort of place where he might be happily and peacefully married to Charity. And broke, too.

"Frank Pagan has a history of curious behavior," Korn said. "I assume you've read his file."

"Yes, sir."

"He should have been put out to pasture a long time ago. But who can understand the British? Instead of firing Pagan when he didn't fit in at Scotland Yard, they gave him his own little dominion with his own powers of rulership. Crazy. And now he has to go and have a breakdown in the U.S.A."

A breakdown. Zuboric flexed his fingers. The Director was silent for some time. It was spooky and unnerving.

"A Lone Ranger complex," Korn finally said, sighing, shaking his head. "Didn't you notice? Didn't you see the signs?"

Zuboric stared at the floor. If he admitted he'd seen signs of what Korn called a breakdown, then it would be tantamount to confessing his lack of insight into human behavior and consequently an inability to predict situations. If he didn't admit it, then he was damned on the grounds of insensitivity. Either way he was lost. He opened his mouth to say something, but Korn cut him off.

"The point is, he's out there somewhere," and one of the Director's white hands flew up in the direction of the map. "Presumably with the intention of capturing Jig. If he succeeds, well, that would be an unacceptable state of affairs. How would we look then, Zuboric? How would the Bureau look if this lone man brought in Jig?"

Zuboric shook his head. He knew the answer to that question.

"Does Pagan know something we don't?" Korn asked.

"Not to the best of my knowledge, sir." But Zuboric wasn't sure. Lately he'd had the disturbing feeling that Pagan was hiding something, although he hadn't been able to put his finger on it.

Leonard M. Korn sat down and said nothing for a time. Then, "The point is, Zuboric, Pagan's expendable. Just as expendable as Jig."

Expendable. Zuboric thought the word had a fine ring to it. He liked the idea of it being applied to Pagan. When he thought of Frank Pagan attacking Tyson Bruno he was enraged. Apart from the assault on a federal agent, Pagan had made Zuboric's operation look very bad indeed, clumsy and inept.

"What I'm saying, Arthur, is that while Frank Pagan doesn't rank priority as far as I'm concerned, it wouldn't be altogether a tragedy if he had an accident of some kind during the course of our investigation." Korn shrugged. "If he gets in our way, that is."

A death warrant, Zuboric thought.

"On the other hand, it would be more *tidy* if he was simply bundled up and shoved on to a plane for Heathrow." The Director ran a hand over his shaved head. "I really don't care one way or another. You do understand what I'm saying, don't you?"

"Yes, sir." Zuboric moved his feet around.

"His photograph has been circulated to everyone involved in this operation," the Director said. "Let's talk about something else. Let's talk about you, Arthur."

Here it comes, Zuboric thought. His heart fluttered. He knew that Korn had something in mind for him, perhaps one of those banishments into exile for which the Director was notorious. If it wasn't the bat caves of Carlsbad, it could be the frozen tundra of the Dakotas. He suddenly had an insight into Korn's powers. This small man, with the shaven head and the voice that barely rose above a whisper, was privy to all manner of confidential information, and had all kinds of power over others. At a whim, he could consign you to oblivion, ruin your career, wreck your whole life. With the stroke of a pen, Leonard M. Korn could make it seem as if you'd never existed. Zuboric wondered what that sort of power did to a person.

"I think you need to spend a little time out of the city, Arthur. Rural Connecticut might be pleasant." Korn smiled, a sly little expression. "Our President has a brother, as you know."

Zuboric wondered where this was leading.

"It appears that Kevin Dawson and his family are planning to take a trip this afternoon. The President wasn't specific when he talked to me." Korn paused. He took a pen from the pocket of his suit and fiddled with it. "Whatever. Our President seems a little anxious about brother Kevin's safety these days. Don't ask me why. Perhaps it's an occupational hazard of being a Dawson. Somebody's always got it in for you. Anyhow, the upshot of this is that I agreed to provide a little extra protection for brother Kevin and his offspring. Namely, you."

"Me?" Zuboric wasn't sure if this assignment meant exile and removal from the Jig affair or something else. You could tell nothing from the Director's face, which was inscrutable in the way of most men who have played political games all their lives.

"It's a simple matter. There are already three Secret Service men deployed at the Dawson house. Our President feels a little added security wouldn't be a bad thing. He turned, of course, to the Bureau with this request. He trusts the Bureau." Korn stood up, looking at Zuboric. "Naturally, the Secret Service would know about your presence, and so would Kevin Dawson. You'd simply keep a low profile around the household, and when the time came for the family to leave for the airport you'd escort them. That's all there is to it."

Zuboric relaxed a little. It wasn't banishment entirely. And even if it was exile, it wasn't going to be a very long one. It would give him a day away from Jig and Frank Pagan and anything else pertaining to twisted Irish matters. He could stand around the Dawson house in Connecticut and think up ways to persuade Charity to marry him.

"The Dawsons plan to leave at four. You could get up to New Rockford by early afternoon if you left now."

"Do I go alone?" Zuboric asked.

"Take Bruno with you," Korn answered. "Presumably he needs a break from the city as much as you."

Zuboric moved toward the door. He saw a flurry of white-shirted agents in the corridor. From somewhere came the clacking of a printer. Phones were ringing in offices. One Irish killer had created all this bedlam. One man. Zuboric turned, looked back once at Leonard Korn, then stepped out into the corridor. The countryside was suddenly very appealing to him.

"Remember, Zuboric. Keep your profile so low your chin is scraping the ground. Understand?"

"Understood," Zuboric said.

Leonard M. Korn watched the agent leave. When the door closed, the Director removed his jacket and hung it neatly over the back of the chair. He rolled his sleeves up, turning each cuff exactly four times. He looked at the blank TV, a small portable, which he'd had placed in the corner of the room. The White House was going to issue an official statement some time today. Not Thomas Dawson himself, but one of his faceless spokesmen. The subject would be the presence in America of the IRA terrorist known as Jig and the bombing of the church in White Plains. It would mention how the Federal Bureau of Investigation was currently pursuing every available lead. There might even be a confident hint that the capture of Jig was imminent.

The prospect of all this publicity satisfied Leonard M. Korn. But he gained even more satisfaction from the fact that Thomas Dawson had capitulated, that all the needless secrecy was at an end. There was still something else that made Korn feel very good about himself—Thomas Dawson had telephoned him not more than an hour ago with the request to supply, as *quietly* as possible, a little extra protection for brother Kevin. Korn, even as he wondered why Kevin might need extra muscle, had asked no questions. He knew the President had reasons of his own for not drawing on the Secret Service pool, and he suspected that they had to do with his nervousness about this whole Irish situation, but he wasn't going to examine them. Later, if he thought it necessary, a little exploratory surgery into the life of brother Kevin might be useful. It would do no harm to know why Kevin needed added protection. But for the moment he'd agreed gladly, almost obsequiously, to the request, understanding that some kind of trade-off had been made with the President.

Thomas Dawson had given Korn his manhunt.

And he'd quietly given Tommy Dawson, in the process of tit for tat, favor for favor, two FBI agents. It was called backscratching and it was how Washington worked. A handshake, a tacit agreement, a little discretion. And *voilà!* You had a system that functioned. Besides, it was always a pleasure to oblige the person in the White House, even if all you were doing was supplying two agents, both of whom were tired and angry and no longer needed at the heart of things.

ROSCOMMON, NEW YORK

Celestine Cairney picked up the telephone on the second ring. She was seated at the kitchen table, a phone book open in front of her and a cigarette burning down inside an ashtray. When she heard Patrick Cairney's voice, she picked up the cigarette and tilted her chair back at the wall and held the receiver in a hand that had become moist.

"You sound like you're miles away." It was the first thing that came into her mind.

"New York City isn't so far," he answered.

She stared up at the ceiling where a wintry fly, black and glossy, circled the unlit fluorescent light strip. She tried to picture Patrick now, his surroundings, what he was wearing. But no images came to her.

"You called yesterday, didn't you? But you just hung up."

Cairney said he hadn't. There was a voice behind him, background noise, a man shouting something about eggs over easy. So he was in a restaurant, a café, somewhere. She shut her eyes tightly and sucked cigarette smoke deep inside her chest, then tried to relax as she exhaled, stretching her legs, letting one arm hang limply from her side. But there was turmoil within.

"I wanted to talk to my father," Cairney said.

Celestine said nothing for a long time. That wasn't why he'd really called. She wasn't convinced by him. He'd called because he needed to hear her voice as much as she needed to hear his. She wanted to say this, but she didn't. She wanted to say *I want you, Patrick. Before it becomes impossible.*

"Are you still there?" he asked.

"Yes."

"Something's wrong, isn't it?"

"Yes."

"Is it my father?"

Celestine made a pattern with the telephone cord, pressing it against her thigh, pushing it deep into the soft flesh in an absentminded fashion. She felt a catch in her throat, like a small air pocket, a vacuum lodged there. She opened her eyes and looked round the stainless-steel kitchen. Her heartbeat was loud in the hollow of her chest.

In a very deliberate voice she heard herself say, "He had an attack last night."

"Is it serious?"

"Tully said so. I had to call him in."

"How bad is serious?"

"Bad enough. Tully says one of the lungs is completely collapsed and the other isn't doing too well."

"He ought to be in a hospital."

"Tully doesn't want him moved just yet," Celestine said. She looked through the open kitchen doorway into the hall. The silences of the big house seemed ominous to her just then, shadows and still places and huge empty rooms. It was like a child's idea of a haunted house, phantoms on stairways, apparitions in windows.

She said, "If he gets stronger, he can be moved. But not before." She raised her hand, slipped it beneath her blouse, pressed the palm flat against her stomach and made small circular strokes.

"*If* he gets stronger?" Cairney asked.

"Patrick, this is touch and go. This is a bad situation. He can hardly breathe. Tully has him inside a portable oxygen tent."

"Is Tully still there? I'd like to talk to him."

"He left an hour ago."

"Is he coming back?"

"He said later." She was quiet. She raised her legs, propped her feet up on the table so that her skirt slid back. She wore no underwear. She imagined Patrick Cairney touching her between the legs.

"Can you come home?" she asked.

Cairney sighed. "Maybe tomorrow. I'm not sure yet."

"It would mean a great deal to Harry if he could see you."

"I know."

"Your own father has to be more important than some goddam gathering of academics." She raised her voice. She hadn't intended to. But she had to show him that she was unhappy and frayed and couldn't handle this situation on her own.

"I'll do what I can," he said.

"Of course you will."

The voice of the operator came on the line, asking in a faintly metallic way for Cairney to insert more money. But then the line was dead and Cairney was gone. Celestine replaced the receiver, stood up, wandered around the kitchen. She paused by the window, which had a view of the woodlands behind the house.

Then she stared down at the open telephone book on the table. All morning long she'd been calling different educational institutions, colleges and universities throughout the state. She'd even contacted a group that called itself the Archaeological Society of New York. One polite voice after another had told her what she needed to know.

There was no symposium anywhere at the time. Not in New York City, not in the suburbs, not in any of the large or small cities of the state, not even in any of the obscure colleges that proliferated in rural areas. There was no such thing as the event Patrick Cairney claimed to be attending. If she'd had doubts about him before, she had absolutely none now.

She lit another cigarette.

She stepped out of the kitchen and stood in the hallway, looked up the staircase, which ascended by stages into gloom. She felt extremely tense as she gazed upward. He would come home. Because he felt guilty about what had happened, because he wanted to see her again, and because of his father. Yes, he'd come back. He had good reasons. And what would she do then?

Only what she had to. There was no choice.

She put her foot on the first step. A small web of smoke drifted away from her lips. She raised her face when she heard a sound from the top of the stairs. Harry stood up there in his bathrobe, his bare flesh the color of paper.

She smiled up at him. He was whistling quietly to himself. His white hair was wet from the shower, and the smell of his aftershave was strong enough to reach her at the foot of the stairs.

"By God, I can smell spring this morning," he said. He'd been morose for most of last night, distant and preoccupied in a place where she couldn't reach. But now, even if he was forcing it slightly, he seemed cheerful.

"It's in the air," she replied.

"My stomach's rumbling. There's nothing quite like spring to stoke an old man's appetite."

She watched him descend. He seemed almost sprightly today. There was a slight lift to his step. When he was halfway down he spread his arms and rolled his eyes and in a fake Irish baritone sang, "*I shall tell her all my love, all my soul's adoration. And I think she will hear me and not say me nay.*"

Celestine clapped and said it was a good impersonation of an Irish barroom singer. Harry put his arms around her and hugged her strongly as he finished his song.

"*It is this that gives my soul all its joyous elation. As I hear the sweet lark sing in the clear air of day.*"

T WENTY-TWO

Frank Pagan drove through the business district of New Rockford, noticing banks and insurance offices and real-estate brokers as well as the usual fast-food franchises with signs that created an ungodly jumble along the road. The sign that welcomed you said New Rockford had a population of some 57,540 souls.

Beyond the business district were suburbs of frame houses. Here and there a flagpole protruded from a house or stood unadorned in the middle of a lawn. There was a sense of neatness and quiet patriotism here, a orderly world well preserved. But then appearances changed, and the grids of the streets yielded to pockmarked dead ends, alleys, abandoned warehouses, weeds, after which woodland stretched away for mile after mile.

Pagan parked the Cutlass outside an industrial park and studied the street map he'd bought in the town. He made a circle with a ballpoint pen, folded the map, drove the car onto the thruway and continued until he came to Leaf Road, which was the exit he wanted. It began promisingly enough, then dwindled to a one-vehicle thoroughfare with a barbed-wire fence running along one side. Beyond, punctuated by the occasional meadow, were tree-covered hills, which seemed to gather all the available sunlight and squander it, so that the prevalent impression was of shadows and dank places. It wasn't an encouraging landscape.

When a house came in view, Pagan slowed the car. It was a large, ungainly house, set some way from the road at the end of a driveway. It was overlooked by a series of small hills. There was no number anywhere, no name. If this was the wrong house, then he would simply ask directions and leave.

He turned the car into the driveway.

Before he had gone twenty feet a man wearing a dark suit and black glasses emerged from a clump of shrubbery and waved him to stop. Pagan braked. He had an uncomfortable moment when it crossed his mind that the man might be associated with the FBI— but then he realized he was being paranoid. Zuboric couldn't have traced him here. How could he?

Pagan rolled his window down and smiled. He was about to ask if somebody called Dawson lived here when he saw a gun in the man's hand. A very large gun, trained directly on Pagan's forehead.

The man, who was built like a weight lifter, reached for the car door and opened it and Pagan got out with absolutely no reluctance at all. A second figure, somewhat taller than the first but with exactly the same kind of shades, appeared at Pagan's side. Pagan was expertly frisked, then pushed face first against the side of the Olds. Whoever they were, these characters had done a certain amount of frisking in their time. Pagan wondered how long it might take him to reach his own gun, if the situation called for it. His pistol was in the glove compartment and too far away. It was a maxim of his that a gun was useful only in direct proportion to its proximity. And his was at present redundant.

"Get his ID," the taller man said.

The other, waving the gun near Pagan's face, plunged his hand inside Pagan's jacket and took out his wallet.

The taller man reached for the wallet and flipped it open. "He's a long way from home," he said.

"Yeah," the other man said. "You ever seen ID like this before, Marco?"

Marco stepped so close Pagan could smell his aftershave. "Never did," he said.

"Me neither." The wallet was flipped shut. "We got absolutely no way of knowing if it's authentic."

"I came to see Dawson," Pagan said.

Marco laughed. "They all say that, don't they, Chuckie?"

"Mr. Dawson doesn't just see people who wander in off the street, fella," Chuckie said.

"Unhappily, I didn't have time to make an appointment."

"Call the cops," Marco said.

"Before you call anybody, you'd better tell Dawson I'm here, because he's going to be damned unhappy with you if he doesn't get to hear what I have to say."

Marco came closer. He pushed his knee into the back of Pagan's leg, pressing deep into the crook. Pagan was obliged to bend under the pressure. He loathed being shoved around, and if it had been Marco alone he might have taken a swing.

"I don't have the time nor the inclination for this kind of intimacy, Marco." Pagan spoke in his best accent, trying hard to sound the way Foxie did. He wasn't very good with upper-class accents, and he wouldn't have convinced anyone in the gentlemen's clubs along Pall Mall or Piccadilly, but neither Chuckie nor Marco could tell he was faking it. It was a strange thing about Americans. They had a kind of self-imposed sense of inferiority, possibly some old colonial hangover, that put them in awe of Oxford tones, as if the accent of a BBC newscaster were the way God talked. Pagan had noticed this phenomenon before. It worked now, at least to the extent of Marco removing the pressure from Pagan's leg.

"Buddy, you and a thousand other guys come here wanting to see *Mister* Dawson," Chuckie said. "Your fancy ID isn't going to cut it here, bozo."

Pagan turned around to face the pair. "Look. Take my ID card. Show it to him. Tell him it has to do with certain Irish funds. Do that for me."

"Irish funds?"

"You heard me."

Marco reached out and took Pagan's ID. He flexed the powder-blue plastic card between thumb and forefinger, as if he meant to snap it in half. Then he glanced at Chuckie, who shrugged. It was a bad moment for Pagan. If either of these characters took the trouble to run his name through a computer, and if he was already imprisoned in the complicated circuitry of the FBI's electronic brain, then he was in deep trouble. The only thing to do was to be insistent with Marco and Chuckie. And authoritative, if he could summon the dignity for a decent performance.

"If Dawson doesn't want to see me, I'll be happy to let you turn me over to any cops you like," he said. He sounded as if he had a plum in his throat. "But I know he'll want to talk to me. It's up to you."

Marco hummed. He looked at Chuckie again. The black glasses glinted, four somber disks.

"I'll take your card inside, fella," he said. "But Chuckie here is going to keep his gun pointed right at your brain, understand?"

Pagan nodded. Marco, who obviously didn't want Pagan to think he was a softie just because he'd consented to something, performed his knee trick again, only this time he pressed so hard that Pagan had to go down on all fours.

"Understand?" Marco asked.

"I understand," Pagan replied. He felt like a barnyard animal pawing earth.

"If he moves, shoot him, Chuckie."

Chuckie said he'd be glad to. Pagan rose slowly, watching Marco go off in the direction of the house, which was very still, silent, the windows reflecting the glacial sun. He moved his feet in an uneasy manner. Marco could at this very moment be running his name across the telephone wires and into the ear of a computer operator. That would be the end of this solo performance, Pagan thought. He brushed little streaks of mud from his overcoat and waited.

Marco appeared in the doorway of the house. He waved an arm. Chuckie, who still had his gun trained on Pagan, jerked his head.

"Move," Chuckie said.

Pagan moved. Chuckie walked behind him. When they reached the house Marco said, "He'll see you."

Pagan smiled. Marco ushered him inside and across the hallway with a great show of reluctance. Outside a closed door Marco paused and slipped off his black glasses and stared at Pagan with eyes that were almost the same color as the lenses.

"We'll be right here, Pagan," he said. "Right on this spot."

"Of course," Pagan said.

"Go in."

Pagan pushed the door open and stepped inside a large sitting room, which was furnished in a fussy Victorian way, heavy furniture and bell jars, and which was scented with violets. Children's toys and books were scattered on the floor, as if there had been small untidy intruders in the museum. A blind was drawn halfway down on a window, tinting the room a faint yellow. The man who stood by the fireplace cleared his throat and looked at Pagan unsmilingly. Kevin Dawson was taller than his photographs suggested. He held Pagan's ID card in one hand.

"Let's get one thing straight. I don't know anything about any Irish funds," Dawson said.

The defense of ignorance. Kevin Dawson talked like a man conscious of a hidden tape recorder, somebody who wanted to leave an exonerating cassette for posterity. He understood Dawson's attitude—after all, the brother of the President of the United States couldn't confess to a complete stranger that he had any involvement with the finances of the IRA. There were laws against the unreported export of huge sums of cash. And Kevin Dawson couldn't be seen to break the law.

"So why did you agree to see me?" Pagan asked.

"Your ID made me curious," Dawson said. "But if you've come here to question me, I think you're going to be very frustrated."

"I'm not the one who's going to be frustrated," Pagan said. He moved to the window and looked out beyond the trees at the surrounding hills. It was a view he found depressing and somehow fascinating in a melancholic way. He rapped his fingertips on the pane of glass. "I don't give a damn one way or another about IRA money or the misguided people who collect the stuff. I'm only interested in Jig, who is either going to come here looking for you, or else is on his way to a place called Roscommon to see Harry Cairney. I'm guessing here, but I may be completely wrong. If he *does* come here, I want to be someplace nearby. I don't want your buffoons out there getting him first."

"Hold on, Pagan. You're losing me. I don't know anything about the IRA. I don't know who Jig is. The only connection I have with Ireland is that I'm third-generation American-Irish. That and the fact I've visited the place a couple of times. Nothing more."

Pagan smiled. Dawson's deadpan expression wasn't very successful. The man was palpably uneasy. If he was in control of himself, it was only with a great effort. There was sweat on his upper lip.

"Regardless of what you say, Jig's going to get here sooner or later. He wants his money back, and he's not going to be in the most pleasant frame of mind by this time," Pagan said.

Kevin Dawson made a small gesture with one hand, a flutter. "I don't know anything about any money."

"That's what you say. But Jig isn't going to believe that one."
Pagan glanced through the window again. This whole side of the
house was exposed to the hills. And something about those hills
kept drawing him. The shaded pockets in the landscape, the sunlight. They had a certain mysterious quality, similar to the landscape
of the English Lake District, which Pagan had always found brooding and hostile. A landscape for poets and manic depressives.

But it wasn't just those qualities that made him keep looking up
there. He was thinking about something else. He placed an index
finger on the glass and drew a tiny circle, which he peered through
as if it were the sight of a gun.

"Good view," he said.

"Some people think it's too severe," Dawson remarked.

Dawson moved to the mantelpiece and adjusted a photograph.
Pagan saw that it was of two girls, presumably Dawson's daughters.
Dawson turned around, faced Pagan. "This Jig," he said, then paused
a moment. "Do you have any hard evidence he's in this vicinity? Or
is it only guesswork?"

"Nicholas Linney wouldn't think it was guesswork," Pagan said.

"Who?"

"It doesn't matter." Pagan glanced back up into the hills. Sunlight
turned to deep shadow in the high hollows. Dawson was a very
poor liar. He didn't have the flair for it. Therefore he had no future
in politics, Pagan thought. "How did you get into it in the first place?"

"Into what?"

"You know what I'm talking about. How did you get into the
patriot game?"

"When did I stop beating my wife?" Dawson said. "It's that kind
of a question."

Pagan felt a small flare of anger. People like Dawson played at
being Irish. They bought their way into it from the safety of their
big houses in America. They sent money as if they were investing
in offshore developments. Well, their houses just weren't so safe
anymore. "Do you have any idea of the sheer human misery your
money can buy in Ireland? Do you know what explosive devices can
do to a person? Have you ever seen the victim of a machine gun?
Or did you just get caught up in the *romance* of it all?" And Pagan
made the word "romance" sound obscene. "If people like you didn't
send money there in the first place, maybe there wouldn't be weapons, and maybe we'd be moving in the direction of some kind of
peace. Who knows?"

"There are always going to be weapons," Dawson said.

Pagan shrugged. "Here's the funny consequence of it all, Dawson. If you run into Jig, you'll be looking directly down the barrel of a gun that you probably paid for yourself. How does that thought grab you?"

"Is your lecture over?" Dawson asked.

"It's over," Pagan replied. Ease off, he told himself. You're here looking for Jig, not to moralize on terror in Ireland. He felt a cord of tension at the side of his head. There was stress in him, and fatigue, and he felt like a traveler who wasn't sure he'd come to the right place anyhow. No, he couldn't afford to go off at tangents like that. He'd come too far and he had the feeling, that astonishing light bulb of intuition, that he was on the right track.

"I'm sorry if I can't help you," Dawson said. "Maybe you'll have better luck at the other place you mentioned."

"You mean Roscommon?" Pagan asked.

"I believe that's what you said. Roscommon."

"Where Harry Cairney lives. But you don't know that name either, do you?"

Dawson shook his head. "I know it in a political context. That's all."

"And I suppose Jock Mulhaney means nothing to you?"

"He's some kind of union figure," Dawson said.

"You might say that."

Dawson stepped toward the door. He pulled it open, looked at Pagan with a smile that was almost all desperation. He couldn't be honest, couldn't admit his connections. Denials were vouchers for limited amounts, valid for limited durations. And no matter how hard Dawson denied his involvement, it wasn't going to make a damn bit of difference to Jig. If Jig came here and somehow sneaked past Mannie and Moe outside, if he got into the house and confronted Dawson, he wasn't going to be even remotely convinced by Dawson's squeaky claims of innocence.

"Good luck, Pagan," Kevin Dawson said.

"I wish you the same, only more of it."

Pagan stepped out into the hallway where the two bodyguards were waiting for him. Behind him, the door of the room closed, and Kevin Dawson was gone.

"We'll see you out," Marco said.

"No need." Pagan headed to the door. Chuckie and Marco tailed him anyhow.

Outside in the thin light Pagan studied the view of the hills again. They seemed to him the most interesting aspect of his visit to this place.

FROM the place where he lay concealed in the hills, Patrick Cairney stared down at the house below. He saw Frank Pagan walk to his car.

Frank Pagan. Always Frank Pagan. Always one step behind him. He wondered where Pagan's information came from. Maybe Mulhaney had talked. Maybe Mulhaney had told Pagan the same thing as he'd told Cairney. *Kevin Dawson took the money. Dawson is the one.*

Ten minutes ago he'd seen Pagan arrive. There had been a confrontation with the two men who guarded the house, then Pagan had gone indoors. Had he come to warn Kevin Dawson about Jig? Was that it?

Now he saw Pagan get inside the car, then drive along the narrow road. Cairney followed him with the binoculars until he was out of sight. He swung the glasses back toward the house and tried to concentrate on how he was going to get inside. He had to get past the two guards. How, though? And how long was it until nightfall now? His body was cold, and he felt cramped. He lowered the binoculars and looked along the ridge, his eye sweeping the wintry trees and the dead grass that swayed limply in the wind. He couldn't concentrate. His mind kept slipping away from him and the wind made him shiver.

There were spectral images. *His father trapped under an oxygen tent like something immersed in ectoplasm.* He couldn't shake this one loose. Harry Cairney, close to the end of his life, propped up inside an oxygen tent with tubes attached like tendrils to his body. There was a terrifying sadness inside Patrick Cairney, and a sense of loss—it came from the thought that he might never see Harry again. It didn't matter whether he loved his father or not. It didn't matter whether he even respected the man. Like any son facing the imminent death of his father, he felt he was about to lose some essential part of himself.

One of the men below stood against the hood of the car and smoked a cigarette. The other wandered around the side of the house, then returned. They stood together, both now leaning against the car, and they presented an impenetrable obstacle between Cairney and the house. Cairney focused on the house, the two men, but still the landscape wouldn't yield up an easy way to get inside that place down there.

Think. Think hard. The money might be inside that house and you're lying up here wondering about your father and your thoughts won't make a damn bit of difference whether he lives or dies.

His truant attention strayed again, and he was thinking about Roscommon once more, seeing Celestine sit by the sickbed of his father. Maybe she spoke softly to the old man. Maybe she was reading to him. Or perhaps she just sat there watching him motionlessly, her hands in her lap and her lovely face expressionless and her hair pulled back so that she looked gaunt and distressed and prepared for the ultimate grief.

Cairney focused on the man below. His head pounded now, and his hands, when he lowered the binoculars, shook visibly. He sat back against the side of the hollow, wondering at the responses of his own body. It was as if strange blood flowed in his veins and the heart that pumped so loudly in his chest were not his own. He was seized with the feeling that he shouldn't be here in this place at all, that he should never have been sent from Ireland unless it was to kill a specific target, a certain individual. Unless it was to do the very thing he did best, better than anyone else.

Why didn't you send somebody else, Finn? Was your precious Jig the only candidate?

He crawled to the lip of the hollow. From where he was he could see almost the whole length of the hills. Slopes swooped down into shadows where the sun didn't go. These shadowy places, like sudden pools of unexpected water, troubled him. He wasn't quite sure why.

And then, because he understood how to read landscapes, how to tell human movement from the motion of the wind, how to feel when a landscape had been subtly altered, he knew.

NEW YORK CITY

At ten minutes past two, the Reverend Ivor McInnes entered the office of a car-rental company on East Thirty-eighth Street. He spoke to the clerk at the desk, a young man with red hair arranged around his skull like a corona. McInnes reserved a 1986 Continental because he liked the idea of traveling in some comfort. He looked at the desk clock as the clerk filled out the various papers. He was glad it was one of those digital affairs. He didn't think he could tolerate the idea of watching the agonizing movements of a second hand. It was twenty past two by the time the young man completed the copious paperwork. McInnes said he'd pick the car up around six. He had to return to his hotel first and pack.

He left the agency at approximately two-thirty. He thought of Seamus Houlihan and the others as he stepped out on the street. They'd be taking up their positions by this time.

He walked slowly along the street, looking now and then in the windows of stores. He felt the way he had done before White Plains, except it was heightened somehow.

In about twenty minutes, if the information he had received was correct—and he had absolutely no reason to doubt it, because of its reliable source—the vehicle would be making a turn into the isolated stretch of road where Houlihan and his men were waiting.

Twenty minutes.

Twenty long minutes.

McInnes reached the intersection of Thirty-eighth Street and Fifth Avenue. He looked in the window of a jewelry store. Rings, necklaces, bracelets. It would take his mind off it all if he went inside and lost himself in browsing through the glittering array. Nineteen minutes. He wandered between the glass cases, tracked by a sales clerk who insisted on pointing out the merits of this or that stone.

McInnes stopped in front of an emerald ring. He asked the clerk to bring it out and show it to him. The clerk said it was an excellent piece and any woman would be *delirious* to have it. Ivor McInnes held the stone up to the light. Its greenness was stunning and deep. McInnes closed his hand over the ring. The stone felt very cool against his skin.

"I'll have it," he said. *Eighteen minutes.*

"Excellent choice," the clerk said. "Cash or credit card?"

"Cash."

The clerk, who was a small man with eyes that themselves resembled gems, smiled. "Is it a gift, sir? Shall I gift wrap it?"

"Why don't you?" McInnes said. As he watched the clerk cut gift paper with long scissors, he stared across the floor to where there was a clock display. All kinds of time pieces hung on the wall, every last one of them showing a different time. The effect was of stepping outside the real world and into one where the passage of seconds and minutes and hours couldn't be measured with any semblance of accuracy. McInnes had to look away. Real time was important to him now.

Seventeen minutes.

He tried not to think about time. He tried to put it out of his mind. But it kept returning to him and his nervousness increased. Sixteen minutes. Sixteen minutes and it would be all over. And by tomorrow, if everything went as planned, he'd be out of the country entirely.

NEW ROCKFORD, CONNECTICUT

John Waddell crouched in the shrubbery. He held an M-16 against his side. He glanced out across the clearing at the place where Rorke and McGrath were concealed, but he couldn't see them. He felt Houlihan tap him lightly on the shoulder and he turned. The big man was offering him something, and it took Waddell a moment to realize it was a stick of chewing gum. Waddell shook his head.

"Helps you relax," Houlihan said.

Waddell looked through the barren trees. He had the odd feeling that he wasn't here, that some other entity had been substituted for him and that the real John Waddell was back in Belfast, strolling across Donegall Square and wondering where he'd stop for a pint of Smithy's. But Houlihan nudged him, and the illusion disintegrated.

"Are you all right, Waddy?" the big man asked.

"Fine," John Waddell said.

"Gun loaded?"

Waddell nodded. He looked down at the M-16 in his hands.

Seamus Houlihan, who also held an M-16, tapped his fingers against the stock. This drumming increased Waddell's anxiety. He looked up at the sky. Clouds drifted in the region of the sun.

Houlihan looked at his wristwatch. "Two-forty," he said. "Ten minutes."

Waddell tightened his grip on his gun. What he hoped for was that something unexpected might happen and that the exercise would have to be postponed. A freak storm, for example. Or the appearance of other people. But this was such a damned lonely place he couldn't imagine anybody coming here by choice. And what kind of vehicle could it possibly be that made a stop here anyhow? He tried to slacken his grip on the gun but his fingers remained tight and stiff.

Houlihan made a sniffing sound. He wiped the back of his sleeve over the tip of his nose and cleared his throat. Waddell thought for a moment that he detected a certain jumpiness in Seamus, but he decided he was wrong. The big man never showed any unease at times like this. He was always cool. Always in control. Chewing gum, looking composed—Jesus, Seamus might be contemplating a stroll on a Sunday afternoon. Waddell felt a branch brush his face, and he was startled.

"You're a twitchy wee fucker," Houlihan said.

"I'm okay," Waddell replied.

"Look, there's nothing to be nervous about. Point the bloody gun when I tell you, and fire. That's all. Nothing to it."

Ten minutes, Houlihan had said.

Waddell wondered how long ten minutes could be. He glanced at Seamus, then he looked through the trees. "I wish to God we were out of here," he said. "Out of this whole bloody country."

"Soon." Houlihan removed his chewing gum and flicked it away.

"How soon?"

Seamus Houlihan, keeper of secrets, didn't answer. He checked his gun, traced a finger along the barrel. What did it take to be that relaxed? Waddell wondered. What kind of ice water ran in Seamus's veins?

"Five more minutes," Houlihan said.

Eternity. Waddell wanted to urinate. He concentrated on his weapon, wishing it were lighter, less of a burden. The weight of the thing made it all the more menacing.

"Four," Houlihan said.

By Jesus, he was going to count the bloody minutes down! Waddell tried not to listen. Houlihan could keep his countdown to himself. Waddell preferred to hear nothing.

"Three."

Waddell saw McGrath's face briefly across the clearing. Then it was gone. Momentarily a cloud masked the sun.

Two.

In the distance there was the sound of a vehicle.

"It's early," Houlihan said, swinging his weapon into a firing position. "Get ready."

The sound grew. Waddell held his gun at his side and waited. The vehicle seemed to strain, gears clanking and grinding, as it came closer. Waddell stared beyond the clearing but he couldn't see the vehicle yet because there was a bend in the road. As the motor labored and whined, the noise grew. Waddell gripped his gun tightly.

"Ready," Houlihan said.

Waddell shook his head. No, he thought.

No.

"Ready," Houlihan said again.

Waddell—baffled by the sense of unreality he suddenly felt, almost as if time and motion had ceased to exist and the whole world had frozen in its flight path and he was the only person left alive—stared at the vehicle as it appeared in front of him. It was a big yellow school bus, and it was coming to a dead stop in the clearing, and the faces pressed to the windows were those of children, and they were smiling even as Houlihan stood up in the shrubbery and leveled his weapon at them.

F R A N K   P A G A N   drove two miles from the house of Kevin Dawson, then turned the Oldsmobile off the road and down a dirt track that led between the wooded hills. When the car would go no farther, when the track had become too narrow and rutted and overgrown with weeds, he got out, taking his gun from the glove compartment. It had been a long time since he'd climbed any hills and he wasn't sure his physical condition was terrific, but he was going up anyway. He went between the trees, straining over fallen logs and mounds of wet, dead leaves that had been buried under snow since fall. Here and there patches of old snow, hard as clay, still clung to the ground.

Halfway up the hill Pagan had to stop and catch his breath. He leaned against a tree trunk. The sun, trapped between spidery branches, was a frozen, listless globe. When he'd been staring at these hills from the window of Kevin Dawson's living room, Pagan had imagined that this landscape was the perfect one for Jig. There were pockets in which to hide, trees and shrubbery for cover. If Jig wanted to observe the Dawson household, what more suitable place from which to do it? He knew that if *he* were Jig, this was the kind of spot he'd have come to without hesitation. But that was only a guess. Just the same, Pagan felt he had nothing to lose by climbing up here, save perhaps the future use of lungs and legs.

He climbed again. There were no tracks, no pathways, only the sullen trees pressing against him and crisp twigs cracking underfoot. His breath hung on the air like cobwebs. Up and up and up. Any higher, he thought, and he'd need an oxygen mask, a Tibetan guide, and dried food for a week. When he reached the crest, he realized he hadn't climbed very far at all. He could see the road below and, off to his left about a mile, Kevin Dawson's house, which looked isolated in the landscape. Ahead of him, running the entire length of the range, was more woodland. He paused, looking down the slopes. There were a thousand places where Jig could hide and wait for the right time to make a move on Dawson's house.

Pagan blew on his hands for warmth. A gnawing wind had begun to rush across the slopes, carrying smells of moss and deadwood and rotted leaves. He moved through the trees, gazing down every so often. From certain places the Dawson house couldn't be seen because trees obscured the view. But here and there, in clearings, every detail of the structure could be observed in miniature. Windows, eaves, smoke rising from a chimney.

It was a lifeless landscape, almost morbid in its quiet and lack of color. He walked a little farther, then stopped again, wishing he had paid more attention to the art of tracking and reading signs when he'd been a Boy Scout. How many stories could a crushed leaf or a broken branch tell you if you knew how to interpret the damn things? A decent Boy Scout could find a whole bloody library of information in this place. But Pagan, a city boy, had never had any great affinity for rustic places.

He kept moving. The wind came up, blowing directly into his face and shaking all kinds of sounds out of the trees. Pagan turned his face away from the fullness of the blast, which whipped his hair and his coat.

Then the wind died and the place was still again.

Pagan moved quietly. Underfoot, dead leaves crackled, frail wood popped. It was impossible to stir in these woods without announcing yourself.

He came now to a hollow in the land, a scoop masked by crisscrossing branches. Somebody could conceal himself successfully in such a place. Pagan looked beyond the hollow. There, immediately below on the other side of the road, was Kevin Dawson's house. The perfect view. But the hollow was empty and still.

He went down carefully, his gun held forward.

He didn't register the noise he heard. It was a whisper on the far edges of his awareness. He thought it might have been an animal, a rabbit emerging from a thicket. He was about to turn his face around when he heard the voice say, "Toss the gun a few feet to your side, Pagan. If you don't, you get a bullet in the back of your head."

Pagan threw the gun a couple of feet away. He saw Jig come forward to pick it up.

"I heard you coming. I heard you coming for the last twenty minutes."

Pagan stared at his own gun in the man's hand. Fool, he thought. You should have finished reading Baden-Powell's *Scouting for Boys*. You should have studied tracking and bent blades of grass and little heelmarks in the soil and all the rest of it.

Jig said, "A brass band would have made less noise. Put your hands in the air where I can see them, then have a seat."

Pagan did as he was told. He sat down inside the hollow and stared at Jig, who had a gun in either hand. Pagan wondered if this was the place, this lonely ridge overlooking a lonely house, where he would die.

U N T I L he saw the yellow school bus rolling toward the clearing and understood he was meant to open fire on the vehicle as soon as it stopped, John Waddell had never thought of himself as a terrorist. In his world, terrorists were always Arabs who blew up airports and planes, or IRA fanatics who planted bombs inside supermarkets and pubs. But suddenly, as if he had been given a stunning insight into his own condition, he realized he was no better than any of the thugs who committed these outrages. He wasn't a soldier in a credible struggle, he wasn't in the glorious vanguard of Ulster freedom, he wasn't even a *man*, because a man didn't fire an automatic weapon at a crowd of kids in a school bus. It was a monster's work. All the sensations that had been depressing him since White Plains became more strident, more compelling. What business did he have firing a fucking gun at a bunch of kids?

He watched the bus pull into the clearing and stop, and he heard the hiss of the automatic door as it slid open. he was conscious of a light-blue car behind the bus, smoke from its exhaust rising into the frigid air. There was a man inside the car although Waddell hardly registered this fact because he was drawn to the faces of the children at the windows. A boy of about eleven appeared in the door of the bus, satchel over his shoulder. He was about to step down from the doorway but he hesitated, turning to say something to a friend. There was laughter and a good-natured insult and somebody tossed a rolled-up ball of paper at the boy's head.

Houlihan, thus far unseen by the kids in the bus or the driver of the blue car, was standing with the M-16 in firing position. Waddell was screaming inside. He wanted to stop this whole thing before it started, but now Seamus Houlihan was snapping at him to stand up and start firing, and the hell of it was he couldn't move, didn't want to move, wanted to remain crouched in the damned shrubbery and make believe this was all a nightmare. The kids all had the same face, and it was the face of John Waddell's own dead son, and he couldn't bear the image.

He looked up at Houlihan, and he shook his head.

"Get up. Get up on your fucking feet, goddam you."

Waddell stared at the big man with his mouth open.

"Fucking eedjit," Houlihan said. He poked Waddell in the chest with the barrel of the weapon and John Waddell understood that Seamus, his friend, his avenging angel, his mentor, would blow him away without even thinking about it.

Houlihan pulled the gun back, swung around, and opened fire. From the bushes at the other side of the clearing Rorke and McGrath began their volley as well. Waddell watched in white terror as the windows of the yellow bus exploded. He heard the shrieks of children and saw the boy in the doorway fall forward, lying half in and half out of the vehicle. He saw the driver of the vehicle slide out of her seat and disappear in a sudden spray of blood. The firing continued, on and on and on, until there wasn't a window remaining on the bus and the yellow panels had been riddled with holes. But now Waddell understood something else. The man in the light-blue car was shooting back. He'd crawled out of the car and was concealed now behind the vehicle, a pistol in his hand, and every so often he'd send a shot into the trees. Houlihan changed his magazine and started firing again. Waddell stared at the bus. It was shattered, a great yellow shell, and now there were no faces at the windows, only jagged slices of glass hanging in frames at angles that defied gravity.

Houlihan made a roaring sound. A battle cry. He was firing at the blue car with a savage determination. Waddell heard the shots ricochet off the metal. Then he stared down at the gun in his hands. He realized he should have shot Houlihan. It was the sane thing to do. He should have turned the weapon on the big man before all this started, but now it was too damned late.

Houlihan grunted, fired, his whole body shaking from the relentless kick of the gun. Waddell saw the blue car catch fire and explode all of a sudden. One moment it was there, the next it had gone up in a cloud of flame and smoke. And then there was a secondary explosion, louder than the first, and the clearing was showered with glass and plastic. The driver of the car lay facedown some yards from the yellow bus.

It was over.

The clearing was silent. The whole afternoon, so sulfuric and cold, was terribly silent.

John Waddell dropped his weapon. He felt Houlihan grab him and pull him to a standing position. He was cuffed roughly by the big man, stinging blows that made his eyes water and brought blood into his mouth.

"You're a dead man, Waddy," Houlihan said.

John Waddell said nothing.

Houlihan had an odd little grin on his face. "It's war, John. It's this bloody war. And I can't have a man beside me who doesn't have the guts for it. You understand that, don't you?"

John Waddell nodded his head slowly. He looked in the direction of the dead boy who lay in the doorway of the yellow bus. His satchel had burst open and sheets of colored paper spilled from it. Waddell thought he'd never seen anything as sad as that. He turned back to look at Houlihan, and he understood, in the final moments of his life, that Seamus was fighting a war that he never wanted to see finished. For as long as he lived, Seamus Houlihan would never be able to liberate himself from this conflict. He was trapped in violence because he was consumed by his love for it.

"Maybe you'll go to heaven," Houlihan said. He'd taken his pistol from his belt, and he pressed it against John Waddell's heart, and he pulled the trigger quickly. Waddell fell into the shrubbery, where he lay with his face turned up toward the sun.

TWENTY-THREE

"What now?" Frank Pagan asked, looking up at Jig who stood on the rim of the hollow.

Jig's expression was grim. "I'm thinking of shooting you" was what he said in the voice Pagan had heard a thousand times on tape. The accent was not exactly Irish. Nor was it American. It came somewhere between the two. It was the accent of a man who was neither one thing nor the other, as if he'd spent much of his life wandering indecisively between two nations. And the face, which Pagan had tried to imagine so many times and which he'd glimpsed only briefly before at St. Finbar's, was handsome and yet inflexible, almost as if all the muscles were locked in place. It was not the kind of face one could envisage smiling in a relaxed fashion, or in calm repose. The eyes were vigilant and guarded, the mouth defiant. Jig reminded Pagan right then of something wild, a creature forever conscious of traps and pitfalls, who sees enmities everywhere, who expects hostilities. But there was another quality, one so hidden it was difficult to detect at all, and Pagan had a problem defining it. In some other circumstances, he thought that this face—at present so hard and set—might be capable of showing sensitivity and concern. But not now. Certainly not now.

"Let me know what you decide," Pagan said.

"However, I'm not in the habit of shooting defenseless people, Pagan. Unless they're guilty of crimes against Ireland."

"Am I included in that category?" Pagan asked. He stared past Jig and up into the trees through which the afternoon sun created white flickers. He had to gather his thoughts, all his resources, and decide how he might turn this situation to his advantage. It was a possibility that seemed ludicrously, laughably, slim.

"As far as I'm concerned, you're just another English policeman. And that's enough to make you guilty."

"What about two young Cambodian girls in a house in Bridge-hampton? What crimes had they committed against Ireland?"

Jig was quiet a moment. "They were killed by a man called Linney."

"It's not what the FBI believes, Jig."

"I don't give a damn what the FBI believes. The same applies to you, Pagan. I've never been interested in what people say or believe about me." The wind, blowing down through the trees, stirred Jig's tightly curled hair almost as if a hand had passed over his skull. Pagan thought he had never seen a person as tense as this one. You could almost see glowing wires just beneath the surface of his skin.

"The FBI also believes you were responsible for the explosion in White Plains."

"What explosion?"

"You've been out of touch, Jig. Somebody blew up a Presbyterian church in White Plains. They made a pretty thorough job of it. Then they called the FBI to claim it as an IRA score. And where the FBI is concerned, you're the only known IRA factor in the vicinity; ergo, you're the one responsible." Pagan looked to see what effect this information would have on Jig.

Jig's expression didn't change. "I've never been in White Plains," he said, without any emotion in his voice. "I'd have no reason to blow up a church, Presbyterian or otherwise."

"They also claimed you killed a man called Fitzjohn in Albany."

"I get around, don't I?"

"It would seem so."

"I haven't been in Albany either."

"Tell that to Leonard Korn. I understand he's a good listener."

Jig stared at Pagan. "I don't know of any authorized IRA activities in this country that would involve bombing. It doesn't make sense."

"My feeling exactly," Pagan said. "What makes it even more interesting in the case of Fitzjohn is that he was a member of the Free Ulster Volunteers. But it gets better still."

"I'm listening."

Pagan said, "Ivor McInnes is in New York City."

"And what is that holy man doing there?"

"I'm not absolutely sure. But I have the feeling he could clear up some of the mystery if only he would talk. Ivor can be very close-mouthed when he wants to be. He knows a hell of a lot more than he's prepared to say. Whatever's going on, Ivor has a dirty finger in it somehow."

Jig's face changed slightly. The set of his mouth altered, but Pagan couldn't tell what it meant. He even wondered if any of what he was talking about interested Jig remotely. The man's mind was seemingly elsewhere, his manner distracted. It was the house below, Pagan realized. All Jig's focus was fixed there.

Then Jig turned to look at Pagan. "I'm wondering why you're here on your own, Pagan. I'm wondering if maybe there aren't more of you up in these hills and you're sitting here smugly waiting for them to turn up. Don't you have a little gang of associates? On Canal Street, you said you had a score of men."

"I dumped the Bureau."

"Did you now?"

"They want your balls nailed to Leonard Korn's bulletin board. Which made me a little unhappy. I have my own ideas about justice." Pagan paused a moment. "They're turning over every stone they can find. It has all the makings of a massive manhunt. After all, you're a killer. And you can't hide under the umbrella of Irish romanticism, not after the barbarism in White Plains."

"Irish romanticism," Jig said disdainfully. "There's no such thing, Pagan. Is Belfast romantic? Are checkpoints romantic? Do you find anything enchanting in the sight of a country that's dying from schizophrenic hatred?" He looked down at the guns he held in both hands, turning them over, examining them in a thoughtful way.

He said, "So the mighty FBI is looking for me, is it? I don't know if I should feel proud or humbled by the notion."

"Nervous would be a more practical response," Pagan said. He was wondering how he could get the weapons away from Jig. Idle speculation. There was no way in the world Jig was going to be fooled by a surprise attack.

Jig pressed the barrel of one of the guns against the side of his face and scratched. "You could be telling me a complete fairy tale, Pagan. You could be sitting here right now and making all this up. You could be thinking that some convoluted story about bombings and murder and an FBI manhunt might fluster me enough that I'll call off my mission and go home quietly. You obviously know what I'm looking for in this country, and it would suit your purpose—and your government's—if I didn't find it. No money, therefore no weapons. The Cause would be strapped for cash, which would delight Whitehall."

Pagan shook his head. "The only way I want you to go home is handcuffed to me."

Jig smiled for the first time. "How do you propose to accomplish that?"

Pagan stood up. "Let me put it another way, Jig. If you decide to go down to see Kevin Dawson, you're dead. You're finished. There's absolutely no way in the world you're going to get within a hundred feet of that house without somebody blowing your bloody head off. I know that for a fact. Your only real chance is with me, Jig. I'm the only person who believes you're not the monster the FBI is itching to kill."

"And what makes you think so highly of me, Pagan?"

"I know you. I've studied you. I know how you operate, and I know how you kill. I also know that you're out of your depth in this country, Jig. Too much is stacked against you here. This isn't your kind of operation. This isn't the old one-two, the quick in and out that you're used to." Pagan made a sweeping gesture with his hand. "This isn't some bloody hapless English politician walking home from his club or some future ambassador stepping out of his mews cottage and into his Jaguar. This is something else altogether."

"What exactly are you saying, Pagan? That I give myself up to you? I'm standing here with two guns in my possession and I'm supposed to give myself up to an *unarmed* man because he's got some intriguing stories to tell? Back to Britain and a cozy berth in one of Her Majesty's lodging houses? I came here to recover some lost property, Pagan. I don't intend to go home without it."

"It isn't going to be a matter of just that, Jig. You're looking at the prospect of going home inside a plain wooden box. Take another look down at that house, Jig. There are two Secret Service men with guns they're just aching to fire. Be realistic."

"You call it realistic to listen to your story?"

"It's the truth."

"I'm never sure what it means when people say they're telling the truth, Pagan. I've heard a lot of different truths lately."

Frank Pagan was silent. If he were in Jig's shoes, would he have believed the narrative? Probably not. Probably he'd have reacted in precisely the same way, with incredulity. In Jig's profession, the only counsel you ever listened to was your own.

Pagan turned and looked down at the stretch of road that lay between the hills and Kevin Dawson's estate. In the distance there was the sound of a car. He narrowed his eyes and looked off in the direction of the noise. He saw a car come into view at a place where the road ran between the folds of hills.

"Give me the glasses a moment," he said.

Jig, slipping one of the guns inside the waistband of his pants, passed the binoculars to him. Pagan held them up to his eyes and saw the car approach the entrance to the Dawson estate where it was stopped, just as Pagan himself had been, by the Secret Service men. Pagan tightened his grip on the glasses. He saw two men get out of the car. One was Tyson Bruno. The other Artie Zuboric. Pagan thrust the binoculars back at Jig, who held them to his face and studied the scene below.

"Surprise, surprise," Pagan said.

"The tall one is a friend of yours," Jig said.

"Zuboric. You saw him at St. Finbar's Mission. The other is an FBI agent called Tyson Bruno."

Jig lowered the glasses. He looked at Frank Pagan. His face was unrevealing. Pagan was suddenly aware of how close Jig stood to him. How very near the weapons were. One frantic grab, he thought. He rejected the idea immediately. One frantic grab was likely to be his last.

He said, "The only reason I can think of for that pair to be coming here is that somehow they know you're in the vicinity. Which means we can expect even more men turning up pretty damn soon. Now do you see? There's no way into that house. What makes it worse from your point of view is that they apparently know you're around. So what happens when more men arrive and suddenly these hills are swarming with people who all want a piece of you? What happens when it's open season on Jig?"

Jig said nothing. He sat down and frowned. Pagan was puzzled by the sudden appearance of Zuboric and Bruno. Did they *really* know Jig was in the vicinity? Or had they come here expecting to find only Frank Pagan? How could they have known that Pagan was here, though? Unless Dawson had made a phone call to somebody in authority, but the timetable was all wrong. If Dawson *had* called the FBI, there hadn't been time for Zuboric and his sidekick to get here from New York City. Mysteries.

"Even if I believed your story," Jig said, "what difference would it make? Even if everything you said is true, do you think it would make me roll over like some lame dog and let you take me back home for my own protection?"

"You might find things a little different at home," Pagan said. "Especially now."

"Meaning what?"

"Meaning simply that you might find yourself out in the cold with your own people. After all, you blew up a church and a whole bunch of innocent people along with it. You might find a change in the tide. Some people will go along with a hero only so far. They tend to dislike it when they find their hero is capable of the same scummy acts as any ordinary thug, no matter what side he happens to be on."

"You can't goad me, Pagan."

"I wasn't aware of trying."

"I had nothing to do with that church."

"I know that. But what does my opinion count for? People died in that explosion. Innocent kids as well as adults. People who had nothing on their minds except the usual Sunday rapport with God."

Jig looked through the binoculars at the house. Pagan thought of a man calculating the movements of his own future, weighing this possibility against that one, trying to decide on a course of action.

"It doesn't matter a shit if I happen to believe you, Jig. The FBI has other ideas. Soon the public will have those ideas as well. And the public is notoriously fickle, my friend. You're a hero one day, the next you stink. The great Jig is reduced to killing harmless people. The bold Irish assassin turns common gangster. It's going to make nice reading. How does that make you feel?"

Pagan wondered what Jig's reputation meant to the man. Did the newspaper articles and the songs sung in Irish bars and the reverence afforded Jig mean anything to him? Was his ego such that he couldn't allow his reputation to be eroded by the actions of other people?

Pagan waited for his words to sink into Jig's brain.

"What do you really want, Pagan?"

"Two things."

"What two things."

"First, I'd like to know who's going around committing these acts you're being blamed for. And I keep coming back to good old Ivor. It was courtesy of the Free Ulster Volunteers that I found out you were in America in the first place. And it's a fair bet that Ivor was instrumental in making sure I received that bit of information. If he knew that much, maybe he knows why Fitzjohn was killed and why somebody bombed the church." Pagan paused. He had one more dart to shoot in Jig's direction. "Maybe he even knows something about that lost property of yours."

Jig passed his gun from one hand to the other. If this last remark of Pagan's swayed him any, he certainly didn't show it. "That's a lot of ifs, Pagan."

"I agree. But what else is there?"

"You think you can make him talk?"

"Between us, I suspect we could get something out of him."

"Between us? You're actually asking for my help?"

Pagan shrugged. "Don't you *want* to know who's been taking your name in vain? Don't you want to know if McInnes has any information about your money?"

Jig affected to ignore this question. "What's the second thing?"

"You know what that is."

"Me," Jig said.

"Correct."

Jig stared off into the trees. "You've got to understand one thing, Pagan. I'll never let you take me. No matter what."

Pagan nodded. "You're the man with the weapons. I make it a cardinal rule never to argue with guns."

Jig looked back down the slopes toward the road. Pagan tried to imagine the inner workings of the man. Obviously Jig suspected a trap. But at the same time perhaps he was beginning to realize the hopelessness of getting access to Kevin Dawson. On the other hand, maybe he didn't know the meaning of hopelessness, maybe he had such a supreme belief in his own capabilities that he didn't think in terms of insuperable obstacles. But it didn't work that way, not in the real world. Not when you were faced with determined people who wanted nothing but your death.

"If I understand you, Pagan, you're calling a truce," Jig said.

"In a way."

"I don't like truces. Especially when I have all the advantages."

"Take your pick." Pagan gestured toward the house.

Jig turned his face from the anxious wind that came fretting once again down the slopes.

"Go down there," Pagan said. "See if you can get an interview with Kevin Dawson. Try it. I wish you all the luck in the world."

Jig stared at Frank Pagan. "Do you really think it matters to me if I get the blame for things I didn't do? Do you think I *care* about anything so bloody shallow as my reputation? If some group of IRA idiots has gone free-lance, that's not my problem. Whatever blame attaches to my name is irrelevant in the long run. Personalities don't enter into this."

The old terrorist cant, Pagan thought with some disappointment. The usual humbug of the fanatic. History is more important than people. Movements outweigh personalities. Pawns in the larger game. Et cetera and amen. He had expected something more out of Jig, although he wasn't sure what exactly. In his experience of terrorists, they were mainly men and women who approached life without humor. They were emotional fuck-ups. And even when they experienced human feelings that weren't related to their particular cause, they didn't know what to do with them. Maybe Jig came into that category.

He said, "I misjudged you, then. I thought you'd see it as your problem, Jig."

"We don't have matching objectives, Pagan. And we don't come from the same perspective."

Pagan sat down. "Fine," he said. "But what if the people who attacked the church are going to kill again? What if they already have? What if it's something even more monstrous than the church this time? Whatever it is, Jig, it's going to be attributed to you as surely as if you'd left your fucking fingerprints at the scene. And when Jig gets tainted by these actions, how does it reflect on the things he's supposed to stand for? How does it rub off on his Cause? The plain fact is, Jig, somebody's out there making a fucking asshole out of you and every bloody thing you stand for." Pagan was quiet for a time. "Okay. Go down there to Dawson's house. Be a martyr. Isn't that what the Cause expects of you anyhow? Doesn't the Cause expect all its good soldiers to die totally fucking senseless deaths?"

Jig wandered to the edge of the hollow. For a second Pagan thought he was about to step down the slopes and between the trees and, as if it were a personal act of defiance, like a unicyclist setting out on a frayed wire, go immediately in the direction of the house. But then he stopped and stood motionless. Pagan wondered what was going on in his mind now. Had anything Pagan said made a dent? Was he going to agree to the truce? It was a desperate kind of proposal, Pagan realized. But he had no other cards to play. It was reasonable to assume that Jig wouldn't be happy with any activities that sullied his precious Cause, but would he go as far as Pagan wanted him to? If he did, and if they went after Ivor the Terrible together—and the idea of nailing Ivor appealed greatly to Pagan, with or without Jig's help—it would at least have the advantage of keeping Jig within Pagan's reach. It wasn't much, but it was something as far as Frank Pagan was concerned. And down the line somewhere he'd have to make his play, he'd have to get the weapons away from Jig. If an opportunity occurred it was going to be a small one and he'd have to be alert and act faster than he'd ever acted in his life. Jig wasn't going to doze off, that was certain.

From somewhere down the road, like the cry of a wounded animal, there was a noise that echoed through the hills. Jig tilted his head, listening.

Frank Pagan stood up.

The noise was growing shriller, more urgent. Pagan looked off into the distance, where he saw red and blue flashing lights creating a small extravaganza against the backdrop of the dour hills.

"Looks like more reinforcements," Pagan said, wondering about all this activity. "I suppose we can expect the cavalry next."

There was a very thin smile on Jig's face, but the eyes were deadly serious. He continued to look at Pagan and the look was one of scrutiny, uncertainty, like that of a man testing the ground beneath him for the presence of a mine.

He said, "The air around here is unhealthy."

Pagan agreed. "And getting worse."

"Remember what I said, Pagan. You don't take me. Under any circumstances."

"I've got that."

"Don't let it slip your mind. You're dead if you do."

"I like living," Pagan said.

Jig looked one last time back down at the estate. Then he sighed and asked, "You really think Ivor McInnes knows, do you?"

"I'd bet on it."

Jig was silent a second. Then, "What hotel is he staying at?"

ARTIE ZUBORIC didn't like the Secret Service because he thought its agents had an overblown concept of their own importance. They guarded presidents and visiting heads of state, admittedly, but Zuboric thought they had it easy when you got right down to it. He stood outside Kevin Dawson's house in the company of Tyson Bruno and felt frustrated because the two SS characters who'd greeted him had told him in a rather airy fashion to keep himself occupied in the grounds. There was more than a little condescension in their manner. This was their little world, and they didn't like intruders because they could look after Dawson damn well by themselves, and besides, they considered the FBI screw-ups in general.

Zuboric stood with his hands on his hips and gazed at the house. The two SS characters stood some distance away, smoking cigarettes and looking extremely proprietorial. They hadn't even allowed Zuboric inside the house, and so far there hadn't been any sign of Kevin Dawson.

Zuboric turned and examined the hills. Tyson Bruno cleared his throat and said, "I keep thinking about that fucker. The way he decked me. I should never have let that happen."

Zuboric shook his head. He hadn't thought of anything except Frank Pagan during the drive up here. He looked at Tyson Bruno and said, "Enjoy the countryside."

"I hate the fucking countryside," Bruno answered.

Zuboric looked back at the house. He felt he should have been invited inside and introduced to Dawson, which was what his position merited. Instead, he was being left out in the cold. All because the SS guys protected Kevin Dawson with the zealous tenacity of insecure lovers. "Let's walk," he said. "Take a look around."

They walked between the trees as far as the narrow road. Dawson's estate was about eighty acres, most of it meadow but wooded here and there. It seemed to Zuboric that it was secure, given the vigilance of the Secret Service fatheads, which prompted the question of why he'd been sent up here in the first place. He felt like an underused extra in a movie, a body, something superfluous.

Tyson Bruno lit a cigarette. "I'd rather be back in the center of things," he said. "Do you think this is Magoo's way of punishing us?"

Zuboric didn't answer. He was looking at the house. Smoke rolled down the roof, blown out of the chimney by a gust of wind. So far as pastoral prettiness was concerned, this whole area wasn't exactly in the blue-ribbon class. It was too forlorn, too uninviting. He stuck his hands in the pockets of his coat. He was thinking of Pagan again, and he'd resolved not to because it created a knot of sheer anger in the middle of his brain.

He tried to relax but Pagan came again, returning to his thoughts like a ghost you couldn't exorcize. He would have liked to see Pagan one more time, just one more time, and give the man a dose of some very bad medicine. He'd never trusted Pagan from the beginning, never warmed to the guy, and now he was filled with a churning need for revenge that might have to go unsatisfied unless he happened to run into the limey again. After all, hadn't Korn practically given the green light to the final solution of the Pagan problem?

"Magoo thinks we screwed up, so he's giving us a little taste of exile. Call it a warning," Bruno said.

Zuboric frowned. So far as he was concerned the assignment wasn't such a bad one and certainly couldn't be construed as a severe knuckle rapping. After all, Kevin Dawson was the President's brother, and Magoo wouldn't take that fact lightly. On the other hand, the Director's inscrutability was legend. You didn't make it to the top if you were an easy guy to figure. Zuboric gazed up into the hills, then looked back at Tyson Bruno, who appeared quite uncomfortable.

"Spooky landscape," Bruno said. "What makes a guy want to live way out here anyhow?"

Zuboric shrugged. "Privacy, I guess."

Tyson Bruno made a snorting sound of derision. It was clear he didn't think much of privacy. He tightened his drab plaid scarf at his neck and narrowed his eyes as he looked across Dawson's estate. In Zuboric's mind, Tyson Bruno was a perfect example of the old school, a graduate of the J. Edgar Hoover Academy for numbskulls. He was dependable up to a point, but not very inventive. Until Frank Pagan had come along, he'd been a rather reliable watchdog. Frank fucking Pagan. Ireland, fucking Ireland. He found himself wishing that the whole goddam island would sink under a tidal wave, drowning Frank Pagan with it and all the problems he'd laid, like so much crap, on Zuboric's doorstep. Problems Artie most certainly didn't need. He had a whole shitload of his own. Charity had started talking about some rich physician who was paying a lot of attention to her lately. How could Zuboric compete with that?

Zuboric walked between the trees. At his side, Tyson Bruno was scanning the landscape, his head swiveling on the thick stalk of his neck. He reminded Zuboric of a bullfrog in certain ways.

"I could use a nip of gin," Bruno said. "This damn cold is getting to me."

Zuboric stopped quite suddenly. In the distance he'd heard something, a sound that never failed to raise the level of his adrenaline. It was the shrill siren of a police car, and it was growing louder, sending scared birds whining out of branches. Zuboric turned his face toward the road. He could see flashing lights, two small points a couple of miles down the road.

He leaned against the trunk of a tree and watched. The cop car was still blasting its siren as it swung into the driveway and went toward the house, where the two SS agents were already taking up a defensive position behind their car, weapons drawn. The police vehicle came to a halt, the siren died. It was all very quick. Two uniformed cops jumped out of the car. The SS men, trusting nobody, especially callers in uniform—who could easily have been fakes—emerged with their guns ready.

"What the fuck," Bruno said.

Zuboric, who knew the signs of trouble when he saw them, started to walk back toward the house. The cops and the agents, having apparently arrived at an understanding, had gone inside the house already. Even before Zuboric had reached the house, Kevin Dawson was hurrying out, the agents flapping behind him. All three got into the Secret Service car, which whipped past Zuboric at top speed and tore down the driveway, spewing dirt as it traveled.

Puzzled, Zuboric looked at the two uniformed cops. He flashed his ID and asked what was going on. The two state policemen appeared flustered and uncertain.

The older of the pair studied Zuboric's ID a second. His hand trembled.

"I can't really describe it" was what he said, and his voice, like his hand, shook.

PATRICK CAIRNEY shaded his eyes against the harsh afternoon sun that burned against the windshield of the Dodge Colt. He glanced at Pagan, who was behind the wheel, then looked down at the gun in his lap. As he did so, he remembered something Finn had once said about how the Cause would one day wither because it lacked nobility. And it lacked nobility because it had no heroes anymore. *I'll make my own bloody hero out of Jig,* Finn said. My own bloody hero. What would Finn think of him now that he'd entered into this pact with Pagan? Would he call it an error of judgment, damned from the very beginning?

Finn's advice might have been to withdraw from the vicinity of Dawson until the heat had gone out of the situation and an approach to Dawson involved less risk. Maybe. But Finn would also have been angry about somebody maligning the Cause by blowing up a church. And Finn's outbursts of anger were fierce things to behold, as if the whole person were on the volcanic rim of exploding into lava. Finn might have done precisely the same thing as Jig was doing now. *Let's find out what bloody McInnes is up to and put a stop to that bastard once and for all.*

Cairney turned the gun over in his hand. He was unsure of the decision he'd made. Thoughts crowded him, cramped him. His sick father. The missing money. The possibility that Ivor McInnes might know something about it. The notion that Pagan could be setting a trap.

And Celestine. The last thought he wanted or needed right then. But there she was, her face floating through his mind, the remembered feel of her mouth, the vibrant warmth of the woman. There she was, a bright, enticing intruder on his thoughts. He closed his eyes for a second. The retreat into darkness. The calm center of himself. It wouldn't come. He couldn't find it.

He opened his eyes, looked at Frank Pagan's face as Pagan drove the winding road that led narrowly through the hills. He suspected Pagan was telling the truth about McInnes being in New York and the attack on the church, but he wasn't certain if Ivor McInnes knew anything about the money. How the hell could he? And how could the FUV have informed Pagan about the American trip anyway—something only he and Finn knew about?

This last question buzzed in his head. The obvious answer—that there was a traitor within the ranks of the Association of the Wolfe—was disheartening. But Frank Pagan might have been lying from start to finish, fabricating everything he'd said. He'd have to be wary from here on in, supersharp, each one of his senses prepared for some sudden occurrence—a move from Pagan, a car following too close behind, anything. If Pagan was as tenacious as he thought, this truce was going to be as substantial as ice in springtime. And if it melted—if it melted he'd shoot Frank Pagan without any further thought.

What had Pagan said? *Be a martyr? Isn't that what the Cause expects of you anyhow?* That remark had stung Cairney more than anything else, because Pagan had somehow managed to center in on the one thing that was anathema to Jig—the idea of martyrdom, the notion that that was what the Cause was all about finally. To succeed you had to be dead. To win you had to have died a soldier's death. A loser's death. To win you had to have old women light penny candles to your memory in cold churches and old men drink Guinness over your sanctified name. The old Irish ways, your name immortalized in song and dredged up on every anniversary of your death, which was usually premature and always fruitless.

And something else Pagan had said had struck a chord inside him. *You're out of your depth in this country, Jig. Too much is stacked against you.* Maybe. But it didn't matter now. It was too late for it to matter. Finn had sent him into this, Finn with his hopes and ambitions, his conviction that Jig could do anything. He'd prove Finn right in the end. When he went back to Ireland with the money it would prove that Finn's decision to send Jig to America had been the right one all along, that Finn's faith in him was completely justified.

"I wonder why Kevin Dawson left in such a hurry," Pagan said. He was turning the Dodge into a sharp bend, driving in a fashion that was a little cavalier. The squeal of tires on pavement seemed to delight him.

Cairney said nothing. He'd been just as curious as Pagan at the sight of Dawson hurrying out of the house and racing off in a car with the two Secret Service men. Shortly after, the FBI agents and the two state cops had also departed. If Cairney had been indecisive about his next step, then the knowledge that Kevin Dawson had left the house made his mind up for him. What was the point of watching an empty house when you had no way of knowing if and when Dawson was coming back?

Pagan swung the Dodge into a hairpin turn and looked at Cairney as he did so. "Does my driving make you nervous?"

Cairney shook his head. He wouldn't give the Englishman any small satisfaction. Pagan, as if Cairney's refusal to be upset rattled him, put his foot harder on the gas pedal and the car went whining into the next turn. Pagan took his hands from the wheel for a second. The speedometer was approaching seventy-five and the small Dodge was quivering.

Cairney pressed his gun hard into Pagan's ribs. "I see how it would suit you if we were pulled over by the highway patrol. But I don't think I'd care for that personally. Anyway, guns behave unpredictably at high speeds, Pagan. Keep that in mind. Never play games with me."

Pagan caught the wheel, braked gently, and the car slowed. "I'll drive like a senile dowager," he said.

Cairney pulled the gun back from Pagan's body. "So long as we have an understanding."

Pagan nodded. "I'm sure we have," he said. He was concerned about the tension in Jig, the extreme wariness. He didn't like the proximity of the gun either, the way Jig had it pointed directly at his side. He sighed, jabbed the radio, heard only static. Jig reached out and turned the radio off.

"Let's get some ground rules straight up front, Pagan. No noise. No music. No conversation. If we get to New York and I find out all this is bullshit, you're dead. On the other hand, if Ivor *does* know something, I decide the next step. Is that clear?"

"Clear," Pagan said, thinking how he wasn't cut out for this chauffeur business. He hated being in an inferior position.

On either side of the road now the hills were flattening, drifting down gently into meadows. Road signs appeared, indicating the thruway some miles ahead. Older signs pointed out back roads, cattle crossings, deer warnings. Everything was lit by the same filmy ivory sunlight, which had an illusory quality. Here and there an old farmhouse or barn was visible, framed by trees. There was a bucolic assurance about everything, a timelessness.

The road curved suddenly, a long sweeping turn that almost took Pagan by surprise. He braked lightly as he took the Dodge into the curve. And then, surprised by what he saw ahead of him, he slowed the speed of the car so abruptly that Jig was momentarily thrown forward. Not enough to make him careless with the gun, but enough to irritate him.

"For God's sake, Pagan—"

And then Jig saw what it was that had so surprised Frank Pagan, and his first thought was that if *this* was the trap, then it was elaborate and cunning, involving all kinds of incongruous vehicles—a shattered school bus, a sedan that issued a thin cloud of smoke, a couple of state police cruisers, two ambulances, and several other vehicles all parked carelessly around the pathetic relic of the yellow bus, whose windows had been broken and side panels blitzed. Then Jig became conscious of something else, the sight of bodies lying in a clearing between the trees, with men in white coats hovering over them. The realization that many of these bodies were unmistakably children caused his heart to freeze. He put his hand involuntarily up to his mouth. *Kids.* And his mind was spinning back to a street scene he'd once witnessed in the Shankill Road area of Belfast when two kids, both bloodied from random gunfire, had been stretched out on a sidewalk, small casualties of a conflict that was beyond their understanding—but that had been only two kids, now he was staring at about ten, a dozen, he wasn't sure. He heard his own blood pound inside his skull, and ice laid a terrible film the length of his spine.

Pagan was traveling past the scene at about ten miles an hour. A cop came across the road and waved an arm impatiently at the Dodge, gesturing for it to pass and mind its own goddam business. Pagan's nostrils filled with the stench of burning rubber and gasoline.

"Keep moving," Cairney said. He poked the gun into Pagan's hip, concealing the weapon under the folds of his overcoat.

Pagan winced. "I've got no bloody intention of stopping. Do you imagine I'm going to try and turn you over to some local cop? Take the fucking gun away from me."

Pagan pressed his foot on the gas pedal as the car drew closer to the cop. Smoke drifted thickly across the road, obscuring the cop for a moment. When it cleared the policeman was about fifteen feet away, still waving his arm. Pagan stared past him at the clearing. What the hell had happened here? It looked as if the school bus had been used for target practice. It was an unreal scene, yet the air of authentic tragedy hung over it. Those small bodies under sheets. The ambulance lights flashing. The men sifting around the wreckage. Pagan's eye was drawn quickly to an area at the rear of the clearing.

Artie Zuboric was standing there, ash colored, his usually upright body set in a slouch, as if the weight of whatever had happened in this place were too heavy for him. At the center of the clearing, flanked by his Secret Service men and a group of cops, stood Kevin Dawson.

"Jesus Christ," Pagan said, horrified by the scene, by the awful expression on Dawson's face.

Jig, who had also recognized Dawson, asked, "What the hell's going on here?" And his voice was hushed, his question phrased in a tone Pagan hadn't heard from him before.

Pagan barely had time to absorb the whole situation before the scene dwindled in the rearview mirror and was finally lost beyond a curve in the road. But the look on Dawson's face stayed with him. It was that of a man shattered, a man bewildered by events that defy description, someone who has seen his world tilted on its axis.

It was grief.

It was a look Frank Pagan had seen on his own face, when reflections in mirrors threw back the countenance of a stranger undergoing an impossible trauma, an experience beyond the language of loss. It was an alien voice whispering in your brain over and over and over *Roxanne is gone, gone, gone.*

Dawson's daughters, Pagan thought.

It struck Pagan then with the force of a hammer.

Somebody had ambushed that school bus, which must have had the Dawson girls on board, otherwise why would Kevin Dawson be there looking so utterly grief stricken?

Somebody.

Dear God. He felt his stomach turn over.

Somebody, he thought again. It was violence as pointless and as brutal as that done to the church in White Plains. And what he heard suddenly was Ivor McInnes's voice saying *If it's the IRA, it's not going to stop with some church. Once those fellows get the taste of blood, they don't know when to stop.*

Pagan had a raw sensation in his heart.

There is going to be a telephone call. A man will speak in an Irish accent. He'll say that the bus was attacked by members of the Irish Republican Army.

And Jig, who was still looking at Pagan, still waiting for an answer to the question he'd asked minutes before, was going to be blamed for this new monstrosity. It had all the texture of the completely inevitable. Jig would be blamed, then crucified.

Pagan thumped his foot down hard on the gas pedal. Had Ivor McInnes known about this outrage? If he'd known, as Frank Pagan felt he did, about an IRA presence in the U.S.A., had he also known that *this* was going to happen?

A small nerve began to work in Pagan's cheek as he thought of McInnes, that smug, bloody man with his poisonous hatreds. And something moved through Pagan's brain, an anger he hadn't felt in years, a turmoil of rage, a searing emotion that he couldn't bring entirely under control. He knew this much—he knew he was looking forward to tearing that mask away from Ivor's face and getting down to the truth of things. It would be a slippery descent, because in McInnes's world truth was never something you ascended to, it was a quality concealed in deep places, dank places, down at the fetid bottom of the man's heart.

"I asked you a question," Jig said. "What the hell do you think *happened* back there?"

"I can only guess," Pagan said.

"Let me hear it anyway."

Frank Pagan told him.

HARRISON, NEW YORK

Seamus Houlihan called the FBI from a phone booth at a shopping plaza at twenty minutes past five. The man he spoke with attempted unsuccessfully to keep Houlihan talking. But Houlihan delivered his terse message without hesitation, then hung up. He looked across the plaza to the place where the yellow Ryder truck was parked. It was strange, Houlihan thought, not to see John Waddell's face staring out through the windshield. Waddy had deserved to die, it was as simple as that. Like Fitzjohn, he'd been weak when strength was needed.

Houlihan entertained no regrets at the act. There was hardly anything in his life he regretted. Since Waddell had been his friend, though, he felt it was his duty to give the man a decent burial. That was the very least he could do. He had, after all, his own sense of honor.

He paused, staring into the window of a Carvel ice-cream shop. He went inside, ordered a single scoop of vanilla. He had to repeat his order three times because the eedjit girl behind the counter didn't understand his accent. He came out, licking the ice cream, which was too soft for his taste. By the time he reached the Ryder truck the ice cream was already melting, running down the sleeve of his jacket. He tossed the cone away in disgust.

He gazed a moment at the discarded confection. It created a bright white puddle on the concrete. He thought of McInnes's instructions to discard all weapons at the time of getting rid of the truck. They were to be cleaned thoroughly of all fingerprints and then dumped in some isolated place, after which Houlihan and the others were to return to Canada, and from there back to Ireland. The part Houlihan didn't like was throwing the weapons away, especially his own handgun, a Colt Mark V he'd become attached to. What did McInnes know anyhow? The man wasn't out here doing the fucking dirty work, was he? He wasn't getting his hands grubby. He'd probably never even fired a gun in his whole bloody life, so how could he understand the personal relationship you could develop with a weapon? Besides, what would happen if the weapons were dumped and *then* a bad situation cropped up? You'd be totally naked, wouldn't you?

Houlihan made up his mind to disobey McInnes. It made him feel good. It gave him a pleasing sense of his own authority. He'd keep the guns, *all* the guns, until he was good and ready to toss them. And he wouldn't tell McInnes about this decision when he telephoned him next time. He looked at his watch. He had thirty minutes to kill before he was due to call the Reverend again.

He reached up and opened the door of the cab and slid in behind the wheel.

"What's next?" Rorke asked.

"Another phone call, then a good night's sleep" was how Seamus Houlihan answered.

TWENTY-FOUR

In his room at the Essex House Ivor McInnes stared at the TV.

A man named Lawrence W. Childes was speaking from the colored screen. The President's press officer, he was a solemn figure whose gatherings with the press were reminiscent of a convention of undertakers. He told the assembled journalists that the government had learned of the presence of the Irish assassin Jig in the United States. That Jig, working either alone or with a group of fellow IRA terrorists, had been responsible for the bombing of the Memorial Church in White Plains. That Irish terrorism, so long contained within the borders of the United Kingdom, had come to the U.S.A. He spoke of an extensive ongoing investigation being conducted by the FBI in association with a variety of local law enforcement agencies. He was convinced that Jig would soon be apprehended and brought to justice.

After the introductory remarks, Childes was besieged by questions. Hands were upraised, papers clutched and shaken, cameras thrust forward, as journalists vied for attention. Lawrence W. Childs accepted a question from a fat woman with an Irish name. She represented a wire service. She wanted to know why the Irish were operating within the continental United States, a question Childes hummed at but couldn't answer.

McInnes had been packing his suitcase on the bed. He stopped, moving a little closer to the TV. The fat woman was still pursuing her line of inquiry despite the protests of other journalists who, like hopeful adolescent suitors, had claims of their own to press for Childes's attention.

I have no information, Ms. McClanahan.

All of a sudden Irish terrorists start operations inside our borders and you don't know why? What exactly is this administration hiding, Mr. Childes?

McInnes smiled. He folded a shirt, put it inside the suitcase. He knew that this press conference was going absolutely nowhere, no matter how shrill were the hyenas of the media in their full-blooded curiosity. He rolled a necktie, placed it neatly beside the shirt. The radio clock on the bedside table said it was 6:39. Since Houlihan had already called, McInnes knew the big man had succeeded in the afternoon's endeavor and had made his call to the FBI on schedule. Which meant that either Lawrence W. Childes wasn't being entirely open with the press or else the information about the school bus hadn't reached him yet. Maybe it had been decided, at levels above and beyond Childes, that an attack on schoolkids wasn't something the American public was geared as yet to hear. What difference did it make? McInnes asked himself. Sooner or later news of the latest outrage would reach them, because a thing like that couldn't be contained forever.

McInnes adjusted the volume control.

A man with a florid face, a boozer's face, was asking if there were any important political figures in the congregation of Memorial Church at the time of the bombing.

So far as we can tell, the answer is negative, Childes replied.

Then what we're talking about is plain random violence and destruction?

It would appear that way.

McInnes placed a pair of pants on top of the shirt. Then he picked up the folder that contained the notes he'd made on the history of Ulster workers in the construction of the railroad and put it inside a side pocket of the suitcase. He went into the bathroom and splashed some cold water on his face, and when he returned the press conference was still in progress.

Graf, Detroit Free Press. Is there any evidence to suggest that the IRA plans future attacks?

We have no such evidence at this time, Mr. Graf.

But why would they come into this country just to blow up one church and then leave again?

As I said, we have no evidence to support the view that the IRA plans further terrorist activities.

McInnes sat on the edge of the bed. He saw Lawrence W. Childes move away from the podium, and he gathered that the press conference had come to an abrupt end. There was one of those uncertain moments when the cameraman loses his focus and the camera swings wildly, shooting a ceiling, an empty doorway, the faces of flustered journalists—but then Childes was back behind the podium again, holding a sheet of paper in one hand. He was calling for quiet and the picture was steady now.

McInnes leaned toward the TV.

Lawrence W. Childes said that he had just learned of a new development. He cleared his throat and read.

At approximately two-fifty this afternoon a school bus was attacked outside New Rockford, Connecticut, by gunmen who claim to be members of the Irish Republican Army.

On board this bus were the nieces of the President of the United States. The President has no statement to make at this time.

There was a long silence. Then the questions, held in check a moment by the fragile seawall of concern and decency and outright shock, came bursting forward. Were the Dawson girls injured? How many were on board the bus? What was the number of casualties? Was this the same group that had destroyed the church in White Plains? Was this the work of Jig? Lawrence Childes, face drained and voice shaking, clasped his hands and said that he had no information to add to what he'd already said. Tracked by reporters, who now showed all the demeanor of crazed ladies at a hat sale, he moved away from the podium. Security officers blocked the newsmen as Lawrence Childes vanished down a hallway without looking back.

McInnes turned the TV off.

There. It was out now. It was common knowledge.

And McInnes experienced a feeling that was jubilation suffused with relief. The road had been mapped and traveled and was behind him now. He had won. He zipped up his suitcase, then turned the small key in its lock. He tossed the key in the air and snapped it up in his hand as it fell back down. He uttered a small whoop of exhilaration.

It was out now and all America knew it. The Irish Republican Army had blown up a church and then attacked a school bus. The IRA had sunk to a level that defied description. Already, McInnes was anticipating the next day's headlines and editorials, the anger and dismay that would yield to the call for blood, for violent responses to violent men, an eye for an eye. He could hear the knives being released from their sheaths and sharpened. Revenge, when it came, would be devastating.

He didn't hear the knock on his door at first. Even when he became conscious of it, it barely registered. An intrusion from another world. He turned. Whatever it was, whoever, he could handle it. He could handle anything now. There was nothing that wasn't beyond his capabilities.

He opened the door. Somehow he wasn't altogether astonished to see Frank Pagan. The presence of a second man, somebody McInnes had never seen before, did surprise him, but he quickly took it in his stride. He was in a place where even Frank Pagan couldn't harm him.

"Why, Frank," he said. "And you've brought a friend. How very nice."

Pagan's face was dark. His forehead was broken into deep ridges and his jaw was set at a belligerent angle. His large hands were clenched and they hung at his sides, as if restraining them required effort. The other man had drawn a gun. Curiously, though, he didn't aim it directly at McInnes. Instead, he seemed to point into the space between Pagan and McInnes as if he wanted to cover both men. McInnes stepped back.

"Talk to me," Pagan said. "Start at the beginning and talk to me."

"We've talked already," McInnes replied. He glanced at his suitcase.

"Packed, are we? Ready to leave?" Pagan asked.

"Quite ready." McInnes looked briefly at the gun in the young man's hand. "There's nothing left for me to do here."

"Wrong, Ivor. You've got unfinished business."

McInnes shook his head. "Tell your friend to put his gun away, Frank."

"I can't tell him anything like that," Pagan said. He widened his eyes and smiled. "Bad manners on my part. I forgot to introduce you. Ivor McInnes, meet Jig."

McInnes felt a pulse throb at the back of his throat. He looked into the young man's eyes, which were harder even than Pagan's, and had an odd sideways quality, a shiftiness. McInnes wondered how this state of affairs added up. Pagan and Jig. Now there was a combination that God and Scotland Yard and the FBI hadn't exactly intended. How had it come about that Frank Pagan and Jig were together? How had this pair managed to find one another, and who was the quarry, who the hunter now? It wasn't supposed to happen like this. Not at all.

"Jig isn't pleased, Ivor," Pagan said. "He isn't pleased at all. Which goes for me too."

McInnes saw a narrowing of Jig's eyes. It was hardly perceptible, but it was as obvious as a neon sign to McInnes.

"I'm sure you're making some kind of sense, Frank," he said. "But it escapes me."

Jig spoke for the first time. "Tell us about the church, McInnes. Tell us about the school bus."

"Terrible things," McInnes said, shaking his head.

"We're all agreed that they're terrible things," Pagan said. "But we haven't come here to make little sympathetic noises, McInnes."

"What do you know?" Jig asked.

"What do I know?" McInnes smiled. "Only what I see on TV."

"Try again," Pagan said.

There was a smell of violence about both Pagan and the other man, and nothing quickened the brain quite like that odor. McInnes stepped to the window and looked out at the park. The ghost of a decision was beginning to take shape at the back of his mind. Sometimes, from out of nowhere, he had an inspiration, a flash, an insight that seemed to transcend the usual labored workings of logical thought. He had one now.

Pagan stepped closer to him. And then one of Pagan's hands was clamped on his shoulder, turning McInnes around as if he were nothing more than a sack of frail kindling.

McInnes hated violence. On one broad level it was a political tool of some use, but when it descended to the personal arena it was loathsome. It wasn't even cowardice on his part either. He'd boxed one year when he'd been a university student in Liverpool, accumulating a fair record, but something about crunching his glove into an opponent's face had repelled him. As indeed he was repelled now by the way Pagan was holding him.

"We're reduced to this, are we?" he asked.

Pagan held a fist beneath McInnes's jaw. "This is nothing," Pagan said. "I haven't even worked up a sweat yet, Ivor."

"I don't think there's any need for this, Frank."

Before McInnes could say anything, Pagan had swung the fist in a low trajectory. It dug into the fleshy lower part of McInnes's belly, doubling him over, expelling all the air from his lungs and causing his eyes to register fiery sparks.

McInnes gasped and sat down on the bed and blinked up at Frank Pagan.

"It's like I said, Ivor. We don't have time for any further bullshit. It's pain and more pain from here on in."

Through layers of pain, McInnes realized he had perceived the outline of a plan that would serve two purposes at once. It would get Pagan off his back, which was admittedly a priority right now. But more than that, it would rid him of Seamus Houlihan, whose work was finished and whose continued existence could easily become an embarrassment over the long run. Besides, Seamus had shown a tendency to take the initiative in situations where invention on his part wasn't needed. The man was a thug, a cold-blooded killer, and McInnes perceived no kind of future for such a man in his scheme of things. Houlihan was like some kind of primitive weapon that Ivor McInnes had no further use for.

Frank Pagan reached down and grabbed the lapels of McInnes's jacket.

"Easy," McInnes said.

"Don't stop me, Ivor. Not unless you've got something sensible to say."

McInnes raised a hand defensively.

"Do we talk, Ivor?" Pagan asked.

McInnes nodded. He was struggling to catch his breath. The lie that had presented itself to him was ingenious, all the more so since it would contain elements of truth. All the best lies had fragments of truth in them.

"We talk," he said.

Pagan folded his arms against his body. Jig, who had been observing this situation without comment, still had his gun trained in front of him.

McInnes rubbed his stomach where it hurt. He turned the lie around in his mind, preparing to float it in front of these two hostile men. "I heard a story in Belfast," he said. "I have my sources, you know."

"Go on," Pagan urged. His tone was skeptical.

"Give me a minute, Frank. Breathless." McInnes stood up now, just a little unsteady. He took a couple of deep breaths. "I heard an interesting little yarn about a group of disaffected IRA men who were planning an action in America." McInnes paused, looking first at Pagan, then at Jig. Both of them were bloody poker players, he decided.

"It appears that this IRA cell, unhappy because money wasn't coming down the pipeline as fast as they wanted it, decided to branch out. Well, you have some idea of how the IRA is, don't you? They're forever splitting into factions. They're always squabbling and going for each other's throats. Anyhow, this group, which needed finances for various projects—presumably of a criminal nature—came up with the notion of doing a couple of outlandish things in America. The idea behind their thinking was quite simple. They felt that if they went off at a tangent in America, they'd be making a point with the powers back in Ireland. It would be a form of blackmail, you see. They'd come here and make a mess, which would be like holding a pistol to the head of the people in the IRA who mind the purse. Are you with me?"

Frank Pagan didn't move a muscle. No nod, no expression. McInnes swallowed and continued. "This little group of the disaffected decided on outrages. Human outrages. Acts that would alienate public opinion. A church would be first. What's more innocent than a church, after all? Then they thought of the answer to that one, didn't they? They came up with something even more vile. A school bus. Better yet, what if that particular bus carried two rather important children? You see the wicked way some people think."

"Spare me the moral judgments, Ivor."

"Well, apparently they've come here and they succeeded in doing what they set out to do. Now they think they'll go home and suddenly the purse-strings will be wide open for them because if they're not, then it's an easy matter to come back to the United States and do something else." McInnes paused. He wished he had a litmus paper he could dip into Frank Pagan's brain to check the effect of his story on the man. "You understand what I'm telling you, don't you?"

Pagan said nothing.

McInnes went on, "Blackmail, Pagan. Blackmail on a terrible scale. You and I might not understand that way of thinking, but certain people come to it quite naturally. And the people responsible for these horrors are quite capable of anything. As you well know."

"Where do you fit in, Ivor?"

McInnes stood up, a little shaky. A lie was always more convincing if it involved a detail that cast the liar himself in a bad light. And this was the tactic McInnes pursued now. "I know how some people perceive me, Frank. They think that because I'm socially and philosophically opposed to Catholicism, I'm behind Protestant violence."

"Get on with it, Ivor."

"You're an impatient man, Frank Pagan."

"You have that effect on me."

McInnes smiled slightly. "Well, to be perfectly honest, I saw an opportunity to do myself some good. Call it selfish thinking. I'm not without a certain vanity, after all. Most people have some. What I genuinely believed was that I could come here, make contact with these people and perhaps negotiate something that wouldn't involve the violence we've seen in the last few days. In other words, I misled myself into thinking I could contact these men and reason with them. It didn't matter that I was on a different side from them. The point was, I thought I could sway them, I thought I could make a gesture that had nothing to do with the partisan nature of life in Ireland. I believed I could spare the United States a taste of the strife that has torn Ireland apart for so long."

McInnes paused. He stared at Frank Pagan with a look of grief and misery in his eyes.

"I failed, obviously."

"You thought you could be a saint, did you?"

"Not a saint, Frank. Just the voice of reason."

"The voice of reason," Pagan said flatly. "Do I applaud now?"

"Applaud?"

"Quite a little performance, Ivor."

"You don't believe me?"

"In another world I might. In a world where cows played bagpipes and money grew on trees, I might be convinced."

McInnes shrugged. "I'm telling you the truth." He looked at Jig, who had been listening motionless to the story.

Pagan said, "Let me see if I can get this straight, Ivor. You came after these men, without telling anyone in authority, because you imagined you could do your Henry Kissinger bit and get them to sit down like reasonable men at a table? You imagined some bloodthirsty IRA characters were going to pay attention to the man they think of as the Protestant anti-Christ?"

"I thought I could do myself some good," McInnes said. "Call me vain. Call me egocentric. Call it a normal human response."

"Call it bullshit," Frank Pagan said.

McInnes looked down at the floor. He felt suddenly very calm, in control of things. Even the sight of Frank Pagan's incredulous face didn't trouble him.

"You asked for the truth," McInnes said.

"And what did I get? Tripe."

"Have it your own way, Frank."

Pagan glanced at Jig, then said, "What about Fitzjohn? How does he fit into this fable of yours?"

McInnes looked sheepish. "I'm afraid I lied to you there, Frank."

"Well, knock me down with a feather," Pagan said.

"Fitzjohn was acting on my instructions to arrange a meeting between myself and this IRA faction."

"Your personal emissary."

"Exactly."

"And?"

"They killed him. They aren't reasonable men. I thought they were. But I was wrong again. Poor Fitzjohn."

Frank Pagan sat down on the bed now. "If any of what you're telling us is true, you're covered in blood. You're up to your thick neck in blood. You claim you knew in advance of situations that could have been prevented if you'd gone to the authorities. Jesus Christ, we're talking about innocent kids here! We're talking about kids traveling home on a school bus."

"Ask yourself this. Would the authorities have listened to me?"

"I don't believe a word of this. That's the problem I'm having, Ivor," Pagan said.

Jig moved slowly across the floor. McInnes imagined that the gun in the young man's hand was going to come up through the air and smack him straight across the face and he braced himself for it. But it didn't happen.

Jig asked, "How did your source happen to come upon all this information in the first place?"

McInnes's mind was like a needle laying threads across what had already been embroidered. He knew how he could convince Jig of his story at least. He knew which name to drop into the conversation for maximum effect. He said, "I can't reveal that. But I can tell you this much. A man called Padraic Finn was in control of finances, which didn't please certain people. It obviously didn't please the faction I'm talking about, the ones who are here in America right now."

"Finn?" Jig asked.

"That's right."

Jig stared at McInnes. There was a flicker of interest in his eyes now. "How did your source know about Finn?"

McInnes smiled in a weary way. "There's a very old craft called infiltration, Jig. No doubt you're familiar with it."

Jig absently fiddled with the tuner of the bedside radio. "What do you know about the missing money?"

"Money?" McInnes replied.

"Money from the *Connie O'Mara*," Pagan said.

"I'm a couple of steps behind you," McInnes said in a puzzled way. "You're talking in another language."

There was silence inside the room.

"I don't believe Finn was infiltrated," Jig said finally.

McInnes gazed down at his suitcase. "He wasn't just *infiltrated*, my friend. No, it was more than that."

Jig stared at McInnes. "What more?"

"This same IRA faction *murdered* Padraic Finn at his home in Dun Laoghaire."

Jig didn't move. McInnes saw the face change. He saw the lips open and the skin turn white. He saw all the light sucked from the eyes, drawn backward into some unfathomable area of the skull. McInnes had never seen a face alter so quickly, so profoundly.

Jig shoved his gun directly at McInnes's head, the barrel pressing into a spot just above McInnes's ear.

"You lying bastard, McInnes."

McInnes tried to move away from the weapon, but Jig was pressing it hard.

"I'm not lying," McInnes said.

"They *couldn't* infiltrate Finn. They *couldn't* murder him."

"But they did. They went at night to his house. They'd already bribed the watchman, George Scully. With nobody to protect the house, it must have been easy for them."

Jig took the gun from McInnes's head as suddenly as he'd placed it there. He opened his mouth to say something, but no words came. He was like a man trying to still some awful internal turmoil to which he was totally unaccustomed. A man experiencing some new and terrifying sensation that he couldn't name, couldn't identify, didn't want to believe.

"No," Jig said, and his voice was hollow.

McInnes said, "I know where these killers are. Their leader is somebody called Houlihan. There are four in this group, so far as I know. They travel in a rented Ryder truck. And they're presently staying at a place called the River View Motel near Hastings." McInnes paused. He could see that Jig was absorbing this information quietly, but Frank Pagan—ah, always the skeptic—was looking incredulous, a big frown distorting his features.

McInnes thought a moment about Houlihan and the others. It was *perfect*. If there was a confrontation in the course of which Houlihan and his pals were killed, it would be splendid. What did it matter if they were later discovered, after fingerprints were run through computers, to be Free Ulster Volunteers and not IRA? He'd simply say he was mistaken, if Pagan asked. He'd simply say he'd received the wrong information and had passed it along in good faith, that he'd believed the men in the River View Motel were IRA. Pagan couldn't prove otherwise. He could interrogate until doomsday, but he couldn't prove a damn thing. There was just no way. And, since Houlihan had dumped the guns and the remote-control devices that triggered the explosives, there was absolutely *nothing* to tie some dead FUV men into the barbarism in New Rockford or the bombing in White Plains. All anybody would ever know was that four men from Ulster, their purpose in America mysterious, had been killed in a motel in Hastings, New York.

The weakness in this scheme was the possibility of Pagan taking prisoners—the slight chance that Houlihan or one of the others might talk. But it was such an unlikely possibility that McInnes dismissed it. For one thing, Houlihan and the others would never talk. Houlihan's strange moral code precluded betrayal, no matter the circumstances. He'd never give anything away. He was a miser when it came to revealing information. He'd never say anything about his reason for being in the U.S.A. Even if he wanted to talk, was he likely to *admit* that he'd gunned a school bus and bombed a church?

But it would never come to that, because McInnes knew Houlihan well enough to guess that Seamus, even though he'd dumped the incriminating automatic weapons, wasn't going to discard his beloved handgun quite so promptly—he'd never go anywhere without his pistol. Which was fine. The handgun had played no part in the attack on the school bus. And if the pistol was all he had, Seamus would gladly go into battle. He'd never turn his back on a good fight, especially if he still had his precious handgun. And Seamus would never be captured because he'd rather blow out his own brains than go back to jail again. Anyhow, if the expression on Jig's face meant anything, the possibility of prisoners being taken was remote, a courtesy that Jig in his present mood wouldn't entertain. The young man had a desperate killing look. He was ready to do violence. He was ready to kill. The battle was inevitable and, to McInnes's way of thinking, a neat solution to his problems with Seamus Houlihan and the FUV. But it would be the last one. After this, he thought, there would be no more violence.

Jig picked up the telephone. McInnes watched him. The hand that held the receiver was tense, skin drawn, knuckles bleached. McInnes heard the young man ask for a phone number in Ireland.

After about thirty seconds Jig hung up.

"No answer?" McInnes asked. He thought, *Dead men don't answer telephones.*

Jig appeared not to have heard the question. He once more picked up the telephone and asked for the number of the River View Motel.

McInnes smiled. "You don't think Houlihan registered under his own name, do you?"

Jig said, "It's easy to find out if a party of men arrived in a Ryder truck." His voice was clipped, shorn of intonation, like that of a deaf person who has never learned the nuances of speech.

McInnes stretched out one hand. "Go ahead," he said. "You'll find out I've been telling the truth."

Frank Pagan stared at Jig. "You can't be giving serious consideration to any of this shit," he said in dismay.

Jig said nothing. He dialed the number.

McInnes smiled at Pagan, who had the look of a man chewing on fragments of an electric light bulb, a trick he'd never master no matter how long and hard he worked at it.

NEW ROCKFORD, CONNECTICUT

Artie Zuboric had very little experience of handling grief, his own or anyone else's. Now, as he stood in the living room of Kevin Dawson's house in the company of Tyson Bruno and the two Secret Service men, he was conscious of a tide of grief flowing throughout this large house.

Upstairs, in a darkened bedroom, Kevin Dawson was standing at the bedside of his sedated wife, Martha, holding her hand and muttering something unintelligible over and over. Earlier, Zuboric had looked inside the bedroom through the open door, but his awareness of pain was too much for him.

In the hallway outside the living room people came and went. Physicians. Family members. Employees in one or other of the Dawson industries. There was word that Thomas Dawson himself was on his way here. Zuboric went over to the fireplace and looked at the framed photographs of the two Dawson girls on the mantelpiece, but he couldn't bring himself to look for long. He stepped out into the hallway and stood at the foot of the stairs. Tyson Bruno came out to join him.

Neither man spoke for a very long time. Grief, Zuboric noticed, imposed silences, made you speak only when you had to and then in hushed whispers. Grief was like sitting in the reading room of a large library. He glanced up the long staircase a moment. He was anxious to be out of this place, out in the cold night air, but instructions had come directly from Korn that he was to stay where he was until the Director himself had arrived. Already, the site of the attack was being combed thoroughly by a dozen FBI agents and a score of state cops, all feverishly working under floodlights. Forensic experts were going over the bus in punctilious detail. But what could that tell them except what they already knew—that twelve children out of a total of eighteen on the wretched bus had been murdered, including the daughters of Kevin and Martha Dawson?

"It's a fucking nightmare," Tyson Bruno said.

Zuboric wandered to the front door of the house. He pushed it open. It was a nightmare all right, and it made him horribly impatient. Somewhere in the darkness was the man responsible for it all. Somewhere there was Jig. Zuboric wondered what kind of man was capable of an act like the massacre of schoolkids. He knew terrorists courted indecency with a passion. He knew they understood no limits. But *this*. This was something else.

Tyson Bruno came and stood beside him. "I'm thinking," he said quietly. "I'm thinking Korn's going to be a very angry man, Artie. He sends us up here to keep an eye on Dawson, and what happens?" Bruno made a sweeping gesture with one plump hand.

"He can hardly blame us for this," Zuboric answered. "Christ, we weren't responsible for looking after that school bus. That wasn't our brief, Ty."

"Tell that to Korn," Bruno said. "He's going to be looking for heads to roll. And we're the most convenient ones."

Zuboric drew a fingertip through his moustache. He felt most uneasy. It was more than the grief that eddied through this house. It was more than the wall-to-wall misery of this place. There was an element of truth in what Tyson Bruno said. The Director, who took every dent in the FBI armor personally, who saved grievances the way some men collect baseball cards, would need a scapegoat or two. It didn't matter in the long run that guarding a school bus hadn't ever been mentioned. The Director had one of those selective memories that could reach back and revise any conversation. The Director could say that he'd told Zuboric to protect the bus. Zuboric wouldn't put that kind of thing beyond the man. The Bureau was everything. People didn't matter. They were nothing more than fuses that burned out and could be replaced.

Zuboric stepped out of the house. He scanned the bleak darkness and the cars parked outside. "It's the wrong time to start thinking about our own skins," he said.

"It's never the wrong time for that," Tyson Bruno replied.

Zuboric made an impatient gesture with his hand. That was something else about grief. It precluded all other matters and feelings, regardless of their importance. You went into a state of suspended animation. Everything was put on hold. You couldn't act. Couldn't think.

A sound by the living-room door made him turn around. He saw the two Secret Service men coming out of the room. They moved almost in unison, like a married couple who have become attuned to one another's vibrations over the years. They carried with them a scent of cologne, somewhat stale, as if it had been trapped in their suits for a very long time. Without their dark glasses, their faces looked strange and blank, a pair of unfinished masks.

The one called Marco stepped outside the house and lit a cigarette. Zuboric had to move aside to let him pass. The other, Chuckie, remained just inside the door, drawing the night air deeply into his lungs.

"It's a hell of a thing," Marco said.

There was a muted murmur of agreement among the four men.

Then silence. Marco pulled on his cigarette and said, "They were the prettiest kids. Given the fact they were Dawsons and got a lot of attention, they were damned nice. Jesus." He dropped his cigarette and crushed it with unrestrained energy. "I'd like to get the guy that did this."

Zuboric looked away. There was a half-moon over the hills.

Marco said, "It's sickening. That's what it is. It's like somebody kicked me in the gut. I can't get over the feeling." He blinked out at the sky. "Some motherfucker comes here and shoots up a bus. I keep thinking, what the fuck has Ireland got to do with those two kids, huh? What did they know from Ireland, for fuck's sake? And not just those two. A whole gang of kids."

Chuckie blew his nose into a big white handkerchief. Zuboric thought the moon was the saddest he'd ever seen.

"Poor Jack Martyns," Chuckie said, referring to his dead Secret Service colleague. "He thought he had it easy. Went to school every day. Came home at three every afternoon. What a schedule. Nothing to do but look after a couple of kids."

Marco furrowed his brow and sighed. "Jack was a good man."

Zuboric now caught another scent on the air. It was that of cognac, and it came over strongly on Chuckie's breath. This pair had been drinking on the sly. That's why they were suddenly loose and communicative and open.

Marco smoked a second cigarette. Two people came down the stairs and went silently out in the direction of their car. Zuboric recognized the woman as Kevin Dawson's younger sister, Elaine, who was always in the newspapers because of her celebrated boyfriends. He didn't recognize the guy who went with her, though. Tinted glasses, silver hair, prosperous. He looked just like all of Elaine's other boyfriends.

Zuboric watched the beige Rolls-Royce slide softly down the driveway. Marco was still puffing furiously on his cigarette and Chuckie was studying the center of his large handkerchief. They put Zuboric in mind of two uncles at the funeral of nieces they'd never known very well. They had been drinking to accelerate their feelings and open their pores up in general.

Marco said, "Yeah, it's a kick in the gut okay."

Chuckie agreed. He folded his handkerchief. "I was wondering about that guy who came this afternoon."

Marco made a loose little gesture with his shoulders. "What about him?"

"Well, it was kinda coincidental," Chuckie said. "He comes here, talks to Kevin Dawson. Next thing we know, the bus is attacked.

Who the hell was he? I mean, what the hell did he want anyhow?"

"Okay, I'm with you," Marco said in the unfocused way of a man who has drunk one small glass too many. "The Englishman."

"Englishman?" Zuboric asked. He had a strange feeling, almost as if a hatpin had been pushed into his heart. "What Englishman?"

Both Chuckie and Marco surveyed Zuboric coolly. They appeared to have forgotten his existence and now, forcibly reminded of it, weren't altogether pleased by the fact.

Marco stubbed his half-smoked cigarette underfoot. "Okay. An English guy comes here. Shows us some fancy ID. Wants to see Mr. Dawson on urgent business. Mr. Dawson says it's fine. They talk in private for a while. Then the limey leaves."

"What *Englishman*?" Zuboric asked.

"The name was Pagan," Chuckie said.

"Pagan?" Zuboric asked. "*Frank* Pagan?"

"Friend of yours?" Chuckie asked.

"What did he talk about with Dawson?"

"Don't know," Chuckie said. "It was behind closed doors. Seemed like it was urgent, though."

Zuboric looked at Tyson Bruno. They he studied the flight of stairs that led up to the other rooms of the house.

Bruno shook his head. "I don't think you should, Artie. Bad timing."

Zuboric barely listened to his colleague. He was already moving quickly toward the stairs, wondering how he could approach Kevin Dawson, how he could get to a man who was totally lost in grief, how he could find out what Frank Pagan had been doing here only a few hours ago and whether there was any kind of information on the face of the whole planet that might redeem him in the thunderous eyes of Leonard M. Korn.

Grief or no grief, it was worth a shot.

NEW YORK CITY

Ivor McInnes stood in the lobby of the Essex House and dialed the telephone number of the River View Motel in Hastings-on-Hudson.

A man's surly voice came on the line. "River View."

"Connect me with Mr. Houlihan, please."

"Uno momento."

McInnes waited. When he heard Houlihan's harsh accent he said, "This is the last call I'll make until we meet in Canada, Seamus. I have to be absolutely sure you've followed all my instructions to the letter."

"Don't I always follow your bloody instructions?" Houlihan asked.

"Not always." McInnes saw a lovely girl in a knee-length fur coat wander down the lobby. He watched the loose motion of her body under the folds of the coat. He imagined the bareness of her back and the way her spine would fall in diminishing ridges to her buttocks. She smiled at him in an absent fashion. He was reminded of another smile, another face.

"This is important, Seamus," he said.

Houlihan sighed but said nothing.

"You've dumped everything I told you to dump?"

"We got rid of the remote-control devices yesterday. Nobody's ever going to find them. Nobody's ever going to pin that church on us."

"I'm talking about the guns, Seamus."

Houlihan paused before answering. "They're gone," he said.

"Every gun?"

"Every last one."

"Are you absolutely positive?"

"Is there a point to this conversation?" Houlihan asked.

"Did you toss your handgun as well?"

"I did. With great regret."

McInnes caught it then. The lie in the big man's voice. Seamus still had his pistol. Therefore he'd fight. "You're clean then."

"As a fucking penny whistle."

"There's absolutely nothing left that can connect you with any of your recent activities?"

"Not a damn thing," Houlihan said.

McInnes was quiet for a moment. Then he said, "You did a wonderful job, Seamus. See you in Canada."

He hung up, smiling. The girl had gone now. The lobby was empty. McInnes felt a deep glow of anticipation. He had almost reached the end of it all now. Only the final pieces remained to be put in place.

IN the rear seat of the helicopter Thomas Dawson sat huddled inside his overcoat. Below, there was one of those staggering views of Manhattan, all lights, like a huge cathedral of electricity. He closed his eyes and sat with his head tipped back. He wasn't looking forward to an encounter with his brother's anguish. He patted his gloved hands against his knees and sighed and gazed out of the window again as the chopper banked abruptly, swinging away from the canyons of the city.

There had been a great deal of sorrow in the Dawson family history. His older brother, Joseph, to take one example, had shot himself through the head with a revolver at the age of twenty-three because he'd been depressed over some affair of the heart that hadn't worked out. And his youngest sister, Sarah, had died in a sanitorium from an overdose of heroin. But there had never been anything quite like this, the deaths of two small children in the most violent way imaginable. Sarah and Joseph had been neurotic, highly strung, the kind of people who perceived every slight in the most magnified fashion and perhaps their self-inflicted deaths were not so terribly surprising.

But the two girls—

Dear Christ, they'd been nothing but innocent children! What had they *ever* done to deserve such deaths? Dawson, not unnaturally, searched his mind for somebody he might blame for this tragedy. It was easy to say that he might have done more personally, could have been more persistent in forcing Kevin to take his family out of the country. He might also have acted more decisively in dealing with the presence of Jig. By the same token, the FBI could have been more vigilant, worked a little harder at bringing Jig to justice. When you started down the blame trail, it was hard to stop. Kevin himself—for God's sake, he should have seen the danger in his involvement with the Irish. Now, if he understood that at all, it was just too damned late. Goddammit. You could lay blame all over the place with thick brushstrokes, but nothing would ever restore those two small girls to life.

Thomas Dawson took out a cigarette and lit it. He exhaled the smoke slowly in the direction of his fellow passenger, Leonard M. Korn, who'd come aboard in Manhattan.

"We could have done more," Dawson said. He couldn't keep a certain quiver out of his voice. "God, we should have done more."

Korn said nothing. He nodded his shaven head. He wasn't a man who felt the kind of pity most human beings do, but in the presence of Thomas Dawson's obvious grief, he was touched a little. It wasn't his main concern at this moment, however. He was also thinking of ways in which he might perform some damage control. Admittedly, the Secret Service had been directly responsible for the two children, but there *had* been an FBI presence in the vicinity, and that was bad. He'd have the scalps of the two agents, of course. He'd nail them to a wall in public. But this kind of bloodletting would go only so far to protect the Bureau from charges of negligence. There was really only one thing that might turn the situation around somewhat.

And that was the death of Jig.

Korn looked at the President. "We weren't prepared for terrorism from this quarter," he said. "From the Libyans, of course. From some of the Arab countries, certainly. We routinely keep such people under scrutiny. But the Irish . . ." And he flapped one of his small white hands.

Thomas Dawson wasn't interested in what Korn had to say. He was remembering the previous summer when he'd taken his nieces out on the presidential yacht and they'd cruised Chesapeake Bay. He was remembering a quality in those girls that had struck him as rather un-Dawsonlike. They were without guile, that's what it was. You couldn't imagine them conspiring about anything. This had to be on account of Martha's influence. Dawson gulped down more smoke, which was harsh at the back of his throat. He wondered how Martha was doing. She was a steadfast little woman, one with reserves of strength, but how could anybody pull out of a situation like this?

The Dawsons would survive. They always did. They had their own shock absorbers for family tragedies. They retrenched, regrouped, and came out stronger in the end. But there was a very bad time ahead. He stared from the window. The lights of Manhattan had gone and there were stretches of black landscape below.

"We could have done more," he said again. He wasn't really speaking to Leonard Korn, but rather to himself. As far as he was concerned, Korn's career was coming dangerously close to an end.

Korn could see, even in the darkened cabin, that Thomas Dawson had all the mannerisms of a shell-shocked man. The tremor in the fingers, the toneless voice, the way his eyes were quite without life.

"I give you my solemn vow, Mr. President," Korn said, "that we'll settle this Irish business—"

Thomas Dawson interrupted. "The British have been saying the same thing for centuries, Korn. And what have they actually achieved?" Dawson turned so that the instrument lights around the pilot's seat threw eerie little colors, stark reds and chill greens, against his face. "The answer is nothing. In several centuries, the British have accomplished absolutely nothing."

Korn chewed on a fingernail. It was hard to talk to a man in Thomas Dawson's present distraught condition.

The President put out his cigarette and continued to speak in the same unemotional voice. "Tomorrow, the next day, I'll meet with the British and Irish ambassadors. I won't push the matter too strongly—at least not yet—but I'm coming very close to recommending that they consider some form of American assistance in combating the IRA."

"An American presence?" Korn asked. "In Ireland?"

Thomas Dawson nodded. "A handful of advisers, in the beginning. People with some expertise in counterterrorist tactics. Twenty, say. Twenty-five. Whatever the situation calls for. Later, of course, we could add to that number if need be."

Korn asked, "Will the Irish and the British accept this?"

Dawson shrugged. "Who knows? It's a friendly suggestion. One ally to a couple of others. They haven't exactly handled it well on their own, have they? Besides, I'm not talking about sending in armed forces. Advisers only. There's a big difference."

Korn sat back in his seat. He wasn't interested in the President's plans for Ireland.

Thomas Dawson said nothing more on the subject. He was conscious of the helicopter losing height. He looked out of the window and saw, like a submarine rising on an empty dark sea, the pale lights of an isolated dwelling. And then he was dropping toward it, down and down to his brother's house of sorrow.

TWENTY-FIVE

HASTINGS, NEW YORK

The River View Motel was a brown brick building located five miles from State Highway 87. It was inappropriately named. Unless you had an excellent telescope and a forty-foot-high platform on which to stand, you'd never get a glimpse of any river. The view, such as it was, was obstructed by the rooftops of surrounding houses and by trees. Seamus Houlihan stood on the balcony outside of his room and looked out across a concrete forecourt at two small neon lights that said OFFICE and VACANCY. He saw the shadow of the man who sat behind the window down there. Then, changing his angle of vision, he saw the yellow truck. It was the only vehicle in the whole bloody place. Scratched and dented and splattered with mud, it resembled some old wagon of war.

Houlihan leaned against the rail. So far as he could tell this place had no other residents besides himself and Rorke and McGrath. He yawned, turned around, stepped inside his room. He locked the door, sat down in his armchair, picked up his M-16 from the floor and wondered why bloody McInnes had been so insistent when he'd called awhile back. The man had turned into a nag. He was like an old woman, Houlihan thought. Worrying over this, over that, fretting and whining. He'd be taking up crochet next. Dump the weapons indeed!

Houlihan heard Rorke and McGrath move along the balcony. They knocked quietly on his door. He got up, slid the chain, let them come inside. Rorke was carrying a six-pack of Genesee Cream Ale, and McGrath had a pint of Johnny Walker Red Label.

Houlihan produced a deck of cards from his duffel bag and shuffled them. "Want to play a few hands?" he asked.

"Aye, why not," McGrath said. He and Rorke sat down at the small table by the window. Houlihan popped one of the beers and proposed a game of three-card brag, nothing wild.

They played a hand for American pennies and Houlihan won it with a queen high. Rorke had a ten, and McGrath the worst hand possible in brag, a five high. Houlihan smiled and sipped his beer, which tasted like soapsuds in his mouth.

Rorke dealt a second hand, which Houlihan also won, this time with a pair of eights.

"Shitty cards," McGrath said, turning over a four, a six, and a nine.

McGrath dealt another hand. Houlihan received three threes, called a prile, the highest hand in the game. He had quite a collection of pennies by this time, a small coppery heap in front of him.

"You're a lucky sod," McGrath said.

Houlihan scooped the pennies toward himself. He liked the simple pleasure of winning.

Rorke yawned. McGrath shuffled his feet. Neither of them ever enjoyed playing cards with Houlihan for long. Seamus had a way of always winning. When he started to lose he'd begin to cheat, palming cards in the most obvious fashion. Nobody ever complained when he cheated.

From the forecourt below the window there was the sound of a car. Houlihan stepped to the drapes, parted them deftly, saw a small red car go past the truck and then it disappeared around the other side of the building. After that there was silence again. Houlihan dropped the curtains back in place.

"Anything wrong?" Rorke asked.

"Just a car," Houlihan replied.

McGrath ran a tattooed hand through his short brown hair. "I don't mind saying, I'll be glad when we're out of this place. It gives me the willies being the only people in this whole dump."

Even though the car had gone, force of habit kept Houlihan listening. He experienced a small shrill sensation of unease, and he had been trusting such instincts for a long time now. He reached down and picked up his automatic weapon, a movement that was almost involuntary.

He looked at the other two men. "Where are your guns?" he asked.

"In our room," Rorke replied.

"Get them and come back here."

"Get them?" Rorke asked.

"Do as I tell you."

Both men turned toward the door.

"One of you," Houlihan said. "It doesn't take two men to pick up the weapons."

McGrath went outside, closing the door behind him. Houlihan, stepping back to the drapes, saw him move along the balcony. Outside, the forecourt was still, lit only by a couple of pale lamps and the neon signs burning above the office.

"What's wrong?" Rorke wanted to know.

Houlihan didn't answer. He wasn't sure anyhow. There were times when he had feelings he just couldn't explain. Some people called it a sixth sense, but to Seamus Houlihan it was nothing more than a survivor's caution. One time, in Armagh Jail, he'd known in advance that some Catholics were lying in wait for him in the lavatories. Nobody had actually told him this. He hadn't seen anything unusual either. It had simply *occurred* to him. There had been a slight pricking sense of danger, nothing he could truly identify, but he'd heeded the sensation with enough attention that when he stepped into the lavatories he was armed with a lead pipe wrapped in a rag. The Catholics had been there all right, but when they saw what he was carrying they dispersed quickly. Consequently, Seamus had a healthy respect for his own antennae. With his fingers holding the drapes about a half inch apart he scanned the forecourt.

"What's wrong?" Rorke asked again.

"Probably nothing," Houlihan answered. "But I'm not in the business of taking chances."

"HOW do you know this isn't an elaborate trap?" Pagan asked. "How do you know that this isn't something McInnes and I cooked up between us? We play out a dramatic scene. I get to punch Ivor. But it's all fake. It's all done for the purpose of luring you here to Arsehole-on-the-Hudson so we can kill you. How do you know that isn't true?"

Patrick Cairney stared through the windshield of the Dodge at the

side of the motel building. He wasn't really listening to Frank Pagan. He was looking up at the balcony. At the lighted windows of
one room. There was a pain inside him that throbbed endlessly. He
shut his eyes a second, and what he saw pressed behind his lids
was Finn, Finn the indestructible, the immortal. Finn in his baggy
cords, standing by the window in the room of harps. Finn's finger
tunelessly plucking strings. Everywhere he searched his mind he
saw images of Finn.

Cairney opened his eyes and stared hard at the yellow rectangle
of window above. When he'd called the house in Dun Laoghaire,
an unfamiliar voice had answered the telephone. Not Finn. Finn,
who always answered the phone himself because there was never
anybody else in the house to do it, would have picked up the receiver *if he'd been there to do it.* And he wasn't. The strange voice had
been hard and sharp and edgy. *Who is this? Who's calling?* Patrick
Cairney had a mental image of Garda officers going through the
house, and somewhere lay Finn's body covered in a plastic sheet,
surrounded by photographers and fingerprint men and all the other
officials who attended so clumsily to violent death. A murder investigation, Finn's house ransacked by careless fingers, files opened and
read, correspondence analyzed for clues.

Finn was dead.

Patrick Cairney tried not to think. But this one incontrovertible
fact kept coming back at him. Again and again. It surged up out of
all the hollows he felt inside. It echoed, died, returned with vigor.
Finn was dead. He'd never felt loneliness like this before.

"You haven't answered my question," Pagan said.

Cairney couldn't take his eyes from the window. He needed to
kill. It was the first time in his life that he felt he really *needed* to
shed blood. Beyond that lighted window were the men who had
slain Finn. The butchers. "McInnes is telling the truth. This isn't
a trap."

Frank Pagan sighed. It was when McInnes had mentioned Finn
that the atmosphere of the room in the Essex House had changed.
Jig bought the whole story. Everything. Lock and stock and all the
rest of it. He remembered Finn's name from his files, recalled the
mystery of the man who was said to have controlled the finances of
the IRA, and what he wondered about now was the nature of the
relationship between Jig and Finn. Ever since McInnes had pronounced the man dead, ever since that phone call had been placed
to Ireland, Jig had gone into a place that was beyond Pagan's reach.

A place where with every passing moment it seemed to Pagan that something quite volcanic was going on inside of the man. Pagan thought about taking his chance now, grabbing the gun in Jig's hand and seizing it. But he wasn't going to be lulled by Jig's apparent distraction or the volatile nature of his mood.

Cairney said, "McInnes was right about Finn. He was right about the Ryder truck."

"He said four men checked into this hotel. The guy at the desk says three."

"McInnes got his numbers wrong. That's all."

Pagan asked, "Have you ever heard of this Houlihan?"

Cairney pressed his fingertips to his eyes. There was a dull pain behind them. He thought he heard the sound of his whole life collapsing inside him. "Pagan, I don't know the name of every person associated with the IRA. We're talking about a large and secretive organization arranged in cells. It's highly unlikely that I'd know the man."

Patrick Cairney continued to study the motel. A balcony ran the length of the upper floor, studded here and there with dim overhead lights. Across the forecourt two neon signs shimmered. One read VACANCY. The tension he felt was strong, like acid rising inside him. He tried to relax, tried to put his mind in a place beyond Finn. There isn't time for this, he thought. Finn wouldn't want you to grieve over him. What Finn would want is retribution, plain and simple. *Get on with it, boy. Don't dwell on death. People come and people go, only the Cause remains.* All at once Cairney was standing in Glasnevin Cemetery and Finn was handing him a revolver, and Cairney wished now that he'd reached out—just once in the whole time he'd known Finn—and goddam *held* him. On that day. Or any other. Just once. Somewhere. But death took everything away, sealed all the hatches, killed all the possibilities, and whatever he felt now for Finn could never be said.

"You've only got McInnes's word," Pagan said, with the air of a man making one last plea that he knows in advance will be useless. "You've only got his word that the men in this motel are responsible for all the violence. In my book, Jig, that's a damn frail thing to go on."

Cairney looked at Pagan. "Your own story was also frail, if you remember. And I accepted it, didn't I? I accepted the story you told me about McInnes, didn't I? It was me who decided to take a chance on you, Pagan, and go back to New York City."

"There's a difference," Pagan said. "I don't lie."

Cairney returned his eyes to the balcony. Then he glanced across the parking area at the yellow truck. It dully reflected the neon signs. "So what now?" Pagan asked. "Do you go in? Is that your scheme? Do you go in with your six-gun drawn and your fingers crossed?"

Pagan lowered his face wearily against the rim of the steering wheel. He was tired of arguing the case against McInnes. Besides, Jig was running this show. Jig had the guns. It was Jig's baby. And if Jig wanted to believe Ivor, if he wanted to believe that the men inside this motel were some renegade faction of the IRA, well, that was the way it was going to be, and there was nothing Pagan could do or say to change it.

Cairney tapped the barrel of his gun against the dash, a quiet little tattoo. "You're going in with me."

"Right," Pagan said. "Unarmed, of course."

Cairney reached inside the pocket of his overcoat and took out Pagan's gun, the Bernardelli.

"I can't do this alone," Cairney said.

Pagan stared at his own gun. He made no move to take it from Jig's hand.

Cairney realized that this gesture could easily backfire. He was holding the gun out, reaching across a gulf that was far more than the handful of inches separating him from Frank Pagan. But what was the alternative? If he went in alone against the three men, his chances were very thin. Besides, that would entail leaving Frank Pagan right here in the car—and Pagan might just sneak away to make a phone call, bringing in reinforcements. It was possible. Cairney, who knew he was gambling, dangled the Bernardelli in the air.

"I can't do this alone," he said again.

"Goddam," Pagan said.

"I *need* you, Pagan. Take the gun."

"Then what?"

Cairney said, "I don't think you're going to shoot me in the back, Pagan. You had a chance at that already on Canal Street."

Pagan still didn't take the weapon. He kept his hands clamped to the wheel.

Cairney thrust the Bernardelli forward. "There are three men in this place, Pagan. They shot up a school bus, and they bombed a church. More than that, they killed Padraic Finn. That's all I need to know."

Pagan suddenly hated the idea that he was transparent to Jig. Jig saw straight through him. Jig understood there was no way in the world, given Pagan's private code of behavior—which was bound up with such antiquated notions as decency and honor and justice, the very sounds of which suggested they belonged in their own room in the British Museum—that Pagan would turn the weapon on him. Frank Pagan wished he were devious, that he had hidden lodes of cunning and could simply take his gun back and shoot Jig through the eyes and drive away from this place, forgetting the three men allegedly responsible for so many deaths. Praise from the Yard. Love and kisses from Furry Jake. Fuck them. Fuck them all. He didn't need their pressures. He'd do this thing his own way. And if it meant going up to that balcony with Jig, then that's what he'd do.

He raised his hand, brought it out toward the gun, didn't touch it.

"Imagine this, Jig," he said. "We go in there. There's gunplay. We come out again intact. What then? Do you expect me to hand this weapon back like a good little boy? Because I have no bloody intention of doing that."

Cairney didn't respond to the question. He couldn't see that far into the future. Nor did it matter. He turned his face back up to the balcony.

"It's one of those unanswerable questions, is it?" Pagan asked. "We play it as it comes."

"There's no other way."

Pagan took the pistol from Jig's fingers.

Jig opened the door of the Dodge. The night air that came in was cold and smelled of damp leaves and the musty odor of the river. Honor and decency and a sense of justice, Pagan thought. They weren't always wonderful qualities to bring into a situation, but they were inherent in him, a perception that irritated him. Why couldn't he have been more *sly*? He opened his own door now and stared up in the direction of the balcony. Another man might simply have shot Jig there and then. But he wasn't that man, nor could he ever be.

A figure appeared overhead.

Cairney and Pagan, drifting into the gloom beneath the balcony, heard the footsteps rap on concrete. There was the sound of a key turning in a lock, a door opening, closing. Some yards away a flight of iron stairs led to the upper story. Cairney and Pagan moved quietly toward them.

Jig started to climb. Pagan was surprised by the way the man moved, swiftly and yet without a whisper of sound. He was like a bloody shadow rising, something created by the moon amid latticed metalwork. He appeared not to have substance, weight. Pagan felt clumsy and leaden and *old* by comparison. When they reached the balcony Jig stopped. Two windows threw light out at an oblique angle ten yards ahead of them.

Pagan pressed himself flat against the wall, echoing the way Jig moved. He didn't like the idea of creeping toward the windows where the lights now seemed rather bright to him. If *he* had been running this show, he might have chosen to wait outside in the parked car until morning, when at least there would be the definite benefit of visibility.

There was a noise from along the balcony. A door swung open. Framed faintly by electricity from the room behind him, a man appeared. He was holding what looked like two automatic rifles, one stuck under either arm. He struggled to remove a key from his pocket, which he did in an awkward way, then he turned and somehow contrived to lock the door.

When he'd done this to his satisfaction he started to move toward the place where Pagan and Jig stood. Then, seeing them for the first time, he stopped dead. His features were indistinct but Pagan had the impression that the man's mouth hung open in astonishment.

For a long moment there was no movement. It seemed to Pagan that the place had been drained of air, that there was nothing to breathe. Then the man stepped forward and, as if it were the most natural thing in the whole world to be carrying automatic weapons under your arms, moved to the door of the room adjacent to the one he'd just left. He raised his knee and rapped it upon the wood panels.

Somebody opened the door from inside. Pagan saw a heavy shadow fall across the threshold. The character holding the weapons made to step inside when Jig, suddenly going down on one knee like a determined marksman, fired off a shot. Pagan heard it whine in the dark, glancing against concrete. The man with the weapons turned and faced them and this time Pagan was certain that the expression on his face was one of pure astonishment. The man dropped one of the rifles and clutched at the other, trying to swing it into a firing position. Before he could even get a decent grip on the gun, Jig had shot him.

The man was knocked sideways, sprawling against the handrail. The rifle flew out of his arms and clattered across the balcony.

Somebody ducked out of the room, grabbed both the automatic weapons up, then vanished back inside, slamming the door shut.

All this happened so swiftly that Pagan felt like a spectator at a deadly game. He looked at the body lying halfway along the balcony, face tipped back, legs crooked. Jig was still incautiously pressing forward, his spine flat against the wall. There was more determination than foresight in the way Jig was conducting business here, and Pagan didn't like it, but he felt trapped inside a sequence of events over which he had no control. He weighed his own gun in his hand and realized that the back of Jig's skull made a perfect target for him. The simplest thing in the world, he thought. One shot. One well-placed shot. *Finis.* But it wasn't simple at all.

He saw Jig going toward the light that spilled out of the open doorway five yards ahead. Pagan crouched and followed.

SEAMUS HOULIHAN shoved one of the weapons into McGrath's arms. It was rammed with such force into McGrath's body that the man was momentarily winded.

"Who the fuck is out there?" McGrath asked. His face was white. One minute there had been cards and beer and the prospect of going home to Ireland, the next gunfire.

"The enemy," Houlihan replied. He went closer to the door, opened it a fraction.

"What bloody enemy?" McGrath asked.

"You name it, McGrath. People like you and me don't have many friends." Houlihan sniffed the air coming in through the open door. He could see, even though the angle was narrow, the outline of Rorke's body lying some feet away on the balcony. When he'd stepped outside a moment ago to retrieve the weapons there hadn't been time to assess the strength of the enemy. Houlihan had been conscious only of the need to get the guns as fast as he could, which he'd done successfully because the enemy was concentrating on Rorke at that point.

Seamus Houlihan picked up the pint of Johnny Walker from the table, took a long swallow, then slid the bottle to McGrath. McGrath drank. When he was finished he set the bottle down on top of the playing cards. He noticed that his last hand, which had gone unplayed, was a reasonable flush. Good hand. But Houlihan would have beaten it somehow. The big man always did.

"We better get the fuck out of here," Houlihan said.

McGrath appeared hesitant. "We don't know how many are out there," he said.

"Does it make any difference? Do you want to sit here and let them come for you? Fuck that!" For a long time now Houlihan had expected to die a violent death. His whole world had been so circumscribed by violence that the notion of a peaceful death, of slipping away in his sleep, was a bad joke. His father had been shot in a street brawl in Derry. His brother, Jimmy Houlihan, had been blown up inside a Protestant bar in Belfast at Christmas, 1975. Why would he expect his own end to be any different? He clutched the M-16, checked the clip.

He'd gone out once before, and his luck had held. But he wasn't going to risk going out again unless he had the gun blazing in front of him. He had absolutely no fear of death. It neither mystified nor terrified. He had chosen combat as a way of life, and the simple fact was that you lived through combat or you died in the throes of it. Death had no metaphysical implications for him. He believed more in an M-16 than in any God. He was thinking suddenly about Waddy, who'd held some superstitious beliefs, and what he hoped was that he could live through any forthcoming conflict because he'd promised himself that he'd give Waddy a decent burial. Poor wee Waddy.

Houlihan went closer to the door. It occurred to him for the first time that he and the others had been sold out. And that the seller had to be McInnes. Even this realization neither distressed nor surprised him. In his world treachery was just another fact of life. People said one thing, then did the opposite. It had always been this way, and it always would be. He just wished he'd been better prepared. But at least he hadn't obeyed Ivor's demand to toss the guns. At least there was that, and he was glad he'd made that decision. He looked out into the darkness. There was perfect silence. The night held all sounds like a bloody miser, giving nothing away. He glanced at McGrath, whose face was colorless. Then he turned his eyes back to the door.

He heard something then.

It was barely audible, but there it was.

A movement on the balcony. Leather on concrete.

McGrath whispered, "There could be twenty men out there."

"Either we go out or we sit back and let them come in," Houlihan said. He stepped toward the doorway.

"Who goes first?" McGrath asked.

"We go together."

McGrath moved to Houlihan's side.

"Just think," Houlihan said with a smile. "If you were a Catholic you'd be crossing yourself right now."

FRANK PAGAN saw the shadow fall in the doorway. He brought his pistol up, caught his breath, waited. He stared at the shadow, which was massive and still. Jig, who was perhaps two feet in front of him, stopped moving. The open door was three or four yards away at most.

Pagan lost his concentration a second. He wasn't sure why. Tension probably. He gazed down at the motel office where the two neon lights had gone out. Had the clerk gone to sleep? Had he slept through the sound of Jig's gun? Lucky man. It was another world down there, something that came to Pagan as if through filters, gauzy and indistinct. He stared back along the balcony at the dead man, who lay in his very awkward position. Death could be highly unflattering. Pools of liquid, urine and blood, had gathered around the body. Frank Pagan thought he could catch the odor of urine from where he stood.

The shape in the doorway appeared to grow, but then Pagan realized it wasn't a solitary shadow at all, it was the darkness cast by two men who stood very close together. He tightened his grip on his gun. Fear, he understood, didn't have that legendary cold touch at all—rather, it was a warm thing, the temperature of your blood rising and the surface of your skin turning hot.

The shapes moved again. Deliberately, slowly. Pagan glanced at Jig, who was going down as close to the balcony floor as he could. Frank Pagan did likewise, feeling hard concrete against his face.

And then the silhouettes took on flesh and substance, emerging from the doorway, turning from two ghostly things to forms that had an imposing reality about them. The sound of Jig's gun was suddenly loud, ferocious in Pagan's ears, and he must have flinched or briefly closed his eyes because when he looked again and fired his own gun he was aware of a man falling back into the doorway and the fierce rattle of an automatic weapon, which sprayed the air randomly as the man went on falling. The second man, who had been behind the first, shot from his hip in a series of small flashes, and Pagan heard Jig groan, a sound that was less one of pain than of surprise.

Pagan rolled on his side and fired his handgun again even as the automatic weapon continued to stutter, pocking the concrete and zinging off the handrail, creating a tympany of destruction. Pagan kept rolling and turning until his body was jammed against the metal rail. His eyes were filled with dust and small chips of shattered concrete and he had difficulty focusing, but he understood that the one man left standing had either used up the clip in his gun or the damned thing had jammed on him and he was now reaching into the pocket of his seaman's coat for something else, another clip maybe, another weapon. Pagan didn't wait to find out. He fired quickly, striking the tall man somewhere in the region of the shoulder. The man spun around and, clutching his shoulder, began to move along the balcony in the direction of the stairs.

Pagan got to his feet. He was conscious of several things simultaneously. The man running. The fact that the two lights below had come on.

And Jig, sitting with his back to the wall, his head tilted back and his mouth open in pain.

Pagan gaped at him a moment and then raw toward the stairs, which the man in the seaman's jacket was already descending loudly. Pagan's feet encountered the M-16 the man had discarded, which slid away from him on contact and went out beneath the rail to clatter on the court below.

The running man was heading for the yellow truck. He stopped suddenly, took a gun from the pocket of his jacket, turned and fired. A window exploded in a place just beyond Frank Pagan's skull. Pagan reached the bottom of the stairs, and the man fired again—a hasty shot that went off harmlessly into the darkness. Now the man was reaching up to the door of the cabin, apparently fumbling with a key in the lock. Pagan ducked beneath the overhang of the balcony where he was absorbed by shadows, and he took very careful aim. His shot went wide, hammering into the side panel of the truck.

He moved out from under the shadows and took aim again. Before he could get a shot off, the big man had fired twice in rapid succession. Both shots went whining past Pagan's head. Then the big man was climbing up into the cabin of the truck, grunting as he moved.

Pagan leveled his pistol.

This time his shot struck the man directly in the side of the face. He staggered out of the cab, flailing his arms as he fell to the concrete. There was one terrible cry of pain and then a silence that stretched through the night.

Now, Pagan thought. *Now Jig.*

He raced up the stairs.

There was no sign of Jig.

Pagan looked the length of the balcony. The two dead figures lay where they had fallen, one slumped in the open doorway of the room, the other close to the rail.

But no Jig.

Frank Pagan hurried to the other end of the balcony. He realized there was a thin trail of blood underfoot, which must have spilled from the place where Jig had been hit. He reached the stairs. Then stopped.

The red Dodge was pulling out of the parking lot below. Pagan saw the taillights dwindling as the vehicle moved away.

Pagan went quickly down the stairs. He sprinted toward the yellow truck. The keys dangled from the door lock. He climbed up into the cabin, stuck the key in the ignition, turned it, listened to the big engine come to life. As he backed the ungainly vehicle out of the forecourt he thought he knew where Jig was headed. It was inevitable. Since he couldn't go back to Kevin Dawson's, and since he wasn't likely to go into hiding and leave his quest for the missing money in some unacceptable limbo, that left only one place—the last address of all.

Roscommon, New York. The home of Senator Harry Cairney. Where else would he possibly go after Mulhaney and Linney? Where else after Kevin Dawson?

Pagan found Highway 9, which went north. This truck was no match for the Dodge, which meant Jig would reach Roscommon before he could. But there was nothing he could do about that. He'd drive as hard as he possibly could and hope that whatever wounds Jig had sustained would slow his progress north.

When he reached a sign that said Tarrytown, he became conscious of something that lay on the floor of the cab, something bulky stuck between seat and dash. At first he assumed it was a sack of some kind, but when he passed under the sudden glare of a roadside light, he realized that his guess was quite wrong.

This particular sack had eyes.

Shocked, Pagan braked very hard, pulled to the side of the road. He turned on the overhead light. The face he saw half turned away from him was chalk white and ghastly. The eyes were open in a way that suggested some cruel realization at the abrupt end of a life. They had about them a certain knowing quality. The mouth was twisted and stiff and the one hand that was visible was bent in a spastic fashion. Frank Pagan reached out and touched the side of the corpse's jaw, almost as if to reassure himself that this figure had once been flesh and blood and not always the wax effigy it resembled now. A ghoulish moment. He pulled his hand away quickly.

He recognized the man. And as he did so, as he realized that this was the body of one John Waddell, whom he had interviewed last year in connection with the murder of an IRA member in London, he perceived a pattern in events, a meaning in the mosaic that was Ivor McInnes's bizarre story, a flood of understanding. He wondered how he could possibly have missed the truth for so long. Because like most truths, it had been self-evident all the way along.

Blind, Frank.

Very blind of you.

He dragged the body out of the truck and laid it among a clump of bushes at the edge of the highway. And then he was driving again, thinking of Ivor McInnes and the man's scheme, which was luminous in its simplicity and savage in its execution.

T WENTY-SIX

ROSCOMMON, NEW YORK

Celestine Cairney had been unable to sleep. It was five past three and totally dark when she decided she'd tossed and turned on the bed long enough. She got up, went to the window, looked out across the blackness of Roscommon. Earlier, there had been a wisp of a moon in the sky, but even that had gone and the waters of the lake were invisible. She sat in the window seat and listened to the uneven sounds of Harry breathing.

She looked at the luminous figures on the dial of her watch. When you were excited, when anticipation touched you like this, time had a way of prolonging itself. She got up from the seat and moved through the darkness of the bedroom. She rubbed her hands together because she was tense. She wanted Patrick Cairney to come. She wanted to see Patrick Cairney alone.

She caught this thought and held it.

She was remembering Patrick Cairney again as she'd seen him that night in his bedroom. And suddenly she felt sad. There were times when you wished everything had been different. Birth and circumstances, the history of your heart, every damn thing about you.

She sat in the armchair in front of the cold fireplace, legs crossed, placing her hands flat on her stomach. Her nipples were hard, and the very soft hairs that grew on the lower part of her belly stirred.

Patrick Cairney.

She wanted him to be the first to get here.

"Can't sleep?" Harry's voice startled her.

"A little restless," she said. She lowered her hands to her side and clutched the silk of her nightgown, bunching it in the palms of her hands. It felt like Patrick Cairney's flesh to her.

Harry turned on the bedside lamp. He reached out for a Kleenex and blew his nose. It was a trumpeting sound, an old man's sound. Even this room smelled like an old man's flesh. She had the urge to get up and throw the windows open and let the cold Roscommon night perfume the air with winter.

"Come here," Harry said.

She rose slowly, went to the bed, looked down at him. He wore maroon pajamas with his monogram stitched into the breast pocket. HC, in fine gold thread.

"A kiss," the old man said.

She lowered her face, brushed her lips against his, stepped back from the bed. "Get some sleep. You need it."

"What about you?"

"Don't worry about me."

Harry Cairney watched her with eyes that never ceased to be adoring. She rearranged the bed sheets, turned off the lamp, returned to the window. The room seemed even darker than it had before. She placed one hand under the cushion of the window seat, where she'd concealed Harry's old Browning, and she removed it. There was a terrifying certainty about the gun, the weight of it, the hardness in her hands. She turned it over a couple of times, then returned it to its hiding place.

Make him come here, she thought.

Just make him come here.

Soon. Soon now. Soon she'd be gone from this house.

She laid her cheek against the glass and looked out across the night, and thought how hard she'd tried to pretend she cared for Harry Cairney. And how close she'd come to the peril of actually believing she felt something, when all she carried in her heart for him was no more feeling than a slug had when it slunk insensately through blades of grass and left a trail of crystal. When you pretend to be something for long enough, you become that thing.

But she'd done her duty. She could always say that about herself.

POUGHKEEPSIE, NEW YORK

Patrick Cairney pulled into a closed gas station and turned off the engine of the car. The pain he felt was searing, as if the flesh were peeling away from the bone. He reached down and turned up the left leg of his pants and gasped because even something so simple as the brush of clothing against the wound was excruciating. He drew his hand back up. It was covered in blood. He knew that a bullet had passed through, close to the shinbone, burrowing a ragged hole in his flesh. Pretty soon he'd feel numbness around the wound, and then there would be the sensation of uselessness in the limb. He wondered how much blood he might have lost since leaving the River View Motel.

He struggled to take off his coat, which he tossed into the rear seat. Then he removed his shirt and tugged at the sleeve, managing to separate it from the rest of the garment. With this improvised bandage twisted around a ballpoint pen he found in the glove compartment, he made a very crude tourniquet he applied to the wound. It was extremely painful to do so, but he realized his choices were more than a little limited. He could bleed to death or he could attempt to stem the flow of blood with anything he had at hand—and hope he'd make it to Roscommon before he became weak and delirious.

He rolled the window down and breathed night air deeply into his lungs. He had to keep a very clear head. When he reached Roscommon he'd make up some kind of story—something about an accident. He wasn't sure quite what yet. That was the easy part anyway.

For a moment he sat with his eyes closed and his head tipped back against the seat. It was odd how, when he thought of Finn now, he was unable to bring into his mind an image of the man's face. It was lost to him suddenly. He could hear the voice still and he imagined he was listening to Finn whispering quietly in his ear. *I asked too much of you this time. I sent you in there on a wing and a prayer. I was only thinking of the money. I wasn't thinking about the danger to you. Nobody could have done anything better in the terrible circumstances. I'm sorry, boy.*

Cairney shook his head, opened his eyes.

Roscommon. He'd go there and see his father. He'd go there and heal for a time. It was a safe place for him now. He'd avoid Celestine. He wouldn't think about her. When he passed her in the hallway or ran into her at mealtimes he'd be polite but aloof. She'd get the message quickly.

Goddam, the pain was agonizing. He bit on his lower lip hard. There was a way to transcend this kind of pain, if he could only reach inside himself deeply enough. The trick was to remove yourself from your physical cage and soar. To cross that bridge between the corporeal and the spiritual. To divide yourself.

Bullshit. Pain was pain, no matter what you tried to think.

Groaning, he retrieved his overcoat and drew it around his shoulders. Then he turned the engine on. You're young and strong and the wound will mend. And after that you can go looking for Finn's money again.

Finn's money, he thought. He'd been sidetracked, detoured, that was all. When he'd healed, he'd go back to Kevin Dawson's house. And if Dawson didn't have the money, then the President's brother might be able to give him a lead to the character Mulhaney had called the Old Man. When his wound was better, he'd go back out again, he'd find the money and take it back to the house in Dun Laoghaire.

The empty house.

The room of muted harps. Finn's old wall posters, collected over the years. There were a couple from the Irish general election in 1932. END UNEMPLOYMENT! VOTE FIANNA FAIL. VOTE CUMANN NA NGAEDHEAL! Cairney recalled them with clarity, the way he remembered the whole whitewashed house, the airy rooms, the crooked hallway, the stairs that went up to Finn's immaculately spartan bedroom, which was like a monk's cell. But he still couldn't see Finn's face. He wondered if he'd ever be able to bring it to mind again or if, like the man himself, it was lost to him for all time.

He drove the car out of the gas station and headed back in the direction of the highway. For the next twenty miles he wasn't even conscious of the pain. He'd found a useful trick to deal with it. He kept thinking of his father, the sickbed, the claustrophobic enclosure of an oxygen tent—and these images dispelled at least some of his own anguish.

Not all. Just some. Maybe enough to keep him plugging through the miles still ahead.

DANBURY, CONNECTICUT

Inside the diner, Artie Zuboric waited impatiently for Tyson to finish his coffee but Bruno was obviously reluctant to hurry. He'd
been like this all the way from Kevin Dawson's place, hemming and
hawing, wondering aloud if what they were doing was the right
thing. It never occurred to Bruno that what they were doing was the
only thing and that questions of right and wrong didn't come into it.

Tyson Bruno dropped a sugar lump into his coffee and said, "When
Korn finds we've split, he's going to shit bricks."

Zuboric was tired of hearing his colleague talk about the things
Leonard M. Korn was going to do. "Look, you want out, that's fine
by me. I'll go on alone."

Tyson Bruno shook his head. "I've come this far."

Zuboric was very anxious to be on his way, but Bruno had insisted they stop for coffee. Now, though, Zuboric felt the kind of
urgency that had the relentless quality of a runaway train. He knew
he'd overstepped his authority, that he'd defied the personal instructions of the Director, but he hadn't seen much point in hanging
around Dawson's house and waiting for Korn to show up just to
vent his considerable wrath on himself and Bruno.

This was all or nothing time now.

It had taken nerve to walk away from the situation. But then his
own reserves of nerve had astonished him. He'd *actually* gone upstairs in the Dawson home and *interrupted* Kevin in the middle of
his grief, gently taking him aside, pulling him away from the figure
of his sedated wife, saying he had a couple of questions to ask and
they had to be answered even though the time was wrong, but the
process of justice couldn't wait, sorry sorry, a million apologies, but
that's how it had to be. Zuboric didn't want to go through all that
again ever. Kevin Dawson had responded to the questions like a
man submerged in ten feet of stale green water.

"If we bring in Jig . . ." Zuboric started to say.

Bruno interrupted. "If we bring in Jig we'll get medals. And if we
also happen to bring in Frank Pagan, hey, write your own citation."
A bruised little smile appeared in the middle of Tyson Bruno's face.
"But you can't open a bank account with ifs, Artie. First off, you got
to keep in mind that Kevin Dawson wasn't exactly at his best when

you talked to him. The man's in an awful lot of pain and turmoil. In that condition, you don't always get your facts right. Second, you could be making a trip way out to the sticks for absolutely nothing, because by the time you get there Jig might have been and gone, and Frank Pagan as well. If either of them was ever headed there in the first place, that is."

"I've got nothing to lose," Zuboric said. "Neither have you." And he thought of Charity Zuboric taking off her copious bra and her G-string for the gratification of sick old men.

Tyson Bruno finished his coffee, pushed his cup aside. "That's the truest thing you ever said."

Zuboric started to get up. Tyson Bruno tugged at his coat sleeve. "I want you to know it took a lot of balls to talk to Kevin Dawson the way you did."

"I did what I had to," Zuboric answered.

Both men stepped outside into the parking lot of the diner.

"It would be neat if we happened to find both these guys in the same place," Bruno remarked as they reached the car.

Zuboric said nothing. He surreptitiously patted his shoulder holster, a man taking inventory of himself. He got inside the car on the passenger side and Tyson Bruno sat behind the wheel.

"Drive," Zuboric said. "Drive like your life depends on it."

"It does," Bruno said.

RHINEBECK, NEW YORK

The old guy in the twenty-four-hour convenience store did everything slowly and deliberately. When he said the word "Roscommon" Pagan thought he counted at least fourteen syllables.

"You mean old Franz's place," the man said. "Used to belong to a brewer before Harry Cairney come along."

"That's the place," Pagan said.

"Can't figure why you'd want to go there this time of day."

"I'm looking for a friend." Pagan kept the impatience out of his voice.

The old guy stepped out of the store to the sidewalk. The cold apparently didn't bother him. "Go down thataway," he said, pointing one long bony finger down the main street of Rhinebeck, which was sleepy and clean. "You want three-oh-eight for five miles. There's a crossroads down there. You take the left fork. Quiet road. There's no signs. Keep going maybe two miles. You can't miss it. Big house about a hundred yards back from the road."

Frank Pagan thanked the old man and went toward the truck. He climbed up inside the cab and turned the key in the ignition. His whole body, still shaking from the vibrations of the vehicle and all the miles he'd traveled, felt like a tuning fork. Fatigue gnawed at him. There was some small corner of his brain that was still alert, but it was like a room lighted only by a twenty-watt bulb. It was a room occupied by two people. Jig sat in one corner. Ivor McInnes, the Terrible, was silent and surly in another. *I know what you're up to, Ivor,* Pagan thought. And all your silences, all your denials, won't save your white Presbyterian arse now.

But first there was Jig.

He backed the truck up, headed out through Rhinebeck, passing the unlighted windows of small stores. He adjusted his rearview mirror, catching a quick flash of his own reflection. He looked like something disinterred and carted home by a dog and dumped in the middle of the Persian rug to the general dismay of the whole family.

Frank Pagan, an old bone.

But an old bone with a mission.

ROSCOMMON, NEW YORK

There was a weak suggestion of dawn in the sky when Patrick Cairney drove through the gates of Roscommon and passed the security jeep that was parked between the trees. The driver of the jeep recognized him and waved him to continue.

Cairney, who felt disoriented because the pain in his leg had been crippling for the last twenty miles, slowed the car in front of the house. He made no move to get out at once. He reached down and grabbed the leg, massaging it lightly, trying to ease the pain with his fingertips. The cuffs of his pants were soaked with blood, his sock squelched inside his shoe, and there was barely any feeling left in the limb itself. It might have been a stranger's leg, a graft that hadn't worked. He pushed the car door open and got out awkwardly, standing in front of the steps that led up to the front door. The injured leg pulsated, several scalding little spasms. Cairney moved toward the steps, dragging one foot.

She materialized there in the shadows, a sudden bright specter in the gloom. She wore a blue robe and her hair was tied up on her scalp with a simple rose-colored ribbon. Cairney stared at her expressionlessly. He didn't move. Nor did he want her to see him in pain because he didn't need her concern or any offer of assistance. He didn't want her to touch him, a supportive hand on his elbow, the nearness of her body, her perfume, anything. No contact. No connection.

He gazed at her. She was standing very still, her arms at her side. She looked remote. He had absolutely no way of knowing if she was pleased to see him. But then she wasn't *going* to smile, was she? There was a sick man inside the house, it wasn't a situation for merriment or pleasure. It wasn't a time for happy reunions, even if he'd wanted one.

He moved up on to the first step.

It was a brave effort, but he couldn't pull it off. The leg buckled under him and he went down, and suddenly she was coming down the steps toward him, her arm held out and her look one of worry.

She saw the blood on his clothes. She went down on one knee and moved the cuff of his pants aside and her touch, which he still didn't want, was pleasantly cool, almost a cure in itself. She raised her face, looked at him. Cairney closed his eyes. Pain could be seductive at one end of its spectrum, it could lull you out of your body, carry you away into a numb place.

"What happened?" she asked.

"I had an accident."

"We better get you indoors," Celestine said. She helped him stand, let him support the weight of his body against her. They went up the steps, bound together as surely as if they'd been roped one against the other. She aided him inside, took him along the hallway, made him lie down on the living-room sofa. His blood came through the useless tourniquet and soaked the velvet material of the couch.

She decided to undo the tourniquet he'd created. She tossed aside the bloodstained ballpoint pen, the sleeve of the shirt, and then she was studying the raw wound itself. She saw at once that it was a gunshot wound, but she didn't say anything. She looked at him, and what she felt was pity for him.

She didn't want to feel such a thing. If she entertained pity, then it would only make everything more difficult. She lowered her eyes and examined the wound again. She touched it gently. Cairney winced, drawing his leg aside.

"Sorry," she said.

He struggled to control the pain. "How is he?"

"As well as can be expected."

"I need to see him."

"It can wait."

Cairney moved his leg. Celestine pressed firmly on his shoulders. "Stay where you are," she said.

"I can get up. I can make it upstairs."

"Patrick," with a warning in her voice.

Cairney swung his leg to the floor. She wasn't going to stop him from going upstairs. He tried to stand, but the leg gave way and he had to sit down again.

"I told you," she said.

Cairney stared at her. He hated feeling so damned feeble in front of her. He hated the idea of being at her mercy.

She said, "There's a way to take your mind off pain, Patrick."

She undid the buttons of her robe and leaned toward him, her small breasts swinging very slightly.

Cairney caught her by the hair and turned her face to one side. Her ribbon came undone and the hair spilled out over his hand and he remembered how, when she'd come to his bedroom, she'd woven that same hair around his penis in a gesture that was perhaps the most intimate he'd ever experienced. Desire and pain. There was a strange interlocking of sensations inside him right then, as if desire and pain had fused together in one feeling that was indescribable and fresh and beyond any emotion he'd ever registered. He shut his eyes, let his hand fall away from her hair, felt her fingers move over his thighs.

"Trust me," she said.

It was a whisper, barely audible. He felt her breasts against the palms of his upturned hands.

She undid his belt slowly. Then she slid her fingers against his groin.

"Trust me," she said again.

He felt her mouth, the slight friction of lips, the motion of her tongue. He retreated into the darkness of himself, a refuge of pleasure, a place where all the pains subsided like dead tides. She was climbing up into his lap, and he could feel the edge of her open robe rub the side of his face, then she was taking his hand and directing it between her legs, where she was moist and warm and open for him.

He opened his eyes, looked directly into her face. There was a quality of opaque glass to her beauty, he thought. Just as you thought you could see straight into her, a glaze moved over her eyes, leaving you with nothing.

"Love me," she said. "Love me just one time."

He closed his eyes again and felt himself float out through the estuaries of pain as if on some very frail raft of himself. He wasn't thinking now of Finn nor of the sick man who lay upstairs at this very moment nor of the money stolen from the doomed *Connie O'Mara*, he wasn't thinking, he was out of the range of his own thoughts, beyond the radar of conscience or guilt, moving his hips while Celestine tilted her head back and her hair toppled in disarray over her bare shoulders. It was a fragile moment, and an intense one, and he wanted to believe he was capable of this treachery, that nothing else mattered to him except this woman who straddled him now and in whose body he had lost himself. That the man who lay ill upstairs meant absolutely nothing to him. He had lost Finn—what was the loss of his father compared to that? Besides, he had spent years creating and maintaining fictions. What was one more? He could imagine he loved her, and that love was a form of salvation. He could imagine all the events of recent days collapsing behind him into oblivion. Here and now, nothing else.

And then it passed. The moment was gone. Cairney sighed and fell motionless against the back of the sofa.

Celestine stared at him. She was also conscious of a precious moment passing away. She had an empty feeling, a realization that this particular segment of time was never going to come again, no matter how long she might live. And it couldn't be otherwise. She slid away from him, lowered herself to the carpet, looked up at his face.

"I asked too much," she said very quietly. "Or maybe I didn't ask enough. Go see your father now."

How could he go upstairs and into the old man's sick room with the smell of Celestine on his fingers? How could he stand by the bed and look into that dying face and not feel the weight of a terrible guilt? He stared down at his wound. Dear God, he'd been so determined to avoid this woman, so intent on staying away from her—and then this had happened, this travesty, this bastard intimacy.

His father's wife.

He stood up slowly.

The leg didn't yield this time. But his eyesight blurred, and he felt very weak.

He turned toward the door, where he stopped and looked back at her. "There's a name for people like us," he said.

"I'm sure there is." Kneeling on the floor, her robe open, Celestine looked impossibly lovely. He understood he was always going to see her the way she was right then. She had a curious smile on her face.

"It was my last chance," she added. "I didn't want to waste it."

That finality in her voice. It was odd. He wanted to know what she meant by her statement, but he didn't ask. He didn't think he could stand the sound of his own voice.

He began to move toward the stairs. He climbed slowly, stiffly, hearing the sound of Celestine at his back.

"I'm sorry," she said.

She caught up with him on the landing. Ahead, the door of Harry Cairney's bedroom lay half open. Celestine reached for him, caught him by the wrist.

"I'm sorry," she repeated.

"You don't have to be. It takes two." He paused. "In this case, the wrong two."

He moved toward the bedroom door. He raised his hand to the wood and pushed the door open very quietly.

"You don't understand," she said. "How could you?"

FRANK PAGAN saw the jeep come out of the trees toward him. It moved quickly, blocking the truck on the driveway, then it stopped. Two men stepped out of the vehicle. They carried shotguns and moved cautiously but with a certain dead-eyed determination. Pagan saw a grim quality about the men. Like security guards everywhere, they had enemies all over the place. A mailman, a delivery boy, a milkman—anybody who came to this place was a possible carrier of destruction.

Pagan took his gun out of his pocket and held it concealed between his knees. He gazed past the oncoming guards into the first few bars of dawn that had slunk across the sky, and he thought it was a hell of a way to begin a new day. Two men with shotguns. He hoped it wasn't downhill from here.

He didn't move. He didn't roll his window down. He just watched them coming. They wore plaid jackets and had baseball caps, and they reminded Pagan of archetypes in the American nightmare, those rednecks who seasonally take to the forests and wage a bloody one-sided war on anything with four paws or a beak. Beyond them, through bare trees, he saw the house itself, a big gray stone building that lacked the one quality every country house should have—enchantment.

His attention was drawn back to the two men.

They approached the cab of the truck. One of the men rapped on the glass with the barrel of his shotgun. It was an ominous gesture. Frank Pagan braced himself. He smiled, reached for the door handle, hesitated. He wasn't going to let such a trivial matter as two men with shotguns spoil his day.

He turned the handle. This was going to take all the scattered elements of his concentration. This was going to need everything he could find in himself.

"Where the hell do you think you're going, buddy?" one of the men asked.

Now! Pagan shoved with all his might and the door flew open, swinging back swiftly on its hinges. It hit the first man with terrific force in the dead center of his chest, and the window smashed into his face, and he dropped to his knees, clutching himself and groaning. It was a violent collision of metal and glass and bone, and Pagan felt the connection shudder through him. The second guard quickly brought his shotgun up, but he was a pulse too slow because Frank Pagan was already out of the cab and pointing his gun at the man in a deliberate way, the expression on his face as severe and forbidding as he could make it.

"I'll use it," Pagan said. "Make no mistake."

The guard with the shotgun appeared subdued. His look suggested that of a hunter confronted by a duck with an M-16. He stared into Pagan's pistol and dropped his weapon and stepped back from it, raising his hands in the air.

"Cooperation," Pagan said. "I like that."

The man who'd gone down was staring up at Pagan through eyes that showed nothing but intense pain. Pagan kicked both fallen shotguns into the shrubbery and said, "Get up."

Moaning, the guard got to his feet. He was a short man and he moved with uncertainty, in the manner of somebody betrayed by his limbs. He wouldn't stop groaning as he shuffled. He raised a hand to his nose and touched it in a tentative way, afraid that it had been broken. Pagan saw slicks of blood gather in his nostrils.

"Get inside the truck," Pagan said. "Both of you."

He herded the guards forward, unlocked the rear door of the truck, pushed them inside. They complained and threatened, telling him what terrible things they were going to do to him when they got out. He slammed the door behind them, locked it, smiled to himself. He hadn't altogether lost his touch, which was a nice thing to know. When he had to act, he could still be swift and purposeful. There was no better way to begin a day than with some striking insight into your own capabilities. To know that, despite the oncoming winter of forty, a season he feared would be drab and filled with dread, you still had the fire inside.

He turned away from the truck, listening to the muffled noise of the imprisoned guards beating on the interior panels, and walked quickly up the driveway to the house. Outside, he saw Jig's red car parked at an awkward angle near the foot of the steps. He paused then, noticing that the front door of the house lay open. He didn't care for the open door. It suggested that the inhabitants of the place had become so distracted by other things that they'd forgotten to close it behind them. Distracted by what, though?

Pagan, whose recent surge of adrenaline was fading, stood very still at the bottom of the steps. He stared up at the gray windows of the house, which reflected very little of the dawn light. It really wasn't a welcoming kind of house. The windows suggested dark rooms beyond them, large rooms with high ceilings. Pagan just knew there would be chilly crawl spaces and an arctic attic, and, in the dead of winter, the whole house would have corners that no heat could ever reach.

He had to go inside. He had to get out from under the windows, which were beginning to make him feel vulnerable. He went up the steps slowly, stepped inside the large hallway, stopped. There was a silence in the place, the kind of quiet that breeds indefinable fears. Pagan looked in the direction of the staircase, an ornate mahogany construction that went up and up into shadows.

PATRICK CAIRNEY stopped as soon as he entered the room. *This was all wrong, this was all somehow askew, his expectations wrenched out of sync with reality. There was no oxygen tent, no tubes and appendages, no sick man lying on the bed.* Harry Cairney was kneeling on the floor by the fireplace, stuffing rolled-up newspapers into a grate that was creating black smoke. He was trying to build a fire, and the stereo was playing an old John McCormack recording, which filled the room with a familiar melancholy.

She was lovely and fair as the rose of the summer
Yet 'twas not her beauty alone that won me. . . .

It was totally wrong.

Patrick Cairney stood still. He clenched his hands at his side. The song, usually so sentimental and sweet, struck him with terror. He stared at the back of his father's head, conscious of Celestine moving in the corner of his vision, stepping across the room toward the window. Patrick Cairney felt very cold all at once, and the pain in his leg flared up again with renewed ferocity. He had the sensation of drifting inside a dream, when all your known realities and all your expectations are perceived through the misshapen reflections of trick mirrors, beveled surfaces, frosted glass.

Harry Cairney turned. His face was lit by surprise. "Patrick!" he said. "Dear God, nobody told me you were coming!" He dropped newspapers and matches in a flurry and stepped across the room and embraced his son and held him for a long time. Patrick Cairney clasped his father and it was still dreamlike. Even the touch of the old man had no real substance, no depth.

"Patrick, Patrick," the old man said. "Welcome back. Welcome home."

Patrick Cairney stared over his father's shoulder at Celestine, who was framed by the window. He couldn't read her face. Suddenly he wanted to know what was written there, what her expression said. He thought of the lie she'd told him about his father's sickness, and it made him feel as if his heart were squeezed in a vise. There was something wrong here, very wrong, and he couldn't figure it out. He'd been lured back to Roscommon. He'd fallen into some awful trap. And even though he knew this, he couldn't find the resources in himself to respond to the bewilderment of the situation.

He closed his eyes a moment, feeling his father's breath on the side of his face. The old man smelled of burned newspapers and spent matches.

Harry Cairney released his son, stepped back.

"Celestine knew you were coming, didn't she?" Harry asked. "This is one of her surprises, isn't it?"

"She knew," Patrick Cairney said. He heard his own voice echo inside his head. It was the sound of something stirring at the end of a long tunnel.

"She's always surprising me." And Harry Cairney smiled across the room at his wife. She was standing beside the window seat.

Patrick Cairney reached out and hugged his father again. He held him very tightly this time.

"You'll suffocate me," the old man said, laughing.

Patrick Cairney slackened his hold. It seemed to him that the only real thing in this room, the only anchor, was his father. He felt the pain burn, rising the whole length of his leg. He fought to gain control over it, but his will wasn't fully functioning.

Celestine, he thought. *What have you done?*

Harry Cairney took a step back, studied his son, noticed the bloodsoaked cuff of the pants. "Jesus. What happened to you?"

"I had an accident," Patrick said.

Celestine moved at the window.

> *Oh, no, 'twas the truth in her eyes ever beaming*
> *That made me love Mary, the Rose of Tralee. . . .*

There was the wretched scratching sound of the needle being struck across the surface of the record and the song stopped. Both Patrick Cairney and his father looked in Celestine's direction. The silence in the room was suddenly overwhelming. Nobody moved. Celestine created a slim shadow against the window.

"Why did you do that?" Harry Cairney asked. He went to the record player and took the disc off and examined it. "You've ruined it, for God's sake. Do you know how hard it is to get a duplicate of that particular recording?"

Celestine said, "I don't care."

The look on her face was one Patrick Cairney hadn't seen before. It was fearfully cold, and ruthless, and there was a tiny spark of amusement in the eyes.

He also saw the gun in her hand, concealed by the folds of her robe.

Dizzy, he reached for the back of a chair and leaned against it and the pain in his leg went shooting up into his skull, where it was molten and white hot like lead in a furnace.

"What are you doing with my gun?" Harry Cairney asked.

Celestine pointed the Browning directly at her husband. "Harry. Dear Harry. Have you met John Doyle?"

Patrick Cairney gripped the back of the chair. He had the strange impression that the ceiling was lowering itself, that the room was diminishing and the walls were going to crush him.

"John who?" the old man asked.

"Your son," Celestine said. "John Doyle. Also known as Jig."

Harry Cairney laughed. "What the hell has gotten into you?"

Celestine looked at Patrick Cairney. Her face seemed to him as though it were a fuzzy television image traveling through miles of static. He had no control over his pain now. Wave after wave, each one sickening and depleting, surged through him.

"Pat," Celestine said. "Didn't you know your father headed the organization that raised funds for the IRA? Didn't you guess that your own father was on your wanted list? Doesn't it strike you as superbly ironic, Jig? Doesn't it strike you as funny?"

Patrick Cairney shook his head, glanced at his father. *The Old Man*, he thought. Harry Cairney raised an arm slowly, turned his hand over in a little gesture of puzzlement.

"You don't know what you're saying, Cel."

"But I do, Harry." Celestine smiled. "Ask your son. Ask him if he's Jig."

Harry Cairney looked at his son. He opened his mouth, but he didn't say anything. He couldn't bring himself to talk. He gazed down at the blackened blood staining Patrick's leg, then raised his eyes to the boy's face. Jig, he thought. The whole thing was some terrible mistake, a joke, any moment now Celestine would pull the trigger of the gun and a flag would pop out with the words *Ha ha, fooled you*, but it wasn't April the First, and the way his wife looked didn't seem remotely whimsical to him.

Patrick Cairney said, "You're lying, Celestine."

She tossed her hair back with a gesture of her head that reminded Cairney of a small girl bothered by flies. "You're careless, Patrick. You carry a passport made out in the name of John Doyle. You don't take the precautions you should. You're not as good as people say you are. The great Catholic avenger. The Irish freedom fighter. But you're weak, Patrick. Weak where it really matters. Shall I tell your father how weak you really are? Would you like that?"

Cairney stared at her. He understood that it didn't matter to her whether she hurt Harry or not. "I'd prefer it otherwise," he said feebly.

The old man had a fleck of spit at the cranny of his mouth. He reminded Patrick Cairney of a man plunged down in the center of some totally unfamiliar spectator sport whose rules he has to guess.

He stepped toward his wife and asked, "Even if he happens to have a passport in somebody else's name, how the hell does that make him Jig?"

"Because Jig travels under that name at times."

The old man's face was suddenly florid. "How do you know that? How do you know any of this?"

Celestine ignored his question. The look on her face dismissed him, relegated him to some unimportant corner of her life. She turned her attention to Patrick Cairney.

"I liked the archaeological symposium bit," she said. "It's a pretty good cover. It explains all the trips you must take if anybody ever asked, but it's fake. Totally fake. Tell your father, Patrick. Tell him the truth."

Cairney felt the room spin around. He wondered how much blood he'd actually lost. He wanted to sit down but didn't move. He had the feeling that if he did sit he'd never rise again. He gazed at the gun in Celestine's hand and experienced an odd little hallucinatory moment when it seemed to him that metal and skin had become fused together. He blinked, rubbed his eyes, focused on Celestine's face, trying to associate what he saw there with the woman who'd whispered *Trust me, trust me* on the sofa downstairs. He had the thought that if she was capable of sexual treachery, what else could she bring herself to do? There were no limits, no boundaries. Anything was possible.

"You've been wasting your time from the start, Jig," she said. "It's been a lost cause from the beginning. But you must be used to lost causes by this time. You'll never see that money, Jig. You know that, don't you?"

Harry Cairney, who felt betrayed by all his senses, couldn't take his eyes from his wife. "What do you know about the money?" he asked.

"Harry, Harry," she answered. "We used your boat to steal it."

"My boat?"

Celestine shrugged. "Why not? You hardly ever find any use for it, do you?"

Harry Cairney was trembling. "Who used the boat? Who are you talking about?"

"Ask your son," Celestine said.

"I'm asking you," the old man said. "I'm asking my wife."

"Your wife," Celestine said.

"Yes. My wife." The old man held his arms out. "The woman I love."

"Funny. I never really thought of you as my husband."

Harry Cairney was moving forward, propelled by notions of love, convinced even now that all this was a travesty, some kind of breakdown on Celestine's part, something he could put right the way he'd put things right all his life. In his time he'd been capable of fixing anything. It didn't matter what. And he could fix this, whatever it was. Hadn't some of the most powerful men in the whole goddam nation come to him at one time or another and asked him to bail them out of their problems?

"I don't want to hear that, I don't want to hear you say that kind of thing." He had both hands extended in front of himself. "We've been happy. I know we have."

"Dear Harry," she said. "We've had our moments. But they're finished now."

"What are you saying?"

Celestine was very quiet. Patrick Cairney watched her, knew what was coming, understood he was powerless to do anything about it. He watched Celestine shoot the old man through the side of the neck.

Harry Cairney cried out and dropped to the floor, turned over on his back, raised one hand up in Celestine's direction, and then he was finally still. Celestine turned the gun toward Patrick.

Cairney said, "You're on their side."

"The right side, Jig. The side of the angels."

Cairney knelt beside the body of the old man. He lightly touched the side of his father's jaw. There was a grief in him, but he realized he wasn't going to live long enough to express it. The tightness behind his eyes, the awful parched sensation in his throat. *Do something.*

"You were the bonus," Celestine said. "I never expected you. Not in this house."

Without looking at her Cairney said, "They put you here. You told them about the money. The ship."

"Yes," she said quietly. "I told them a lot of things, Patrick. I told them about the money. The route taken by the *Connie*. It wasn't difficult to find out. Your father always thought he was such a hotshot at keeping secrets, but he wasn't. Not really." She paused a moment. Then, "I also told them about the route taken by a certain school bus—that New England trip I mentioned, remember? Does that surprise you, Jig?"

A school bus. Cairney felt very cold. He was fumbling toward the sense of it all, groping for a revelation that he knew was going to be denied him.

He opened his eyes, turned his face toward her. "Who the fuck are you?" he asked, thinking maybe, just maybe, he could fish his weapon out of his pocket, if he could be quick enough, slick, but even as he reached for it she took one step forward and fired her gun a second time.

Cairney didn't feel the entrance of the bullet into his chest. He fell back, knocking a chair over as he dropped, and he lay facedown on the rug. He was barely conscious of hearing her footsteps as she approached him.

She bent down to touch the nape of his neck. "We had some moments too," she whispered.

CALMLY, carefully, Celestine Cairney changed her clothes. She stepped out onto the landing, without once looking at the two figures who lay on the bedroom floor. The heels of her boots made soft clicking noises on wood floorboards as she entered Patrick Cairney's bedroom. She stood by the window, gazing out a moment.

She saw a car come up to the front of the house.

She pressed her face against the glass, then she turned away. It was time now. It was time to leave this place.

She opened the closet in Patrick's bedroom and began to remove old books, boxes that contained ancient board games, a battered microscope, running shoes, a football, crumpled pennants, a dusty framed wall map with the title LEGENDARY IRELAND in Celtic script. *The relics of Jig,* she thought.

There was a satchel stored at the very back of the closet. She reached for it and drew it toward her. And then she turned around and, with one last glance at Patrick Cairney's bed, she left the room.

T WENTY-SEVEN

Frank Pagan was standing at the foot of the stairs when he heard the first gunshot. When he heard the second, he turned and moved back along the hallway. He stepped inside the living room and closed the door, leaving only a small space through which he could observe the staircase. It was a limited field of vision, but it was infinitely more safe than doing something completely reckless, like charging up the stairs with his gun in his hand. If he waited here, sooner or later Jig was going to come down. He wondered about the gunfire. He assumed that Jig had had to shoot Senator Cairney, although he couldn't understand why *two* shots had been fired.

He waited.

The room in which he stood was elegantly furnished. There were old prints on the walls, each depicting a Dublin scene at the turn of the century. Kingstown Pier. The Custom House on the banks of the Liffey. Horse-drawn carriages on St. Stephen's Green. He glanced at them a moment, then returned his attention to the stairs.

Pagan heard a sound from above. A door opened and closed faintly, a slight noise diminished by the mass of the house. Then there were footsteps for a moment. After that there was silence again.

Pagan waited. Earlier, when he'd been poking cautiously through the downstairs rooms, he thought he'd heard a man's upraised voice, but he hadn't been certain. The brickwork of this old house trapped sounds and diffused them and created auditory illusions. He passed his pistol from one hand to the other because there was a sudden small cramp in his fingers. The palms of his hands were sticky with sweat.

Now he heard footsteps in the hallway. They were coming from the front door, not from the stairs as he'd expected. He couldn't see anything in that direction. He heard them come close to where he stood. Heavy steps. A man's steps. They stopped some feet from the door behind which he was standing.

Frank Pagan held his breath, listened. Now there was more movement, from the stairs this time. He glanced up into the dark-brown shadows.

The person coming down wasn't Jig and it wasn't Senator Harry Cairney either. Wrong sex.

It was a woman dressed in black cord pants and a black leather jacket. She wore tinted glasses and her yellow hair was held up by a black ribbon. In one hand she carried a small overnight bag, also black, in the other a large satchel. She created a somber impression as she moved, taking the stairs slowly. Where the hell was Jig? Pagan wondered. And who was this woman?

She reached the bottom step, where she set her bag down and took off her dark glasses. Her smile was suddenly radiant. She had the bluest eyes Pagan had ever seen. She held her arms out. The man who had entered from Pagan's blind side stepped forward and Pagan could see him for the first time, and he felt a certain voltage around his heart.

"Celestine," the man said.

His voice was unmistakable.

Pagan watched as the couple embraced. There was laughter, the kind of laughter you associate with a reunion. There was relief and happiness in the sound and a maudlin tinge.

"Too long, too bloody long," the man said.

"Yes," the woman whispered. "Far too long."

The woman slid her glasses back over her eyes.

The man made a gesture toward the stairs.

"It's over," the woman said.

"Both of them?"

"Both of them."

The man laughed again. "You were right about Jig then," he said. "You're a bloody wonder. You know that?" The man was quiet before he added, "I think I'd like to go upstairs, take a look at the body. I'd like to be sure."

The body, Frank Pagan thought. Was he talking about Jig? Jig's body? Pagan felt a cold hand inside his brain.

The woman turned and looked up the flight of stairs. "Take my word for it. He's dead. Let's get the hell out of here. I've been in this place too bloody long. I want to go home to Ireland."

The big man reached down to pick up the overnight bag.

Frank Pagan stepped out from behind the door, holding his pistol in front of him.

The big man turned around, saw Pagan, and for a second his expression was one of disbelief, but it changed to a restrained kind of amusement. "Frank Pagan," he said. "I can't seem to shake you."

"People always tell me I've got a dogged quality, Ivor," Pagan replied.

"People are right." Ivor McInnes sighed and turned to the woman. "This, my dear, is Frank Pagan. I mentioned him to you once or twice, I believe."

The woman removed her glasses and stared at Pagan. She didn't say anything. She gazed at Pagan's gun, then turned her face back to McInnes. She shrugged, almost as if Pagan's presence made no difference to her.

Ivor McInnes was still smiling. "What brings you all the way up here to this wild place, Frank?"

"Jig," Pagan said. He found it difficult to take his eyes away from the woman's face. She had a rare beauty that seemed somehow innocent to him, and he couldn't begin to imagine what her association with McInnes might be. There was intimacy between them, in the way they stood close together, the way they'd embraced before. And, almost as if some of this woman's beauty had affected Ivor McInnes, the man looked suddenly handsome there in the hall, distinguished and proud and pleased.

"Jig's dead," McInnes said. "And his father along with him."

"His father?" Pagan asked.

"Senator Harry Cairney."

Pagan was quiet. The fact that Harry Cairney was Jig's father took a very long time to make its way into that part of his brain that absorbed information. It had to pass through filters of disbelief first. It had to make its way around the confusion of emotions Pagan felt at the news of Jig's death. Disappointment. Anger. And sorrow— was there just a touch of sorrow in there or was he simply sad that the chance to take Jig back to London with him had gone? He wasn't sure of any of his feelings right then.

"I see it perplexes you, Frank," McInnes said.

"To put it mildly."

McInnes shook his head and made a long sighing sound. "It would seem that neither man knew of the other's activities," he said. "It's what you might call a lack of communication. The son doesn't know what the father's doing. And the father has no idea about his son. Ah, modern families."

Pagan didn't say anything for a while. He'd come a long, long way to take Jig back to England, and now there was nothing left of that ambition. But there was Ivor still, and Ivor would have to suffice. There was also this woman, Ivor's accomplice. Somehow, though, he felt strangely empty. He felt he was moving through the demands imposed upon him by a role, a job of acting, doing the things expected of him even if his heart wasn't entirely in it. He'd been after Jig too long, and now Jig was gone.

He looked at the woman and said, "You killed them."

The woman gave him a look of mild disgust. "Do you expect me to admit that?"

Frank Pagan didn't know what to expect. He stared at her a moment, then turned toward Ivor. If he couldn't have Jig, then by Christ he'd bring McInnes to some kind of justice.

He said, "I almost didn't see your plan, Ivor. I almost missed it. I was looking for the complex when I ought to have been looking for something simple."

Ivor McInnes moved just a little closer to the woman, cupping her elbow in the palm of his hand.

"You brought your thugs into this country," Pagan said. "You orchestrated acts of violence and placed the blame on the IRA."

"Is that what you think, Frank?"

"It's what I *know*," Pagan said. He was hoarse all at once, depleted. "I only fully realized it when I found the body of John Waddell. You lied to me from the start, McInnes. And then you compounded your lies with even more lies. Bullshit about trying to make some kind of peace with an IRA faction. I never bought that story. Jig did. But not me. Unfortunately, I was in no position to argue with him at the time. You set out to discredit the IRA in the most callous way imaginable. You set out to turn public opinion totally against them by directing the FUV to act as it did."

McInnes was quiet for a moment. He said. "Northern Ireland is a sad society, Frank. You've been there. You've seen it. You've seen what happens when warring factions can't find a peace plan. And the sorry thing about it is that there's no possibility of any peace in the future unless the IRA is squashed."

"Along with the Free Ulster Volunteers," Pagan said.

"I agree with you, Frank. In the Ireland I want, there's no place for hoodlums." McInnes glanced at the woman. "When you want to provoke outrage, you strike at the innocent, Pagan. It does no good in this day and age to assassinate a president. People expect that kind of atrocity. They're numbed by that. But blow up a church and then massacre some children on a school bus, and suddenly you've got the public attention. They howl. Jesus, how they howl. And then they strike back with a vengeance at the perpetrators. In this case, Frank, the Irish Republican Army is the culprit."

Pagan felt a numbness in the hand that held the gun. He was thinking now of the school bus and the dead children and the fact that Jig had been murdered, and all the deaths congealed inside him, a knot in the center of his chest. He realized he wanted to kill McInnes then and there. Shoot the man on the precise spot where he now stood. Shoot him directly between the eyes. All along McInnes had been manipulating events, plotting destruction.

"You knew the names of the Fund-raisers, didn't you, Ivor?"

"Of course I did." McInnes smiled at the woman. "Mrs. Harry Cairney kept me well informed."

"Mrs. Cairney?" Pagan asked.

The woman smiled coldly at Pagan from behind her dark glasses. Frank Pagan wondered what inestimable treasons had been going on in this large gloomy house.

"You could have made my life easier if you'd supplied me with the names, Ivor," he said.

"I'm not in the business of making my enemies' lives easier, Frank. Why tell you their names? It was nice to think of you busily running around trying to find out. It kept your mind off me for a while."

"And you knew Jig was coming to the States," Pagan said.

"All along, Frank. From the moment Finn first sent him. We knew he was coming here to find the money. We told you about that. We wanted you to have a gift from your friends inside the FUV, Frank. We wanted you to come over here and catch him. We were much too busy to be sidetracked into getting him ourselves. Besides, we didn't have the expertise for that. And I assumed you did. You and the FBI. But you failed to catch him. You let me down there. It doesn't matter now, of course. We didn't expect to find Jig was part of this particular household, but you know what they say about gift horses. And Jig did us a favor by rendering the Fund-raisers obsolete." McInnes was lightly rubbing the woman's neck. "Besides, Jig wasn't what I was after. Jig was only a part of a larger entity. I want the IRA in its entirety, Frank. Not just one assassin."

Pagan said nothing. He kept looking at the woman's expressionless face. *Mrs. Harry Cairney.*

McInnes looked suddenly solemn. "The trouble is, Frank, your government hasn't done a damn thing about the IRA. They pussyfoot around the problem. They send in bloody soldiers, young kids who're too scared to act. And then when they do get their hands on the IRA, it's your court system that protects the bastards. It's your courts that say these gangsters have rights. They can't be hanged. They can't be flogged. They can't be tortured. Good heavens, don't lay a hand on them or else they'll be sending out for their lawyers and making depositions to the bloody Court of Human Rights in Strasbourg. Jesus Christ! The IRA aren't people, Pagan. They aren't human beings. They're rodents. And you people don't have a clue about what to do with them."

Rodents, Pagan thought.

McInnes said, "I'm sick and tired of violence, Pagan. I want an end to it. I want an end to the IRA. I want to see peace in Belfast and through the rest of Ireland. And if the British can't do it, then perhaps the Americans will."

The Americans. Frank Pagan rubbed the corner of an eye. Here he was now, standing on the precipice of Ivor's dream and looking down a dark slope into the abyss. "Was that it, Ivor? You brought violence into the United States because you hoped it would outrage Americans enough that they'd send some troops over there to wipe out the IRA?"

"It's going to happen," McInnes said. "People in this country are sick to death of terrorists and their threats. They're tired of all the anti-American activities that go on throughout the world. The Americans hate two things, Frank. They hate being put on the defensive, especially in their own country. And they hate to be inconvenienced. My God, do they ever hate that! They can't go to Europe, because they're afraid. They can't cruise the Med, because the bloody Libyans will likely hijack their ships. They can't do business in the Middle East without fearing for their lives. They're tired of it all, Frank. And now they're ready to hit back. And they've got a target all set up for them. The IRA. It's going to happen because there's a weak President in the White House who's going to be swayed by public outrage. A man who's personally suffering at this very moment from his own loss. His two nieces, Frank. His brother's children. The IRA killed his own flesh and blood. Tell me he won't react to *that*."

Pagan thought McInnes had to go down as the worst kind of monster. The monster who dreams and who doesn't care what his dreams destroy or who they touch or the lives they shatter. He thought about Kevin Dawson for a second. He thought about dead kids and a shattered school bus and a silent country house near New Rockford, Connecticut. For the rest of his life Kevin Dawson would have only pictures of his daughters to look at. Pictures on a mantelpiece.

"You want your own fucking little Vietnam in Ireland."

"I don't think so," McInnes said. "It wouldn't take the Americans long to crush the IRA."

"No, Ivor," Pagan replied. "It would take forever. You don't see very far, do you? The IRA would thrive in the end because it's always thrived in one form or another. The English couldn't kill it. The Irish themselves couldn't stamp it out. It passes between father and son. It goes from one generation to the next. The Americans might subdue them for a while, but sooner or later the Americans would have to go home. That is, if the governments of Ireland and Britain approved of this hypothetical intervention in the first place, which is highly unlikely."

"No, Frank. It's the logical step for this country. And do you think the governments of Ireland and Britain are going to turn down a helping hand when it comes to a problem they've been battling with miserable success one way or another for centuries? I don't think so."

Pagan was quiet again. Ivor's dream, grandiose, elaborate, made a jarring sound inside his head. He said, "If it hadn't been for your own troops killing Fitzjohn in Albany and calling the FBI, the name of the Free Ulster Volunteers wouldn't ever have entered into the picture, would it?"

McInnes nodded. "It was a bad moment for me, but it doesn't matter now," he said.

The woman, who'd been listening to this in a distant kind of way, tugged at McInnes's sleeve impatiently. McInnes looked at her, taking his hand away from her neck. It suddenly occurred to Frank Pagan that this pair expected to walk out of the house and take their leave as if nothing had ever happened here, as if McInnes had nothing to answer for.

McInnes said, "You'll excuse us now, Pagan."

"Don't make me laugh, Ivor. Where the hell do you think you're going?"

McInnes looked at the gun. "I haven't seen my wife in two long years, Frank."

"Your *wife*?"

McInnes slung an arm round the woman's shoulder. Pagan couldn't see her expression for the dark glasses.

"You sound surprised, Frank."

"You said she was Mrs. Cairney."

"So I did, so I did." McInnes smiled. "You can figure it out for yourself, Frank. I know you're capable of it. But you shouldn't sound so surprised. Why shouldn't an old warhorse like me have a wife as beautiful as Celestine?"

A match made in hell, Pagan thought. He stared at McInnes's large hand on the woman's shoulder.

"Two years is a long time," McInnes said. "And I've come a long way to take her back home, Frank. I'm sure you understand."

"The only thing I understand is that you're going straight to jail," Pagan said.

"I don't think so." McInnes smiled. It was an infuriating little movement of the lips. "For one thing, Frank, you've got nothing in the way of evidence that links me with anything. For another, my dear wife here had no part in the tragedy that took place in this house. Father finds out about son, shoots son, turns gun on himself. You've seen the headlines before, I'm sure."

"There are some corpses in Hastings," Pagan said. "The valiant men of the Free Ulster Volunteers. The people you betrayed. How would you explain them away?"

"Do I have to? They had nothing to do with me. Show me a connection, Frank."

Pagan hesitated. He saw it now. He saw the flaw in Ivor's scheme, and he circled it in his mind briefly before pouncing on it joyfully. "They had *guns,* Ivor. Presumably the same guns used in the attack on the school bus."

"Guns?" McInnes appeared surprised. "They didn't have any guns!"

"What's the matter, Ivor? Did you expect them to be unarmed? Was that what you wanted? That they wouldn't have anything that might tie them to the school bus? Tough shit. What happened? Did they decide not to follow your orders?"

McInnes said, "They were supposed to get rid of the goddam weapons."

"Terrible how unreliable the hired help is these days," Pagan said. "It isn't going to be difficult to show that these men weren't members of the IRA. As soon as they're fingerprinted and run through the computer, everybody's going to know that they were connected with the FUV. Fingerprints and weapons will prove conclusively that the attacks weren't carried out by anyone associated with the Irish Republican Army. *How does that grab you, Ivor?* If only they'd tossed their weapons away, everything would have been neatly blamed on the IRA."

McInnes was quiet for a time. He seemed rather pale to Pagan. "It might change things a little," he said and there was a certain raspiness in his voice.

"It might change things quite a lot," Pagan said. He was savoring this moment, the punctured expression on Ivor's craggy face, the way the man's mouth had slackened, his smile erased. "It demolishes your notion of blaming the IRA. And there goes your case, Ivor. If you hadn't betrayed your own chums in Hastings, my friend, you might *just* be able to walk out of here. But you were so bloody anxious to get rid of your own thugs you didn't stop to think. You didn't want them around as a potential embarrassment, did you? You slipped up there. You should have let your killers leave the country."

The woman asked, "Is he serious, Ivor?"

"Deadly," Pagan replied. "Don't you hear it? That long-drawn-out sound of a man's scheme dying?"

McInnes made a small fumbling gesture with his hand. He looked lost, but then he appeared to gather himself together again.

"It could still work," McInnes said. "I know it could still work."

"Ivor," Pagan said. "It's not going to work."

"Jesus," McInnes said angrily. "I'm telling you it could still work. I'll think of a way. I'll think of something."

"How, Ivor? How is it going to work now? You can't think of anything that could make it plausible now. There are corpses in Hastings. You can't fucking wish them away, Ivor."

The woman placed her hand on McInnes's wrist as if to calm him down. She had a small smile on her face. "They still can't link you with any killings," she said. "They can't tie you into anything that's happened, Ivor."

Pagan looked at her. It was obvious she provided some kind of support system for McInnes, which made her as crazy as he was. The little wife comforting the distraught husband, laying out his slippers in front of the fire and massaging his weary shoulders. The lethal little woman. But Ivor looked despairing again, a chess player who has overlooked some simple strategy, who has made a bad pawn move at a bad time.

Pagan thought for a moment. "Even if you could walk out of here, I could make a case, Ivor. You know I could do it. I'd backtrack. I'd go over all your movements. All your associations. I'd go back ten years if I had to, but you know I'd make a damn good case. There are links between you and the killers because somewhere you had to sit down and plan this whole thing out with them. I'd find those links. And when I did, I'd squeeze you like a fucking cherry."

The woman said, "We're going. We're leaving, Ivor."

"I have a gun," Pagan said.

The woman slipped off her glasses. There was a cruelty somewhere in that beauty. The mouth was heartless. The eyes seemed subtly insane. "Use it then, Mr. Pagan."

She linked her arm through McInnes's.

"Use it," she said again. "Shoot me."

Frank Pagan marveled at her calm. He raised the gun, leveled it. He didn't want these people dead. He wanted them tried and imprisoned. Imprisoned for a very long time, the rest of their lives. Death was altogether too quick, too generous.

The woman smiled at him. "Good-bye, Mr. Pagan."

"I'll shoot," Pagan said.

The woman, who had infinitely more nerve than McInnes, put

her hands on her hips. It was a gesture of defiance. She had seen into the heart of Frank Pagan, and she understood that he wasn't capable of cold-blooded murder. She knew she was free, that all she had to do was walk with Ivor McInnes to the door.

The smile on her face chilled Pagan.

"Good-bye," she said again.

Ivor McInnes placed his arm once more around the woman's shoulder.

And then he lurched suddenly, sinking to his knees, a horrified expression on his face. His face traveled down the length of the woman's leg as he slipped. Blood spilled from the side of his jaw. The woman screamed. She turned, kneeled alongside McInnes, and then the back of her scalp was shattered with a sound Frank Pagan could *feel* in his own head. She toppled forward over the body of McInnes, and she lay there motionless, hands outstretched.

Pagan turned and looked up the flight of stairs.

The shots had come from the landing up there. From the shadows. Pagan thought he saw somebody move. He went toward the stairs quickly.

I T was Finn's voice Jig heard, it was Finn's voice inside his head. A sea breeze, a gull's wing, it floated through his brain with a soft insistence, quiet and reassuring and coming from a place nearby. *Even when you don't think you've got it, boy, you'll always find some strength from somewhere.*

The strength.

He didn't have any strength left.

What life he still had was going out like the tide in Dublin Bay.

He didn't hear the shots he fired, nor the sound of the gun slipping out of his fingers and toppling down the stairs. He didn't feel any kind of pain. He saw Celestine, the lovely, venomous Celestine, look clumsy in death.

Dying isn't any great business. When you took the oath, you commited yourself to death. It's nothing to fear because it's been a close companion all along.

Dear Finn. He had loved Finn more than he'd ever loved his father. More than any other human being.

Jig closed his eyes. He lay down on the landing. He wondered what death was going to be like.

It was all weariness now, and fatigue such as he'd never felt before. He didn't see Frank Pagan come up the stairs, didn't hear him. He didn't feel Frank Pagan's fingers touch his arm.

And he never heard Frank Pagan turn away and go back down the stairs because all the doors to his mind had closed tight shut and there was only darkness—and somewhere, at the very last, a sweet note that might have been plucked on the string of a harp, one of Finn's harps, echoing and echoing, then finally silent and still.

FRANK PAGAN opened the dead woman's satchel, looked inside, saw what he guessed was there all along, then went out onto the steps of the house. Over the lake lay some low clouds, heavy and thick. Pagan walked toward the shore, moving very slowly. He had a bad taste in his mouth and his head felt as if it were filled with stones. When he reached the reeds at the shoreline he sat down.

He tossed a pebble out into the water lethargically. He was beyond tiredness now. His condition felt more serious. There was a numbness inside him. It was almost as if he were out of contact with himself. He couldn't get in touch with ground control. He heard the lyrics of a song he'd listened to only a day or so before on his car radio.

> *With your long blond hair and your eyes of blue*
> *The only thing I ever get from you*
> *Is sorrow. . . .*

Celestine Cairney. Sorrow and treachery.

Treachery, he thought. It bruised you, left you shaken. It shouldn't have surprised you, but it always did. Call me naïve, Pagan thought. What is it about you that keeps bringing you back to the untenable idea that the human soul is not so awful as it sometimes seems?

He flipped another stone out into the somber lake.

He would go home, and he'd take nothing with him, unless you counted a narrative of deception and violence. At least it was something he didn't have to declare at Customs. And he was dissatisfied too, because the total story eluded him. The bits and pieces you could put together only after you'd started to dig around. He wasn't sure he had the energy for that. He wasn't certain he had the inclination to go around tagging the corpses, trying to understand the roles of people who no longer had any part left to play.

He thought of Jig's face in death. How to describe that? Composed? Indifferent? He wasn't sure. He shut his eyes and felt the frosty morning breeze scurry across the surface of the lake, blowing through his hair, against his face. It might have been refreshing in other circumstances. But not now. He hardly felt it.

He opened his eyes when he heard the sound of footsteps coming toward him. The swishing of reeds. He saw Artie Zuboric and Tyson Bruno looming up, two men in a raging hurry, flustered and out of breath. Artie's moustache hadn't been combed, and it drooped sadly. Tyson Bruno needed a shave. His jaw looked like sandpaper.

Pagan smiled at them. "Welcome," he said.

Zuboric took a gun out of his raincoat. "You're up shit creek, Frank."

"A place I know well," Pagan replied. He turned away from the two agents and looked out at the gloomy lake. He was going to pretend that Zuboric didn't have a gun in his hand. He wanted to see how far that might get him. A little make-believe.

But Zuboric wasn't going to be ignored. He shoved the barrel of the gun into the back of Frank Pagan's neck.

"Artie, please," Pagan said. "It's a tender spot."

"I'm trying to think of one good reason why I shouldn't shoot you."

"I'll give you one," Pagan said. "I don't want to die."

"Not good enough, Frankie. Not convincing."

Pagan pushed the gun away with his fingers. He hated anyone calling him Frankie.

Tyson Bruno, no doubt remembering the day Pagan struck him, plucked a reed out of the ground and bent it between his hands. "Shoot him," he said with a certain exuberance. "You've got the authorization to do it. Shoot him. Nobody's going to give a fiddler's fuck anyway."

Zuboric poked the gun back into the nape of Pagan's neck. Frank Pagan stood up, feeling the edge of irritation. These characters had quite spoiled his lakeside meditation.

"One fucking good reason," Zuboric said again.

Pagan stared into the agent's face. He didn't like what he saw there. Meanness, a lack of imagination, a narrow human being at best. Artie and Tyson, a couple of lovely specimens. Pagan looked out once more across the water. He wasn't absolutely sure if Zuboric intended to use the gun. He had no confidence in his own predictions when it came to Zuboric.

"You been in the house?" Pagan asked.

"Not yet."

Pagan smiled. "You should. Jig's dead."

"Dead? How?"

"Does it matter?" Pagan asked. He had a thought just then. It was cynical and thoroughly without any redeeming qualities, unless you happened to be Artie Zuboric. When it occurred to him he wanted to laugh out loud. But Artie had a gun, and Pagan didn't want to make any sound the agent might misinterpret. He didn't want to die right here and now.

"Artie," he said. "How would you like to be a hero?"

Zuboric looked mystified. "What are you trying to say?"

"How would you like to be known as the man who killed Jig?"

Zuboric said nothing. He was scrutinizing Pagan, his whole face filled with mistrust.

"You'd like that, wouldn't you, Artie? Think of it. Think of the fame. Your standing in Korn's eyes. Your stock would go up overnight. You'd be a big bloody hero."

"I'm not with you," Zuboric said.

"It's dead simple. I saw you do it, after all. I'm your eyewitness. Jig was about to kill me, when all of a sudden you just popped up and saved my life."

"Are you serious?"

"Never more so, my old dear. Never more so."

Tyson Bruno cleared his throat. "It sounds like bullshit to me. I'd shoot the sonofabitch, Artie."

"Wait," Zuboric said.

"It's a nifty idea," Pagan remarked. "I'll tell you what. For good measure, I'll throw in Ivor McInnes as well. I'll say you gunned him down because he drew a pistol on you."

Zuboric narrowed his eyes. "McInnes?"

"Absolutely." Pagan looked at Tyson Bruno. "You could pick up a consolation prize, Ty. We can say you were forced to shoot McInnes's wife because she'd just shot Senator Cairney. Christ, there are enough bodies to go around. Regular funeral parlor up there."

"Senator Cairney?" Bruno asked.

"The very same," Pagan said.

"Hold on," Zuboric said. "Just wait a minute. What about ballistics tests? They'll find out I never fired this gun at anybody."

"A piece of cake," Pagan said. "It's all a question of logic. Who had what gun and why. I don't think such a story is beyond us, is it? Not if we put our heads together. It's no sweat."

"I still don't like it." Tyson Bruno snapped another reed. He folded it between his hands and blew into it, creating a humming sound.

"Ty. Think. Merit badges. Maybe promotion. A raise in salary. A leg up the ladder. Advancement."

Zuboric had a curious smile on his face. There was a faraway look in his eyes. "How can we trust you, Pagan?"

Frank Pagan shrugged. "You've got two choices. You can shoot me. Or you can use me to back up the authentic story of your heroic deeds. What's it to be, Arthur?"

Zuboric was silent. He was looking at Tyson Bruno. There was some form of mutual decision-making going on here. Pagan stared up at the sky. A sound forced its way through the cover of clouds, throaty and deep. There, far over the trees on the other side of the lake, two helicopters appeared. Whirring, skimming treetops, they were coming in toward Roscommon like a pair of enormous gnats.

"Visitors," Pagan said. "Friends of yours?"

Zuboric peered up. Tyson Bruno did likewise, making slits of his puffy eyes. The helicopters came in across the lake, rippling the water into tiny whirlpools. They were traveling very low.

The chopper in front banked slightly. There was the unmistakable sight of Leonard Korn's shaven head in the cabin. He was gesticulating, pointing down toward the three men bunched by the edge of the lake.

"Your Master," Pagan said. "Better make up your mind quickly."

"One thing, Frank. Why don't you want credit for Jig yourself?"

Credit, Pagan thought. It was a funny word. "I couldn't do that," he replied. "I couldn't deprive you, Artie."

Zuboric nodded. "Okay. It's a deal. Tyson?"

Bruno looked suddenly quite brutal. "It's okay with me. But there's something I got to settle first."

"Like what?" Zuboric asked.

"I owe this sonofabitch," and Tyson Bruno turned to Pagan, making a hammer out of his fist and raising it in the air with the intention of bring it down somewhere on Pagan's face.

Frank Pagan reached up and caught Bruno's fist in his hand and twisted, just enough to make Bruno gasp and step back.

"Not today, Ty," Pagan said. "I'm not in the mood. Believe me."

There was a wicked look in Pagan's eye, a murderous light that made Tyson Bruno refrain from trying a second time.

"Besides," Pagan added, "I make it a point not to fight with heroes."

Zuboric and Tyson Bruno looked at one another as if to be sure they had reached agreement regarding Pagan's proposition. They had. Then they turned and started to walk toward the house.

As Pagan watched them move away, he remembered the satchel in the house. He remembered how it lay alongside Celestine's body. It contained several million dollars of IRA money. He considered calling out to the two agents, but he didn't. Let them discover it themselves. Let them decide what to do with all that cash. He thought he knew anyhow. They were about to become heroes, after all. And heroes deserved something more in the way of remuneration than any salary the FBI might provide. He shrugged and looked up at the helicopters. Jig's cash. And Jig was dead. The fate of the money— money that had brought death and treachery, and, for himself, a depression he couldn't shake, an isolation that penetrated him, money that was bloody and tainted and only valuable now to men without scruples—didn't matter a damn to him.

He saw the choppers come in low over the front lawn just as Zuboric and Bruno disappeared through the open doorway and were swallowed by the gloomy interior of the house. He sat down among the reeds. The surface of Roscommon Lake, recently disturbed by the great blades of the helicopters, was placid again, and as desolate as Frank Pagan felt himself.

EPILOGUE

On the evening before St. Patrick's Day, Frank Pagan went inside a bar on the West Side of Manhattan that belonged to a man who had made a good living out of performing Irish folk songs in a rich baritone voice. Pagan ordered a Guinness and scanned the large room. There was a great deal of easy laughter in this place. If there was any tension, if anybody had paid any mind to the editorial writers who had called for the cancellation of the St. Patrick's Day Parade this year, it didn't show. You might just as well have tried to cancel New Year's Eve. Everybody here was having a fine old time.

On a small stage behind Pagan a fiddler was tuning up his instrument. Pagan turned to watch. The fiddler, a tiny man with large ears, had a gnomelike demeanor. When he played the fiddle, his stubby little fingers danced in a blur. Pagan, who had booked a flight for London first thing in the morning, closed his eyes and listened to the opening bars of "The Rose of Aranmore." Somebody at the back of the room sang the lines

But soon I will return again
To the scenes I loved so well

Where many an Irish lass and lad
Their tales of love do tell.

It was a thing about the Irish. They were always leaving Ireland
and then composing homesick songs, songs filled with the prospect
of a return to their birthland. A melancholy crowd, he thought. They
were never entirely at home anywhere. And even if they did return
to Ireland after years of exile, they were usually eager to be gone
again as soon as they could. Who could figure them out?

He finished his drink, decided to have a second. Only four days
had passed since the events at Roscommon. In that brief period of
time Leonard Korn had been quoted as saying that only the "tenacity" of the Federal Bureau of Investigation had brought about a res-
olution to an unhappy business, a senator from Arkansas had
introduced a bill in the House calling for tougher screening when it
came to Irish immigrants and their political affiliations, sanctimo-
nious editorialists everywhere had demanded a moratorium on Irish
public assemblies for an indefinite period, and investigative reporters, like the good little hotshots they were, had gone scurrying off
to dig into the lives of Ivor McInnes and Patrick Cairney and anybody else who might have been associated with them.

Pagan was tired. For four days he hadn't been able to rid himself
of a disturbing sense of hollowness. It was as if something quite
important had gone out of him. Energy, dedication to his work, he
couldn't pin it down. He read the signs in himself and decided they
were nothing more than the responses of a man burned out by the
events in which he'd participated. What he needed was a vacation
from his life, a period where he wouldn't be Frank Pagan at all, but
some anonymous tourist with a camera, somebody strolling a sunlit
Caribbean beach and sipping tall drinks on a terrace while a great
red sun went falling into the blue horizon. A little amnesia. A place
where he might forget the question and answer sessions with Leonard Korn that had occupied the last couple of days. *Had he really seen
Zuboric shoot Jig? How far was Jig standing from Zuboric when the fatal
shot was fired? How did he explain the fact that Zuboric had killed Jig with
an old Browning registered to Senator Harry Cairney?* Korn liked the role
of Grand Inquisitor. But the Director was too carried away by the
possibility of public rapture to be really good in the part. If there
were holes in the story—which was reluctantly narrated by a weary
Frank Pagan, who wasn't good at lies and told them with a kind of

white-hot resentment of the FBI because he had nothing but contempt for that organization and the man who ran it—Korn didn't pay them the kind of close attention he might have because Leonard M. Korn needed a convincing story that put the FBI in a good light more than he needed the truth. Pagan supplied the flattering light, wondering all the while how Jig would have reacted to the fable that he'd been killed by a valiant FBI man in the line of duty. Maybe it was best that nobody knew he'd been shot by his own bigamous stepmother. God knows, there was scandal enough in all of this.

Arthur Zuboric had enjoyed his moment in the sun. He'd been called a hero, a description he modestly turned aside. He was only doing his job, he'd said to the reporters who'd clamored around him. *But why was he retiring?* they wanted to know. Artie said it was time to take a long break. Besides, he had money from his pension, and he could live for a time before making a career decision. *A long vacation?* Yes, Artie had said. Perhaps a month or two in Rio might be nice, especially in the company of Charity, his new fiancée. Tyson Bruno, who was uncommunicative and therefore unattractive to reporters, had taken an extended leave of absence and was said to be fishing in the wilds of Canada.

Pagan smiled. Rio. Canada. Faraway places.

He turned his glass around in his hand. The fiddle music was strident and loud in his ears. He thought about the Dawsons. The press had been very subdued about Kevin and Martha, apparently respecting their need for privacy, although there was a spate of articles about the lack of security afforded the unfortunate Dawson girls. Kevin and his wife had gone into seclusion at some country estate in Virginia. If the reporters knew of Kevin Dawson's association with Irish matters, they were discreet enough not to write about it.

Pagan shut his eyes a moment. A beach was a tempting prospect. But he wouldn't want to vacation alone. He was afraid of solitude suddenly. He'd had enough of it. He looked at his wristwatch, took another sip of his drink.

The other Dawson, Thomas, was off in the Southwest somewhere, campaigning under the rubric of law and order, and generally bearing up under what one journalist called "the stress of recent grief." He had given an interview to *Newsweek* on the Irish question, during the course of which he wondered about the possibility of the United States playing a greater role in bringing peace to Ireland. He wasn't specific, for which all of his advisers were thankful.

Pagan shook his head. The world moves on, he thought. It keeps turning. And you couldn't keep the Irish down for very long.

The fiddler had begun to play that great Irish weepy "The Rose of Tralee." Sometimes Pagan thought that there were only about twenty Irish songs in existence and they just kept circulating endlessly. The crowd in the bar was singing along with the musician. Pagan finished his drink. Tomorrow, London. A report for the Under-Secretary. Question and answer sessions. Reporters at the airport. He couldn't shake the feeling he'd come all this way for nothing. Screw London. Why didn't he change his plans? If he decided to step on another plane destined for a remote sunny place, what could anybody do to stop him? London seemed a drab prospect to him now, a cold season, wet streets and rooftops, sad little parks.

He looked inside his glass. He wondered if you could possibly tell your future from the pattern left by the froth of a Guinness. *You're going on a long journey, Frank.*

He pushed his empty glass away. He was thinking of Ivor McInnes and the woman called Celestine. Foxie, who had done some legwork in London, had called with the information that Ivor had indeed married the woman in a private ceremony in the Ulster town of Enniskillen in 1978. As for Celestine, it appeared that she'd been born in Belfast but raised in Boston by Irish-American parents, both of whom were fervent anti-Catholics. What she had drummed into her from the start was hatred. The hard-line stuff. Catholics are evil. They breed like rabbits. One day they'll dominate the world. We have to do something about them. Celestine Cunningham, as she was known, went back and forth between America and Ireland, where she became attached to the concept of Protestant supremacy in Ulster. She had bought the whole package, hatreds intact, bigotries in place. She was naturally suited to Ivor. And she was a natural for the Free Ulster Volunteers—indeed, their only female member. Northern Ireland wasn't a place where women went in great numbers into terrorist groups. Their role was expected to be more domestic.

Celestine and Ivor McInnes. Pagan tried to imagine the inner workings of Ivor McInnes. It was tough. Pagan could see the obsession somewhat, but he knew his insights were superficial and limited. There was no way in the world he could grasp the depths of Ivor, the Byzantine workings of the brain, nor did he understand what the heart was made of. There had to be as much patience as there was loathing for Ivor. That plan of his, for instance. Devious, time-consuming, having to make each play slowly. The bigamous marriage of Celestine to Harry Cairney—how long had it taken for McInnes to orchestrate that affair? He had somehow contrived to put Celestine Cunningham in Boston, in a position where she'd inevitably meet Harry Cairney and where her beauty would overwhelm the old man to the extent that he'd want to marry her. Pagan supposed that he might never know now how McInnes had latched on to Harry as one of the Fund-raisers in the first place. Maybe it had started with nothing more than a rumor, an item of gossip produced by one of McInnes's sources of intelligence, a thin possibility that Celestine, as soon as she was ensconced at Roscommon as the bride of the former senator, confirmed for him. It had to be a strange precarious existence for the woman, watching Harry's activities, listening, spying, and then somehow reporting back to Ivor. Clandestine phone calls. Secret letters. Pagan realized he'd never know the extent of the communication between them.

He wondered if there ever were moments in McInnes's life when he lay awake thinking about his absent wife or if his cause was more important than the matter of sexual jealousy. Did he lie in a dark room and envisage his wife in Senator Cairney's bed? Did he sweat and clutch the bed sheets and stare at the window in anger and envy? Or was he more pragmatic than that, more patient, was his love for the woman subjugated to her usefulness to him? Pagan would never know.

And Jig.

Frank Pagan didn't want to think about Jig. He ordered a third Guinness, sipped it slowly. He could see, if he wanted to, the set of Jig's face as he lay dead at Roscommon. He could see the blood soak into the rug and the closed eyelids and the way the shadows on that landing left small scarlike marks across the skin. But these were images and had nothing to do with the substance of the man. And besides, he didn't want to entertain them. All he knew was that in some inexplicable way he felt a strange sense of loss. Strange because he hadn't known Jig well. Hadn't really known him at all.

He drank from his glass.

The fiddler was playing "The Mountains of Mourne." Pagan thought he could have taken bets on that one. Later, it would be "Kevin Barry" and "Galway Bay," and "Johnny, I Hardly Knew Ye."

He didn't intend to hang around for those tunes. He looked at his watch. He'd finish his drink, and if nothing had happened by then he'd leave. He didn't care if he never heard another Irish tune. He drained his glass, reluctant to set it down and go. But he couldn't linger here.

He thought of how Foxie had told him that all the known members of the Free Ulster Volunteers were being rounded up in Ireland and questioned about the *Connie O'Mara* and the missing money. The money, Pagan thought. Long gone. Artie was on his way to Rio and Tyson Bruno was in Canada and the money had disappeared in such a manner that soon it would have the substance of legend and, like any lost treasure, attract all kinds of crackpots who claimed they had half of a map to its burial place and needed only the other section to disinter the cash. They came out of the woodwork when huge sums of money were inexplicably missing.

He saw his face in the bar mirror and thought, *Pale, Pagan. Far too white.* He wanted sand castles and tides and exotic drinks and a woman's mouth.

He turned around when he felt the girl's hand on his sleeve.

She said, "Sorry I'm late. I couldn't get my money to add up. I was short about nine dollars."

"A hanging offense," Pagan said.

She nudged him and smiled. "It's quite serious." She removed her shoulder bag, which somehow managed to slip out of her grasp and tumble on the bar, where it fell open, showering out tubes of lipstick, a wallet, combs, bobby pins, and tissues.

"Christ," she said. "It's like I can't help myself. Butterfingers."

"It's endearing. Don't worry about it."

The girl scooped up the items back inside her purse. Pagan, thinking about his beach, turning over the sorry prospect of London in his mind, asked her what she wanted to drink.

"Something green," she said.

"Green?"

"For St. Patrick's Day."

Pagan looked into her eyes. He felt a strong affection for this clumsy girl. He placed his hand over hers, surprised by his movement, his boldness. It was strange to be touching a woman after so long a time. It was strange and exciting and it took his breath away.

"You're not Irish, are you?" he said.

"With a name like Mindi Straub? You've got to be kidding."

"So why a green drink?"

"Everybody's a little bit Irish on St. Patrick's Day," she replied.

Pagan put his hand inside the pocket of his coat. He took out an emerald ring he'd found in the hallway of the house at Roscommon. It had been lying close to the body of Ivor McInnes, hidden in the shadows of the staircase. He wasn't even sure now why he'd bothered to pick it up. He didn't know to whom it had belonged. It was a souvenir he didn't want to keep.

"This is green," he said. He gave it to the girl. "I want you to have it."

She held it in the palm of her hand and smiled. "I can't accept this."

"Why not?"

"I hardly know you."

Pagan was silent for a while. Before the night was out, he would somehow remedy that situation. He reached for her hand and closed her fingers gently over the ring.

"Keep it," he said.

"Are you sure?"

"It's the appropriate color."

The girl smiled at him. "Are you a little bit Irish too?" she asked.

Pagan considered this question for a time before he said, "Only a little."

"GUM!" yelled Ruben.
It tended to make a mess.

"JULIUS!" shouted Mom.

CRINKLE
WRACKLE
CRACKLE ————————————

SMAK SMAK ————————————

SMIK SMAK ————————————

CRINKLE WRACKLE
CRACKLE ————————————

STUUURCH... STUUUURCH... STUUUURCH... ————

SNAP! ————————————

CRINKLE WRACKLE
CRACKLE ————————————

CRINKLE WRACKLE CRACKLE ————————————

PUFF — SPLATT ————————————

SHUFF... UFF... WHUFF...

SHUFF... UFF... WHUFF...

SHUFF... UFF...
WHUFF...

Then...

"Ruben, fetch Grammy's purse! It's time to say good-bye," Mom said.

BUNK!

THUMP!

THUMP!

THUNK!

GUM

RUB
DUB
DUB

SCRUB
SCRUB
SCRUB

But...

"RUBEN!"

"Let's see what we can do with three pieces," said Ruben. "Look out for Mom, okay?"

He blew a bubble as big as Great Uncle Stu!

"Watch this, Julius! I'm a natural, really. . . ."

He blew a bubble as big as a birdhouse!

"Hey!"

"You're a *good* pig, Julius!

Ever see me blow a bubble?" Ruben asked.
"This is how the big pigs blow a bubble, Julius."

Ruben was still learning.

But on his next try, he blew a bubble
as big as a juice box.

However...

PEEK!

TIP
TIP

SQUIG - SQUIG - SNATCH!

"No more gum!" Mom said.

"No more gum," Ruben mumbled.

Fortunately, this wasn't the first piece of gum
Ruben had gotten stuck in Mom's knitting.
He knew *just* what to do.

"Ruben! My blanket!" Mom yelled.

Uh-oh.

"Not in Mom's blanket!" Ruben cried.

STUUUUUUUUURCH

"Hang on, Julius!"

But Ruben couldn't stop yet. . . .

"Just once more, Julius," Ruben whispered.
"Mom won't know. You hold this end. . . ."

"I hope you're not playing with your gum, Ruben," said Mom. "If you do, the gum will go right in the trash!

And let's put my new blanket back on the chair, okay?"

STUUURCH... STUUURRRCH

STUFF!
STUFF!

"This is how the big pigs stretch a piece of gum, Julius," Ruben said.

I'll just sit *and* chew, Ruben thought, wrapping up in a warm blanket.

"Give him one more chance, dear," Grammy said. "You swallowed many a piece of gum when you were a piglet."

Mom reluctantly agreed.

CRINKLE
WRACKLE
CRACKLE

"Pleeeease!" Ruben begged.

"I *promise* not to swallow another one."

But...

GULP!

Uh-oh.

"I accidentally swallowed my gum. Can I have another piece, Grammy?" Ruben asked.

"Good gravy!" Mom said. "You only had that gum two minutes and you've already broken the rules. I'm sorry, there will be no more gum for you today."

He chewed in
super-slow motion.

He chewed in *full-tilt, fast motion!*

He chewed balancing on his head.

He chewed lying down.

Then, all right ones.

SMAK
SMAK
SMIK
SMAK

He swapped sides.

First, all left chews.

Ruben loved chewing. "This is how the big pigs chew, Julius," Ruben said between smacks.

SMAK

SMAK

SMIK

SMAK

SMAK

SMAK

SMIK

SMAK

"Ruben!" Mom yelled. "Settle down!" Grammy had
an idea:

Gum wasn't often allowed. It tended to make a mess.

"You know the rules," Mom said. "Don't swallow your
gum. Don't play with your gum. And don't blow big,
sticky bubbles with your gum.

Be *careful*."

THUMP!

Ruben played Superpig.

Ruben always got to be Superpig.

Julius was always his sidekick, Squeal.

"C'mon, Squeal! To the rescue!!" Ruben shouted.

Julius was playing with his cars and trucks.
Ruben played along.

"Watch this, Julius! I'm an ambulance!"

WAOOO! WAOOO! WAOOO! WAOOO! WAOOO!

"Ruben, can you be a little quieter?" Mom asked.

"Aw, Mom!" Ruben said. "When's the rain gonna end?"
"Not for a while, Ruben. Why don't you play with Julius?"

WHUMP!

Ruben stared out the living room window.

The trouble at the Figgs' house began one rainy day when Grammy was over for tea.

Mom was knitting a blanket for Julius.

TROUBLE GUM

SHUFF...
UFF...
WHUFF...

Matthew Cordell

FEIWEL AND FRIENDS
New York

For Romy

A FEIWEL AND FRIENDS BOOK
An Imprint of Macmillan

Library of Congress Cataloging-in-Publication Data

Cordell, Matthew,
Trouble Gum / Matthew Cordell. — 1st ed.
p. cm.
Summary: Playing indoors with his little brother on a rainy day, a rambunctious
young pig causes a ruckus and then breaks his mother's three chewing gum rules.
ISBN: 978-0-312-38774-7
[1. Chewing gum—Fiction. 2. Behavior—Fiction. 3. Brothers—Fiction.
4. Pigs—Fiction.] I. Title. PZ7.C815343Tr 2009 [Fic]—dc22
2008048140

Book design by Rich Deas
Feiwel and Friends logo designed by Filomena Tuosto

First Edition: 2009

10 9 8 7 6 5 4 3 2 1

www.feiwelandfriends.com